RANDOM HOUSE

LARGE PRINT

Also by Haruki Murakami Available from Random House Large Print

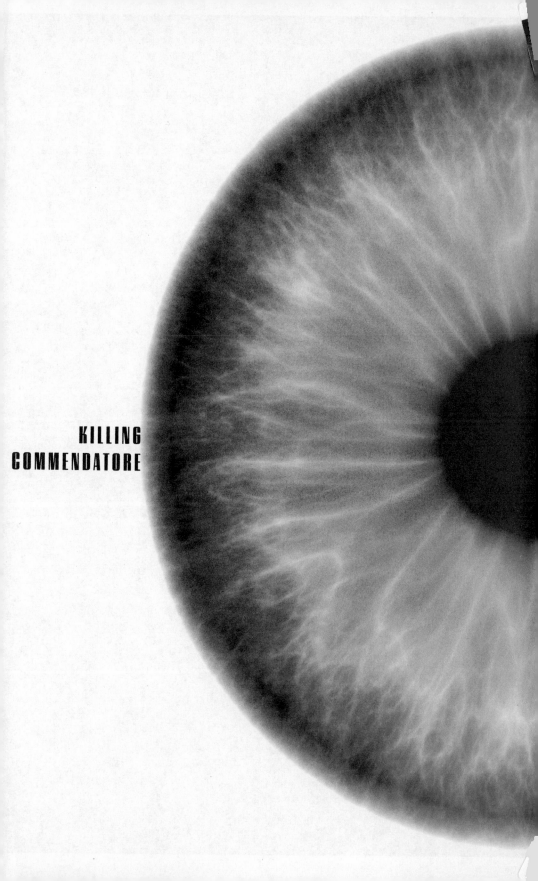

KILLING
COMMENDATORE

HARUKI MURAKAMI

KILLING

R A N D O M H O U S E
LARGE PRINT

COMMENDATORE

Translated from the Japanese by Philip Gabriel and Ted Goossen

Translation copyright © 2018 by Haruki Murakami

Published in the United States of America by Random House Large Print in association with Alfred A. Knopf, a division of Penguin Random House LLC, New York, New York. Originally published in Japan in two volumes, titled **Kishidancho goroshi: Dai ichi-bu, Arawareru idea hen** and **Kishidancho goroshi: Dai ni-bu, Utsurou metafa hen** by Shinchosha Publishing Co., Ltd., Tokyo, in 2017. Copyright © 2017 by Haruki Murakami

Cover images: (blue canvas) Alis Photo/Alamy; (eye) Science Photo Library/Alamy
Cover design by Chip Kidd

Frontmatter images: (moon) Stocktrek Images, Inc./Alamy; (eye) Science Photo Library/Alamy

The Library of Congress has established a Cataloging-in-Publication record for this title.

ISBN: 978-1-9848-9190-7

www.penguinrandomhouse.com/large-print-format-books

FIRST LARGE PRINT EDITION

Printed in the United States of America

10 9 8 7 6 5 4 3 2 1

This Large Print edition published in accord with the standards of the N.A.V.H.

PART I

THE IDEA MADE

VISIBLE

Prologue

oday when I awoke from a nap the faceless man was there before me. He was seated on the chair across from the sofa I'd been sleeping on, staring straight at me with a pair of imaginary eyes in a face that wasn't.

The man was tall, and he was dressed the same as when I had seen him last. His face-that-wasn't-a-face was half hidden by a wide-brimmed black hat, and he had on a long, equally dark coat.

"I came here so you could draw my portrait," the faceless man said, after he'd made sure I was fully awake. His voice was low, toneless, flat. "You promised you would. You remember?"

"Yes, I remember. But I couldn't draw it then because I didn't have any paper," I said. My voice, too, was toneless and flat. "So to make up for it I gave you a little penguin charm."

"Yes, I brought it with me," he said, and held out his right hand. In his hand—which was extremely long—he held a small plastic penguin, the kind you often see attached to a cell phone strap as a good-luck charm. He dropped it on top of the glass coffee table, where it landed with a small **clunk**.

"I'm returning this. You probably need it. This little penguin will be the charm that should protect those you love. In exchange, I want you to draw my portrait."

I was perplexed. "I get it, but I've never drawn a portrait of a person without a face."

My throat was parched.

"From what I hear, you're an outstanding portrait artist. And there's a first time for everything," the faceless man said. And then he laughed. At least, I think he did. That laugh-like voice was like the empty sound of wind blowing up from deep inside a cavern.

He took off the hat that hid half of his face. Where the face should have been, there was nothing, just the slow whirl of a fog.

I stood up and retrieved a sketchbook and a soft pencil from my studio. I sat back down on the sofa, ready to draw a portrait of the man with no face. But I had no idea where to begin, or how to get started. There was only a void, and how are you supposed to give form to something that does not exist? And the milky fog that surrounded the void was continually changing shape.

"You'd better hurry," the faceless man said. "I can't stay here for long."

My heart was beating dully inside my chest. I didn't have much time. I had to hurry. But my fingers holding the pencil just hung there in midair, immobilized. It was as though everything from my wrist down into my hand were numb. There were several people I had to protect, and all I was able to do was draw pictures. Even so, there was no way I could draw him. I stared at the whirling fog. "I'm sorry, but your time's up," the man without a face said a little while later. From his faceless mouth, he let out a deep breath, like pale fog hovering over a river.

"Please wait. If you give me just a little more time—"

The man put his black hat back on, once again hiding half of his face. "One day I'll visit you again. Maybe by then you'll be able to draw me. Until then, I'll keep this penguin charm."

Then he vanished. Like a mist suddenly blown away by a freshening breeze, he vanished into thin air. All that remained was the unoccupied chair and the glass table. The penguin charm was gone from the tabletop.

It all seemed like a short dream. But I knew very well that it wasn't. If this was a dream, then the world I'm living in itself must all be a dream.

Maybe someday I'll be able to draw a portrait of nothingness. Just like another artist was able to complete a painting titled **Killing Commendatore**. But to do so I would need time to get to that point. I would have to have time on my side.

IF THE SURFACE IS FOGGED UP

From May until early the following year, I lived on top of a mountain near the entrance to a narrow valley. Deep in the valley it rained constantly in the summer, but outside the valley it was usually sunny. This was due to the southwest wind that blew off the ocean. Moist clouds carried by the wind entered the valley, bringing rain as they made their way up the slopes. The house was built right on the boundary line, so often it would be sunny out in front while heavy rain fell in back. At first I found this disconcerting, but as I got used to it, it came to seem natural.

Low patches of clouds hung over the surrounding mountains. When the wind blew, these cloud fragments, like some wandering spirits from the past, drifted uncertainly along the surface of the mountains, as if in search of lost memories. The pure white rain, like fine snow, silently swirled around on the wind. Since the wind rarely let up, I could even get by in the summer without air conditioning.

The house itself was old and small, but the garden in back was spacious. Left to its own devices it was a riot of tall green weeds, and a family of cats made its home there. When a gardener came over to trim the grass, the cat family moved elsewhere. I imagine they felt too exposed. The family consisted of a striped mother cat and her three kittens. The mother was thin, with a stern look about her, as if life had dealt her a bad hand.

The house was on top of the mountain, and when I went out on the terrace and faced southwest, I could catch a glimpse of the ocean through the woods. From there the ocean was the size of water in a washbowl, a minuscule sliver of the huge Pacific. A real estate agent I know told me that even if you can see a tiny portion of the ocean like I could here, it made all the difference in the price of the land. Not that I cared about an ocean view. From far off, that slice of ocean was nothing more than a dull lump of lead. Why people insisted on having an ocean view was beyond me. I much preferred gazing at the surrounding mountains. The mountains on the opposite side of the valley were in constant flux, transforming with the seasons and the weather, and I never grew tired of these changes.

Back then my wife and I had dissolved our marriage, the divorce papers all signed and sealed, but afterward things happened and we ended up making a go of marriage one more time.

I can't explain it. The cause and effect of how this all came about eluded even those of us directly involved, but if I were to sum it up in a word, it would come down to some overly trite phrase like "we reconciled." Though the nine-month gap before the second time we married (between the dissolution of our first marriage and the beginning of our second marriage, in other words) stood there, a mouth agape like some deep canal carved out of an isthmus.

Nine months—I had no idea if this was a long period or a short period for a separation. Looking back on it later, it sometimes seemed as though it lasted forever, but then again it passed by in an instant. My impression changed depending on the day. When people photograph an object, they often put a pack of cigarettes next to it to give the viewer a sense of the object's actual size, but the pack of cigarettes next to the images in my memory expanded and contracted, depending on my mood at the time. Like the objects and events in constant flux, or perhaps in opposition to them, what should have been a fixed yardstick inside the framework of my memory seemed instead to be in perpetual motion.

Not to imply that all my memories were haphazard, expanding and contracting at will. My life was basically placid, well adjusted, and, for the most part, rational. But those nine months were different, a period of inexplicable chaos and confusion. In all senses of the word that period was the exception, a time unlike any other in my life, as though I were a swimmer in the middle of a calm sea caught up in a mysterious whirlpool that came out of nowhere.

That may be the reason why, when I think back on that time (as you guessed, these events took place some years ago), the importance, perspective, and connections between events sometimes fluctuate, and if I take my eyes off them even for a second, the sequence I apply to them is quickly supplanted by something different. Still, here I want to do my utmost, as far as I can, to set down a systematic, logical account. Maybe it will be a wasted effort, but even so I want to cling tightly to the hypothetical yardstick I've managed to fashion. Like a helpless swimmer who snatches at a scrap of wood that floats his way.

When I moved into that house, the first thing I did was buy a cheap used car. I'd basically driven my previous car into the ground and had to scrap it, so I needed to get a new one. In a suburban town, especially living alone on top of a mountain, a car was a must in order to go shopping. I went to a used Toyota dealership outside Odawara and found a great deal on a Corolla station wagon. The salesman called it powder blue, though it reminded me more of a sick person's pale complexion. It had only twenty-two thousand miles on it, but the car had been in an accident at one point so they'd drastically reduced the sticker price. I took it for a test drive, and the brakes and tires seemed good. Since I didn't plan to drive it on the highway much, I figured it would do fine.

Masahiko Amada was the one who rented the house to me. We'd been in the same class back in art school. He was two years older, and was one of the few people I got along well with, so even after we finished college we'd occasionally get together.

After we graduated he gave up on being an artist and worked for an ad agency as a graphic designer. When he heard that my wife and I had split up, and that I'd left home and had nowhere to stay, he told me the house his father owned was vacant and asked if I'd like to stay there as a kind of caretaker. His father was Tomohiko Amada, a famous painter of Japanese-style paintings. His father's house (which had a painting studio) was in the mountains outside Odawara, and after the death of his wife he'd lived there comfortably by himself for about ten years. Recently, though, he'd been diagnosed with dementia, and had been put in a high-end nursing home in Izu Kogen. As a result, the house had been empty for several months.

"It's up all by itself on top of a mountain, definitely not the most convenient location, but it's a quiet place. That I guarantee for sure," Masahiko said. "The perfect environment for painting. No distractions whatsoever."

The rent was nominal.

"If the house is vacant, it'll fall apart, and I'm worried about break-ins and fires. Just having someone there all the time will be a load off my mind. I know you wouldn't feel comfortable not paying any rent, so I'll make it cheap, on one condition: that I might have to ask you to leave on short notice."

Fine by me. Everything I owned would fit in the trunk of a small car, and if he ever asked me to clear out, I could be gone the following day.

I moved into the house in early May, right after the Golden Week holidays. The house was a one-story,

Western-style home, more like a cozy cottage, but certainly big enough for one person living alone. It was on top of a midsized mountain, surrounded by woods, and even Masahiko wasn't sure how far the lot extended. There were large pine trees in the back garden, with thick branches that spread out in all directions. Here and there you'd find stepping stones, and there was a splendid banana plant next to a Japanese stone lantern.

Masahiko was right about it being a quiet place. But looking back on it now, I can't say that there were "no distractions whatsoever."

During the eight months after I broke up with my wife and lived in this valley, I slept with two other women, both of whom were married. One was younger than me, the other older. Both were students in the art class I taught.

When I sensed that the timing was right, I invited them to sleep with me (something I would normally never do, since I'm fairly timid and not at all used to that sort of thing). And they didn't turn me down. I'm not sure why, but I had few qualms about asking them to sleep with me, and it seemed to make perfect sense at the time. I felt hardly a twinge of guilt at inviting my students to have sex with me. It seemed as ordinary as asking somebody you passed on the street for the time.

The first woman I slept with was in her late twenties. She was tall with large, dark eyes, a trim waist, and small breasts. A wide forehead, beautiful straight hair, her ears on the large side for her build. Maybe not exactly a beauty, but with such distinctive features that if you were an artist you'd want to draw her. (Actually I am an artist, so I did sketch her a number of times.) She had no children. Her husband taught history at a private high school, and he beat her. Unable to lash out at school, he took his frustrations out at home. He was careful to avoid her face, but when she was naked I saw all the bruises and scars. She hated me to see them and when she took off her clothes, she insisted on turning off the lights.

She had almost no interest in sex. Her vagina was never wet and penetration was painful for her. I made sure there was plenty of foreplay, and we used lubricant gel, but nothing made it better. The pain was terrible, and it wouldn't stop. Sometimes she even screamed in agony.

Even so, she wanted to have sex with me. Or at least she wasn't averse to it. Why, I wonder? Maybe she wanted to feel pain. Or was seeking the **absence** of pleasure. Or perhaps she was after some sort of self-punishment. People seek all kinds of things in their lives. There was one thing, though, that she wasn't looking for. And that was **intimacy**.

She didn't want to come to my house, or have me come to hers, so to have sex we always drove in my car to a love hotel near the shore. We'd meet up in the large parking lot of a chain restaurant, get to the hotel a little after one p.m., and leave before three. She always wore a large pair of sunglasses, even when it was cloudy or raining. One time, though, she didn't show up, and she missed art class too. That was the end of our short, uneventful affair. We slept together four, maybe five times.

The other married woman I had an affair with had a happy home life. At least it didn't seem like her family life was lacking anything. She was forty-one then (as I recall), five years older than me. She was petite, with an attractive face, and she was always well dressed. She practiced yoga every other day at a gym and had a flat, toned stomach. She drove a red Mini Cooper, a new car she'd just purchased, and on sunny days I could spot it from a distance, glinting in the sun. She had two daughters, both of whom attended a pricey private school in upscale Shonan, which the woman was a graduate of too. Her husband ran some sort of company, but I never asked her what kind of firm it was. (Naturally I didn't want to know.)

I have no idea why she didn't flatly turn down my brazen sexual overtures. Maybe at the time I had some special magnetism about me that pulled in her spirit as if (so to speak) it were a scrap of iron. Or maybe it had nothing to do with spirit or magnetism, and she'd simply been needing physical satisfaction outside marriage and I just happened to be the closest man around.

Whatever it was, I seemed able to provide it,

openly, naturally, and she commenced sleeping with me without hesitation. The physical aspect of our relationship (not that there was any other aspect) went smoothly. We performed the act in an honest, pure way, the purity almost reaching the level of the abstract. It took me by surprise when I suddenly realized this, in the midst of our affair.

But at some point she must have come to her senses, since one gloomy early-winter morning, she called me and said, "I think we shouldn't meet anymore. There's no future in it." Or something to that effect. She sounded like she was reading from a script.

And she was absolutely right. Not only was there no future in our relationship, there was no real basis for it, no **there** there.

Back when I was in art school I mainly painted abstracts. Abstract art is a hard thing to define, since it covers such a wide range of works. I'm not sure how to explain the form and subject matter, but I guess my definition would be "paintings that are nonfigurative images, done in an unrestrained, free manner." I won a few awards at small exhibitions, and was even featured in some art magazines. Some of my instructors and friends praised my work and encouraged me. Not that anyone pinned his hopes on my future, but I do think I had a fair amount of talent as an artist. Most of my oil paintings were done on very large canvases and required a lot of paint, so they were expensive to create. Needless to say, the possibility of laudable people appearing, ready to purchase an unknown artist's massive painting to hang on the wall at their home, was pretty close to zero.

Since it was impossible to make a living painting what I wanted, once I graduated, I started taking commissions for portraits to make ends meet. Paintings of so-called pillars of society—presidents of companies, influential members of various institutes, Diet members, prominent figures in various locales (there were some differences in the width of these "pillars"), all painted in a figurative way. They were looking for a realistic, dignified, staid style, totally utilitarian types of paintings to be hung on the wall in a reception area or a company president's office. In other words, my job compelled me to paint paintings that ran totally counter to my artistic aims. I could add that I did it **reluctantly,** and that still wouldn't amount to any artistic arrogance on my part.

There was a small company in Yotsuya that specialized in portrait commissions, and through an introduction by one of my art school teachers, I signed an exclusive contract with them. I wasn't paid a fixed salary, but if I turned out enough portraits, I made plenty for a young, single man to live on. It was a modest lifestyle—I was able to rent a small apartment alongside the Seibu Kokubunji railway line, usually managed to afford three meals a day, would buy a bottle of inexpensive wine from time to time, and went out on the occasional date to see a movie. Several years went by, and I decided that I'd focus on portrait painting for a fixed period, and then, once

15

I'd made enough to live on for a while, I'd return to the kind of paintings I really wanted to do. Portraits were just meant to pay the rent. I never planned to paint them forever.

But once I got into it, I discovered that painting **typical** portraits was a pretty easy job. When I was in college I'd worked part-time for a moving company, and at a convenience store, and compared to those jobs, painting portraits was, physically and emotionally, much less of a strain. Once I got the hang of it, it was just a matter of repeating the same process again and again. Before long, I was able to finish a portrait quickly. Like flying a plane on autopilot.

After I'd been rather indifferently doing this work for about a year, I learned that my portraits were gaining some acclaim. My clients were really satisfied with my work. Obviously, if customers complain about the finished portraits, then not much work will come your way, and your contract with the agency might even get terminated. Conversely, if you have a good reputation, you get more work and your fees go up with each painting. The world of portrait painting is a fairly serious profession. I was still a beginner, but I was getting more and more commissions, and could charge higher fees with each work. The agent in charge of my portfolio was impressed, and some of my clients even glowingly commented that I had a "special touch."

I couldn't figure out why the portraits were being received so well. I was less than enthusiastic, just trudging through one assignment after another.

Truthfully, I can't recall the face of a single person whose portrait I painted. Still, as my ultimate goal was to become a serious artist, once I took up my brush and faced a canvas I couldn't bring myself to paint something completely worthless, no matter what type of painting it was. To do so would tarnish my sense of artistry, and show contempt for the kind of professional I was hoping to be. Even if I painted a portrait that I didn't love, at least I never felt embarrassed about the work I'd completed. You could call it professional ethics, I suppose. For me, it was just something I felt compelled to do.

One other aspect of my portrait painting was that I insisted on following my own approach. I never used the actual person as a model. When I got a commission I would meet with the client, just the two us, to talk for an hour or so. I wouldn't do any rough sketches at all. I would ask a lot of questions, and the client would respond. When and where were you born? What kind of family did you grow up in? I asked what kind of childhood they had, what school they attended, what sort of work they did, what kind of family they had now, how they had achieved their present position. Typical questions. I'd ask about their daily life and interests, too. Most people were happy, even enthusiastic, to talk about themselves. (Most likely no one else wanted to hear those things.) Sometimes the hour interview would stretch to two, even three hours. After this I would ask to borrow five or six casual snapshots of the person, just unposed, ordinary snapshots. And occasionally I would use my own small camera and take a few close-ups from different angles. That's it.

Most clients seemed concerned. "Aren't I supposed to sit still and pose for the portrait?" they'd ask. From the outset, they were resigned to enduring a long painting process. Artists—even if no one wore those silly berets anymore—were supposed to stand, brush in hand before the canvas, brow furrowed, as the model sat there, trying to sit up straight. Perfectly still. Clients were imagining the kind of scene they'd seen a million times in movies.

Instead of answering, I would ask them, "Do you want to do it that way? Being a painter's model is hard work if you're not used to it. You have to hold the same pose for a long time, and it's boring and your shoulders will really ache. Of course, if that's how you'd like to do it, I'd be happy to oblige."

Predictably, ninety-nine percent of my clients declined. Most all of them were busy people with busy lives, or else elderly people who had retired. They all preferred, if possible, to avoid such pointless asceticism.

"Meeting you and talking together is all I need," I would say, putting them at ease. "Whether I have a live model or not won't affect the result at all. If you find you're dissatisfied with the painting, I'll be happy to do it over again."

After this I'd spend about two weeks on the portrait (though it would take several months for the paint to fully dry). What I needed was less the actual person in front of me than my vivid memories of that person. (Having the subject present, truth be told, actually interfered with my ability to complete the portrait.) These memories were three-dimensional, and all I had to do was transfer them to canvas. I seem to have been born with that sort of powerful visual memory—a special skill, you might label it—and it was a very effective tool for me as a professional portrait artist.

It was critical to feel a sense of closeness, even just a little, toward the client. That's why during our initial one-hour meeting I tried so hard to discover, as much as I could, some aspects of the client that I could respond to. Naturally, this was easier with some people than with others. There were some I'd never want to have a personal relationship with. But as a **visitor** who was with them for only a short time, in a set place, it wasn't that hard to find one or two appealing qualities. Look deep enough into any person and you will find something shining within. My job was to uncover this and, if the surface is fogged up (which was more often the case), polish it with a cloth to make it shine again. Otherwise the darker side would naturally reveal itself in the portrait.

So, before I knew it, I had become an artist who specialized in portraits. And I became fairly known within this particular, rather narrow field. When I got married, I ended my exclusive contract with the company in Yotsuya, became independent, and—through an agency specializing in the art business—received individual commissions to do portraits for even higher fees. The agent in charge, a capable, ambitious person, was ten years older than me. He encouraged me to be independent and take my work even more seriously. After that point, I painted portraits of numerous people (mostly in the financial and political worlds, celebrities in some cases, though I'd never heard of most of them) and made a decent income. Not that I became a great authority in the field or anything. The world of portraiture is totally different from that of the **artistic** art world. And different from photography too. There are a lot of photographers specializing in portraits who are held in high esteem and whose names are well known, but you don't find that with portrait artists. Very seldom is one of our works seen in the world at large. They aren't featured in art magazines or hung in galleries. Instead they're hung in reception areas somewhere, forgotten, gathering dust. If anyone happens to look at those paintings carefully (someone with time on his hands), they still aren't about to ask about the artist's name.

Occasionally I've thought of myself as a high-priced artistic prostitute. I use all the techniques at my disposal, as conscientiously as I can, in order to satisfy my client. I possess that sort of talent. I'm a professional, but that said, it doesn't mean I mechanically follow a set procedure. I do put a certain amount of feeling into my work. My fees aren't cheap, but my clients all pay without any complaints. The sort of people I take on as clients aren't the kind to worry about price. People learned of my skill through word of mouth, and I had an unending line of clients, my appointment book always jam-packed. But inside me I felt no desire whatsoever. Not a shred.

I hadn't become that sort of artist, or that type of person, because I'd wanted to. Carried along by circumstances, I'd given up doing paintings for myself. I'd married and needed to make a stable income, but that wasn't the only reason. Honestly, I'd already lost the desire to paint for myself. I might have been using marriage as an excuse. I wasn't young anymore, and something—like a flame burning inside me—was steadily fading away. The feeling of that flame warming me from within was receding ever further.

I should have washed my hands of that person I'd become. I should have stood up and done something about it. But I kept putting it off. And before I got around to it, the one who gave up on it all was my wife. I was thirty-six at the time.

2

THEY MIGHT ALL GO
TO THE MOON

I am very sorry, but I don't think I can live with you anymore," my wife said in a quiet voice. Then she was silent for a long while.

This announcement took me by complete surprise. It was so unexpected I didn't know how to respond, and I waited for her to go on. What she'd say next wasn't going to be very upbeat—I was certain about that—but waiting for her to continue was the most I could manage.

We were seated across from each other at the kitchen table. A Sunday afternoon in the middle of March. Our sixth wedding anniversary was the middle of the following month. A cold rain had been falling since morning. The first thing I did when I heard her news was turn toward the window and check out the rain. It was a quiet, gentle rain, with hardly any wind. Still, it was the kind of rain that carried with it a chill that slowly but surely seeped into the skin. Cold like this meant that spring was still a long ways off. The orangish Tokyo Tower was visible through the misty rain. The sky was bereft of birds. All of them must have quietly sought shelter.

"I don't want you to ask me why. Can you do that?" my wife asked.

I shook my head slightly. Neither yes nor no. I had no idea what to say, and just reflexively shook my head.

She had on a thin, light purple sweater with a wide neckline. The soft strap of her white camisole was visible beside her collarbone. It looked like some special kind of pasta used in some specific recipe.

Finally, I was able to speak. "I do have one question, though," I said, gazing blankly at that strap. My voice was stiff, dry, and flat.

"I'll answer, if I can."

"Is this my fault?"

She thought this over. Then, like someone who has been underwater for a long time, she finally broke through to the surface and took a deep, slow breath.

"Not directly, no."

"Not **directly**?"

"I don't think so."

I considered the subtle tone of her voice. Like checking the weight of an egg in my palm. "Meaning that I am, **in**directly?"

She didn't answer.

"A few days ago, just before dawn, I had a dream," she said instead. "A very realistic dream, the kind where you can't distinguish between what is real and what's in your mind. And when I woke up that's what I thought. I was certain of it, I mean. That I can't live with you anymore."

"What kind of dream was it?"

She shook her head. "I'm sorry, but I can't tell you that here."

"Because dreams are personal?"

"I suppose."

"Was I in the dream?" I asked.

"No, you weren't. So in that sense, too, it's not your fault."

Just to make sure I got it all, I summarized what she'd just said. When I don't know what to say I have a habit of summarizing. (A habit that, obviously, can be really irritating.)

"So, a few days ago you had a very realistic dream. And when you woke up you were certain you can't live with me anymore. But you can't tell me what the dream was about, since dreams are personal. Did I get that right?"

She nodded. "Yes. That's about the size of it."

"But that doesn't explain a thing."

She rested her hands on the tabletop, staring down at the inside of her coffee cup, as if an oracle was floating there and she was deciphering the message. From the look in her eyes the words must have been very symbolic and ambiguous.

My wife puts great stock in dreams. She often makes decisions based on dreams she had, or changes her decisions accordingly. But no matter how crucial you think dreams can be, you can't just reduce six years of marriage to nothing because of one vivid dream, no matter how memorable.

"The dream was just a trigger, that's all," she said,

as if reading my mind. "Having that dream made lots of things clear for me."

"If you pull a trigger, a bullet will come out."

"Excuse me?"

"A trigger is a critical part of a gun. 'Just a trigger' isn't the right expression."

She stared at me silently, as if she couldn't understand what I was getting at. I don't blame her. I couldn't understand it myself.

"Are you seeing someone else?" I asked.

She nodded.

"And you're sleeping with him?"

"Yes, and I feel bad about it."

Maybe I should have asked her who it was, and when it had started. But I didn't want to know. I didn't want to think about those things. So I gazed again outside the window at the falling rain. Why hadn't I noticed all this before?

"This was just one element among many," my wife said.

I looked around the room. I'd lived there a long time, and it should have been familiar, but it had now transformed into a scene from a remote, strange land.

Just one element?

What does that mean, just one? I gave it some thought. She was having sex with some man other than me. But that was "just one element." Then what were all the others?

"I'll move out in a few days," my wife said. "So you don't need to do anything. I'm responsible, so I should be the one who leaves."

"You already decided where you're going to go?"

She didn't answer, but seemed to have already decided on a place. She must have made all kinds of preparations before bringing this up with me. When I realized this, I felt helpless, as if I'd lost my footing in the darkness. Things had been steadily moving forward, and I'd been totally oblivious.

"I'll get the divorce procedures going as quickly as I can," my wife said, "and I'd like you to be responsive. I'm being selfish, I know."

I turned from the rain and gazed at her. And once again it struck me. We'd lived under the same roof for six years, yet I knew next to nothing about this woman. In the same way that people stare up at the sky to see the moon every night, yet understand next to nothing about it.

"I have one request," I ventured. "If you'll grant me this, I'll do whatever you say. And I'll sign the divorce papers."

"What is it?"

"That **I'm** the one who leaves here. And I do it today. I'd like you to stay behind."

"Today?" she asked, surprised.

"The sooner the better, right?"

She thought it over. "If that's what you want," she said.

"It is, and that's **all** I want."

Those were my honest feelings. As long as I wasn't left behind alone in this wretched, cruel place, in the cold March rain, I didn't care what happened.

"And I'll take the car with me. Are you okay with that?"

I really didn't need to ask. The car was an old, stick-shift model a friend of mine had let me have for next to nothing back before I got married. It had well over sixty thousand miles on it. And besides, my wife didn't even have a driver's license.

"I'll come back later to get my painting materials and clothes and things. Does that work for you?"

"Sure, that's fine. By 'later,' how much later do you mean?"

"I have no idea," I said. I couldn't wrap my mind around the future. There was barely any ground left under my feet. Just remaining upright was all I could manage.

"I might not stay here all that long," my wife said, sounding reluctant.

"Everyone might go to the moon," I said.

She seemed not to have caught it. "Sorry?"

"Nothing. It's not important."

By seven that evening I'd stuffed my belongings into an oversized gym bag and thrown that into the trunk of my red Peugeot 205. Some changes of clothes, toiletries, a few books and diaries. A simple camping set I had always had for hiking. Sketchbooks and a set of drawing pencils. Other than these few items, I had no idea what else to take. It's okay, I told myself, if I need anything I can buy it somewhere. While I packed the gym bag and went in and out of the apartment, she was still seated at the kitchen table. The coffee cup was still on top of the table, and she continued to stare inside it . . .

"I have a request, too," she said. "Even if we break up like this, can we still be friends?"

I couldn't grasp what she was trying to say. I'd finished tugging on my shoes, had shouldered the bag, and stood, one hand on the doorknob, to stare at her.

"Be friends?"

"I'd like to meet and talk sometimes. If possible, I mean."

I still couldn't understand what she meant. Be friends? Meet and talk sometimes? What would we talk about? It's like she'd posed a riddle. What could she be trying to convey to me? That she didn't have any bad feelings toward me? Was that it?

"I'm not sure about that," I said. I couldn't think of anything more to say. If I'd stood there a whole week, running this through my head, I doubt I'd have found anything more to add. So I opened the door and stepped outside.

When I left the apartment I hadn't given any thought to what I was wearing. If I'd had on a bathrobe over pajamas, I probably wouldn't have noticed. Later on, when I looked at myself in a full-length mirror in a restroom at a drive-in, I saw I had on a sweater that I favored while working, a gaudy orange down jacket, jeans, and work boots. And an old knit cap. There were white paint stains here and there on the frayed, green, round-neck sweater. The only new item I had on were the jeans, their bright blue too conspicuous. A random collection of clothes, but not too peculiar. My one regret was not having brought a scarf.

When I pulled the car out from the parking lot underneath the apartment building, the cold March rain was still falling. The Peugeot's wipers sounded like an old man's raspy, hoarse cough.

I had no clue where to go, so for a while I drove aimlessly around Tokyo. At the intersection at Nishi Azabu, I drove down Gaien Boulevard toward Aoyama, turned right at Aoyama Sanchome toward Akasaka, and after a few more turns found myself in Yotsuya. I stopped at a gas station and filled up the tank. I had them check the oil and tire pressure for me, and top off the windshield washer fluid. I might be in for a very long trip. For all I knew I might even go all the way to the moon.

I paid with my credit card, and headed down the road again. A rainy Sunday night, not much traffic. I switched on an FM station, but it was all pointless chatter, a cacophony of shrill voices. Sheryl Crow's first CD was in the CD player, and I listened to the first three songs and then turned it off.

I suddenly realized I was driving down Mejiro Boulevard. It took a while before I could figure out which direction I was going—from Waseda toward Nerima. The silence got to me and I turned on the CD again and listened to Sheryl Crow for a few more songs. And then switched it off again. The silence was

29

too quiet, the music too noisy. Though silence was preferable, a little. The only thing that reached me was the scrape of the worn-out wipers, the endless hiss of the tires on the wet pavement.

In the midst of that silence I imagined my wife in the arms of another man.

I should have picked up on that, at least, a long time ago. **So how come I didn't think of it?** We hadn't had sex for months. Even when I tried to get her to, she'd come up with all kinds of reasons to turn me down. Actually, I think she'd lost interest in having sex for some time before that. But I'd figured it was just a stage. She must be tired from working every day, and wasn't feeling up to it. But now I knew she was sleeping with another man. When had that started? I searched my memory. Probably four or five months ago, would be my guess. Four or five months ago would make it October or November.

But for the life of me I couldn't recall what had happened back in October or November. I mean, I could barely recall what had happened yesterday.

I paid attention to the road—so as not to run any red lights, or get too close to the car in front of me—and mentally reviewed what had happened last fall. I thought so hard about it that it felt like the core of my brain was going to overheat. My right hand unconsciously changed gears to adjust to the flow of traffic. My left foot stepped on the clutch in time with this. I'd never been so happy that my car was a stick shift. Besides mulling over my wife's affair, it gave me something to do to keep my hands and feet busy.

So what had happened back in October or November?

An autumn evening. I'm picturing my wife on a large bed, and some man undressing her. I thought of the straps on her white camisole. And the pink nipples that lay underneath. I didn't want to visualize all this, but once one image came to me, I couldn't stop. I sighed, and pulled into the parking lot of a drive-in restaurant. I rolled down the driver's-side window, took a deep breath of the damp air outside, and slowly got my heart rate back to normal. I stepped out of the car. With my knit cap on but no umbrella I made my way through the fine drizzle and went inside the restaurant. I sat down in a booth in the back.

The restaurant was nearly empty. A waitress came over and I ordered coffee and a ham-and-cheese sandwich. As I drank the coffee I closed my eyes and calmed down. I tried my best to erase the image of my wife and another man in bed. But the vision wouldn't leave me.

I went to the restroom, gave my hands a good scrub, and checked myself in the mirror over the sink. My eyes looked smaller than usual, and bloodshot, like a woodland animal slowly fading away from famine, gaunt and afraid. I wiped my hands and face with a thick handkerchief, then studied myself in the full-length mirror on the wall. What I saw there was an exhausted thirty-six-year-old man in a shabby, paint-spattered sweater.

As I gazed at my reflection I wondered, **Where am I headed?** Before that, though, the question was

Where have I come to? Where **is** this place? No, before that even I needed to ask, **Who the hell** am I?

As I stared at myself in the mirror, I thought about what it would be like to paint my own portrait. Say I were to try, what sort of self would I end up painting? Would I be able to find even a shred of affection for myself? Would I be able to discover even one thing shining within me?

These questions unanswered, I returned to my seat. When I finished my coffee the waitress came over and refilled my cup. I asked her for a paper bag and put the untouched sandwich in it. I should be hungry later on. But right now I didn't want to eat anything.

I left the drive-in, and drove down the road until I saw the sign for the entrance to the Kan-Etsu Expressway. I decided to get on the highway and head north. I had no idea what lay north, but somehow I got the sense that heading north was better than going south. I wanted to go somewhere cold and clean. More important than north or south, however, was getting away from this city.

I opened the glove compartment and found five or six CDs inside. One of them was a performance of Mendelssohn's Octet by I Musici. My wife liked to listen to it when we went on drives. An unusual setup with a double string quartet, but a beautiful melody. Mendelssohn was only sixteen when he composed the piece. My wife told me this. A child prodigy.

What were you doing when you were sixteen?

I called up the past. When I was sixteen I was crazy over a girl in my class.

Did you go out with her?

No, I barely said a word to her. I just looked at her from a distance. I wasn't brave enough to speak up. When I went home I used to sketch her. I did quite a few drawings.

So you've done the same thing from way back when, my wife said, laughing.

True, I've done the same thing from way back when.

True, I've done the same thing from way back when, I said, mentally repeating the words I'd spoken to her.

I took the Sheryl Crow CD out of the player and slipped in an MJQ album. **Pyramid.** I listened to Milt Jackson's pleasant, bluesy solo as I headed down the highway toward the north. I'd make the occasional stop at a service area, take a long piss, and drink a couple of cups of hot black coffee, but other than that I drove all night. I drove in the slow lane, only speeding up to pass trucks. I didn't feel sleepy, strangely enough. It felt like I'd never be sleepy again in my whole life. And just before dawn I reached the Japan Sea coast.

In Niigata I turned right and drove north along the coast, from Yamagata to Akita Prefecture, then through Aomori into Hokkaido. I didn't take any highways, and drove leisurely down back roads. In all senses of the word I was in no hurry. When night came I'd check in to a cheap business hotel or run-down Japanese inn, flop down on the narrow bed, and sleep. Thankfully I can fall asleep right away just about anywhere, in any type of bed.

On the morning of the second day, near Murakami City, I phoned my agent and told him I wouldn't be able to do any portrait painting for a while. I had a few commissions I was in the middle of, but wasn't in a place where I could do any work.

"That's a problem, since you've already accepted the commissions," the agent said, his tone harsh.

I apologized. "There's nothing I can do about it. Could you tell the clients I got in a car accident or something? There are other artists who could take over, I'm sure."

My agent was silent for a time. Up till now I'd never missed a deadline. He knew how seriously I took my work.

"Something came up, and I'll be away from Tokyo for a while. I'm sorry, but in the meantime I can't do any painting."

"How long is 'for a while'?"

I couldn't answer. I switched off the cell phone, found a nearby river, parked my car on the bridge over it, and tossed that small communication device into the water. I felt sorry toward him, but I had to get him to give up on me. Have him think I'd gone to the moon or something.

In Akita I stopped at a bank, withdrew some cash, and checked my balance. There was still a decent amount in my personal account. Credit card payments were automatically deducted . . . For the time being I had enough to continue my trip. I wasn't using that much each day. Gas money, nights in business hotels, that's about the size of it.

At an outlet store outside Hakodate I purchased a simple tent and a sleeping bag. Hokkaido in early spring was still cold, so I also bought some thermal underwear. Whenever I arrived in a place, I looked for an open campground, set up my tent, and slept there, in order to save money. Hard snow still covered the ground and the nights were cold, but because I'd been spending nights in cramped, stuffy business hotel rooms I felt relieved and free inside the tent. Hard ground below, the endless sky above. Countless stars sparkling in the sky. That and nothing else.

For the next three weeks I wandered all over Hokkaido in my Peugeot. April came, but it looked like the snow wasn't going to melt anytime soon. Still, the color of the sky visibly changed, and plants began to bud. Whenever I ran across a small town with a hot springs I'd stay in an inn there, enjoy the bath, wash my hair and shave, and have a decent meal. Even so, when I weighed myself I found I'd lost eleven pounds.

I didn't read any newspapers or watch TV. My car radio had started acting up from the time I arrived in Hokkaido, and soon I couldn't hear anything on it at all. I had no clue what was happening in the world at large, and didn't care to know. I stopped once in Tomakomai and did laundry at a laundromat. While I waited for the clothes to finish I went to a nearby

35

barbershop and got a haircut and shave. At the shop I saw the NHK news on TV for the first time in a long while. I say "saw," but even with my eyes closed I could hear the announcer's voice, whether I wanted to or not. From start to finish, though, the news had nothing to do with me, like events happening on some other planet. Or else some fake stories somebody had cooked up for the fun of it.

The only news story that hit home was a report on a seventy-three-year-old man in Hokkaido who'd gone mushroom gathering in the mountains and been attacked and killed by a bear. When bears wake from hibernation, the announcer said, they're hungry and irritable and very dangerous. I slept in my tent sometimes, and when the mood struck me I took walks in the woods, so it wouldn't have been strange if I were the one who'd been attacked. It **just happened** to be that old man who got attacked, and not me. But even hearing that news I felt no sympathy for the old man who'd been so cruelly butchered by a bear. No empathy came to me for the pain and fear and shock he must have experienced. I felt more sympathy for the bear. No, "sympathy" isn't the right word, I thought. It's more like a feeling of complicity.

Something's wrong with me, I thought as I stared at myself in the mirror. I said this aloud, in a small voice. It's like something's messed up with my brain. **Better not get near anyone.** For the time being, at least.

Toward the latter half of April I was sick and tired of the cold, so I bid Hokkaido farewell and crossed back over to the mainland. I drove from Aomori to Iwate, from Iwate to Miyagi, along the Pacific coast. The weather got more springlike the farther south I drove. And all the while I thought about my wife. About her, and the anonymous hands caressing her this very moment in bed somewhere. I didn't want to think about it, but I couldn't think of anything else.

The first time I met my wife was just before I turned thirty. She was three years younger than me. She worked in a small architecture firm in Yotsuya, held a second-level architect certificate, and was a former high school classmate of the girl I was dating at the time. She had straight hair, wore little makeup, and had rather calm-looking features (her personality was not all that calm, but I only understood that later on). My girlfriend and I were on a date and happened to run into her at a restaurant. We were introduced, and I basically fell for her right then and there.

She wasn't exactly a standout in terms of looks. There wasn't anything at all wrong with her appearance, but neither was there anything about her that would turn any heads. She had long eyelashes, a thin nose, was on the small side, and her hair, which fell to her shoulder blades, was beautifully styled. (She was very particular about her hair.) On the right side of her full lips was a small mole, which moved in marvelous ways whenever her expression changed. It lent her a slightly sensual air, but again this was only if you paid close attention. Most people would see the girl I was going out with at the time as far more beautiful. But even so, one look was all it took for me to fall for her, like I'd been struck by lightning. Why? I wondered. It took a few weeks for me to figure out the reason. But then it suddenly hit me. She reminded me of my younger sister, who had died. Reminded me very clearly of her.

Not that they looked alike on the outside. If you were to compare photos of the two of them, most people would be hard-pressed to find any resemblance. Which is why at first I didn't see the connection either. It wasn't anything specific about her looks that made me remember my younger sister, but the way her expression changed, especially the way her eyes moved and sparkled, was amazingly like my sister's. It was like magic or something had brought back the past, right before my very eyes.

My sister had also been three years younger than me, and had a congenital heart valve problem. She'd had numerous operations when she was little, and though they were successful, there were lingering aftereffects. Her doctors had no idea if those aftereffects would get better on their own, or cause some life-threatening issues. In the end, she died when I was fifteen. She'd just entered junior high. All her short life she'd battled those genetic defects, but never failed to be anything other than positive and upbeat. Until the very end she never grumbled or complained, and always made detailed plans for the future. That she would die so young was not something she factored into her plans. She was naturally bright, always with outstanding grades (a lot better a child than I was). She had a strong will, and always stuck to whatever she decided to do, no matter what. If she and I ever quarreled—a pretty rare occurrence—I always gave in. At the end she was terribly thin and drawn, yet her eyes remained animated, and she was still full of life.

It was my wife's eyes, too, that drew me to her. **Something** I could see deep in them. When I first saw those eyes, they jolted me. Not that I was thinking that by making her mine I could restore my dead sister or anything. Even if I'd wanted to, I could imagine the only thing that would lead to was despair. What I wanted, or needed, was the spark of that positive will. That definite source of warmth needed to live. It was something I knew very well, but that was, most likely, missing in me.

I managed to get her contact info, and asked her on a date. She was surprised, of course, and hesitated. I was, after all, her friend's boyfriend. But I kept at it. I just want to see you, and talk, I told her. Just meet and talk, that's all. I'm not looking for anything else. We had dinner in a quiet restaurant, and talked about all kinds of things. Our conversation was a little nervous and awkward at first, but then became more animated. There was so much I wanted to know about her, and I had plenty to talk about. I found out that her birthday and my sister's were only three days apart.

"Do you mind if I sketch you?" I asked.

"Right here?" she asked, glancing around. We were seated at the restaurant, and had just ordered dessert.

"I'll finish before they're back with dessert," I said.

"Then I guess I don't mind," she replied doubtfully.

I took out the small sketchbook I always carried with me, and quickly sketched her face with a 2B pencil. As promised, I finished before our desserts arrived. The important part was, of course, her eyes. That's what I wanted to draw most. Back within those eyes there was a deep world, a world beyond time.

I showed her the sketch, and she seemed to like it.

"It's very full of life."

"That's because **you** are," I said.

She gazed for a long time at the sketch, apparently taken with it. As if she were seeing a self she hadn't known before.

"If you like it, I'll give it to you."

"I can have it?" she said.

"Of course. It's just a quick sketch."

"Thank you."

After this we went on more dates, and eventually became lovers. It all happened so naturally. My girl-friend, though, was shocked that her friend stole me away. She was probably thinking that we might get married. So of course she was upset (though I doubt I ever would have married her). My wife, too, was going out with someone else at the time, and their breakup wasn't easy either. There were other obstacles to overcome, but the upshot was that half a year later we were married. We had a small party with a handful of close friends to celebrate, and settled into a condo in Hiroo. Her uncle owned the condo and gave us a good deal on rent. I used one small room as my studio and focused on my portrait work. This was no longer just a temporary job. Now that I was married I needed a steady income, and other than portrait painting I had no means of earning a decent living. My wife commuted from our place by subway to the architecture firm in Yotsuya. And it sort of naturally came about that I was the one who took care of everyday housework, which I didn't mind at all. I never minded doing housework, and found it a nice break from painting. At any rate it was far more pleasant to do housework than commute every day to a job and be forced to do work behind a desk.

I think for both of us our first few years of marriage were calm and fulfilling. Before long we settled into a pleasant daily rhythm. On weekends and holidays I'd take a break from painting and we'd go out. Sometimes to an art exhibition, sometimes hiking outside the city. At other times we'd just wander around town. We had intimate talks, and for both of us it was important to regularly update each other. We spoke honestly, and openly, about what was going on in our lives, exchanging opinions, sharing feelings.

For me, though, there was one thing I never opened up about to her: the fact that her eyes reminded me so much of my sister who'd died at twelve, and that that was the main reason I'd been attracted to her. Without those eyes I probably never would have tried to win her over as eagerly as I did. But I felt it was better not to tell her that, and until the very end I didn't. That was the sole secret I kept from her. What secrets she may have kept from me—and I imagine there were some—I have no idea.

My wife's name was Yuzu, the name of the citrus fruit used in cooking. Sometimes when we were in bed I'd call her Sudachi, a similar type of fruit, as a joke. I'd whisper this in her ear. She'd always laugh, but it upset her all the same.

"I'm not Sudachi, but Yuzu. They're similar but not the same," she'd insist.

When did things start to go south for us? As I drove on, from one roadside restaurant to another, one business hotel to another, randomly moving from point A to point B, I thought about this. But I couldn't pinpoint where things had begun to go wrong. For a long time I was sure we were doing fine. Of course, like many couples, we had some issues and disagreements. Our main issue was whether or not to have children. But we still had time before we had to make a final decision. Other than that one problem (one we could postpone for the time being), we had a basically healthy marriage, on both an emotional and physical level. I was sure of that.

Why had I been so optimistic? Or so stupid? It's like I'd been born with a blind spot, and was always missing something. And what I missed was always the most important thing of all.

In the mornings, after I saw my wife off to work, I'd focus on my painting, then after lunch would take a walk around the neighborhood, do some shopping while I was at it, and then get things ready for dinner. Two or three times a week I'd go swimming in a nearby sports club. When my wife got back we'd have a beer or some wine together. If she called me saying she had to work overtime and would grab something near the office, I'd sit by myself and have a simple dinner alone. Our six years together were mostly a repeat of those kinds of days. And I was basically okay with that.

Things were busy at the architecture firm, and she often had to work overtime. I gradually had to eat dinner alone more often. Sometimes she wouldn't get back until nearly midnight. "Things have gotten so hectic at work," she'd explain. One of her colleagues suddenly changed jobs, she said, and she had to pick up the slack. The firm was reluctant to hire new staff. Whenever she came home late, she was exhausted and would just take a shower and go to sleep. So the number of times we had sex went way down. Sometimes she even had to go in on days off, too, to finish her work. Of course I believed her. There wasn't any reason not to.

But maybe she wasn't working overtime at all. While I was eating dinner alone at home, she may have been enjoying some intimate time in a hotel bed with a new lover.

My wife was outgoing. She seemed quiet and gentle but was sharp and quick-witted, and needed situations where she could be more social and gregarious. And

I wasn't able to provide those. So Yuzu went out to eat a lot with women friends (she had lots of friends) and would go out drinking with work colleagues (she could hold her liquor better than me). And I never complained about her going out on her own and enjoying herself. In fact I might have encouraged it.

When I think about it, my younger sister and I had the same kind of relationship. I've always been more of a stay-at-home type, and when I got back from school I'd hole up in my room to read or draw. My sister was much more sociable and outgoing. So our everyday interests and activities didn't overlap much. But we understood each other well, and valued each other's special qualities. It might have been pretty unusual for an older brother and younger sister the ages we were, but we talked over lots of things together. Summer or winter, we'd climb up to the balcony upstairs where we hung our laundry, and talk forever. We loved to share funny stories, and often had each other in stitches.

I'm not saying that's the reason why, but I felt secure about the relationship my wife and I had. I accepted my role in our marriage—as the silent, auxiliary partner—as natural, self-evident even. But maybe Yuzu didn't. There must have been aspects of our marriage that dissatisfied her. She and my sister were, after all, different people with different personalities. And of course, I wasn't a teenage boy anymore.

.   .   .

By May I was getting tired of driving day after day. And sick of the same thoughts looping endlessly around in my head. The same questions spun around in my brain, with no answers in sight. Sitting all day in the driver's seat had given me a backache, as well. A Peugeot 205 is an economy car, and the seats weren't exactly high quality, the suspension noticeably worn out. All the road glare I'd stared at for hours was giving me chronic eyestrain. I realized I'd been driving pretty much nonstop for over a month and half, restlessly moving from one spot to another as if something were chasing me.

I ran across a small, rustic therapeutic hot springs in the mountains near the border between Miyagi and Iwate, and decided to take a break. An obscure hot springs tucked away deep in a valley, with a small inn that locals would stay in for days to rest and recuperate. The room rate was cheap, and there was a communal kitchen where you could cook simple meals. I enjoyed soaking in the baths and sleeping as much as I wanted. I sprawled on the tatami, read, and recovered from the exhaustion of all that driving. When I got tired of reading I'd take out my sketchbook and draw. It had been a long time since I'd felt like drawing. I started off sketching flowers and trees in the garden, then drew the rabbits they kept there. Just rough pencil sketches, but people were impressed. Some asked me to draw their portraits. Fellow lodgers, and people who worked at the inn. People just passing through my life, people I'd never see again. And if they asked, I'd give them the sketches.

Time to get back to Tokyo, I told myself. Going on like this would get me nowhere. And I wanted to paint again. Not commissioned portraits, or rough sketches, but paintings I could really concentrate on, and undertake for myself. Whether this would work out or not I had no clue, but it was time to take the first step.

I'd planned to drive my Peugeot across the Tohoku region and return to Tokyo, but just before Iwaki, along Highway 6, my car breathed its last. There was a crack in the fuel line and the car wouldn't start. I'd done hardly any maintenance on the car up till then, so I couldn't complain when it gave out. The one lucky thing was that the car gave up the ghost right near a garage where a friendly mechanic worked. It was hard to get parts for an old Peugeot in a place like that, and would take time. Even if we repair it, the mechanic told me, it's likely something else will soon go wrong. The fan belts looked sketchy, the brake pads were ready to go, and the suspension was nearly shot. "My advice? Put it out of its misery," he said. The car had been with me for a month and a half on the road, and now had nearly seventy-five thousand miles on the odometer. It was sad to say goodbye to the Peugeot, but I had to leave it behind. It felt like the car had died in my stead.

To thank him for disposing of the car for me, I gave the mechanic my tent, sleeping bag, and camping equipment. I made one last sketch of the Peugeot, and then, shouldering my gym bag, boarded the Joban Line and went back to Tokyo. From the station I called Masahiko Amada and explained my situation. My marriage fell apart and I went on a trip for a while, I told him, but now I'm back in Tokyo. Do you know of any place I could stay? I asked.

I do know of a good place, he said. It's the house my father lived in for a long time by himself. He's in a nursing home in Izu Kogen, and the house has been unoccupied for a time. It's furnished and has everything you'd need, so you don't have to get anything. It's not exactly a convenient location, but the phone works. If that sounds good, you should try it out.

That's perfect, I told him. I couldn't have asked for more.

And so my new life, in a new place, began.

3

JUST A PHYSICAL REFLECTION

A few days after I'd settled into my new mountain-top house outside Odawara, I got in touch with my wife. I had to call five times before I finally got through. Her job always kept her busy, and apparently she was still getting home late. Or maybe she was with someone. Not that that was my business anymore.

"Where are you now?" Yuzu asked me.

"I've moved into the Amadas' house in Odawara," I said. Briefly I explained how I came to live there.

"I called your cell phone many times," Yuzu said.

"I don't have the cell phone anymore," I said. That phone might have washed into the Japan Sea by then. "I'm calling because I'd like to go pick up the rest of my things. Does that work for you?"

"You still have the key?"

"I do," I said. I'd considered tossing the key into the river, too, but thought better of it since she might want it back. "But you don't mind if I go into the apartment when you're not there?"

"It's your house too. So of course it's okay," she said. "But where have you been all this time?"

Traveling, I told her. I told her how I'd been driving alone, going from one cold place to the next. How the car had finally given out.

"But you're okay, right?"

"I'm alive," I said. "The car was the one that died."

Yuzu was silent for a while. And then she spoke. "I had a dream the other day with you in it."

I didn't ask what kind of dream. I didn't really care to know about me appearing in her dream. She didn't say any more about it.

"I'll leave the key when I go," I said.

"Either way's fine with me. Just do what you like."

"I'll put it in your mailbox when I leave," I said.

There was a short pause before she spoke.

"Do you remember how you sketched my face on our first date?"

"I do."

"I take it out sometimes and look at it. It's really well done. I feel like I'm looking at my real self."

"Your real self?"

"Right."

"But don't you see your face every morning in the mirror?"

"That's different," Yuzu said. "My self in the mirror is just a physical reflection."

After I hung up I went to the bathroom and looked at my face in the mirror. I hadn't looked at myself straight on like that for ages. My self in the mirror is just a physical reflection, she'd said. But to me my face in the mirror looked like a virtual fragment of my self that had been split in two. The self there was the one I **hadn't chosen**. It wasn't even a physical reflection.

·   ·   ·   ·

In the afternoon two days later I drove my Corolla station wagon to the apartment in Hiroo, and gathered my possessions. It had been raining since morning that day, too. The underground parking lot beneath the building had its usual rainy-day odor.

I took the elevator upstairs and unlocked the door, and when I went inside for the first time in nearly two months I felt like an intruder. I'd lived there almost six years and knew every inch of the place. But I no longer was part of this scene. Dishes were stacked up in the kitchen, all dishes she had used. Laundry was drying in the bathroom, all her clothes. Inside the fridge it was all food I'd never seen before. Most were ready-made food. The milk and orange juice were different brands from what I bought. The freezer was packed with frozen food. I never bought frozen food. A lot of changes in the two months I'd been away.

I was struck by a strong urge to wash the dishes stacked up in the sink, bring in the laundry drying and fold it (and iron it if I could), and neatly rearrange the food in the fridge. But I did none of this. This was someone else's house now. I shouldn't poke my nose in where I didn't belong.

My painting materials were the bulkiest possessions I had. I tossed my easel, canvas, brushes, and paints into a large cardboard box. Then turned to my clothes. I've never been one to need a lot of clothes. I don't mind wearing the same clothes all the time. I don't own a suit or necktie. Other than a thick winter coat, it all fit into one suitcase.

A few books I hadn't read yet, and about a dozen CDs. My favorite coffee cup. Swimsuit, and goggles, and swim cap. That was about all I felt I needed. Even those I could get along without if need be.

In the bathroom my toothbrush and shaving kit were still there, as well as my lotion, sunscreen, and hair tonic. An unopened box of condoms, too. But I didn't feel like taking all that miscellaneous stuff to my new place. She could just get rid of it.

I packed my belongings in the trunk of the car, went back to the kitchen, and boiled water in the kettle. I made tea with a tea bag, and sat at the table and drank it. I figured she wouldn't mind. The room was perfectly still. The silence lent a faint weight to the air. As though I were sitting alone, at the bottom of the sea.

All told, I was there by myself in the apartment for about a half hour. No one came to visit, and the phone didn't ring. The thermostat on the fridge turned off once, then turned back on once. In the midst of the silence I perked up my ears, probing what I sensed in the apartment, as if measuring the depths of the ocean with a sinker. No matter how you looked at it, it was an apartment occupied by a woman living alone. Someone busy at work who had next to no time to do any housework. Someone who took care of any errands on the weekends when she had free time. A quick visual sweep of the place showed that everything there was hers. No evidence of anyone else (hardly any evidence of me anymore, either). No man was stopping by here. That's the impression I got. They must have seen each other elsewhere.

I can't explain it well, but while I was in the apartment I felt like I was being watched. Like someone was observing me through a hidden camera. But that couldn't be. My wife is a major klutz when it comes to equipment. She can't even change the batteries in a remote control. No way could she do something as clever as setting up and operating a surveillance camera. It was just me, on edge.

Even so, while I was in the apartment I acted as if every single action of mine was being recorded. I did nothing extra, nothing untoward. I didn't open Yuzu's desk drawer to see what was inside. I knew that in the back of one of the drawers of her wardrobe, where she had her stockings, she kept a small diary and some important letters, but I didn't touch them. I knew the password for her laptop (assuming she hadn't changed it), but didn't even open it. None of this had anything to do with me anymore. I washed the cup I'd drunk tea in, dried it with a cloth, put it back on the shelf, and turned off the lights. I went over to the window and gazed at the falling rain for a while. The orangish Tokyo Tower loomed up faintly in the distance. Then I dropped the key in the mailbox and drove back to Odawara. The trip was only an hour and a half, but it felt like I'd taken a day trip to a far-off foreign land.

·   ·   ·

The next day I called my agent. I'm back in Tokyo, I told him, and I'm really sorry, but I don't plan to do any more portrait painting.

"You're never going to do any more portraits? Is that what you're telling me?"

"Most likely," I said.

He didn't say much. No complaints, nothing in the way of advice. He knew that once I said something, I didn't back down.

"If you ever find yourself wanting to do this work again, call me anytime," he said at the end. "I'd welcome it."

"Thank you," I said.

"Maybe it isn't my place to say this, but how are you planning to make a living?"

"I haven't decided," I admitted. "I'm by myself, so I don't need much to live on, and I've got a bit of savings."

"Will you still paint?"

"Probably. There isn't much else I know how to do."

"I hope it works out."

"Thanks," I said once more. And tagged on a question that had just occurred to me. "Is there anything I should make sure to keep in mind?"

"Something you should make sure to keep in mind?"

"In other words—how should I put it—any advice from a pro?"

He thought it over. "You're the type of guy who

takes longer than other people to be convinced of anything. But long term, I think time is on your side."

Like the title of an old Rolling Stones song.

"One other thing: I think you really have a special talent for portraiture. An intuitive ability to get straight to the heart of the subject. Other people can't do that. Not using that talent would be a real shame."

"But right now painting portraits isn't what I want to do."

"I get that. But someday that ability will help you again. I hope it works out."

Hope it works out, I thought. Good if time is on your side.

On the first day I visited the house in Odawara, Masahiko Amada—the son of the owner—drove me there in his Volvo. "If you like it, you can move in today," he said.

We took the Odawara-Atsugi Road almost to the end and, when we exited, headed toward the mountains along a narrow, paved farm road. On either side, there were fields, rows of hothouses for growing vegetables, and the occasional grove of plum trees. We saw hardly any houses, and not a single traffic signal. Finally we drove up a steep, winding slope in low gear for a long time, until we came to the end and arrived at the entrance to the house. There were two stately pillars at the entrance, but no gate. And no wall, either. It seemed the owner had planned to add a gate and wall but thought better of it. Maybe halfway through he'd realized there was no need. On one of the pillars was a magnificent nameplate with AMADA on it, almost like some business sign. The house beyond was a small Western-style cottage with a faded brick chimney sticking out of the flat roof. It was a one-story house, but the roof was unexpectedly high. In my imagination I'd been taking it for granted that a famous painter of Japanese-style paintings would live in an old Japanese-style dwelling.

We parked in a spacious covered driveway by the front door, and when we opened the car doors some screeching black birds—jays, I imagine—flew off from a nearby tree branch into the sky. They seemed none too happy about us intruding on their space. The house was pretty, surrounded by woods with a variety of trees, with only the west side of the house open to a broad view of the valley.

"What do you think? Not much here, is there?"

I stood there, gazing around me. He was right, there wasn't much there. I was impressed that his father had built a house in such isolated surroundings. He really must have wanted nothing to do with other people.

"Did you grow up here?" I asked.

"No, I've never lived here very long. Just came to stay over occasionally. Or visited on summer holidays when we were escaping the heat. I had school, and grew up in our house in Mejiro with my mother. When my father wasn't working he'd come to Tokyo and live with us. Then come back here and work by himself. I went out on my own, then ten years ago my mother died, and ever since he's been living here by himself. Like someone who's forsaken the world."

A middle-aged woman who lived nearby had been watching the house, and she came over to explain some things I needed to know. How the kitchen operated, how to order more propane and kerosene, where various items were kept, which days the trash was picked up and where to put it. The artist seemed to have led a very simple solitary existence, with very little equipment or appliances, so there wasn't much for a lecture. If there's anything else you need to know, just give me a call, the woman said (though I actually never called her, not even once).

"I'm very happy someone will be living here now," she said. "Empty houses get dilapidated, and they're unsafe. And when they know no one's at home, the wild boar and monkeys get into the yard."

"You do get the occasional wild boar or monkey around here," Masahiko said.

"Be very careful about the wild boars," the woman explained. "You see a lot of them in the spring around here when they root for bamboo shoots. Female boars with young are always jumpy, and dangerous. And you need to watch out for hornets, too. There've been people who've been stung and died. The hornets build nests in the plum groves."

The central feature of the house was a fairly large living room with an open-hearth fireplace. On the southwest side of the living room was a spacious roofed-in terrace, and on the north side was a square studio. The studio was where the master had done his painting. On the east side of the living room was a compact kitchen with dining area, and a bathroom. Then a comfortable master bedroom and a slightly smaller guest bedroom. There was a writing desk in the guest bedroom. Amada seemed to enjoy reading, as the bookshelves were stuffed with old books. He seemed to have used this room as his study. For an older house, it was fairly neat and clean, and comfortable looking, though strangely enough (or perhaps not so strangely) there was not a single painting hanging on the walls. Every wall was completely bare.

As Masahiko had said, the place had most everything I'd need—furniture, electric appliances, plates and dishes, and bedding. "You don't need to bring anything," he'd told me, and he was right. There was plenty of firewood for the fireplace stacked up under the eaves of the shed. There was no TV in the house (Masahiko's father, I was told, hated TV), though there was a wonderful stereo set in the living room. The speakers were huge Tannoy Autographs, the separate amplifier an original vacuum tube Marantz. And he had an extensive collection of vinyl records. At first glance there seemed to be a lot of boxed sets of opera.

"There's no CD player here," Masahiko told me. "He's the sort of person who hates new devices. He only trusts things from the past. And naturally there's not a trace of anything to do with the Internet. If you need to use it, the only choice is to use the Internet café in town."

"I don't have any real need for the Internet," I told him.

"If you want to know what's going on in the world, then the only choice is to listen to the news on the transistor radio on the shelf in the kitchen. Since we're in the mountains the signal isn't great, but you can at least pick up the NHK station in Shizuoka. Better than nothing, I suppose."

"I'm not that interested in what's going on in the world."

"That's fine. Sounds like you and my father would get along fine."

"Is your father a fan of opera?" I asked.

"Yes, he paints Japanese paintings, but always liked to listen to opera while he painted. He went to the opera house a lot when he was a student in Vienna. Do you listen to opera?"

"A little."

"I'm not into it at all. Way too long and boring for me. There are a lot of records, so feel free to listen to them as much as you'd like. My father has no need of them anymore and I know he'd be happy if you listened to them."

"No need of them?"

"His dementia's getting bad. Right now he doesn't know the difference between an opera and a frying pan."

"Vienna, you said? Did he study Japanese painting in Vienna?"

"Nobody's that eccentric—to go all the way to Vienna to study Japanese painting. My father originally worked on Western painting. That's why he went to study in Vienna. At the time he did very cutting-edge modern oil paintings. But after he came back to

Japan he suddenly switched styles, and began painting Japanese-style. Not totally unheard of, I suppose. Going abroad awakens your own ethnic identity or something."

"And he was very successful at it."

Amada made a small shrug. "According to the public he was. But from a child's perspective, he was just a grouchy old man. All he thought about was painting, and did exactly as he pleased. No trace of that now, though."

"How old is he?"

"Ninety-two. When he was young he was apparently pretty wild. I never heard the details."

I thanked him. "Thank you for everything. I'm really grateful. This really helps me out."

"You like it here?"

"Yes, I'm really happy you're letting me stay."

"I'm glad. Though I'm hoping you and Yuzu can get back together again."

I didn't respond. Masahiko himself wasn't married. I'd heard a rumor he was bisexual, though I didn't know if it was true or not. We'd known each other for a long time, but had never spoken about it.

"Are you going to keep doing portraits?" Amada asked as we were leaving.

I explained how I'd made a clean break with portrait painting.

"Then how are you going to make a living?" Amada asked, the same thing my agent had wanted to know.

I'll cut back on expenses and get by on my savings for a while, I replied, echoing my first answer. I also wanted to try painting whatever I wanted, something I hadn't been able to do for ages.

"Sounds good," Amada said. "Do what you like for a while. But would you consider teaching art part time too? There's this arts-and-culture center near Odawara Station and they have painting classes. Most of them are for children, but they have some community art classes for adults set up as well. They teach sketching and watercolor, but not oil painting. The man who runs the school knows my father, he's not really in it for the money. And he needs a teacher. I'm sure he'd be overjoyed if you'd help out. It doesn't pay much, but you could make a little extra to live on. You'd only need to teach twice a week, and it shouldn't be too much trouble."

"But I've never taught painting, and don't know much about watercolors."

"It's simple," he said. "You're not training professionals. You just teach the basics. You'll pick it up in a day. Teaching children should be good for you, too. And if you're going to live up here all by yourself, you have to get down off the mountain a couple of times a week and be with other people, even if you don't want to, or else you'll go a little stir-crazy. Don't want you ending up like **The Shining**."

Masahiko screwed up his face like Jack Nicholson. He's always been good at impressions.

I laughed. "I'll give it a try. Whether I'll do a good job or not, I don't know."

"I'll get in touch with him and let him know," he said.

Then Masahiko drove me to the used Toyota dealership next to the highway, where I paid cash for the Corolla station wagon. My life alone on a mountaintop in Odawara began that day. I'd been on the move for nearly two months, but now I'd take up a sedentary life. It was quite a switch.

Starting the following week, I began teaching art classes on Wednesdays and Fridays at the arts-and-culture center near Odawara Station. There was a perfunctory interview beforehand, but Masahiko's introduction meant that I was as good as hired already. I was to teach two classes for adults, plus one for children on Fridays. I quickly got used to teaching the kids. I enjoyed seeing the paintings they did, and, as Masahiko said, it was a good stimulus for me as well. I quickly got to be friends with the children. All I did was go around the room, check on the paintings they did, give them a few words of technical advice, find good points about their paintings, and praise and encourage them. My approach was to have them paint the same subject matter several times, to instill in them the idea that the same object could appear quite different if viewed from a different angle. Just as people had many facets, so too did objects. The kids immediately picked up on how fascinating this could be.

Teaching adults was a bit more of a challenge. The students were either elderly retirees, or housewives whose children were grown and in school, and had time on their hands. As you might imagine, they weren't as adaptable as the kids, and when I pointed out something, they didn't easily accept my suggestions. A few of them, though, were willing to learn, and there were a couple who did some pretty appealing paintings. Whenever they asked, I gave them helpful pointers, but for the most part I let them paint however they liked. I confined myself to praising them whenever I found something nice about what they'd done. That seemed to please them. I figured it was enough for them to simply enjoy painting.

And I started sleeping with two housewives, both of whom attended the art classes and received my so-called instruction. Both my students, in other words, and incidentally both fairly decent painters. It's hard for me to tell whether that was something permissible for a teacher—even a casual teacher like me with no proper license. I basically think mutually consenting adults having sex isn't a problem, though certainly society might frown at this kind of relationship.

I'm not trying to excuse my actions, but at the time I really didn't have the mental wherewithal to decide whether I was right or wrong. I was desperately clinging to a scrap of wood that had been swept away. In pitch-black darkness, not a single star, or the moon, visible in the sky. As long as I clung to that piece of wood I wouldn't drown, but I had no clue where I was, where I was heading.

It was a couple of months after I'd moved there that I discovered Tomohiko Amada's painting **Killing Commendatore**. I couldn't know it at the time, but that one painting changed my world forever.

4

FROM A DISTANCE, MOST THINGS LOOK BEAUTIFUL

One sunny morning near the end of May I carried all my painting materials into the studio Mr. Amada had been using, and for the first time in what seemed like forever stood before a brand-new canvas. (Nothing of the master's painting materials was left in the studio. I assume that Masahiko had packed them all away somewhere.) The studio was a large, square room sixteen feet on a side, with a wood floor and white walls. The floor was bare wood, with not a single rug. There was a large open window on the north side, with simple white curtains. The window on the east side was smaller, with no curtains. As elsewhere in the house, there was nothing hanging on the walls. In one corner of the room was a large porcelain sink for washing away paint. The sink must have been in long use, for its surface was dyed with a mix of different colors. Next to the sink was an old-fashioned kerosene stove, and there was a large ceiling fan. A worktable and a round wooden stool. A compact stereo set was on a built-in shelf so he could listen to opera while painting. The wind blowing in the open window carried with it the fresh fragrance of trees. This was, without doubt, a space for an artist to focus on his work. Everything you might need was here, and not one thing extra.

Now that I had this environment to work in, the feeling of **wanting to paint something** grew stronger, like a quiet ache. And there were no limits on the amount of time I could spend for myself. No need any longer to paint things I didn't want to in order to earn a living, no more obligation to prepare dinner for my wife when she came home. (Not that I minded making dinner, though that didn't change the fact that it was an obligation.) And it wasn't just preparing meals—I had the right to stop eating altogether and starve if I felt like it. I was utterly free to do exactly what I wanted, without worrying about anybody else.

In the end, though, I couldn't paint a thing. No matter how long I stood in front of the canvas and stared at that white, blank space, not a single idea of what to paint came to me. I had no clue where to begin, how to start. Like a novelist who has lost words, or a musician who has lost his instrument, I stood there in that bare, square studio, at a complete loss.

I'd never felt that way before, not ever. Once I faced a canvas, my mind would immediately leave the horizon of the everyday, and **something** would well up in my imagination. Sometimes it would be a productive image, at other times a useless illusion. But still, something would always come to me. From there, I'd latch onto it, transfer it to the canvas, and continue to develop it, letting my intuition lead the way. If I did it that way, the work completed itself.

But now I couldn't see **anything** that would provide the initial spark. You can have all the desire and ache inside you want, but what you really need is a concrete starting point.

I would get up early in the morning (I generally always wake before six), brew coffee in the kitchen, and then, mug in hand, pad off to the studio and sit on the stool in front of the canvas. And focus my feelings. Listen closely to the echoes in my heart, trying to grasp the image of something that had to be there. But this always ended in a fruitless retreat. I'd try concentrating for a while, then plunk down on the studio floor, lean back against the wall, and listen to a Puccini opera. (I'm not sure why, but all I seemed to listen to then was Puccini.) **Turandot**, **La Bohème**. I'd sit there, staring at the languidly rotating ceiling fan, waiting for an idea or motif to come to me. But nothing ever came. Just the early-summer sun that rose sluggishly in the sky.

What was the problem? Maybe it's because I'd spent so many years doing portraits for a living. Maybe that diminished any natural intuition I had. Like sand slowly washed away by the tide. Somehow the flow of my life had gone off in the wrong direction. I needed time, I thought. I had to be patient. **Make time be on my side.** Do that, and I was sure to seize the right flow. That channel would surely come back to me. Truthfully, though, I wasn't sure it ever would.

It was during this period, too, that I slept with the two married women. I think I was looking for some kind of inner breakthrough. Come what may, I wanted to break out of the rut I was in, and the only way for me to do so was to jolt my psyche, give it a prod (it didn't matter what kind). Plus I'd started to tire of being alone. And it had been a long time since I'd slept with a woman.

It occurs to me now that my days back then were pretty strange. I'd wake up early, go into that small square, white-walled studio, have no ideas for what to paint as I stared at the blank canvas, then flop down on the floor and listen to Puccini. When it came to the realm of creativity, I was basically facing a pure nothingness. When Claude Debussy had writer's block while composing an opera, he wrote, "Day after day I produce **rien**—nothingness." That summer was the same for me—day after day I took part in **producing nothingness**. Perhaps I was quite used to facing nothingness day after day—though I wouldn't go so far as to say we were intimate.

About twice a week in the afternoon, the second of the married women would drive to my place in her red Mini. We'd go straight to bed and make love. In the early afternoon we'd devour each other's flesh. What this produced was, of course, not nothingness. No doubt about it, actual flesh-and-blood bodies were involved. Bodies you could actually touch with your hands, every inch, even run your lips over them. In this way, as if I'd flipped a switch on my consciousness, I began moving between an ambiguous, vague **rien** and a vivid, living reality. The woman said her husband hadn't made love to her in nearly two years. He was ten years older than she was, and busy with work, never returning home until late at night. She tried many ways of enticing him, but nothing seemed to rouse his interest.

"I wonder why. I mean, you have such a lovely body," I said.

She gave a small shrug. "We've been married over fifteen years and have two kids. I guess I'm no longer as fresh as I used to be."

"You seem plenty fresh to me."

"Thanks. Though that makes it sound like I'm being recycled or something."

"Like recycling resources?"

"Exactly."

"It's a very precious resource, though," I said. "Contributes to society, too."

She giggled. "As long as you sort everything correctly."

A little while later, we eagerly set out to sort out resources once more.

Truthfully I wasn't all that drawn to her as a person at first. In that sense there was a different tone about our relationship than with the women I'd dated. She and I had almost nothing in common to talk about. There was hardly anything about our present lives, or our personal histories until then, that overlapped. I'm not generally a talkative person, so when we were together, she did most of the talking. She'd tell me personal things and I'd make the appropriate responses, giving my feedback, I guess you'd call it, though it was hardly a real conversation.

This was a first for me. With other women, I'd always been attracted to their personalities. Physical relationships came later, something that accompanied the initial appeal . . . That was the usual pattern. But not with her. With her the physical came first. Not that I'm complaining. When I was with her I could enjoy the act in a pure, unfettered way. And I think she could, too. She came many times as we made love, and I came many times too.

She told me this was the first time since she got married that she'd slept with another man. I had no reason to doubt her. And for me, too, this was the first time I'd slept with another woman since I got married. (No, actually there was one exception, when I shared a bed with another woman. Not that it was something I was looking for. I'll get into that later on.)

"But my friends the same age, all of them are married but most of them are having affairs," she said. "They talk about it a lot."

"Recycling," I said.

"I never imagined I'd join them."

I gazed up at the ceiling and thought about Yuzu. Was she off somewhere, in bed with somebody?

After the woman left, I felt at loose ends. The bed still showed the hollows where she had lain. I didn't feel like doing anything, so I lay out on a lounge chair on the terrace and killed time reading a book. All the books on Mr. Amada's bookshelf were old, among them a few unusual novels that would be hard to get hold of these days. Works that in the past had been pretty popular but had been forgotten, read by no one. I enjoyed reading this kind of out-of-date novel. Doing so let me share—with this old man I'd never met—the feeling of being left behind by time.

As the sun set, I opened a bottle of wine (drinking wine was my one and only luxury at the time, though of course this was inexpensive wine) and listened to some old LPs. The record collection was comprised entirely of classical music, the majority of which was opera and chamber music. All of them looked like they'd been lovingly cared for, without a single scratch. During the day I listened to opera, while at night I favored Beethoven and Schubert string quartets.

Having a relationship with that older married woman, being able to hold a real live woman in my arms regularly, brought me a certain level of calm. The soft touch of a mature woman's skin eased the pent-up emotions I'd had. At the very least, while I made love to her I was able to shelve the doubts and problems I'd been carrying around. Yet I still wasn't able to come up with an idea of what to paint. Occasionally in bed I'd do a pencil sketch of her in the nude. Most of these were pornographic. Pictures of my cock inside her, or her sucking me off. The sketches made her blush, but she enjoyed looking at them. I imagine that if these had been photos most women wouldn't have liked them, and would even have been disgusted with the man who made them, and on their guard. But I found that with rough sketches, if they were done well, women were actually happy to see them. Because they had the warmth of life in them—or, at least, they didn't have a mechanical coldness. But still, no matter how well I managed these sketches, not even a fragment of an image of what I really wanted to paint came to me.

The kind of paintings I did as a student, so-called abstracts, no longer appealed to me. My heart wasn't drawn to them anymore. Looking back on it now, I see that what I'd been wrapped up in back then was nothing more than the pursuit of form. Back when I was young, I was completely drawn to the beauty of form, and to balance. Nothing wrong with that. But in my case I didn't reach the soulful depth that should lie beyond. Now I see it very clearly, but at the time, all I could grasp was the **appeal** of shape at a superficial level. Nothing really moved me. My paintings were **smart** but nothing more.

And now I was thirty-six. Forty was just around the corner. I felt that by the time I turned forty, I'd have to secure my own unique artistic world. Forty was a sort of watershed for people. Once you get past that age, you can't keep going on as you were before.

I still had four years to go, but I knew that those four years might flash by in an instant. Painting portraits for a living had taken me on a wide detour. Somehow I had to get time on my side once again.

While I lived in that house in the mountains I found myself wanting to know more about Tomohiko Amada. I'd never been interested in Japanese-style painting, and though I'd heard the name Tomohiko Amada, and he happened to be my friend's father, I had no idea what kind of person he was, or what kind of paintings he did. He might be a heavyweight in the world of Japanese painting, but he had totally stayed out of the limelight, turning his back on his worldly renown, and alone, quietly—or one might say stubbornly—focused on creating his art. This was about the extent of what I knew about him.

But as I listened to his record collection on the stereo he'd left behind, borrowed his books, slept in his bed, made meals every day in his kitchen, and used his studio, I gradually became more interested in Tomohiko Amada as a person. Something close to curiosity, you could say. The path he'd taken aroused my interest—the way he'd been focused on modernist painting, traveled all the way to Vienna to study, then after returning to Japan made a sudden return to Japanese-style painting. I didn't know the details, but in general you would think that it couldn't have been very easy for someone who'd done Western painting for so long to shift over to Japanese-style painting. You'd need to decide to abandon all the techniques you'd spent so much time and effort mastering, and begin again from zero. Despite this, Tomohiko Amada had chosen that arduous path. There must have been a compelling reason.

One day, before my art class, I went to the Odawara city library to search out collections of Tomohiko Amada's artwork. Probably because he was an artist living in the area, the library had three beautiful volumes of his work. One of them included some of the Western paintings he'd done in his twenties as reference material. What surprised me was that the series of Western-style paintings he'd done as a young man reminded me somewhat of the abstract paintings I'd done myself in the past. The style wasn't specifically the same (in the prewar period he'd been heavily influenced by Cubism), yet his stance of "greedily pursuing form" in no small way had something in common with my own approach. As you might expect from someone who went on to become a first-class artist, his paintings also had much more depth and persuasive power than mine. Technically, too, there were things about them that were, simply, astounding. I imagine they must have been highly acclaimed at the time. Still, there was **something missing**.

I sat there in the reading room at the library and carefully examined his works for a long time. So what was it that was lacking from his work? I couldn't pinpoint it. But if I had to give an opinion, I'd say they were paintings that **weren't really necessary**. The kind of paintings that, if they disappeared somewhere forever, wouldn't put anybody out. A cruel way of putting it, perhaps, but it's the truth. From the present perspective, some seventy years on, I could see that quite well.

I turned the pages and followed along, in chronological order, to see how he shifted gears to become a painter of Japanese-style art. In his early period these works were still a bit awkward, imitating the methods of previous artists, but then gradually, and undeniably, he discovered his own unique style. I could see how it progressed. A bit of trial and error at times, but no hesitation. After he took up painting Japanese-style art, his works all had something unique that only he could paint, and he himself was well aware of this. He always strode confidently toward the core of that special **something**. No more did you get the impression, as with his Western paintings, of something missing. It was less a shift and more akin to a conversion.

Like most artists of Japanese-style paintings, at first Tomohiko Amada painted realistic scenery and flowers, but eventually (and there must have been some motive for this) he began painting scenes from ancient Japan. Some were themes from the Heian and Kamakura periods, but what he was most fond of was the Asuka period at the beginning of the seventh century, specifically the period when Prince Shotoku Taishi, the legendary regent, was alive . . . On his canvases he boldly, minutely, reproduced the scenery, historical events, and lives of the people of that period. Naturally he had never witnessed those scenes in reality with his own eyes. But with his inner eye he **saw** them, clearly and vividly. Why he chose the Asuka period, I have no idea. But that became his own special period, done in an inimitable style. And with the passage of time his technique in painting Japanese-style paintings became even more refined.

If you pay close attention you can see that from a certain point on he painted exactly what he wanted to paint. From then on his brush seemed to freely leap across the canvas. The wonderful part about his paintings was the use of blank space. Paradoxically, the best part was what was **not** depicted. By not painting certain things he clearly accentuated what he **did** want to paint. This is undoubtedly one of the areas that Japanese painting excels at. At least I'd never seen such bold use of blank space in any Western paintings. Seeing this, I could somehow understand why Tomohiko Amada converted to painting Japanese art. But what I didn't understand was exactly when and how he made that daring conversion and put it into practice.

According to his brief biography at the end of the book, he was born in the mountainous Aso district in Kumamoto. His father was a great landowner, an influential local figure, and his family was quite affluent. He was always artistically talented and distinguished himself while still quite young. He graduated from the Tokyo Fine Arts School (later Tokyo University of the Arts), and with great expectations for his career studied abroad in Vienna from the end of 1936 to 1939. At the beginning of 1939, before World War Two began, he boarded a passenger ship from Bremen and returned to Japan. Hitler was in power during this time. Austria was annexed by Germany, the so-called **Anschluss** taking place in March 1938. And the young Tomohiko Amada was right there in Vienna in the midst of this turbulent period. He must have witnessed a number of historical events at that time.

So what happened to him then?

I read through a long essay in one of the collections titled "Theory of Tomohiko Amada," only to find that almost nothing was known about his time in Vienna. The essay went into great detail about his career as a painter of Japanese-style paintings after he returned to Japan, yet there was only vague, baseless speculation about the motives and details of the conversion he must have experienced during his time in Vienna. What he had done in Vienna, and what had led him to his dramatic conversion, remained a mystery.

Tomohiko Amada returned to Japan in February 1939, and settled into a rented house in Sendagi in Tokyo. By this point he had completely abandoned Western painting. But he still received an allowance every month from his family, so he wanted for nothing. His mother, in particular, doted on her son. During this period he was, apparently, studying Japanese-style painting on his own. A number of times he tried to have established painters take him under their wing, but it never worked out. Tomohiko was, from the first, not exactly the humblest of people. Maintaining calm, friendly ties with others was not his forte. Isolation from others was a leitmotif that ran through his entire life.

With the attack on Pearl Harbor in 1941, Japan entered an all-out war, and Amada left turbulent Tokyo and moved back to his parents' home in Aso. As the second son, he avoided all the problems involved in succeeding to his father's estate, and was given a small house with a maid, and lived a quiet life there pretty much isolated from the war. For better or worse, he had a congenital lung defect and thus there was no worry he would be drafted. (Though this could have been the excuse they used for the public, and his family may have worked behind the scenes to make sure he didn't have to be a soldier.) He also avoided the severe food shortages and near starvation that plagued most Japanese citizens at the time. Living deep in the mountains of rural Japan, unless some major mistake was made he could also be pretty certain that no U.S. planes would be dropping any bombs on them. So until the surrender in 1945 he lived, holed up alone, deep in the mountains of Aso. His ties with society were severed, and he devoted himself entirely to mastering the techniques of Japanese-style painting. He didn't display a single work during this time.

For Tomohiko Amada, after being in the spotlight as a promising painter of Western art, and then going to study in Vienna, it must have been a trying experience to maintain total silence for over six years, forgotten by the art world. But he was not the type to easily lose heart. When the long war was finally over, and as people struggled to recover from the chaos, a reborn Tomohiko Amada debuted again, this time as an up-and-coming painter in the Japanese style. One by one he displayed the works he'd completed during the war. This was the period when most artists, having painted stirring propaganda pieces, were forced to take responsibility for their actions and, under the watchful eye of the Occupation, were fairly compelled into retirement. Which is precisely why Tomohiko's works, revealing the possibility of a revolution in Japanese painting, garnered so much attention. The times, one could say, were his ally.

There was little to say of his career after this time. Once an artist is successful, his life is often quite boring. Of course there are some artists who, once they are successful, head straight toward a colorful downfall, but Tomohiko Amada wasn't one of them. He won countless awards over the years (though he turned down the Order of Cultural Merit award from the government, claiming it would be "distracting") and became very famous. Over the years the price for his works rose, and most were displayed in public exhibitions. There was no end to the number of commissions, and he gained a high reputation abroad, too. Smooth sailing all around. The artist himself, though, avoided center stage, and turned down any official positions. He also refused any invitations, domestic or international. Instead he stayed holed up alone in the mountaintop house in Odawara (the house I was now living in) painting whatever he liked.

Now he was ninety-two and in a nursing home in Izu Kogen, and no longer knew the difference between an opera and a frying pan.

I shut the book of paintings and returned it to the library counter.

When the weather was good I liked to lie on a lounge chair out on the terrace after dinner and enjoy a glass of white wine. And as I gazed at the twinkling stars to the south, I would consider what lessons I might draw from Tomohiko Amada's life. Naturally there should be a few lessons I should learn. The courage not to fear a change in one's lifestyle, the importance of having time on your side. And above all, discovering your own uniquely creative style and themes. Not an easy thing, of course. Though if you make a living creating things, it's something you have to accomplish no matter what. If possible, before you turn forty . . .

But what kind of experiences did Tomohiko Amada have in Vienna? What scenes did he witness? And most of all, what exactly made him decide to lay down his oil paintbrush forever? I pictured red-and-black Nazi swastika flags fluttering over a street in Vienna, a young Tomohiko Amada walking down that street. For some reason the season is winter. He has on a thick coat, a scarf, and a cloth cap pulled down low. His face isn't visible. A streetcar rounds the corner and approaches in the newly falling sleet. As he walks, he exhales white breath into the air like the very embodiment of silence. The Viennese are in warm cafés, sipping coffee with a spot of rum.

I tried visualizing his later paintings of Japanese scenes in the Asuka period overlapping with this old Viennese street scene. But my imagination was unequal to the task, and I couldn't discover any similarities between the two.

My terrace faced the narrow valley to the west, and across the way was a range of mountains about the same height as mine. And on the slopes of those mountains were a number of houses with generous space separating them, surrounded by lush greenery. To the right, diagonally across from the house I was living in, was a particularly striking modern-style house. The mountaintop house, built of white concrete and plenty of bluish tinted glass, was so elegant and luxurious the word "mansion" seemed a better term. It was built in three levels that ran along the slope. Most likely some first-rate architect had designed it. There are lots of summer homes in this area, but someone seemed to live in this house all year long, with lights on behind the windows every night. Of course it could be that the lights were on timers as a safety precaution. But I gathered otherwise, since the lights came on and turned off at different times, depending on the day. Sometimes all the lights were on at once and the windows were lit like brilliant window displays on a main street, while at other times the whole house sank back into darkness, the only light a faint glow from lanterns in the yard.

Sometimes a person would appear on the deck that faced my direction (the one that resembled the top deck of an ocean liner). At twilight I would often see the figure of whoever lived there. I couldn't tell if it was a man or a woman. The silhouette was small and usually backlit and in shadow. But from the outline of the silhouette, and the movements, my guess was that it was a man. And this person was always alone. Perhaps he didn't have any family.

What kind of person lived in a place like that? In spare moments I tried to imagine. Did this person really live all by himself on this out-of-the-way mountaintop? What sort of work did he do? No doubt his life in that chic, glass-enclosed mansion was one of luxury and ease. He couldn't be commuting every day to Tokyo from such an inconvenient spot. He must be living a life free of worries. But viewed from his perspective, looking at me from his side of the valley, I might appear to also be living a life of ease and leisure. From a distance, most things look beautiful.

That evening the figure appeared again. Like me, he sat, barely moving, in a chair out on the deck. As if he too was gazing at the twinkling stars, mulling over something. Thinking, no doubt, about things for which there was no answer, no matter how hard you thought about them. At least that's how he looked to me. Everybody has something they speculate and wonder about, no matter how blessed their circumstances. I raised my wineglass a couple of inches, a secret gesture of solidarity to this person across the valley.

Naturally at the time I never imagined that this person would soon enter my life and change its direction entirely. Without him, none of the events that happened to me would have ever taken place. At the same time, if he hadn't been there I might very well have lost my life in the darkness, with no one ever the wiser.

Our lives really **do** seem strange and mysterious when you look back on them. Filled with unbelievably bizarre coincidences and unpredictable, zigzagging developments. While they are unfolding, it's hard to see anything weird about them, no matter how closely you pay attention to your surroundings. In the midst of the everyday, these things may strike you as simply ordinary things, a matter of course. They might not be logical, but time has to pass before you can see if something is logical.

Generally speaking, whether something is logical or isn't, what's meaningful about it are the effects. Effects are there for anyone to see, and can have a real influence. But pinpointing the cause that produced the effect isn't easy. It's even harder to show people something concrete that caused it, in a "Look, see?" kind of way. Of course there is a cause somewhere. Can't be an effect without a cause. You can't make an omelet without breaking some eggs. Like falling dominoes, one domino (cause) knocks over the adjacent domino (cause), which then knocks over the domino (cause) next to it. As this sequence continues on and on, you no longer know what was the original cause. Maybe it doesn't matter. Or people don't care to know. And the story comes down to "What happened was, a lot of dominoes fell over." The story I'll be telling here may very well follow a similar route.

In any case, the first things I want to describe— the first two dominoes I have to bring up, in other words—are the mysterious neighbor who lived on the mountaintop across the valley, and the painting titled **Killing Commendatore**. I'll start with the painting.

5

HE HAS STOPPED BREATHING ...
HIS LIMBS ARE COLD

The first thing I found odd after I moved into the house was the utter lack of any paintings. Not only were none hanging on the walls, but there wasn't a single painting of any kind even stuffed away in a shed or closet. No paintings by Tomohiko Amada, but none by any other artists either. Every wall was bare, with no traces even of nails that might have once been used to hang paintings. Artists almost always had at least some paintings around them—their own paintings, or those by other artists. Before they knew what had hit them, they'd be surrounded by all kinds of paintings, like when you endlessly shovel the snow but it keeps on piling up.

Once when I called Masahiko about something else, I happened to raise the topic. How come there's not a painting of any kind in this house? Did somebody take them away, or there weren't any to begin with?

"My father didn't like keeping his own paintings around," Masahiko said. "He'd call up his art dealers when he finished a work and leave it with them. If he wasn't happy with a painting, he burned it in the incinerator in the yard. So it's not so strange that there's not a single one of his paintings there."

"He didn't own any paintings by other artists either?"

"He owned a handful. An old Matisse or Braque and the like. All of them small paintings he bought in Europe before the war. He got them from acquaintances, and they weren't so expensive at the time. Now, of course, they would bring a hefty price. When he went into the nursing home I took all those paintings to an art dealer I know and let him handle them. Can't leave them sitting there in an empty house now, can I? I imagine they're in a special air-conditioned art storage warehouse. Apart from those, I've never seen any other artists' works in the house. To tell the truth, my father didn't much like other artists. And they didn't like him either. A lone wolf, you might call him, or if we're not being nice about it, a misfit."

"Your father was in Vienna from 1936 to 1939, wasn't he?"

"Right, he was there for about two years. I don't know why he chose Vienna, since the artists he liked were mainly French."

"And then he returned to Japan and suddenly switched to Japanese-style paintings," I said. "Why do you think he made such a monumental decision? Did something unusual happen while he was abroad?"

"Hmm. It's a mystery. My father never spoke much about his time in Vienna. Occasionally he'd talk about things nobody cared about—the Vienna zoo, or food, or the opera house. But when it came to talking about himself, he was a man of few words. And I never dared to ask him. We mostly lived apart, and rarely saw each other. He was less like a father to me than an uncle who came to visit every once in a while. When I got to junior high he seemed even more annoying, and I avoided contact with him. When I went into the art institute, too, I never consulted him about it. It's not like our family was complicated, though it wasn't exactly a normal family either. You get the general idea?"

"I do."

"Anyway, my father's memories of the past are all gone now. Or have sunk away into deep mud. He won't answer you, no matter what you ask. He doesn't even know who I am. Probably doesn't even know who **he** is. Sometimes I think I should have asked all kinds of things before he got this way. Well, it's too late now."

Masahiko was silent for a time, lost in thought. "Why do you want to know that?" he finally asked. "Did something spark an interest in him?"

"Not particularly," I said. "It's just that, living in this house, I sense something like your father's shadow lurking about. I also did a little research into his life at the library."

"My father's shadow?"

"Like a reminder of his existence, maybe."

"Don't you find that a little creepy?"

Over the phone I shook my head. "No. Not at all. It's just like the presence of Tomohiko Amada is still hovering over things. Like it's in the air."

Masahiko was lost in thought again. "My father lived in that house for a long time, and did a lot of work there," he said, "so maybe his presence remains. Who knows? To tell the truth, that's why I don't want to go near the place."

I listened without comment.

"Like I said before," he went on, "to me, Tomohiko Amada was basically just a grouchy old man I knew. Always holed up in his studio, painting, with a sour look on his face. He didn't talk much, so I had no idea what was on his mind. When we were under the same roof my mom always told me, 'Don't bother your father when he's working.' I couldn't run around or yell or anything. The world saw him as a famous artist, but to a little kid, he was simply a pain. Plus when I decided to go into art myself, having him as a father was a burden. Every time I introduced myself people would ask if I was related to Tomohiko Amada. I even thought about changing my name. I realize now he wasn't such a bad person, really. I suppose he showed me affection in his own way. Though he wasn't the type to show unconditional love toward a child. But that can't be helped. Painting was always his top priority. That's what artists are like."

"I suppose so," I said.

"I could never be an artist," Masahiko said with a sigh. "That might be the only thing I learned from my father."

"Didn't you tell me before that when he was young he was pretty wild and did whatever he liked?"

"By the time I was big, he wasn't like that anymore,

but when he was young he played around a lot apparently. He was tall, good-looking, a young guy from a wealthy family, and a talented painter. How could women not be drawn to him? And he was certainly fond of the ladies. Rumor is that he had some affairs that his family had to pay to clear up. But my relatives said that after he returned from his time abroad, he was a different person."

"A different person?"

"After he returned to Japan, he didn't play around anymore, and just stayed at home focusing on his painting. And he didn't socialize anymore. After he got back to Tokyo he was a bachelor for a long time, but once he could earn a good living painting, like the idea had just occurred to him, he suddenly and unexpectedly married a distant relative back home. For all the world like he was balancing the account book of his life or something. It was a late marriage for him. And then I was born. I have no clue if he ever played around with other women after he got married. Though I can say that he no longer made a show of having a good time."

"Quite a change."

"His parents were really happy, though, at how he'd changed. No more messy affairs for them to clean up. But none of our relatives could tell me what had happened to him in Vienna, or why he rejected Western painting in favor of Japanese-style art. When it came to those things my father's mouth was clamped shut, like an oyster at the bottom of the sea."

And even if you pried open that shell now, there

would be nothing inside. I thanked Masahiko and hung up.

It was by total coincidence that I discovered the painting by Tomohiko Amada, the one with the unusual title, **Killing Commendatore.**

Sometimes in the middle of the night I'd hear a faint rustling sound from the attic above the bedroom. At first I thought it must be mice, or a squirrel that had found its way into the attic. But the sound was clearly not that of a rodent's feet scurrying around. Nor that of a slithering snake. It sounded more like oil paper being crumpled up. Not loud enough to keep me from sleeping, but it did concern me that there was some unknown creature in the house. I figured it might be an animal that could cause some damage.

After searching around, I located the opening to the attic in the ceiling in the back of the guest bedroom closet. I lugged over the aluminum ladder from the storage shed and, flashlight in one hand, pushed open the cover. I timidly stuck my head through and looked around. The attic was bigger than I'd thought, and dark. A small amount of sunlight filtered in through the small vent holes on either side. I shone the flashlight around but didn't see anything. At least nothing was moving. I took the plunge and hauled myself up into the attic.

The place smelled dusty, but not enough to bother me. The attic was apparently well ventilated and there wasn't much dust on the floor. Several thick beams hung low on the ceiling, but as long as I avoided them I could walk around okay. I edged forward and checked both vents. Both were covered with screens so no animals could get in, but the screen on the north vent had a gap in it. Something might have knocked against it and ripped it. Or else an animal had intentionally ripped the wire to get inside. Either way, the opening was large enough for a smallish animal to easily scramble in.

I spotted the culprit I'd been hearing at night, silently settled on top of a beam in the dark. It was a small, gray horned owl. The owl's eyes were closed and it seemed to be sleeping. I switched off my flashlight and stood away to silently observe without frightening it. I'd never seen a horned owl up close before. It looked less like an owl than like a cat with wings. It was a beautiful creature.

The owl most likely rested here during the day and then at night went out the vent hole to hunt for prey in the mountains. The sound of it going in and out must have been what woke me. No harm done. Having an owl in the attic also meant I needn't worry about mice and snakes settling in. I figured I should just leave it be. I felt close to the little owl. Both of us just happened to be borrowing this house and sharing it. It could have the run of the attic as far as I was concerned. I enjoyed observing it for a time, then tiptoed back where I'd come from. That's when I discovered the large wrapped package near the entrance.

One look told me it was a wrapped-up painting. About three feet in height and five feet in length, it was wrapped tightly in brown Japanese wrapping paper, with string tied several times around it. Nothing else was in the attic. The faint sunlight filtering in from the vent holes, the gray horned owl on top of a beam, the wrapped painting propped up against a wall. The combination felt magical, somehow, and captivated me.

I gingerly lifted the package. It wasn't heavy—the weight of a painting set in a simple frame. The wrapping paper was slightly dusty. It must have been placed here, out of anyone's sight, quite some time ago. A name tag was attached tightly with wire to the string. In blue ballpoint ink was written **Killing Commendatore**. The writing was done in a very careful hand. Most likely this was the title of the painting.

Naturally, I had no clue why that one painting would be hidden away in the attic. I considered what I should do. Obviously the correct thing to do would be to leave it where it was. This was Tomohiko Amada's house, not mine, the painting clearly his possession (presumably it was one that he himself had painted), one that, for whatever reason, he had hidden away so no one would see it. That being the case, I thought I shouldn't do anything uncalled for, and should let it continue to silently share the attic with the owl. I should just leave it be.

That made the most sense, but still I couldn't suppress the curiosity surging up inside. The words in (what appeared to be) the title—**Killing**

Commendatore—grabbed me. What kind of painting could it be? And why did Tomohiko Amada have to hide away **this** painting alone in the attic?

I picked up the painting and tested to see if it could squeeze through the opening to the attic. Logic dictated that a painting that had been brought up here shouldn't have any problem being carried down. And there was no other entrance to the attic. But still I checked to see if it would squeeze through. As expected, it was a tight fit, but when I held it diagonally, it squeezed through the square opening. I imagined Tomohiko Amada carrying the painting up to the attic. He must have been by himself then, carrying around some secret inside him. I could vividly imagine the scene, as if I were actually witnessing it.

I don't think Amada would be angry if he found out I'd brought the painting down from the attic. His mind was buried now in a deep maelstrom, according to his son, "unable to distinguish an opera from a frying pan." He would never be coming back to this home. And if I left this painting in an attic with the screen over the vent hole ripped, mice and squirrels might gnaw away at it someday. Or else bugs might get to it. And if this painting really was by Tomohiko Amada, this would be a substantial loss to the art world.

I lowered the package on top of the shelf in the closet, gave a little wave to the horned owl huddled on the beam, then clambered down and quietly shut the lid to the entrance.

I didn't unwrap the painting right away. I left that brown package propped up against the wall in the studio for several days. And I sat on the floor, gazing vaguely at it. It was hard for me to decide whether I should unwrap it or not. I mean, it belonged to somebody else, and whatever positive spin you might try to put on it, I didn't have the right to unwrap it. If I wanted to, at least I should get permission from his son, Masahiko. I'm not sure why, but I didn't feel like letting Masahiko know the painting existed. I felt like it was something personal, just between me and Tomohiko Amada. I can't explain why. But that's how I felt.

I stared at the painting (my assumption, of course, that it was actually a painting)—wrapped in Japanese paper and tied tightly with string—so hard I almost burned a hole in it, and after running the next step through my mind, over and over, I finally decided to unwrap it. It was no contest: my curiosity won out over any sense of etiquette or common sense. Whether this was the professional curiosity of an artist, or simple personal curiosity, I couldn't say. Whatever, I just had to see what was inside. I don't care what anyone says, I told myself. I brought over scissors, cut the tightly bound string, and peeled away the brown wrapping paper. I took my time, and did it carefully, in case I needed to rewrap it again later on.

Underneath the layers of wrapping paper was a painting in a simple frame, wrapped in a soft white cloth like bleached cotton. I gently lifted off that cloth, as carefully as if I were removing the bandages from a burn victim.

What was revealed under the white cloth was, as expected, a Japanese-style painting. A long, rectangular painting. I stood it up on a shelf, stood back a bit, and studied it.

It was Tomohiko Amada's work, no doubt about it. Clearly done in his style and inimitable technique, with his signature bold use of space and dynamic composition. The painting depicted men and women dressed in the fashions of the Asuka period, the clothes and hairstyles of that age. But the painting startled me nonetheless. What it depicted was so violent it took my breath away.

As far as I knew, Tomohiko Amada hardly ever painted pictures that were harsh and violent. Maybe never. His paintings mostly summoned up feelings of nostalgia, gentleness, and peace. Occasionally they would take up historical events as his theme, but the people depicted in them generally faded away into the overall composition. They were shown as part of a close community in the midst of the abundant natural scenery of ancient times, esteeming harmony above all. Ego was submerged in the collective will, or absorbed into a calm fate. And the circle of life was quietly drawn closed. For Tomohiko Amada that very well may have been utopia. Over the years he continued to depict that world from all sorts of angles, all sorts of perspectives. Many called his style a "rejection of modernity" or a "return to antiquity." Of course there were some who criticized it as escapist. In any case, after he returned to Japan from studying in Vienna he abandoned modernist oil painting, and shut himself away inside that kind of serene world, without a single word of explanation or justification.

But this painting titled **Killing Commendatore** was full of blood. Realistic blood flowing all over. Two men were fighting with heavy, ancient swords, in what seemed to be a duel. One of the men fighting was young, the other old. The young man had plunged his sword deep into the old man's chest. The young man had a thin black mustache and wore tight-fitting light-greenish clothes. The old man was dressed in white and had a lush white beard. Around his neck was a necklace of beads. He had dropped his sword, which had not yet struck the ground. Blood was spewing from his chest. The tip of the sword must have pierced his aorta. The blood had soaked his white clothes, and his mouth was twisted in agony. His eyes were wide open, staring in disbelief into space. He realized he was defeated. But the real pain had yet to hit him.

For his part, the young man's eyes were cold, fixed on his opponent. Not a sign of regret in those eyes, not a hint of confusion or fear, or a trace of agitation. Totally composed, those eyes were simply watching the impending death of another, and his own unmistakable victory. The gushing blood was nothing more than proof of that, and elicited no emotional reaction whatsoever.

Honestly, until then I had thought of Japanese-style paintings as static and formulaic, their techniques and subject matter ill-suited to the expression of strong emotion. A world that had nothing to do with me. But looking now at Tomohiko Amada's **Killing Commendatore** I realized that had been nothing but prejudice on my part. In Amada's depiction of the two men's violent duel to the death was something that shook the viewer to the core. The man who won, the man who lost. The man who stabbed and the man who was stabbed. My heart was captured by the discrepancy. There is something very special about this painting, I thought.

There were a few other figures nearby watching the duel. One was a young woman. She had on refined, pure white clothes. Her hair was done up, with a large hair ornament. She held one hand in front of her mouth, which was slightly parted. She looked like she was about to take a deep breath and let out a scream. Her lovely eyes were wide open.

And there was another young man there. His clothes were not as splendid. Dark clothes, bereft of any ornaments, the kind of outfit designed to be easy to move around in. On his feet were plain-looking zori sandals. He looked like a servant. He had no long sword, just a short sword hanging from his waist. He was short and thickset, with a scraggly beard. In his left hand he held a kind of account book, like a clipboard that a company employee nowadays might have. His right hand was reaching out in the air as if to grab something. But it couldn't grab anything. You couldn't tell from the painting if he was the servant of the old man, or of the young man, or of the woman. One thing that was clear, though, was that this duel had taken place quickly, and neither the woman nor the servant had expected it to happen. Both of their faces revealed an unmistakable shock at the sudden turn of events.

The only one of the four who wasn't surprised was the young man doing the killing. Probably nothing ever took him by surprise. He was not a born killer, and he didn't enjoy killing. But if it served his purpose he wouldn't hesitate to kill. He was young, burning with idealism (though of what kind I have no idea), a man overflowing with strength. And he was skilled in the art of wielding a sword. Seeing an old man past his prime dying by his hand didn't surprise him. It was, in fact, a natural, rational act.

There was one other person there, an odd observer. The man was at the bottom left of the painting, much like a footnote in a text. His head was peeking out from a lid in the ground that he had partially pushed open. The lid was square, and made of boards. It reminded me of the attic cover in this house. The shape and size were identical. From there the man was watching the people on the surface.

A hole opening up to the surface? A square manhole? No way. They didn't have sewers back in the Asuka period. And the duel was taking place outdoors, in an empty vacant lot. The only thing visible in the background was a pine tree, with low-hanging branches. Why would there be a hole with a cover there, in the middle of a vacant lot? It didn't make any sense.

The man who was sticking his head out of the hole was weird looking. He had an unusually long face, like a twisted eggplant. His face was overgrown with a black beard, his hair long and tangled. He looked like some sort of vagabond or hermit who'd abandoned the world. In a way he also looked like someone who'd lost his mind. But the glint in his eyes was surprisingly sharp, insightful, even. That said, the insight there wasn't the product of reason, but rather something induced by a sort of deviance—perhaps something akin to madness. I couldn't tell the details of what he was wearing, since all that I could see was from the neck up. He, too, was watching the duel. But unlike the others, he showed no surprise at the turn of events. He was a mere observer of something that was supposed to take place, as if checking all the details of the incident, just to be sure. The young woman and the servant weren't aware of the man with the long face behind them. Their eyes were riveted on the bloody duel. No one was about to turn around.

But who **was** this person? And why was he hiding beneath the ground back in ancient times? What was Tomohiko Amada's purpose in deliberately including this uncanny, mysterious figure in one corner of the painting, and thus forcibly destroying the balance of the overall composition?

And why in the world was this painting given the

title **Killing Commendatore**? True, an apparently high-ranking person was being killed in the picture. But that old man in his ancient garb certainly didn't deserve to be called a commendatore—a knight commander. That was a title clearly from the European Middle Ages or the early modern period. There was no position like that in Japanese history. But still Tomohiko Amada gave it this strange-sounding title— **Killing Commendatore**. There had to be a **reason**.

The term "commendatore" sparked a faint memory. I'd heard the word before. I followed that trace of memory, as if tugging a thin thread toward me. I'd run across the word in a novel or drama. And it was a famous work. I knew I'd seen it somewhere . . .

And then it hit me. Mozart's opera **Don Giovanni**. In the beginning of that opera was a scene, I was sure, of **Killing Commendatore**. I went over to the shelf of records in the living room, took out the boxed set of **Don Giovanni**, and read through the accompanying commentary. And sure enough, the person killed in the opening scene was the Commendatore. He didn't have a name. He was simply listed as "Commendatore."

The libretto was in Italian, and the old man killed in the beginning was called **Il Commendatore**. Whoever translated the libretto into Japanese had rendered it as **kishidancho**—literally, "the knight commander"—and that had become the standard term in Japanese. I had no clue what sort of rank or position the term "commendatore" referred to in reality. The commentary in a few other boxed sets didn't elaborate. He was merely a nameless commendatore appearing in the opera with the sole function of being stabbed to death by Don Giovanni in the opening of the opera. And in the end he transformed into an ominous statue that appeared to Don Giovanni and took him down to hell.

Pretty obvious, if you think about it, I thought. The handsome young man in this painting is the rake Don Giovanni (Don Juan in Spanish) and the older man being killed is the honored knight commander. The young woman is the Commendatore's beautiful daughter Donna Anna, the servant is Don Giovanni's man, Leporello. What he had in his hands was the detailed list of all the women Don Giovanni had seduced up until then, a lengthy catalog of names. Don Giovanni had forced himself on Donna Anna, and when her father confronted him with this violation, they had a duel, and Don Giovanni stabbed the older man to death. It's a famous scene. Why hadn't I picked up on that?

Probably because Mozart's opera and a Japanese-style painting depicting the Asuka period were so remote from each other. So of course I hadn't been able to make the connection. But once I did, everything fell into place. Tomohiko Amada had "adapted" the world of Mozart's opera into the Asuka period. A fascinating experiment, for sure. That, I recognized. But why was that adaptation **necessary**? It was so very different from his usual style of painting. And why did he tightly wrap the painting and hide it away in the attic?

And what was the significance of that figure in the bottom left, the man with the long face sticking his head out from underground? In Mozart's **Don Giovanni** no one like that appeared. There must have been a reason Tomohiko Amada had added him. Also in the opera Donna Anna didn't actually witness her father being stabbed to death. She was off asking her lover, the knight Don Ottavio, for help. By the time they got back to the scene, her father had already breathed his last. Amada had—no doubt for dramatic purposes—subtly changed the way the scene played out. But there was no way the man sticking his head out of the ground was Don Ottavio. That man's features weren't anything found in this world. It was impossible that this was the upright, righteous knight who could help Donna Anna.

Was he a demon from hell? Scouting out the situation in anticipation of dragging Don Giovanni down to hell? But he didn't look like a demon or devil. A demon wouldn't have such strangely sparkling eyes. A devil wouldn't push a square wooden lid up and peek out. The figure more resembled a trickster who had come to intervene. "Long Face" is what I called him, for lack of a better term.

For a few weeks I just silently stared at that painting. With it in front of me, I couldn't bring myself to do any painting of my own. I barely even felt like eating. I'd grab whatever vegetables were in the fridge, dip them in mayo, and chew on that, or else heat up a can of whatever I had on hand. That's about the size of it. All day long I'd sit on the floor of the studio, endlessly listening to the record of **Don Giovanni**, staring enthralled at **Killing Commendatore**. When the sun set, I'd have a glass of wine.

The painting was amazing. As far as I knew, though, it wasn't reprinted in any collection of Amada's work, which meant no one else knew it existed. If it were made public it would no doubt become one of his best-known paintings. If they held a retrospective of his art, it wouldn't be surprising if this was the painting used on the promotional poster. This wasn't simply a painting that was wonderfully done, though. The painting was brimming with an extraordinary sort of energy. Anyone with even a little knowledge of art couldn't miss that fact. There was something in this painting that appealed to the deepest part of the viewer's heart, something suggestive that enticed the imagination to another realm.

I couldn't take my eyes off the bearded Long Face on the left side of the painting. It felt like he'd opened the lid to invite me, personally, to the world underground. No one else, just **me**. I couldn't stop thinking about what sort of realm lay beneath. Where in the world had he come from? And what did he do there? Would that lid be closed up again, or would it be left open?

As I stared at the painting I listened to that scene from **Don Giovanni** over and over. Act 1, scene 3, soon after the overture. And I nearly memorized the lyrics and the lines.

DONNA ANNA: Ah, the assassin
has struck him down! This
blood . . .
this wound . . . his face
discolored with the pallor of
death . . .
He has stopped breathing . . .
his limbs are cold.
Oh father, dear father, dearest
father!
I'm fainting . . . I'm dying!

6

AT THIS POINT HE'S
A FACELESS CLIENT

Summer was winding down when the call came in from my agent. It had been a while since anyone had called me. The summer heat still lingered during the day, though when the sun set the air in the mountains was chilly. The noisy clamor of the summer cicadas was slowly fading away, but now a chorus of other insects had taken their place. Unlike when I lived in the city, I was surrounded by nature now and one season freely chipped away at portions of the preceding one.

We brought each other up to date, though there wasn't much to tell on my end.

"How's your painting coming along?" he asked.

"Slowly but surely," I said. This was a lie, of course. It was more than four months since I'd moved here, yet the canvas I'd prepared was still blank.

"Glad to hear it," he said. "I'd like to see how you're doing sometime. Maybe there's something I can do to help out."

"Thanks. We'll do that sometime."

Then he told me why he'd called. "I have a request. Are you sure you're not willing to do one more portrait? What do you think?"

"I told you I've given up doing portraits."

"I know. But the fee this time is unbelievable."

"Unbelievable?"

"It's amazing."

"How amazing?"

He told me the figure. I nearly let out a whistle of surprise. "There have got to be a lot of other people besides me who specialize in portraits," I replied calmly.

"There aren't all that many, really, though there are a few besides you who are fairly decent."

"Then you should ask them. With a fee like that anybody would jump at the chance."

"The thing is, the other party specifically asked for **you**. That's their condition. No one else will do."

I shifted the phone to my left hand and scratched behind my right ear.

The agent went on. "The person saw several portraits you've done and was very impressed. He felt that the vitality in your paintings can't easily be found elsewhere."

"I don't get it. How could an ordinary person have seen **several** of my portraits? It's not like I have a one-man show at a gallery every year."

"I really don't know the details," he said, sounding perplexed. "I'm just passing along what the other party told me. I told him up front that you were no longer doing portraits. I said you seemed pretty firm about it, and even if I asked you you'd most likely turn him down. But he wouldn't give up. That's when this figure came up."

I mulled over the offer. Honestly, it was a tempting amount. And I felt a bit of pride that someone saw that much value in my paintings—even if it was work I'd done half mechanically for money. But the thing was, I'd sworn I'd never paint commissioned portraits again. When my wife left me it spurred me to start over again, and I couldn't reverse my decision just because somebody was willing to shell out a pile of money.

"Why is he being so generous?" I asked.

"Even though we're in a recession, there are still people who have so much money they don't know what to do with it. There are a lot of people like that—ones who made a killing in online stock trading, or tech entrepreneurs. And getting a portrait done is something they can write off as a business expense."

"Write off?"

"In their accounts a portrait isn't included as a work of art but as office equipment."

"Talk about heartwarming," I said.

But even if they have tons of excess cash, and even if they can write it off as a business expense, I can't see entrepreneurs or people who've made a fortune trading stocks online wanting to have their portraits painted and hung on their company walls as **office equipment**. Most of these are young people decked out at work in faded jeans, sneakers, worn T-shirts, and Banana Republic jackets, proud to be drinking Starbucks from a paper cup. An imposing oil portrait didn't fit their lifestyle. But there are all kinds in the world. You can't generalize. It's not necessarily true that no one wants to be painted sipping Starbucks (or whatever) coffee (Fair Trade beans only, of course) from a paper cup.

"But there's one condition," the agent said. "The other party wants you to use the client as a live model, and paint when you're actually together. They'll make the time to do that."

"But I don't work that way."

"I know. You meet the client but don't have them model for you. That's your way of working. I told them that. They said they understood but they'd like you to make an exception and paint the client live and in person. That's the other party's condition."

"What's the purpose?"

"I don't know."

"That's a pretty odd request. Why would they insist on that? You'd think they'd be happy not to actually have to sit for the portrait."

"I agree it's unconventional. But it's hard to complain about the fee."

"I'm with you there—hard to complain about the fee," I agreed.

"It's all up to you. It's not like you're being asked to sell your soul or anything. You're a very skilled portrait painter, and they're counting on that skill."

"I feel like a retired hit man in the mob," I said. "Like I'm being asked to whack one more target."

"Though no blood's going to be shed. What do you say—will you do it?"

No blood's going to be shed, I silently repeated. The painting **Killing Commendatore** came to mind.

"What sort of person is the one I'd paint?" I asked. "Actually, I don't know."

"You don't even know if it's a man or a woman?"

"I don't. I haven't heard a thing about the sex or age or name. At this point he's a totally faceless client. A lawyer saying he was representing the client called me. That's the 'other party' I spoke with about it."

"Do you think it's legit?"

"I don't see anything suspect about it. The lawyer works at a reputable firm and said they'll transfer an advance as soon as you accept."

Phone in hand, I sighed. "This is kind of sudden, and I don't think I can give you an answer right away. I need time to think."

"Understood. Think about it as long as you need. It's not an urgent job, the other party said."

I thanked him and hung up. I couldn't think of anything else to do so I went to the studio, turned on the light, plunked myself down on the floor, and stared vaguely at **Killing Commendatore**. After a while I started to get hungry and went to the kitchen, piled a plate with Ritz Crackers and ketchup, and went back to the studio. I dipped the crackers in the ketchup and munched them as I went back to staring at the painting. Nothing about that food tasted good. It was, if anything, pretty awful. But taste wasn't the issue. Keeping hunger at bay for a while was the priority.

That's how much the painting drew me in, from the overall composition to the small details. It truly held me captive. After a few weeks of exhaustive gazing at the painting, I ventured closer to it to inspect each detail. What most caught my attention were the expressions on each of the five people's faces. I did minute pencil sketches of each of them. From the Commendatore, to Don Giovanni, Donna Anna, Leporello, and Long Face. Just like a reader might carefully copy down in a notebook each word and phrase he liked in a book.

This was the first time I'd ever sketched figures from a Japanese-style painting, and it was far more difficult than I'd expected. Japanese painting emphasized lines, and tended to be more flat than three-dimensional. Symbolism was emphasized over reality. It's inherently impossible to transfer a painting done from that perspective into the grammar of Western painting, though after much trial and error I was able to do a fairly decent job of it. Calling it "recasting" might be a bit much, but it was necessary to interpret and translate the painting in my own way. Which necessitated grasping the intent that went into the original painting. I had to come to an understanding of Tomohiko Amada, his viewpoint as an artist, and the kind of person he was. Figuratively speaking, I had to put myself in his shoes.

After I'd done this for a while, the thought struck me: maybe doing a portrait again wasn't such a bad idea. I mean, my painting wasn't going anywhere. I couldn't even get a hint of what I should paint, or what I wanted to paint. Even if I wasn't too keen on the job, getting my hands moving again wouldn't be a bad thing. If I kept on like this, unable to draw a thing, I might find myself unable to paint ever again. **Maybe I wouldn't even be able to paint a portrait.** The fee, of course, was also pretty tempting. My living expenses at this point were minimal, but my pay from the art classes wasn't enough to cover them. I'd gone on that long trip, bought a used Corolla station wagon, and my savings were diminishing. So a sizable fee like the one I'd get from doing the portrait was, admittedly, very appealing.

I called my agent and told him that just this one time, I would take on the job. Naturally, he was happy to hear this.

"But if I have to paint the client in person, that means I need to travel to wherever he is," I said.

"No need to worry about that. The other party will come to your place in Odawara."

"To Odawara?"

"That's right."

"He knows where I'm living?"

"He apparently lives nearby. He even knows that you're living in Tomohiko Amada's place."

This left me speechless. "That's strange. Hardly anybody knows I'm living here. Especially that I'm in Amada's house."

"I didn't know that either," the agent said.

"Then how does that person know?"

"I have no idea. But you can find out just about anything from the Internet these days. For people who know their way around it, privacy is a thing of the past."

"Is it just a coincidence that that person lives near

me? Or was the fact that I live nearby one of the reasons he chose me?"

"That, I couldn't say. When you meet the client, if there's something you want to know, you can ask."

"I'll do that," I said.

"So when can you start?" he asked.

"Anytime," I said.

"All right, I'll let them know, and get back to you," the agent said.

After I hung up I went out to the terrace, settled into the lounge chair, and thought about how things had turned out. The more I mulled it over, the more questions I had. First off, it bothered me that the client knew I was living here, in this house. It was like I was under surveillance, with somebody watching my every move. But why would anyone have that much interest in a person like me? Plus the whole thing sounded too good to be true. The portraits I'd done were certainly well received. And I had a certain amount of confidence in them. But these were, ultimately, the kind of portraits you could find anywhere. No way could you ever call them "works of art." And as far as the world was concerned I was a completely unknown artist. No matter how many of my paintings someone had seen and liked (not that I accepted that story at face value), would that person really shell out such an enormous fee?

A thought suddenly struck me, out of nowhere: Could the client be the husband of the woman I was having an affair with? I had no proof to go on, yet the more I thought about it the more it seemed like a real possibility. When it came to an anonymous neighbor who was interested in me, that's all I could come up with. But why would her husband go to the trouble and expense of paying a huge fee to have his wife's lover paint his own portrait? It didn't add up. Unless he was some weird pervert or something.

Fine. If that's how things are working out, then just go with the flow. If the client has some hidden agenda, just let it play out. That was a much more sensible thing to do than remaining as I was, stuck, deadlocked in the mountains. Curiosity was also a factor. What kind of person **was** this client? What did he want from me in exchange for the huge fee? I had to discover what motivated him.

Once I'd made up my mind I felt relieved. That night, for the first time in a while, I fell into a deep sleep right away, with no thoughts buzzing around in my head. At one point I felt like I heard the rustling of the horned owl in the middle of the night. But that might have just been a piece of a fragmentary dream.

FOR BETTER OR FOR WORSE, IT'S AN EASY NAME TO REMEMBER

My agent in Tokyo called a few more times, and we decided that I would meet our mystery client on Tuesday afternoon of the following week. (At that point the client's name was still not revealed.) I had them agree to my usual procedure, wherein, on the first day, we simply met and talked together for an hour or so, before we embarked upon a drawing.

As you might imagine, painting a portrait requires the ability to accurately grasp the special features of a person's face. But that's not all. If it were, you'd end up with a caricature. To paint a vibrant portrait you need the skill to discover what lies at the core of the person's face. A face is like reading a palm. More than the features you're born with, a face is gradually formed over the passage of time, through all the experiences a person goes through, and no two faces are alike.

On Tuesday morning I straightened up the house, picked some flowers from the garden and put them in vases, moved the **Killing Commendatore** painting out of the studio into the guest bedroom, and wrapped it up again in brown paper. I didn't want anyone else seeing it.

At five past one p.m. a car drove up the steep slope and parked in the covered driveway at the entrance. A heavy, brazen-sounding engine echoed, like some giant animal giving a satisfied purr from deep inside a cave. A high-powered engine. The engine shut off, and quiet again settled over the valley. The car was a silver Jaguar sports coupe. Sunlight from between the clouds reflected brightly off the long, brightly polished fenders. I'm not that into cars, so I don't know which model this was, but my guess was that it was the latest model, the mileage in the four digits, the price twenty times what I paid for my used Corolla station wagon. Not that this surprised me. The client was, after all, willing to pay such a huge fee to have a portrait done. If he'd appeared at my door in a massive yacht, it wouldn't have been surprising.

The person who got out of the car was a well-dressed middle-aged man. He had on dark-green sunglasses, a long-sleeved white cotton shirt (not simply white, but a pure white), and khaki chinos. His shoes were cream-colored deck shoes. He was probably a shade over five feet seven inches tall. His face had a nice, even tan. He gave off an overall fresh, clean feel. But what struck me most on this first encounter was his hair. Slightly curly and thick, it was white down to the last hair. Not gray or salt-and-pepper, but a pure white, like freshly fallen, virgin snow.

He got out of the car, closed the door (which made that special pleasant **thunk** expensive car doors make when you casually shut them), didn't lock it but put the key in his trouser pocket, and strode toward my front door—all of which I watched from a gap in the curtains. The way he walked was quite lovely. Back straight, the necessary muscles all equally in play. I figured he must work out regularly, and pretty hard training at that. I stepped away from the window, sat in a chair in the living room, and waited for the front doorbell to ring. Once it did, I slowly walked to the door and opened it.

When I opened the door the man took off his sunglasses, slipped them into the breast pocket of his shirt, and without a word held out his hand. Half reflexively I held out my hand, too. He shook it. It was a firm handshake, the way Americans do it. A little too firm for me, not that it hurt or anything.

"My name is Menshiki. It's very nice to meet you," the man said in a clear voice. The sort of tone a lecturer would make at the beginning of his talk to test the microphone and introduce himself at the same time.

"The pleasure's mine," I said. "Mr. Menshiki?"

"The **men** is written with the character in **menzeiten**—the one that means 'avoidance'—and the **shiki** is the character **iro**, for 'color.'"

"Mr. Menshiki," I repeated, lining the two characters up in my mind. A strange combination.

"'Avoiding colors,' is what it means," the man said. "An unusual name. Other than my relatives I rarely run across anyone who shares it."

"But it's easy to remember."

"Exactly. It's an easy name to remember. For better or for worse." The man smiled. He had faint stubble from his cheeks to his chin, but I don't think he'd simply left off shaving. When he'd shaved he'd left an exact, calculated amount of stubble. Different from his hair, his beard was half black. I found it odd that only his hair was pure white.

"Please come in," I said.

Menshiki gave a small nod, removed his shoes, and stepped inside. The way he carried himself was charming, though I could sense a bit of tension. Like some large cat taken to a new place, each movement was careful and light, his eyes darting quickly around to take in his surroundings.

"A comfortable-looking place," he said after sitting down on the sofa. "Very relaxed and quiet."

"Quiet it certainly is. But kind of inconvenient when you have to go shopping."

"I would imagine for someone in your field it's an ideal environment."

I sat down in the chair across from him.

"I heard that you live nearby, Mr. Menshiki?"

"Yes, that's right. It would take a while to walk here, though as the crow flies it's actually pretty near."

"**As the crow flies**," I said, repeating his words. There was a somehow strange ring to the expression. "But how near is it, actually?"

"Close enough that if you wave your hand here you could see it."

"You can see your house from here?"

"Exactly."

I wasn't sure how to respond, and Menshiki asked, "Would you like to see my house?"

"If I could, yes," I said.

"Do you mind if we go out on the terrace?"

"Please, go right ahead."

Menshiki got up from the sofa and went straight from the living room to the terrace. He leaned out over the railing and pointed across the valley.

"You see that white concrete house over there? The one on top of the mountain, with the shiny windows?"

I was speechless. That was the house, that smart, elegant house I often looked at when I went out at sunset onto the terrace to enjoy a glass of wine. The large house that stood out from all the rest, diagonally to the right from mine.

"It's a little far, but if you made a big wave with your hand you could say hello," Menshiki said.

"But how did you know I was living here?" I asked, resting my hands on the railing.

He looked puzzled. He wasn't really fazed, just displaying a puzzled look. Not that his expression seemed contrived. He'd simply wanted to throw in a pause before responding.

"One aspect of my job is gathering all kinds of information," he said. "That's the sort of business I'm in."

"Is it tech related?"

"That's right. Or more precisely, that's also one aspect of my work."

"But hardly anyone knows yet that I'm living here."

Menshiki smiled. "Saying hardly anyone knows means, paradoxically, that there are some who **do**."

I looked over again at that exquisite white concrete

building across the valley, and once more studied the man beside me. He was, most likely, the one who appeared almost every evening on the deck of that house. When I thought of it, his shape and movements all fit that silhouette perfectly . . . It was hard to figure out his age. That snow-white hair made me think he must be in his late fifties or early sixties, though his skin was lustrous and tight, and wrinkle free. His deep-looking eyes had the youthful twinkle of a man in his late thirties. All of which made guessing his age a tough call. I would have accepted anything between forty-five and sixty.

Menshiki went back to the sofa in the living room, and I sat down again across from him.

"Do you mind if I ask a question?" I finally ventured.

"Ask away," he said, beaming.

"Is there some connection between the fact that I live near your house and your decision to ask me to paint your portrait?"

A slight look of confusion came over him. And when he looked confused, several tiny wrinkles appeared at the corners of his eyes. Charming wrinkles. His features, viewed individually, were all quite attractive—the eyes almond shaped and slightly deep set, the forehead noble and broad, the eyebrows thick and nicely defined, the nose thin and a nice size. Eyes, eyebrows, and nose that perfectly fit his smallish face. His face was a bit small, yet too broad in a way, and from a purely aesthetic viewpoint was a little imbalanced. The vertical and horizontal were out of sync, though this disparity wasn't necessarily a defect. It's what gave his face its distinctiveness, since it was this imbalance that conversely gave the viewer a sense of calm. If his features had been too perfectly symmetrical people might have felt a bit of antipathy, or wariness, toward him. But as it was, his ever-so-slightly unbalanced features had a calming effect on anyone meeting him for the first time. They broadcast, in a friendly way, "It's all good, not to worry. I'm not a bad person. I don't plan to do anything bad to you."

The pointed, largish tips of his ears were slightly visible through his neatly trimmed hair. They conveyed a sense of freshness, of vigor, reminding me of spry little mushrooms in a forest, peeking out from among the fallen leaves on an autumn morning, just after it had rained. His mouth was broad, the thin lips neatly closed in a line, diligently prepared to, at any moment, break into a smile.

One could call him handsome. And he actually was. Yet his features rejected that sort of casual description, neatly circumventing it. His face was too lively, its movements too subtle to simply abide by that label. The expressions that rose on his features weren't calculated, but looked more like they'd arisen naturally, spontaneously. If they weren't, then he was quite the actor. But I got the impression that wasn't the case.

When I observe the face of a person I've met for the first time, from habit I sense all sorts of things. In most cases there's no tangible basis for how I feel. It's nothing more than intuition. But that's what helps me as a portrait artist—that **simple intuition**.

"The answer is yes, and no," Menshiki said. His hands on his knees were wide open, palms up. He turned them over.

I said nothing, waiting for his next words.

"I do worry about who lives in the neighborhood," Menshiki went on. "No, not worry, exactly. It's more like I'm **interested**. Especially when it's someone I see now and then across the valley."

It's a little too great a distance to say we actually **see** each other, I thought, but didn't say anything. Maybe he had high-powered binoculars and had been secretly observing me? I kept that thought to myself. I mean, what possible reason could he have to observe a person like **me**?

"And I learned that you had moved in here," Menshiki continued. "I found out you're a professional portrait artist, and that aroused my interest enough to seek out a few of your paintings. At first I saw them on the Internet. But I wasn't satisfied, so I went to see three actual paintings."

That had me puzzled. "You saw the actual paintings?"

"I went to see the people who had modeled for you and asked them to let me see the portraits. They were happy to show me them. It seems like people who sit for portraits are really pleased to show them off. I got a strange sensation when I saw the actual paintings up close and compared them to the faces of the people. It's like I couldn't tell which one was real anymore. How should I put it? There's something about your paintings that strikes the viewer's heart from an unexpected angle. At first they seem like ordinary, typical portraits, but if you look carefully you see something hidden inside them."

"Something hidden?" I asked.

"I'm not sure how to put it. Maybe the real personality?"

"Personality," I mused. "**My** personality? Or the **subject's?**"

"Both, probably. They're mixed together, so elaborately intertwined they can't be separated. It's not something you can overlook. Even if you just glance at the paintings as you pass by, you feel like you've missed something, and you can't help but come back and study them carefully. It's that indefinable **something** that drew me to them."

I was silent.

"And I had this thought: This is the person I want to paint my portrait. No matter what. I got in touch with your agent right away."

"Through an intermediary."

"Correct. I normally use an intermediary, a law office. It's not that I have a guilty conscience or anything. I just like to protect my anonymity."

"And it's an easy name to remember."

"Exactly," he said, and smiled. His mouth spread wide, the tips of his ears quivered ever so slightly.

"There are times when I don't want my name to be known."

"Still, the fee is a little too much," I said.

"Price is always relative, determined by supply and demand. Those are basic market principles. If I want to buy something and you don't want to sell it, the price goes up. And in the opposite case, the price goes down."

"I understand market principles. But is it really necessary for you to go to all that length to have me paint your portrait? Maybe I shouldn't say this, but a portrait isn't something a person really **needs**."

"True enough. It's not something you need. But I'm also curious about what sort of portrait you'd do if you painted me. I want to find that out. You could think of it another way, namely that I'm putting a price on my own curiosity."

"And your curiosity doesn't come cheap."

He smiled happily. "The purer the curiosity is, the stronger it is. And the more money it takes to satisfy it."

"Would you care for some coffee?" I asked.

"That would be nice."

"I made it a little while ago in the coffee maker. Is that okay?"

"That's fine. I'll take it black, if you don't mind."

I went into the kitchen, poured coffee into two cups, and carried them back out.

"I notice you have a lot of opera recordings," Menshiki said as he drank the coffee. "You're a big opera fan?"

"Those aren't mine. The owner of this place left them. Thanks to them, though, I've listened to a lot of opera since I came here."

"By owner you mean Tomohiko Amada?"

"That's right."

"Do you have a favorite?"

I gave it some thought. "These days I've been listening to **Don Giovanni** a lot. There's a bit of a reason for that."

"What kind of reason? I'd like to hear, if you don't mind?"

"Well, it's personal. Nothing important."

"I like **Don Giovanni** too, and listen to it a lot," Menshiki said. "I heard it once in a small opera house in Prague. This was back just after the fall of the communist regime.

"I'm sure you know this," he continued, "but **Don Giovanni** was first performed in Prague. The theater was small, and so was the orchestra, and none of the singers were famous, yet it was a wonderful performance. They didn't have to sing really loud like in a big opera house, and could express their feelings in a very intimate way. Impossible at the Met or La Scala. There you need a well-known singer with a booming voice. Sometimes the arias in those big opera houses remind me of acrobatics. But what operas like Mozart's need is intimacy, like music. Don't you think so? In that sense the performance I heard in Prague was the ideal **Don Giovanni**."

He took another sip of coffee. I said nothing, observing his actions.

"I've had the opportunity to hear performances of **Don Giovanni** all over the world," he went on. "In Vienna, Rome, Milan, London, Paris, at the Met, and even in Tokyo. With Abbado, Levine, Ozawa, Maazel, and who else? . . . Georges Prêtre, I believe. But the **Don Giovanni** I heard in Prague is the one that, strangely enough, has stayed with me. The singers and conductor weren't people I'd ever heard of, but outside, after the performance, Prague was covered in a thick fog. There weren't many lights back then and the streets were pitch black at night. As I wandered down the deserted cobblestone streets I suddenly ran across a bronze statue. Whose statue, I have no idea. But he was dressed as a medieval knight. The thought struck me that I should ask him out to dinner. I didn't, of course."

He smiled again.

"Do you often go abroad?" I asked.

"Sometimes for work I do," he said. As if a thought occurred to him, he remained silent. I surmised that he didn't want to talk specifics about his job.

"So, what do you think?" Menshiki asked, looking me right in the eye. "Did I pass the test? Will you paint my portrait?"

"I'm not testing you. We're just getting together for a talk."

"But before you begin a painting you always meet and talk with the client. I heard that if you don't like the person, you won't paint his portrait."

I glanced over toward the terrace. A large crow had settled on the railing, but as if sensing my gaze, he spread his glossy wings and took off.

"I guess that's possible, but fortunately I haven't met anyone I don't like yet."

"I hope I'm not the first," Menshiki said with a smile. His eyes, though, weren't smiling. He was serious.

"Don't worry. I would be more than pleased to paint your portrait."

"That's wonderful," he said. He paused. "This is kind of selfish of me, but I have a little request myself."

I looked straight at him again. "What kind of request?"

"If possible I'd like you to paint me freely, and not worry about the usual conventions involved in doing a portrait. I mean, if you want to paint a standard portrait, that's fine. If you paint it using your usual techniques, the way you've painted till now, I'm all right with that. But if you do decide to try out a different approach, I'd welcome that."

"A different approach?"

"Whatever style you like is entirely up to you. Paint it any way you like."

"So you're saying that, like Picasso's painting during one period, I could put both eyes on one side of the face and you'd be okay with that?"

"If that's how you want to paint me, I have no objections. I leave it all up to you."

"And you'll hang that on the wall of your office."

"Right now I don't have an office per se. So I'll probably hang it in my study at home. As long as you have no objection."

Of course I had none. All walls were the same

as far I was concerned. I mulled all this over before replying.

"Mr. Menshiki, I'm grateful to you for saying that, for telling me to paint in whatever style I want. But honestly nothing specific pops into my head at the moment. You have to understand, I'm merely a portrait painter. For a long time I've followed a set pattern and style. Even if I'm told to remove any restrictions, to paint as freely as I want, the restrictions themselves are part of the technique. So I think it's likely I'll paint a **standard** portrait, the way I have up till now. I hope that's all right with you?"

Menshiki held both hands wide. "Of course. Do what you think is best. The only thing I want is for you to have a totally free hand."

"One other thing: if you're going to pose for the portrait, I'll need you to come to my studio a number of times and sit in a chair for quite a while. I'm sure your work keeps you quite busy, so do you think that'll be possible?"

"I can clear my schedule anytime. I was the one, after all, who asked that you paint me from real life. I'll come here and sit quietly in the chair as long as I can. We can have a good long talk then. You don't mind talking?"

"No, of course not. Actually, I welcome it. To me, you're a complete mystery. In order to paint you, I might need a little more information about you."

Menshiki laughed and quietly shook his head. When he did so, his pure white hair softly shook, like a winter prairie blowing in the wind.

"I think you overestimate me. There's nothing particularly mysterious about me. I don't talk much about myself because telling all the details would bore people, that's all."

He smiled, the lines at his eyes deepening. A very clean, open smile. But that can't be all, I thought. There was something hidden inside him. A secret locked away in a small box and buried deep down in the ground. Buried a long time ago, with soft green grass now growing above it. And the only person in the world who knew the location of the box was Menshiki. I couldn't help but sense, deep within his smile, a solitude that comes from a certain sort of secret.

We talked for another twenty minutes or so, deciding when he would come here to model, and how much time he could spare. On his way out, at the front door, he once more held out his hand, quite naturally, and I took it without thinking. A firm handshake at the beginning and end of an encounter seemed to be Menshiki's way of doing things. He slipped on his sunglasses, took the car keys from his pocket, boarded the silver Jaguar (which looked like some well-trained, slick, oversized animal), and gracefully eased down the slope, as I watched from the window. I went out on the terrace and gazed at the white house on the mountain he was heading back to.

What an unusual character, I thought. Friendly enough, not overly quiet. But it was as if he hadn't said a single thing about himself. The most I'd learned was that he lived in that elegant house across the valley, did work that partly involved the Internet, and frequently traveled abroad. And that he was a big fan of opera. Beyond that, though, I knew very little. Whether or not he had a family, how old he was, where he was from originally, how long he'd lived on that mountain. He hadn't even told me his first name.

And why be so insistent on me being the one to paint his portrait? I'd like to think it was because I had talent, something obvious to anyone who saw my work. Yet it was clear that this was not his sole motivation for commissioning me to do the painting. It seemed true that portraits I'd done had drawn his attention. That couldn't be a complete lie. But I wasn't naive enough to accept everything he told me at face value.

So—what did this man, Menshiki, want from me? What was his endgame? What sort of scenario had he prepared for me?

Even after we had talked, I still had no idea how to answer these questions. The mystery, in fact, had deepened. Why, for one thing, did he have such amazingly white hair? That kind of white wasn't exactly normal. I recalled an Edgar Allan Poe short story in which a fisherman gets caught up in a massive whirlpool and his hair turns white overnight. Had Menshiki experienced something just as terrifying?

After the sun set, lights came on in the white concrete mansion across the valley. Bright lights, and plenty of them. It looked like the kind of house designed by a self-assured architect unconcerned about things like the electric bill. Or perhaps the client was overly afraid of the dark and requested the architect to build a house where lights could blaze from one end to the other. Either way, viewed from afar, the house looked like a luxury liner silently crossing the ocean at night.

I sprawled out on the chair on the terrace and, sipping white wine, gazed at those lights. I was half expecting Menshiki to come out on his terrace, but that evening he didn't appear. But if he had, how should I have acted? Wave my hand in a big gesture of greeting?

I figured that, in time, my questions would be answered. That's about all I could expect.

8

A BLESSING IN DISGUISE

After my Wednesday-evening art class, when I taught an adult class for about an hour, I stopped by an Internet café near Odawara Station and did a Google search for the name Menshiki. I came up empty-handed. There were lots of online articles with the character **men** in them, as in **unten** men**kyo**—driver's license—and the **shiki** appeared in ones about partial color-blindness—shiki**jaku**. But there didn't seem to be any information out there in the world about a Mr. Menshiki. His statement that he took anonymity seriously seemed, indeed, to be the case. I was assuming, of course, that Menshiki was his real name, but my gut told me he wouldn't lie about something like that. It didn't make sense for him to tell me where he lived but not tell me his real name. And unless he had some compelling reason, it seemed to me that if he were to make up a phony name, he would choose one that was more common and didn't stand out so much.

When I got back home I called Masahiko Amada. After chatting a bit I asked if he knew anything about the man named Menshiki who lived across the valley.

I described the white concrete house on the mountain. He had a vague memory of it.

"Menshiki?" Masahiko asked. "What kind of name is that?"

"It's written with the characters that mean 'avoiding colors.'"

"Sounds like a Chinese ink painting."

"But white and black are counted as colors," I pointed out.

"In theory, I suppose. . . . Menshiki? I don't think I've heard the name. I wouldn't know anything about anyone living on a mountain across the valley. I mean, I don't even know the people living on **your** side of the valley. Is there something going on between the two of you?"

"We sort of connected," I said. "And I was wondering if you knew anything about him."

"Did you check online?"

"I did a Google search but struck out."

"How about Facebook or other social media?"

"I don't know much about those."

"While you were asleep with the fish in the Dragon King's palace, like in the fairy tale, culture has forged on ahead. Not to worry—I'll check them for you. If I find anything, I'll give you a call."

"Thanks."

Masahiko was suddenly silent. On the other end of the phone it felt like he was contemplating something.

"Hold on a sec. Did you say Menshiki?" Masahiko asked.

"That's right. Menshiki. The **men** in **menzeiten**—'avoidance'—and the **shiki** in 'color'—**shikisai**."

"**Menshiki** . . . ," he said. "You know, I do remember now hearing that name before. Maybe I'm just imagining it."

"It's such an unusual name I'd think if you heard it once you wouldn't forget it."

"Agreed. Which is why maybe it's stuck in a corner of my mind. But I can't remember when I heard it, or in what context. It feels like when you have a small fishbone stuck in your throat."

If you remember, let me know, I said. Will do, Masahiko promised.

I hung up and then had a light meal. While I was eating, a call came in from the married woman I was having an affair with. Do you mind if I come to your place tomorrow afternoon? she asked. No problem, I replied.

"By the way, do you know anything about a person named Menshiki?" I asked. "He lives in the neighborhood."

"Menshiki?" she repeated. "Is that the last name?"

I explained how it was written.

"I've never heard of him," she said.

"You know that white concrete house across the valley from me? He lives there."

"I remember that house. The one you see from the terrace that really stands out."

"That's his house."

"Mr. Menshiki lives there?"

"That's right."

"So what about him?"

"Nothing, really. I just wanted to know if you knew him or not."

Her voice grew one tone darker. "Does that have something to do with me?"

"No, nothing to do with you."

She sighed, as if in relief. "Well, I'll see you tomorrow afternoon. Probably about one thirty."

"I'm looking forward to it," I said. I hung up and finished eating.

The call from Masahiko came a little while after that.

"It seems like there are a few people with the name Menshiki in Kagawa Prefecture down in Shikoku," Masahiko said. "Perhaps this Mr. Menshiki has roots in Kagawa. But I couldn't find any information anywhere on a Menshiki living now around Odawara. What's his first name?"

"He didn't tell me. I don't know what kind of work he does, either. Something tech related. If his lifestyle is any indication, he must be doing pretty well. That's all I know. I don't even know how old he is."

"I see," Masahiko said. "In that case, that might be the best you can do. Information is, after all, a product, and if you pay enough you can neatly cover your tracks. Even truer if the person knows a lot about technology."

"You mean Mr. Menshiki erased his footprints?"

"Could be. I spent a lot of time online, searching through sites, and didn't get a single hit. It's such an eye-catching name, yet there's not a thing online. Which is all pretty strange. I know you're a little naive when it comes to things like this, but for someone who is fairly active in society to completely block any information about themselves and have nothing at all get out on the web—that's no mean feat. Even information on you, and on me, is out there and available. There's information on me I didn't even know. If that's true for nobodies like us, you can imagine how much harder it is for some big shot to erase their digital presence. Like it or not, that's the world we live in. What about you? Have you checked out the information that's out there on you?"

"No, never."

"You should keep it that way."

"That's the plan," I told him.

One aspect of my job is gathering all kinds of information. That's the sort of business I'm in. Those were Menshiki's own words. If he could get hold of information that easily he could probably erase it as well.

"By the way, Mr. Menshiki said he looked me up on the Internet and saw a few of my portraits there," I said.

"And?"

"And he asked me to paint his portrait. He said he liked the portraits I've done."

"But you turned him down because you're no longer in the portrait business. Correct?"

133

I was silent.

"Are you telling me you didn't?" he asked.

"Actually, I didn't turn him down."

"How come? Weren't you set on not doing any more?"

"The fee is pretty hefty, that's why. I thought it might be okay to do one more portrait."

"For the money?"

"That's a big reason. I'm making hardly any money anymore, and I have to think about how I'm going to make a living. My expenses right now are minimal, but still, with one thing and another the money keeps flowing out."

"Huh. So, how much is the fee?"

I named the amount. Masahiko let out a whistle.

"Wow," he said. "That certainly makes it worth taking on. I bet you were surprised when you heard how much he'd pay?"

"Yeah, of course I was."

"Maybe I shouldn't say this, but there can't be any other odd people out there willing to pay that much for one of your paintings."

"I know."

"Don't get me wrong, I'm not saying you're not a talented artist. You do solid work, and people recognize that. I think you're about the only one of our classmates from our art school class who's managed to make a living doing oil paintings. What level of living we're talking about, I have no idea, but anyway it's admirable what you've accomplished. But honestly?

You're no Rembrandt, or Delacroix. Or even Andy Warhol."

"I'm well aware of that."

"If you are, then you understand how exorbitant that fee is he's offering, right?"

"Of course I do."

"And just **by chance** he lives near you."

"Exactly."

" 'By chance' is putting it mildly."

I didn't say anything.

"There might be something else to it. Didn't that cross your mind?" he asked.

"Sure, I thought about it. But what else there could be, I have no clue."

"So you accepted the job?"

"I did. I start the day after tomorrow."

"Because the fee's so good?"

"The fee's a big part of it. But that's not all. There are other reasons," I said. "Honestly, I want to see how things are going to play out. See with my own eyes why he's willing to pay so much. And if there're really other motives at work, I want to find out what they are."

"I see," Masahiko said, and paused. "Well, if there are any new developments, let me know. I'm intrigued."

Just then I recalled the horned owl.

"I forgot to mention it, but there's a horned owl living in the attic," I said. "A little gray horned owl that sleeps on a beam during the day. At night it goes out the vent hole and hunts. I don't know how long it's been here, but it seems to have roosted."

"In the attic?"

"I heard a sound from the ceiling, so I climbed up during the day to check on it."

"Really. I didn't know you could access the attic."

"There's an opening in the closet in the guest bedroom. It's a tight space, though. Smaller than what you might think of as an attic. But just the right size for an owl to roost in."

"That's a good thing, though," Masahiko said. "With an owl there, no mice or snakes will get in. I've heard it's a lucky omen to have an owl roosting in a house."

"Maybe that lucky omen brought me that high portrait fee."

"That would be nice if it did," he laughed. "You know the English expression 'a blessing in disguise'?"

"Languages aren't my strong suit."

"A camouflaged blessing. A blessing that's changed appearance. At first glance it seems unfortunate, but it turns out to bring you happiness. There are things that should be the opposite, too, of course. In theory."

In theory, I repeated to myself.

"Better keep your eyes open," he said.

"Will do," I said.

At one thirty the next day she came to see me, and as always we headed straight for bed. While we had sex we hardly said a word. It was raining that afternoon, an unusually heavy shower for autumn, more like a midsummer downpour. Heavy raindrops, carried on the wind, rapped against the window, and I think there were a few flashes of lightning, too. A thick bank of dark clouds passed over the valley, and when the rain let up, the mountains had taken on a darker hue. Flocks of birds that had taken shelter from the rain somewhere now twittered back and were busily hunting down insects. Right after rain was the perfect lunchtime for them. The sun shone from breaks in the clouds, making the raindrops on all the tree branches sparkle. While it had been raining we were deep into making love, and I had barely given the falling rain a second thought. And just as we were finishing, the rain abruptly stopped. Almost as if it were waiting for us.

We lay naked in bed, wrapped in a thin bedcover, talking. Mostly we talked about the grades her two daughters were getting in school. The older girl was good at school and had very good grades. She was a placid child who never caused any trouble. The younger daughter, in contrast, hated to study and would never settle down at her desk to do homework. But she was cheerful and upbeat, and quite good-looking as well. Self-assured, popular, good at sports. Maybe we should give up on having her do well at school, her mother said, and let her go into the entertainment field? I'm thinking of eventually putting her into one of those schools that train child entertainers, she said.

If you think about it, it was kind of strange. I was

lying there next to a woman I'd known for only about three months, listening to her talk about her daughters, whom I'd never laid eyes on. She was even asking me my opinion on what sort of path they should take in life. And the two of us there, without a stitch on. Admittedly, though, not a bad feeling, to take a random peek into the lives of people I hardly knew. Brushing past the lives of people I would never have anything to do with. Their lives felt right before me, yet also far away. As she talked, the woman toyed with my now flaccid penis, which was slowly coming back to life.

"Have you been painting anything these days?" she asked.

"Not really," I answered honestly.

"No creative urge welling up?"

I hesitated. ". . . Well, tomorrow I have to start on a commission I got."

"You're going to paint on commission?"

"That's right. Have to earn some money sometimes."

"What sort of commission?"

"A portrait."

"Is it, by any chance, a portrait of that person you mentioned on the phone yesterday, Mr. Menshiki?"

"It is," I said. She was so sharp at times it took me by surprise.

"And you want to know something about this Mr. Menshiki, right?"

"At this point he's a mystery. I met him once and we talked, but I still have no idea what sort of person he is. I like to know what kind of person I'm going to paint."

"You should just ask him directly."

"He might not give me a straight answer," I said. "He might only tell me what he wants me to know."

"I could look into it for you," she said.

"You can do that?"

"I might have an idea."

"There were zero hits on him on the Internet."

"The Internet doesn't work well in the jungle," she said. "The jungle has its own communications network. Signaling with drums, tying a message around a monkey's neck."

"I don't know much about the jungle, I'm afraid."

"When civilization's devices don't operate, it's worth trying drums or a monkey."

My penis had now grown fully erect under her soft, busy fingers. She skillfully and greedily began to use her lips and tongue, and a meaningful silence descended upon us for a while. As the birds outside chirped and went about the work of making a living, the two of us began a second round of sex.

After our long second bout of lovemaking, punctuated by an intermission, we climbed out of bed, lazily gathered our clothes from the floor, and dressed. We went out to the terrace and, sipping hot herb tea, gazed across the valley at the large white concrete house there. We sat side by side on the weathered wooden deck chairs and breathed in deeply the fresh dampness of the mountain air. Through the woods to the southwest was a small patch of sparkling ocean, a mere fragment of the enormous Pacific. The mountain slopes around were already dyed with autumn colors, minute gradations of yellow and red, with an intrusion of green from the clumps of evergreens. The mix of these vivid colors made the white concrete of Menshiki's house stand out all the more. It was an almost obsessive white that looked like it would never be dirtied or treated with contempt by such things as wind, rain, dust, or even time itself. **White is a color, too**, I thought distractedly. Definitely not the lack of color. We sat there on the lounge chairs for a long time without saying a word, silence an entirely natural companion.

"Mr. Menshiki in his white mansion," she said after a while. "Sounds like the beginning of an amusing fairy tale."

But what awaited me was, of course, not some "amusing fairy tale." Or a blessing in disguise, either. But by the time that became clear to me, there was no turning back.

9

EXCHANGING FRAGMENTS
WITH EACH OTHER

On Friday at one thirty Menshiki appeared in the same Jaguar. The deep roar of the engine as it climbed the steep slope grew louder as it approached, and finally came to a stop in front of the house. As before, he shut the door of the car with the same solid sound, and removed his sunglasses and slipped them into the breast pocket of his jacket. An exact repeat of the previous visit. This time, though, he wore a white polo shirt with a blue-gray cotton jacket, cream-colored chinos, and brown leather shoes. He was so impeccably dressed that he could have been a model in a magazine, though he didn't give the impression that it was all **too perfect**. It looked casual, and naturally neat. And that abundant white hair of his was, like the walls of his mansion, a pure, unadulterated white. Just as I had the first time, I watched him approach through a gap in the curtains.

The front doorbell rang and I opened it and let him in. This time he didn't hold his hand out to shake mine. He just looked me in the eye, and gave a small smile and a brief nod of greeting. I breathed a sigh of relief. I'd been a bit anxious that every time we met I'd have to go through one of his firm handshakes.

Once again, I showed him into the living room and had him sit on the sofa. And brought out two cups of freshly brewed coffee from the kitchen.

"I didn't know what I should wear," he said, sounding apologetic. "Is this outfit all right?"

"It doesn't matter at this point. We can decide at the end how you should be dressed. A suit, or shorts and sandals, we can adjust the clothes later on however we want."

Or show you holding a Starbucks cup, I added to myself.

"Knowing you're going to be modeling makes you anxious. I know I won't have to take off all my clothes, but it still makes me feel like I'm being stripped down."

"You could be right. Models for paintings sometimes pose nude—in most cases actually nude, in some cases more metaphorically. The artist wants to view the model's essence, meaning he has to strip away the clothed, outer appearance. To do that, of course, takes great powers of observation and a sharp intuition."

Menshiki spread his hands on his lap and seemed to be inspecting them. He then looked up. "I heard that you don't use a live model when you paint a portrait."

"That's right. I meet the subject once and have a long talk with him, but don't have him model live for me."

"Is there a reason for that?"

"No real reason. I've just found, through experience, that things go more smoothly that way. When we first meet I concentrate as much as I can, trying to get a take on the subject's looks, expressions, quirks, and tendencies, and brand those into my memory. Once I've done that, it's just a question of reproducing them from memory."

"That's very intriguing," Menshiki said. "So, days later you take the memory you've burned into your brain, rearrange all that as an image, and reproduce it as a work of art. You must have a gift to do that—to have such extraordinary visual recall."

"I wouldn't call it a gift, exactly. More of a skill set, I'd say."

"Maybe that's why, when I saw some of the portraits you've done, I sensed something unique in them. Compared with other standard portraits—portraits done purely as commodities. The way everything's reproduced so vividly, you might say . . ."

He took a sip of coffee, took a light-cream linen handkerchief from his jacket pocket, and wiped his mouth. "But this time, unusually, you'll be using a model—with me in front of you, in other words—as you do the portrait."

"Exactly. At your request."

He nodded. "Truthfully, I was curious. About how it feels to become part of a painting, right in front of your eyes. I wanted to actually experience it. Not simply have my painting done, but to experience it as a kind of exchange."

"An exchange?"

"Between the two of us, you and me."

143

I was silent. The meaning of the expression "an exchange" eluded me for a moment.

"We exchange parts of us with each other," Menshiki explained. "I offer something of myself, and you offer something of yourself. It doesn't have to be something valuable. It can be simple, like a kind of sign."

"Like children exchange pretty seashells?"

"Exactly."

I thought about this. "Sounds interesting, but the problem is I don't have any nice seashells to offer you."

"You're not so comfortable doing it this way? Are you intentionally avoiding that kind of exchange? Is that why you don't use live models? If that's true, then I can—"

"No—that's not it. I don't use models because I don't need them. That's all. I'm not trying to avoid an interchange between people. I've studied painting for a long time, and have used live models more times than I can remember. If you don't mind the drudgery of sitting still in a hard chair for hours at a time, I'm totally fine with you posing for me."

"I don't mind," Menshiki said, spreading his palms up, lightly lifting them upward. "Then why don't we commence the drudgery?"

We went into the studio. I brought over a dining room chair and had Menshiki sit in that. I let him assume whatever posture he wanted. I sat on an old wooden stool facing him (no doubt the stool To-mohiko Amada used when he painted), and started sketching with a soft pencil. I needed to decide on a basic approach of how I was going to reproduce his face on canvas.

"Is it boring to sit there? If you'd like, we could listen to some music," I said.

"If it doesn't bother you, I'd love to hear some music," Menshiki said.

"Why don't you choose something from the shelf in the living room."

He spent about five minutes perusing the selection of records and returned with a four-disc boxed set of LPs of Georg Solti conducting a performance of Richard Strauss's **Der Rosenkavalier**. The orchestra was the Vienna Philharmonic, the singers Régine Crespin and Yvonne Minton.

"Do you like **Der Rosenkavalier**?" he asked me.

"I've never heard it."

"It's an unusual opera. The plot's critical, of course, like with all operas, but with this one even if you don't know the plot it's easy to give yourself over to the music and be completely enveloped by that world. The world of supreme bliss Strauss achieved at the peak of his powers. When it was first performed, people criticized it as nostalgic, unadventurous even, where in reality the music is quite progressive and un-inhibited. He was influenced by Wagner, but Strauss creates his own strange, unique musical realm. Once you get into this music you can't get enough of it. I usually prefer Karajan's or Erich Kleiber's version, and have never heard Solti's. If it's all right with you, I'd like to take this opportunity to hear it."

"Of course. Let's listen to it."

He placed the record on the turntable, lowered the needle, and carefully adjusted the volume on the amp. He went back to his chair, settled into a proper pose, and concentrated on the music flowing from the speakers. I did some quick sketches in my sketchbook of his face from several angles. His face was overall nicely put together, the features distinctive enough that I didn't find it hard to capture the unique details of each. In the space of thirty minutes I completed five sketches from different angles. But when I examined them again, I was struck by an odd, helpless feeling. My sketches had accurately captured what was distinctive about his face, yet there was nothing about them beyond the sense that they were **well-done drawings**. They were all oddly shallow and superficial, devoid of depth. They were no different from caricatures drawn by some street artist. I tried doing a few more sketches, with basically the same result.

For me, this was pretty unusual. I had years of experience reconstructing people's faces in a drawing, and flattered myself that I was good at it. Whether with a pencil or a paintbrush I could almost always come up with several mental images of what I was after with no trouble. I rarely struggled to decide on the composition of a painting. But now, with Menshiki as my model, not a single image came to me.

Perhaps I was overlooking something important. I couldn't help but think that. Maybe Menshiki was adeptly hiding it from me. Or maybe it didn't exist in him to begin with.

When the B side of the first of the four records in **Der Rosenkavalier** set finished I gave up, shut my sketchbook, and laid down my pencil. I lifted the needle, took the record off the turntable, and returned it to the boxed set. I glanced at my watch and sighed.

"I'm finding it very hard to draw you," I admitted.

He looked at me in surprise. "In what way?" he asked. "Are you saying there's some pictorial issue with the way I look?"

I shook my head slightly. "No, it's not that. Of course there's nothing wrong with your face."

"Then what's making it hard?"

"I wish I could tell you. It just feels that way. Maybe we still haven't **exchanged** enough yet, as you put it. Haven't traded enough seashells."

Menshiki smiled, looking a bit perplexed. "Is there anything I can do to help?"

I stood up from the stool, went over to the window, and watched the birds flying over the woods.

"Mr. Menshiki, if it's all right with you, could you give me a little more information about yourself? I know next to nothing about you."

"Of course. I'm not trying to hide anything. No

outrageous secrets or anything I'm trying to keep from you. I can tell you just about everything. What sort of information were you thinking of?"

"Well—for starters, I don't even know your full name."

"That's right!" he said, looking a bit surprised. "Now that you mention it, you're absolutely right. I was so caught up in talking I forgot to give this to you."

He took a black leather holder from a pocket of his chinos and removed a business card. He handed me the card, and I read it. The thick white card simply read:

免色　　渉
WATARU MENSHIKI

On the back was an address in Kanagawa Prefecture, a phone number, and an email address. That was all. No company name or title.

"The **wataru** in my name is the character that means 'to cross a river,'" Menshiki said. "I don't know why I was given that name. I've never had much to do with water."

"The name Menshiki isn't one you see very often."

"I heard our family's roots are in Shikoku, but I

have no connection to Shikoku at all. I was born and raised in Tokyo, all my schooling was in Tokyo. And I prefer soba noodles to udon, which Shikoku is famous for." Menshiki laughed.

"May I ask how old you are?"

"Of course. I turned fifty-four last month. How old do I look to you?"

I shook my head. "Honestly, I had no idea. That's why I asked."

"It must be this white hair," he said with a smile. "People often tell me they can't tell my age because of the white hair. You often hear about people whose hair turned white overnight because they were terrified. People often ask if that's what happened with me, but I never had such a traumatic experience. I just tended to have a lot of white hair, ever since I was young. By the time I was in my mid-forties it was completely white. It's weird, though, since my grandfather, father, and two older brothers are all bald. In the whole family I'm the only one who has completely white hair."

"If you don't mind me asking, what sort of work are you involved in?"

"I don't mind at all. It's just—hard to talk about."

"If you'd rather not . . ."

"It's a little embarrassing, actually," he said. "Right now I'm not working at all. Not that I'm getting unemployment insurance or anything, but officially I'm unemployed. I spend a few hours each day online in my office in stock trading and currency exchange, though we're not talking large amounts. More a hobby or to kill time. Training to keep my mind active. Like a pianist practices scales every day."

Menshiki took a quiet, deep breath and recrossed his legs. "In the past I started and ran a tech-related company, but not long ago I decided to sell all my stock and step down. The buyer was a major telecommunications company. That sale meant I have enough savings to live on for a while. I used that opportunity to sell my house in Tokyo and move here. Basically, I'm retired. My savings are divided among several overseas banks, and I move those around depending on variable exchange rates, so I make a bit of a profit that way."

"I see," I said. "Do you have a family?"

"No family. I've never been married."

"So you live in that huge house all by yourself?"

He nodded. "I do. At this point I have no household staff. I've lived by myself for a long time and am used to doing housework. But since it's such a big place, I can't clean it all myself, so I hire a cleaning service to come in once a week. Other than that, I pretty much take care of everything. What about you?"

I shook my head. "I've been on my own less than a year. Still an amateur."

Menshiki gave a slight nod, but didn't ask any questions or offer any comments. "Are you close to Tomohiko Amada?" he asked.

"No, I've never even met him. I was with his son in art school, and through that connection he asked me if I wanted to take care of the vacant house.

Some things came up in my life and I didn't have any place to live then, so I decided to accept the offer. For the time being."

Menshiki gave a few more small nods. "It's not very convenient for anyone working at a regular job, but for folks like you two, I imagine it's a wonderful environment."

I gave a forced smile. "We might both be painters, but Tomohiko Amada and I are on totally different levels. It's embarrassing to even be mentioned in the same breath as him."

Menshiki raised his head and looked at me, his eyes serious. "It's too soon to say that. You might become a well-known artist someday."

There was nothing I could say to that, so I was silent.

"Sometimes people go through huge transformations," Menshiki said. "They obliterate the style they've worked in, and out of the ruins they rise up again. Tomohiko Amada was that way. When he was young he painted Western-style work. You've heard about this, I'm sure?"

"I have. Before the war he was a promising young painter of Western-style art. But after he came back from studying in Vienna he changed to being a Japanese-style artist, and after the war was amazingly successful."

"The way I see it," Menshiki said, "there's a point in everybody's life where they need a major transformation. And when that time comes you have to grab it by the tail. Grab it hard, and never let go. There are some people who are able to, and others who can't. Tomohiko Amada was one who could."

A major transformation. The words suddenly made me think of **Killing Commendatore**. And the young man stabbing the Commendatore to death.

"Do you know much about Japanese-style painting?" Menshiki asked.

I shook my head. "I'm basically a layman. I attended lectures on it when I was in art school, but that's the extent of my knowledge."

"This is a very basic question, but how is Japanese art defined, professionally?"

"It's not so easy to define. It's usually taken to mean paintings done using glue and pigment and foil leaf. And done not with a paintbrush, but with a writing brush. In other words Japanese paintings are defined mainly by the materials used to paint them. The transmission of ancient, traditional techniques is one feature, though there are lots of Japanese paintings done using avant-garde techniques, and with colors, too, there is a lot of use of new materials. So the definition has steadily become increasingly vague. But as far as Tomohiko Amada's paintings go, they're classic Japanese art. Archetypal, you might call them. They're done in a style that's recognizably his own, of course. I just mean as far as techniques are concerned."

"So you're saying that if the definition based on materials and techniques gets vague, all you're left with is the mental aspect, right?"

"Maybe so. But the mental aspect of Japanese paintings isn't easily defined. They are, from the beginning, rather eclectic."

"By eclectic you mean . . . ?"

I searched the depths of memory and recalled what I'd learned in art history class. "The Meiji Restoration took place in the latter half of the nineteenth century, and along with other aspects of Western culture Western art also was introduced into Japan, but until then the genre of 'Japanese painting' didn't actually exist. The term didn't even exist. Just like up till then the name of the country, Japan, was hardly ever used. With the appearance of Western art from abroad, the concept of Japanese art was born as a way of asserting something that could be distinguished as standing in opposition to Western art. What had existed up until then in various forms and styles was, for the sake of simplicity, lumped together under the new name of 'Japanese painting.' Of course, there were some types of painting that were excluded from that and fell into decline. Chinese ink paintings, for instance. The Meiji government established and cultivated so-called Japanese painting as a kind of national art, as part of Japanese cultural identity that could stand shoulder to shoulder with Western culture—the 'Japanese spirit' part of the popular slogan at the time—'Japanese Spirit with Western Learning.' What had been everyday designs, arts and crafts designs such as paintings on folding screens and **fusuma** sliding doors and bowls and plates, were now set in frames and featured in art exhibitions. To put it another way, items done in a natural style as part of everyday life were now accommodated to the Western system and elevated to the status of 'works of art.'"

I paused for a moment and studied Menshiki's face. He seemed to be listening closely to what I said. I went on.

"Tenshin Okakura and Ernest Fenollosa were at the forefront of this movement. What happened with art could be counted as one of the amazing success stories during this period when aspects of Japanese culture were rapidly being reconfigured. A similar process was taking place in the worlds of music, literature, and thought. It must have been a pretty hectic time for Japanese back then, since they had tons of important work they had to accomplish in a very short period of time. Looking back on it now, I'd say we did a pretty clever and skillful job of it. The merging and compartmentalizing of Western aspects and non-Western aspects took place very smoothly. Maybe Japanese are intrinsically suited to that kind of process.

"So Japanese painting wasn't clearly defined originally. You might say it was a concept based on a vague consensus. There wasn't initially a clear division, and it only came about tangentially, when external and internal pressure created one."

Menshiki seemed to be considering all this. "It might have been vague," he finally said, "but this was a consensus born of necessity, right?"

"Exactly. A consensus arising out of necessity."

"Not having a set framework was both a strength and a weakness of Japanese painting. Could we interpret it this way?"

"I think so."

"But when we look at a painting, in most cases we have the sense whether it's a Japanese painting or not. Right?"

"That's right. There's an intrinsic method used. A kind of trend, or tone. And a tacit, shared understanding. It's hard sometimes to define it, though."

Menshiki was silent for a while. "If a painting is non-Western, then does it have the form of a Japanese painting?"

"Not necessarily," I replied. "In principle there are Western paintings that have a non-Western form."

"I see," he said. He tilted his head ever so slightly. "But if it's a Japanese painting, then to some extent it will have a non-Western form about it. Would that be accurate?"

I gave it some thought. "Put that way, yes, you could say so. I hadn't thought about it that way, to tell you the truth."

"It's self-evident, but still difficult to put into words."

I nodded in agreement.

He paused for a moment, and then went on. "If you think about it, it's akin to defining yourself as compared with another person. The difference is self-evident, but still difficult to verbalize. As you said, you can perhaps only understand it as a kind of tangent produced when external and internal pressure combine to create it."

Menshiki gave a slight smile. "Fascinating," he added in a small voice, as if to himself.

What are we talking about? I suddenly thought. An intriguing topic in its own right, but what significance did this conversation hold for him? Was it mere intellectual curiosity? Or was he testing my intellect? What was the point?

"By the way, I'm left-handed," Menshiki said at one point, as if he'd just recalled this fact. "I don't know if that will be helpful, but it's another piece of information about me. If I'm told to go left or right, I always choose left. It's become a habit."

It was finally near three o'clock, and we set the date and time of our next session. He would come to my house in three days, on Monday at one p.m. As he did this day, we would spend two hours together in my studio, and I would attempt to sketch him again.

"I'm in no rush," Menshiki said. "As I said in the beginning, take as much time as you need. I have all the time in the world."

And then he left. Through the window I watched him get into his Jaguar and drive away. I picked up all the sketches I'd done of him, studied them for a time, then tossed them aside.

A terrible silence descended over the house. Now alone, it was as if the silence had become all the more weighty. I went out on the terrace and there was no wind, the air jelly-thick and chilly. It felt like it was going to rain.

I sat down on the living room sofa, reviewing the conversation Menshiki and I had had, in order. How we'd talked about posing for a portrait. About Strauss's opera **Der Rosenkavalier**. About how Menshiki had started a tech company, sold off his stock, and with the sizable profit retired young. How he lived all alone in that huge house. His first name was Wataru. Written with the character that means "to cross a river." He'd always been a bachelor, and his hair had turned white early on. He was left-handed and was now fifty-four. How Tomohiko Amada had made a bold pivot, how one should grab opportunity by the tail and never let go. The definition of Japanese painting. And finally, about the relationship between Self and Other.

What in the world did he want from me?

And why wasn't I able to do any decent sketches of him?

The answer was simple, really. **Because I had not yet grasped what lay at the core of his being.**

After talking with him I felt uneasy. Yet at the same time, my curiosity about him had grown all the stronger.

Thirty minutes later heavy drops of rain began to fall. The little birds had by then already vanished.

10

AS WE PUSH OUR WAY THROUGH THE LUSH GREEN GRASS

When I was fifteen my younger sister died. It happened very suddenly. She was twelve then, in her first year of junior high. She had been born with a congenital heart problem, but since the time she was in the upper grades of elementary school she hadn't shown any more symptoms, and our family had felt reassured, holding out the faint hope that her life would go on, without incident. But in May of that year her heartbeat became more irregular. It was especially bad when she lay down, and she suffered many sleepless nights. She underwent tests at the university hospital, but no matter how detailed the tests the doctors couldn't pinpoint any changes in her physical condition. The basic issue was supposed to have been resolved back when she'd had her operations, and the doctors were baffled.

"Avoid strenuous exercise, and follow a regular routine, and things should settle down soon," the doctor said. That was probably all he could say. And he wrote out a few prescriptions for her.

But her arrhythmia didn't settle down. As I sat ~ross from her at the dining table I often looked ~er chest and imagined the defective heart inside it. Her breasts were beginning to noticeably develop. Her heart might have problems, but her flesh continued growing nonetheless. It felt strange to see my little sister's breasts grow by the day. Up till then she'd just been a little child, but now she'd suddenly had her first period, and her breasts were slowly starting to take shape. Yet within that tiny chest, my sister's heart was defective. And even a specialist couldn't pinpoint the defect. That fact alone had my brain in constant turmoil. I spent my adolescence in a state of anxiety, fearful that, at any moment, I might lose my little sister.

My parents told me to watch over her, since her body was so delicate. While we attended the same elementary school I always kept my eye on her. If need be, I was willing to risk my life to protect her and her tiny heart. Though the opportunity never presented itself.

She was on her way home from junior high one day when she collapsed and lost consciousness while climbing the stairs at Seibu Shinjuku Station. She was rushed by ambulance to the nearest emergency room. By the time I got home and then raced to the hospital, her heart had already stopped. It all happened in the blink of an eye. That morning we'd eaten breakfast together, said goodbye to each other at the front door, me going off to high school, she to junior high. And the next time I saw her she'd stopped breathing. Her large eyes were closed forever, her mouth slightly open as if she were about to say something. Her developing breasts would never grow.

The next time I saw her she was in a coffin. She was dressed in her favorite black velvet dress, with a touch of makeup, her hair neatly combed. She had on black patent-leather shoes and lay faceup in the modestly sized coffin. The dress had a white lace collar, so white it looked unnatural.

Lying there, she appeared to be peacefully sleeping. Shake her lightly and she'd wake up, it seemed. But that was an illusion. Shake her all you want, but she would never awaken again.

I didn't want my sister's delicate little body to be stuffed into that cramped, confining box. Her body should be laid to rest on a much more spacious place. In the middle of a meadow, for instance. We would wordlessly go to visit her, pushing aside the lush green grass as we went. The wind would slowly rustle the grass, and birds and insects would call out from all around her. The raw smell of wildflowers would fill the air, pollen swirling. When night fell, the sky above her would be dotted with countless silvery stars. In the morning a new sun would make the dew on the blades of grass sparkle like jewels. But in reality she was packed away in some ridiculous coffin. The only decorations were ominous white flowers that had been snipped by scissors and stuck in vases. The narrow room had fluorescent lighting that was drained of color. From a small speaker set into the ceiling came the artificial strains of organ music.

I couldn't stand to see her be cremated. When the ꞏoffin lid was shut and locked, I couldn't take it anymore and left the cremation room. I didn't help when the family ritually placed her bones inside a vase. I went out into the crematorium courtyard and cried soundlessly by myself. During her all-too-short life, I'd never once helped my little sister, a thought that hurt me deeply.

After my sister's death, our family changed. My father became even more taciturn, my mother even more nervous and jumpy. Basically I kept on with the same life as always. I joined the mountaineering club at school, which kept me busy, and when I wasn't doing that I started oil painting. My art teacher recommended that I find a good instructor and really study painting. And when I finally did start attending art classes, my interest became serious. I think I was trying to keep myself busy so I wouldn't think about my dead sister.

For a long time, I'm not sure how many years, my parents kept her room exactly as it was. Textbooks and study guides, pens, erasers, and paper clips piled on her desk, the sheets, blankets, and pillows on her bed, her laundered and folded pajamas, her junior high school uniform hanging in the closet—all untouched. The calendar on the wall still had her schedule written in her tiny writing. It was left at the month she died, as if time had frozen solid at that point. It felt as if the door would open at any moment and she'd come inside. When no one else was at home I'd sometimes go into her room, sit down on the neatly made bed, and gaze around me. But I never touched anything. I didn't want to disturb, even a little, any of the silent little objects left behind, signs that my sister had once been among the living.

I often tried to imagine what sort of life my sister would have had if she hadn't died at twelve. Though there was no way I could know. I couldn't even picture how my own life would turn out, so I had no idea what her future would have held. But I knew that if only she hadn't had a problem with one of her heart valves, she would have grown to be a capable, attractive adult. I'm sure many men would have loved her, and held her gently in their arms. But I couldn't picture any of that in detail. For me, she was forever my little sister, three years younger, who needed my protection.

For a time after she died I drew sketches of her, over and over. Reproducing in my sketchbook, from all different angles, my memory of her face, so I wouldn't forget it. Not that I was about to forget her face. It will remain etched in my mind until the day I die. What I sought was not to forget the face I remembered at that point in time. In order to do that, I had to give form to it by drawing. I was only fifteen then, and there was so much I didn't know about memory, drawing, and the flow of time. But one thing I did know was that I needed to do something in order to hold on to an accurate record of my memory. Leave it alone, and it would disappear somewhere. No matter how vivid a memory, the power of time was stronger. I knew this instinctively.

I would sit alone in her room on her bed, drawing

her, sketching her face over and over. I tried to re-produce onto the blank paper how she looked in my mind's eye. I lacked experience then, and the requisite technical skill, so it wasn't an easy process. I'd draw, rip up my effort, draw and rip up, endlessly. But now when I look at the drawings I did keep (I still treasure my sketchbook from back then), I can see that they are filled with a genuine sense of grief. They may be technically immature, but it was a sincere effort, my own soul trying to awaken my sister's. When I looked at those sketches, I couldn't help but cry. I've done countless drawings since, but never again has any-thing I've drawn brought me to tears.

There's one other effect my sister's death had on me—a very severe case of claustrophobia. Ever since I saw her be placed in that cramped little coffin, the lid shut and locked tight, and taken away to the crematorium, I haven't been able to go into tight, enclosed places. For a long time I couldn't take elevators. I'd stand in front of an elevator and all I could think about was it automatically shutting down in an earthquake, with me trapped inside that confined space. Just the thought of it was enough to send me into a choking sense of panic.

These symptoms didn't appear right after my sis-ter's death. It took nearly three years for them to sur-face. The first time I had a panic attack was soon after I started art school, when I had a part-time job with a moving company. I was the driver's assistant in a covered truck, loading boxes and taking them out, and one time I got mistakenly locked inside the empty cargo compartment. Work was done for the day and the driver was checking to see if anything was left behind in the cargo compartment. He forgot to make sure if anyone was still inside, and locked the door from the outside.

About two and half hours passed until the door was opened and I was able to crawl out. That whole time I was locked inside a sealed, cramped, totally dark place. It wasn't a refrigerated truck or anything, so there were gaps where air could get in. If I'd thought about it calmly, I would have known I wouldn't suffocate.

But still, a terrible panic had me in its grip. There was plenty of oxygen, yet no matter how deeply I breathed in, I wasn't able to absorb it. My breathing got more and more ragged and I started hyperventilating. I felt dizzy, like I was choking, and was overwhelmed by an inexplicable panic. It's okay, calm down, I told myself. You'll be able to get out soon. It's impossible to suffocate here. But logic didn't work. The only thing in my mind was my little sister, crammed into a tiny coffin, and hauled off to the crematorium. Completely terrified, I pounded on the walls of the truck.

The truck was in the company parking lot, and all the employees, their workday done, had gone home. Nobody noticed that I wasn't around. I pounded like crazy, but no one seemed to hear. If I was unlucky I might be shut inside until morning. At the thought of that, it felt like all my muscles were about to disintegrate.

It was the night security guard, making his rounds of the parking lot, who finally heard the noise I was making and unlocked the door. When he saw how agitated and exhausted I was, he had me lie down on the bed in the company break room. And gave me a cup of hot tea. I don't know how long I lay there. But finally my breathing became normal again. Dawn was coming, so I thanked the guard and took the first train of the day back home. I slipped into my own bed and lay there, shaking like crazy for the longest time.

Ever since then, riding elevators has triggered the same panic. The incident must have awoken a fear that had been lurking within me. And I have little doubt this was set off by memories of my dead sister. And it wasn't only elevators, but any enclosed space. I couldn't even watch movies with scenes set in submarines or tanks. Just imagining myself shut inside such confined spaces—**merely** imagining it— made me unable to breathe. Often I had to get up and leave the theater. If a scene came on of someone shut away in a confined space, I couldn't stand to watch. That's why I seldom watched movies with anyone else.

One time on a trip to Hokkaido I had no choice but to stay overnight in one of those capsule hotels. My breathing became labored, and I couldn't sleep, so I went outside and spent the night inside my car. It was early spring in Hokkaido, still quite cold, and the whole night was like a nightmare.

My wife often kidded me about my panic attacks. When we had to go to a floor high up in a building she would precede me in the elevator and would wait there, enjoying me huffing and puffing my way up sixteen or so flights of stairs. But I never explained to her why I had that phobia. I just told her I've always had a fear of elevators.

"Well, it might be healthier for you to walk," she said.

I also had a feeling akin to fear about women with larger than normal breasts. I don't know if that has anything to do with my sister, or the way her breasts were just beginning to develop when she died. Still, I've always been attracted to women with more modest breasts, and every time I see them, every time I touch them, I remember my sister . . . Don't get me wrong, I wasn't sexually interested in my sister. I think I was just looking for a certain type of scene. A finite scene, lost and never to return.

On Saturday afternoon my hand was resting on the chest of my married lover. Her breasts weren't particularly small, or large. Just the right size, they fit neatly into my palm. Her nipples were still hard in my hand.

She'd never come to my house on a Saturday. She always spent the weekends with her family. But that weekend her husband was on a business trip to Mumbai and her two daughters were staying over at their cousin's house in Nasu in Tochigi. So she came to my place. And like we did on weekday afternoons, we leisurely enjoyed sex. Afterward we lay there in a lazy, indolent silence. Like always.

"Would you like to hear what the jungle grapevine turned up?" she asked.

"Jungle grapevine?" I suddenly couldn't think of what she was talking about.

"Don't tell me you forgot? The mystery man in the big white house across the valley. You asked me to look into this Mr. Menshiki the other day."

"Ah, that's right. Of course I remember."

"I found out a little bit about him. One of my housewife friends lives near him, and she could gather some info on him. Would you like to hear it?"

"Of course."

"Mr. Menshiki bought that house with the gorgeous view about three years ago. Another family was living in it before then. They're the ones who built the house, but those original owners only lived there about two years. One sunny morning they suddenly packed up all their belongings and left, and Menshiki took their place. He bought the house, which was practically brand-new. How that all came about, though, nobody knows."

"So he didn't build the house himself," I said.

"That's right. He moved into a container that was already there. Like a quick-witted hermit crab."

That was unexpected. I'd been positive he was the one who built that house. That's how closely I'd linked his image—probably corresponding to his wonderfully white hair—with that white mansion on top of the mountain.

She continued. "Nobody knows what kind of work he does. What they do know is that he never commutes to work. He stays in his house all day, probably on his computer. His study is full of those devices. Nowadays if you know what you're doing, you can find out most everything online. A man I know is a surgeon who works entirely from home. He's crazy about surfing and doesn't want to leave the ocean."

"A surgeon can work entirely from home?"

"They send him all the images and information about the patients, which he analyzes and then creates the protocols for the operations, sends these to the on-site staff, and monitors the operations remotely, sometimes giving them advice. Sometimes he uses a remote magic hand device to actually perform operations. That kind of thing."

"What an age we live in," I said. "I wouldn't like to have anyone operate on me like that."

"I wonder if Mr. Menshiki is doing something similar," she said. "No matter what kind of work he's doing, he's pulling in enough income. He lives alone most of the time in the huge house, occasionally goes on long trips. Probably trips abroad. In his house he has a home gym with lots of exercise machines, where he works out whenever he has a chance. There's not an ounce of fat on him. He mostly prefers classical music, and has a substantial listening room. A pretty luxurious life, wouldn't you say?"

"Where'd you get all these details?"

She laughed. "You seem to underestimate women's information-gathering skills."

"You could be right."

"He has four cars altogether. Two Jaguars and a Range Rover. Plus a Mini Cooper. He seems to like British cars."

"Mini Coopers are made by BMW these days, and I believe Jaguar was purchased by an Indian corporation. So it's hard to call either of them British cars."

"The Mini he drives is an older version. And whatever corporation bought Jaguar, it's still a British car."

"Did you find out anything else?"

"Hardly anybody ever comes to the house. Mr. Menshiki prefers solitude. He likes to be alone, likes to listen to classical music and read a lot. He's single and well off, yet almost never brings women home. For all appearances he lives a very simple, orderly life. Makes you think he might be gay. Though there's some evidence that points in the other direction."

"I'm thinking you must have a well-placed source of information."

"She's not there now, but until not long ago he had a maid who'd come in a few times a week. She's the one who took out the garbage, went shopping for him at the local supermarket, where there were other housewives from the neighborhood and they'd start chatting."

"I see," I said. "That's how the jungle grapevine gets formed."

"You got it. According to her, there's a kind of **forbidden chamber** in the house. He instructed her never to enter it. He made it quite clear."

"Sounds like Bluebeard's castle."

"Exactly. People often say that, right? That every house has a skeleton in the closet."

That reminded me of the painting **Killing Commendatore** hidden away in the attic. That might be a skeleton hidden in a closet too.

She went on. "The woman never did find out what was in that mystery room. It was always locked. But anyway, that maid doesn't work there anymore. Maybe she got fired for being a bit too talkative. He seems to be doing all the housework himself now."

"He told me the same thing. That aside from a once-a-week cleaning service he takes care of all the household chores himself."

"He seems very touchy about his privacy."

"Be that as it may, but isn't the fact that you and I meet like this spreading through your jungle grapevine?"

"I doubt it," she said in a quiet voice. "First of all, I'm very careful that it doesn't. And second, you're a little different from Mr. Menshiki."

"Meaning . . . ," I said, translating this into words that were easy to understand, ". . . that there are things about him that lend themselves to rumor, but not with me."

"We should be thankful for that," she said cheerily.

After my little sister died all kinds of things started to go wrong. The metalworking company my father operated went downhill, and he was so busy dealing with that he hardly ever came home. The atmosphere at home became strained. Long, heavy silences reigned over the house. It hadn't been that way when my sister was still alive. I wanted to get away from it all, and got even more absorbed in painting as a way to escape. Eventually I decided to attend art school and major in painting. My father was dead set against it. You can't earn a decent living painting, he argued. And I don't have the money to help raise an artist. The two of us argued about it. My mother intervened to smooth things over, and though somehow I was able to attend art school, my father and I never did reconcile.

If only my sister hadn't died, I sometimes thought. If she'd lived, my family would have been so much happier. Her sudden disappearance made our family fall apart. Our home became a site where people lashed out and hurt each other. I felt helpless, knowing I could never fill in the hole my sister had left behind.

I stopped drawing pictures of her. After I entered art school the things I wanted to paint were phenomena and objects that didn't have intrinsic meaning. Abstract paintings, in other words. Things in which all sorts of meanings were encoded, where new semantic meaning arose from the interweaving of one sign and another. I plunged into a world that aimed at that type of completeness, and was able to breathe normally for the first time in forever.

Creating those kinds of paintings, though, didn't lead to any decent jobs. I graduated, but as long as I stuck to abstract painting my father was right—I had

171

no hope of earning any money. So in order to make a living (I'd already left my parents' home and needed to earn money for rent and food) I was compelled to take on portrait work. By doing a conventional job, painting those utilitarian paintings, I was somehow able to survive as an artist.

And now I was about to paint a portrait of Wataru Menshiki. The Wataru Menshiki who lived in the white mansion on top of the mountain across the way. The white-haired man the neighbors had heard all sorts of rumors about, this clearly intriguing person. He had picked me out, hired me for a huge fee to paint his portrait. But what I discovered was that at this point I **wasn't even able to paint a portrait.** Even that kind of conventional, utilitarian art was beyond me. I'd truly become hollow, an empty shell.

We should wordlessly go to visit her, pushing our way through the lush green grass. This random thought struck me. If we could, how truly wonderful that would be.

11

THE MOONLIGHT SHONE
BEAUTIFULLY ON EVERYTHING

The silence woke me. That happens sometimes. A sudden sound will cut the silence, waking a person, and sometimes a sudden silence will cut through sounds, waking you.

I shot awake and glanced over at my bedside clock. The digital display read 1:45. After a moment I remembered that it was 1:45 a.m. on Saturday night, or rather early Sunday morning. Earlier that afternoon I had spent time with my married lover in this bed. She went home before evening, I'd had a simple dinner, read for a while, and gone to sleep after ten. I'm generally a sound sleeper, and don't wake up until the morning light wakes me. So having my sleep interrupted like that in the middle of the night was unusual.

I lay there in the darkness wondering why I'd awakened at this hour. It was a typical, quiet night. The nearly full moon was a huge round mirror floating in the sky. The scenery on earth was whitish, as if washed with lime. But nothing else seemed out of the ordinary. I half sat up and listened carefully. And finally realized something **was** different from usual. **It was too quiet.** The silence was too deep. It was a fall night, yet no insects were chirping. Since the house was built in the mountains, after sunset the insects invariably started their ear-splitting chirping, a chorus that went on until late at night. (It really surprised me to learn this, since until I lived here I always thought they only chirped early in the evening.) The sound was so piercing it made me think that insects had conquered the world. But this night, when I woke up, there was not a single screech or chirp. It was disconcerting.

Once awake, I found it hard to get back to sleep. I reluctantly crawled out of bed, and threw a light cardigan over my pajama top. I went to the kitchen, poured myself some Scotch, added a few ice cubes from the ice maker, and drank it. I went onto the terrace and gazed at the lights of the houses through the woods. Everyone seemed to be asleep, no lights on anywhere in any houses. All I saw was a scattering of tiny security lights. The area around Menshiki's house across the valley, too, was surrounded by darkness. And like before, there were no insects chirping. Had something happened to them?

After a while I heard a sound I wasn't used to. Or perhaps **felt** like I heard it. A very faint sound. If the insects had been chirping as loudly as usual I probably never would have caught it. But the profound silence that reigned allowed it to reach me, though barely. I held my breath and strained my ears. It wasn't the chirp of any insects. Not a naturally occurring sound. It was the sound some implement or tool might make, a kind of jingling sound. The sound a bell, or something close to it, might make.

There would be a pause, then the sound. A deep silence, then that sound ringing out a few times, then deep silence once more. As if someone were patiently sending out an encoded message. But it wasn't repeated at regular intervals. Sometimes the silence in between rings was longer, sometimes shorter. And it didn't ring the same number of times. I couldn't tell if their regularity was intentional or capricious. At any rate, it was such a faint sound that if I hadn't focused and listened hard I wouldn't have caught it. But once aware of it, in the deep silence of the middle of the night, with the moonlight so unnaturally bright, that unidentified sound irretrievably ate its way into my awareness.

I was flustered, wondering what it could be, then decided to just go outside and see. I wanted to trace the source of that mysterious sound. Someone, somewhere, was ringing **something or other**. I'm not bold. But going out into the dark night alone then didn't frighten me. Curiosity won out over my fears. And the weirdly bright moonlight might have encouraged me, too.

With an oversized flashlight in my hand, I unlocked the front door and stepped outside. A single light above the entrance threw out a yellowish tint. A swarm of flying insects was drawn to that light. I stood there, ears perked up, trying to see what direction that sound was coming from. It really did sound like a bell, but not an ordinary one. It had a deeper, dull, uneven ring. Maybe it was some special percussion instrument. But what was it, and why would someone be ringing it in the middle of the night? The only residence in the vicinity was the house I was living in. If indeed someone nearby was ringing that bell, it meant they were trespassing.

I looked around to see if anything could serve as a weapon. All I had in my hand was a long cylindrical flashlight. Better than nothing. I grasped the flashlight tightly and headed toward the sound.

I turned left from the front door, which led me to a small set of stone steps. I climbed up the seven steps and entered the woods. I walked up the gentle upward-sloping path that cut through the trees, and before long came to a clearing where there was a small shrine. Masahiko had said that the shrine had been there for a very long time. He didn't know the origins of it, but in the mid-1950s when his father had purchased the house and land from an acquaintance, the shrine already existed . . . On top of a flat stone was a sanctuary with a simple triangular roof—or, more accurately, a small wooden box made to look like a sanctuary. It was about two feet high and a foot and a half wide. It had originally been painted, though by now the color had mostly worn off, leaving one to imagine what it had once been. In the front was a small double door, and I had no idea what sort of offering was set up inside. I didn't check, but probably there wasn't anything enshrined inside. In front of the doors was an empty white ceramic pot. Rainwater had accumulated, then evaporated, over and over, leaving a number of dirty stained lines inside. Tomohiko Amada had left the shrine as it was. Not bringing his hands together in prayer as he passed it, not cleaning it, he simply let it be, swept by rain and wind. For him it must have been not a shrine, but just a plain, spare box.

"He had no interest in faith or worship or the like," his son had explained. "He didn't care a wit about things like divine punishment or retribution or anything. He said those were stupid superstitions, and looked down on them. It wasn't that he was brazen about it, it's just that he's always held to an extremely materialist view of things."

Masahiko had shown me the shrine the first time he took me to see the house. "You don't find many houses these days that come with their own shrine," he laughed, and I agreed.

"When I was a kid, though," Masahiko went on, "it creeped me out to have that kind of weird thing on our property. So when I stayed over I avoided coming near here," he said. "Even now, to tell the truth, I'd rather not go near it."

I wasn't a person who often thought in materialistic terms, but just like his father, Tomohiko Amada, having the shrine nearby didn't bother me. People in the past set up shrines in all kinds of places, much like the little Jizo and Dosojin statues you see next to roads in the countryside. This shrine blended naturally into the scenery in the woods, and when I went on walks I often passed in front of it but never gave it much thought. I never prayed to it, or made any offerings. And I didn't feel anything significant about having that sort of thing on the property where I was living. It was just part of the kind of scenery you'd find anywhere.

The bell-like sound seemed to be coming from near that shrine. Once I set foot in the woods, the tree branches above me blocked the moonlight and everything got suddenly darker. I carefully made my way forward, lighting the path with the flashlight. The wind would occasionally pick up, as if remembering to blow, rustling the thin layer of leaves on the ground. The woods at night felt totally different from walking there in the daytime. The place was operating under the principles at work at night, and those principles didn't include me. That said, I didn't feel particularly afraid. Curiosity spurred me on. I felt compelled to locate where that strange sound was coming from. I tightly gripped the heavy cylindrical flashlight, its weight calming me.

The horned owl might be in these woods some-where, I thought. Hidden in the darkness on a branch, waiting for its prey. It would be nice if it were nearby. In a way that owl was my friend. But I didn't hear anything that sounded like the hooting of an owl. The night birds, like the insects, were keeping quiet.

As I made my way forward, the bell-like sound became ever clearer. It continued to ring out inter-mittently, irregularly. The sound seemed to be com-ing from behind the little shrine. It sounded much closer, but was still muffled, like it was filtering out from deep inside a narrow cave. The silence between each ring had grown longer, and the number of rings was decreasing. As if the person ringing the bell had grown weak, become worn out.

The area around the shrine had been cleared and the moonlight shone beautifully on everything. Stepping silently, I walked over behind the shrine. There was a tall thicket of pampas grass and, led by the sound, I pushed my way into the thicket. There I found a small mound of square stones casually piled up, a kind of ancient burial mound. Though perhaps it was too small to be called that. At any rate, I had never noticed it was there before. I'd never gone behind the shrine, and even if I had, the mound was hidden in the midst of the pampas grass. You weren't going to see it unless you had some reason to wade into the thicket.

I approached the mound and shone my flashlight directly upon it. The stones were old, but weren't in their natural form, and had clearly been chiseled into squares. They had been carried up onto the mountain and piled up behind the shrine. The stones were of different sizes, most of them covered in moss. There wasn't any visible writing or designs on them. There were twelve or thirteen stones altogether, by my count. In the past, the mound might have been taller and more orderly, but maybe an earthquake had made part of it crumble. The bell-like sound somehow seemed to be filtering out from the cracks between those stones.

I lightly rested my foot on top of the stones and searched for the source of that sound. But no matter how bright the moonlight, it was next to impossible to locate it in the dark of night. And what if I did happen to locate it? What then? I couldn't lift these heavy stones myself.

At any rate it seemed like someone below the stone mound was ringing the bell. I was sure of it. But **who**? It was at this point that an enigmatic fear began to well up inside me. Instinct told me not to get any closer to the source of that sound.

I left, and with the bell ringing behind me hurried back along the path through the woods. Moonlight filtering through the branches cast a suggestive mottled pattern on my body. I emerged from the woods, rushed down the seven stone steps, got back to the house, went inside, and locked the door. I walked to the kitchen, poured a glass of whiskey straight, no ice, no water, and gulped it down. I could finally breathe a sigh of relief. I took my glass of whiskey out to the terrace.

From the terrace I could hear the bell only faintly. If I hadn't listened carefully I wouldn't have been able to catch it. But the point was, the sound continued. The interval of silence between each ringing of the bell was definitely lengthening. I listened to that irregular repetition for some time.

What in the world lay beneath the stones of that mound? Was there a space there, and somebody locked inside who was ringing that bell, or whatever it was? Maybe it was a signal for help. But no matter how much I thought it over, I couldn't think of a single plausible explanation.

I might have thought about it for a long time. Or maybe it was but a moment. I had no idea. My sense of time had vanished. Glass of whiskey in hand, I sank back into the lounge chair, shuffling back and forth in the maze of consciousness. And then it hit me. The bell had stopped. Everything was enveloped in a profound silence.

I stood up, went into the bedroom, and looked at the digital clock. It was 2:31 a.m. I didn't know the precise time the bell had started ringing, but since it had been 1:45 when I woke up, I surmised the bell had gone on ringing for at least forty-five minutes. Soon after the mysterious sound ceased, the insects began chirping again, as if probing the new silence that had arisen. As if all the insects in the mountains had been patiently waiting for the sound of that bell to stop. Holding their breath, cautiously assessing the situation.

I went back to the kitchen, rinsed out my glass, then slipped back into bed. By this time the autumn insects were a lusty chirping chorus. I should have been too worked up to sleep, but the straight whiskey did the trick and I fell asleep as soon as my head hit the pillow. A long, deep sleep, bereft of dreams. When I woke again it was already bright outside the bedroom.

That day, before ten a.m., I walked out again to the little shrine in the woods. I couldn't hear that enigmatic sound, but I wanted to study the shrine and

181

stone mound once more in the daylight. I found a stout oak walking stick in Tomohiko Amada's umbrella stand and took that with me. It was a sunny, pleasant morning, the clear autumn sunlight throwing the shadows of leaves across the ground. Birds with sharp bills flitted busily from one branch to another, squawking as they searched for fruit. Up above, a straight line of pitch-black crows was winging its way off somewhere.

The little shrine looked worn and shoddy in the daylight. Bathed in the bright, whitish light of the nearly full moon the shrine had looked deeply meaningful, even a bit ominous, yet now in the light of day it seemed like nothing more than a faded, seedy-looking wooden box.

I went behind the shrine, shouldered my way through the tall thicket of pampas grass, and emerged in front of the stone mound. It seemed completely transformed from the night before. What I saw before me now were merely square moss-covered stones long abandoned in the mountains. In the moonlight it had appeared like part of ancient historical ruins, covered with a mythic slime. I stood on top of the mound and perked up my ears, but couldn't hear a thing. Other than the screech of insects and the occasional bird chirp, it was silent all around.

From far away came the bang of what I took to be a shotgun. Someone might be hunting birds in the mountains. Or else it was one of those automatic devices set up by farmers to shoot blanks to scare away sparrows, monkeys, and wild boar. Either way, the sound echoed with the feeling of autumn. The sky was high, the air slightly humid, and sounds carried well. I sat down on top of the stone mound and thought about the space that might exist beneath. Was someone really under there, ringing a bell, calling out for help? Were they like me, back when I worked for the moving company and got locked inside the truck and pounded on the side panels as hard as I could, hoping someone would rescue me? The image of someone locked up in a cramped dark space put me on edge.

After a light lunch I changed into work clothes (and by that I mean things I didn't mind getting dirty), went into the studio, and once more tried my hand at Wataru Menshiki's portrait. I had to dispel the image of someone shut away in an enclosed space, hoping for help, and the chronic sense of suffocation that induced in me. I had to keep my hands busy, and painting was the only solution. This time I put aside my sketchbook and pencil. They wouldn't help, I figured. I readied my paints and paintbrushes, stood facing the canvas, and, gazing deep into that blank space, I focused on Menshiki. I stood erect, focused my concentration, and pruned away any extraneous thoughts.

A white-haired man with young-looking eyes who lived in a white mansion on a mountain. He spent most of his time at home, had what appeared to be a hidden room, and owned four British cars. How had he moved when he was here? What kind of expressions did he have on his face, what was his tone of voice, what did he look at and with what sort of look in his eyes, how did he move his hands? I recalled each and every detail. It took a while, but all the fragments started to fall into place. In my mind now, a three-dimensional, organically constructed sense of the man began to come together.

With small brushstrokes I transferred the image of Menshiki that arose from this directly onto the canvas, without the usual rough sketch. The Menshiki in my mind was facing forward, face slightly tilted to the left, his eyes looking a bit in my direction. For some reason I couldn't picture any other angle his face should be. To me, **that** was Wataru Menshiki. He had to have his face slightly tilted to the left. And had to have both eyes looking a bit in my direction. I'm in his field of vision. No other composition would accurately capture him.

I stepped away from the canvas and studied the simple composition I'd done, pretty much with a single brushstroke. It was just a temporary line drawing, but I could sense from that outline a budding, living organism. With that as the starting point, it would naturally expand from there. Something was reaching out a hand—but what was it?—and had flipped a switch inside me. A sort of vague sensation, as if an animal hibernating deep within me had finally recognized that the season had arrived, and was slowly brushing aside the cobwebs of sleep.

I washed the paint off the brush in the sink and lathered my hands with oil and soap. I was in no hurry. This was plenty for today. It was best to not rush the work. When Mr. Menshiki next came to see me, as a live model, I could then flesh out this outline. I had a premonition that this painting was going to be very different from any portrait I'd ever done before. And this painting required the flesh-and-blood Menshiki.

Which was very odd, I thought.

How had Menshiki known that?

In the middle of the night I suddenly shot awake again. The clock next to my bed read 1:46, almost exactly the same time as the night before. I sat up in bed, listening carefully in the dark. No insects chirping; it was silent all around. As if I were at the bottom of a deep sea. A repeat of the previous night. But now it was dark outside my window. That was the only difference from the night before. Thick clouds covered the sky, completely hiding the nearly full autumn moon.

Everything was in total silence. No, that wasn't entirely true. Of course it wasn't. That silence wasn't total. When I held my breath and listened carefully I could catch the faint sound of the bell wending its way past the deep silence. In the dark of night someone was ringing that bell-like object. As on the night before, it was a fragmented, intermittent sound. And now I knew exactly where the sound was coming from. From the woods, underneath that stone mound. There was no need to check it. What I didn't know, though, was **who was ringing that bell, and to what end?** I got out of bed and padded out to the terrace.

There was no wind, but a fine rain had started to fall. An invisible silent rain wetting the ground. Lights were on over in Mr. Menshiki's mansion. From over here, across the valley, I couldn't see what was going on inside his house, but he seemed to still be awake. It was unusual to see the lights on this late at night. As the fine drizzle wet me, I gazed at those lights, listening to the faint tinkling of the bell.

The rain started to pick up and I went back inside, but couldn't go back to sleep, so I sat on the sofa in the living room and turned the pages of a book I'd been reading. Not a particularly difficult book, but no matter how I focused nothing registered. I was merely tracing the words from one line to the next. Still, it was better than simply sitting there listening to the bell. I guess I could have put on some music to drown out the sound, but I didn't feel like it. I had to hear it. **Because that was a sound directed at me.** I understood that. And as long as I didn't do something about it, it would no doubt go on ringing forever. Suffocating me every night, robbing me of a good night's sleep.

I have to do something. Take some action to stop that sound. To do that, I first had to understand the meaning and purpose of that sound—of that signal that was being sent out. Why was somebody sending out from this mysterious place a signal to me every single night, and who was it? But I felt too choked, my mind too confused, for logical thought. There was no way I could handle this alone. I had to talk to somebody about it. And at this point I could only think of one person.

I went back out on the terrace and looked over at Mr. Menshiki's mansion. Now the lights were all out, with just a glimmer of outdoor lanterns in the garden.

The bell stopped ringing at 2:29 a.m., almost the same time as the night before. Soon after the bell stopped the insects' chirping returned. And as if nothing had happened, the autumn night was once more filled with the clamor of nature's chorus. Everything was a repeat of the previous night.

I went back to bed and went to sleep listening to the insects. I felt confused and anxious, but like on the night before, I soon fell asleep. Plunged into a deep, dreamless sleep.

12

LIKE THAT NAMELESS MAILMAN

Rain started falling early in the morning, and stopped before ten. Slowly, the sun began to peek out. Moist wind from the sea slowly pushed the clouds off to the north. And at one p.m., on the dot, Menshiki showed up at my place. The time signal on the radio and the front doorbell sounded at almost precisely the same moment. Many people are punctual, but seldom do you find anyone that precise. And it wasn't that he stood in front of the door, patiently waiting for the appointed time, timing his ringing of the front doorbell with the second hand on his watch. He drove up the slope, parked in his usual spot, and headed toward the front door at his usual pace and stride, and at almost the same instant he pushed the button for the front doorbell the time signal on the radio chimed. Pretty impressive.

I showed him into the studio, and had him sit on the same dining room chair as before. I put Richard Strauss's **Der Rosenkavalier** on the turntable and lowered the needle. I started at the point we'd ended up with last time. Everything was a repeat of the previous sitting. The only difference was that this time I didn't offer him a drink, and instead had him pose for me. I had him seated on the chair, facing forward, looking to the left, his eyes slightly facing toward me. That's what I wanted from him this time.

He followed my instructions exactly, but it still took a while until he got the position and pose right. The angle and look in his eyes wasn't exactly the way I wanted them. The way the light struck, too, wasn't like my mental image. I don't usually use a model, but once I do, I tend to have a lot of demands. Menshiki very patiently followed my nagging directions. He never looked put out, never complained. I pegged him as a person experienced in putting up with all sorts of trials and difficulties.

When he finally got the pose right I said, "I'm very sorry, but try to hold that pose without moving."

Menshiki said nothing, only his eyes indicating that he understood.

"I'll try to finish as quickly as I can. It might be hard, but please be patient."

Once again he nodded with his eyes. He kept his gaze still, his body unmoving, literally not moving a muscle. He did have to blink a few times, but I couldn't even tell if he was breathing. He was so still he looked like a lifelike statue. I couldn't help but be impressed. Even professional art models find it hard to get to that point.

As Menshiki endured posing, I worked on the canvas as quickly and efficiently as I could. I concentrated, eyeing his figure, and moved my brush as my intuition dictated. I was using black paint on the white canvas, and with a single fine brushstroke fleshed out

189

the outline of his face I'd already drawn. No time even to re-grip the brush. In a limited amount of time I had to capture the various elements that made up his face and get them down on canvas. At a certain point the process switched over to something close to autopilot. It's important to bypass your conscious mind and get your eye and hand movements in sync. There's no time to consciously process every single thing your gaze takes in.

This demanded a very different type of process from me compared with the numerous portraits I'd done up till then—the countless "business items" I'd leisurely painted based solely on memory and photographs. In about fifteen minutes I'd gotten him from the chest up on canvas. It was just a rough, incomplete outline, but at least I was able to capture an image that seemed to breathe a sense of vitality, one that managed to scoop out and capture the sort of internal movement that gave birth to who this person was. If this were an anatomical drawing, though, it would be just the bones and muscles, the internal part alone boldly laid bare. It needed actual flesh and skin laid on over it.

"Thank you, you've been very patient," I said. "That's enough for today. You can take it easy now."

Menshiki smiled and relaxed his pose. He stretched his hands above him and took a deep breath. He slowly massaged his face with his fingers to loosen up the tense muscles. I stood there taking a few deep breaths. It took a while for my breathing to return to normal. I was exhausted, like a sprinter who'd just finished a race. I'd had to work speedily, with intense concentration, and with no room for compromise, something I hadn't experienced for quite some time. I'd had to flex long-dormant muscles, and though I felt tired, it also felt good.

"Like you said, sitting for a painting is a lot harder work than I'd imagined," Menshiki said. "When I think about you painting me, it feels like my insides are slowly being scraped away."

"The official view in the art world is that it's not being scraped away but rather transplanted to a different place," I said.

"Transplanted to a more permanent, lasting place?"

"Yes, if the painting is a true work of art."

"Like, for instance, the nameless mailman who lives on in Van Gogh's portrait of him?"

"Exactly."

"He probably had no idea that, well over a century later, countless people around the world would visit art museums, or look through art books, and gaze intently at his portrait."

"I'm sure he never had a clue."

"It was some odd painting done in a corner of a shabby country kitchen, painted by a man who, whichever way you look at it, was a little off."

I nodded.

"It's kind of weird," Menshiki said. "Something that, on the face of it, shouldn't be so lasting ends up having permanent value."

"Not something that happens every day."

I suddenly thought of **Killing Commendatore**.

Through Tomohiko Amada's hand, was the Commendatore given permanent life, even though he was stabbed to death in the painting? And who was this Commendatore anyway?

I offered Menshiki some coffee. That would be nice, he replied, and I went to the kitchen and made a fresh pot. Menshiki remained on the chair in the studio, listening to the opera record. The coffee was ready as the B side of the record came to an end, and we went into the living room to drink it.

"So, does it look like you can do a good portrait of me?" Menshiki asked as he delicately sipped his coffee.

"I'm not sure yet," I answered honestly. "I don't know if it will turn out well. The way I've painted portraits up till now has been so different from this."

"Because you're using an actual model this time?" Menshiki asked.

"That's one reason, but only a part of it. I don't know why, but it's like I'm not able anymore to paint the sort of conventional portraits I've done up till now. I need a different method and procedure, but those are still out of reach. I'm still fumbling in the dark."

"Which means you really are changing. And I'm the catalyst for that change—wouldn't you say?"

"You may be right."

Menshiki thought for a while before speaking. "As I told you before, it's entirely up to you what style of painting you do. I'm a person who's always seeking change, always in flux. And it's not like I'm hoping you'll paint some conventional portrait. Any style, any concept is fine. What I want is for you to depict me exactly as you see me. The methods and procedure are up to you. I'm not hoping I live on like that mailman from Arles. I'm not that ambitious. I just have a healthy curiosity to see what sort of painting will emerge from this."

"I appreciate your saying that. I just have one request," I said. "If I can't come up with a satisfactory painting, then I'd like to forget the whole thing."

"You won't give me the painting then?"

I nodded. "I'll return the advance, of course."

"All right," Menshiki said. "I'll let you be the final judge. Though I must say I have a strong hunch it's not going to turn out that way."

"I hope your hunch turns out to be correct."

Menshiki looked me in the eyes. "But even if the painting's never completed, I'd be very happy if, in some way, I'm able to help you change. Truly."

"By the way, Mr. Menshiki," I said, broaching the topic a little while later, "there's something I wanted to get your advice on. Something personal, nothing to do with the painting."

"Of course. I'll be happy to help if I can."

I sighed. "It's kind of a weird story. I might not be able to tell the whole story in the right order, so it makes sense."

"Take your time, tell it in whatever order is easiest for you. And then we'll consider it together. The two of us might come up with a good idea that you couldn't come up with on your own."

So I told him the story, start to finish. How I suddenly woke up just before two a.m. and heard a weird sound in the darkness. A faint, far-off sound that I could only catch because the insects had stopped chirping. A sound like someone ringing a bell. When I tried to trace the source, it seemed to be coming from between the cracks in a stone mound in the woods behind my house. That mysterious sound continued for some forty-five minutes, intermittently, with irregular intervals of silence between. Finally it stopped completely. The same thing happened two nights in a row—two nights ago and last night. Someone might be ringing that bell-like thing from underneath the stones. Maybe sending out a distress call. But could that be possible? I was starting to doubt my own sanity a little. Was I just imagining things?

Menshiki listened to my story without comment, and remained silent even after I finished. He'd listened intently to what I'd said, and I could tell he was thinking deeply about it.

"A fascinating story," he said a little while later. He lightly cleared his throat. "As you said, it's certainly out of the ordinary. I wonder . . . if possible, I'd like to hear the sound of that bell myself, so could I come over tonight? If you don't mind?"

This took me by surprise. "Come all the way over here in the dead of night?"

"Of course. If I hear the bell too, that would prove you're not hallucinating. That's the first step. If it is an actual bell, then let's try to locate the source, the two of us. Then we can think about what to do next."

"True enough—"

"If you don't mind, I'll come over here tonight at twelve thirty. Does that work for you?"

"That's fine, but I don't want to put you out—"

A pleasant smile graced his lips. "Not to worry. If I can help you, nothing would make me happier. Plus, I'm a very curious person. What that bell in the middle of the night might mean, and if someone is ringing it, who that is—I'm dying to know. You feel the same way, don't you?"

"Of course—" I said.

"Then let's go with that. I'll see you tonight. And there's something else I thought of."

"Excuse me?"

"I'll tell you about it later. I have to make sure of something first."

Menshiki got up from the sofa and held out his right hand. I shook it. As always, a firm handshake. He looked happier than usual.

After he left I spent the rest of the afternoon in the kitchen cooking. Once a week I prepare all my meals. I put them in the fridge or freezer, then get by on these for the week. This was my meal-prep day. For dinner that evening I added macaroni to some boiled sausage and cabbage. Plus a tomato, avocado, and onion salad. In the evening I lay on the sofa as always, reading while listening to music. After a while I stopped reading and thought about Menshiki.

Why had he looked so happy when we said goodbye? Was he **really** so pleased to be able to help me out? Why? I didn't get it. I was just a poor, unknown artist. My wife of six years had left me, I didn't get along with my parents, had no set place to live, no assets, and was simply hanging out in a friend's father's house. Menshiki, in contrast (not that there was any need to make a comparison), had been successful at business at a young age, and made enough to live comfortably for the rest of his days. At least that's what he had told me. He was good-looking, owned four British cars, and lived in luxury in a huge mountaintop mansion without, apparently, doing any real work. So why would a person like that be interested in someone like me? And why would he make time in the dead of the night to help me out?

I shook my head and went back to reading. Thinking about it wasn't going to get me anywhere. It was like trying to put together a puzzle that was missing some pieces. I could think all I wanted and never arrive at any conclusion. But I couldn't help but think about it. I sighed, and put the book on the tabletop again, closed my eyes, and listened to the music. Schubert's String Quartet no. 15, played by the Vienna Konzerthaus Quartet.

Since coming here, I'd listened to classical music every day, most of it German (or Austrian), since the majority of Tomohiko Amada's record collection consisted of German classical music. His collection included the obligatory nods to Tchaikovsky, Rachmaninoff, Sibelius, Vivaldi, Debussy, and Ravel, but that's all. Since he was an opera fan there were, as you might expect, some recordings by Verdi and Puccini. But compared to the substantial lineup of German opera he didn't seem as enthusiastic about these.

I imagined Amada had intense memories of his time studying in Vienna, which may have accounted for the deep absorption in German music. Or it could have been the opposite. Maybe his love of German music had come first, and that's why he had chosen to study in Vienna instead of France. I had no way of knowing which had come first.

Either way, I was in no position to complain that German music was the preferred type in this house. I was a mere caretaker, and they were kind enough to let me listen to the records there. And I enjoyed listening to the music of Bach, Schubert, Brahms, Schumann, and Beethoven. Not forgetting Mozart, of course. Their music was deep, amazing, and gorgeous. Up to then in my life I'd never had the opportunity to really settle down and listen to that type of music. I'd always been too busy trying to make a living, and didn't have the wherewithal financially. So I decided that, as long as I'd been provided this wonderful opportunity, I'd listen to as much music here as I could.

After eleven I fell asleep for a while on the sofa listening to music. I might have slept for about twenty minutes. When I woke up the record was over, the arm back in its cradle, the turntable not moving. There were two players in the living room, one an automatic, the other an old-school manual type, but to play it safe—so I could fall asleep listening, in other words—I generally used the automatic. I slipped the Schubert record back in its jacket, and returned it to its designated spot on the record shelf. From the open window I could hear the clamor of insects. Since they were still making a racket, I wouldn't be hearing the sound of the bell quite yet.

I warmed up coffee in the kitchen and munched on a few cookies. And listened intently to the noisy insect ensemble that enveloped the mountains. A little before twelve thirty I heard the Jaguar slowly making its way up the slope. As it changed direction, the pair of yellow headlights lit up the window. The engine finally cut out, and I heard the usual solid **thunk** as the door shut. I sat on the sofa, sipping coffee, getting my breathing under control, waiting for the front doorbell to ring.

13

AT THIS POINT IT'S MERELY A HYPOTHESIS

We sat in chairs in the living room, drank our coffee, and talked, killing time until **that time** rolled around. At first we chatted about inconsequential things, but after a curtain of silence descended on us Menshiki, a bit hesitantly, yet resolutely, asked, "Do you have any children?"

The question took me by surprise. He didn't seem the type to ask that kind of question—especially of someone he didn't know well. He seemed more the I-won't-stick-my-nose-in-your-business-if-you-won't-stick-yours-in-mine type of person. At least that's the way I read him. But when I looked up and saw his serious expression, I knew it wasn't an impulsive question. He'd been thinking of asking me this for a long time.

I responded. "I was married for six years, but we didn't have any children."

"You didn't want any?"

"I was fine either way. But my wife didn't want any," I said. I didn't, though, get into the reason she gave. Even now I'm not sure that it reflected her true feelings.

Menshiki seemed hesitant, but forged ahead. "This

might sound rude, but have you ever considered that there might be another woman somewhere, other than your wife, who secretly had a child of yours?"

I looked him full in the face again. What a strange question. I rummaged around, pro forma, through a few drawers of memory, but came up empty-handed. I hadn't had sex with all that many women until then, and even if something like that had taken place, I think I would have heard about it.

"I guess it's possible, in theory. But realistically—commonsensically, you might say—it's not."

"I see," Menshiki said. He quietly sipped his coffee, thinking deeply.

"Why do you ask?" I ventured.

He looked out the window, silent for a time. The moon was visible, not as weirdly bright as two days ago, but still plenty bright. Scattered clouds slowly wended their way from the sea toward the mountains.

Menshiki finally spoke up. "As I mentioned before, I've never been married. I've always been a bachelor. Work kept me busy all the time, that's one reason, but it's also because living with someone else didn't fit my personality and lifestyle. I'm sure this sounds pretty stuck-up, but I'm the type who can only live alone. I have almost no interest in lineage or relatives. I've never thought I'd like to have children. There's a personal reason for that, mostly because of my home environment when I was growing up."

He paused, took a breath, then went on.

"But a few years ago I began to think that I might

actually have a child. Or I should say, I was compelled to think that way."

No comment from me.

"I find it strange myself that I'm opening up to you, about this kind of personal matter. I mean, we just met." The faintest of smiles rose to Menshiki's lips.

"I'm okay with it, as long as you are."

Ever since I was little, for some reason people have tended to open up to me about the most unexpected topics. Maybe I have an innate ability to draw out secrets from strangers. Or maybe I just seem like a good listener, I don't know. Either way, I don't remember it ever working to my advantage. After people tell me their secrets, they always regret it.

"This is the first time I've ever told anybody this," Menshiki said.

I nodded and waited for more. Everyone says the same thing.

Menshiki began his story. "This happened fifteen years ago, when I was going out with a woman. I was in my late thirties then, she was in her late twenties. She was a beautiful, attractive woman, extremely bright. I was serious about our relationship, though I'd made it clear to her there was no chance of us getting married. I don't plan to ever marry anyone, I told her. I didn't want her to have any false hopes. If she ever found someone else she wanted to marry, I would step aside without a word. She understood exactly how I felt. While we went out—for about two and half years—we got along really well. We never argued, even once. We traveled together to lots of places, and she'd often stay over at my place. She even kept a set of clothes there."

He seemed to be contemplating something, then continued his story.

"If I were a normal person, or closer to being normal, I wouldn't have hesitated to marry her. But—" He paused here and let out a small breath. "But the upshot was I chose the kind of life I have now, a quiet life all by myself, and she chose a healthier life for herself. In other words, she got married to another man who was closer to being normal than me."

Until the very end, however, she didn't disclose to him the fact that she was getting married. The last time he saw her was a week after her twenty-ninth birthday (the two of them had dined out at a restaurant in Ginza on her birthday, and later on he recalled how unusually quiet she'd been). He was working in an office in Akasaka then and she'd called him saying she wanted to see him and talk, and asked if she could see him right away. Of course, he replied. She'd never visited his workplace even once, but he hadn't thought it odd. His office was a small place, just him and a middle-aged woman secretary. So he didn't need to worry about anyone else if she stopped by. There had been a time when he'd managed a large company with lots of employees, but at this point he was developing a new network by himself. His usual approach was to work quietly by himself to develop a new business strategy; then, when he began implementing the plan, he would aggressively employ a broad range of talent.

It was just before five p.m. when his girlfriend showed up. They sat down together on his office sofa to talk. He'd had the secretary in the next room go home. It was his normal routine to continue working alone in the office after his secretary left for the day. Often he'd be so engrossed in his work that he'd stay all night. His idea was for the two of them to go to a nearby restaurant and have dinner, but she turned that down. I don't have time today, she said, I have to meet somebody in Ginza.

"You said you had something you wanted to talk about," he said.

"No, I don't have anything to really talk about," she said. "I just wanted to see you."

"I'm glad you came," he said, smiling. It had been some time since she'd spoken so openly to him. She generally spoke in a more indirect, roundabout way. He had no idea what this portended.

She moved over on the sofa and sat down in his lap. She put her arms around him and kissed him. A serious, deep kiss, tongues entwined. She reached out and undid Menshiki's belt. She took out his already erect penis, holding it in her grasp for a time. Then she leaned forward and wrapped her mouth around it. She slowly ran the tip of her long tongue around it. Her tongue was smooth and hot.

This all came out of nowhere. She was usually more passive when it came to sex—especially oral sex—and when it came to doing it, or having things done to her, he'd always felt a slight resistance on her part. But now here she was taking the lead. What's come over her? he wondered.

She suddenly stood up, tossed aside her expensive black pumps, briskly lowered her stockings and panties, again sat down on his lap, and now guided his penis inside her. Her vagina was wet, and moved smoothly, naturally, like some living being. The whole sequence had happened so quickly (and was so unlike her, since she was always so calm and deliberate). Before he realized it, he was deep inside her, that smooth wall completely enveloping his penis, squeezing him silently yet insistently.

This was unlike any sex he'd ever had with her. It was at once hot and cold, hard and soft. It was a strange, contradictory sensation, as if he were being simultaneously accepted and rejected. He had no idea what that meant. She straddled him, and like a person on a small boat being tossed around by the waves, moved violently up and down. Her black hair tossed about, supple as a willow branch in a strong wind. She lost control, her gasps growing ever louder. Menshiki wasn't sure if he had locked the office door or not. He felt he had, but also that he'd forgotten to. But this wasn't the time to go check.

"Shouldn't we use a condom or something?" he managed to ask. She was always careful about contraception.

"It's okay—today," she gasped in his ear. "Don't worry about a thing."

Everything about her was different from usual, as if a totally different personality dormant inside her had awoken and hijacked her body and soul. Menshiki imagined that today must be some sort of special day for her. There was so much that men can't fathom about women's bodies.

Her movements became increasingly frenzied. There was nothing he could do but make sure not to interfere with what she desired. They neared climax. He couldn't hold back, and ejaculated, and in time with that she let out a short screech like some foreign bird, and her womb, as if waiting for that instant, greedily absorbed his semen. A muddied image occurred to him of himself, in the darkness, being devoured by a greedy beast.

After a while she stood up, as if pushing his body aside, and silently adjusted the hem of her dress, stuffed the stockings and panties that had fallen to the floor in her handbag, and hurried off to the bathroom, bag in hand. She didn't come out for a long time. He was beginning to get worried that something had happened to her when she finally emerged. Her clothing and hair were neatly arranged now, her makeup redone. Her usual calm smile graced her lips.

She gave Menshiki a light peck on the lips, and told him she had to go, since she was already late. And she hurried out of the office, without looking back. He could still recall the click of her pumps as she left.

That was the last time he ever saw her. All contact ceased. He'd call her, and write, but never got a response. And two months later she got married. He heard about this from a mutual friend, after the fact. The friend found it odd that Menshiki was not invited to the wedding ceremony, and, in particular, that he had no idea she was getting married. He'd always thought that Menshiki and the woman were good friends (they'd always been very discreet about their relationship, and no one else had known they were lovers). Menshiki didn't know the man she married. He had never even heard his name. She hadn't told Menshiki she was planning to marry, nor even hinted at it. She just disappeared from his world without a word.

That violent embrace on the sofa at his office, Menshiki realized, must have been her final, farewell act of love. Afterward he went over those events, over and over in his mind. Even after a long time had passed, those memories remained amazingly distinct and clear. The creak of the sofa, her hair whirling around her, her hot breath in his ear—it all came back to him.

So did Menshiki regret losing her? Of course not. He wasn't the type to have regrets. He knew very well he wasn't suited to family life. No matter how much he loved someone, he still couldn't share his life with them. He needed solitary time every day to concentrate, and he couldn't stand it when someone's presence threw off his concentration. If he lived with someone he knew he would end up detesting them. Whether it was his parents, a wife, or children. He

feared that above all. He wasn't afraid of loving someone. What he feared was growing to hate someone.

For all that, he had loved her very deeply.
He'd never loved any other woman so deeply, and
probably never would again. "Even now there's a special spot inside me just for her," Menshiki said. "A
very real spot. You might even call it a shrine."

A shrine? This struck me as an odd choice of words.
But for him it was likely the right way of putting it.

Menshiki ended his story there. He'd told this private
tale in great detail, yet I got little sense of it being
sexual. It was more like he'd read aloud from a medical report. Or maybe it really was that sort of dispassionate experience for him.

"Seven months after the wedding she gave birth
to a baby girl in a hospital in Tokyo," Menshiki continued. "Thirteen years ago. I heard about this birth
much later from someone."

Menshiki stared down at his now empty coffee
cup, as if nostalgic for some past age when it had been
full of hot coffee.

"And that child might possibly be my own," he
said, seemingly forcing out the words. He looked at
me, like he wanted to hear my opinion.

It took me a while to grasp what he was trying
to say.

"Does the timeline fit?"

"It does. It coincides perfectly. The child was born

nine months after she came to my office. She must have picked the day she was most fertile to come see me and—how should I put it?—deliberately **gathered** my sperm. That's my working hypothesis. From the beginning she wasn't expecting to marry me, but had decided to have my child. I figured that's what happened."

"But you can't confirm that," I said.

"Of course. At this point it's merely a hypothesis. But I do have a sort of basis to say this."

"That was a pretty risky experiment for her, wasn't it?" I pointed out. "If the blood types didn't match it might come out that the father was someone else. Would she risk that?"

"My blood is type A. Most Japanese are A, and I think she is too. As long as they didn't have some reason to run a full-blown DNA test, the chances are slim that the secret would come out. That much she could figure out."

"But on the other hand, unless you ran an official DNA test you wouldn't be able to determine if you're the girl's biological father or not. Right? Or else you ask her mother directly."

Menshiki shook his head. "It's no longer possible to ask the mother. She died seven years ago."

"That's terrible. She was still so young," I said.

"She was walking in the woods and was stung by hornets and died. She was allergic to them. By the time they got her to the hospital she'd stopped breathing. Nobody knew she was so allergic to their stings.

Maybe she didn't even know herself. She left behind her husband and daughter. Her daughter is thirteen now."

About the same age my little sister was when she died, I thought.

"And you have some sort of basis for conjecturing that this girl is your daughter. Is that what you're saying?"

"Some time after she died I suddenly received a letter from the deceased," Menshiki said in a quiet voice.

One day a large envelope, with a return receipt, arrived at his office from a law firm he'd never heard of. Inside was a typed two-page letter (with the letterhead of the law firm) and a light pink envelope. The letter from the law firm was signed by a lawyer. The lawyer's letter read: **Ms. **** entrusted me with this letter while she was still alive. Ms. **** left instructions with me to send this letter to you in case of her death. She added a note to the effect that the letter should be for your eyes only.**

That was the gist of the lawyer's letter. The circumstances leading to her death were described simply, in a businesslike manner. Menshiki was speechless, but finally pulled himself together and snipped open the second envelope. The letter inside was handwritten in blue ink, on four sheets of stationery. The handwriting was exquisite.

Dear Mr. Menshiki,

I don't know what month or year it is now, but if you are reading this it means I am no longer among the living. I'm not sure why, but I've always had the feeling I'd depart this world at a relatively young age. Which is why I made full preparations like this for after my death. If all this ends up being wasted, of course nothing could be better—but when all is said and done since you are reading this letter it means that I've already passed away. The thought leaves me very, very sad.

The first thing I'd like to say in advance (maybe it's something I really don't need to say) is that my life has never been of much consequence. I'm well aware of that. So it seems fitting for someone like me to quietly exit the world without making a big deal of things, without any uncalled-for pronouncements. But there is one thing I need to tell you alone. My conscience is telling me that if I don't, I may forever lose the chance to treat you fairly. So I've left this letter with a lawyer I know and trust with instructions to pass it on to you.

Suddenly leaving you like that, and marrying someone else, and not saying a word to you about it beforehand—I am deeply sorry about all of it. I can imagine how shocked and upset you must have been. But you're always so calm, so maybe it didn't shock you, or bother you. At any rate, that was the only path I could follow. I won't get into details here, but I do want you to understand that. I was left with hardly any other choice.

But one choice was left to me. A choice that was condensed in one event, in one act. Do you remember the last time I saw you? That evening in early fall when I suddenly came to your office, maybe I didn't seem like it, but I was at my wit's end then, completely driven into a corner. I no longer felt like I was myself anymore. But even in that confused state of mind, the act I did was utterly intentional. And I've never, ever regretted it. This was something profoundly important in my life. Something far surpassing my own existence.

I am hoping that you will understand my intentions, and ultimately forgive me. And I pray that none of this will cause you, personally, any harm. Since I know very well how much you dislike those kinds of things.

I wish you a long and happy life. And I hope that what a truly wonderful person you were will be passed along, in all its richness, for a long time to come.

* * * *

Menshiki read the letter over so many times that he memorized it all (and he recited it to me without faltering). All sorts of emotions and suggestions played back and forth through the letter—light and dark, shadow and sunlight—creating a complex, hidden picture. Like a linguistics scholar researching an ancient language no one speaks anymore, he spent years considering the possibilities concealed in the letter's contents. Extracting each word and phrasing, recombining them, intertwining them, shifting their order. And he arrived at one conclusion alone: that the baby girl she gave birth to seven months after she got married was, he was now certain, conceived in that office, on that leather sofa, with him.

"I asked a law office I knew to investigate the daughter she left behind," Menshiki said. "Her husband was fifteen years older than she was, worked in real estate. Or, rather, he was the son of a local landowner and managed the land and properties he'd inherited from his father. He had some other real estate holdings, too, of course, but wasn't that ambitious when it came to expanding the business. He had enough assets to live on comfortably without working. The daughter's name was Mariye. The husband had not remarried after his wife's accidental death seven years ago. The husband has an unmarried younger sister who lives with them and takes care of the household. Mariye is in her first year at a local public junior high."

"And have you met this girl, Mariye?"

Menshiki was silent as he chose his words. "I've seen her from a distance many times. But never spoken with her."

"And what did you think when you saw her?"

"Did she look like me? I couldn't say. If I think there's a resemblance then everything about her resembles me, but if I don't think that way then I don't see a resemblance at all."

"Do you have a photo of her?"

Menshiki silently shook his head. "No, I don't. I could get one easily enough, but that's not what I was after. What good is carrying around a photo of her in my wallet going to do? What I'm after is—"

But nothing came after this. He was silent, the quiet buried in the lively buzz of the hordes of insects outside.

"But you told me earlier, Mr. Menshiki, that you were totally uninterested in blood relations."

"True enough. I've never cared about lineage. In fact, I've lived my life trying to avoid that as much as I could. My feelings haven't changed. But still, I find I can't take my eyes off this girl, Mariye. I simply can't stop thinking about her. There's no reason for it, but still . . ."

I couldn't find the right words to say.

Menshiki continued. "I've never had this experience before. I've always been very self-controlled, even proud of it. But sometimes now I find it painful to be alone."

I went ahead and said what was on my mind. "Mr. Menshiki, this is just a hunch on my part, but it seems like there's something you want me to do in regard to Mariye. Or am I overthinking things?"

After a pause Menshiki nodded. "I'm not sure how I should put this—"

· · ·

I realized at that instant that the clamor of insects had completely stopped. I looked up at the clock on the wall. It was just past one forty. I held a finger up to my lips, and Menshiki stopped in midsentence. And the two of us listened carefully in the still of the night.

14

BUT SOMETHING THIS
STRANGE IS A FIRST

Menshiki and I stopped talking, and sat still, listening carefully. The insects had stopped chirping, just like they had two days ago, and again yesterday. In the midst of that deep silence I could again make out the tinkling of the bell. It rang a few times, with uneven periods of silence in between before ringing once again. I looked over at Menshiki, seated across from me on the sofa. I could tell he was hearing the same sound. He was frowning. He lifted up his hands on his lap, his fingers moving slightly in time to the ringing of the bell. So this wasn't an auditory hallucination.

After listening intently to the bell for two or three minutes, Menshiki slowly rose from the sofa.

"Let's go where that sound's coming from," he said drily.

I picked up my flashlight. He went outside and retrieved a large flashlight from his Jaguar. We climbed the seven steps and walked into the woods. Though not as bright as two days before, the autumn moonlight clearly lit the path for us. We walked in back of the little shrine, pushing aside pampas grass as we went, and emerged in front of the stone mound.

And again we perked up our ears. No doubt about it, the sound was coming from the cracks between the stones.

Menshiki slowly circled the mound, cautiously shining his flashlight into the cracks between the stones. But nothing was out of the ordinary, just a jumble of old, moss-covered stones. He looked over at me. In the moonlight his face resembled some mask from ancient times. Perhaps my face looked the same?

"When you heard the sound before, was it coming from here?" he whispered.

"The same place," I said. "The exact same spot."

"It sounds like someone underneath the stones is ringing a bell," Menshiki said.

I nodded. I felt relieved to know I wasn't crazy, but I had to admit that the unreality of the situation had now, through Menshiki, taken on a reality, creating a slight gap in the seam of the world.

"What should we do?" I asked Menshiki.

He shone his flashlight on where the sound was coming from, his lips tight as he considered the situation. In the still of the night I could almost hear the wheels turning in his mind.

"Someone might be seeking help," Menshiki said quietly, as if to himself.

"But who could have possibly gotten under these heavy stones?"

Menshiki shook his head. He had no idea either.

"Anyway, let's go back to the house," he said. He lightly touched my shoulders from behind. "At least we've pinpointed the source of the sound. Let's go home and talk it over."

We cut through the woods and came out onto the empty space in front of the house. Menshiki opened the door of his Jaguar and returned the flashlight. In its place he took out a small paper bag. We went back inside the house.

"If you have any whiskey, could I have a glass?" Menshiki asked.

"Regular Scotch okay?"

"Of course. Straight, please. With a separate glass of water, no ice."

I went into the kitchen and took a bottle of White Label from the shelf, poured some into two glasses, and took them and some mineral water out to the living room. We sat across from each other without speaking, and drank our straight whiskey. I went back to the kitchen to get the bottle of White Label and poured him a refill. He picked up the glass but didn't drink any. In the silence of the middle of the night, the bell continued to ring out intermittently. A small sound, but with a delicate weight one couldn't fail to hear.

"I've seen a lot of strange things in my time, but something this strange is a first," Menshiki said. "Pardon me for saying this, but when you first told me about this I only half believed you. It's hard to believe something like this could actually happen."

Something in that expression caught my attention. "What do you mean, could actually happen?"

Menshiki raised his head and looked me in the eyes.

"I read about this sort of thing in a book once," he said.

"You mean hearing a bell from somewhere in the middle of the night?"

"No, what they heard was a gong, not a bell. The kind of gong they would ring along with a drum when searching for a lost child. In the old days it was a small Buddhist altar fitting that you would hit with a wooden bell hammer. You'd strike it rhythmically as you chanted sutras. In the story someone heard that kind of gong ringing out from underground in the middle of the night."

"Was this a ghost story?"

"Closer to what's called a tale of the mysterious. Have you ever read Ueda Akinari's book **Tales of the Spring Rain**?" Menshiki asked.

I shook my head. "I read his **Tales of Moonlight and Rain** a long time ago. But I haven't read that one."

"**Tales of the Spring Rain** is a collection of stories Akinari wrote in his later years. Some forty years after he finished **Tales of Moonlight and Rain**. Compared with that book, which emphasized narrative, **Tales of the Spring Rain** was more an expression of Akinari's philosophy as a man of letters. One strange story in the collection is titled 'Fate over Two Generations.' The main character experiences something like what you're going through. He's the son of a wealthy farmer. He enjoys studying, and one night he's reading late when he hears a sound like a gong coming from underneath a rock in the corner of the garden. Thinking it odd, the next day he has people dig it up, and they find a large stone underneath. When they move that stone they find a kind of coffin with a stone lid. Inside that they discover a fleshless emaciated person, like a dried fish. With hair down to his knees. Only his hands are still moving, striking a gong with a wooden hammer. It was a Buddhist priest who long ago chose his own death in order to achieve enlightenment, and had himself buried alive in the coffin. This act was called **zenjo**. The mummified dead body was unearthed and enshrined in a temple. Another term for **zenjo** is **nyujo**, meaning a deep meditative practice. The man must have originally been quite a highly revered priest. As he had hoped, his soul reached nirvana, and the soul-less physical body alone continued to live on. The main character's family had lived on this plot of land for ten generations, and this burial must have taken place before that. In other words, several centuries before."

Menshiki ended there.

"So you're saying the same sort of thing took place around this house?" I asked.

Menshiki shook his head. "If you think about it, it's not possible. This was just a take on the supernatural written in the Edo period. Akinari knew that this tale had become part of folk legend and he adapted it and created the story 'Fate over Two Generations.'

219

What I'm saying is, the story does have strange parallels with what we're experiencing now."

He lightly shook his glass of whiskey, the amber liquid quietly oscillating in his hand.

"So after he was unearthed, what happened?" I asked.

"The story took off in strange directions," Menshiki replied, sounding hesitant to go into it. "Ueda Akinari's worldview late in his life is deeply reflected in that story. A quite cynical view of the world, really. Akinari had a complicated background, a man who went through a lot of troubles in his life. But rather than hearing me summarize, I suggest you read the story yourself."

Menshiki took an old book out of the paper bag he'd brought inside from the car, and handed it to me. A volume from a collection of classical Japanese literature. The book contained the entire text of Akinari's two most famous books, **Tales of Moonlight and Rain** and **Tales of the Spring Rain**.

"When you told me what was going on here, right away I recalled this story. Just to be sure, I reread the copy I had on my shelves. I'll give you the book. If you'd like, please take a look. It's a short tale and doesn't take long to read."

I thanked him and accepted the book. "It's all pretty strange," I said. "Kind of unbelievable. Of course I'll read it. But apart from all that, what am I actually supposed to **do**? I don't think I can just leave things the way they are. If somebody really is buried beneath those rocks, ringing a bell or gong or whatever, sending out a call for help every night, we have to help get him out."

Menshiki frowned. "But the two of us would never be able to move that pile of stones."

"Should we report it to the police?"

Menshiki shook his head a few times. "The police won't be any help. Once you report that you're hearing a bell ringing from under stones in a woods in the middle of the night, they're not going to take you seriously. They'll just think you're crazy. It could make things worse. Better not go there."

"But if that bell keeps ringing every night, I don't think my nerves can take it. I can't get much sleep. All I can do is move out of this house. That sound is definitely trying to tell us something."

Menshiki considered this. "We'll need a professional's help to move those rocks," he said. "There's a man I know pretty well who's a local landscape designer. He's used to moving heavy rocks in landscaping. If need be, he could arrange for a small backhoe. Then it'd be easy to move the rocks and dig a hole."

"Okay, but I see two problems with that," I said. "First, I'd have to get permission to do that work from the son of the owner. I can't decide anything on my own. And second, I don't have the funds to hire someone to do that kind of job."

Menshiki smiled. "Don't worry about the money. I'll take care of that. What I mean is, that designer owes me one, and I think he'll do it at cost. Don't worry about that. As for Mr. Amada, why don't you get in touch with him? If you explain the situation,

I think he'll give permission. If somebody really is shut away underneath those rocks and we just leave him to his fate, Mr. Amada will be liable for it as the property owner."

"But to ask you, an outsider, to go to all that trouble—"

Menshiki spread his hands wide on his lap, as if catching the rain. His voice was quiet.

"I mentioned this before, but I'm a very curious person. I'd like to find out how this odd story will play out. It's not something you run across every day. So, like I said, don't worry about how much it'll cost. I understand you have your own position to consider, but let me arrange everything."

I looked Menshiki in the eye. There was a keen light there I hadn't seen before. Those eyes told me that no matter what happened he was going to pursue it to the very end. If you don't understand something, then stick with it until you do—that seemed to be Menshiki's basic approach to life.

"Okay," I said. "Tomorrow I'll get in touch with Masahiko."

"And I'll contact the landscape designer," Menshiki said. He paused. "By the way, there's one thing I wanted to ask you."

"Yes?"

"Do you often have these kinds of—what should I say?—paranormal experiences?"

"No," I said. "This is a first. I'm a very ordinary person who's lived a very ordinary life. That's why I find it all so confusing. What about you, Mr. Menshiki?"

A faint smile rose to his lips. "I've had many strange experiences. I've seen things common sense can't explain. But something **this** strange is a first."

After this we sat there in silence, listening to the ringing of the bell.

As always the bell stopped completely a little after 2:30. And the mountains were again blasted with the buzz of insects.

"I'd best be going," Menshiki said. "Thank you for the whiskey. I'll get in touch soon."

Under the moonlight Menshiki got into his glossy silver Jaguar and drove off. He gave a short wave out the open window and I waved back. After the sound of his engine had faded away down the slope, I remembered that he'd had a glass of whiskey (the second glass he hadn't touched), but his face hadn't turned red at all, his speech and attitude no different than if he'd drunk water. He must be able to hold his liquor. And he wasn't driving far. It was a road that only local residents used, and at this hour there wouldn't be any cars coming the other direction, or any pedestrians.

I went back inside, rinsed out our glasses in the kitchen sink, and went to bed. I thought about people coming with heavy equipment to move the stones behind the little shrine, and digging a hole. It was hard to picture it as real. Before that happened, I needed to read the Ueda Akinari story he'd mentioned, "Fate over Two Generations." But I'd leave everything for tomorrow. Things would look different in the light of day. I switched off the bedside light, and to the background noise of buzzing insects, I fell asleep.

· · ·

At ten a.m. I called Masahiko Amada's office and explained the situation. I didn't bring up Ueda Akinari, but told him how I'd had an acquaintance over to make sure that bell ringing in the middle of the night wasn't just an auditory illusion I was having.

"That is really creepy," Masahiko said. "But do you really believe there's someone underneath those stones ringing a bell?"

"I don't know. But I can't just ignore it. I hear it every single night."

"What will you do if, when you dig it all up, something weird emerges?"

"What do you mean, something weird?"

"I don't know," he said. "Some mysterious thing that's best left alone."

"You should come at night sometime and hear that sound. If you heard it yourself you'd understand why I can't just let it be."

Masahiko sighed deeply on the other end of the line. "No thanks," he said, "I'll pass. I've always been a bit of a coward. I hate scary stories, anything frightening. No thanks. I'll leave it all up to you. It's not going to bother anyone if you move those old stones and dig a hole. Do whatever you like. Just make sure not to unearth anything weird, okay?"

"I don't know how it's going to turn out, but once I know, I'll be in touch."

"If it were me, I'd just wear earplugs," Masahiko said.

After I hung up I sat in a chair in the living room and read the Ueda Akinari story. I read it first in the original classical Japanese, then in the contemporary-language version. A couple of details were different, but as Menshiki had said there was a strong resemblance between the story and what I was experiencing here. In the story the character heard the gong sounding at two o'clock in the morning, about the same time. But what I heard wasn't a gong but a bell. In the story the buzz of insects didn't stop. The protagonist hears the gong mixed in with the sound of the insects. But these small details aside, what I experienced was exactly the same as in the story. It left me dumbfounded, in fact, at how close the two were.

The unearthed mummy was completely dried up, just its hand doggedly moving, striking the gong. A terrifying vitality made the hand move almost mechanically. No doubt this priest gave up the ghost while reciting sutras and beating out a rhythm on the gong. The main character put clothes on the mummy and poured water on his lips. Before long he was able to eat some thin rice gruel and gradually put on flesh. Finally he recovered to the point where he looked like a normal human being. But you got no sense from him at all of a priest who had attained enlightenment. No intelligence or wisdom, and not a hint of dignity. And he had lost all memory of his former life. He couldn't recall, even, why he'd gone underground like that for so very long. He ate meat now, and had a considerable sexual appetite. He got married, and managed to make a living doing menial work. People nicknamed him "Nyujo no Josuke"— Josuke, the meditation guy. His pathetic figure made the villagers lose all respect for Buddhism. Is this the kind of wreck you end up as, they wondered, after all the strict ascetic training he went through, risking his life in pursuit of Buddhism? They started to despise faith, and stopped going to temple. That was Ueda's story. As Menshiki had said, the story reflected the author's cynical worldview. It's not merely some tale of the supernatural.

For all that, Buddhist teachings were in vain. That man must have been underground, ringing that gong, for well over a hundred years. Yet nothing miraculous came of it, and people were fed up that all that came from it were bones.

I reread the short story "Fate over Two Generations" several times and found myself utterly confused. Say we used heavy equipment to move the stones, dug up the soil, and what emerged was a bony, pathetic mummy, then how was I supposed to handle that? Would I be responsible for resuscitating him? Was it wiser, as Masahiko had advised, to not meddle, and simply plug up my ears and leave it all alone?

But even if I wanted to do that, I couldn't simply make it go away. I would never be able to escape that sound, no matter how tightly I plugged up my ears. And say I moved somewhere else; that sound might follow me. Plus, like Menshiki, I was curious. I had to find out what lay hidden beneath those stones.

In the afternoon Menshiki called me. "Did you get Mr. Amada's permission?"

I told him pretty much everything about my conversation with Masahiko. And how he'd told me to handle it any way I wanted.

"I'm glad," Menshiki said. "I've arranged things with the landscape designer. I didn't tell him about the mysterious sound. I just asked him to move some stones out in the woods and then dig a hole there. It was a sudden request, but his schedule happened to be free, so if you don't mind, he'd like to come and look over the site this afternoon and start work tomorrow morning. Is it all right with you that he comes to check out the work site?"

"He can come over whenever he wants," I said.

"After he inspects the site, he'll arrange for the equipment he needs. The work itself should be done in a few hours. I'll be present when they're working," Menshiki said.

"I'll be there, too. When you find out what time they'll start, let me know," I said. "By the way," I added, remembering, "about what we were talking about last night, before we heard that sound . . ."

Menshiki didn't seem to follow. "I'm sorry, you mean—"

"It was about the thirteen-year-old girl, Mariye. You said she might be your real daughter. We were

227

talking about her when we heard the bell, and that's as far as we got."

"Ah yes," said Menshiki. "Now that you mention it, we did talk about that. I'd totally forgotten. Yes, we should talk about that again sometime. But there's no rush. We can talk about it again once we take care of the matter at hand."

After that I couldn't concentrate. I tried reading, listening to music, cooking, but all I could think of was what lay beneath those ancient stones in the woods. I couldn't shake the thought of a blackened mummy, shriveled up like a dried fish.

15

THIS IS ONLY THE BEGINNING

Menshiki called me that night to let me know that the work would begin the next morning, Wednesday, at ten.

Wednesday morning it was drizzling off and on, but not hard enough to delay the work. It was a fine rain, and a hat or raincoat with a hood was enough. No need for an umbrella. Menshiki had on an olive-green rain hat, the kind the British might use for duck hunting. The leaves of the trees, starting to turn fall colors, took on a dull color from the nearly invisible rain that soaked them.

The workers used a flatbed truck to move in a small backhoe. A very compact piece of equipment, with a tight turning radius, made to work in confined spaces. There were four workers altogether—one backhoe operator, one foreman, and two additional workers. The shovel operator and the foreman drove the truck. They all had on matching blue rainwear, jackets and trousers, and muddy thick-soled work boots, and wore protective helmets made of heavy-duty plastic. Menshiki and the foreman were apparently acquainted, and they talked for a while, the two of them beaming, next to the little shrine. I could tell, though, that the foreman remained on his best behavior toward Menshiki.

Menshiki must have had a lot of clout to arrange for this many people and equipment in such a short time. I watched this whole process half impressed, half bewildered. I had a slight sense of resignation, too, as if everything were already out of my hands. Like when I was a child and the little kids would be playing some game and bigger kids would come around and take over. I remembered that feeling.

They started the operation by using shovels and some material and boards to create a flat foothold for the backhoe to move, and then they began to actually remove the stones. The backhoe soon trampled down the thicket of pampas grass surrounding the mound. Menshiki and I stood to one side watching as they lifted the stones from the mound one by one and moved them to a spot a little ways away. There wasn't anything special about the operation. Probably the same sort of operation that takes place every day, all around the world. The workers looked ordinary too, like they were matter-of-factly following procedures they'd done a thousand times. Occasionally the backhoe operator would stop and call out in a loud voice to the foreman, but it didn't seem like there was any problem. They just exchanged a few words, and he didn't switch off the engine.

But I couldn't calmly watch the operation. Each time one of the square stones was removed, my anxiety only deepened. It was like some dark secret that I'd hidden away for years was being revealed, layer by layer, by the powerful, insistent tip of that machine. The problem lay in the fact that even I didn't know what secret I was hiding. Several times I felt I had to get them to stop the operation. Bringing in some large machinery like this backhoe couldn't be the solution. As Masahiko had told me on the phone, all "mysterious things" should be left buried. I was seized by the urge to grab Menshiki's arm and shout, "Let's stop this! Put the stones back where they were."

But of course I couldn't do that. The decision had been made and the work begun. Several other people were already involved. A not-insubstantial sum of money was changing hands (the amount was unclear, but I assumed Menshiki was footing the bill). We couldn't just stop at this point. The work continued, beyond my will.

As if he knew what I was going through, at a certain point Menshiki came over beside me and lightly patted me on the shoulder.

"There's nothing to worry about," he said in a calm voice. "It's going smoothly. It'll all be finished soon."

I nodded in silence.

Before noon all the stones had been moved. The ancient stones that had been piled in a jumble in a crumbling mound were now piled up in a neat, official-looking pyramid a little ways away. The fine drizzle silently fell on the pile. Even after removing all those stones, though, the ground hadn't appeared. Below the stones lay more stone. These stones were flat and had been methodically laid out there like a square stone flooring. The whole thing was about six feet on each side.

"I wonder why it's like that," the foreman said after coming over to where Menshiki was. "I was sure that the stones were just piled up on top of the ground. But they weren't. There seems to be an open space underneath that stone slab. I inserted a thin metal rod into a gap and it went down pretty far. Not sure yet how deep it goes, though."

Menshiki and I gingerly tried standing on top of the freshly uncovered slab. The stones were darkly wet and slippery in spots. Though they'd been artificially cut and evened up over time, the edges had become more rounded off, with gaps between the stones. The nightly sound of the bell must have filtered out through those gaps. And air could probably get in through those too. I crouched down and stared through a gap inside, but it was pitch black and I couldn't make out a thing.

"Maybe they used flagstones to cover up an ancient well. Though for a well, its diameter is a bit big," the foreman said.

"Can you remove these flagstones?" Menshiki asked.

The foreman shrugged. "I'm not sure. We hadn't planned on this. It'll make things a little complicated, but I think we can manage it. Using a crane would be our best bet, but we'd never get one in here. Each stone doesn't look that heavy. And there's a gap between them, so with a little ingenuity I think we can manage with the backhoe. We're coming up on our lunch break, so I'll work out a good plan then and we'll get to work in the afternoon."

Menshiki and I went back to the house and had a light lunch. In the kitchen I threw together some simple ham, lettuce, and pickle sandwiches and we went out on the terrace to eat as we watched the rain.

"This whole operation is delaying what we should be working on, finishing the portrait," I said.

Menshiki shook his head. "There's no rush with the portrait. Our first priority is solving this weird matter. Then you can get back to work on the painting."

Did this man **seriously** want his portrait painted? I couldn't help but wonder. This doubt had been smoldering in a corner of my mind from the very start. Did he **seriously** want me to paint his portrait? Wasn't he just using the portrait as a mere pretext, and had some other reason for getting to know me?

But what could it be? I couldn't figure it out. Was his goal unearthing what was under those stones? This didn't make sense. He hadn't known about them. That was something unforeseen that only came up after we started on the portrait. Still, he seemed overly enthusiastic about digging them up. And he was shelling out quite a bit of money for the operation, even though it had nothing to do with him.

As I was mulling over all this Menshiki asked, "Did you read the story 'Fate over Two Generations'?"

"I did," I told him.

"What did you think? A very strange tale, isn't it?" he said.

"It certainly is," I said.

Menshiki looked at me for a while, then said, "To tell the truth, that story has tugged at me for a long time. It's one of the reasons this discovery has aroused my interest."

I took a sip of coffee and wiped my mouth with a paper napkin. Two crows, cawing at each other, winged their way across the valley, undeterred by the rain. Wet by the rain, their wings would only grow a deeper black.

"I don't know much about Buddhism," I said to Menshiki, "so I don't understand all the details, but doesn't a priest doing a voluntary burial—this **nyujo**—mean he chooses to go into a coffin and die?"

"Exactly. **Nyujo** originally means 'attaining enlightenment,' so they have the term **ikinyujo**—'living **nyujo**'—to distinguish the two. They make a stone-lined underground chamber and insert a bamboo pipe to allow in air. Before a priest does **nyujo** he maintains a fruitarian diet for a set time so his body won't putrefy but will become nicely mummified."

"Fruitarian?"

"Just eating grasses and nuts and berries. They eat no cooked foods whatsoever, starting with grains. In other words, a radical elimination of all fats and moisture from the body. Changing the makeup of the body so it can easily mummify. And after purifying his body, the priest goes underground. In the darkness there the priest fasts and recites sutras, hitting a gong in time to that. Or ringing a bell. And people can hear the sound of that gong or bell through the vent hole. But at some point the sounds stop. That's the sign that he's breathed his last. And over a period of time the body gradually turns into a mummy. The custom is to un-earth the body after three years and three months."

"Why would they do that?"

"So the priests could practice austerity to the point of becoming self-mummified. Doing that al-lows them to reach enlightenment and to arrive at a realm beyond life and death. This also connects up with mankind's salvation. So-called Nirvana. The un-earthed enlightened monk, the mummy, is kept at a temple, and through praying to it people are saved."

"In reality it's a kind of suicide."

Menshiki nodded. "Which is why in the Meiji pe-riod the practice of self-burial was outlawed. People who helped in the process could be arrested for aid-ing and abetting suicide. The truth is, though, priests continued to follow the practice in secret. That's why there may be quite a few cases of priests being buried but never unearthed by anyone."

"Are you thinking that stone mound is the remains of a secret burial of that kind?"

Menshiki shook his head. "We won't know until we actually remove the stones. But it's possible. There's no bamboo tube there, but the way it's constructed, air could get in through the gaps, and you can hear sounds from inside too."

"And you're saying that someone is still alive un-derneath those stones and is ringing a gong or bell every night?"

Menshiki shook his head again. "That obviously doesn't make any sense."

"Reaching Nirvana—is that different from merely dying?"

"It is. I'm not all that familiar with Buddhist doctrine, but as far as I understand, Nirvana is found beyond life and death. You could see it as the idea that even if the flesh dies and disappears, the soul goes over to a place beyond life and death. Worldly flesh is nothing more than a temporary dwelling."

"Even if a priest were, through burial alive, to reach Nirvana, is it possible for him to rejoin his physical body?"

Menshiki said nothing and looked at me for a while. He took a bite of his ham sandwich, and a sip of coffee.

"What you're saying is—"

"I didn't hear that sound until four or five days ago," I said. "I'm certain of that. If the sound had been there I would have noticed. Even if it was small, it's not the kind of sound I would have missed. I only started hearing it a few days ago. What I mean is, even if there's somebody underneath those stones, that person hasn't been ringing the bell for a long time."

Menshiki returned his coffee cup to the saucer and studied the pattern on the cup. "Have you seen a real mummified priest?" he finally said.

I shook my head.

"I've seen several. When I was young I traveled around Yamagata Prefecture on my own and saw a few that were preserved in temples there. For some reason there are a lot of these mummified priests in the Tohoku region, especially in Yamagata. Honestly, they're not very nice to look at. Maybe it's my lack of faith, but I didn't feel very grateful when I saw them. Small, brown, all shriveled up. I probably shouldn't say this, but the color and texture reminded me of beef jerky. The physical body really is nothing more than a fleeting, empty abode. That, at least, is what these mummies teach us. We may do our utmost, but at best we end up as no more than beef jerky."

He picked up the ham sandwich he'd been eating and gazed at it intently for a moment. As if he were seeing a ham sandwich for the first time in his life.

He went on. "At any rate, let's wait till after lunch for them to move those stones. Then we'll know more, whether we want to or not."

We went back to the site in the woods just after one fifteen. The crew had finished lunch and were hard at work. The two workmen put wedge-like metal implements in the gaps between the stones, and the backhoe used a rope to pull those and raise the stones. The workmen then attached ropes to the dug-up stones, and the shovel hauled these up. It was time consuming, but one by one the stones were steadily unearthed and moved off to the side.

Menshiki and the foreman were deep in conversation about something for a while, but then he came back to join me.

"As they thought, the stones aren't all that thick.

Looks like they'll be able to remove them," he explained. "There seems to be a lattice-shaped lid underneath all the stones. They don't know what it's made of, but that lid supported the stones. After they remove all the stones on top they'll need to take off that lid. They don't know yet if they can. It's impossible to guess what lies beneath that. It'll take a while for them to remove all the stones, and once they've made more progress they'll call us, so they said they'd like us to wait in the house. If you don't mind, let's do that. Standing around here isn't going to help."

We walked back home. I should have used the extra time to continue work on the portrait, but I didn't feel I'd be able to concentrate on painting. The operation out in the woods had me on edge. The six-foot-square stone flooring that had emerged from underneath the mound of crumbling old stones. The solid lattice lid. And the space that seemed to lie below it. I couldn't erase these images from my mind. Menshiki was right. Until we settled this matter we wouldn't be able to move forward on anything else.

"Do you mind if I listen to music while we wait?" Menshiki asked.

"Not at all," I said. "Play whatever record you'd like. I'll be in the kitchen preparing some food."

He chose a recording of Mozart. A sonata for piano and violin. The Tannoy Autograph speakers weren't very showy, but gave out a deep, steady sound. The perfect speakers for classical music, especially for listening to vinyl records of chamber music. As you might expect of old speakers, they were well suited to a vacuum-tube amp. The pianist was Georg Szell, the violinist Rafael Druian. Menshiki sat on the sofa, eyes closed, and gave himself over to the music. I listened to it from a little ways off, making tomato sauce. I'd bought a lot of tomatoes and had some left over and wanted to make some sauce before they went bad.

I boiled water in a large pan, parboiled the tomatoes and removed the skins, cut them with a knife, removed the seeds, crushed them, put them in a large skillet, added garlic, and simmered it all with olive oil, let it cook well. I carefully removed any scum on the surface. Back when I was married I often made sauce like this. It takes time and effort, but basically it's an easy process. While my wife was at work I'd stand alone in the kitchen, listening to music on a CD while I made it. I liked to cook while listening to old jazz. Thelonious Monk was a particular favorite. **Monk's Music** was my favorite of his albums. Coleman Hawkins and John Coltrane played on it, with amazing solos. But I have to admit that making sauce while listening to Mozart's chamber music wasn't bad either.

It was only a short while ago that I'd been cooking tomato sauce in the afternoon while enjoying Monk's unique offbeat melodies and chords (it was only half a year ago that my wife and I had dissolved our marriage), but it felt like something that had taken place ages ago. A trivial historical episode a generation ago that only a handful of people still remembered. I suddenly wondered how my wife was. Was she living with another man now? Or was she still living by herself in that apartment in Hiroo? Either way, at this time of day she would be at work at the architectural firm. For her, how much of a difference was there between her life when I was there, and her life now without me? And how much interest did she have in that difference? I was sort of half thinking about all this. Did she have the same feeling, that our days spent together seemed like something from the distant past?

The record was over, the needle making a popping sound as it spun in the final groove, and when I went to the living room I found Menshiki asleep on the sofa, arms folded, leaning over slightly to one side. I lifted the needle up from the spinning disc and switched off the turntable. Even when the steady click of the needle stopped, Menshiki continued to sleep. He must have been very tired. He was faintly snoring. I left him where he was. I returned to the kitchen, shut off the gas under the skillet, and drank a big glass of water. I still had time on my hands, so I began to fry some onions.

When the phone rang Menshiki was already awake. He was in the bathroom, washing his face with soap and gargling. The call was from the foreman at the work site, so I handed the phone to Menshiki. He said a few words, and then said that we would be right over. He handed the phone back.

"They're almost done," he said.

Outside it had stopped raining. Clouds still covered the sky, but it was lighter out now. The weather seemed to be steadily improving. We hurried up the steps and through the woods. Behind the little shrine the four men were standing around a hole, staring down into it. The backhoe's engine was off, nothing was moving, the woods strangely hushed.

The stones had been neatly removed, exposing the hole below. The square lattice lid had been taken off too, and laid to one side. It was a thick, heavy-looking wooden cover. Old, but not rotted at all. After that the circular stone-lined room below was visible. It was under six feet in diameter, about eight feet deep, and was enclosed by a stone wall. The floor seemed to be dirt. Not a single blade of grass grew there. The stone room was completely empty. No one there calling for help, no beef jerky mummy. Just a bell-like object lying on the ground. Actually less like a bell than some ancient musical instrument with a stack of tiny cymbals. A wooden handle was attached, about six inches long. The foreman shone a floodlight down on it.

"Was this all that was in there?" Menshiki asked him.

"Yes, that's it," the foreman said. "Like you asked, we left it just as we found it, after we took off the stones and lid. We haven't touched a thing."

"That's strange," Menshiki said, as if to himself. "So there really wasn't anything else at all?"

"I called you right after we lifted off the lid. I haven't been down inside. This is exactly the way it was when we uncovered it," the foreman said.

"Of course," Menshiki said, in a dry voice.

"It might have been a well originally," the foreman said. "It looks like it was filled in, leaving the hole. But it's too wide for a well, and the stone wall around it is so elaborately constructed. It couldn't have been easy to build. I suppose they must have had some important purpose in mind to construct something that took this much time and effort."

"Can I go down and check it out?" Menshiki asked the foreman.

The foreman was a little unsure. With a hard face, he said, "I think I should go down first. Just in case. If it's all clear, then you can climb on down. Does that sound good?"

"Of course," Menshiki said. "Let's do that."

One of the workmen brought over a folding metal ladder from the truck, opened it up, and lowered it down. The foreman put on his safety helmet and climbed down the eight feet to the dirt floor. He looked around him for a while. He gazed up, then shone his flashlight on the stone wall and the floor, closely checking everything. He carefully observed the bell-like object that lay on the dirt floor. He didn't touch it, though, just observed it. He rubbed the soles of his work boots a few times against the dirt floor, kicking his heel against it. He took a few deep breaths, smelling the air. He was only in the hole for about five or six minutes, then slowly clambered up the ladder to ground level.

"It doesn't seem dangerous. The air's good, and there aren't any weird bugs or anything. And the footing is solid. You can go down now if you'd like," he said.

Menshiki removed his rainwear to make it easier to move around, and in his flannel shirt and chinos, he hung his flashlight by a strap around his neck and climbed down the metal ladder. We watched in silence as he descended. The foreman shone the floodlight below Menshiki's feet. Menshiki stood still at the bottom of the hole for a while, waiting, then reached out and touched the stone wall, and crouched down to check out what the dirt floor felt like. He picked up the bell-like object on the ground, shone his flashlight on it, and gazed at it. Then he shook it a few times. When he did, it was unmistakably the same bell sound I'd heard. No doubt about it. In the middle of the night someone had been ringing it here. But that **someone** was no longer here. Only the bell was left behind. As he studied the bell Menshiki shook his head a few times, evidently puzzled. Then he carefully studied the surrounding wall again, as if looking for a secret entrance and exit. But he found nothing of the sort. He looked up at us at ground level. He seemed totally confused.

He stepped onto the ladder and held out the bell toward me. I bent over and took it from him. A dampness penetrated deep into the ancient wooden handle. As Menshiki had done, I tried shaking it a few times. It sounded louder and clearer than I'd expected. I didn't know what it was made of, but the metal portion wasn't damaged at all. It was dirty, for sure, but not at all rusted. I couldn't figure out how it had remained rust-free despite being underground in damp soil for years.

"What **is** that?" the foreman asked me. He was in his mid-forties, short but with a sturdy build. Suntanned, with a bit of stubble on his face.

"I'm not sure. Maybe some kind of Buddhist implement or something," I said. "Whatever it is, it's certainly from ancient times."

"Is this what you were looking for?" he asked.

I shook my head. "No, we were expecting something else."

"At any rate, it's a strange place," the foreman said. "I can't explain it, but there's a mysterious feeling about it. Who would make this kind of place, I wonder—and why? This was a long time ago, and it must have been quite a task to haul the stones all the way up the mountain and stack them up."

I didn't say anything.

Menshiki finally climbed up out of the hole. He called the foreman over to his side, and they talked for a long time. I stood there, bell in hand, next to the hole. I pondered climbing down into this stone-lined chamber, but then thought better of it. I wasn't as hesitant as Masahiko, but I did decide it was better not to do anything uncalled for. If things could be left alone, the smart thing might be to do so. I placed the bell, for the time being, in front of the little shrine, and wiped my palm on my pants a couple of times.

Menshiki ambled over. "We'll have them do a more thorough examination of that stone-lined chamber," he said. "At first glance it looks like just a hole, but I'll have them check it all out from one end to the other. They might discover something. Though I sort of doubt it." He looked at the bell I'd placed in front of the shrine. "It's odd that this bell's the only thing left. Since someone had to be inside there in the middle of the night ringing the bell."

"Maybe the bell was ringing by itself," I ventured.

Menshiki smiled. "An interesting theory, but I doubt it. For whatever purpose, someone was sending out a message from down inside that hole. A message to you, or maybe to us. Or to people in general. But whoever it was has vanished like smoke. Or else slipped away from there."

"Slipped away?"

"Slipped right past us."

I couldn't understand what he was getting at.

"Because the soul isn't something you can see," Menshiki said.

"You believe in the existence of the soul?"

"Do you?"

I didn't have a good answer.

"I believe that it's not necessary to believe in the soul's existence. But turn that around and you come to the belief that there's no need to **not** believe in its existence. A kind of roundabout way of putting it, but do you understand what I'm getting at?"

"Sort of," I said.

Menshiki picked up the bell from where I'd placed it in front of the shrine. He held it out and rang it several times. "A priest probably breathed his last there, underground, ringing this bell and chanting sutras.

All alone, shut away in the pitch-black darkness, that heavy lid in place, in the bottom of a sealed well. And most likely all in secret. I have no idea what sort of priest he was. A respectable priest, or merely some fanatic. Either way, someone constructed a stone tumulus on top of it. I don't know what happened after that, but people then completely forgot he'd been voluntarily buried under here. Then a big earthquake occurred at some point, and the mound collapsed until it was just a pile of stones. It could have been during the Kanto earthquake of 1923, since certain areas around Odawara suffered real damage back then. And everything was swallowed up into oblivion."

"If that's true, then where did the priest who died there—the mummy, I mean—disappear to?"

Menshiki shook his head. "I don't know. Maybe at some point someone dug up the hole and took him away."

"To do that they'd have to move all these stones and then pile them up again," I said. "And then who was ringing the bell yesterday in the middle of the night?"

Menshiki shook his head again, and smiled faintly. "Good grief. We used all this equipment to move the stones and open up the chamber, and in the end all we found out for sure is that we don't know a single thing. All we managed to get was an old bell."

They examined the stone chamber thoroughly, and merely determined that there were no hidden devices anywhere. This was merely a round hole, lined with a stone wall, 8.2 feet deep with a diameter of 5.9 feet (they made precise measurements). Finally, they loaded the backhoe up onto the truck bed, and the workers collected all their tools and left. All that remained was the open hole and the metal ladder. The foreman was kind enough to leave it behind. They also laid several thick boards on top of the hole so no one would fall into it by mistake. They left some heavy stones on top to weigh the boards down so they wouldn't blow away in a strong wind. The wooden lattice cover was too heavy to lift, so they left it on the ground nearby and covered it with a plastic tarp.

Before they left, Menshiki told the foreman not to mention this operation to anyone. It had archaeological significance, and he wanted, he said, to keep it from the public until the time was right to announce the find.

"Understood," the foreman said with a serious expression. "We'll leave it all here. And I'll warn the others not to say anything about it."

After the workers and heavy machinery had left and the mountains were blanketed in their usual stillness again, the dug-up area looked like skin after a major operation, shabby and pitiful. The formerly vigorous clump of pampas grass had been trampled down beyond recognition, the ruts left by the backhoe like stitches left behind in the dark, damp soil. The rain had cleared up completely, though the sky was still covered by an unbroken layer of monotonously gray clouds.

When I looked at the pile of stones now stacked up on another piece of ground, I couldn't help but think, We should never have done this. We should have left them the way they were. On the other hand, though, the indisputable fact was that it was something we **had** to do. I couldn't go on listening to that strange sound night after night. But if I hadn't met Menshiki, I never would have had the means to dig up that hole. It was only because he had arranged for the workers, and had paid for the whole thing— I had no clue how much it cost—that the operation had been possible.

But meeting Menshiki and, as a result, having this large-scale excavation take place—was it really all just coincidence? Had it all just fallen together by chance? Weren't things just a little **too** convenient? Hadn't the scenario been all planned out in advance? With all these unanswered doubts, I went with Menshiki to the house. He carried the bell we'd unearthed. He never let go of it the whole time we were walking. As if trying to read, from the touch of it, some kind of message.

As soon as we got back inside Menshiki asked, "Where should I put this bell?"

Where indeed? I had no idea. For the time being, I decided to place it in the studio. Having that weird object under the same roof didn't sit well with me, but that said, I couldn't just toss it outside. It was, no doubt, a valuable Buddhist implement, imbued with a certain soulfulness, so I couldn't just neglect it. I decided to put it in the sort of neutral zone of the studio, which felt like a separate annex. I cleared a space on the long, narrow shelf used for painting materials and placed it there. Next to the large mug used to hold brushes, it even looked like some specialized painting tool.

"What a strange day," Menshiki said.

"I'm sorry you had to use up your entire day for this," I said.

"No, don't apologize. It's been very interesting," Menshiki said. "And this isn't the end of it, I would imagine."

Menshiki had an odd look on his face, as if gazing far away.

"Meaning something else is going to happen?" I asked.

Menshiki chose his words carefully. "I can't explain it well, but I get the feeling that this is only the beginning."

"Only the beginning?"

He held his palms upward. "I'm not sure, of course. Maybe that'll be it, and we'll just be left thinking what a strange day that was. That would probably be the best outcome. But nothing's been resolved. The same questions remain. And these are **very important** questions. That's why I have a hunch that something else is going to happen."

"Something connected to that stone-lined chamber?"

Menshiki gazed outside for a moment before he

spoke. "I don't know what's going to happen. It's just a hunch."

And of course it turned out as he'd felt—or predicted—it might. Like he said, that day was only the beginning.

16

A RELATIVELY GOOD DAY

That night I had trouble sleeping. I was anxious whether the bell I'd left in the studio would start ringing in the middle of the night. If it did, then what would I do? Pull the covers up over my head and pretend not to hear anything until the next morning? Or take my flashlight and go to the studio to check it out? And what would I find there?

Unable to decide how I should react, I lay in bed reading. But even after two a.m. the bell hadn't rung. All I heard was the usual drone of insects. As I read my book I checked the clock next to my bed every five minutes. When the digital display read 2:30 I finally breathed a sigh of relief. The bell wouldn't be ringing tonight, I figured. I closed the book, turned out the bedside light, and went to sleep.

The next morning when I woke up before seven, the first thing I did was go check on the bell. It was as I'd left it the night before, on the shelf. Brilliant sunlight illuminated the mountains, and the crows were in the midst of their usual noisy morning routine. In the light of day the bell didn't look ominous at all. It was nothing more than a simple, well-used Buddhist implement from the past.

I went back to the kitchen, brewed coffee in the coffee maker, and drank it. Heated up a scone that had gotten hard in the toaster and ate it. Then went out to the terrace, breathed in the morning air, leaned against the railing, and looked over at Menshiki's house across the valley. The large tinted windows glistened in the morning sun. Probably one of the tasks included in the once-per-week cleaning service was to clean all the windows. The glass was always clean and shiny. I looked over there for a while, but Menshiki didn't appear. We still hadn't yet reached the point where we waved at each other across the valley.

At ten thirty I drove my car to the supermarket to buy groceries. I came back, put them away, and made a simple lunch, a tofu and tomato salad with a rice ball. After I ate, I had some strong green tea. Then I lay down on the sofa and listened to a Schubert string quartet. It was a beautiful piece. According to the liner notes on the jacket, when it was first performed there was quite a backlash among listeners, who felt it was "too radical." I don't know what part was radical, but something about it must have offended the old-fashioned people of that time.

As one side of the record ended I suddenly got very sleepy, so I pulled a blanket over me and slept for while on the sofa. A short but deep sleep, probably about twenty minutes. It felt like I had a few dreams, but when I woke up I couldn't remember them. Those kinds of dreams—the kind where all sorts of unrelated fragments are mixed together. Each fragment has a certain gravitas, but by intertwining they canceled each other out.

I went to the fridge and drank some cold mineral water straight from the bottle and managed to chase away the dregs of sleep that remained like scraps of clouds in the corners of my body. I felt a renewed awareness of the reality that I was living, alone, in the mountains. I lived here by myself. Some sort of fate had brought me to this special place. I remembered the bell. In the weird stone chamber deep in the woods, who in the world had been ringing that bell? And where on earth was that person now?

By the time I had changed into my painting outfit, gone into the studio, and stood looking at Menshiki's portrait, it was past two p.m. Normally I worked in the morning. From eight to noon was the time I could focus best on painting. I liked the sort of domestic quiet at those times. After moving to the mountains I'd grown fond of the brilliant and pure air that the teeming nature around me provided. Working at the same time in the same place each day has always held a special meaning for me. Repetition created a certain rhythm. But this day, partly because I hadn't slept well the night before, I spent the morning without accomplishing anything. Which is why I went to the studio in the afternoon.

I sat on my round work stool, arms folded, and from a distance of some six feet gazed at the painting

I'd begun. I'd started by using a thin brush to outline Menshiki's face, then with him modeling before me for fifteen minutes also used black paint to flesh this out. This was just a rough framework at this point, though it gave rise to a productive flow. A flow that had its source in Wataru Menshiki. This was what I needed most.

As I stared hard at this black-and-white framework, an image of a color I should add came to me. The idea sprang up suddenly, all on its own. The color was like that of a tree with its green leaves dully dyed by rain. I mixed several colors together and created what I wanted on my palette. After much trial and error, I finally arrived at what I'd pictured and, without really thinking, added the color to the line drawing I'd done. I had no idea myself what sort of painting would emerge from this, though I did know that that color was going to be a vital grounding for the work. Gradually this painting was beginning to stray far afield from the format of a typical portrait. But even if it doesn't turn out as a portrait, I told myself, that was okay. As long as there was a set flow, all I could do was go with it. What I wanted now was to paint what I wanted to paint, the way I wanted to paint it (something Menshiki wanted as well). I could think about the next step later on.

I was simply following ideas that sprang up naturally inside me, with no plan or goal. Like a child, not watching his step, chasing some unusual butterfly fluttering across a field. After adding this color to the canvas I set my palette and brush down, again sat down on the stool six feet away, and studied the painting straight on. This is indeed the right color, I decided. The kind of green found in a forest wet by the rain. I nodded several times to myself. This was the kind of feeling toward a painting I hadn't experienced for ages. Yes—this was it. This was the color I'd wanted. Or maybe the color the framework itself had been seeking. With this color as the base, I mixed some peripheral, variant colors, adding variation and depth to the painting.

And as I gazed at the image I'd done, the next color leaped up at me. Orange. Not just a simple orange, but a flaming orange, a color that had both a strong vitality and also a premonition of decay. Like a fruit slowly rotting away. Creating this color was much more of a challenge than the green. It wasn't simply a color, but had to be connected with a specific emotion, an emotion entwined with fate, but in its own way firm, unfluctuating. Making a color like that was no easy task, of course, but in the end I managed. I took out a new brush and ran it over the surface of the canvas. In places I used a knife, too. **Not thinking** was the priority. I tried to turn off my mind, decisively adding this color to the composition. As I painted, details of reality almost totally vanished from my mind. The sound of the bell, that gaping stone tomb, my ex-wife sleeping with some other man, my married girlfriend, the art classes I taught, the future—I thought of none of it. I didn't even think of Menshiki. What I was painting had, of course, started out as his portrait, but by this point my mind was even clear of the thought of his face. Menshiki was nothing more than a starting point. What I was doing was painting for me, for my sake alone.

I don't remember how much time passed. By the time I looked around, the room had gotten dim. The autumn sun had disappeared behind the western mountains, yet I was so engrossed in my work I'd forgotten to switch on a light. I looked at the canvas and saw five colors there already. Color on top of color, and more color on top of that. In one section the colors were subtly mixed, in another part one color overwhelmed another and prevailed over it.

I turned on the ceiling light, sat down again on the stool, and looked at the painting. I knew the painting was incomplete. There was a wild outburst to it, a type of violence that had propelled me forward. A wildness I had not seen in some time. But something was still missing, a core element to control and quell that raw throng, an idea to bring emotion under control. But I needed more time to discover that. That torrent of color had to rest. That would be a job for tomorrow and beyond, when I could return to it under a fresh, bright light. The passage of the right amount of time would show me what was needed. I had to wait for it, like waiting patiently for the phone to ring. And in order to wait that patiently, I had to put my faith in time. I had to believe that time was on my side.

Seated on the stool, I shut my eyes and took a deep breath. In the autumn twilight I could clearly sense something within me changing. As if the structure of my body had unraveled, then was being recombined in a different way. But why **here**, and why **now**? Did meeting the enigmatic Menshiki and taking on his portrait commission result in this sort of internal transformation? Or had uncovering the weird underground chamber, and being led there by the sound of the bell, acted as a stimulus to my spirit? Or was it that I'd merely reached an unrelated turning point in my life? No matter which explanation I went with, there didn't seem to be any basis for it.

"It feels like this is just the beginning," Menshiki had said as we parted. Had I stepped into this **beginning** he'd spoken about? At any rate, I'd been so worked up by the act of painting in a way I hadn't in years, so absorbed in creating, that I'd literally forgotten the passage of time. As I stowed away my materials, my skin had a feverish flush that felt good.

As I straightened up, the bell on the shelf caught my eye. I picked it up and tried ringing it a couple of times. The familiar sound rang out clearly in the studio. The middle-of-the-night sound that made me anxious. Somehow, though, it didn't frighten me anymore. I merely wondered why such an ancient bell could still make such a clear sound. I put the bell back where it had been, switched off the light, and shut the door to the studio. Back in the kitchen, I poured myself a glass of white wine and sipped it as I prepared dinner.

Just before nine p.m. a call came in from Menshiki.

"How were things last night?" he asked. "Did you hear the bell?"

I'd stayed up until two thirty but hadn't heard the bell at all, I told him. It was a very quiet night.

"Glad to hear it. Since then has anything unusual happened around you?"

"Nothing particularly unusual, no," I replied.

"That's good. I hope it continues that way," Menshiki said. A moment later he added, "Would it be all right for me to stop by tomorrow morning? I'd really like to take another good look at the stone chamber if I could. It's a fascinating place."

"Fine by me," I said. "I have no plans for tomorrow morning."

"Then I'll see you around eleven."

"Looking forward to it," I said.

"By the way, was today a good day for you?" Menshiki asked.

Was today a good day for me? It sounded like a sentence that had been translated mechanically by computer software.

"A relatively good day," I replied, puzzled for a moment. "At least, nothing bad happened. The weather was good, overall a pleasant day. What about you, Mr. Menshiki? Was today a good day for you?"

"It was a day when one good thing happened, and so did one not-so-good thing," Menshiki replied. "The scale is still swinging, unable to decide which one was heavier—the good or the bad."

I didn't know how to respond to that, so I stayed silent.

Menshiki went on. "Sadly, I'm not an artist like you. I live in the business world. The information business, in particular. In that world the only information that has exchange value is that which can be quantified. So I have the habit of always quantifying the good and the bad. If the good outweighs the bad even by a little, that means it's a good day, even if something bad happened. At least numerically."

I still had no idea what he was getting at. So I kept my mouth closed.

"By unearthing that underground chamber like we did yesterday, we must have lost something, and gained something. What did we lose, and what did we gain? That's what concerns me."

He seemed to be waiting for me to reply.

"I don't think we gained anything you could quantify," I said after giving it some thought. "At least right now. The only thing we got was that old Buddhist bell. But that probably doesn't have any actual value. It doesn't have any provenance, and isn't some unique antique. On the other hand, what was lost can be clearly quantified. Before long, you'll be getting a bill from the landscaper, I imagine."

Menshiki chuckled. "It's not that expensive. Don't worry about it. What concerns me is that we haven't yet taken from there **the thing we need to take**."

"The thing we need to take? What's that?"

Menshiki cleared his throat. "As I said, I'm no artist. I have a certain amount of intuition, but unfortunately I don't have the means to make it concrete. No matter how keen that intuition might be, I still can't turn it into art. I don't have the talent."

I was silent, waiting for what came next.

"Which is why I've always pursued quantification as a substitute for an artistic, universal representation. In order to live properly, people need a central axis. Don't you think so? In my case, by quantifying intuition, or something like intuition, through a unique system, I've been able to enjoy a degree of worldly success. And according to my intuition . . ." he said, and was silent for a time. A very dense silence. "According to my intuition, we should have got hold of something from digging up that underground chamber."

"Like what?"

He shook his head. Or at least it seemed that way to me from the other end of the phone line. "I still don't know. But I think we have to know. We need to combine our intuition, allow it to pass through your ability to express things in concrete form, and my ability to quantify them."

I still couldn't really grasp what he was getting at. What was this man talking about?

"Let's see each other again tomorrow at eleven," Menshiki said. And quietly hung up.

Soon after he'd hung up, I got a call from my married girlfriend. I was a little surprised. It wasn't often that she'd get in touch at this time of night.

"Can I see you tomorrow around noon?" she asked.

"I'm sorry, but I have an appointment tomorrow. I made it just a little while ago."

"Not another woman, I hope?"

"No. It's with Mr. Menshiki. I'm painting his portrait."

"You're painting his portrait," she repeated. "Then the day after tomorrow?"

"The day after tomorrow's totally free."

"Great. Is early afternoon okay?"

"Of course. But it's Saturday."

"I'll manage it."

"Did something happen?" I asked.

"Why do you ask?" she said.

"You don't often call me at this time of day."

She made a small sound at the back of her throat, as if making a minor adjustment in her breathing. "I'm in my car now, by myself. I'm calling from my cell."

"What are you doing in the car all alone?"

"I just wanted to be by myself in the car, so that's where I am. Housewives sometimes do these things. Is that a problem?"

"No problem. No problem at all."

She sighed, the kind of sigh that condensed a variety of sighs into one. And then she said, "I wish you were here with me. And that we could do it from behind. I don't need any foreplay. I'm so wet you could slip right inside. I want you to pound me, hard and fast."

"Sounds good to me. But a Mini is too small inside to pound you hard like that."

"Don't expect too much."

"Let's figure out a way."

"I want you to knead my breast with your left hand and rub my clit with your right."

"What should my right foot be doing? I could manage to use it to adjust the car stereo. You don't mind a little Tony Bennett?"

"I'm not joking here. I'm totally serious."

"I know. My bad. Serious. Got it," I said. "Tell me, what are you wearing right now?"

"You want to know what clothes I'm wearing?" she asked enticingly.

"I do. My procedure might change depending on what you have on."

Over the phone she gave me a detailed rundown on the clothes she had on. It always surprised me, the variety of clothes mature women wore. Orally, she took these off, one by one.

"So, did that get you hard?" she asked.

"Like a hammer," I said.

"You could pound a nail?"

"You bet."

There are hammers in the world that need to pound in nails, and nails that need to be pounded by hammers. Now who said that? Nietzsche? Or was it Schopenhauer? Or maybe nobody said it.

Over the phone line, we entwined bodies in a way that felt so real. Phone sex was definitely a first for me, with her—or with anyone, for that matter. Her descriptions were so detailed, so arousing, that these imaginary sex acts were, in part, more sensual than what we could do with our actual bodies. Words can sometimes be so direct, sometimes so erotically suggestive. At the end of this exchange, I unexpectedly climaxed. And she seemed to have an orgasm as well.

We said nothing, catching our breath.

"I'll see you Saturday, then," she said after she seemed to have pulled herself together. "I have something to tell you about our Mr. Menshiki, too."

"You got some new information?"

"A bit of new information I gathered through the jungle grapevine. But I'll wait to see you to tell you. While we're probably doing something naughty."

"You going home now?"

"Of course," she said. "I'd better be getting back."

"Drive carefully."

"Right. I need to take care. I'm still sort of shuddering down there."

I stepped into the shower and used soap to clean my penis. I changed into pajamas, threw on a cardigan, and with a glass of cheap white wine in hand went out onto the terrace and gazed off in the direction of Menshiki's house. The lights were still on in his massive, pure-white mansion across the valley. The lights seemed to be on all over the house. What he was doing over there (most likely) all by himself, I had no idea. Seated at the computer, perhaps, engaged once more in quantifying intuition.

"A relatively good day," I said to myself.

And an odd day at that. What kind of day tomorrow would bring I had no clue. Suddenly I remembered the horned owl up in the attic. Was today a good day for it, too? Then I recalled that for horned owls, the day was now only beginning. During the day they slept in dark places. And come night, they set out to the woods in search of prey. That was a question a horned owl should be asked early in the morning. The question of "Was today a good day?"

I went to bed, read a book for a while, then turned off the light at ten thirty and went to sleep. Since I slept, without waking even once, until just before six the next morning, I imagine that the bell didn't ring during the middle of the night.

17

HOW COULD I MISS SOMETHING THAT IMPORTANT?

never could forget the last words my wife said when I left our home: "Even if we break up like this, can we still be friends? If possible, I mean." At the time (and for a long time after), I couldn't understand what she was trying to say, what she was hoping for. I was confused, as if I'd put some totally tasteless food into my mouth. The best I could say was, "Well, who knows." And those were the last words I said to her face-to-face. Pretty pathetic, as final words go.

Even after we broke up, it felt like my wife and I were still connected by a single living tube. An invisible tube, but one that was still beating slightly, sending something like hot blood traveling back and forth between our two souls. I still had that sort of organic sensation. But before long, that tube would be severed. And if it was bound to be cut sometime, I needed to drain the life from that faint line connecting us. If the life was drained from it, and it shriveled up like a mummy, the pain of it being severed by a sharp knife would be that much more bearable. To do so, I needed to forget about Yuzu, as soon as I could, as much as I could. That's why I never tried to contact her. After I came back from my trip and went to pick up some belongings back at the apartment, I did call her once. I needed to get all my painting materials I'd left behind. That was the only conversation I had with Yuzu after we broke up, and it didn't last long.

We officially dissolved our marriage, and I couldn't contemplate the thought of us remaining friends. We'd shared so many things during our six years of marriage. A lot of time, emotions, words and silence, lots of confusion and lots of decisions, lots of promises and lots of resignation, lots of pleasure, lots of boredom. Naturally each of us must have had inner secrets, but we even managed to find a way to share the sense of having something hidden from the other. With us there was a gravitas of place that only the passage of time can nurture. We did a good job of accommodating our bodies to that sort of gravity, maintaining a delicate balance. We had our own special local rules that we lived by. And there was no way we could get rid of all that history, jettison the gravitational balance and local rules, and live simply as **good friends**.

I understood that very well. That's the conclusion I came to after thinking about it during that lengthy trip. I invariably came to the same conclusion: it was best to keep Yuzu at a distance and break off contact. That made the most sense. And that's what I did.

And for her part Yuzu didn't contact me either. Not a single phone call, not one letter. Even though she was the one who said she wanted to **remain friends**. That hurt far more than I'd expected. Or more precisely, what hurt me was actually **me**, myself. In the midst of that continuing, unsettled silence my feelings, like a heavy pendulum, a razor-sharp blade, made wide swings between one extreme to the other. That arc of emotions left fresh wounds in my skin. And I had only one way of forgetting the pain. And that was, of course, by painting.

Sunlight filtered in silently through the studio window. From time to time a gentle breeze rustled the white curtains. The room had an autumn-morning scent. After coming to live on the mountain I'd grown sensitive to the changes in smells from one season to another. Back when I lived in the city I'd hardly ever noticed those.

I sat on the stool, and gazed for a long time at the portrait of Menshiki I'd begun. This was the way I always began work, reevaluating with new eyes the work I'd done the previous day. Only then could I pick up my brush.

Not bad, I thought. Not bad at all. The colors I'd created completely enveloped the original framework of Menshiki I'd done. The outline of him in black paint was hidden now behind those colors. Though concealed, I could still make it out. I would have to once more bring that outline into relief. Transform a hint into a statement.

There was no guarantee, of course, that the painting would ever be complete. It was still inchoate, something missing. Something that should be there was appealing to the nonvalidity of absence. And that missing element was rapping on the glass window separating presence and absence. I could make out its wordless cry.

Focusing so hard on the painting had made me thirsty, so I went into the kitchen and drank a large glass of orange juice. I relaxed my shoulders, stretched both arms high above my head, took a deep breath, and exhaled. I went back to the studio and sat down on the stool and studied the painting. Refreshed, I focused again. But something was different from before. The angle I was looking at the painting from was clearly not the same as it had been a few minutes before.

I got down from the stool and checked its location. It was in a slightly different spot from when I'd left the studio earlier. The stool had clearly been moved. But how? When I'd gotten down from the stool, I hadn't moved it. That I was sure of. I'd gotten down gingerly in order not to move the stool, and when I'd come back I'd also been careful not to move it when I sat down. I remembered these details because I'm very sensitive about the position and angle I view paintings from. I have a set position and angle that I always use, and like batters who are very particular about their stance in the batter's box, it bothers me to no end if things are off, even by a fraction.

But now the stool was eighteen inches away from where it had been, the angle that much changed. All I could think was that while I'd been in the kitchen drinking orange juice and taking deep breaths, someone had moved the stool. Someone had gone into the studio, sat on the stool to look at the painting, then got down from the stool before I came back, and silently slipped out of the room. And that's when—whether intentionally or it just worked out that way—they moved the stool. But I'd been out of the studio at most five or six minutes. Who in the world would go out of their way to do something like that—and why? Or had the stool moved on its own?

My memory must be messed up. I'd moved the stool but forgotten that I had. That's all I could think. Maybe I was spending too much time alone. The order of events in my memory was getting muddled.

I left the stool in the spot where I'd found it—in other words, a spot twenty inches away from where it had been, and at a different angle. I sat down on it and studied Menshiki's portrait from that position. What I saw was a slightly different painting. It was the same painting, of course, but it looked ever so different. The way the light struck it was not the same as before, and the texture of the paint, too, looked changed. There was something decidedly animated and alive in the painting. But also something still lacking. The direction of that lack, though, wasn't the same as before.

So what was different about it? I brought my focus to bear on the painting. The difference must be speaking to me, trying to tell me something. I had to discover what was being hinted at by the difference. I took a piece of white chalk and marked the position of the three legs of the stool on the floor (location A). Then I moved the stool back twenty inches to the side to its original position (location B), and marked that, too, with chalk. I moved back and forth between the two positions, studying the one painting from the different angles.

Menshiki was still in both paintings, but I noticed that his appearance was strangely different depending on the two angles. It was as if two different personalities coexisted within him. Yet both versions of Menshiki were missing something. That shared lack unified both the A and B versions of Menshiki. I had to discover what it was, as if it were triangulated between position A, position B, and myself. What could that shared absence be? Was it something that had form, or something formless? If the latter, then how was I to give it form?

Not an easy thing to do, now is it, someone said.

I clearly heard that voice. Not a loud voice, but one that carried. Nothing vague about it. Not high, not low. And it sounded like it was right next to my ear.

I involuntarily gulped and, still seated on the stool, slowly gazed around me. I couldn't see anyone else there, of course. The clear morning light filled the floor like pools of water. The window was open, and from far off I could faintly hear the melody played by a garbage truck. It was playing "Annie Laurie" (why the garbage trucks in Odawara played a Scottish folk song was a mystery to me). Beyond that, I couldn't hear a thing.

Maybe I was just imagining things. Maybe it was

my own voice I was hearing, a voice welling up from my unconscious. But what I'd heard sounded odd. **Not an easy thing to do, now, is it?** Even unconsciously, I wouldn't talk to myself like that.

I took a deep breath and from my perch on the stool again looked at the painting, focusing my attention on the work. It must have just been my imagination.

Is it not obvious? someone now said. The voice was right beside my ear.

Obvious? I asked myself. What's so obvious?

What you must discover, can you not see, is what it is about Mr. Menshiki that is not present here, someone said. As before, a clear voice. A voice with no echo, like it was recorded in an anechoic chamber. Each sound clear as crystal. And like an embodied concept, it had no natural inflection.

I looked around again. This time I got down from the stool and went to check in the living room. I checked every room, but nobody else was in the house. The only other creature there was the horned owl in the attic. The horned owl, of course, couldn't talk. And the front door was locked.

First the stool moving on its own, and now this weird voice. A voice from heaven? Or my own voice? Or the voice of some anonymous third party? Something was clearly wrong with my mind. Ever since I had started hearing that bell, I'd begun having doubts about whether my brain was functioning normally. With the bell, at least, Menshiki had been there and had heard the same sound, which proved that it wasn't an auditory hallucination. My hearing was working fine. Okay, so what could this mysterious voice be?

I sat back down on the stool and looked at the painting.

What you must discover, can you see, is what Mr. Menshiki has that is not here. Sounded like a riddle. Like a wise bird deep in the forest showing lost children the way home. **What Menshiki has that is not here**—what could that be?

It took a long time. The clock silently, regularly, ticked away the minutes, the pool of light from the small east-facing window silently shifted. Colorful, agile little birds flew onto the branches of a willow, gracefully searched for something, then flew away with a twitter. White clouds, like round slates, floated over the sky in a row. A single silver plane flew toward the sparkling sea. A four-engine propeller SDF plane, on antisubmarine patrol. Keeping their ears and eyes sharp and watchful, making the latent manifest, was their daily job. I listened as the engine drew closer and then flew away.

And finally, a single fact struck me. Literally as plain as day. Why had I forgotten this? What Menshiki had that my portrait of him did not—it was all clear to me now. **His white hair.** That beautiful white hair, as pure white as newly fallen snow. Menshiki without that white hair was unimaginable. How could I miss something that important?

I leaped up from the stool, went to my paint box and gathered up the white paint, picked a brush, and, without thinking, thickly, vigorously spread it on the canvas. I used a knife too, even my fingertip at one point. For fifteen minutes I painted, then stood back from the canvas, sat down on the stool, and checked out my work.

And there, before me, was Menshiki the person. Without a doubt, he was in the painting now. His personality—no matter what that was made up of—was integrated, manifested in the painting. I had no handle on the person named Wataru Menshiki, and knew barely a thing about him. But as an artist I had captured him on canvas, as a synthesized image, as a single, indivisible package. Alive and breathing within the painting. Even the riddles about him were present.

Still, no matter how you looked at it, this was no **portrait**. I'd succeeded (at least I felt I had) in artistically bringing the presence of Wataru Menshiki into relief on canvas. But the goal wasn't to depict his outer appearance. That wasn't the goal at all. That was the big difference between this work and a portrait. What I'd created was, at heart, a painting I'd done **for my own sake**.

I couldn't predict if Menshiki would accept this painting as his **portrait**. It might be light-years away from the kind of painting he'd been expecting. He'd told me to paint it any way I liked, and didn't have any special requests about the style it was done in. But just **possibly**, there might be some element in the painting, something negative, that he himself didn't want to recognize. Not that I could do anything about that now. Whether he liked the painting or not, it was already out of my hands, beyond my will.

Seated on the stool, I kept staring at the portrait for nearly another half hour. I had painted it, that much I knew, but the end product outstripped the bounds of any logic or understanding I possessed. How had I painted something like that? I couldn't even recall now. I stared dumbfounded at the painting, my feelings swinging from intimacy to total alienation. But one thing was sure—the colors and form were perfect.

Maybe I was on the verge of finding an exit, I thought. Finally able to pass through the thick wall that stood in my way. But still, things had only begun. I had only just managed to grasp a kind of clue as to how to proceed. I would have to be extremely careful. Telling myself this, I went over to the sink and methodically cleaned the paint from the brushes and painting knife. I washed my hands with oil and soap. Then I went to the kitchen and drank several glasses of water. I was parched.

All well and good, but who had moved the stool in the studio? (It had most definitely been moved.) And who had spoken in my ear in that strange voice? (I had clearly heard the voice.) And who had suggested to me what was missing from the painting? (A suggestion that had clearly been effective.)

In all likelihood it was me—I'd done this myself. I'd unconsciously moved the stool, and given myself the suggestion about how to proceed. In a strange, roundabout way I must have freely intertwined my conscious and subconscious . . . I couldn't think of any other explanation. Though of course this couldn't be the case.

At eleven, I was seated on a straight-backed chair, sipping hot tea and randomly mulling over things, when Menshiki's silver Jaguar drove up. I'd been so wrapped up in painting that the appointment we'd made the day before had completely slipped my mind. Not to mention the auditory illusion, or the voice I must have imagined.

Menshiki? Why is **he** here?

"I'd really like to take a good look at the stone chamber again if I could," Menshiki had said over the phone. As I listened to the now familiar growl of the V8 engine come to a halt, it all came back to me.

18

CURIOSITY DIDN'T JUST
KILL THE CAT

I went outside to greet Menshiki. It was the first time I'd done so. I didn't have any particular reason, it just turned out that way. I wanted to get outside, stretch my legs, breathe some fresh air.

Those round slate-shaped clouds still floated in the sky. Lots of these clouds formed far off in the sea, then were slowly carried on the southwest wind, one by one, toward the mountains. Did those beautiful, perfect circles form naturally, not from any practical design? It was a mystery. For a meteorologist maybe it was no mystery at all, but it was for me. Living on this mountaintop, I found myself attracted to all sorts of natural wonders.

Menshiki had on a collared dark-red sweater, light and elegant. And well-worn jeans, so light blue they looked ready to fade away. The jeans were straight leg, made of soft material. To me (and I might be overthinking things) he always seemed to intentionally wear colors that made his white hair stand out. This dark-red sweater went very well with his white hair. His hair always was at just the right length. I had no idea how he kept it that way, but it was never any longer or shorter than it was right now.

"I'd like to go and look into the pit right away, if it's okay with you?" Menshiki asked. "See if anything's changed."

"Okay by me," I said. I hadn't been back, either, in the woods since that day. I wanted to see how things were, too.

"Sorry to bother you, but could you bring me the bell?" Menshiki asked.

I went inside, took down the ancient bell from the studio shelf, and returned.

Menshiki took a large flashlight from the trunk of his Jaguar and hung it from a strap around his neck. He set off for the woods, me tagging along. The woods seemed even a deeper color than before. In this season, every day brought changes to the mountains. Some trees were redder, others dyed a deeper yellow, and some stayed forever green. The combination was truly beautiful. Menshiki, though, didn't seem to care.

"I looked into the background of this land a little," he said while he walked. "Who owned it up till now, what it was used for, that sort of thing."

"Did you find out something?"

Menshiki shook his head. "No, next to nothing. I was expecting that it might have been some religious site, but according to what I found that wasn't the case. I couldn't find out any background as to why there would be a small shrine and stone tumulus here. It was apparently just an ordinary piece of mountainous land. Then it was partly cleared and a house was built. Tomohiko Amada purchased the land along with the house in 1955. Prior to that, a politician had used it as a mountain retreat. You probably haven't heard of him, but he held a Cabinet position back before the war. After the war he essentially lived in retirement. I couldn't trace back who owned the place before that."

"It's a little strange that a politician would go to the trouble of having a vacation home in such a remote place."

"A lot of politicians had retreats here back then. Prince Fumimaro Konoe, prime minister just before World War Two, had a summer retreat just a couple of mountains over from here. It's on the way to Hakone and Atami, and must have been a perfect spot for people to gather for secret talks. It's hard to keep it secret when VIPs get together in Tokyo."

We moved the thick boards that lay covering the hole.

"I'm going to go down inside," Menshiki said. "Would you wait for me?"

"I'll be here," I said.

Menshiki climbed down the metal ladder the contractor had left for us. The ladder creaked a bit with each step. I watched him from above. When he got to the bottom he took the flashlight from around his neck, switched it on, and carefully checked his surroundings. He rubbed the stone wall, and pounded his fist against it.

"This wall is solidly made, and pretty intricate," Menshiki said, looking up at me. "I don't think it's just some well that's been filled in halfway. If it was a well, it would just be a lot of stones piled up on top of each other. They wouldn't have done such a meticulous job."

"You think it was built for some other purpose?"

Menshiki shook his head, indicating that he had no idea. "Anyway, the wall is made so you can't easily climb out. There aren't any spaces to get a foothold. The hole's less than nine feet deep, but scrambling to the top wouldn't be an easy feat."

"You mean it was built that way, to be hard to climb up?"

Menshiki shook his head again. He didn't know. No clue.

"I'd like you to do something for me," Menshiki said.

"What would that be?"

"Would it be an imposition for you to pull up the ladder, and put the cover on tight so no light gets in?"

That left me speechless.

"It's okay. Don't worry," Menshiki said. "I'd like to experience what it's like to be shut up here, in the bottom of the dark pit, by myself. No plans to turn into a mummy yet, though."

"How long do you plan to be down there?"

"When I want to get out, I'll ring the bell. When you hear the bell, take off the cover and lower down the ladder. If an hour passes without you hearing the bell, come and remove the cover. I don't plan to be down here over an hour. Please don't forget that I'm down here. If you did forget, I really **would** turn into a mummy."

"The mummy hunter becomes a mummy."

Menshiki laughed. "Exactly."

"There's no way I'll forget. But are you sure it's okay, doing that?"

"I'm curious. I'd like to try sitting for a while at the bottom of a dark pit. I'll give you the flashlight. And you can hand me the bell."

He climbed halfway up the ladder and held out the flashlight for me. I took it, and held out the bell. He took the bell and gave it a little shake. It rang out clearly.

"But if—just supposing—I were attacked by vicious hornets on the way and fell unconscious, or even died, then you might never be able to get out of here. You never know what's going to happen in this world."

"Curiosity always involves risk. You can't satisfy your curiosity without accepting some risk. Curiosity didn't just kill the cat."

"I'll be back in an hour," I said.

"Watch out for the hornets," Menshiki said.

"And you take care down there in the dark."

Menshiki didn't reply, and just looked up at me, as if trying to decipher some meaning in my expression as I gazed down at him. There was some kind of vagueness in his eyes, like he was straining to focus on my face, but couldn't. It was an uncertain expression, not at all like him. Then, as if reconsidering things, he sat down on the ground and leaned against the curved stone wall. He looked up and raised his hand a little. **All set**, he was telling me. I yanked up the ladder, pulled the thick boards over so they completely covered up the hole, and set some heavy stones on top of that. A small amount of light might filter in through narrow cracks between the boards, though inside the hole should be dark enough. I thought about calling out to Menshiki from on top of the cover, but thought better of it. What he wanted was solitude and silence.

I went back home, boiled water, and made tea. I sat on the sofa and picked up where I'd left off in a book. I couldn't focus on reading, though, since my ears were alert for the sound of the bell. Every five minutes I checked my watch, and imagined Menshiki, alone in the bottom of that dark hole. What an odd person, I thought. He uses his own money to hire a landscape contractor, who uses heavy equipment to move that pile of stones and open up the entrance to that hole. And now Menshiki was confined there, all by himself. Or rather, deliberately **shut away in there** at his own request.

Whatever, I thought. Whatever necessity or intentions motivated it (assuming there was some kind of necessity or intention), that was Menshiki's problem, and I could leave it all up to him. I was an unthinking actor in someone else's plan. I gave up reading the book, lay down on the sofa, closed my eyes, but of course didn't fall asleep. This was no time to be sleeping.

An hour passed without the bell ringing. Or maybe I'd somehow missed the sound. Either way, it was time to get that cover off. I got up off the sofa, slipped on my shoes, and went outside and into the woods. I was a bit apprehensive that hornets or a wild boar might appear, but neither did. Just some tiny birds, Japanese white-eyes, flitted right past me. I walked through the woods and went around behind the shrine. I removed the heavy stones and took off just one of the boards.

"Mr. Menshiki!" I called out into the gap. But there was no response. What I could see of the hole from the gap was pitch dark, and I couldn't make out his figure there.

"Mr. Menshiki!" I called again. But again no answer. I was getting worried. Maybe he'd vanished, like the mummy that should have been there had vanished. I knew it wasn't logically possible, but still I was seriously concerned.

I quickly removed another board, and then another. Finally the sunlight reached to the bottom of the pit. And I could see Menshiki's outline seated there.

"Mr. Menshiki, are you okay?" I asked, relieved.

He looked up, as if finally coming to, and gave a small nod. He covered his face with his hands, as if the light was too bright.

"I'm fine," he answered quietly. "I'd just like to stay here for a little longer. It'll take time for my eyes to adjust to the light."

"It's been exactly an hour. If you'd like to stay there longer I could put the cover on again."

Menshiki shook his head. "No, this is enough. I'm

okay now. I can't stay any longer here. It might be too dangerous."

"Too dangerous?"

"I'll explain later," Menshiki said. He stroked his face hard with both hands, as if rubbing something away from his skin.

Five minutes later he slowly got to his feet and clambered up the metal ladder I'd let down. Once again at ground level he brushed the dirt off his pants and looked up at the sky with narrowed eyes. The blue autumn sky was visible through the tree branches. For a long time he gazed lovingly at the sky. We lined up the boards and covered the hole as before, so no one would accidentally fall into it. Then we put the heavy stones on top. I memorized the position of the stones, so I'd know if anyone moved them. The ladder we left inside the pit.

"I didn't hear the bell," I said as we walked along.

Menshiki shook his head. "I didn't shake it."

That's all he said, so I didn't ask anything more.

We walked out of the woods and headed home. Menshiki took the lead as we walked and I followed behind. Without a word he put the flashlight back in the trunk of the Jaguar. We then sat down in the living room and drank hot coffee. Menshiki still hadn't said a thing. He seemed preoccupied. Not that he wore a serious expression or anything, but his mind was clearly in a place far away. A place, no doubt, where only he was allowed to be. I didn't bother him, and let him be. Just like Doctor Watson used to do with Sherlock Holmes.

During this time I mentally went over my schedule. That evening I had to drive down the mountain to teach my classes at the local arts-and-culture center near Odawara Station. I'd look over paintings students had done and give them advice. This was the day when I had back-to-back children's and adults' classes. This was just about the only opportunity I had to see and speak with living people. Without those classes I'd probably live like a hermit up here in the mountains, and if I went on living all alone, I'd likely start to lose my mind, just as Masahiko said.

Which is why I should have been thankful for the chance to come in contact with the real world. But truth be told, I found it hard to feel that way. The people I met in the classroom were less living beings than mere shadows crossing my path. I smiled at each one of them, called them by name, and critiqued their paintings. No, critique isn't the right term. I just praised them. I'd find some good component to each painting—if there wasn't, I'd make up something—and praise them for a job well done.

So I had a pretty good reputation as a teacher. According to the owner of the school, many of the students liked me. I hadn't expected that. I'd never once thought I was suited to teaching. But I didn't really care. It was all the same to me whether people liked me or didn't. I just wanted things to go smoothly in the classroom, without any hitches, so I could repay Masahiko for his kindness.

I'm not saying every person felt like a shadow to me. I'd started seeing two of my students. And after starting a sexual relationship with me, the two women both dropped out of my art class. They must have found it awkward. And I did feel some responsibility for that.

Tomorrow afternoon, I'd see the second girl-friend, the older married woman. We'd hold each other in bed and make love. So she was not just a passing shadow, but an actual presence with a three-dimensional body. Or perhaps a passing shadow with a three-dimensional body. I couldn't decide which.

Menshiki called my name, and I came back to the present with a start. I'd been completely lost in thought, too.

"About the portrait," Menshiki said.

I looked at him. His usual cool expression was back on his face. A handsome face, always calm and thoughtful, the kind that relaxed others.

"If you need me to pose for you, I wouldn't mind doing it now," he said. "Continue from where we left off, maybe? I'm always ready."

I looked at him for a while. **Pose?** It finally dawned on me—he was talking about the portrait. I looked down, took a sip of the coffee, which had cooled down, and after gathering my thoughts, put the cup back on the saucer. A small, dry clatter reached my ears. I looked up, faced Menshiki, and spoke.

"I'm very sorry, but today I have to go teach at the arts-and-culture center."

"Oh, that's right," Menshiki said. He glanced at his watch. "I'd totally forgotten. You teach art at the school near Odawara Station, don't you. Do you need to leave soon?"

"I'm okay, I still have time," I said. "And there's something I need to talk with you about."

"And what would that be?"

"Truthfully, the painting is already finished. In a sense."

Menshiki frowned ever so slightly. He looked straight at me, as if checking out something deep inside my eyes.

"By painting, you mean my portrait?"

"Yes," I said.

"That's wonderful," Menshiki said. A slight smile came to his face. "Really wonderful. But what did you mean by 'in a sense'?"

"It's hard to explain. I've never been good at explaining things."

"Take your time and tell it to me the way you'd like to," Menshiki said. "I'll sit here and listen."

I brought the fingers of both of my hands together on my lap.

Silence descended as I chose my words, the kind of silence that makes you hear the passing of time. Time passed very slowly on top of the mountain.

"I got the commission from you," I said, "and did

the painting with you as model. But to tell the truth, it's not a **portrait**, no matter how you look at it. All I can say is it's a **work done with you as model**. I can't say how much value it has, as an artwork, or as a commodity. All I know for sure is it's **a work I had to paint**. Beyond that I'm clueless. Truthfully, I'm pretty confused. Until things become clearer to me it might be best to keep the painting here and not give it to you. I'd like to return the advance you paid. And I am extremely sorry for having used so much of your valuable time."

"In what way is it—not a portrait?" Menshiki asked, choosing his words deliberately.

"Up till now I've made my living as a professional portrait painter. Essentially in portraits you paint the subject the way he wishes to be portrayed. The subject is the client, and if he doesn't like the finished work it's entirely possible he might tell you, 'I'm not going to pay money for this.' So I try not to depict any negative aspects of the person. I pick only the good aspects, emphasize those, and try to make the subject appear in as good a light as I can. In that sense, in most cases it's hard to call portraits works of art. Someone like Rembrandt being the exception, of course. But in this case, I didn't think about you as I painted, but only about myself. To put it another way, I prioritized the ego of the artist—myself—over you, the subject."

"Not a problem," Menshiki said, smiling. "I'm actually happy to hear it. I told you I didn't have any requests, and wanted you to paint it any way you liked."

"I know. I remember it well. What I'm concerned about is less how the painting turned out and more about **what I painted there**. I put my own desires first, so much that I might have painted something I shouldn't have. That's what I'm worried about."

Menshiki observed my face for a time, and then spoke. "You might have painted something inside me that you shouldn't have. And you're worried about that. Do I have that right?"

"That's it," I said. "Since all I thought of was myself, I loosened the restraints that should have been in place."

And maybe extracted something from inside you that I shouldn't have, I was about to say, but thought better of it. I kept those words inside.

Menshiki mulled over what I'd said.

"Interesting," he finally said, sounding like he meant it. "A very intriguing way of looking at things."

I was silent.

"I think my self-restraint is pretty strong," Menshiki said. "I have a lot of self-control, I mean."

"I know," I said.

Menshiki lightly pressed his temple with his fingers, and smiled. "So that painting is finished, you're saying? That **portrait** of me?"

I nodded. "I feel it's finished."

"That's wonderful," Menshiki said. "Can you show me the painting? After I've actually seen it, the two of us can discuss how to proceed. Does that sound all right?"

"Of course," I said.

I led Menshiki to the studio. He stood about six feet in front of the easel, arms folded, and stared at the painting. There was the portrait that he'd posed for. No, less a portrait than what you might call an **image** that formed when a mass of paint hit the canvas. The white hair was a violent burst of pure white. At first glance it didn't look like a face. What should be found in a face was hidden behind a mass of color. Yet beyond any doubt, the reality of Menshiki the person was present. Or at least I thought so.

He stood there, unmoving, gazing at the painting for the longest time. Literally not moving a muscle. I couldn't even tell if he was breathing or not. I stood a little ways away by the window, observing him. I wondered how much time passed. It seemed almost forever. As he observed the painting, his face was totally devoid of expression. His eyes were glazed, flat, clouded, like a still puddle reflecting a cloudy sky. The eyes of someone who wanted to keep others at a distance. I couldn't guess what he might be thinking, deep in his heart.

Then, like when a magician claps his hands to bring a person out of a hypnotic spell, he stood up straight and trembled slightly. His expression returned, as did the light in his eyes. He slowly walked over to me, held out his right hand, and rested it on my shoulder.

"Amazing," he said. "Truly outstanding. I don't know what to say. This is exactly the painting I was hoping for."

I could tell from his eyes that he was saying how he honestly felt. He was truly impressed, and moved, by my painting.

"The painting expresses me perfectly," Menshiki said. "This is a portrait in the real sense of the word. You didn't make any mistake. You did exactly what you should have."

His hand was still resting on my shoulder. It was just resting there, yet I could feel a special power radiating from it.

"But what did you do to discover this painting?" Menshiki asked me.

"Discover?"

"It was you who did this painting, of course. You created it through your own power. But you also discovered it. You found this image buried within you and drew it out. You **unearthed** it, in a way. Don't you think so?"

I suppose so, I thought. Of course I moved my hands, and followed my will in painting it. I was the one who chose the paints, the one who used brushes, knives, and fingers to paint the colors onto the canvas. But looked at from a different angle, maybe all I'd done was use Menshiki as a catalyst to locate something buried inside me and dig it up. Just like the heavy equipment that moved aside the rock mound behind the little shrine, lifted off the heavy lattice cover, and unearthed that odd stone-lined chamber. I couldn't help but see an affinity between these two similar operations that took place in tandem. Everything that had happened had started with Menshiki's appearance, and the ringing of the bell in the middle of the night.

Menshiki said, "It's like an earthquake deep under the sea. In an unseen world, a place where light doesn't reach, in the realm of the unconscious. In other words, a major transformation is taking place. It reaches the surface, where it sets off a series of reactions and eventually takes form where we can see it with our own eyes. I'm no artist, but I can grasp the basic idea behind that process. Outstanding ideas in the business world, too, emerge through a similar series of stages. The best ideas are thoughts that appear, unbidden, from out of the dark."

Menshiki once more stood before the painting and stepped closer to examine the surface. Like someone reading a detailed map, he studiously checked out each and every detail. He stepped back nine feet, and with narrowed eyes gazed at the work as a whole. His face wore an expression close to ecstasy. He reminded me of a carnivorous raptor about to latch onto its prey. But what was the prey? Was it my painting, or me myself? Or something else? I had no idea. But soon, like mist hovering over the surface of a river at dawn, that strange expression like ecstasy faded, then vanished. To be filled in by his usual affable, thoughtful expression.

He said, "Generally I avoid saying anything that smacks of self-praise, but honestly I feel kind of proud to know that I didn't misjudge things. I have no ar-

tistic talent myself, and have nothing to do with creating original works, but I do know outstanding art
when I see it. At least I flatter myself that I do."

Somehow I couldn't easily accept what Menshiki
was telling me, or feel happy to hear it. It may have
been those sharp, raptor-like eyes that bothered me.

"So you like the painting?" I asked again to make
sure.

"That goes without saying. This is truly a valuable
painting. I'm overjoyed that you came up with such
a powerful work using me as the model, as the motif.
And of course it goes without saying that as the one
who commissioned the painting, I'll take it. Assuming that's all right with you?"

"Yes. It's just that I—"

Menshiki held up a hand to cut me off. "So, if you
don't mind, I'd like to invite you to my house to celebrate its completion. Would that be all right? It will
be, like the old expression, a cozy little get-together.
As long as this isn't any trouble for you, that is."

"None at all, but you really don't need to do this.
You've done so much already—"

"But I'd really like to. I'd like the two of us to celebrate the completion of the painting. So won't you
join me for dinner at my place? Nothing fancy, just
a simple little dinner, just the two of us. Apart from
the cook and bartender, of course."

"Cook and bartender?"

"There's a French restaurant I like near Hayakawa
harbor. I'll have the cook and bartender over on their
regular day off. He's a great chef. He uses the freshest

fish and comes up with some very original recipes. Actually, for quite some time I've been wanting to invite you over, and have been making preparations. But with the painting done, the timing couldn't be better."

It was hard to keep the surprise from showing on my face. I had no idea how much it would cost to arrange something like that, but for Menshiki, it must be a regular occurrence. Or at least something he was accustomed to arranging . . .

Menshiki said, "How would four days from now be? Tuesday evening. If that's good for you, I'll set it up."

"I don't have any particular plans then," I said.

"Tuesday it is, then," he said. "Also, could I take the painting home with me now? I'd like to have it nicely framed and hanging on the wall by the time you come over, if that's possible."

"Mr. Menshiki, do you really see your face within this painting?" I asked again.

"Of course I do," Menshiki said, giving me a wondering look. "Of course I can see my face in the painting. Very distinctly. What else is depicted here?"

"I see," I said. What else could I say? "You're the one who commissioned the work, so if you like the painting, it's already yours. Please do what you'd like with it. The thing is, the paint isn't dry yet, so be extremely careful when you carry it. And I think it's better to wait a little longer before framing it. Best to let it dry for about two weeks before doing that."

"I understand. I'll handle it carefully. And I'll wait to have it framed."

293

At the front door he held out his hand and we shook hands for the first time in a while. A satisfied smile rose to his face.

"I'll see you Tuesday, then. I'll send a car over around six."

"By the way, you aren't inviting the mummy?" I asked Menshiki. I don't know why I said that. The mummy just suddenly popped into my head, and I couldn't help myself.

Menshiki looked at me searchingly. "Mummy? What do you mean?"

"The mummy that should have been in that chamber. The one that must have been ringing the bell every night, and disappeared, leaving the bell behind. The monk who practiced austerity to the point of being mummified. I was thinking maybe he wanted to be invited to your place. Like the statue of the Commendatore in **Don Giovanni**."

Menshiki thought about this, and a cheerful smile came over him as if he finally got it. "I see! Just like Don Giovanni invited the statue of the Commendatore, you're wondering how would it be if I invited the mummy to our dinner?"

"Exactly. It might be karma, too."

"Sounds good. Fine with me. It's a celebration, after all. If the mummy would care to join us, I will be happy to issue the invitation. Sounds like we'll have a pleasant evening. But what should we have for dessert?" He smiled happily. "The problem is, we can't see him. Makes it hard to invite him."

"Indeed," I said. "But the visible is not the only reality. Wouldn't you agree?"

Menshiki gingerly carried the painting outside. He took an old blanket from the trunk, laid it on the passenger seat, and placed the painting down on top so as not to smear the paint. Then he used some thin rope and two cardboard boxes to secure the painting so it wouldn't move around. It was all cleverly done. He always seemed to carry around a variety of tools and things in his trunk.

"Yes, what you said may be exactly right," Menshiki suddenly murmured as he was leaving. He rested both hands on the leather-covered steering wheel and looked straight up at me.

"What I said?"

"That sometimes in life we can't grasp the boundary between reality and unreality. That boundary always seems to be shifting. As if the border between countries shifts from one day to the next depending on their mood. We need to pay close attention to that movement, otherwise we won't know which side we're on. That's what I meant when I said it might be dangerous for me to remain inside that pit any longer."

I didn't know how to respond, and Menshiki didn't go any further. He waved to me out the window, revving the V8 engine so it rumbled pleasantly, and he and the still-not-dry portrait vanished from sight.

19

CAN YOU SEE ANYTHING BEHIND ME?

A t one p.m. on Saturday afternoon my girlfriend drove over in her red Mini. I went out to greet her when she arrived. She had on green sunglasses and a light-gray jacket over a simple beige dress.

"You want to do it in the car? Or do you prefer the bed?" I asked.

"Don't be silly," she laughed.

"Doing it in the car doesn't sound so bad. Figuring out how to manage it in a cramped space."

"Someday soon."

We sat in the living room and drank tea. I told her about how I'd just managed to finish the portrait (or portrait-like painting) of Menshiki I'd been struggling with. And how it was totally different from any of the portraits I'd done professionally. Her interest seemed piqued.

"Can I see the painting?"

I shook my head. "You're a day late. I wanted to get your opinion on it, but Mr. Menshiki already took it home. The paint wasn't completely dry yet, but it seemed like he wanted to take possession as soon as he could. He seemed worried somebody else might take it away."

"So he liked it."

"He said he did, and I don't have any reason to doubt him."

"The painting's successfully completed, and the person who commissioned it likes it. So all's well that ends well?"

"I guess," I said. "And I'm happy with it. I've never done that type of painting before, and I think it's opened up some new possibilities."

"A new style of portrait?"

"I'm not sure. This time, I arrived at that method by using Mr. Menshiki as my model. But maybe it's just coincidence that it was the framework of a portrait that proved to be the entranceway to that. I don't know if the same method would be valid if I tried it again. This might have been a special case. Having Mr. Menshiki as my model may have exerted a special power. But the important thing is I'm dying to do some serious painting now."

"Well, congratulations on finishing the painting."

"Thanks," I said. "I'll also be receiving a fairly hefty payment."

"The munificent Mr. Menshiki," she said.

"And he invited me over to his place to celebrate the painting. Tuesday evening, we'll have dinner together."

I told her about the dinner that was planned. Nothing about inviting the mummy, though. A dinner for two, with a professional cook and bartender.

"So you'll finally set foot in that chalk-white mansion, won't you," she said, sounding impressed. "The

297

mysterious mansion of the man of mystery. I'm so curious. Make sure to keep your eyes open, and observe what kind of place it is."

"As much as my eyes can take in."

"And remember exactly what sort of food was served."

"Will do," I said. "You know, the other day you mentioned getting new information about Mr. Menshiki."

"That's right. Through the jungle grapevine."

"What kind of information?"

She looked a little confused. She picked up her cup and took a sip of tea. "Let's talk about that later," she said. "There's something I'd like to do before that."

"Something you'd like to do?"

"Something I hesitate to put into words."

We moved from the living room into the bedroom. Like always.

During the six years I lived my first married life with Yuzu (my former marriage, is what it might best be called), I never had a sexual relationship with any other women, not even once. Not that the opportunity didn't present itself, but during that period I was much more interested in living a peaceful life with my wife than seeking greener pastures elsewhere. And as far as sex was concerned, regular lovemaking with Yuzu more than satisfied me.

But then at a certain point, out of the blue (to me at least) she announced that she couldn't live with me any longer. An unshakable conclusion, no room for negotiation or compromise. I was shaken, with no clue how to respond. Left speechless. But I did understand one thing: **I can't stay here anymore.**

So I threw some belongings into my old Peugeot 205 and set off on an aimless journey. For a month and a half at the beginning of spring I wandered through northern Japan—Tohoku and Hokkaido— where it was still cold. Until my car finally broke down for good. Every night on the trip I remembered Yuzu's body. Every single detail. How she'd react when I touched certain spots, what sort of cry she made. I didn't want to remember this, but I couldn't help it. Occasionally, as I traced those memories, I'd ejaculate. Another thing I didn't particularly want to do.

But during that long trip I only slept with one actual woman. A truly weird turn of events ended with me spending the night with a young woman I'd never seen before. Not that it was something I was looking for.

This was in a small town in Miyagi Prefecture along the coast. As I recall, it was near the border with Iwate, but I was on the move then and had passed through a number of towns that all blurred into one. My mind wasn't in a place where I could remember their names. I do recall that it had a big fishing harbor. Though most of the towns in that region had harbors. And I remember how everywhere I went the smell of diesel oil and fish tagged along.

On the outskirts of town, near the highway, was a chain restaurant, and I was eating dinner there by myself. It was about eight p.m. Shrimp curry and house salad. There were only a handful of other customers. I was in a table next to the window, reading a paperback book while I ate, when a young woman abruptly sat down across from me. No hesitation, no asking permission, without a word she sat down onto the vinyl-covered seat like it was the most natural thing in the world.

I looked up, surprised. Of course I didn't recognize her. It was the first time I'd ever laid eyes on her. It was all so sudden I didn't know what to think. There were any number of unoccupied tables, and no reason for her to share mine. Maybe that's how they did things in this town? I put down my fork, wiped my mouth with the paper napkin, and gazed at her, bewildered.

"Pretend like you know me," the girl said. "Like we were meeting up here." Her voice was, if anything, a bit husky. Or maybe tension made a voice temporarily hoarse. I detected a slight Tohoku accent.

I put the bookmark in my book and shut it. The woman seemed to be in her mid-twenties. She had on a white blouse with a round collar and a navy-blue cardigan. Neither one very expensive looking, or very fashionable. Ordinary clothes, like what you'd wear when you went shopping at the local supermarket. Her hair was black, cut short, with bangs falling to her forehead. She had on hardly any makeup. On her lap was a black cloth shoulder bag.

There was nothing special about her face. Pleasant enough features, but they didn't leave a strong impression. The kind of face that, if you saw her on the street, you'd forget as soon as you passed by. Her thin lips were taut, and she was breathing through her nose. Her breathing was a bit ragged, the nostrils expanding a tiny bit, then contracting. A small nose, out of balance with the size of her mouth. As if the person molding her out of clay halfway through and decided to scrape some off the nose.

"You understand? Pretend like you know me," she repeated. "Don't look so surprised."

"Okay," I answered, not knowing what was going on.

"Just keep on eating," she said. "And pretend to be talking to me like we know each other?"

"What about?"

"You're from Tokyo?"

I nodded. I picked up my fork and ate a mini tomato. Then drank some water.

"I could tell by the way you talk," the woman said. "But why are you here?"

"Just passing through," I said.

A waitress in a ginger-colored uniform came over, lugging a thick menu. The waitress had mammoth breasts, the buttons on her uniform ready to burst. The girl across from me didn't take the menu. She didn't even glance at the waitress. Staring straight at me she just said, "Coffee and cheesecake." Like she was giving me the order. The waitress nodded without a word. Still lugging the menu, she left.

"Are you in some kind of trouble?" I asked.

She didn't respond. She just stared at me, like she was evaluating my face.

"Can you see anything behind me? Is anybody there?" the woman asked.

I looked behind her. Just ordinary people eating in an ordinary way. No new customers had come in.

"Nothing. Nobody's there," I said.

"Keep an eye out for a little longer," she said. "Tell me if you see anything. Keep on talking like nothing's happened."

Our table looked out on the parking lot. I could see my decrepit, dusty little old Peugeot parked there. There were two other cars. A small silver compact, and a tall black minivan. The minivan looked new. They'd both been parked there for a while. No new cars had driven in. The woman must have walked. Or else someone gave her a ride here.

"Just passing through?" the woman asked.

"That's right."

"Are you on a trip?"

"You could say that," I said.

"What kind of book are you reading?"

I showed her the book. It was Ogai Mori's **Abe Ichizoku,** a samurai tale written over a hundred years before.

"**Abe Ichizoku,**" she intoned. She handed the book back. "How come you're reading such an old book?"

"It was in the lounge of a youth hostel I stayed at in Aomori not long ago. I leafed through it, thought it was interesting, and took it with me. In exchange, I left a couple of books I'd finished reading."

"I've never read **Abe Ichizoku**. Is it interesting?"

I'd read it once and was rereading it. The story was

pretty interesting, but I couldn't figure out why, and from what sort of stance, Ogai had written it, or felt compelled to write that kind of tale. But explaining that would take too long. This wasn't a book club. And this woman was just bringing up random topics so our conversation seemed natural (or at least so that it looked that way to the people around us).

"It's worth reading," I said.

"So what sort of work?" she asked.

"You mean the novel?"

She frowned. "No. I don't care about that. I mean **you**. What kind of work do **you** do for a living?"

"I paint pictures," I said.

"You're an artist," she said.

"You could say that."

"What sort of paintings?"

"Portraits," I said.

"By portraits you mean those paintings you see hanging on the wall in the president's office in companies? The ones where big shots look all full of themselves?"

"That's right."

"That's your specialty?"

I nodded.

She said no more about painting. She might have lost interest. Most people in the world, unless they're the ones being painted, have zero interest in portraits.

Right then the automatic door at the entrance slid open and a tall, middle-aged man came in. He had on a black leather jacket and a black golf cap with a golf company's logo on it. He stood at the entrance, gave the whole diner a once-over, chose a table two over from ours, and sat down, facing us. He took off his cap, finger-combed his hair a couple of times, and carefully studied the menu the busty waitress brought over. His hair was cut short, and had some white mixed in. He was thin, with dark, suntanned skin. His forehead was lined with a series of deep, wavy wrinkles.

"A man just came in," I told her.

"What does he look like?"

I gave her a quick description.

"Can you draw him?" she asked.

"You mean a likeness?"

"Yes. You're an artist, aren't you?"

I took a memo pad from my pocket, and, using a mechanical pencil, quickly sketched the man. Even added some shading. While I drew it I didn't need to glance over at him. I have the ability to grasp the features of a person quickly and etch them into my memory. I passed the drawing across the table to her. She took it, and stared at it, eyes narrowed, for a long time, like a bank teller examining dubious handwriting on a check. Finally she laid the memo page on the table.

"You're really good at drawing," she said, looking at me. She sounded genuinely impressed.

"It's what I do," I said. "So, do you know this man?"

She didn't reply, just shook her head. Her lips tight, her expression unchanged. She folded the drawing up twice, and stuffed it away in her shoulder bag.

I couldn't figure out why she would keep something like that. She should have just crumpled it up and thrown it away.

"I don't know him," she said.

"But you're being followed by him. Is that what's going on?"

She didn't reply.

The same waitress brought over her coffee and cheesecake. The woman kept quiet until the waitress had left. She sliced a bite of the cheesecake with her fork, then pushed it from side to side on the plate. Like a hockey player practicing on the ice before a game. She finally put the piece in her mouth and, expressionless, chewed slowly. Once she finished it she poured a hint of cream into her coffee and took a sip. She nudged the plate with the cheesecake to one side, as if it was no longer needed.

A white SUV had joined the cars in the parking lot. A stocky, tall car, with solid-looking tires. Apparently driven by the man who'd just come in. He'd parked the car facing in, not backing into the spot as was more usual. On the cover of the spare tire attached to the luggage compartment were the words SUBARU FORESTER. I finished my shrimp curry. The waitress came over to take away the plate, and I ordered coffee.

"Have you been traveling for a long time?" the woman asked.

"It'll be a long trip," I said.

"Is it fun to travel?"

I'm not traveling for fun, is how I should have

answered. But that would have made things long and complicated.

"Sort of," I answered.

She stared at me, like studying some rare animal. "You sure are a man of few words."

It depends on who I'm talking with, is how I should have answered. But going there would have also made things long and complicated.

The coffee came, and I drank some. It tasted like coffee, but it wasn't all that good. But at least it was coffee, and piping hot. After this no other customers came in. The salt-and-pepper-haired man in the leather jacket, in a voice that carried, ordered a Salisbury steak and rice.

A string-section version of "Fool on the Hill" came over the sound system. Did John Lennon write that song, or Paul McCartney? I couldn't remember. Probably Lennon. This kind of random thought rattled around in my head. I had no idea what else I should think about.

"Did you come here by car?"

"Um."

"What kind of car?"

"A red Peugeot."

"What district is the license plate?"

"Shinagawa," I said.

Hearing that, she frowned, as if she had a bad memory associated with a red Peugeot with Shinagawa plates. She tugged down the sleeves of her cardigan and checked that the buttons on her white shirt were done all the way up. She wiped her mouth with a paper napkin. "Let's go," she suddenly said.

She drank a half glass of water and stood up. She left her coffee, only one sip taken, and cheesecake, only one bite taken, on the tabletop. Like the remains after a terrible natural disaster.

Not knowing where we were going, I stood up after her, took the bill from the table, and paid at the register. The woman's order was included, but she didn't say a word of thanks, or make a move to pay her share.

As we left, the man with the salt-and-pepper hair was eating his Salisbury steak, seemingly bored by it all. He looked up and glanced in our direction, but that was all. He looked down at his plate again and went on eating, with knife and fork, his face expressionless. The woman didn't look at him at all.

As we passed by the white Subaru Forester, a bumper sticker on it with a picture of a fish caught my eye. Probably a marlin. Of course, I had no idea why he had to have a sticker with a marlin on it on his car. Maybe he worked in the fishing industry, or was a fisherman.

The woman didn't tell me where we were going. She sat in the passenger seat and gave me clipped directions. She seemed to know the roads. She must have been from that town, or else had lived there a long time. I drove the Peugeot where she told me to go.

We drove along the highway for a while out of town and came to a love hotel with a gaudy neon sign. I parked there as directed and cut the engine.

"I'm staying here tonight," she announced. "I can't go home. Come with me."

"But I'm staying in another place tonight," I said. "I've already checked in and put my luggage in the room."

"Where?"

I gave the name of a small business hotel near the railway station.

"This place is a lot better than that cheap place," she said. "Your room there must be shabby and no bigger than a closet."

Right she was. A shabby room the size of a closet was an apt description.

"And they don't like women checking in by themselves here. They're on guard against prostitutes. So come with me."

Well, at least she's not a hooker, I thought.

At the front desk I paid in advance for one night (again, no word of thanks from her) and got the key. Once in the room she filled up the bathtub, switched on the TV, and adjusted the lighting. The bathtub was spacious. It was definitely a lot more comfortable than the business hotel. She seemed to have come here—or someplace like it—many times before. She sat on the bed and took off her cardigan. Then removed her white blouse and her wraparound skirt. And took off her stockings. She had on very simple white panties. They weren't particularly new. The kind your ordinary housewife would wear when she went shopping at the neighborhood supermarket. She neatly reached behind her and unhooked her bra, folded it, and set it next to a pillow. Her breasts weren't particularly big, or particularly small.

"Come over here," she said to me. "Since we're in a place like this, let's have sex."

That was the one and only sexual experience of my whole long trip (or wanderings). Wilder sex than I'd expected. She had four orgasms in total, every single one genuine, if you can believe it. I came twice, but oddly enough didn't feel much pleasure. It was like while I was doing it with her, my mind was elsewhere.

"I'm thinking maybe it's been a long time since you had sex?" she asked me.

"Several months," I answered honestly.

"I can tell," she said. "But how come? You can't be that unpopular with women."

"There's a whole bunch of reasons."

"You poor thing," she said, and gently stroked my neck. "You poor thing."

You poor thing, I thought, repeating the words to myself. Put that way I really did feel like I was a person to be pitied. In an unknown town, in some random place, with no clue what was going on, naked in bed with a woman whose name I didn't even know.

We had a few beers from the fridge, in between rounds. It was about one a.m. when we finally slept.

When I woke up the next morning she was nowhere to be seen. She left no note or anything behind. I was alone in the overly huge bed. My watch showed seven thirty, and it was light outside. I opened the curtain and saw the highway running alongside the ocean. Huge refrigerated trucks transporting fresh fish roared up and down the road. The world is full of lonely things, but not many could be lonelier than waking up alone in the morning in a love hotel.

A thought suddenly struck me, and I hurriedly checked my wallet in my pants pocket. Everything was still there. Cash, credit cards, ATM card, license, everything. I breathed a sigh of relief. If my wallet had been gone I would have freaked. These sorts of things **did** happen, and I needed to be careful.

She must have left early in the morning, while I was sound asleep. But how had she gotten back to town (or back to where she lived)? Had she walked, or called a taxi? Not that it made any difference to me. Pointless speculation.

I returned the room key at the front desk, paid for the beers we'd drunk, and drove the Peugeot back to town. I needed to get the luggage I'd left at the business hotel near the station, and pay for the one night. Along the way into town I passed by the chain restaurant I'd gone to the night before. I stopped and ate breakfast there. I was starving, and was dying for some coffee. Just before I pulled into the parking lot I saw the white Subaru Forester. Parked nose in, with that marlin bumper sticker. The same Subaru Forester from the night before. The only difference was where it was parked. Which made sense. No one spent the whole night in a place like that.

I went inside the restaurant. As before, hardly any customers. Like I expected, the same man from last night was at a table, eating breakfast. The same table as the night before, wearing the same black leather jacket. Like last night, the same black golf cap with the Yonex logo resting on the tabletop. The only difference from last night was the folded morning newspaper on top of the table. A plate of toast and scrambled eggs was in front of him. It was probably just served, steam still rising from the coffee. As I passed him, the man glanced up and looked me in the face. His eyes were even sharper and colder than the night before. There was a sense of criticism in them, or at least that's what it felt like.

I know exactly where you've been and what you've been up to, he seemed to be telling me.

That's the whole story of what happened to me in that small town along the seacoast in Miyagi. Even now I have no idea what that woman, with her petite nose and perfect teeth, wanted from me. And it was never clear to me if that middle-aged guy with the white Subaru Forester was really following her, or if she was running from him. Whatever was going on, I happened to be there, and through an odd series of events spent the night in a garish love hotel with a woman I'd just met, and had a one-night stand, the wildest sex I'd ever had. But I still can't recall the name of the town.

"Could I get a glass of water?" my married girlfriend said. She'd just woken up from a short postcoital nap.

It was early afternoon, and we were in bed. While she slept I stared at the ceiling and recalled the events in that small fishing town. It was only a half a year before, but it seemed like events from the distant past.

I went to the kitchen, poured mineral water into a large glass, and returned to bed. She drank down half of it in a single gulp.

"Now, about Mr. Menshiki," she said, placing the glass on the nightstand.

"Mr. Menshiki?"

"The new information I got about Mr. Menshiki," she said. "What I said I'd tell you later?"

"Your jungle grapevine."

"Right," she said, and drank more water. "According to my sources, your friend Mr. Menshiki spent quite a long time in Tokyo Prison."

I sat up and looked at her. "Tokyo Prison?"

"Yeah, the one in Kosuge."

"For what crime?"

"I don't know the details, but I imagine it had something to do with money. Tax evasion, money laundering, insider trading—something of that sort, or perhaps all of them. He was imprisoned six or seven years ago. Did Mr. Menshiki tell you what kind of work he does?"

"He said it was dealing with tech, and information," I said. "He started a company, and some years ago sold the stock for a high price. He's living now on the capital gains."

"'Dealing with information' is a pretty vague way of describing it. Nowadays there're hardly any jobs not connected with information."

"Who told you about him being in prison?"

"A friend of mine whose husband's in finance. But I don't know how much of that information is true. Someone heard it from someone, and passed it along to someone else. You know how it is. But from what I can make of it, it doesn't seem groundless."

"If he was in Tokyo Prison that means that he was put there by the Tokyo district prosecutor."

"In the end they found him not guilty, is what I heard," she said. "Still, he was in detention for a long time, and had to endure a very intense investigation. They extended his incarceration a number of times, and wouldn't grant bail."

"But he won in court."

"That's right. He was prosecuted, but wasn't given a jail sentence. He apparently remained totally silent during the investigation."

"My understanding is that the Tokyo district prosecutors are the cream of the crop," I said. "A proud lot. Once they set their sights on someone, they have solid evidence before they arrest them and charge them. Their win rate in court is really high. So the investigation they did while he was in detention couldn't have been half-baked. Most people break down under that kind of scrutiny, and sign whatever the prosecutors want them to. Ordinary people wouldn't be able to stay silent under that kind of pressure."

"Still, that's what Mr. Menshiki did. He must have a strong will and a sharp mind."

Menshiki wasn't your average person, that was for sure . . . A strong will and a sharp mind were indeed part of his repertoire.

"There's one thing I don't get," I said. "Whether it is for tax evasion or money laundering or whatever, once the Tokyo district prosecutor arrests you, it's reported on in the newspapers. And with an unusual name like Menshiki, I would remember the case. I used to be a pretty avid reader of newspapers."

"I don't know about that. There's one other thing—I mentioned it before—but he bought that mountaintop mansion three years ago. Almost forcing the owners to sell. Other people were living there then, and they had no intention at all of selling the house they'd just built. But Mr. Menshiki offered them money—or maybe pressured them in some other way—and drove them out. And then he moved in, like some mean-spirited hermit crab."

"Hermit crabs don't drive away what's living in a shell. They just quietly take over the leftover shell of a dead shellfish."

"But there must be some hermit crabs that are mean."

"I don't get it," I said, trying to avoid a debate over the ecology of hermit crabs. "If what you're saying is true, why would Mr. Menshiki insist so strongly that it had to be **that house**? So much so that he drove the residents out and took over? That must have taken a lot of money and effort. And that mansion is really too gaudy, too conspicuous, to suit him. It's a wonderful house, for sure, but I just don't think it fits his tastes."

"Plus it's too big. He doesn't have a maid, lives alone, hardly ever has guests over. There's no need to live in such a huge place."

She drank the rest of the water.

"There must be some special reason why it had to be that house," she went on. "I have no idea why, though."

"Anyway, he's invited me over to his place on Tuesday. Once I actually visit I might learn more."

"Make sure you check out the secret locked room, the one like Bluebeard's castle."

"I'll remember to," I said.

"For the time being, things have worked out well."

"Meaning—?"

"You finished the painting, Mr. Menshiki liked it, and you got a hefty payment for it."

"I guess so," I said. "I guess it did work out. I'm relieved."

"Felicitations, maestro," she said.

It was no lie to say that I felt relieved. It was true that I'd finished the painting. And true that Menshiki had liked it. And also true that I was happy with the painting. And equally true that this resulted in a nice, healthy amount of money coming my way. For all that, though, I couldn't feel totally pleased with the way things had worked out. So much around me was still up in the air, left as is, with no clues to follow. The more I wanted to simplify my life, the more disjointed it seemed to become.

As if searching for clues, I almost unconsciously reached out to hold my girlfriend. Her body felt soft, and warm. And damp with sweat.

I know exactly where you've been and what you've been up to, the man with the white Subaru Forester said.

20

THE MOMENT WHEN EXISTENCE AND NONEXISTENCE COALESCE

The next morning I woke up at five thirty. It was Sunday morning. It was still pitch dark outside. After a simple breakfast in the kitchen I changed into work clothes and went into the studio. As the eastern sky grew brighter, I switched off the light, threw open the window, and let chilly, fresh morning air into the room. I took out a fresh canvas and set it on the easel. The chirping of birds filtered in through the open window. The rain during the night had thoroughly soaked the trees. The rain had stopped just a while before, bright gaps in the clouds showing. I sat down on the stool, and, sipping hot black coffee from a mug, stared at the empty canvas before me.

I've always enjoyed this time, early in the morning, gazing intently at a pure white canvas. "Canvas Zen" is my term for it. Nothing is painted there yet, but it's more than a simple blank space. Hidden on that white canvas is what must eventually emerge. As I look more closely, I discover various possibilities, which congeal into a perfect clue as to how to proceed. That's the moment I really enjoy. The moment when existence and nonexistence coalesce.

But on this day I knew from the beginning what I

would be painting. Emerging from this canvas would be a portrait of the middle-aged man with the white Subaru Forester. Up to this moment the man had been patiently waiting, inside me, to be painted. And I had to paint his portrait not for anyone else (not by commission, not to earn a living) but for myself. Just as I had painted Menshiki's portrait, in order to make visible his reason for being—or at least the meaning it had for me—I had to paint him in my own way. I'm not sure why. But it had to be done.

I closed my eyes and called to mind the figure of the man with the white Subaru Forester. I could distinctly recall the minutest details of his features. Early that second day he'd looked straight at me from his seat in the restaurant. The morning paper on the tabletop was folded, white steam rising from his cup of coffee. The bright morning light shining in the large window, the restaurant filled with the clatter of cheap tableware. That whole scene came back in every detail. And in the midst of that scene the man's face began to show some expression.

I know exactly where you've been and what you've been up to, his eyes told me.

This time I began with a rough draft. I stood up, grabbed a stick of charcoal, and stood before the canvas. On the blank space I created the spot where the man's face would go. With no plan, without thinking, I drew in a single vertical line. A single line, the focal point from which everything else would emerge. What would emerge was the face of a thin, suntanned man, deep wrinkles on his forehead. Thin, piercing eyes. Eyes used to staring at the far-off horizon. Eyes dyed the color of the sky and sea. Hair cut short, dotted with white. My guess, a taciturn, long-suffering man.

Around that central line I used charcoal to add a few supplementary lines, so the outlines of the man's face would appear. I stepped back to look at the lines I'd done, made a few corrections, and added some new lines. What was important was believing in myself. Believing in the power of the lines, in the power of the space the lines divided. I wasn't speaking, but letting the lines and spaces speak. Once the lines and spaces began conversing, then color would finally start to speak. And the flat would gradually transform into the three-dimensional. What I had to do was encourage them all, lend them a hand. And more than anything, not get in their way.

I kept working until ten thirty. The sun had made a slow crawl to the midpoint in the sky, the gray clouds had broken into thin strands, driven away one after another beyond the mountains. No longer did water drip from the tips of the tree branches. I stepped back and examined the rough sketch I'd done from various angles. What I saw was the face of the man I'd remembered. Or rather the framework that should abide in that face. But there were a few too many lines. I needed to do some trimming. Subtraction was the order of the day. But that was for tomorrow. Best to end this day's work here.

I put down the now shorter stick of charcoal, and washed my smudged hands in the sink. As I dried my hands with a towel, my eyes came to rest on the bell on the shelf in front of me, and I picked it up. I shook it, and the sound was terribly light, dry, and outdated. I couldn't believe it was an enigmatic Buddhist implement that had been underground for ages. It sounded so different from what I'd heard in the middle of the night. No doubt the pitch black and stillness had added to the depth and clarity of the sound, and made it carry farther.

The question of who could possibly have been ringing that bell in the middle of the night remained an unsolved mystery. Though someone must have been down in the hole every night ringing it (sending out what had to be some kind of message), whoever it was had vanished. When we uncovered the hole, all that was there was this bell. The whole thing was baffling. I placed the bell back on the shelf.

After lunch I went outside and into the woods out back. I had on a thick gray hooded windbreaker, and paint-stained sweatpants. I followed the damp path to the small shrine, and walked around behind it. The thick board cover over the hole was piled with fallen leaves of different colors and shapes. Leaves soaked by last night's rain. Since Menshiki and I had visited two days before, no one else seemed to have touched the cover. I wanted to make sure of that. I sat down on the damp stones, and, listening to the calls of birds overhead, I gazed for a while at where the hole was.

In the silence of the woods it felt like I could hear

the passage of time, of life passing by. One person leaves, another appears. A thought flits away and another takes its place. One image bids farewell and another one appears on the scene. As the days piled up, I wore out, too, and was remade. Nothing stayed still. And time was lost. Behind me, time became dead grains of sand, which one after another gave way and vanished. I just sat there in front of the hole, listening to the sound of time dying.

What would it feel like to sit at the bottom of that hole, all alone, I wondered. Being shut away by oneself in a cramped dark space. Menshiki had even given up his flashlight and the ladder. Without the ladder, without someone's help (specifically **mine**) it would be nearly impossible to escape from there. Why did he have to go to the trouble of putting himself into such a predicament? Did being down in that dark hole remind him of his solitary time behind bars in Tokyo Prison? There was no way I could know that, of course. Menshiki lived his own life, in his own way.

I could say only one thing for sure. I **would never be able to do that**. Nothing scared me more than dark, confined spaces. Put me in a place like that, and I wouldn't be able to breathe, I'd be so terrified. Even so, I was drawn to that hole. Drawn **very strongly**. So much so it felt like the hole was beckoning to me.

I sat next to the hole for a good half hour. Then I stood up and walked home through the sunlight that filtered down through the trees.

·   ·   ·

After two p.m. I had a call from Masahiko Amada. He had an errand to run near Odawara and wondered if he might drop by. Of course, I told him. I hadn't seen him in a while. He drove up just before three. He brought a bottle of single-malt whiskey as a present. I thanked him. Good timing, since I'd almost run out of whiskey. As always he was stylishly dressed, neatly shaved, wearing glasses I'd seen before, with shell-rimmed frames. He looked nearly the same as he had in the past, though admittedly his hairline was beating a slow-motion retreat.

We sat in the living room and caught up. I told him how the landscapers had used heavy equipment to dig up the stone mound. How after that, a hole just under six feet in diameter had emerged. Nine feet deep, surrounded by a stone wall. A heavy lattice cover was over it, and when that was removed, all we found was an old Buddhist implement like a bell. He listened intently as I told him the story. But he didn't say he wanted to see the hole. Or the bell.

"After that I take it you didn't hear the bell at night?"

"I don't hear it anymore," I said.

"That's great," he said, sounding a bit relieved. "I can't handle those kind of spooky things. I try to avoid them at all costs."

"Let sleeping dogs lie?"

"Exactly," Masahiko said. "I leave that hole up to you. Do whatever you like."

I told him how now, for the first time in what seemed like forever, I had the urge to paint. How ever since I finished Menshiki's portrait two days ago, it was like some blockage had been removed. I felt like I was discovering a new, original style, using portraits as a motif. I'd started the painting as a portrait, but what had eventually emerged was far from a conventional likeness. Even so, it was in essence still a portrait.

Masahiko wanted to see Menshiki's portrait, but when I told him I'd already given it to him, he was disappointed.

"But the paint can't be dry yet, can it?"

"He said he'd make sure it dries properly," I said. "He seemed eager to have the painting as quickly as possible. I don't know, maybe he was worried I might change my mind and not give it to him."

"Hmm," Masahiko said, impressed. "Do you have any new work, then?"

"I started on something this morning," I said. "But it's still just a charcoal sketch, so even if you saw it, it wouldn't mean anything."

"That's okay. Would you mind showing it to me?"

I took him into the studio and showed him the sketch for **The Man with the White Subaru Forester**. It was just a rough sketch in charcoal, but Masahiko stood in front of the easel, arms folded, a hard look on his face.

"Interesting," he said a little later, squeezing the words out between his teeth.

I was silent.

"It's hard to tell how it's going to develop, but it certainly does look like someone's portrait. Like the

root of a portrait. A root buried deep in the ground."
He was silent for a time.

"In a very deep, dark place," he went on. "And this
man—it **is** a man, right?—is angry about something?
What is he blaming?"

"You got me. I haven't got that far."

"You haven't got that far," Masahiko repeated in
a monotone. "But there really is a deep anger and
sadness here. And he can't spit it out. The anger is
swirling around inside him."

In college Masahiko was in the oil painting department, though to be blunt about it, he wasn't
known as a great painter. He was skilled enough, but
his work lacked depth, something he himself admitted. He was, however, blessed with the skill of being
able to instantly evaluate other people's paintings. So
whenever I felt stuck doing one of my own paintings,
I'd ask his opinion. His advice was always accurate
and impartial, as well as practical. And thankfully he
had no sense of jealousy or rivalry. I guess this was
part of his personality, something he was born with.
I always could believe what he told me. He never
minced words, but had no ulterior motives, so oddly
enough even when his criticism was pretty scathing,
I never felt upset.

"When you finish this painting, before you give
it to anyone else, could you let me take a look at it,
even just for a minute?" he asked, eyes never leaving
the painting.

"Sure," I said. "No one commissioned me to do

this. I'm just painting it for myself. I don't plan to turn it over to anyone."

"You want to do your **own** painting now, right?"

"Seems that way."

"It's a portrait of sorts, but not a **formal** portrait."

I nodded. "You could put it that way, I suppose."

"You might be . . . discovering a new destination for yourself."

"I'd like to think so," I said.

"I saw Yuzu the other day," Masahiko said as he was leaving. "Happened to bump into her, and we talked for a half hour or so."

I nodded but said nothing. I had no idea what I should say, or how I should react.

"She seemed fine. We didn't talk about you much. It was like we both wanted to avoid the topic. You get it, that feeling? But at the end she did ask about you. What you're doing, that kind of thing. I told her you were painting. I don't know what kind of paintings, I said, but I said you're holed up on a mountaintop and painting something."

"I'm alive, at least," I said.

Masahiko seemed to want to say something more about Yuzu but thought better of it, and clammed up. Yuzu had always liked him and had apparently gone to him for advice. Probably things that had to do with the two of us. Just like I often went to him for advice about paintings. But Masahiko didn't tell me anything. He was that kind of guy. People often sought his advice, but he kept it all inside. Like rain running down a gutter and into a rainwater tank. It doesn't leave there, doesn't spill over the sides. He probably adjusted the amount of water inside as needed.

Masahiko didn't seem to ask anyone else for advice about his own troubles. He must have had plenty, as the son of a famous artist who went to art school but wasn't blessed with much talent as an artist. There must have been things he wanted to talk over. I've known him for a long time, but I don't recall ever hearing him complain about anything, even once. That's the type of man he was.

"Yuzu had a lover, I think," I went ahead and said. "During the last part of our marriage she stopped having sex with me. I should have known something was going on."

It was the first time I'd confessed this to anyone. I had kept it all inside until this moment.

"I see," was all Masahiko said.

"But you already knew that much, didn't you?"

He didn't respond.

"Am I wrong?" I asked again.

"There are things people are better off not knowing. That's all I can say."

"But whether you know it or not, it ends up the same. Sooner or later, suddenly or not suddenly, with a loud knock or a soft one, that's the only difference."

Masahiko sighed. "Yeah. You might be right. Whether you knew about it or not, the end result is the same. But still, there are things I can't talk about."

I was silent.

"No matter how things end up, everything has both a good and bad side. I'm sure breaking up with Yuzu was hard on you. And I feel for you. I really do. But because of that you've finally begun painting what you want to paint. You've discovered your own style. A kind of silver lining, wouldn't you say?"

Maybe he was right. If I hadn't split up with Yuzu—I mean, if Yuzu hadn't left me—I'd probably still be painting run-of-the-mill portraits to make a living. But that wasn't a choice I made **myself**. That's the important point.

"Try to look on the bright side," Masahiko said as he was leaving. "This might sound like dumb advice, but if you're going to walk down a road, it's better to walk down the sunny side, right?"

"And the cup still has one-sixteenth of the water left."

Masahiko laughed. "I like your sense of humor."

I hadn't said it to be humorous, but didn't comment.

Masahiko was silent for a time, and then spoke up. "Do you still love Yuzu?"

"I know I have to forget her, but my heart's still clinging to her and won't let go. That's just the way it is."

"You don't plan to sleep with other women?"

"Even if I did, Yuzu would always come between me and the other woman."

"That's a problem," he said. He rubbed his forehead with his fingertips. He really did look perplexed.

He got in his car and prepared to drive away.

"Thanks for the whiskey," I said. It was not yet five p.m. but the sky was pretty dark. The season when the night gets longer with each passing day.

"Actually, I wanted to have a drink with you," he said, "but I'm driving. Someday soon let's go out and do some serious drinking together. It's been ages."

"We'll do it soon," I said.

There are things people are better off not knowing, Masahiko had said. Maybe so. There are probably things people are better off not hearing, as well. But they can't go forever without hearing them. When the time comes, even if they stop their ears up tight, the air will vibrate and invade a person's heart. You can't prevent it. If you don't like it, then the only solution is to live in a vacuum.

It was the middle of the night when I woke up. I fumbled for the light next to my bed and looked at the clock. The digital readout showed 1:35. I could hear the bell ringing. **That bell**, no mistake. I sat up and listened to where the sound was coming from.

The bell started ringing again. Someone was ringing it in the middle of the night—and it was much louder, much clearer than ever.

21

IT'S SMALL, BUT SHOULD YOU CUT WITH IT, BLOOD WILL CERTAINLY COME OUT

I sat upright in bed, and in the dark of night I held my breath and listened to the sound of the bell. Where could the sound be coming from? It was louder than before, and clearer. No doubt about it. And it was coming from an entirely new direction.

The bell was ringing inside this house. I could come to no other conclusion. And from a jumble of memories came the recollection that the bell had been resting on a shelf in my studio for a few days. After we uncovered that hole I'd put the bell there myself.

The sound of the bell was coming from the studio. Absolutely no doubt.

But what should I do? I was shaken, and scared. Something truly weird was taking place inside this house, under the same roof. It was the middle of the night, in an isolated house in the mountains, and I was all alone. I couldn't help but be afraid. When I thought about it later, I think my confusion surpassed my fear at that point. The human brain is probably constructed that way. All the emotions and feelings you have are mobilized to blunt, or mitigate, fear and distress. Like at a fire, where every single container that can hold water is put to use.

I tried to gather my thoughts and figure out what to do. One choice was to pull the covers over my head and go back to sleep. The method Masahiko advocated, to ignore the inexplicable. Switch your mind off, see nothing, hear nothing. The problem was, there was no way I could go back to sleep. Even if I put my head under the covers, stopped up my ears, and switched off my mind, there was no way I could ignore the bell when it rang out this clearly. Because it was ringing inside this very house.

As always, the bell rang intermittently a few times, then came a short silence, then the bell rang out again. The silence in between was never uniform, each time a little shorter or longer than before. There was a strange human feel to that lack of uniformity. The bell wasn't ringing by itself. No device was being used to ring it. Someone was holding it and ringing it. It was sending out a message.

If I can't escape it, then all I can do is get the facts. If this keeps up, then I'll never get to sleep and my life will be totally upended. I decided to take the initiative and find out what was happening in the studio. A bit of anger was included in this—why did I have to go through this? And of course there was a dash of curiosity thrown in as well. I wanted to be certain, with my own eyes, what was going on here.

I got out of bed and threw on a cardigan over my pajamas. I grabbed a flashlight and went out to the front entrance. I grabbed the oak walking stick that Tomohiko Amada had left behind in an umbrella stand. A sturdy, heavy stick. I didn't think it would be useful, but holding something in my hand bucked up my courage. I had to be ready for anything.

Needless to say, I was scared. I was barefoot, but could barely feel the floor. My body was stiff, as if every bone in my body creaked with each step. Someone must have snuck into the house. And that someone was ringing the bell. And it must be the same person who was ringing the bell at the bottom of the hole. Who—or **what**—that was, I couldn't predict. Was it a mummy? Say I set foot in the studio and really did confront a mummy—a shriveled-up man the color of beef jerky—shaking the bell, how should I react? Smack him with Tomohiko Amada's walking stick?

No way, I thought. **I can't do that.** The mummy would have to be a Buddhist priest who'd mummified himself. We weren't talking about a zombie.

Okay, so what should I do? I was still confused. Or rather, my confusion had grown worse. If I had no good way of dealing with the situation, did that mean I'd have to resign myself to sharing the house with a mummy? Putting up with that bell at the same time every night?

I suddenly thought of Menshiki. This problem had arisen because of him. Because he'd done things he shouldn't have. Because he'd used heavy equipment to move the stone mound and uncover the mysterious hole, some unknown being had entered this house along with the bell. I thought of calling him. Despite the late hour I could picture him rushing over in his Jaguar. But I gave up the idea. I didn't have time to wait for him to get ready and drive over. I had to do something **right here, and right now**. I had to make this **my responsibility**.

I steeled myself and stepped into the living room and turned on the light. Even with the light on, the bell kept on ringing. I could clearly hear it coming from beyond the door leading into the studio. I re-gripped the walking stick in my right hand, tiptoed across the large living room, and put my hand on the doorknob of the studio door. I took a deep breath, made up my mind, and turned the knob. As if wait-ing for me to do that, the second I pushed open the door, the bell stopped cold. A deep silence descended.

The studio was pitch black, and I couldn't see a thing. I reached out to the left-hand wall, fumbled for the light switch, and snapped it on. The pendant light on the ceiling came on and the room was suddenly bathed in light. I stood, legs shoulder-width apart, walking stick in hand, ready to respond to anything, and quickly scanned the room. The tension made my throat so parched that I could hardly swallow.

No one was in the studio. No shriveled-up mummy ringing the bell. No one was there. There was the easel standing by itself in the middle of the room, with a canvas on it. In front of the easel was the old three-legged wooden stool. That was all. The studio was deserted. I couldn't hear a single insect. There was no wind. The white curtain hung down at the window, the whole scene bathed in an unearthly silence. The walking stick was shaking, I was so tense. As it shook, the tip of the stick made an irregular click against the floor.

The bell was still on the shelf. I went over and studied it carefully. I didn't pick the bell up, but I didn't see anything different about it. It was the same as when I'd picked it up in the afternoon and returned it to the shelf, with no evidence of having been moved.

I sat on the stool in front of the easel and once more scanned the room, examining every inch of it. But I still didn't see anyone. It was the same scene I was used to. The painting on the easel was the rough sketch I'd begun of **The Man with the White Subaru Forester.**

I glanced at the clock on the shelf. It was exactly 2 a.m. It was 1:35, as I recall, when the bell woke me up, so twenty-five minutes had passed. It didn't feel like that much time had passed. It felt more like five or six minutes. My sense of time was messed up. Or else the passage of time itself was messed up. One of the two.

I gave up, got down from the stool, turned off the light in the studio, went out, and shut the door. I stood in front of the closed door for a while, my ears perked up, but couldn't hear the bell anymore. I couldn't hear anything, only the silence. Hearing silence—this was no play on words. On an isolated mountaintop, silence had a sound. I stood there before the door to the studio and listened to that sound.

Just then I noticed something on the sofa in the living room I hadn't seen before. It was as big as a cushion or a doll. But I had no memory of putting it there. I looked closer and saw it was no cushion or doll. It was a small, living person, about two feet tall. That little person was wearing odd-looking white clothes. And he was squirming around, like he was uncomfortable in his outfit. I'd seen that ancient, traditional garb before. The kind a high-ranking person would have worn in ancient times in Japan. And it wasn't just the clothes—I remembered the person's face, too.

The Commendatore.

My body felt frozen. As if a fist-sized lump of ice were slowly crawling up my spine. The Commendatore from the painting **Killing Commendatore** was sitting on the sofa in my house—or, more precisely, Tomohiko Amada's house—and looking straight at me. The little man was dressed exactly like in the painting, with the same face. As if he'd escaped directly from the painting.

I tried to recall where I'd put it. That's right, I remembered, it was in the guest bedroom. Not wanting anyone visiting the house to see it, I'd wrapped it in brown washi paper and had hidden it there. If this man had escaped, then what had happened to the painting? Was it solely the Commendatore who had vanished from the canvas?

But was that possible? That a person in a picture could escape from it? Of course not. That's impossible. Obviously. No matter what anybody might think . . .

I stood there, rooted to the spot, the thread of

logic lost, random thoughts racing through my head as I gazed at the Commendatore on the sofa. Time temporarily stopped moving forward, shifting back and forth as if waiting for my confusion to subside. I couldn't take my eyes off that bizarre character—all I could think was that he had somehow come from the spirit world. For his part, the Commendatore stared up at me, from the sofa. I had no words, and was silent. The shock must have done it. I was capable of nothing, other than to keep my eyes on him and breathe, my mouth slightly ajar.

The Commendatore didn't take his eyes off me either, and he didn't say a word. His lips were shut tight. On the sofa he flung his short legs out straight in front of him. He leaned back against the sofa, though his head didn't reach to the top. On his feet were oddly shaped shoes. They seemed made out of black leather, the tips pointed and curled upward. At his waist he wore a long sword with a decorated shaft. A long sword, yet of a size to fit his build, so actually nearer in length to a short sword for a normal person. But a lethal weapon all the same. Assuming it was a real sword.

"A real sword it is," the Commendatore said pleasantly, as if reading my mind. His voice carried, despite his small stature. "Affirmative! It's small, but should you cut with it, blood will certainly come out."

Even with this new information, I remained silent. No words came. My first thought was, Oh, so he can talk? My next thought was that he sure had an odd way of speaking. It was not the way ordinary people would speak. But then again, the little two-foot Commendatore was in no way ordinary. So whatever his manner of speech, it shouldn't be surprising.

"In Tomohiko Amada's **Killing Commendatore**, it is indeed me who is impaled by a sword and dies a pitiful death," the Commendatore said. "As my friends are well aware. But have I any wounds that you can see? Negative! No wounds at all. It would be a bother for me to traipse around bleeding, and it would certainly annoy my friends as well. What with blood messing up the carpet and furniture and whatnot. So I left out the stab wound. The one who took the **killing** out of **Killing Commendatore,** that's me. Affirmative! If you need a name for me, my friends can call me the Commendatore."

The way the Commendatore spoke was odd, but he wasn't a poor speaker. In fact he was actually pretty talkative. But I still couldn't get a single word out. Reality and unreality still hadn't come to a mutual understanding inside me.

"Perhaps you will put that stick down?" the Commendatore said. "It is not as though we are about to embark upon a duel . . ."

I looked at my right hand. It was still clutching Amada's walking stick tightly. I let it go . . . The oak stick made a dull **clunk** as it struck the carpet.

"It is not like I escaped from the painting," the Commendatore said, again reading my mind. "Negative! That painting—a fascinating one, by the way—remains intact. The Commendatore is still in the process of being stabbed to death. A huge amount of blood continues to flow from his heart. All I have done is borrow his shape for a while. I need some sort of shape in order to speak with my friends. So for the sake of convenience, I borrowed his form. Is that acceptable to my friends?"

Still not a peep from me.

"Not that anybody really cares. Mr. Amada has gone on to a hazy, peaceful world, and the Commendatore is not trademarked. If I had appeared as Mickey Mouse or Pocahontas, the Walt Disney Company would be only too happy to slap me with a huge lawsuit, but if I am the Commendatore, I think we are safe, my friends."

The Commendatore's shoulders shook as he laughed merrily.

"I would have been okay as a mummy, but if I'd appeared as a mummy all of a sudden in the middle of the night, I am aware that my friends might have been bothered. To see a man all shriveled up like a hunk of beef jerky, ringing a bell in the middle of the night—that would certainly give most people a heart attack."

I nodded almost automatically. True enough—a commendatore was much preferable to a mummy. If he'd been a mummy I might really **have** had a heart attack. But running across Mickey Mouse or Pocahontas ringing a bell in the dark would have been pretty creepy too. A commendatore dressed in Asuka-period costume probably was a better choice.

"Are you a kind of spirit?" I ventured to ask. My voice was hard and hoarse, like a convalescent's.

"An excellent question," the Commendatore said. He held up a tiny white index finger. "An excellent question indeed, my friends. What am I? I am now, for the time being, the Commendatore. Nothing other than the Commendatore. But this form is but temporary. I do not know what I will be next. What am I to begin with? Or I could say, what are **you**, my friends? My friends have your own appearance, but what are **you** to begin with? If you were asked that same question, my friends might indeed be confused, I imagine. It is the same thing with me."

"Can you assume any form you like?" I asked.

"No, it is not that simple. The forms I can take are quite limited. I can't take any form I want. **There is a limit to the wardrobe.** I cannot take on a form unless there is a necessity for it. And the form I could choose now was this pint-sized commendatore. I had to be this small because of the way he was painted. But this attire is highly unpleasant to wear, I am afraid."

He began squirming around in his white costume.

"To return to the pressing question that my friends have pondered—am I a spirit? No, it is nothing like that. I am no spirit. I am just an Idea. A spirit is basically supernaturally free, which I am not. I live under all sorts of restrictions."

I had plenty of questions. Or rather, I **should have had**. But for some reason I couldn't think of a single one. Why did he address me as "my friends"? But that was trivial, not worth asking about. Maybe in the world of an **Idea** there was no second-person singular.

"I have so many kinds of detailed limitations," the Commendatore said. "For instance, I can only take on form for a limited number of hours each day. I prefer the somewhat dubious middle of the night, so mostly shape-shift between one thirty and two thirty a.m. It's too tiring to do it during the day. When I don't have form I take it easy, as a formless Idea, here and there. Like the horned owl in the attic. Also, I cannot go where I am not invited. Whereas when my friends opened the pit and took out the bell for me, I was able to enter this house."

"So you were stuck at the bottom of the pit all this time?" I asked. My voice had improved, but was still a bit hoarse.

"I could not say. I do not have memory, in the exact sense of the term. Though my being stuck in the pit is a fact. I was in the pit and could not escape. But it did not feel inconvenient to me, being shut up in there. I could be stuck in a cramped dark hole for tens of thousands of years and not feel any distress. I am grateful to my friends for getting me out of there. Being free is much more interesting than not being free, needless to say. I am also grateful to that Mr. Menshiki. Without his efforts, the hole never would have been opened up."

I nodded. "That's exactly right."

"I think I must have sensed it. The possibility that the pit would be exhumed, I mean. And must have thought this: The time has come."

"So it was you who began to ring the bell in the middle of the night?"

"Precisely. And the pit was opened. And Mr. Menshiki very kindly invited me to his dinner party."

I nodded again. It was true that Menshiki had invited the Commendatore—though he'd used the word "mummy"—to dinner on Tuesday. Following the example of Don Giovanni's dinner invitation to the bronze statue of Il Commendatore. To him it was probably a bit of a joke. But this was no longer a joke.

"I never take any food," the Commendatore said. "And I do not drink, either. No digestive organs, you see. 'Tis boring if you think about it, since he has gone to the trouble of preparing such a feast. But still I went ahead and accepted. It is not often that an Idea is invited by someone for dinner."

These were the Commendatore's last words that night. He suddenly grew silent and quietly shut both eyes, as if slipping into a meditative state. With his eyes closed, the Commendatore's features took on a contemplative look. His body, too, was completely still. His whole form began to fade, the outline becoming indistinct. And a few seconds later he totally vanished. Reflexively I glanced at the clock. Two fifteen a.m. Most likely his materialization had reached its time limit.

I went over to the sofa and touched the spot where the Commendatore had sat. My hand felt nothing. No warmth, no depression. No evidence at all that anyone had sat there. Ideas most likely had no body heat or weight. That figure was a mere image and nothing more. I sat down next to where he'd been, took a deep breath, and rubbed my face hard.

It felt like it had taken place in a dream. I must have been having a long, very vivid dream. Or maybe this world now was an extension of the dream, one I was shut up inside. But I knew this was no dream. This might not be real, but it wasn't a dream either. Menshiki and I had released the Commendatore—or an Idea taking the appearance of the Commendatore—from the bottom of that strange pit. And that Commendatore—like the horned owl in the attic—had come to inhabit this house. I had no clue what that meant. Or what it would lead to.

I stood up, retrieved Tomohiko Amada's walking stick I'd dropped on the floor, turned off the light in the living room, and returned to my bedroom. It was quiet all around, not a single sound. I took off my cardigan, slipped back into my bed in my pajamas, and lay there thinking about what I should do now. The Commendatore planned to go to Menshiki's house on Tuesday, since Menshiki had invited him to dinner. And what would happen there? The more I thought about it, the more wobbly my brain became, my mind like a dining table with uneven legs.

But before long I grew overpoweringly sleepy. Like every function of my brain was mobilizing to put me to sleep, to pluck me by force from an incoherent, confused reality. And I couldn't resist. Before long I fell asleep. Just before I fell asleep, I thought of the horned owl. How was he doing?

My friends must go to sleep now. It felt like the Commendatore murmured this into my ear.

But that must have been part of a dream.

341

22

THE INVITATION IS STILL OPEN

The next day was Monday. When I woke up the digital clock showed 6:35. I sat up in bed, and reviewed the middle-of-the-night happenings in the studio. The bell ringing, the miniature Commendatore, the strange conversation with him. I wanted to believe it was all a dream. I'd had a very long, real dream—that's all it was. In the light of morning, that's the only way I could see it. I clearly remembered everything that had taken place, and the more I reviewed each and every detail, the more it felt like something that had happened light-years away from reality.

But no matter how hard I tried to see it all as a dream, I knew that it wasn't. **This might not have been real, but it wasn't a dream.** I didn't know what it was, but at any rate it wasn't a dream. It was something altogether different.

I got out of bed, removed the washi paper wrapping from Tomohiko Amada's **Killing Commendatore,** and carried the painting into the studio. I hung it on the wall, then sat on the stool and studied the painting. Like the Commendatore had said the previous night, nothing about the painting had changed.

The Commendatore hadn't escaped from the painting into this world. Like always, the Commendatore was still there, stabbed in the chest, blood pouring out of his heart as he died. He looked up in the air, his mouth open in a grimace, groaning in agony. His hairstyle, the clothes he wore, the long sword he held, even the strange black shoes, were exactly those of the Commendatore who'd appeared here last night. No, to put it in the correct order—chronologically speaking—naturally last night's Commendatore had minutely copied the appearance of the Commendatore in the painting.

It was astounding that the fictional figure that Tomohiko Amada had painted with a Japanese paintbrush and pigment had taken on real form and appeared in reality (or something like reality), moving around under its own willpower in three-dimensional form. But as I stared at the painting, this phenomenon began to seem less and less impossible. That's how vivid and alive Tomohiko Amada's rendering was. The longer I looked at the painting, the less clear was the threshold between reality and unreality, flat and solid, substance and image. Like Van Gogh's mailman, who, the longer you looked, seemed to take on a life of his own. Same with the crows that he painted—nothing but rough black lines, but they really did seem to be soaring through the sky. As I gazed at **Killing Commendatore** I was struck once again with admiration for Amada's gift and craftsmanship as an artist. No doubt that the Commendatore (or Idea, I should say) was equally struck by how amazing and powerful the painting was, and that was why he had "borrowed" the appearance of the Commendatore. Like a hermit crab chooses the prettiest and most sturdy shell to live in.

I studied **Killing Commendatore** for some ten minutes, then went into the kitchen, brewed coffee, and, while listening to the regular news broadcast on the radio, had a simple breakfast. The news was meaningless. Or what I should say is that almost none of the news those days held any meaning for me. Still, listening to the seven a.m. news each day had become part of my routine. It might be a problem if the world was on the brink of destruction and I was the only person unaware of it.

I finished breakfast, and after confirming that that earth, despite all its various troubles, was still spinning away, I headed back to the studio, mug in hand. I drew back the curtain to let in some fresh air, then stood before the canvas and went back to work on my painting. Whether the Commendatore's appearance was real or not, whether he showed up at Menshiki's dinner or not, all I could do in the meantime was focus on the work at hand.

I called to mind the figure of the middle-aged man with the white Subaru Forester. On his table in the restaurant had been a car key with the Subaru logo, a heap of toast, scrambled eggs, and sausage on a plate. Ketchup (red) and mustard (yellow) containers sat alongside. Knife and fork were lined up on the table. He'd yet to start eating. Morning light shone on the whole tableau. As I passed him, the man raised his suntanned face and stared at me.

I know exactly where you've been and what you've been up to, he was informing me. I recognized that heavy, dispassionate light abiding in his eyes. A light I may have seen somewhere else, though when or where I couldn't say.

I was completing that figure and that wordless message in the form of a painting. I started out using a crust of bread as an eraser to get rid of any excess lines from the charcoal framework I'd sketched the day before. After removing all that I could, I again added some lines in black to the black lines that remained. This process took an hour and a half. What emerged on the canvas was (so to speak) a mummified image of the man who drove the white Subaru Forester. The flesh pruned away, the skin dried up like beef jerky, a figure shrunken one whole size. This was depicted through the rough black charcoal lines alone. Just a preliminary sketch, but I could imagine how it linked up with the full painting to come.

"Nicely done," the Commendatore said.

I spun around. The Commendatore was seated on the shelf near the window, facing me, his silhouette distinctly backlit in the morning light. He had on the same ancient white clothes and the same long sword downsized to fit his height. **This is no dream. Of course it isn't**, I told myself.

"I am no dream, I can tell you. Negative. Of course," the Commendatore said, once again reading my thoughts. "I am closer to wakefulness than dream."

I said nothing. From my perch on the stool I gazed at his silhouette.

"I think I said this last night, but it is pretty exhausting for me to materialize when it is bright out like this," the Commendatore said. "But I wanted to watch my friends painting just this once. So I took the liberty of observing while you worked. I hope this does not offend you?"

I had no answer to this either. Whether it offended me or not, how was a real person supposed to reason with an Idea?

Not waiting for my response (or maybe taking what was in my mind as my response), the Commendatore continued. "You are quite a talented painter. Stroke by stroke, the essence of that man is coming out on that canvas."

"Do you know something about him?" I asked, surprised.

"Affirmative," the Commendatore said. "Of course I do."

"Then could you tell me something about him? What kind of person he is, what work he does, what he's doing now?"

"I wonder," the Commendatore said, slightly inclining his head, a hard look coming over his face. When he made that sort of expression he looked like a goblin. Or like Edward G. Robinson from an old gangster movie. Who knows, maybe the Commendatore had "borrowed" that expression from Edward G. Robinson. That wouldn't be impossible.

"There are things in the world my friends are better off not knowing," the Commendatore said, the Edward G. Robinson look plastered on his face.

The same thing Masahiko Amada had said the other day, I recalled. **There are things people are better off not knowing.**

"In other words, you won't tell me the things I'm better off not knowing," I said.

"Affirmative. Even if you hear it from me, the truth is that my friends **already know it.**"

I was silent.

"As my friends paint that picture, you will be subjectively giving form to what my friends already comprehend. Think of Thelonious Monk. Thelonious Monk did not get those unusual chords as a result of logic or theory. He opened his eyes wide, and scooped those chords out from the darkness of his consciousness. What is important is not creating something out of nothing. What my friends need to do is discover the right thing from what is already there."

So he knew about Thelonious Monk.

"Affirmative! And of course I know Edward whatchamacallit, too," the Commendatore said, grabbing hold of my thoughts.

"No matter," the Commendatore continued. "Ah, there is one thing I must raise at this point, as a matter of courtesy. It is about your lovely girlfriend . . . Right, the married woman who drives a red car. Apologies, but I have been watching all you have been doing here. What you all enjoy doing in bed after you take off your clothes."

I stared at him without a word. **What we enjoy doing in bed** . . . To borrow her words for it, **what one hesitates to mention.**

"But you really should not mind. My apologies, but an Idea watches everything that happens. I cannot choose what I watch. But there is nothing to worry about, at all. Sex, radio exercise routines, chimney sweeping, it is all the same to me. Nothing that interesting to see. I just watch."

"There's no notion of privacy in the world of an Idea?"

"Affirmative," the Commendatore said, rather proudly. "Not a speck of that. So if my friends do not mind, then that is all we need to say. So, are you okay with it?"

I shook my head slightly again. How about it? Was it possible to focus while having sex if you knew somebody else was watching the whole time? Could you call up a healthy sexual desire if you knew you were being observed?

"I have a question for you," I said.

"I would be happy to answer if I can," the Commendatore said.

"Tomorrow, on Tuesday, I'm invited to dinner at Mr. Menshiki's. And you're invited as well. Mr. Menshiki used the expression "inviting a mummy," which actually means you. Since at that point you hadn't yet appeared as the Commendatore."

"That does not matter. If I decide to be a mummy, I can do that in a flash."

"No, stay as you are," I said hurriedly. "I would appreciate it if you stay the way you are."

"I will accompany you to Menshiki's house. You will be able to see me, but Menshiki will not. So it does not matter if I am a mummy or a commendatore. Though there is one thing I would like my friends to do."

"And what would that be?"

"My friends should call Menshiki now and make sure the invitation for Tuesday night is still open. When you do, make sure to say, 'It will not be a mummy coming with me that day, but the Commendatore. Would that still be all right?' As I mentioned, I cannot set foot in a place unless I have been invited. The other party needs to invite me, in some form or other say 'Please, come on in.' Once I have been invited, then I can go whenever I feel like it. For this house, that bell over there acted as a substitute invitation."

"I see," I said. The one thing I couldn't have was him turning into a mummy. "I'll call Mr. Menshiki, see if the invitation is still on, and tell him I'd like him to revise the guest list from mummy to Commendatore."

"Affirmative. I would be grateful. Receiving an invitation to a dinner party is quite unexpected."

"I have another question," I said. "Weren't you originally a priest who undertook certain death austerities? A priest who voluntarily was buried under-

349

ground, stopped eating and drinking, and chanted the sutras until you passed away? Didn't you die in the pit while you continued to ring the bell, and eventually turned into a mummy?"

"Hmm," the Commendatore said, and shook his head a little. "Unclear. I can't say, really. At a certain point I became a pure Idea. But I have no linear memory of what I was before that, where I was or what I did."

The Commendatore was silent, staring fixedly into space.

"Anyway, I have to disappear soon," the Commendatore said in a quiet, slightly hoarse voice. "The time during which I can materialize is nearly over. The morning is not my time. Darkness is my friend. A vacuum is my breath. I must be saying goodbye soon. So, thank you in advance for calling Mr. Menshiki."

As if meditating, the Commendatore closed his eyes. His lips were tightly sealed, his fingers locked together, as he steadily grew fainter and then disappeared. Just like the night before. Like fleeting smoke, he silently vanished in the air. In the bright morning sunshine, all that was left was me and the painting I'd started. The outline of the man with the white Subaru Forester glaring at me.

I know exactly where you've been and what you've been up to.

After noon I called Menshiki. I realized this was the first time I'd ever phoned his home. He was the one who always called me. He picked up after six rings.

"I'm glad you called," he said. "I was just about to call you. But I didn't want to bother you while you're working, so was waiting until the afternoon. I remember you mainly work in the morning."

"I just finished for the day," I said.

"Is it going well?" Menshiki asked.

"Yes, I started a new painting. Though I've barely begun."

"That's wonderful. I'm so glad to hear it. By the way, I hung the portrait you painted on the wall of my study, not yet framed. I'm letting it dry there. Even without a frame it looks wonderful."

"About tomorrow . . . ," I said.

"I'll send a car to pick you up at six," he said. "The same car will take you back. It'll just be the two of us, so you don't need to dress up, or bring a gift or anything. Please just come as you are."

"There's one thing I wanted to check with you."

"Yes?"

"The other day you said you wouldn't mind having a mummy join us for dinner, right?"

"I did say that, yes. I remember."

"Is that invitation still open?"

Menshiki considered this for a moment and then gave a cheery laugh. "Of course it is. I meant what I said. The invitation is still open."

"Something happened and the mummy won't be able to come, but instead the Commendatore says he'd like to. Is it all right to invite the Commendatore?"

"Of course," Menshiki said without hesitation. "Like Don Giovanni invited the statue to dinner, I

351

would be pleased to have the Commendatore come to dinner in my humble abode. But unlike Don Giovanni in the opera, I haven't done anything so bad that I deserve to be thrown into hell. At least I don't think I have. After dinner I'm not going to be pulled into hell or anything, I hope?"

"That won't happen," I replied. Though honestly I wasn't all that confident. I couldn't predict anymore what was going to happen next.

"Good. I'm not ready for hell quite yet," Menshiki said cheerily. As you might expect, he was taking it all as a clever joke. "One question, though. As a dead person, Don Giovanni's Commendatore wasn't able to eat earthly food, but what about **this** Commendatore? Should I prepare food for him? Or does he not take any worldly food?"

"There's no need to prepare food for him. He doesn't eat or drink. But it wouldn't be a problem if you set a place for him."

"Because he's basically a spiritual being?"

"I believe so." An Idea and a spirit were a little different, I thought, but I didn't want to get into it.

"I'm fine with that," Menshiki said. "I'll make sure the Commendatore has his own seat at the table. It's an unexpected pleasure to be able to invite the famous Commendatore to dinner in my humble home. It's too bad, though, that he won't be able to sample the food. We'll have some delicious wine as well."

I thanked Menshiki.

"Until tomorrow, then," Menshiki said, and hung up.

That night, the bell didn't ring. The Commendatore must have been tired out from materializing during the day (and answering my questions). Or maybe he no longer felt the need to summon me to the studio. At any rate, I slept a deep, dreamless sleep until morning.

The next morning as I painted in the studio the Commendatore didn't make an appearance. So for two hours, I was able to forget everything and focus on painting. The first thing I did that day was paint over the outline, like spreading a thick slab of butter on toast.

I started with a deep red, an edgy, offbeat green, and a grayish black. These were the colors the man wanted. It took a while to mix the right colors. As I went through this process I put on the record of Mozart's **Don Giovanni**. With that music playing, it felt like the Commendatore would appear behind me at any minute, though he didn't.

That day, Tuesday, the Commendatore, like the horned owl up in the attic, maintained a deep silence. But that didn't bother me particularly. As a flesh-and-blood person, I couldn't worry about an Idea. Ideas had their own way of doing things. And I had my own life. I focused on completing **The Man with the White Subaru Forester**. Whether I was in the studio or out, standing before the canvas or not, the image of the painting was never far from my mind.

According to the radio weather report, there was

supposed to be heavy rain that night in the Kanto-Tokai region. And off to the west the weather was indeed taking a turn for the worse. In southern Kyushu torrential rains had made rivers overflow, and people living in low-lying areas had had to evacuate. People in higher areas were warned to watch out for landslides.

A dinner party on a night when it's going to be pouring, I thought.

I thought of that dark hole in the middle of the woods. That weird stone-lined little chamber that Menshiki and I had exposed to the light of day when we moved the heavy rocks of the mound. I pictured myself sitting alone at the bottom of that pitch-dark hole listening to rain pounding on the wooden cover. I'm shut up inside that hole, unable to escape. The ladder's been taken away, the heavy cover shut tight right above me. And everyone in the world has completely forgotten I've been left behind. Or perhaps they think I'm long dead. But I am still alive. Lonely, but still breathing. All I can hear is the downpour. There's no light. Not a single ray reaches me. The stone wall I'm leaning against is damply cold. It's the middle of the night. All sorts of bugs might ooze their way out.

As this scene took shape in my mind, I gradually found it hard to breathe. I went out to the terrace, leaned against the railing, slowly breathed in the fresh air through my nose, and slowly exhaled through my mouth. As always, I counted the number of breaths and repeated this process at regular intervals. After repeating this for a while, I was able to breathe normally again. The twilight sky was covered in heavy, leaden clouds. The rain was getting closer.

Menshiki's white mansion appeared faintly across the valley. This evening that's where I'll be having dinner, I thought. Menshiki, me, and the famous Commendatore—three of us seated around the dining table.

Affirmative. That is real blood I'm talking about, you know, the Commendatore whispered in my ear.

23

THEY ALL REALLY EXIST

When I was thirteen and my little sister was ten, the two of us traveled by ourselves to Yamanashi Prefecture during summer vacation. Our mother's brother worked in a research lab at a university in Yamanashi and we went to stay with him. This was the first trip we kids had taken by ourselves. My sister was feeling relatively good then, so our parents gave us permission to travel alone.

Our uncle was single (and still is single, even now), and had just turned thirty, I think, at that time. He was doing gene research (and still is), was very quiet and kind of unworldly, though a very open, straightforward person. He loved reading and knew everything about nature. He enjoyed taking walks in the mountains more than anything, which, he said, was why he had taken a university job in rural, mountainous Yamanashi. My sister and I liked our uncle a lot.

Backpacks in tow, we boarded an express train at Shinjuku Station bound for Matsumoto, and got off at Kofu. Our uncle came to pick us up at Kofu Station. He was spectacularly tall, and even in the crowded station, we spotted him right away. He was renting a small house in Kofu along with a friend of his, but his roommate was abroad so we were given our own room to sleep in. We stayed in that house for one week. And almost every day we took walks with our uncle in the nearby mountains. He taught us the names of all kinds of flowers and insects. We cherished our memories of that summer.

One day we hiked a bit farther than usual and visited a wind cave near Mt. Fuji. Among the numerous wind caves around Mt. Fuji there was one in particular that was fairly large. Our uncle told us about how these holes were formed. The caves were made of basalt, so inside you heard hardly any echoes at all, he said. Even in the summer the temperature remained low inside, so in the past people would store ice they'd cut in winter inside the caves. He explained the distinction between the two types of holes: **fuketsu,** the larger ones that were big enough for people to go into, and **kaza-ana,** the smaller ones that people couldn't enter. Both terms were alternate readings of the same Chinese characters meaning "wind" and "hole." Our uncle seemed to know everything.

At the large wind hole, you paid an entrance fee and went inside. Our uncle didn't go with us. He'd been there numerous times, plus he was so tall and the ceiling of the cave so low, he'd end up with a backache. It's not dangerous, he said, so you two go on ahead. I'll stay by the entrance and read a book. At the entrance the person in charge handed us each a flashlight and put yellow plastic helmets on us. There were lights on the ceiling of the cave, but it was still pretty dark inside. The deeper we went inside the cave, the lower the ceiling got. No wonder our lanky uncle had bowed out.

My kid sister and I shone the flashlights at our feet as we went. It was midsummer outside but inside the cave it was chilly. It was ninety degrees Fahrenheit outside, but inside it was under fifty. Following our uncle's advice, we were both wearing thick windbreakers we'd brought along. My sister held my hand tightly, either wanting me to protect her, or else hoping to protect me, one or the other (or maybe she just didn't want to get separated). The whole time we were inside the cave that small, warm hand was in mine. The only other visitors were a middle-aged couple. But they soon left, and it was just the two of us.

My little sister's name was Komichi, but everyone in the family called her Komi. Her friends called her Micchi or Micchan. As far as I know, no one called her by her full name, Komichi. She was a small, slim girl. She had straight black hair, neatly cut just above her shoulders. Her eyes were big for the size of her face (with large pupils), which made her resemble a fairy. That day she wore a white T-shirt, faded jeans, and pink sneakers.

After we'd made our way deeper into the cave my sister discovered a small side cave a little ways off from the prescribed path. Its mouth was hidden in the shadows of the rocks. She was very interested in that little cave. "Don't you think it looks like Alice's rabbit hole?" she asked me.

My sister was a big fan of Lewis Carroll's **Alice in Wonderland**. I don't know how many times she had me read the book to her. Must have been at least a hundred. She had been able to read since she was little, but she liked me to read that book aloud to her. She'd memorized the story, but each time I read it, she still got excited. Her favorite part was the Lobster Quadrille. Even now I remember that part, word for word.

"No rabbit, though," I said.

"I'm going to peek inside," she said.

"Be careful," I said.

It really was a narrow hole (close to a **kaza-ana,** in my uncle's definition), but my little sister was able to slip through it with no trouble. Her upper half was inside, just the bottom half of her legs sticking out. She seemed to be shining her flashlight inside the hole. Then she slowly edged out backward.

"It gets really deep in back," she reported. "The floor drops off sharply. Just like Alice's rabbit hole. I'm going to check out the far end."

"No, don't do it. It's too dangerous," I said.

"It's okay. I'm small and I can get out okay."

She took off her windbreaker, so that she was wearing just her T-shirt, and handed the jacket to me along with her helmet. Before I could get in a word of protest, she'd wriggled into the cave, flashlight in hand. In an instant she'd vanished.

A long time passed, but she still didn't come out. I couldn't hear a sound.

"Komi," I called into the hole. "Komi! Are you okay?"

There was no answer. Without any echo my voice

was sucked right up into the darkness. I was starting to get concerned. She might be stuck inside the
hole, unable to more forward or back. Or maybe she
had had a convulsion inside the hole and lost consciousness. If that had happened I wouldn't be able
to help her. All kinds of terrible scenarios ran through
my head, and I felt choked by the darkness surrounding me.

If my little sister really did disappear in the hole,
never to return to this world again, how would I ever
explain that to my parents? Should I run and tell my
uncle, waiting outside the entrance? Or should I sit
tight and wait for her to emerge? I crouched down
and peered into that hole. But the beam from my
flashlight didn't reach far. It was a tiny hole, and the
darkness inside was overwhelming.

"Komi," I called out again. No response. **"Komi,"**
I called more loudly. Still no answer. A wave of cold
chilled me to the core. I might lose my sister forever. She might have been sucked into Alice's hole
and vanished. Into the world of the Mock Turtle,
the Cheshire Cat, and the Queen of Hearts. A place
where worldly logic didn't apply. No matter what, we
never should have come here.

But finally my sister did return. She didn't back
out like before, but crawled out headfirst. First her
black hair appeared from the hole, then her shoulders and arms. She wriggled out her waist, and finally
her pink sneakers emerged. She stood in front of me,
without a word, stretched, slowly took a deep breath,
and brushed the dirt off her jeans.

My heart was still pounding. I reached out and straightened her disheveled hair. I couldn't quite make it out in the weak light inside the cave, but there seemed to be dirt and dust and other debris clinging to her white T-shirt. I put the windbreaker on her. And handed back her yellow helmet.

"I didn't think you were coming back," I said, hugging her to me.

"Were you worried?"

"A lot."

She grabbed my hand tightly again. And in an excited voice she said, "I managed to squeeze through the narrow part, and then deeper in it suddenly got lower, and down from there it was like a small room. A round room, like a ball. The ceiling's round, the walls are round, and the floor too. And it was so, so silent there, like you could search the whole world and never find any place that silent. Like I was at the bottom of an ocean, in a hollow going even deeper. I turned off the flashlight and it was pitch dark, but I didn't feel scared or lonely. That room was a special place that only I'm allowed into. A room **just for me**. No one else can get there. You can't go in either."

"'Cause I'm too big."

My little sister bobbed her head. "Right. You've gotten too big to get in. And what's really amazing about that place is that it's darker than anything could ever be. So dark that when you turn off the flashlight it feels like you can grab the darkness with your hands. And when you're there in the dark by yourself, it's like your body is gradually coming apart and disappearing. But since it's dark you can't see it happen. You don't know if you still have a body or not. But even if, say, my body completely disappeared, I'd still remain there. Like the Cheshire Cat's grin remaining after he vanished. Pretty weird, huh? But when I was there I didn't think it was weird at all. I wanted to stay there forever, but I thought you'd be worried, so I came out."

"Let's get out of here," I said. She was so worked up it seemed as if she was going to go on talking for-ever, and I had to put a stop to that. "I can't breathe well in here."

"Are you okay?" my sister asked, worried.

"I'm okay. I just want to go outside."

Holding hands, we headed for the exit.

"Do you know?" my sister said in a small voice as we walked so no one else would hear (though there wasn't anyone else around). "Alice really existed. It wasn't made up, it was real. The March Hare, the Walrus, the Cheshire Cat, the Playing Card soldiers— they all really exist."

"Maybe so," I said.

We emerged from the wind hole, back to the bright real world. There was a thin layer of clouds in the sky that afternoon, but I remember how strong the sunlight seemed. The screech of the cicadas was overpowering, like a violent squall drowning every-thing out. My uncle was seated on a bench near the entrance, absorbed in a book. When he saw us, he grinned and stood up.

Two years later, my sister died. And was put in a

tiny coffin and cremated. I was fifteen, and she was twelve. While she was being cremated I went off, apart from the rest of the family, sat on a bench in the courtyard of the crematorium, and remembered what had happened in that wind hole. The weight of time as I waited by that small cave for my little sister to come out, the thickness of the darkness enveloping me, the chill I felt to my core. Her black hair emerging from the hole, then her shoulders. All the random dirt and dust stuck to her white T-shirt.

At that time a thought struck me: that maybe even before the doctor at the hospital officially pronounced her dead two years later, her life had already been snatched from her while she was deep inside that cave. I was actually convinced of it. She'd already been lost within that hole, and left this world, but I, mistakenly thinking she was still alive, had put her on the train with me and taken her back to Tokyo. Holding her hand tightly. And we'd lived as brother and sister for two more years. But that was nothing more than a fleeting grace period. Two years later, death had crawled out of that cave to grab hold of my sister's soul. As if time was up, it was necessary to pay for what had been lent, and the owner had come to take back what was his.

At any rate now, at thirty-six, I realized again that what my little sister had confided to me in a quiet voice in that wind hole was indeed true. Alice really does exist in the world. The March Hare, the Walrus, the Cheshire Cat—they all **really exist**. And the Commendatore too, of course.

· · ·

The weather report was off the mark and we didn't have a rainstorm. Just after five a very light rain began—so fine that you could hardly tell if it was falling or not—and continued till the next morning. Right at six p.m. a large, shiny black sedan slowly made its way up the slope. It reminded me of a hearse, but of course it wasn't one, but the limousine Menshiki had sent for me. A Nissan Infiniti. The driver, in black uniform and hat, alighted from the car and, umbrella in one hand, came over to the front door and rang the bell. I opened the door and he took off his hat and made sure of my name. I left the house and got into the car. I declined the umbrella. It wasn't raining hard enough for one. The driver opened the rear door for me. Once I was inside, he closed it with a solid **thunk** (a little different from the sound of Menshiki's Jaguar). I wore a black, light, round-necked sweater, gray herringbone jacket, dark-gray wool trousers, and black suede shoes. The most formal outfit I owned. At least it didn't have paint stains.

Even after the limo came, the Commendatore still hadn't appeared. And I hadn't heard his voice. So I had no way of making sure he'd remembered the invitation from Menshiki. But he must have. He'd been looking forward to it so much there was no way he'd forgotten.

But I worried for nothing. Soon after the car had set off, I suddenly found the Commendatore, with a nonchalant look on his face, seated beside me. He was dressed in his usual white outfit (looking like it had just come from the cleaners, without a single stain), with the jewel-encrusted long sword at his waist. He was, as always, about two feet high. The whiteness and purity of his clothes stood out even more against the black leather seats of the Infiniti. He stared straight ahead, his arms folded.

"Do not say anything to me," the Commendatore said, as if reminding me. "My friends can see me, but others cannot. My friends can hear me, but others cannot. If you talk to something that cannot be seen, people will think you are very strange. Affirmative? Nod, please, if you understand."

I nodded slightly one time. The Commendatore bobbed his head in response, and afterward sat there silently, his arms folded.

It was dark out. The crows had already withdrawn to their mountain roosts. The Infiniti slowly descended the slope, drove down the road in the valley, and came to a steep slope. It wasn't that long a distance (we were just going to the other side of a narrow valley, after all), but the road was narrow, with plenty of curves. The type of road a driver of a large sedan would not be happy to navigate. The type of road more suited to a four-wheel-drive military vehicle. But the driver's expression didn't change a bit as he calmly handled the car, and we arrived safely at Menshiki's mansion.

The mansion was surrounded by a high white wall, with a solid gate in front. Large wooden double doors painted a dark brown. Like the castle gate in an Akira Kurosawa film set in the Middle Ages. The kind that

365

would look good with a couple of arrows embedded in it. The inside was completely hidden from view. Next to the gate was a plate with the house number, but no nameplate. Probably no need to have one. If someone was going to go to the trouble of coming all the way up to the top of this mountain, they would automatically know this was Menshiki's mansion. The area around the gate was brightly lit by mercury lamps. The driver got out, rang the bell, and spoke for a moment with someone on the intercom. Then he got back in his seat and waited for the gate to open remotely. There were two movable security cameras, one on each side of the gate.

The double doors slowly opened inward, and the driver entered, proceeding leisurely down the curving road on the grounds. The road was a gentle downward slope. I heard the doors close behind us—a heavy sound, as if informing us that there was no return to the world from which we had come. Pine trees lined both sides of the road, all neatly trimmed. The branches were beautifully arranged, like bonsai, and careful measures were obviously taken to keep them from getting any disease. Along the road was also a trim hedge of azaleas. Beyond this there were Japanese roses, and a clump of camellias. The house might be new, but the trees and plants all seemed to have been there since long ago. All of these were beautifully illuminated by garden lanterns.

The road ended in a circular asphalt-covered driveway. As soon as the driver parked, he leaped out the driver's side and opened the back door for me. I looked beside me but didn't see the Commendatore. But I wasn't particularly surprised, and didn't mind. He had his own patterns of behavior.

The taillights of the Infiniti politely and gracefully disappeared into the twilight darkness, leaving me standing there alone. Seen from the front like this, the house looked much cozier and less imposing than I'd expected. When I'd looked at it from across the valley it seemed like an overbearing, gaudy structure. Perhaps the impression changed depending on the angle. The front gate was at the highest point of the mountain, and then, descending the slope, the house was built as if to deliberately make use of the angle of inclination of the land.

On either side of the front door were two old stone statues, a pair of the **komainu** guardian dog figures found in Shinto shrines. On pedestals as well. They might actually have been real **komainu** brought over from somewhere. There were plantings of azaleas at the entrance, too. In May the place must be pretty colorful.

As I slowly walked toward the front door, it opened from inside and Menshiki appeared. He had on a dark-green cardigan over a white button-down shirt, and cream-colored chinos. His pure white hair was, as always, neatly combed and arranged naturally. It felt strange to see Menshiki welcoming me to his own house. I'd always seen Menshiki when he roared up to my house in his Jaguar.

He invited me in and closed the front door. The entrance foyer was spacious and nearly square, with a high ceiling. A squash court could fit inside. The indirect lighting on the wall pleasantly lit the room, and on top of a large octagonal parquet table in the middle of the foyer was a large flower vase, Ming dynasty by the look of it, overflowing with a fresh flower arrangement. A mix of three different types of large flowers (I don't know much about plants so don't know the names). Probably he'd had them specially arranged just for this evening. A frugal college student could manage to live for a month on what Menshiki probably paid the florist. At least I could have, back when I was a student. There were no windows in the foyer, just a skylight in the ceiling. The floor was well-polished marble.

The living room was down three wide steps, and though not quite big enough for a soccer field was definitely large enough for a tennis court. The southeast side was all tinted glass, with a large deck outside. It was dark, so I couldn't tell if you could see the ocean from here, but I imagine you could. On the opposite wall was an open fireplace. It wasn't the cold season yet so there was no fire lit, but firewood was neatly stacked up beside it, so a fire could be started at any time. I don't know who had stacked it up, but it was placed so beautifully it looked like a work of art in itself. There was a mantelpiece above the fireplace, with a row of old Meissen figurines.

The living room floor was also marble, but covered with a variety of rugs. Antique Persian rugs, with such exquisite patterns and colors they looked less like practical objects than artistic handicrafts. I hesitated to step on them. There were several low tables and a scattering of flower vases, all full of fresh flowers. Each vase looked like a valuable antique. It was all in nice taste, and expensive. Here's hoping we don't have a big earthquake, was my thought.

The ceiling was high, the lighting subdued. Refined indirect lighting on the walls, a few floor lamps, and reading lamps on the tables. At the back of the room was a black grand piano. I'd never seen a Steinway concert grand piano in a room like this, one that made it seem smaller than it was. On top of the piano was a metronome and sheet music. Perhaps Menshiki played. Or maybe he invited Maurizio Pollini over for dinner every once in a while.

Overall, though, the room was modestly decorated, and I felt relieved. There was nothing excessive, but it didn't have an **empty** feeling. A comfortable room, despite the size. There was a certain sense of warmth about it, you might say. Half a dozen tasteful paintings graced the walls, all modestly displayed. One of them looked like a real Léger, but I could have been mistaken.

Menshiki motioned me to a large brown leather sofa. He sat on a matching easy chair across from me. The sofa was extremely comfortable, neither too hard nor too soft. The kind of sofa that naturally adjusted to whoever sat on it. Of course if you think about it (not that it was something one had to think about), Menshiki wasn't about to put an uncomfortable sofa in his living room.

As if he'd been waiting for us to get settled, as soon

as we did, a man glided in from somewhere. A stunningly handsome young man. He wasn't so tall, but was slim and had a refined bearing about him. His skin was evenly tanned, with lustrous hair done up in a ponytail. He would look good at the beach, in surfing shorts, carrying a shortboard, though today he was dressed in a clean white shirt and black bow tie. A pleasant smile played about his lips.

"Would you care for a cocktail?" he asked me. "Please order whatever you'd like."

"I'll have a Balalaika," I said, after considering it for a few seconds. Not that I really wanted a Balalaika, but I wanted to test the young bartender to see if he really could make any kind of drink.

"I'll have the same," Menshiki said.

The young man smiled pleasantly and soundlessly withdrew.

I glanced at the spot next to me on the sofa but didn't see the Commendatore. But he had to be here somewhere in the house. He'd ridden with me in the car up to the house, and had come along with me.

"Is something the matter?" Menshiki asked me. He'd followed my glance.

"No, just admiring your gorgeous house."

"It's a little too much, don't you think?" Menshiki said, a smile rising to his face.

"No, it's much more serene than I imagined," I answered honestly. "From a distance it does look a bit luxurious. Like a luxury cruise ship on the ocean. But inside it's surprisingly relaxed. My impression's completely changed."

Menshiki listened and nodded. "I'm happy to hear that, but it took quite a lot of work to get it to that point. I bought the house already built, and when I purchased it, it was pretty gaudy. Flashy, you might say. A man who ran a big-box store built it. The extremes of bad taste of the nouveau riche, you could say, and not my style at all. So I did a huge renovation after I bought it. Which took a lot of time, effort, and money."

As if remembering all that work, Menshiki looked down and sighed. It really must not have suited his taste at all.

"Wouldn't it have been a lot cheaper to build your own house?" I asked.

Menshiki smiled, his white teeth peeking from between his lips. "You're absolutely right. That would have been the sensible thing to do. But I had my own reasons. Reasons why it had to be this house and no other."

I waited for the story to go on, but it didn't.

"Wasn't the Commendatore supposed to be with you tonight?" Menshiki asked.

"I think he'll be along later," I said. "We were together on the trip up to your house and then he suddenly vanished. I think he must be taking a tour of your house. You don't mind, do you?"

Menshiki spread his hands wide. "Of course. Of course I don't mind. He's welcome to look around as much as he likes."

The young man from before appeared, carrying two cocktails on a silver tray. The cocktail glasses were exquisitely cut crystal. Baccarat, would be my guess. They glittered in the light from the floor lamp. Next to them was a Koimari ceramic plate with slices of various cheeses and cashews. There were small monogrammed linen napkins and a set of silver knives and forks. Everything well thought out.

Menshiki and I picked up our cocktail glasses and made a toast. He toasted the completion of his portrait, and I thanked him. We lightly put our lips to the rim of the glasses. A Balalaika is made of one part each of vodka, Cointreau, and lemon juice. A simple concoction, but unless it's as bitingly freezing as the North Pole, it doesn't taste good. If somebody who doesn't have the right touch mixes it, it ends up tasting diluted, watery. This Balalaika was amazingly delicious, with an almost perfect bite to it.

"This is delicious," I said, impressed.

"He's quite good," Menshiki said lightly.

Of course he is, I thought. Menshiki wasn't about to hire a bad bartender. And of course he had Cointreau on hand, antique crystal glasses, and a Koimari serving plate.

As we sipped our cocktails and munched on some nuts, we talked about various topics. Mainly about my painting. He asked what I was working on now and I explained. I told him I was working on a portrait of a man whose name and background I knew nothing about, someone I had encountered in a distant town.

"A portrait?" Menshiki asked, sounding surprised.

"A portrait, but not a typical commercial portrait.

More of an abstract-style portrait, one in which I let my imagination run free. But the motif is definitely a portrait. You might say it's the foundation of the painting."

"Like when you painted my portrait?"

"Exactly. Though this time I wasn't commissioned. It's something I decided to paint on my own."

Menshiki considered this. "Maybe my portrait inspired you to be more creative?"

"No doubt. Though I'm only at the point where my creativity is finally starting to kick in."

Menshiki took another soundless sip of his cocktail, with what I took to be a satisfied gleam deep in his eyes.

"Nothing could make me happier," he said. "The fact that I may have been of help to you, that is. If you don't mind, could I see that new painting when it's finished?"

"I'd be happy to show it to you, provided I'm happy with the result."

I looked over at the grand piano in a corner of the room. "Do you play piano, Mr. Menshiki? That's a beautiful instrument."

Menshiki nodded slightly. "I'm not good, but I do play a little. I took piano lessons as a child. Five or six years from the time I entered elementary school until I graduated. Then I got busy with schoolwork and quit taking lessons. I wish I hadn't, but the piano lessons had worn me out. So my fingers don't move the way I'd like them to, but I'm good at reading sheet music. I play some simple pieces every once in a while just for my own amusement, for a change of pace. I'm not good enough to play for other people, and I never touch the keys when other people are here."

I went ahead and asked a question I'd been wanting to ask for a long time. "Doesn't it feel a little too spacious for you, living in such a big house all by yourself?"

"No, I don't think so," Menshiki replied immediately. "Not at all. I've always preferred being by myself. Consider the cerebral cortex for a moment. Humans are provided with a wonderfully precise and efficient cerebral cortex. But normally we use, at most, less than ten percent of it. We've been divinely provided with this amazing, highly efficient organ, but sadly we haven't the ability to use it completely. You could compare it to a four-person family living in a magnificent, grand mansion but using only one small room. All the other rooms are unused and neglected. When you think that way, it's not so unnatural that I live in this house by myself."

"When you put it that way, I suppose it makes sense," I said. It was an interesting analogy.

Menshiki rolled a few cashews around in his hand for a moment and then spoke. "That highly efficient cerebral cortex might seem wasted at first, but without it we wouldn't be able to think abstract thoughts, or enter the realm of the metaphysical. Even though we use but a small part of it, the cerebral cortex has that capacity. If we could use all the rest of it, what would we be capable of, I wonder. Isn't it fascinating to consider?"

"But in exchange for that efficient brain—the price we paid for that magnificent mansion, in other words—mankind had to neglect all kinds of basic abilities. Right?"

"Exactly," Menshiki said. "Even without abstract thought or metaphysical theorizing, just standing on two legs and using clubs gave mankind more than enough skill to win the race for survival on earth. These other abilities aren't that necessary. And in exchange for our hyper-capable cerebral cortexes, of necessity we have to give up lots of other physical abilities. For example, dogs have a sense of smell several thousand times better than humans, and a sense of hearing tens of times better. But we're able to amass complex hypotheses. We're able to compare and contrast the cosmos and the microcosmos, and appreciate Van Gogh and Mozart. We can read Proust—if you want to, that is—and collect Koimari porcelain and Persian rugs. Not something a dog can do."

"Marcel Proust used a sense of smell inferior to that of a dog's to write his lengthy novel."

Menshiki laughed. "That he did. I'm just speaking in generalities."

"The question then is whether or not an idea can be treated as an autonomous entity or not, right?"

"Exactly."

Exactly, the Commendatore whispered into my ear. But following his earlier warning, I didn't look around me.

•   •   •

After this, Menshiki led me into his study. There were broad stairs that led out of the living room, and we took them to the floor below. Somehow these stairs seemed more than stairs, and part of the habitable space in the house. We went down the hallway past several bedrooms (I didn't count how many, but maybe one of them was the locked "Bluebeard's secret room" my girlfriend spoke of), and at the end was the study. It wasn't an especially big room, but of course, it wasn't cramped either. Built to be just the right amount of space. There were few windows in the study, just long, narrow windows like skylights near the ceiling on one wall. All that was visible from the windows were pine branches and the sky visible through the branches. (The room didn't seem to particularly require sunlight or a view.) Without many windows, the walls were that much bigger. One wall was floor-to-ceiling built-in bookcases, one section of which was for a shelf for CDs. The bookshelves were packed with books of all sizes. There was a wooden stepladder to reach the books on the upper shelves. All the books seemed to have been used at one time or another. It was clear that this was a practical collection used by a devoted reader, not decorative bookshelves.

A large office desk faced away from one wall, with two computers on top, a desktop model and a laptop. There were a couple of cups holding pens and pencils, and a neat pile of paperwork. On another wall was a beautiful, expensive-looking stereo set, and on the opposite wall, facing directly across from the desk, sat a pair of tall, narrow speakers. They were about my height (five feet eight), the cases made of high-quality mahogany. An Art Deco armchair for reading and listening to music was in the middle of the room, and next to it a stainless-steel standing lamp for reading. I imagined that Menshiki spent a large part of his days alone in this room.

My portrait of Menshiki was hanging on the wall, at about eye level, exactly between the two speakers. Bare, not yet framed. It looked like a natural part of the room, as if it had been hanging there for a long time. A painting I'd basically created in one intense sitting, yet in this study that uninhibited aspect of it felt, strangely enough, neatly contained. The unique feeling of the place comfortably stilled the painting's plunge-ahead vigor. And unmistakably concealed within that painting was Menshiki's face. To me, in fact, it looked like Menshiki himself was contained within.

I had most definitely painted that painting, but once it had left my hands and become Menshiki's possession, hanging on his study wall, it had transformed into something beyond my reach. Now it was **Menshiki's painting,** not mine. Even if I tried to comprehend something within it, like a slippery, nimble fish the painting would slip out of my hands. Like a woman who'd once been mine but was now someone else's.

"What do you think? Doesn't it fit this room perfectly?"

Menshiki was referring to the painting, of course. I nodded without a word.

"I tried putting it in lots of different rooms. But in the end I knew this was the best room and the perfect spot for it. The amount of space, the way the light hits it, the whole atmosphere is perfect. What I enjoy most is gazing at the picture from that reading chair."

"Could I give it a try?" I said, pointing to the reading chair.

"Of course. Go right ahead."

I sat down on that leather chair, leaned back into the gentle curve it inscribed, and rested my legs on the ottoman. I brought my hands together on my chest and once more gazed at the painting. As Menshiki said, this was the ideal spot from which to appreciate it. Seen from that chair (a chair so comfortable it left nothing to be desired), my painting hanging on the wall in front of me had a quiet, calm persuasiveness that took me by surprise. It looked like almost a completely different work from when it was in my studio, as if it had acquired, since coming here, its rightful life force. Or something like that. And at the same time it seemed to have severed any contact with me, its creator.

Menshiki used a remote control to turn on some music at just the right low volume. A Schubert string quartet I was familiar with. Composition D804. The sound coming out of those speakers was clear, fine-grained, refined, and elegant. Compared with the sound from the speakers in Tomohiko Amada's home, which had a simpler, unadorned tone, it seemed like different music altogether.

Suddenly the Commendatore was in the room.

He was seated on the stepladder in front of the bookshelves, his arms folded, looking at my painting. When I glanced at him he shook his head slightly, signaling that I shouldn't look at him. I returned my gaze to the painting.

"Thank you very much," I said to Menshiki as I rose from the chair. "That's the perfect place to hang it."

Menshiki beamed and shook his head. "No, I should be the one thanking **you**. Now that it's found a home here, I'm liking it more and more. When I look at it, I feel like I'm standing in front of . . . a special mirror. I'm inside there, but that's not me, entirely. It's a little different me. When I stare at it for a while, a strange feeling comes over me."

As he listened to the Schubert, Menshiki again turned his attention to a silent appraisal of the painting. The Commendatore, still seated on the stepladder, likewise gazed at the painting with narrowed eyes, as if teasingly imitating him (though I doubt that was his intention).

Menshiki glanced over at the clock on the wall. "Let's go to the dining room. Dinner should be just about ready. I do hope the Commendatore shows up."

I looked at the stepladder. The Commendatore was no longer there.

"I think he's already here," I said.

"I'm glad," Menshiki said, sounding relieved. He touched the remote control and stopped the Schubert. "There's a place prepared for him, of course. It's really a shame, though, that he won't be able to enjoy eating the meal."

Menshiki explained that on the floor below where we were currently seated, there was a storehouse, a laundry room, and a gym. The gym was outfitted with all sorts of workout equipment. It had a sound system so he could enjoy music while he exercised. Once a week a trainer came and led him through strength-training exercises. There was also an efficiency-sized residence for a live-in maid. It had a simple kitchen and small bathroom, though nobody was using it at present. There used to be a small indoor pool, but it wasn't very practical and took a lot of upkeep, so he had had it filled in and made into a greenhouse. Some-day he might build a two-lane twenty-five-meter lap pool, he said. If I do, he said, I'd love for you to come over and swim. That would be wonderful, I said.

We headed to the dining room.

24

MERELY GATHERING RAW DATA

The dining room was on the same floor as the study. The kitchen was in back of it. The dining room was a long room, with a large, long table in the middle. The oak table was about four inches thick, and big enough for ten people. A solid table that would look good hosting a banquet for Robin Hood and his men. But it was simply the two of us, Menshiki and myself, not a merry band of outlaws. A place was set for the Commendatore, but he wasn't there. A place mat, silverware, and an empty glass were ready for him, but they were just for show. A courtesy to indicate that was his place.

Like in the living room, one long wall was entirely glass. It looked out over the mountain range beyond the valley. Just as I could see Menshiki's house from mine, my house should be visible from his. The house I lived in, though, was nowhere as big as Menshiki's mansion, and it was a wooden building whose subdued color didn't stand out, so in the dark I couldn't make out where it was. There weren't many homes built here, but in each of the houses that dotted the mountains there were clearly lights on inside. It was dinnertime. People were with their families at the dinner table, about to enjoy a hot meal. I could sense that slight warmth in those lights.

In contrast, on the other side of the valley, Menshiki, I, and the Commendatore were seated at that large table, about to begin an eccentric, formal dinner party. Outside a fine rain continued to silently fall. But there was almost no wind, and it was a typically hushed autumn night. I looked out the window and thought again about the hole. About the lonely stone-lined chamber behind the little shrine. Even as we sat here the hole was there, dark and dank. Memories of that scene brought a special chill to me, deep inside.

"I found this table while traveling in Italy," Menshiki said after I'd complimented it. He didn't sound like he was bragging, simply stating facts. "I ran across it in a furniture store in Lucca, purchased it, and had it shipped here. It's so heavy it was quite a task to transport it."

"Do you go abroad very often?"

His lips twisted up a bit, then relaxed. "I used to. Part business, part pleasure. Not so many opportunities to do so these days. I'm doing a different sort of work now. Plus I no longer like to go out much anymore. Most of the time I'm here."

To indicate more clearly what he meant by "here," he motioned toward the house with his hand. I expected him to add more about this change in his work, but that's all he said. As always, he didn't seem eager to say much about his work, and I didn't press him about it.

"I thought we'd start with some well-chilled champagne, if that's all right with you. You don't mind?"

"Of course not," I said. "I'll leave it all up to you."

Menshiki made a faint motion, and the ponytailed young man came over and poured cold champagne into long narrow flutes. Pleasant little bubbles fizzed up in the glasses, so light and thin they seemed made of high-quality paper. We toasted each other across the table. Then Menshiki respectfully lifted his glass to the unoccupied seat for the Commendatore.

"Thank you so much for coming, Commendatore," he said.

There was, naturally, no reply from the Commendatore.

As he enjoyed the champagne, Menshiki talked about opera. About how, on a trip to Sicily, he saw a spectacular performance of Verdi's **Ernani** at the Catania opera house. The person seated next to him sang along with the performers, all the while snacking on mandarin oranges. And how he'd had some amazing champagne there.

The Commendatore finally made an appearance in the dining room, though not at the seat at the table prepared for him. Given his short stature, he would have only come up to nose level, hidden by the table. Instead he plunked himself down on a kind of display shelf diagonally behind Menshiki. He was about five feet off the floor, lightly swinging his feet clad in those oddly shaped black shoes. I raised my glass slightly to him so that Menshiki wouldn't see. As expected, the Commendatore acted as if he didn't notice.

The meal was served at this point. There was an open serving slot between the kitchen and the dining room and the bow-tied, ponytailed young man brought each dish placed there one by one to our table. For a first course, we had a beautiful dish of organic vegetables and fresh isaki fish. Accompanied by white wine. The ponytailed young man uncorked the bottle as carefully as if he were an explosives expert handling a land mine. No explanation of what kind of wine it was or where it was from, though of course it was superb. Menshiki wasn't about to serve a less-than-perfect wine.

After that we were served a salad of lotus root, calamari, and white beans. Then a sea turtle soup. The fish dish was monkfish.

"It's a bit early in the season for it, but I heard that down at the harbor they got hold of some excellent monkfish," Menshiki said. The fish was certainly fresh and amazing. Firm texture, a refined sweetness, but still a clean aftertaste. Lightly steamed, then served with (what I took to be) a tarragon sauce.

Next came thick venison steaks. There was again an explanation of the special sauce, but it was so full of specialized terms I couldn't remember half of it. At any rate, a wonderfully fragrant sauce.

The ponytailed young man poured red wine into our glasses. Menshiki explained that the bottle had been opened an hour before and decanted.

"It's breathed nicely, and it should be just the peak time to drink it."

I knew nothing about aerating wine, but it had a deep flavor. When your tongue first encountered it, then when you held it in your mouth, and finally when you drank it down, the flavor was different each time. It was like a mysterious woman whose beauty changes slightly depending on the angle and light. The wine left a pleasant aftertaste.

"It's Bordeaux," Menshiki said. "I won't sing its praises. Just know it's a Bordeaux."

"It's the kind of wine that once you started listing its good points, you'd have a long list."

Menshiki smiled. Pleasant wrinkles formed at the corners of his eyes. "You're exactly right. It would be very long if you listed its merits. But I don't particularly like to do that with wines. I'm not good at enumerating the merits of things, no matter what they are. It's just a delicious wine—that's enough, right?"

I had no objections to that.

All this time the Commendatore watched us drinking and eating from his perch on the display shelf. He sat there, unmoving, diligently observing the scene there down to the smallest detail, but didn't seem to have any reaction to what he was seeing. Like he told me once, he merely observes. He doesn't judge, or have any partiality toward it. He's merely gathering raw data.

This might be how he observed me and my girlfriend making love in bed in the afternoons. The thought unsettled me. He'd told me that watching people have sex was for him no different from watching morning radio exercise routines or someone sweeping a chimney. And that might very well be the case. But the fact remained that it was disconcerting to think of being observed.

An hour and a half later, Menshiki and I finally arrived at dessert (a soufflé) and espresso. A long but fulfilling journey. For the first time, the chef came out of the kitchen and over to the dining table. A tall man, in a white chef's outfit. In his mid-thirties would be my guess, with a sparse black beard. He greeted me politely.

"The food was amazing," I told him. "I've hardly ever had anything so delicious."

Those were my honest feelings. I still couldn't believe that a chef who made such exquisite dishes ran a small, unknown French restaurant near the harbor in Odawara.

"Thank you very much," he said, smiling brightly. "Mr. Menshiki's always been very kind to me."

He bowed and returned to the kitchen.

"I wonder if the Commendatore was satisfied, too?" Menshiki said after the chef had left, a concerned look on his face. He didn't appear to be play-acting. He seemed genuinely concerned.

"I'm sure he is," I replied with a straight face. "It's a shame, of course, that he couldn't enjoy the fabulous meal, but he must have enjoyed the atmosphere."

"I do hope so."

Of course I enjoyed it, the Commendatore whispered in my ear.

Menshiki suggested an after-dinner drink, but I declined. I was so full I really couldn't manage anything else. He had a brandy.

"There was something that I wanted to ask you," Menshiki said as he slowly swirled the brandy in the oversized glass. "It's an odd question, and I hope you're not offended."

"Feel free to ask me anything."

He took a small sip of brandy, tasting it. Then quietly laid his glass on the table.

"It's about the pit in the woods," Menshiki said. "The other day I spent about an hour in that stone chamber. No flashlight, seated alone at the bottom of the pit. The cover was on top, and rocks on top of that to hold it down. And I told you, 'Please come back in an hour and get me out of here.' Correct?"

"That's right."

"Why do you think I did that?"

"I have no idea," I answered honestly.

"I needed to do that," Menshiki said. "I can't explain it, but sometimes I need to do **that**. Be left all alone in a cramped, dark, completely silent space."

I was silent, waiting for his next words.

Menshiki continued. "Here's my question to you. During that hour did you ever find yourself, even for a moment, wanting to abandon me in that pit? Tempted to just leave me behind at the bottom of that dark hole?"

I couldn't grasp what he was getting at. "**Abandon you?**"

Menshiki touched his right temple and rubbed it, as if checking out a scar. "This is what I mean. I was at the bottom of that pit, a little less than nine feet deep and six feet across. The ladder had been pulled up. The stones in the wall were all densely laid together, and there was no way to climb up. And the cover was on tight. In mountains like these I could yell at the top of my voice or ring the bell, but no one would ever hear me—though of course **you** might. In other words, I couldn't get back to the surface on my own. If you hadn't come back, I'd have had to stay in the pit forever. Isn't that so?"

"That could be."

The fingers of his right hand were still at his temple. He'd stopped rubbing. "What I'd like to know is whether during that hour the thought ever occurred to you, even for a moment, **I'll just leave that man inside the pit. Leave him the way he is.** Tell me the truth, it won't offend me."

He took his fingers from his temple, reached for the glass of brandy, and again slowly held it up and swirled it. This time, though, he didn't take a sip. Eyes narrowed, he inhaled the aroma and put the glass back on the table.

"That thought never occurred to me," I answered honestly. "**Even for a moment.** All I thought about was that after an hour I had to take the cover off and get you out of there."

"Really?"

"One hundred percent."

"Well, if I had been in your position . . ." Menshiki said, sounding confessional. His voice was quite calm. "I'm sure I would have thought of that. I definitely would have been tempted to leave you inside that pit forever. I would have thought, This is the chance of a lifetime."

No words came to me.

Menshiki said, "Down at the bottom of the pit that's what I was thinking about the whole time. That if I was in your position I would definitely consider it. It's a strange thing. You were the one on the surface and I was the one at the bottom of the pit, but all that time I was picturing me on the surface and you at the bottom."

"But if you'd actually abandoned me in the pit I might have starved to death. I might have turned into an actual mummy, ringing a bell. You're saying you'd be okay with that?"

"It's just a fantasy. Or delusion, perhaps. **Of course** I would never actually do that. I was just imagining the scenario. Just mentally playing with the concept of death. So don't worry. What I mean is, I find it hard to fathom that you didn't feel the same temptation."

I said, "Weren't you afraid, Mr. Menshiki, being down at the bottom of that dark pit all alone? Thinking that I might be tempted to abandon you there?"

Menshiki shook his head. "No, I wasn't afraid. Deep inside me I may have actually been hoping you would."

"**Hoping** I would?" I said, surprised. "That I would leave you down in that pit?"

"Exactly."

"In other words, you were okay with being abandoned down there?"

"Don't get me wrong, it wasn't that I was okay with dying. Even I still have some attachment to this life. And starving to death or dying of lack of water aren't the ways I'd like to go. All I wanted was to **try to get closer to death,** even if just a little more. I know that boundary is a very fine line."

I thought about what he said, though I still couldn't grasp what he meant. I casually glanced over at the Commendatore, still seated on the display shelf. His face was bereft of expression.

Menshiki went on. "When you're locked up alone in a cramped, dark place, the most frightening thing isn't death. The most terrifying thought is that **I might have to live here forever.** Once you think that, the terror makes it hard to breathe. The walls close in on you and the delusion grabs you that you're going to be crushed. In order to survive, a person has to overcome that fear. Which means conquering yourself. And in order to do that, you need to get as close to death as you possibly can."

"But there's a danger to that."

"Like when Icarus flew close to the sun. It's not easy to know how close you can go, where that line is. You put your life at risk doing it."

"But if you avoid approaching it, you can't overcome fear and conquer yourself."

"Precisely. If you can't do that, you can't take your-self to the next level," Menshiki said. He seemed to be considering something. And then suddenly—at least it seemed sudden to me—he stood up, went over to the window, and looked out.

"It's still raining a little, but not so hard. Do you mind going out on the deck? There's something I want to show you."

We walked up the steps from the dining room to the living room and then out to the deck. It was a large deck, with a Mediterranean tiled floor. We went over to the wooden railing and gazed out at the valley. It was like a tourist lookout, and we were afforded a view of the entire valley. A fine rain was still falling, more like mist at this point. The lights were still on in people's homes across the valley. It was the same valley, but viewed from the opposite side like this, the scenery looked transformed.

A section of the deck was roofed over, with a chaise longue beneath it, for sunbathing or perhaps reading. Next to it was a low glass-topped table to put drinks or books on. And also a large planter with a decora-tive green plant, and a tall piece of equipment of some kind, covered in plastic. There was a spotlight on the wall, but it wasn't turned on. The lights in the living room were turned down low.

"I wonder which direction my house is?" I asked Menshiki.

Menshiki pointed to the right. "It's over there."

I stared hard in that direction, but with the lights out and the misty rain I couldn't locate it.

"I can't see it," I told him.

"Just a moment," Menshiki said, and walked over to where the chaise longue was. He removed the plastic cover from the piece of equipment and carried it over. It looked like a pair of binoculars on a tripod. The binoculars weren't big, but looked odd, different from normal ones. They were a drab olive green and the crude shape made it appear like some optical instrument for surveying. He placed this beside the railing, pointed it, and carefully focused.

"Here, take a look. This is where you live," he said.

I squinted through the binoculars. They had a clear field of vision, with high magnification. Not your typical binoculars that you find in a store. Through the faint vale of misty rain the far-off scenery looked close enough to touch. And it definitely was the house I was living in. The terrace was there, the lounge chair I always sat in. Beyond that was the living room, and next to it, my painting studio. With the lights off I couldn't make out the interior, though during the day you probably could. It felt strange to see (or peek into) the place where I lived.

"Don't worry," Menshiki said from behind me, as if reading my mind. "No need to be concerned. I don't encroach on your privacy. I mean, I hardly ever turn these binoculars on your house. Trust me. What I want to see is **something else.**"

"What do you want to see?" I said. I took my eye from the binoculars, turned around, and looked at him. His face was cool, inscrutable as always. At night on the deck, though, his hair looked whiter than ever.

"I'll show you," Menshiki said. With a practiced hand he swung the binoculars slightly to the north and swiftly refocused. He took a step back and said, "Please take a look."

I looked through the binoculars. In the circular field of vision I saw an elegant wooden house halfway up the mountain. A two-story building also constructed to take advantage of the slope, with a terrace facing this direction. On a map it would be my nearest neighbor, but because of the topography there was no road linking us, so one would have to go down to the bottom of the mountain and ascend once more on a separate road to access it. Lights were on in the windows, but the curtains were drawn, and I couldn't see inside. If the curtains were open, though, and the lights on, you would be able to see the people inside. Very possible with binoculars this powerful.

"These are NATO-issue military binoculars. They're not sold anywhere, so it wasn't easy to get hold of them. They're bright, so you can make out images well even in the dark."

I took my eyes away from the binoculars and looked at Menshiki. "This house is **what you want to see?**"

"Correct. But don't get the wrong idea. I'm no voyeur."

He glanced through the binoculars one last time, then put them and the tripod back where they were and placed the plastic cover over them.

"Let's go inside. We don't want to catch cold," Menshiki said. We went back into the living room, and sat on the sofa and armchair. The ponytailed young man sidled over and asked if we'd like anything to drink, but both of us declined.

"Thank you very much for tonight," Menshiki said to the young man. "Feel free to go now." The young man bowed and withdrew.

The Commendatore was now seated on top of the piano. The black Steinway full grand. He looked like he preferred this spot to where he had been sitting before. The jewels on the top handle of his long sword caught the light with a proud glint.

"In that house over there," Menshiki began, "lives the girl who **may be my daughter**. I like to see her, even if it's from a distance."

For quite some time I was speechless.

"Do you remember? What I told you about the daughter my former girlfriend had, after she married another man? That she might be mine?"

"Of course. The woman who was stung by hornets and died. Her daughter would be thirteen. Right?"

Menshiki gave a short, concise nod. "She lives in **that house** with her father. In that house across the valley."

It took a while to put the myriad questions that welled up in my mind in some kind of order. Menshiki waited silently all this time, patiently waiting for my reaction.

I said, "In other words, in order to see that young girl who might be your daughter through the binoculars every day, you bought this mansion directly across the valley. You paid a lot of money and a great deal to renovate this house **for that sole purpose**. Is that what you're saying?"

Menshiki said, "Yes, that's it. This is the ideal spot to be able to observe her house. I had to get this mansion no matter what. There was no other lot around here that I could get a building permit for. And ever since, I've been looking for her across the valley through my binoculars, almost every day. Though I should say that the days I can't see her far outnumber the days I can."

"So you live alone, keeping people out as much as you can, so no one interferes with that pursuit."

Menshiki nodded again. "That's right. I don't want anyone to bother me. No one to disturb things. That's what I'm looking for. I need unlimited solitude. You're the only other person in the world who knows this secret. It wouldn't be good to confess this kind of delicate thing to people."

You got that right, I thought. And this thought occurred to me as well: Then why did you just tell **me**?

"Then why did you just tell me?" I asked Menshiki. "Is there some special reason?"

Menshiki recrossed his legs and looked straight at me. His voice was soft. "Yes, of course there's a reason. I have a special favor to ask of you."

25

HOW MUCH LONELINESS THE TRUTH CAN CAUSE

I have a special favor to ask of you," Menshiki said.

From his tone I guessed he'd been waiting for the right moment to bring this up. And that this was the real reason he had invited me (and the Commendatore) to dinner. In order to reveal his secret and bring up this request.

"If it's something I can help with, of course," I said.

Menshiki gazed into my eyes, and then spoke. "More than something you can help with, it's something only **you** can help with."

I was suddenly dying for a cigarette. When I got married I used that as the incentive to stop smoking, and in the nearly seven years since, I hadn't smoked a single cigarette. It was tough quitting—I'd been a pretty heavy smoker—but nowadays I never had the urge. But at that instant, for the first time in forever, I thought about how great it would be to have a cigarette between my lips and light it. I could hear the scratch of the match.

"What could that possibly be?" I asked. Not that I particularly wanted to know—I'd prefer to get by not knowing—but the way the conversation was going, I had to ask.

"Well, I'd like you to paint her portrait," Menshiki said.

In my head I had to dismantle the context of his words, then reassemble it all. Though it was a very simple context.

"You mean you want me to paint the portrait of this girl who **may be** your daughter."

Menshiki nodded. "Exactly. That's what I want you to do. And not from a photograph, but actually have her pose for you and paint the picture with her as the model. Have her come to your studio, like when you painted me. That's my only condition. How you paint her is up to you—do it any way you want. I promise I won't have any other requests later on."

I was at a loss for words. Several questions immediately occurred to me, and I asked the first one that came to mind. "But how can I convince the girl to do that? I might be her neighbor, but I can't very well just suggest to a young girl I don't know that **I want to paint your portrait, so would you model for me?**"

"No, of course not. That would make her suspicious for sure."

"Then do you have any good ideas?"

Menshiki looked at me for a time, then, like quietly opening a door and tiptoeing into a back room of a house, he slowly opened his mouth. "Actually, you already know her. And she knows you very well."

"I already know her?"

"You do. Her name is Mariye—Mariye Akikawa. **Aki**—the character for 'autumn'—and **kawa**, 'river.' **Mariye** is spelled out in hiragana. You do know her, right?"

Mariye Akikawa. I'd heard the name before, but it felt like some temporary obstruction was keeping me from putting name and face together. Finally the pieces fell into place.

I said, "Mariye Akikawa is in my children's art class in Odawara, isn't she?"

Menshiki nodded. "That's right. Exactly. You're her painting teacher."

Mariye Akikawa was a small, quiet thirteen-year-old girl in the children's art class I taught. The class was for elementary school children, and as a junior high student, she was the eldest, but she was so reserved she didn't stand out at all, even though she was with the younger children. She always sat in a corner, trying to stay under the radar. I remembered her because something about her reminded me of my late sister, and she was about the same age as my sister when she passed away.

Mariye Akikawa hardly ever spoke in class. If I said something to her she just nodded, with barely a word in response. When she absolutely had to say something, she spoke it in such a small voice I often had to ask her to repeat herself. She seemed tense, unable to look me straight in the eye. But she loved painting, and the expression in her eyes radically transformed whenever she held a brush and was working on a canvas. Her gaze became focused, her eyes filled with an intense gleam. And her paintings were quite appealing. Not skilled, exactly, but eye-catching. Her use of colors was especially unique. All in all, a curious sort of girl.

Her glossy black hair fell straight down, her features as lovely as a doll's. So beautiful, in fact, when you looked at her whole face, there was the sense of it being detached from reality. Her features were objectively attractive, but most people would hesitate to label her beautiful. Something—perhaps that special raw, unpolished aspect that certain young girls exude in adolescence—interfered with the flow of beauty that should have been there. But someday that blockage might be removed and she would turn into a truly lovely girl. That was still a ways off, though. Now that I thought of it, my sister's features were similar in that way. I often used to think she didn't appear as beautiful as I knew she could be.

"So Mariye Akikawa **might** be your real daughter. And she lives in the house across the valley," I said. "And I'm to paint a portrait with her as model. That's what you're asking?"

"I'd prefer to see it as a **request,** rather than that I'm **commissioning** the work. And if you're okay with it, once the painting is finished I'd like to buy it and hang it on the wall in this house. That's what I want. Or rather what I'm requesting."

Still, there was something about all this I couldn't quite swallow. I had a faint apprehension that things wouldn't simply end there.

"And that's it? That's all you want?" I asked.

Menshiki slowly inhaled and breathed out. "Honestly, there's one other thing I'd like you to do."

"Which is—?"

"A very small thing." His voice was quiet, but with a certain force behind it. "When she's sitting for the portrait, I'd like to visit you. Make it seem like I just happened to stop by. Once is enough. And it can be for just a short time, I don't mind. Just let me be in the same room as her, and breathe the same air. I won't ask for anything more. And I can assure you I won't do anything to get in your way."

I thought about it. And the more I did, the more uncomfortable I felt. I've never been cut out to act as an intermediary. I don't enjoy getting caught up in the flow of somebody else's strong emotions—no matter what emotions they might be. The role didn't suit me. But the fact was that I also wanted to do something for Menshiki. I had to think carefully about my reply.

"We can talk about that later on," I said. "The first thing is whether or not Mariye will agree to sit for the painting. That's the first step. She's a very quiet girl, like a bashful cat. She might not want to model. Or else her parents might not give permission. They don't really know my background, so they'll be pretty wary, I would imagine."

"I know Mr. Matsushima very well, the man who runs the arts-and-culture center," Menshiki said coolly. "And I'm also, coincidentally, an investor, a financial supporter of the school. I think if Mr. Matsushima puts in a good word, things will go smoothly. You're an upright person, an artist with a solid career, and if he recommends you, I think it will assuage any concerns that her parents might have."

He's already got it all mapped out, I thought. He's already anticipated what might happen, like the opening moves of a game of go. Nothing **coincidental** about it.

Menshiki went on. "Mariye Akikawa's unmarried aunt takes care of her. Her father's younger sister. I believe I mentioned this before, but after Mariye's mother died, this aunt came to live with them and has been like a mother to Mariye. Her father is too busy with work to be very involved. So as long as the aunt is persuaded, things should work out fine. Once she agrees to have Mariye model, I would expect the aunt to accompany her to your house as her guardian. There's no way she'd allow a young girl to go by herself to the house of a man living alone."

"But will she really give permission for Mariye to model?"

"Let me handle that. As long as you agree to paint her portrait, I'll take care of any other practical issues that come up."

I had little doubt he'd be able to "take care of" any of these other "practical issues." That was his forte. But was it good for me to get so deeply involved in those problems—all these complex interpersonal relations? Didn't Menshiki have his own plans and intentions that went beyond what he was revealing to me?

"Can I be totally honest with you?" I said. "Maybe it isn't my place to say this, but I'd like you to hear me out."

"Of course. Say whatever you want."

"Isn't it better, before you put this plan into action, that you determine whether or not Mariye Akikawa really **is** your child? If you find out she isn't, then there's no need to go to all this trouble. It might not be easy, but there has to be a way. I think if anyone could discover that, you could. Even if I paint her portrait, and it's hanging next to yours, that's not going to solve anything."

Menshiki paused before replying. "If I wanted to scientifically determine if Mariye Akikawa is related by blood to me, I could. It might take some effort, but it's not impossible. The thing is—I don't want to."

"Why not?"

"Because whether she's my child or not isn't a de-termining factor."

I gazed at him, mouth shut. He shook his head, his abundant white hair waving, like it was fluttering in the breeze. When he spoke, his voice was calm, like he was explaining to some large, intelligent dog how to conjugate simple verbs.

"I'm not saying either way is fine. It's just that I don't feel like determining the facts. Maybe Mariye Akikawa is my biological child. And maybe she isn't. But what if I do determine that she's my real child— then what? I announce to her that I'm her real father? Try to get custody? I can't do that."

Menshiki shook his head again, rubbing his hands together on his lap like it was a cold night and he was warming himself before a fireplace. He continued.

"Mariye Akikawa is living a peaceful life in that

house with her father and her aunt. Yes, her mother died, but the family—despite some issues her father has—is relatively healthy and functional. She's close to her aunt. She's made a life for herself. If I suddenly appear on the scene announcing that I'm her real father, even if I could prove it scientifically, will that solve anything? The truth will actually confuse things. And it's not going to make anyone happy. Including me."

"So you'd prefer to keep things the way they are, rather than let the truth come out."

Menshiki spread his hands on his lap. "In a word, yes. It took some time for me to arrive at that conclusion, but my feelings are firm. I plan to live the rest of my life holding on to the possibility that **Mariye Akikawa is my real child**. Watching, from a distance, as she grows up. That's enough. Even if I knew for sure she was my child, that wouldn't make me happy. The sense of loss would be all the more painful. And if I knew she **wasn't** my child, that would, in a different sense, also deepen the sense of loss. Or maybe crush me. Either way there's no happy result. Can you follow what I'm trying to say?"

"I think so. At least in theory. But if I were in your position, I'd want to know the truth. Theory aside, it's natural for people to want to know the truth."

Menshiki smiled. "You're still young, so that's why you say that. When you get to be my age, you'll understand how I feel. How much loneliness the truth can cause sometimes."

"So what you're after is not to know the unmitigated truth, but to hang her portrait on your wall, gaze at it every day, and ponder the possibilities. Are you sure that's enough?"

Menshiki nodded. "It is. Instead of a stable truth, I choose unstable possibilities. I choose to surrender myself to that instability. Do you think that's unnatural?"

I did indeed. Or at least I didn't see it as natural. I wouldn't go so far as to call it unhealthy, though. But that was Menshiki's problem, not mine.

I glanced over at the Commendatore seated on top of the Steinway. Our eyes met. He raised both index fingers upward and spread them apart, as if to say, **Let's put that answer on hold**. Then he pointed with his right index finger to a watch on his left wrist. Of course the Commendatore wasn't wearing a watch. He was just pointing to where one would be. And of course what that meant was, **We should be leaving soon**. The Commendatore's advice to me, as well as a warning. I decided to heed it.

"Could I have a little time to get back to you on this? It's a delicate matter, and I need time to consider it."

Menshiki held up his hands from his lap. "Of course. Consider it as long as you'd like. I'm not trying to rush you. I know I may be asking too much."

I stood up and thanked him for the dinner.

"Ah, there's one thing I forgot to tell you," Menshiki said, as if suddenly remembering. "It's about Tomohiko Amada. We talked earlier, didn't we, about how he'd studied abroad, in Austria? About how, just before World War Two broke out, he rushed back home?"

"Yes, I remember."

"I researched it a bit. I'm interested, too, in what was behind all that. It happened a long time ago, and I don't have all the facts, but there were rumors then of some sort of scandal."

"A scandal?"

"That's right. Amada was apparently caught up in an aborted assassination attempt in Vienna. It turned into a political crisis, and the Japanese embassy in Berlin got involved and secreted him back to Japan. According to certain rumors. This was right after the **Anschluss.** You know about the **Anschluss,** I assume?"

"That was when Germany annexed Austria in 1938."

"Correct. Hitler incorporated Austria into Germany. There was a lot of chaos, and the Nazis finally took over all of Austria pretty much by force, and the nation of Austria vanished. This was in March 1938. The place was in turmoil, and in the confusion of the moment a lot of people were murdered. Assassinated, or murdered and made to look like suicides. Or else sent to concentration camps. It was during this time that Tomohiko Amada studied in Vienna. Rumor had it that he fell in love with an Austrian woman and got mixed up with an underground resistance group comprised largely of college students, who plotted to assassinate a high-ranking Nazi official. Not the sort of thing either the German government or the Japanese government would condone, for they'd signed a mutual defense pact only a year and a half before this, and the relationship between the two countries was growing closer all the time. Both were dead set on avoiding anything that would hinder their pact. Though Tomohiko Amada was still young, he had already made a name for himself as an artist in Japan, and his father was a large landowner, a locally politically influential person. A person like that couldn't just be secretly blotted out."

"So Tomohiko Amada was sent back to Japan?"

"Correct. Rescued is more like it. Thanks to the political considerations of higher-ups, he narrowly escaped getting killed. If the Gestapo had gotten hold of him under suspicion of something that serious— even if they hadn't had any clear-cut evidence—that would have been the end of him."

"But the assassination didn't happen?"

"No, it was abortive. There was an informant in the group, and the plan was leaked to the Gestapo. There was a wholesale arrest of the members."

"There would have been a real uproar if they'd gone through with it."

"The strange thing is, there was no talk of it at the time," Menshiki said. "There were whispers about a scandal, but there doesn't seem to be any public record of it. For various reasons, it was covered up."

So the Commendatore in the painting **Killing Commendatore** might represent that Nazi official. The painting might be a hypothetical depiction of the assassination that never actually happened in Vienna in 1938. Amada and his lover were connected with this plot, and then it was discovered by the authorities. The two of them were torn apart, and the woman most likely killed. And after he returned to Japan Amada transferred that horrific experience in Vienna onto the very symbolic canvas of a Japanese-style painting. **Adapting** it, in other words, into a scene from the Asuka period, set over a thousand years ago. **Killing Commendatore** was a painting Tomohiko Amada painted for himself alone. He felt compelled for his own sake to paint it to preserve that awful, bloody memory from his youth. Which is precisely why he never made the painting public, why he wrapped it up tightly and hid it away in the attic.

Perhaps that incident in Vienna was one reason he made a clean break with his career as an artist of Western paintings and converted to Japanese-style painting. He might have wanted to decisively separate himself from the self he used to be.

"How did you find out about all this?" I asked.

"It didn't take a lot of effort on my part. I asked an organization run by an acquaintance to investigate it for me. But it happened such a long time ago, and they can't be held responsible for how much of it is really true. They did check with multiple sources, though, so I think the information can basically be trusted."

"Tomohiko Amada had an Austrian lover. She was a member of an underground resistance group. And he was involved in that assassination plot."

Menshiki inclined his head a bit and then spoke. "If that's true, then it's a pretty dramatic series of events. But most of the people involved are dead by now, so there's no way for us to really know what happened. Facts have a tendency to get embellished, too. At any rate, though, it's pretty melodramatic."

"No one knows how deeply he was involved in that plot?"

"No. We don't know. I've just given it my own dramatic touch. Amada was deported from Vienna, bid his lover farewell—or maybe wasn't even able to do that—was put on a ship in Bremen, and returned to Japan. During the war he remained silent, holed up in rural Aso, then debuted as a painter of Japanese-style paintings soon after the end of the war. Which took people by complete surprise. Another pretty dramatic development."

Thus ended the story of Tomohiko Amada.

The same black Infiniti I'd arrived in was quietly awaiting me in front of the house. A faint drizzle was still intermittently falling, the air wet and chilly. The season when you needed a coat was just around the corner.

"Thank you so much for coming," Menshiki said. "My thanks, too, to the Commendatore."

It is I who should be doing the thanking, the Commendatore murmured in my ear. His voice, of course, was only for me to hear. I thanked Menshiki once more for dinner. It was an amazing meal, I said. I couldn't be more satisfied. The Commendatore seemed grateful as well.

"I hope bringing up all of those boring details after dinner didn't spoil the evening," Menshiki said.

"Not at all. But about your request: I need some time to think about it."

"Of course."

"It takes me time to consider things."

"It's the same for me," Menshiki said. "My motto is: Thinking three times is better than two. And if time allows, thinking four times is better than three."

The driver had the rear door open, waiting. I got inside. The Commendatore should have boarded at the same time, though I didn't see him. The car started up the asphalt slope, drove out the open gate, then proceeded slowly down the mountain. Once the white mansion disappeared from view, everything that happened that night seemed like part of a dream. It was getting harder to distinguish what was normal from what was not, what was real and what was not.

What you can see is real, the Commendatore whispered in my ear. **What you need to do is open your eyes wide and look at it. You can judge it later on.**

Even with my eyes wide open, there could be many things I was overlooking, I thought. I may have actually murmured this aloud, since the chauffeur shot me a glance in the rearview mirror. I closed my eyes and leaned back against the seat. And thought this: How wonderful it would be to put off judging things forever.

I got home a little before ten p.m. I brushed my teeth in the bathroom, changed into pajamas, slid into bed, and fell right asleep. Predictably, I had a million dreams, all of them strange, disconcerting. Swastika flags flying over the streets of Vienna, a huge passenger ship easing out of Bremen harbor, a brass band playing on the pier, Bluebeard's unopened room, Menshiki playing the Steinway.

26

THE COMPOSITION COULDN'T
BE IMPROVED

Two days later I got a call from my agent in Tokyo. They'd received the transfer of funds from Mr. Menshiki, the payment for the painting, and after taking the agent's fee out of it the rest had been deposited into my bank account. When I heard the total amount I was astonished. It was much higher than what I'd originally heard.

"The finished painting was better than he'd anticipated, so he added a bonus. There was a message from Mr. Menshiki requesting that you accept this as a token of his gratitude," my agent said.

I groaned faintly, but no words would come.

"I haven't seen the actual painting, though Mr. Menshiki attached a photo. From the photo, at least, it looks like an amazing work. Something that goes beyond the boundaries of portrait painting, yet remains a convincing portrait."

I thanked him and hung up.

A little while later my girlfriend called. Did I mind if she came over tomorrow morning? That would be fine, I told her. Friday was when I taught art class, but I'd have enough time to make it.

"Did you have dinner at Mr. Menshiki's place?" she asked.

"Yes, a really excellent meal."

"Did it taste good?"

"It was amazing. The wine was great, too, and the food was outstanding."

"What was the house like inside?"

"Beautiful," I said. "It'd take me half a day to describe it all."

"Could you tell me all about it when I see you?"

"Before? Or after?"

"After's good," she said simply.

After I hung up the phone, I went into the studio and looked at Tomohiko Amada's **Killing Commendatore**. I'd seen it so many times, but now, after what Menshiki told me, it took on a strangely graphic reality. This was not simply some historical picture of a past event, reproduced in an old-fashioned format. It felt—from the expressions and movements of each of the four characters (excluding Long Face)—like you could read their reactions to the situation. The young man piercing the Commendatore with his long sword was perfectly expressionless. He'd shut away his heart, hiding his emotions. In the Commendatore's face, one could read the agony as his chest was stabbed, but also a sense of pure surprise, the sense of **How could this possibly be happening?** The young woman watching this take place (in the opera, this character is Donna Anna) was torn apart by violently conflicting emotions. Her lovely face was contorted in anguish, her lovely white hand held to her mouth. The stocky man, a servant by the look of him (Leporello), was gasping for breath, gazing up at the sky. His hand was stretched out as if trying to reach something.

The organization was perfect. The composition couldn't be improved. It was a superb, polished arrangement. Each character maintained a vivid dynamism in their actions, instantaneously frozen in time. And now I saw the events of the aborted assassination that **may** have occurred in 1938 Vienna overlaying the painting. The Commendatore was dressed not in Asuka period costume but in a Nazi uniform. Maybe the black uniform of the SS. And in his chest was a saber or perhaps a dagger. **Perhaps** the one stabbing him was Tomohiko Amada himself. And who was the woman gasping nearby? Was this Amada's Austrian lover? And what was it that was rending her heart in two like that?

I sat on the stool, gazing for a long time at **Killing Commendatore**. My imagination could come up with all sorts of allegories and messages contained therein, but these were, in the final analysis, nothing more than unsubstantiated hypotheses. The background— what I took as background, that is—that Menshiki had talked about was not historical fact, but nothing more than rumor. Or else just a melodrama. Everything remained on the level of **perhaps**.

A thought suddenly struck me: I wish my sister were here.

If Komi were with me, I'd tell her everything that

had happened, and she'd listen quietly, adding an occasional short question. Even with an incomprehensible, mixed-up story like this, I doubt she'd frown or show any surprise. Her calm, thoughtful expression wouldn't change. And after I finished, she'd pause, then give me some useful advice. Ever since we were little we'd had that kind of interaction. But I realized now she'd never come to **me** for advice. As far as I could recall, that had never happened. Why? Maybe she didn't have any major emotional issues? Or maybe she'd decided asking me for advice wasn't going to help? Maybe both, or half of each.

But even if she had been healthy and hadn't died at twelve, the intimate brother-sister relationship we had shared might not have lasted. Komi might have ended up marrying some boring guy, gone to live in a town far away, been run ragged by everyday life, exhausted by raising children, lost her sparkle, and no longer retained the energy to give me advice. No one could say how our lives would have worked out.

The problems my wife and I had had might have stemmed from me unconsciously wanting Yuzu to stand in for Komi. That was never my intention, of course, but now that I thought of it, ever since I lost my sister I may have been seeking, somewhere inside me, a substitute partner I could lean on whenever I was struggling. Needless to say, though, Yuzu wasn't Komi. Their positions, and roles, were vastly different. And so was the history we'd shared.

As I thought about this, I remembered the visit I'd

made to Yuzu's parents' home in Kinuta in Setagaya in Tokyo, before we got married.

Yuzu's father was the branch manager of a large bank. His son—Yuzu's older brother—was also a banker, and worked for the same bank. Both were graduates of the elite economics department of Tokyo University. There seemed to be a lot of bankers in her family. I wanted to marry Yuzu (and of course she wanted to marry me, too), and the visit was for me to convey my intentions to her parents. Any way you looked at it, it was hard to call the half-hour interview I had with her father a friendly visit. I was an unknown artist who worked part-time painting portraits and didn't make what could be called a regular income. A guy with little in the way of future prospects. Not at all the sort of man a top banker like her father would view favorably. I'd anticipated this ahead of time and was dead set on not losing my cool no matter what he said, or how much criticism he heaped upon me. And I was basically the kind of person who could put up with a lot.

Yet as I listened to her father's long-winded sermon, a kind of physical revulsion welled up in me, and I lost it. I felt sick, like I was going to throw up. I stood up before he'd finished and said, I'm sorry, but I need to use the bathroom. I knelt down in front of the toilet bowl, trying to vomit up the contents of my stomach. But I couldn't vomit. Because there was hardly anything in my stomach. Even the gastric juices wouldn't come out. I took some deep breaths and calmed down. I gargled with water to get rid of the bad taste in my mouth, wiped the sweat from my face with a handkerchief, and went back to the living room.

"Are you all right?" Yuzu asked, looking concerned. I must have looked awful.

"A successful marriage is up to the people involved, but I can tell you, this one won't last long. Four, five years at the most." These were her father's parting words to me that day. (I didn't respond.) His spiteful words stayed with me, a kind of curse that remained for a long time to come.

Her parents never did agree to our marriage, but we went ahead and registered it, and officially became a married couple. By this time, I had very little contact with my own parents. Yuzu and I didn't have a wedding ceremony. Our friends rented a small place and held a simple party to celebrate, but that was it. (The person who did the most to make that happen was Masahiko, who was always good at taking care of others.) Despite the inauspicious beginning, we were happy. At least for the first few years, we were definitely happy together. For four or five years, we had no problems between us. But then, like a huge cruising ship in the middle of the ocean turning its rudder, there was a gradual change. I still don't know why. I can't even pinpoint when things began to move in a different direction. What she hoped for in marriage, and what I was looking for, must have been different, and that gap only grew more pronounced over time. And then, before I knew it, she was seeing another man. In the end our marriage only lasted some six years.

I imagine that when her father learned that our marriage had failed, he'd chuckled to himself and thought, I told you so. (Though we had stayed together a year or two beyond what he'd predicted.) It must have pleased him no end that Yuzu had left me. After we'd broken up, had Yuzu reconciled with her family? I had no way of knowing, and didn't really want to know, at that point. This was her business, not mine. But still her father's curse continued to hang over me. Even now, I sensed the vague weight of its presence. I'd been hurt, more than I cared to admit, and had bled. Like the pierced heart of the Commendatore in Tomohiko Amada's painting.

Late afternoon came on, and with it, the early-autumn twilight. The sky turned dark in the twinkling of an eye, the glossy black crows squawking their way across the valley, heading for their roosts. I went out on the terrace, leaned against the railing, and gazed over at Menshiki's house across the way. Several mercury lights were on in his garden, the whiteness of the house rising up in the dusk. I pictured Menshiki out there every night, searching through his high-powered binoculars for Mariye Akikawa. He'd purchased that white house, almost by force, for the sole purpose of doing that. Spent a huge amount of money, made a great deal of effort, all for an overly large house that didn't suit his tastes.

And strangely enough (at least to me it felt strange), I'd begun to feel a closeness to Menshiki, a closeness I'd never felt to anyone before. An affinity—no, a sense of solidarity, really. In a sense, we were very similar—that's what I thought. The two of us were motivated not by what we had got hold of, or were trying to get, but by what we'd lost, what we **did not now have**. I can't say I understood his actions. They were beyond my comprehension. But I could understand what had spurred him on.

I went to the kitchen, took the single malt that Masahiko had given me, and poured a glass on the rocks. I carried the drink out to the living room sofa and selected a record of a Schubert string quartet from Tomohiko Amada's collection, and put it on the turntable. A piece titled "Rosamunde." The same music that had been playing in Menshiki's study. I listened to the music, occasionally clinking the ice in my glass.

The Commendatore never showed up that day. Maybe, like the horned owl, he was quietly resting up in the attic. Even Ideas needed some time off. I didn't do any painting that day, either. I needed some time off as well.

I raised my glass to the Commendatore.

27

EVEN THOUGH YOU REMEMBER
EXACTLY WHAT IT LOOKED LIKE

When my girlfriend came over I told her all about the dinner party at Menshiki's. Leaving out, of course, any mention of Mariye Akikawa, the high-powered binoculars, and the Commendatore having secretly accompanied me. What I described was the dinner menu, the way the rooms were laid out in the house, the kind of furniture—safe subjects. We were in bed, completely naked, after making love for about a half hour. At first it was hard to relax, knowing that the Commendatore must be observing us, but as we got into it, I forgot all about him. If he wanted to watch, let him.

Like a rabid sports fan is dying to know how his favorite team scored in the game the night before, my girlfriend panted over every detail of the dishes we had at dinner. I painstakingly went over the details, as far as I could remember them, from the hors d'oeuvres to dessert, from the wine to the coffee. Even the tableware. I've always been blessed with great visual recall. If I focus on something, even a trivial thing, I can recall the minutest details, even after time has passed. I could reproduce the special features of every dish that was served, as if I were doing a quick sketch. She listened to my descriptions, a spellbound look in her eyes, at times actually gulping back her desire.

"Sounds amazing," she said dreamily. "Someday I'd love to have a wonderful meal like that."

"To tell the truth, though, I don't remember much of what it tasted like," I said.

"You don't remember how the food tasted? But you liked it, right?"

"Yes. It was delicious. That much I remember. But I can't recall the flavors, can't explain it in words."

"Even though you remember exactly what it looked like?"

"I could reproduce exactly what it looked like. I'm a painter—it's what I do. But I can't explain what went into it. Maybe a writer would be able to describe the flavors."

"Weird," she said. "So even when we do **this** together, you could paint a painting of it later on, but you wouldn't be able to reproduce the feeling in words?"

I gathered my thoughts. "You're talking about sexual pleasure?"

"Yes."

"Hmm. You may be right. But I think describing the flavor of a dish is harder than describing sexual pleasure."

"So what you're saying," she said, in a voice as chilly as an early-winter nightfall, "is that the taste of the dishes Mr. Menshiki served you is more exquisite, and deeper, than the sexual pleasure I provide?"

"That's not what I'm saying," I said hurriedly. "It's

not a comparison of the quality of the two, but a question of the degree of difficulty of explaining them. In a technical sense."

"All right," she said. "What I give you isn't so bad, is it? In a technical sense?"

"Of course," I said. "It's amazing. In a technical sense, and all other senses, so amazing I couldn't paint it."

Truthfully the physical pleasure she provided me left nothing to be desired. Up till then I'd had sexual relationships with a number of women—not so many I could brag about it—but her vagina was more exquisite, more wondrously varied, than **any other** I'd ever known. And it was a deplorable thing that it had lain there, unused, for so many years. When I told her this, she didn't look as dissatisfied as you might have thought.

"Really?"

"Really."

She looked at me, dubiously, then seemed to take me at my word.

"So, did he show you the garage?" she asked.

"The garage?"

"His legendary garage with its four British cars."

"No, I didn't see it," I said. "It's such a huge place, and I didn't get a chance to see the garage."

"Hm," she said. "You didn't ask him if he really does own a Jaguar XK-E?"

"No. I didn't think of it. I mean, I'm not really into cars."

"You're happy with a used Corolla station wagon?"

"You got it."

"I'd love to be able to touch a Jaguar XK-E some-time. It's such a gorgeous car. I've been in love with that car ever since I saw it in a film with Audrey Hep-burn and Peter O'Toole when I was a child. Peter O'Toole was driving a bright, shiny Jaguar E. Now what color was it? Yellow, as I recall."

Her thoughts drifted to that sports car she'd seen as a young girl, while what came to my mind was that Subaru Forester. The white Subaru parked in the parking lot on the edge of that tiny town along the coast in Miyagi. Not a particularly attractive ve-hicle. A typical small SUV, a squat little utilitarian machine. I doubt there'd be many people who would unconsciously feel like touching it. Unlike with a Jaguar XK-E.

"So you didn't get to see the greenhouse or the gym either?" she asked me. She was talking about Menshiki's house again.

"No such luck. Didn't get to see the greenhouse, the gym, or the laundry room, the maid's quarters, the kitchen, or the spacious walk-in closet, or the game room with the billiard table. He didn't show them to me."

That evening Menshiki had an important matter he had to talk with me about. He was far too preoc-cupied to give me a leisurely tour of the house.

"Does he really have a huge walk-in closet, and a game room with a billiard table?"

"I don't know. I'm just guessing. It wouldn't be strange if he did, though."

"He didn't show you any of the other rooms besides the study?"

"Yeah. It's not like I'm interested in interior design. What he showed me were the foyer, the living room, the study, and the dining room."

"You didn't try to spot Bluebeard's secret chamber?"

"Didn't have the chance to. And I wasn't about to ask Menshiki, 'By the way, where is the famous Bluebeard's secret chamber?'"

She shook her head a few times, clicking her tongue in frustration. "I tell you, that's what's wrong with men. Don't you have any curiosity? If it were me, I'd want to see every nook and cranny."

"The things men and women are curious about must be different."

"It seems like it," she said, resigned to it. "But that's okay. I should be happy to have gotten a lot of new info about the interior of Mr. Menshiki's house."

I was getting increasingly uneasy. "Getting information is one thing, but it wouldn't be good if this got out to others. Through your jungle grapevine . . ."

"It's all right. No need for you to worry about every little thing," she said cheerily.

She took my hand and guided it to her clitoris. In this way, our two spheres of curiosity once more significantly overlapped. I still had time before I had to go teach. At that point I thought I heard the bell in the studio faintly ringing, but I was probably just hearing things.

.   .   .

After she drove away in the red Mini just before three, I went into the studio, and picked up the bell from the shelf. I couldn't see anything different about it. It had just been quietly lying there. I looked around, but the Commendatore was nowhere to be seen.

I went over to the canvas, sat down on the stool, and gazed at the portrait of the man with the white Subaru Forester that I'd begun. I wanted to consider the direction I should take it in now. But here I made an unexpected discovery.

The painting was **already complete**.

Needless to say, the painting was still unfinished. I had a few ideas I planned to incorporate into it. At this point the painting was nothing more than a rough prototype of the man's face done with the three colors I'd mixed, the colors riotously slapped on over the rough charcoal sketch. In my eyes, of course, I could detect the ideal form of **The Man with the White Subaru Forester**. His face was there in the painting in a latent, trompe l'oeil type of way. But this was only visible to me. It was, at this point, only the foundation for a painting. Merely the hint and suggestion of things to come. But that man—the person I had been trying to paint from memory— was already satisfied with his taciturn form presented there. And maybe dead set against his likeness being made any clearer than it was now.

Don't you touch anything, the man was saying—or maybe commanding—from the canvas. **Don't you add a single thing more**.

The painting was complete as is, incomplete. The

man actually existed, completely, in that inchoate form. A contradiction in terms, but there was no other way to describe it. And that man's hidden form looked out to me from the canvas as if signaling some hard-and-fast idea. Trying hard to get me to understand something. But I still had no idea what that was. This man is alive, I felt. Actually alive and moving.

The paint on the picture was still wet, but I took the canvas down from the easel, turned it facing away, and propped it up against the studio wall, careful not to get paint on the wall. It was harder and harder for me to stand seeing the painting. There was something ominous about it—something I shouldn't know about.

Hovering around the painting was the air of a fishing port. In that air was a mix of smells—the smell of the tide, of fish scales, of diesel engines, of fishing boats. Flocks of birds were screeching, slowly circling on the strong wind. The black golf cap of a middle-aged man who'd probably never played a round of golf in his life. The darkly tanned face, the stringy nape of the neck, the short-clipped hair mixed with gray. The well-used leather jacket. The clatter of knives and forks in the restaurant—that impersonal sound found at chain restaurants around the world. And the white Subaru Forester quietly parked in the lot out front. The sticker of a marlin on the rear bumper.

"Hit me," the woman had said in the middle of sex. Her fingernails were digging deep into my back.

There was a strong smell of sweat. I did as she asked, smacking her face with an open hand.

"Not like that. Don't hold back, hit me harder," the woman said, shaking her head violently. "Harder, **much** harder. Really hit me. I don't care if there's a bruise. Hard enough so my nose bleeds."

I had no desire to hit her. I never had those kind of violent tendencies. Hardly any at all. But she was **seriously** hoping I would **seriously** hit her. What she needed was real pain. So I reluctantly hit her again, a little harder this time. Hard enough to leave a red mark on her. Every time I struck her, her flesh squeezed my penis like a vise. Like a starving animal pouncing on some food.

"Would you choke me a little?" she whispered a little while later. "Use this."

The sound seemed to be coming from another realm. She pulled out a white bathrobe belt from under her pillow. She'd had it there, ready to use.

I refused. I could never do something like that. It was too dangerous. Mess up, and she could die.

"Just pretend," she pleaded, gasping. "You don't need to really choke me, just pretend like you are. Wrap this around my neck and tighten it a little."

I couldn't refuse.

The impersonal clatter of silverware in a chain restaurant.

I shook my head, trying to drive away those memories. It was an incident I didn't care to recall, a memory I'd like to throw away and never have again. But the feel of that bathrobe belt lingered in my hands. The way her neck felt, too. For whatever reason, these stayed with me.

And this man knew. Where I'd been the night before, what I'd done. What I'd been thinking.

What should I do with this painting? Keep it here in the studio, turned toward the wall? Even turned around like that, it still made me uneasy. The only other place to keep it was the attic. The same place Tomohiko Amada had hidden away **Killing Commendatore**. The place to hide away what was in your heart.

In my mind, the words I'd spoken aloud came back to me.

I could reproduce exactly what it looked like. I'm a painter—it's what I do. But I can't explain what went into it.

All sorts of things I couldn't explain were insidiously grabbing hold of me. Tomohiko Amada's **Killing Commendatore** that I'd discovered in the attic, the strange bell left behind inside the gaping stone chamber in the woods, the Idea that appeared to me in the guise of the Commendatore, and the middle-aged man with the white Subaru Forester. And that odd white-haired person who lived across the valley. Menshiki seemed to be enlisting me into some kind of plan he had in mind.

The whirlpool swirling around me was gradually picking up speed. And there was no way for me to turn back. It was too late. That whirlpool was totally soundless. And that weird silence had me scared.

427

28

FRANZ KAFKA WAS QUITE FOND OF SLOPES

That evening I taught a children's art class. The assignment that day was to do rough sketches of people. The children worked in pairs, selecting the type of drawing instruments they wanted from the ones the school had prepared ahead of time (charcoal or various types of soft pencils), and took turns sketching each other in their notebooks. They were limited to fifteen minutes per drawing (I used a kitchen timer to accurately time them). They were supposed to use an eraser as little as they could, and limit themselves to one sheet of paper, if possible.

One by one the children then came to the front of the class, showed us their sketches, and got feedback from the other children. It was a small class, and the atmosphere was congenial. Afterward I went forward and taught them some simple techniques for rough sketches. I explained in general the difference between **croquis**—rough sketches—and **dessan**. A dessan is more of a blueprint for a painting, and requires a certain accuracy. Compared with that, a croquis is a free first impression. You get an impression in your mind and trace the rough outline of it before it disappears. More than accuracy, croquis require balance and speed. Many famous painters actually weren't very skilled at doing croquis. I've always prided myself on being good at drawing these kind of quick sketches.

Finally I chose one of the children to model for me and did a rough sketch of her on the blackboard in white chalk, to show them an actual example. **Wow! You're so fast! It looks just like her!** the children called out, impressed. One of a teacher's important duties is to get children to be genuinely impressed.

Next, I had them change partners and do another croquis, and the second time they were much improved. They absorbed knowledge quickly. This time, the instructor was impressed. Of course some of them were better than others, but that didn't matter. What I was teaching them was less how to draw than a way to view the world.

On this day I selected Mariye Akikawa (intentionally, of course) to serve as model when I drew an example. I did a simple sketch of her from the waist up on the blackboard. It wasn't exactly a croquis, though the elements were the same. I finished quickly, in three minutes. I wanted to use the class to test what kind of painting I could do of her. What I discovered in doing this was that, as a model for a painting, she had a lot of unique possibilities hidden away inside.

I'd never really consciously observed her before, but now, looking at her carefully as the subject of a drawing, I found her face far more intriguing than my original vague impression. It wasn't just that she had lovely features. She was, indeed, a beautiful girl,

429

but a closer observation showed a kind of imbalance at work. And behind that unstable expression there was a latent energy, like some agile animal lurking in the tall grass.

I wanted to see if I could capture that impression, but it was next to impossible to do that in three minutes, in chalk on a blackboard. Basically impossible, I should say. I needed more time to observe her face and dissect all the elements. And I had to know more about this young girl.

I left the chalk sketch of her on the blackboard, and after the children had all left, I stayed behind, arms folded, studying the sketch. I tried to determine if there was anything of Menshiki in her features. But I couldn't decide. I could detect a resemblance in certain features, in others not so much—it could go either way. But if I had to give one feature it would be the eyes, a shared look in their eyes. The distinctive way their eyes would flash for an instant.

If you stare long enough deep into the bottom of a clear spring you discover a kind of lump that emits light. You can't see it unless you look very closely. That lump soon wavers and loses shape. The more carefully you look, the more you start to wonder if it might all be an illusion. But something there is unmistakably glowing. Having done countless portraits of people, occasionally I'll sense someone giving off that **glow**. Not many people have it. But this girl and Menshiki were among these rare few.

The middle-aged receptionist at the school came

into the classroom to straighten up and stood beside me, admiring the drawing.

"That's Mariye Akikawa, isn't it," she said at first glance. "A very nice likeness. It looks like she's about to start moving. It's a waste to have to erase it."

"Thank you," I said. I got up from my desk, picked an eraser, and completely wiped the sketch away.

The Commendatore finally made an appearance the next day (Saturday). It was the first time since Tuesday night at the dinner at Menshiki's that he—to borrow his phrase—**materialized**. I was back from food shopping, in the living room reading a book, when I heard the sound of the bell tinkling from the studio. I went into the studio and found the Commendatore seated on the shelf, lightly shaking the bell next to his ear. As if making sure of the subtle sound. When he spotted me he stopped ringing the bell.

"It's been a while," I said.

"Negative. It has been nothing of the kind," the Commendatore said curtly. "An Idea travels around the world in units of hundreds, thousands of years. A day or two does not count as time."

"How did you like Mr. Menshiki's dinner party?"

"Ah, yes, an interesting dinner that was. I could not partake of the food, of course, but did feast my eyes on it. And Menshiki is a fascinating fellow. Always thinking several steps ahead. And there is much pent up inside him."

"He asked me to do a favor for him."

"Affirmative." The Commendatore gazed at the ancient bell in his hand. He did not seem interested. "I heard it all quite clearly. But it is not something that has much to do with me. It is a practical matter—a worldly matter, you could say—that is between my friends and Menshiki."

"Is it all right if I ask a question?" I said.

The Commendatore rubbed his goatee with his palm. "Affirmative. But I do not know if I will be able to answer."

"It's about Tomohiko Amada's painting **Killing Commendatore**. I assume you know the painting, since you borrowed one of the figures. The painting seems based on an incident in Vienna in 1938. Something Tomohiko Amada himself was involved in. Do you know anything about that?"

Arms folded, the Commendatore thought this over. Finally he narrowed his eyes and spoke.

"There are **plenty** of things in history that are best left in the shadows. Accurate knowledge does not improve people's lives. The objective does not necessarily surpass the subjective, you know. Reality does not necessarily extinguish fantasy."

"Generally speaking," I said, "that might be so. But that painting is calling out to anyone who sees it. I get the sense that Tomohiko Amada painted it to privately capture an event that was essential to him but that he could not share with others. He changed the characters and setting to another age, and made a metaphorical confession, using his newly acquired skills in Japanese-style painting. I even get the feeling that that was the sole reason he abandoned Western painting and converted to Japanese art."

"Cannot you just let the painting speak for itself?" the Commendatore said softly. "If that painting wants to say something, then best to let it speak. Let metaphors be metaphors, a code a code, a sieve a sieve. Is there something wrong with that?"

A sieve? But I let it go.

"No, nothing's wrong with that," I said. "I'd just like to know what made Tomohiko Amada paint it. It's clear that the painting is expecting something. The picture was, without a doubt, painted for a specific purpose."

The Commendatore continued to rub his beard with his palm as if recalling something. "Franz Kafka was quite fond of slopes," he said. "He was drawn to all sorts of slopes. He loved to gaze at homes built on the middle of a slope. He would sit by the side of the street for hours, staring at houses built like that. He never grew tired of it and would sit there, tilting his head to one side, then straightening it up again. A kind of strange fellow. Did you know this?"

Franz Kafka and slopes?

"No, I didn't," I said. I'd never heard of that.

"But does knowing that make one appreciate his works more?"

I didn't respond to his question.

"So you knew Franz Kafka, too? Personally?"

"He does not know about me personally, of course,"

433

the Commendatore said. He chuckled, as if recalling something. This might have been the first time I'd seen him laugh out loud. Was there something about Franz Kafka to make him chuckle?

His expression returned to normal and he went on.

"The truth is a symbol, and symbols are the truth. It is best to grasp symbols the way they are. There's no logic or facts, no pig's belly button or ant's balls. When people try to use a method other than the truth to follow along the path of understanding, it is like trying to use a sieve to hold water. I am telling you this for your own good. Better to give it up. Sadly, what Menshiki is doing is similar to that."

"So no matter what, it's a wasted effort?"

"No one can ever float something full of holes on water."

"So what exactly is Mr. Menshiki trying to do?"

The Commendatore lightly shrugged. Charming lines formed between his eyebrows that reminded me of a young Marlon Brando. I seriously doubted the Commendatore had ever seen Elia Kazan's **On the Waterfront,** but those lines were exactly like Marlon Brando's. Though I had no way of knowing how far he went, when it came to referencing his appearance and features.

He said, "There is very little I can explain to my friends about Tomohiko Amada's **Killing Commendatore.** That is because it is, in essence, allegory and metaphor. Allegories and metaphors are not something you should explain in words. You just grasp them and accept them."

The Commendatore scratched behind his ear with his little finger. Just like a cat will scratch behind its ear before it rains.

"I will, however, tell my friends one thing. Nothing that is enormously significant, but tomorrow night you'll get a phone call. A call from Menshiki. Think things over **very carefully** before you answer. Your answer will be the same no matter how much you think it over, but it is still best to think it over very carefully."

"And it's very important to let the other person know you're thinking things over carefully, isn't it. As a gesture."

"Affirmative. A hard-and-fast rule in business is to never accept the first offer. Remember that, and you will never go wrong." The Commendatore chuckled again. He seemed in an especially good mood today. "Changing topics, but I wondered, is it interesting to touch a clitoris?"

"I don't think you touch it because it's interesting," I said honestly.

"From the sidelines it is hard to understand."

"I don't think I get it, either," I said. So an Idea, too, doesn't necessarily understand everything.

"About time for me to disappear," the Commendatore said. "I have someplace else I need to go. Do not have much time."

And with that the Commendatore vanished. A gradual, phased disappearance, like the Cheshire Cat's. I went to the kitchen, made a simple dinner, and ate. I considered for a moment what "someplace else" an Idea would need to go to. And naturally had no clue.

Like the Commendatore had prophesized, at just past eight the following evening, I got a phone call from Menshiki.

I thanked him again for the dinner party. The food was amazing, I said. It was nothing, he replied. I want to thank **you**, Menshiki said, for letting me have such an enjoyable time. I also thanked him for the payment for the portrait, which was way more than we'd agreed to. Please don't worry about it, Menshiki said modestly. That's only to be expected, for such a wonderful painting. Once we'd finished all these polite exchanges there was a moment of silence.

"By the way, about Mariye Akikawa," Menshiki began, as casually as if discussing the weather. "You remember the other day when I asked if you would have her model for a painting?"

"Of course I remember."

"Yesterday I asked Mariye—actually Mr. Matsushima, the owner of the arts-and-culture center, asked her aunt—if it might be possible—and she agreed to model."

"I see," I said.

"So all the pieces are in place, if you'll agree to paint the portrait."

"But Mr. Menshiki, isn't Mr. Matsushima a bit suspicious that you're involved in this?"

"I've been very careful, so no need to worry. He

sees me as acting as your patron of sorts. I hope you're not offended . . ."

"I don't mind," I said. "But I'm surprised Mariye Akikawa agreed. She's so quiet and docile, and strikes me as a timid girl."

"Honestly, her aunt didn't like the idea at first. She felt nothing good could come from modeling for a painting. I'm sorry if this offends you, as an artist."

"No, most people would feel that way."

"But Mariye herself seemed quite interested in modeling for the painting. She said if you'd paint her she'd be happy to pose. She's the one who persuaded her aunt to agree."

Why, I wondered? Was there some connection with the sketch of her I did on the blackboard? I didn't venture to bring this up with Menshiki.

"Things have worked out perfectly, haven't they?" Menshiki said.

I thought it over. Was this really the perfect way for things to go? Menshiki seemed to be waiting for my opinion.

"Could you tell me more about how this would unfold?"

Menshiki said, "It's very simple. You're looking for a model for a painting. And you think that Mariye Akikawa, from your art class, would be perfect. So you had the owner of the arts-and-culture center, Mr. Matsushima, sound out the girl's guardian, her aunt. That's the story. Mr. Matsushima personally recommended you. Said you have a sterling character, are an enthusiastic teacher, that you're a talented artist with a promising future. I don't appear anywhere in this. I made sure my name didn't come up. Naturally she'll be clothed when she models, and her aunt will accompany her. And you'll finish the sessions by noon. Those are the conditions they laid down. What do you think?"

Following the Commendatore's advice ("Always turn down first offers"), I put on the brakes.

"I don't have any problem with the conditions, but can I have a bit more time to think about this?"

"Of course," Menshiki said calmly. "Think about it as much as you'd like. I'm not trying to rush you. Obviously you're the one who would paint the picture, and if you don't feel like doing it, that's the end of it. I just wanted to let you know that everything's all set, as far as I'm concerned. One more thing, perhaps a little off topic, but I'm planning to pay you fully for the painting."

Things are really moving along here, I thought. Everything's evolving amazingly quickly and smoothly, like a ball rolling down a slope . . . I pictured Franz Kafka seated halfway down the slope, watching the ball roll by. I needed to be cautious.

"Can you give me two days?" I asked. "I should be able to give you an answer then."

"That's fine. I'll call you again in two days," Menshiki said.

We ended the call.

Truth be told, I really didn't need two days to give a reply. I'd already made up my mind. I was dying to paint Mariye Akikawa's portrait. Even if someone tried to stop me, I'd take on the task. The only reason for asking for two extra days was that I didn't want anyone else to dictate the pace of events. I needed to stop and take a deep breath, something instinct—and the Commendatore—had taught me.

It is like trying to use a sieve to hold water, the Commendatore said. **No one ever can float something full of holes on water.**

His words hinted at something, something to come.

29

ANY UNNATURAL ELEMENTS

I spent those two days gazing, back and forth, at the two paintings in my studio—Tomohiko Amada's **Killing Commendatore** and my own painting of the man with the white Subaru Forester. **Killing Commendatore** was hanging now on the white wall of the studio. **The Man with the White Subaru Forester** was in a corner of the studio facing the wall (only when I wanted to look at it did I return it to the easel). Other than gaze at those paintings, I killed time reading books, listening to music, cooking, cleaning, weeding the garden, taking walks nearby. I didn't feel like taking up my paintbrush. The Commendatore didn't appear, and maintained his silence.

As I hiked the mountain roads nearby, I tried to find a place from which I could view Mariye Akikawa's house. But I could never find it. When I saw it from Menshiki's house, I gathered it wasn't far from me, but the topography obstructed my view. As I hiked through the woods I unconsciously was on the lookout for hornets.

What I rediscovered, spending two days gazing at the paintings, was that my feelings were spot on. **Killing Commendatore** wanted me to break its "code," and **The Man with the White Subaru For-ester** wanted the artist (namely me) to not make any more revisions. And both of these appeals were very strong—at least I felt them strongly—and I had to obey. I left **The Man with the White Subaru Forester** as it was (though I did try to fathom the basis for why it wanted to be left as is), and struggled to decipher **Killing Commendatore**. But both paintings were en-veloped in an enigma, as hard as a walnut shell, and I couldn't find the means to crack the shell open.

Without the upcoming portrait of Mariye Aki-kawa to deal with, I might very well have spent my days, ad infinitum, gazing back and forth between these paintings. But in the evening of the second day Menshiki called, and for the time being, at least, the spell was broken.

"Did you make a decision?" Menshiki said, after we'd greeted each other. He was, of course, asking about painting Mariye Akikawa's portrait.

"I'll accept the offer," I replied. "But I do have one condition."

"Which is?"

"I can't predict what kind of painting it will turn out to be. I can't know what style I'll paint it in until Mariye is actually here and I actually begin. If no good ideas come to me, I might not finish. Or it might be finished, but I might not like it. Or you might not like it. So I'd like to do it spontaneously, not because you commissioned it, or because you sug-gested I do it."

A momentary pause, then Menshiki said, probingly, "In other words, if you're not satisfied with the finished painting it won't end up mine, under any circumstances. Is that what you're saying?"

"That's a possibility. Anyway, I'd like to be the one who decides what to do with the painting. That's my condition."

Menshiki gave it some thought before he spoke. "The only thing I can do, I think, is agree. If not accepting that condition means you won't paint it."

"I'm sorry about that."

"So you want to be more free artistically, not bound by the painting being on commission by me, or having any suggestions from me, is that it? Or is the financial aspect the issue?"

"A little bit of both. But what's really important is that I want to do it all more naturally."

"Naturally?"

"I want to get rid of any unnatural elements, as much as I can."

"Meaning . . . ," Menshiki said. His voice had grown a little hard. "That there's something unnatural in my asking you to paint Mariye's portrait?"

It is like trying to use a sieve to hold water, the Commendatore said. **No one can ever float something full of holes on water.**

I said, "What I mean is, with this painting I'd like to be on an equal footing with you, not in a relationship that's mixed up with questions of individual interests. I'm sorry if this sounds rude."

"No, it's not rude at all. It's only natural for people

to be on an equal footing. Feel free to say anything you'd like to me."

"In other words, I'd like to paint the portrait of Mariye Akikawa as a spontaneous act, not one that you had a hand in. Unless I do that, I might not come up with any good ideas about how to paint her. That sort of thing might be a shackle, visible or otherwise."

Menshiki thought about this. "I understand completely," he finally said. "Let's forget about it being a commission. And please forget that I mentioned payment. That was me being overeager, I'm afraid. We can revisit the question of what to do with the painting once it's finished and you show it to me. Of course I'll honor your desires as the artist above all. But how about the other request I had? Do you remember?"

"About you casually stopping by my studio while Mariye is modeling for me?"

"Correct."

I thought it over. "I have no problem with that. I'm acquainted with you, you live in the neighborhood, and just happened to drop by while out for a Sunday stroll. And we just chat for a while. That strikes me as completely natural."

Menshiki seemed relieved. "I'd be very grateful if you'd arrange it. I'll make sure not to get in the way. So can I plan things so that Mariye comes over to your place this Sunday morning, and you'll paint her portrait? Actually Mr. Matsushima will act as intermediary and arrange things between you and the Akikawas."

"That would be fine. Go ahead and set it up. We'll plan on the two of them coming over on Sunday morning at ten, and Mariye will sit for the portrait. I'll be sure to finish up by twelve. It'll take several weeks to finish. Maybe five or six. That's about the size of it."

"I'll be in touch once everything's set."

We'd finished discussing all we needed to.

"Ah, yes," he said, as if suddenly remembering. "I found out a few more things about Tomohiko Amada's time in Vienna. I told you that the failed assassination attempt he was involved in took place right about the time of the **Anschluss,** but actually it was in the early fall of 1938. About half a year after the **Anschluss,** in other words. You know the facts about the **Anschluss,** right?"

"Not in much detail."

"On March 12, 1938, the Wehrmacht smashed across the border with Austria, invaded the country, and soon gained control of Vienna. They threatened President Miklas and made him designate Seyss-Inquart, head of the Austrian Nazi Party, as prime minister. Hitler came to Vienna two days later. On April tenth there was a national referendum, a vote on whether Austria should be annexed by Germany. On the surface it was a free, secret ballot, but the Nazis rigged things so any voter would have to be pretty courageous to vote **nein.** The vote was 99.75 percent **ja** for the annexation. That's how Austria as a nation vanished, reduced to being a part of Germany. Have you ever been to Vienna?"

I'd never been out of the country, let alone to Vienna. I'd never even had a passport.

"Vienna's like no other city in the world," Menshiki said. "You sense it even after being there for a short time. Vienna's different from Germany. The air's different, the people are different. Same with the food and the music. It's a special place for people to enjoy themselves, to love the arts. But back then Vienna was in total chaos, a brutal storm blowing violently through it. And it was exactly this period of upheaval in Vienna that Tomohiko Amada lived through. The Nazis behaved themselves until the national referendum, but after that they revealed their true, brutal nature. The first thing Hitler did after the **Anschluss** was build the Mauthausen concentration camp in northern Austria. It took only a few weeks to complete it. Building it was the Nazis' top priority. In a short space of time, tens of thousands of political prisoners were arrested and shipped off to the camp. Most of those sent to Mauthausen were so-called incorrigible political prisoners or antisocial elements. So their treatment was especially cruel. Lots of people were executed there, or died doing harsh physical labor in the quarries. The label "incorrigible" meant that once you were thrown into that camp, you'd never come out alive. Many anti-Nazi activists weren't sent to the camp, but were tortured and murdered during interrogation, their fate covered up. The aborted assassination attempt that Tomohiko Amada was involved in took place during this chaotic period following the **Anschluss**."

I listened to Menshiki's story without comment.

"But as I mentioned before, there's no public record at all of any abortive assassination attempt on any Nazi VIP from the summer to fall of 1938. Which is pretty strange, if you think about it. If such a plot had really existed, Hitler and Goebbels would have spread the news far and wide and used it for political purposes. Like they did with **Kristallnacht**. You know about **Kristallnacht**, right?"

"The basic facts, yes," I said. I'd seen a movie once that dealt with it. "A German embassy official in Paris was shot and killed by an anti-Nazi Jew, and the Nazis used that as an excuse for fomenting anti-Jewish riots throughout Germany. Lots of businesses run by Jews were destroyed, and quite a few people were murdered. The name comes from the way that the glass from the shattered shop windows glittered like crystals."

"Exactly. That was in November 1938. The German government announced it as spontaneous rioting, when in reality the Nazi government, with Goebbels leading the way, used the assassination to systematically plan this brutality. The assassin, Herschel Grynszpan, carried out the act to protest the cruel treatment of his family as Jews back in Germany. At first he planned to assassinate the German ambassador, but when he couldn't, he instead shot one of the embassy staff who just happened to be there. Ironically, Vom Rath, the staff member he shot, was under surveillance by authorities for anti-Nazi sympathies. At any rate, if there had been a plot at the time to assassinate a Nazi official in Vienna, a similar campaign would definitely have taken place. They would have used it as an excuse to increase the suppression of anti-Nazi forces. At least, they wouldn't have quietly covered up the incident."

"Was there some reason they didn't want it made public?"

"It seems a fact that the incident did take place. Most of the people involved were Viennese college students, and they were all arrested and either executed or murdered. To seal their lips about the plot. One theory is that one of the resistance members was the daughter of a high-ranking Nazi official, and that's why they kept it under wraps. But the facts aren't clear. After the war there was some testimony given about it, but this was all circumstantial evidence, and it's unsure whether any of it is reliable. By the way, the resistance group's name was Candela. In Latin it means a candle shining in the darkness underground. The Japanese word for lantern—**kantera**—derives from this."

"If all those involved in the plot were killed, that means the only survivor is Tomohiko Amada?"

"It does seem that way. Just before the end of the war, the Reich Main Security Office ordered that all secret documents relating to the incident be burned, and the plot was lost to the darkness of history. It would be nice if we could question Tomohiko Amada about the details of what took place, but that would be pretty difficult now."

It would, I said. Up till now Tomohiko Amada had

never spoken of the incident, and his memory had now sunk deep into the thick mud of oblivion.

I thanked Menshiki and hung up.

Even while his memory was still solid, Tomohiko Amada had maintained a firm silence about the incident. He must have had some private reasons for why he couldn't talk about it. Or perhaps when he left the country the authorities had forced him to agree to never speak of it. In place of maintaining a lifelong silence, though, he'd left the painting **Killing Commendatore**. He'd entrusted that painting with the truth he was forbidden to ever speak about, and his feelings about what had occurred.

The next evening Menshiki called again. Mariye Akikawa would be coming to my house the following Sunday at ten a.m., he reported. As he'd mentioned, her aunt would be accompanying her. Menshiki wouldn't be there that first day.

"I'll come by after some time has passed, after she's gotten used to posing for you. I'm sure she'll be nervous at first, and it's better that I don't bother you," he said.

His voice was a little unsteady. That tone put me on edge as well.

"Yes, that sounds like a good idea," I replied.

"Come to think of it, though, I might be the one who's the most nervous," Menshiki said after a little hesitation, sounding as if he were revealing a secret. "I think I said this before, but I've never been near

Mariye Akikawa, not even once. I've only seen her from a distance."

"But if you wanted to get close to her, you could have created an opportunity to do so."

"Yes, of course. If I'd wanted to I could have made any number of opportunities."

"But you didn't. Why not?"

Uncharacteristically, Menshiki took time to choose his words. He said, "I couldn't predict how I'd feel, or what I'd say, if I was close to her. That's why I've intentionally stayed away. I've been satisfied with being on the other side of the valley, secretly watching her from a distance with high-powered binoculars. Is that a warped way of thinking?"

"Not particularly," I said. "But I do find it a bit odd. But now you've decided to actually meet her at my house. Why?"

Menshiki was silent for a time, and then spoke. "That's because you're here, and can act as an intermediary."

"Me?" I said in surprise. "Why me? Not to be rude or anything, but you hardly know me. And I don't know you well either. We only met about a month ago. We live across the valley from each other, but our lifestyles couldn't be more different. So why did you trust me that much? And tell me your secrets? You don't seem the type to give away your inner feelings so easily."

"Exactly. Once I have a secret I lock it away in a safe and swallow the key. I don't seek advice from others or reveal things to them."

"Then how come—I'm not sure how to put this— you've confided in me?"

Menshiki was silent for a time. "It's hard to ex- plain, but I got the feeling the first day I met you that it's all right to let my guard down. Call it intu- ition. And that feeling only grew stronger after I saw my portrait. I decided, **This is a trustworthy person**. Someone who would accept my way of seeing things, my way of thinking. Even if I have a slightly odd and twisted way of seeing and thinking."

A slightly odd and twisted way of seeing and think- ing, I thought.

"I'm really happy you'd say that," I said. "But I don't think I understand you as a person. You go way beyond the scope of my comprehension. Frankly, many things about you simply surprise me. Some- times I'm at a loss for words."

"But you never try to judge me. Am I right?"

That was true, now that he'd said it. I'd never tried to apply some standard to judge Menshiki's words and actions. I didn't praise them, and didn't criticize them. They simply left me, as I'd said, at a loss for words.

"You might be right," I admitted.

"And you remember when I went down to the bot- tom of that hole? When I was down there by myself for an hour?"

"Of course."

"It never even occurred to you to leave me there forever, in that dark, dank hole. Right?"

"True. But that sort of idea wouldn't occur to a normal person."

"Are you sure about that?"

What could I say? I couldn't imagine what lay deep in other people's minds.

"I have another request," Menshiki said.

"And what is that?"

"It's about next Sunday, when Mariye and her aunt come to your place," Menshiki said. "I'd like to watch your house then with my binoculars, if you don't mind?"

"I don't mind," I said. I mean, the Commendatore had watched my girlfriend and me, right beside us, when we'd had sex. Having someone watch my terrace from afar wasn't about to faze me now.

"I thought it'd be best to tell you in advance," Menshiki said, as if excusing himself.

I was impressed all over again how strangely honest he was. We finished talking and hung up the phone. I'd been holding the phone tightly against me, and the spot above my ear ached.

The next morning I received a certified letter. I signed the receipt the mailman held out for me, and got a large envelope. Getting it didn't exactly make me feel cheerful. My experience is that certified mail is never good news.

And as expected, the mail was from a law office in Tokyo, and inside were two sets of divorce papers.

There was also a stamped, self-addressed envelope. The only thing accompanying the forms was a letter with businesslike instructions from the lawyer. It said that all I needed to do was read over the forms, check them, and, if I didn't have any objections, sign and seal one set and send it back. If there are any points that you're uncertain about, the letter said, feel free to contact the attorney in charge. I glanced through the forms, filled in the date, signed them, and affixed my seal. I didn't particularly have any **points that were uncertain**. Neither of us had any financial obligations toward the other, no estate worth dividing up, no children to fight a custody battle over. A very simple, easy-to-understand divorce. Divorce 101, you could say. Two lives had overlapped into one, and six years later had split apart again, that was it. I slipped the documents inside the return envelope and put the envelope on top of the dining room table. Tomorrow when I went to town to teach my art class all I'd need to do was toss it inside the mailbox in front of the station.

That whole afternoon I sort of half-gazed at the envelope on the table, and gradually came to feel like the entire weight of six years of married life was crammed inside that envelope. All that time—time tinged with all kinds of memories and emotions—was stuffed inside an ordinary business envelope, gradually suffocating to death. I felt a weight pressing down on my chest, and my breathing grew ragged. I picked up the envelope, took it to the studio, and placed it on the shelf, next to the dingy ancient bell. I shut the studio door, returned to the kitchen, poured a glass of the whiskey Masahiko had given me, and drank it. My rule was not to drink while it was still light out, but I figured it was okay sometimes. The kitchen was totally still and silent. No wind outside, no sound of cars. Not even any birds chirping.

I had no particular problem about getting divorced. For all intents and purposes we already were divorced. And I had no emotional hang-up about signing and sealing the official documents. If that's what she wanted, fine. It was a legal formality, nothing more.

But when it came to why, and how, things had turned out this way, the sequence of events was beyond me. I understood, of course, that over time, and as circumstances changed, a couple could grow closer, or move apart. Changes in a person's feelings aren't regulated by custom, logic, or the law. They're fluid, unstable, free to spread their wings and fly away. Like migratory birds have no concept of borders between countries.

But these were all just generalizations, and I couldn't easily grasp the individual case here—that **this woman,** Yuzu, refused to love **this man,** me, and chose instead to be loved by someone else. It felt terribly absurd, a horribly ugly way to be treated. There wasn't any anger involved (I think). I mean, what was I supposed to be angry with? What I was feeling was a fundamental numbness. The numbness your heart automatically activates to lessen the awful pain when you want somebody desperately and they reject you. A kind of emotional morphine.

I couldn't easily forget Yuzu. I still wanted her. But say she were living in a place across the valley from my house, and say I owned a pair of high-powered binoculars—would I really try to peer into her daily life through those lenses? I sincerely doubted it. What I mean is, in the first place I wouldn't pick that sort of place to live in. It would be like building a torture rack just for me.

The whiskey did its job and I went to bed before eight and fell asleep. At one thirty a.m. I woke up and couldn't get back to sleep. It was a long, lonely haul until dawn. I didn't read, didn't listen to music, just sat on the sofa in the living room blankly staring out into the empty, dark space. All sorts of thoughts swirled through my head. Most of which I shouldn't have thought about.

I wish the Commendatore were with me, I thought. I wish we could talk about something together. **Anything.** The topic didn't matter. Just hearing his voice would be enough.

But the Commendatore was nowhere to be seen. And I had no way to summon him.

30

IT REALLY DEPENDS
ON THE PERSON

The next afternoon I mailed the divorce papers I'd signed and sealed. I didn't include any letter. I simply tossed the stamped return envelope with the documents into the mailbox in front of the station. Just having that envelope out of the house felt like a burden had been lifted. I had no idea what legal route these documents would take next. Not that it mattered. They could follow whatever path they liked.

And Sunday morning, just before ten, Mariye Akikawa came to my house. A bright-blue Toyota Prius climbed the slope with barely a sound and came to a stop near my front door. In the bright Sunday sunlight, the car sparkled, grandly, vibrantly. Like it was brand-new, just unwrapped. A lot of different cars had found their way to my place recently—Menshiki's silver Jaguar, my girlfriend's red Mini, the chauffeur-driven black Infiniti that Menshiki had sent for me, Masahiko's old black Volvo, and now the blue Toyota Prius that belonged to Mariye Akikawa's aunt. And of course my own Toyota Corolla station wagon (covered with dust for so long I couldn't recall what the original color had been). I imagine people have all sorts of reasons for choosing the car they drive, and of course I had no clue why Mariye's aunt had chosen a blue Toyota Prius. It looked less like a car than a giant vacuum cleaner.

The quiet Prius engine shut off, and the surroundings grew **that much** quieter. The doors opened, and Mariye Akikawa and the woman I took to be her aunt got out. The aunt looked young, though early forties would have been my guess. She had on dark sunglasses and a gray cardigan over a simple light-blue dress. She carried a shiny black handbag and had on low, dark-gray shoes. Good shoes for driving. She shut her door, removed the sunglasses, and put them in her handbag. Her hair fell to her shoulders and was neatly curled (though not with the excessive perfection of someone just emerged from a hair salon). No accessories, other than a gold brooch on her collar.

Mariye had on a black cotton sweater and a brown, knee-length wool skirt. I'd only seen her in her school uniform up till then, and she seemed different. Side by side they looked like a mother and child from a refined, elegant household. Though I knew from Menshiki that they weren't actually mother and child.

As always I observed them through a gap in the curtain. And when the bell rang I went to the entrance and opened the front door.

Mariye's aunt had a very tranquil, calm way of speaking. She had lovely features. Not the kind of beautiful woman that would turn heads, but neat, regular features. A natural, subdued smile graced her lips, like the pale moon at dawn. She was carrying a box of cookies as a present. I was the one who had asked to have Mariye model for me, so there was no reason for her to bring me anything, but she was probably the type of person who'd had it drummed into her since she was little that when you visit someone's house you always should bring along a present. So I simply thanked her and accepted it, and showed the two of them into the living room.

"Our house isn't so far from here, a stone's throw, really, but when you drive it's a roundabout road to get here," the aunt said. (Her name was Shoko Akikawa, she told me, the **sho** written with the character that meant a traditional Japanese pan flute.) "I knew of course that this was Tomohiko Amada's house, but this is the first time I've ever been up here even though we live next door."

"I've been living here, taking care of the place, since this spring," I explained.

"Yes, I heard. I'm glad it turned out we're neighbors. I look forward to getting to know you better."

Shoko bowed deeply and thanked me for teaching Mariye. "My niece really enjoys going to the school, thanks to you," she said.

"I wouldn't say I'm exactly teaching her," I said. "Basically I just enjoy drawing together with all the pupils."

"But I understand you're a very skilled instructor. I've heard many people say that."

That I found hard to believe, but I made no comment, letting these words of praise pass unremarked. Shoko was raised well, a woman who put a premium on social niceties.

Seated side by side like this, the first thing anyone would notice about Mariye Akikawa and her aunt is that their features didn't resemble each other in the slightest. From a little ways off they seemed a well-matched mother and child, but up close it was hard to find anything in common in their appearance. Mariye had lovely features, too, and Shoko Akikawa was without doubt quite attractive, but their features were poles apart. If Shoko Akikawa's features were aiming at gaining a wonderful balance, Mariye Akikawa's aimed at destroying equilibrium, demolishing a set framework. If Shoko Akikawa aimed at a gentle, overarching harmony and stability, Mariye Akikawa sought an asymmetrical friction. Still, one could sense from the mood between them that despite all this they had a warm, healthy relationship. In a sense they were more relaxed around each other than a real mother and daughter. They seemed to maintain a comfortable distance. At least that's the impression I got.

Of course I knew nothing about why a woman like Shoko, beautiful and refined, was still single, and put up with living far off in the hills like this in her older brother's home. Perhaps she'd had a lover, a mountain climber who'd perished in an attempt to reach the summit of Mt. Everest by the most arduous route, and had pledged to remain single forever, cherishing beautiful memories of her lover in her heart. Or perhaps she was having a long-term affair with a charming married man. In any event, it wasn't my business.

Shoko walked over to the windows on the west side and gazed with great interest at the view of the valley from there.

"It's the same mountain we see from our place, but this is a slightly different angle and it doesn't look the same at all," she said, sounding impressed.

Menshiki's huge white mansion glittered on top of that mountain (and he was probably over there watching my house now through his binoculars). How did that mansion appear from her house? I wanted to ask, but it seemed risky to broach that topic right off the bat. It was hard to tell what that might lead to.

Wanting to steer clear of that, I quickly led them into the studio.

"This is where I'll have Mariye model for me," I said to them.

"This must be where Tomohiko Amada did his painting," Shoko said, gazing with great interest around the studio.

"I believe so," I said.

"There's a different feeling here, even from the rest of your house. Don't you think?"

"I'm not sure. Living here day to day, I don't really get that sense."

"What do you think, Mari-chan?" Shoko asked Mariye. "Don't you find there's an unusual sort of feeling to the room?"

Mariye was busy looking around the studio and

didn't reply. She probably hadn't heard her aunt's question. I wanted to hear her reply as well.

"While the two of you are working here, I'll wait in the living room, if that's all right?" Shoko asked.

"It's all up to Mariye. The most important thing is creating an environment where she can feel relaxed. Whether you stay here or not, either way is fine with me."

"I don't want Auntie to be here," Mariye said, the first time she'd opened her mouth that day. She spoke quietly, but it was a terse announcement with no room for negotiation.

"That's fine. I'll do as you'd prefer. I figured that's how it would be, so I brought a book to read," Shoko replied calmly, not bothered by her niece's stern tone. She was probably used to that sort of exchange.

Mariye completely ignored what her aunt said, and crouched down a bit, gazing steadily at Tomohiko Amada's **Killing Commendatore** hanging on the wall. The look in her eyes as she studied this rectangular Japanese painting was intense. She examined each and every detail of the painting, as if etching every element of it in her memory. Come to think of it (I thought), this might be the first time anyone else had ever laid eyes on this painting. It had totally slipped my mind to move the painting somewhere out of sight. Too late now, I thought.

"Do you like that painting?" I asked the girl.

Mariye didn't reply. She was concentrating so much on the painting that she didn't hear my voice. Or did she hear it but was just ignoring me?

"I'm sorry. She really goes her own way some-times," Shoko said, interceding. "She focuses so hard sometimes she blocks out everything else. She's always been that way. With books and music, paintings and movies."

I don't know why, but neither Shoko nor Mariye asked whether the painting was by Tomohiko Amada, so I didn't venture to explain. And of course I didn't tell them the title, **Killing Commendatore**, either. I wasn't too worried that they'd both seen the paint-ing. Neither one probably would notice that this was a special work not included in Amada's oeuvre. Things would be different if Menshiki or Masahiko spotted it.

I let Mariye examine **Killing Commendatore** to her heart's content. I went to the kitchen, boiled water, and made tea. I put cups and the teapot on a tray and carried it to the living room. I added the cookies Shoko had brought as a gift. Shoko and I sat on chairs in the living room and sipped tea while chatting about life in the mountains, the weather in the valley, etc. This kind of relaxed conversation was necessary before I began to work in earnest.

Mariye kept studying **Killing Commendatore** by herself for a while, then finally, like a very curious cat, slowly made her way around the studio, pick-ing things up and checking them out along the way. Brushes, tubes of paint, a canvas, and even the old bell that had been exhumed from underground. She held the bell and shook it a few times. It made its usual light jingling sound.

461

"How come there's an old bell here?" Mariye, facing a blank space, didn't seem to be addressing her question to anyone in particular. She was asking me, of course.

"The bell came nearby, from out of the ground," I said. "I just happened across it. I think it's connected with Buddhism somehow. Like a priest would ring it as he recited sutras."

She rang it again next to her ear. "Kind of a strange sound," she commented.

Once more I was impressed that such a faint sound could have reached out from underground in the woods and found me in the house. Maybe there was some special way of shaking it.

"You shouldn't touch someone else's things without permission," Shoko Akikawa cautioned her niece.

"I don't mind," I said. "It's not valuable."

Mariye seemed to quickly lose interest in the bell. She returned it to the shelf, plunked down on the stool in the middle of the room, and gazed at the scenery out the window.

"If you don't mind, I was thinking of starting," I said.

"All right, then I'll stay here and read," Shoko said, an elegant smile rising to her lips. From her black bag she took out a thick paperback with a bookstore's paper cover. I left her there, went into the studio, and shut the door between it and the living room. Mariye and I were alone in the room.

I had Mariye sit in a dining room chair, one with a

backrest. And I sat on my usual stool. We were about six feet apart.

"Could you sit there for a while for me? You can sit however you'd like. As long as you don't change your position too much, it's okay to move around. No need to sit completely still."

"Is it okay for me to talk while you're painting?" Mariye asked probingly.

"No problem at all," I said. "Let's talk."

"That drawing of me you did the other day was great."

"The one in chalk on the blackboard?"

"Too bad it got erased."

I laughed. "Can't keep it on the blackboard forever. But if you like that kind of thing I can do as many as you want. It's simple."

She didn't reply.

I picked up a thick pencil and used it as a kind of ruler to measure the various elements of her facial features. Different from a croquis, when drawing a dessan you need to take time and make sure you have an accurate grasp of the model's features. No matter what kind of painting it ends up being.

"I think you have a real talent for drawing," Mariye said after a period of silence, as if remembering.

"Thank you," I said. "Hearing that gives me courage."

"You need courage?"

"Sure I do. Everybody needs to have courage."

I picked up a large sketchbook and opened it.

"I'm going to sketch dessan of you today. I enjoy painting with oils directly on a blank canvas, but today I'll stick to drawing detailed dessan. That way I can gradually understand the kind of person you are."

"Understand me?"

"Drawing someone means understanding and interpreting another person. Not with words, but with lines, shapes, and colors."

"I wish I could understand myself," Mariye said.

"I feel the same way," I agreed. "I wish I could understand myself, too. But it's not easy. That's why I paint."

Using a pencil, I quickly sketched her face and figure from the waist up. How to transfer her depth to a flat medium was critical. And how to transplant her subtle movements to something static—that too was vital. A dessan sketch determines the outline of those.

"My breasts are really small, don't you think?" Mariye asked, out of nowhere.

"I wonder," I said.

"They're like bread that didn't rise."

I laughed. "You've just started junior high. I'm sure they'll get bigger. It's nothing to worry about."

"I don't even really need a bra. The other girls in my class all wear bras."

Certainly it was hard to see any development through her sweater. "If it really bothers you, you could always pad your bra," I said.

"You want me to?"

"Either way's fine with me. It's not like I'm paint-

ing you to capture your breasts. You should do whatever you like."

"But don't men like women with big breasts?"

"Not necessarily," I said. "When my younger sister
was about your age, her breasts were small too. But
that didn't seem to bother her."

"Maybe it bothered her, but she just didn't mention it."

"Could be," I said. But I don't think that bothered
Komi. She had other things to worry about.

"Did your sister's breasts get bigger after that?"

My hand continued to move the pencil swiftly
across the page. I didn't respond to her question.
Mariye watched my hand glide along the paper.

"Did her breasts get bigger after that?" Mariye
asked again.

"No, they didn't," I finally gave up and answered.
"My sister died the year she entered junior high. She
was only twelve."

Mariye didn't say anything for a while.

"Don't you think my aunt's really beautiful?"
Mariye said, abruptly changing subjects.

"Yes, she's a very lovely person."

"Are you single?"

"Ah—**nearly**," I responded. Once that envelope
arrived at the law office it'd be completely.

"Would you like to go on a date with her?"

"That would be nice."

"She has big breasts, too."

"I hadn't noticed."

"And they're really nicely shaped. We bathe to-gether sometimes, so I know."

I looked at Mariye's face again. "Do you get along well with your aunt?"

"We fight sometimes," she said.

"About what?"

"All kinds of things. When we have a difference of opinion, or when she makes me mad."

"You're an unusual girl," I said. "You're quite different from when you're in art class. I got the impression you were very quiet."

"In places where I don't want to talk, I don't," she said simply. "Am I talking too much? Would it be better if I stayed quiet?"

"No, not at all. I like talking. Feel free to talk as much as you like."

Of course I welcomed a lively conversation. I wasn't about to stay totally silent for nearly two hours and just paint.

"I can't help thinking about my breasts," Mariye said after a while. "That's all I think about, pretty much. Is that weird?"

"Not particularly," I said. "You're at that age. When I was your age all I thought about was my penis. Whether it was shaped funny, or was too small, whether it was working wrong."

"What about now?"

"You're asking what I think about my penis now?"

"Yeah."

I thought about it. "I don't give it much thought.

It's pretty ordinary, I guess, and hasn't given me any problems."

"Do women admire it?"

"Occasionally there might be one who does. But that might just be flattery. Like when people praise paintings."

Mariye pondered this for a while. Finally she said, "You may be a little strange."

"Really?"

"Normal men don't talk like that. Even my father doesn't say things like that to me."

"I doubt fathers in normal families want to talk about penises with their daughters," I said. All the while my hand continued to move busily over the paper.

"At what age do nipples get bigger?" Mariye asked.

"I'm not really sure. Since I'm a guy. I'd say it really depends on the person."

"Did you have a girlfriend when you were a kid?"

"I had my first girlfriend when I was seventeen. A girl in the same class in high school."

"What high school?"

I told her the name of a public high school in Toshima, in Tokyo. Outside of people who lived in Toshima, probably no one had ever heard of it.

"Did you like school?"

I shook my head. "Not particularly."

"Did you ever see that girlfriend's nipples?"

"Yeah," I said. "She showed them to me."

"How big were they?"

I remembered the girl's nipples. "They weren't especially small, or big. Normal size, I guess."

"Did she pad her bra?"

I tried to recall the bra my girlfriend had worn back then. All I had was a very vague memory of it. What I did recall was how much trouble I had slipping my hand behind her and unhooking it. "No, I don't think she padded it."

"What's she doing now?"

What **was** she doing now? "I don't know. I haven't seen her for a long time. I imagine she's married, maybe with some children."

"How come you don't see her?"

"The last time I saw her, she said she never wanted to see me again."

Mariye frowned. "Was this because there was something wrong with you?"

"I guess," I said. Of course the problem lay with me. No room for doubt there.

Actually, I'd recently had two dreams about this high school girlfriend. In one dream we were strolling along a river on a summer's evening. I tried to kiss her, but her long black hair formed a curtain in front of her face and my lips couldn't touch hers. In the dream she was still seventeen, but I had already turned thirty-six, something I suddenly noticed. And that's when I woke up. It was such a vivid dream. I could still feel her hair on my lips. Before this, I hadn't thought about her for years.

"How much younger than you was your younger sister?" Mariye said, again suddenly changing topics.

"Three years younger."

"You said she died when she was twelve?"

"That's right."

"So that would make you fifteen then."

"Right. I was fifteen. I'd just started high school. And she'd just started junior high. Just like you."

Now that I thought about it, Komi was now twenty-four years younger than me. Since she'd died, every year the age gap only increased between us.

"I was six when my mother died," Mariye said. "She got stung by hornets. When she was walking in the mountains nearby."

"I'm very sorry," I said.

"She had an allergy to hornet stings. They took her by ambulance to the hospital but she was already in shock and went into cardiac arrest."

"Your aunt moved in with you after that?"

"Yeah," Mariye said. "She's my father's younger sister. I wish I'd had an older brother. A brother three years older."

I finished up the first dessan and began a second. I wanted to draw her from several angles. This first day I planned to devote just to sketches.

"Did you ever fight with your sister?" she asked.

"No, I don't recall ever fighting."

"So you got along well?"

"I suppose so. I never considered whether we did or not."

"What does 'nearly single' mean?" Mariye asked, again shifting subjects.

"I'll soon be officially divorced," I said. "We're in

the midst of handling all the paperwork, so that's why it's 'nearly.' "

She narrowed her eyes. "I don't get **divorce**. Nobody I know has ever divorced."

"I don't get it either. I mean, it's the first time I ever got divorced."

"What does it feel like?"

"A bit bizarre, I guess. Like you're walking along as always, sure you're on the right path, when the path suddenly vanishes, and you're facing an empty space, no sense of direction, no clue where to go, and you just keep trudging along. That's what it feels like."

"How long were you married?"

"About six years."

"How old is your wife?"

"She's three years younger." Just a coincidence, but the same age difference as with my sister.

"Do you think you wasted those six years?"

I thought about it. "No, I don't think so. I don't want to think it was all for nothing. We had a lot of good times, too."

"Does your wife think so too?"

I shook my head. "I don't know. I'd hope she would, of course."

"You didn't ask her?"

"No. If I have a chance, maybe I will sometime."

Silence reigned between us for a while. I focused on the dessan, and Mariye Akikawa was lost in serious thought—thoughts about the size of nipples, perhaps, or divorce, or hornets, or maybe something else entirely. Eyes narrowed, lips tight, both hands tightly holding her knees. She'd shifted into that mode, apparently, as I was capturing her earnest expression on the white page of my sketchbook.

Every day, exactly at noon, I could hear a chime from down the mountain. Ringing from some government office, or maybe a school, to announce the time. When I heard it now, I glanced at the clock and finished drawing. I'd managed to complete three dessan during this first session. All of them pretty interesting compositions, each one hinting at something to come. Not bad for a day's work.

Mariye Akikawa had sat on the chair in the studio, posing for me, for over an hour and a half. For the first day, that was enough. For someone not used to it—especially an active, growing child—posing for a painting wasn't easy.

Shoko Akikawa had put on black-framed glasses and was seated on the living room sofa absorbed in reading her paperback. When I came in she took off the glasses and stowed the paperback in her bag. The glasses made her look quite intellectual.

"We're all finished for the day," I said. "If it's all right, could you come again the same day next week?"

"Yes, of course," Shoko said. "It feels really nice to read here. Maybe because the sofa's so comfortable?"

"You don't mind?" I asked Mariye.

Mariye nodded silently. **I don't mind**, it meant.

In front of her aunt she was totally changed, and had become taciturn again. Maybe she didn't like when the three of us were together.

They got into their blue Toyota Prius and drove away. I saw them off at the front door. Shoko, sunglasses on, reached a hand out the window and gave a few short waves goodbye. A small, pale hand. I raised my hand in reply. Mariye tucked in her chin and stared straight ahead. Once the car had disappeared from view down the slope, I went back inside. The house seemed suddenly barren. Like something that should be there wasn't anymore.

An odd pair, I thought, as I stared at the teacups still on the table. There was something peculiar about them. But what, exactly?

I remembered Menshiki. Maybe I should have taken Mariye out on the terrace so he could get a good look at her through his binoculars. But then I rethought that. Why did I have to go out of my way to do that, when he hadn't even asked me to?

Other opportunities would present themselves. No need to rush. Probably.

31

MAYBE A LITTLE TOO PERFECT

That night I got a call from Menshiki. The clock showed that it was past nine. He apologized for calling so late. Something silly came up and I couldn't get free until now, he said. I'm not going to bed for a while, I said, so don't worry about the time.

"So how did things go today? Did it work out well?" he asked.

"It did. I completed a few dessan of Mariye. The two of them will be coming over the same time next Sunday."

"I'm glad," Menshiki said. "By the way, was the aunt favorably disposed toward you?"

Favorably disposed? What a strange way of putting it.

I said, "Yes, she seems like a very nice woman. I don't know if 'favorably disposed' is the right term, but she didn't seem particularly wary."

I summed up what had taken place that morning. Menshiki listened with what seemed like bated breath, apparently trying to absorb as much detailed information as he could. Other than a couple of questions, he hardly said a word, and just listened intently. What sort of clothes the two had on, how they had arrived. How they appeared, what they'd said. And how I'd gone about sketching Mariye Akikawa. I told Menshiki all this, piece by piece. I didn't, though, delve into Mariye's obsession with the size of her breasts. That was best kept between us.

"It might be a little early, then, for me to show up next week?" Menshiki asked me.

"It's up to you. I can't say. I don't have a problem if you come over next week."

On the other end of the line Menshiki was silent. "I'll have to think about it. It's kind of delicate."

"Take your time. It's going to take a while to finish the painting, and there should be plenty of opportunities. Next week, or the week after that—either way's fine with me."

I'd never seen Menshiki so hesitant before. Quickly decisive and never wavering—that was the Menshiki I knew.

I was thinking of asking him if he'd been watching my house with his binoculars this morning. Whether he'd been able to observe Mariye and her aunt. But I thought better of it. As long as he didn't bring it up, it seemed smarter not to mention that topic. Even if the place under surveillance was the house I was living in.

Menshiki thanked me again. "I'm really sorry to ask you to go to all this trouble for me."

I said, "I'm not doing anything for your sake. I'm simply doing a painting of Mariye Akikawa. I'm painting it because I want to. I thought that's how we decided things were going to be. Both the private and public reasons for it. So there's no reason for you to thank me."

"Still, I'm very grateful," Menshiki said quietly. "In **a lot of ways.**"

I didn't really understand what he meant by "a lot of ways," but didn't ask. It was getting late. We said a quick goodbye and hung up. But after I put the phone down, it suddenly occurred to me that Menshiki might be spending a long, sleepless night tonight. I could sense the tension in his voice. He probably had lots of things on his mind.

Not much happened that week. The Commendatore didn't make an appearance, and my girlfriend didn't get in touch. A very quiet week altogether. Autumn steadily deepened around me. The sky opened up, the air clear and crisp, the clouds like beautiful white brushstrokes.

I often studied the three dessan I'd done of Mariye. The different poses, the different angles. I found them fascinating, and suggestive. Though from the beginning I hadn't planned to choose one of them to use as the preliminary design for the painting. The point of doing those three sketches, as she herself had said, was so I could understand the totality of this girl. To internally assimilate her.

I looked at those three dessan over and over again, intently focusing, trying to construct a concrete picture of the girl in my mind. As I did this, I got the distinct sense of Mariye Akikawa's figure and that of my sister getting mixed into one. Was this appropriate? I couldn't say. But the spirits of these two young girls nearly the same age were already, somewhere—probably in some deep internal recesses I shouldn't access—blended and combined. I could no longer unravel those two intertwined spirits.

That Thursday I received a letter from my wife. This was the first time since I'd left home in March that she'd gotten in touch. My name and address and hers were written on the envelope in her familiar, beautiful, steady handwriting. She was still using my last name, I saw. Maybe it was more convenient, somehow, until the divorce became official, to continue to use her husband's last name.

I used scissors to neatly snip open the envelope. Inside was a postcard with a photo of a polar bear standing on top of an iceberg. On the card she'd written a simple message thanking me for signing the divorce papers and mailing them back so quickly.

How are you? I'm managing to get by, nothing to report. I'm still living in the same place. Thank you for mailing back the papers so quickly. I appreciate it. I'll get in touch when there's been progress in the process.

If there's anything you left at the house you need, please let me know. I'll send it to you. At any rate, I hope both our new lives work out.

Yuzu

I reread the letter many times, straining to decipher the feelings hidden behind those lines. But I couldn't detect any implied emotion or intention. She just seemed to be transmitting the clearly stated message that the words conveyed.

One other thing I didn't understand was why it had taken her so long to prepare the divorce papers. It's not that much trouble to get them ready. And she must have wanted to dissolve our relationship as fast as possible. Even so, half a year had passed since I'd left our house. What had she been doing all that time? What had been going through her mind?

I gazed at the postcard with the polar bear, but couldn't read any intentions in that either. Why a polar bear from the North Pole? She probably just happened to have the polar bear card on hand and used it. Most likely that's the case, I figured. Or was she suggesting that my future was like that of the polar bear, stuck on a tiny iceberg, directionless, carried away by the whims of the current? No—that was reading too much into it.

I tossed the card into the envelope and put it inside the top drawer of my desk. Once I shut the drawer it felt like things had progressed one step forward. Like with a **click** the scale had moved one line up. Not that this was my doing. Someone, something, had prepared this new stage in my stead, and I was simply going along with the program.

I recalled how on Sunday I'd talked to Mariye Akikawa about life after divorce.

Like you're walking along as always, sure you're

on the right path, when the path suddenly vanishes, and you're facing an empty space, no sense of direction, no clue where to go, and you just keep trudging along. That's what it feels like.

A directionless ocean current, a road to nowhere, it didn't matter much. They were both the same. Just metaphors. I was experiencing the real thing, and being swallowed up by reality. If I had that, who needs a metaphor?

If I could, I wanted to write a letter to Yuzu to explain the situation I found myself in now. I didn't think I could write something vague like **I'm managing to get by, nothing to report**. Far from it. My honest sense was there was **too much to report**. But if I started writing about every single thing that had happened to me since I started living here, it would spin out of control. The biggest problem was that I couldn't explain well to myself what was happening. At least I knew I couldn't find a consistent, logical context in which to **explain** it all.

So I decided not to write back to Yuzu. If I did start writing there were only two ways to go: either explain everything that had taken place (ignoring logic and consistency), or write nothing. I chose the latter. In a sense I really was the lonely polar bear left behind to drift on an iceberg. Not a single mailbox as far as the eye could see. A polar bear has no way to send a letter, now does he.

·　　·　　·

I remember very well when Yuzu and I first met, and started dating.

On our first date we had dinner, talked about all kinds of things, and she seemed to like me. She said I could see her again. From the first our minds seemed to inexplicably click. Simply put, we seemed a good match.

But it took some time before I actually became her lover. Yuzu had another man she'd been seeing for two years. Not that she was head over heels in love with him.

"He's really handsome. Though a bit boring sometimes," she said.

Very handsome but boring . . . There was no one I knew like that, so I couldn't picture that type of person. What came to mind was a dish of food that looked delicious but ended up tasting bland. Would anyone be happy with that kind of food?

"I've always had a weakness for good-looking men," she said, as if making a confession. "Whenever I meet a handsome man it's like my brain goes out the window. I know that's a problem, but I can't do anything about it. I can't get over that. That might be my biggest weakness."

"A chronic disease," I said.

She nodded. "That could be. An incurable disorder. A chronic disease."

"Not exactly great news for me," I said. Handsome features weren't my strongest selling point.

She didn't deny that, and just laughed happily. At

least she didn't seem bored when we were together. She had a lot to say, and laughed a lot.

So I waited patiently for things to not work out between her and this handsome boyfriend. (He wasn't merely good-looking, but had graduated from a top university and had a high-paying job at a top corporation. I bet he and Yuzu's father got along famously.) All this time she and I talked over all sorts of things, went to all sorts of places. We got to understand each other better. We kissed, held each other, but didn't have sex. Having a physical relationship with several partners at the same time wasn't her style. "I'm a bit old-fashioned that way," she said. So all I could do was bide my time.

This went on for about half a year. For me, it felt like eternity. Sometimes I just wanted to give up. But I managed to hang in there, convinced that someday soon she would be mine.

And finally she and her handsome boyfriend broke up (at least I think they broke up—she never said a word about it, so it was conjecture on my part), and she chose me—not much to look at, not much of a breadwinner—as her lover. Soon after we decided to get married.

I remember very well the first time we made love. We'd gone to stay at a small hot-springs town in the country, and spent our first night together there. Everything went really well. Almost perfect, you could even say. Maybe a little too perfect. Her skin was soft and pale, and silky smooth. The somewhat slick hot mineral water of the hot springs bath, combined with the pale glow of the early-autumn moonlight, may have contributed to the beauty and smoothness of her skin. I held her naked body for the first time, went inside her, she moaned quietly in my ear, and dug her nails hard into my back. The autumn insects were in full chorus then, too. A cool mountain stream burbled in the background. I made a firm pledge to myself then: **Never, ever, let this woman go**. This may have been the most sublime moment of my life up till then. Finally making Yuzu mine.

After I got the short letter from Yuzu I thought about her for a long time. About when we'd first met, that autumn night when we first made love. About how my feelings for her had basically never changed, from the first moment up to the present. Even now I didn't want to lose her. That much was clear to me. I'd signed and sealed the divorce papers, but that didn't change things. No matter how I felt about it, though, the fact was that she'd suddenly left me. Gone far away—probably very far away—where even the most powerful binoculars couldn't afford me a glimpse of her.

Somewhere, while I was oblivious to it, she must have found a new, handsome lover. As always, her **brain went out the window**. I should have picked up on this when she started refusing to sleep with me. **Having a physical relationship with several partners at the same time wasn't her style**. If only I'd thought about it, I soon would have realized that.

A chronic disease, I thought. A serious illness with no prospects for a cure. A physical inclination that doesn't respond to reason.

That night (a rainy Thursday night) I had a long, dark dream.

In that small seaside town in Miyagi I was driving the white Subaru Forester (it was now my car). I had on an old black leather jacket, and a black golf cap with a Yonex logo. I was tall, deeply suntanned, my salt-and-pepper hair short and stiff. In other words, I was the man with the white Subaru Forester. I was stealthily following my wife and the small car (a red Peugeot 205) the man she was having an affair with was driving. We were on the highway that ran along the coast. I saw the two of them go into a tacky love hotel on the outskirts of town. The next day I came up behind my wife and strangled her with a narrow, white belt from a bathrobe. I was used to physical labor and had powerful arms. And as I strangled her with all my might, I screamed something. I couldn't hear what I'd yelled out—a meaningless roar of pure rage. A horrific rage I'd never experienced before had control over my mind and body. White spittle flew as I roared out.

As she desperately gasped for air, I saw my wife's temples convulse a little. I saw her pink tongue ball up and twist inside her mouth. Blue veins rose up on her skin like an invisible-ink map. I smelled my own sweat. An unpleasant smell I'd never smelled before rose up from my body like steam from a hot springs. It reminded me of the stink of some hairy beast.

Don't you dare paint me, I ordered myself. I violently thrust out an index finger at myself in the mirror on the wall. **Don't paint me anymore!**

And there I snapped awake.

I knew now what had frightened me most in bed in that love hotel in the seaside town. Deep in my heart I feared that in the last instant I really would have strangled to death that girl (the young girl whose name I didn't even know). "You can just pretend," she said. But it might not have ended with just that. It might not have ended with **just pretend**. And the reason for that lay inside me.

I wish I could understand myself, too. But it's not easy.

This is what I'd told Mariye Akikawa. I remembered this as I wiped the sweat away with a towel.

The rain let up on Friday morning, the sky turning beautifully sunny. I hadn't slept well, felt worked up, and to calm down went for an hour's walk around the neighborhood later in the morning. I went into the woods, walked behind the little shrine, and checked out the hole for the first time in a long while. It was November now and the wind was much colder than before. The ground was covered with damp, fallen leaves. The hole was, as before, tightly covered over with several boards. Many-colored leaves had piled up on the boards, and there were several heavy stones to hold the boards down. But the way the stones were lined up seemed a little different from when I'd last seen them. Nearly the same, yet ever so slightly positioned differently.

I didn't worry about it. There wouldn't be anyone else other than Menshiki and me who would tramp all the way out here. I pulled away one of the boards and peered down inside, but no one was there. The ladder was leaned up against the wall like before. Like always, that dark, stone-lined chamber lay there, deep and silent, at my feet. I put the board back on top and placed the stone back where it had been.

It didn't bother me, either, that the Commendatore hadn't appeared for a good two weeks. Like he said, an Idea has a lot of business to attend to. Business that transcended time and space.

The following Sunday finally came. A lot of things happened that day. It turned out to be a very hectic day.

32

HIS SKILLS WERE IN
GREAT DEMAND

Another prisoner approached us as we talked. He
was a professional painter from Warsaw, a man of
medium height with a hawk nose and a very black
mustache on his fair-skinned face . . . His distinctive
figure stood out from afar, and his professional status
(his skills were in great demand in the camp) was
evident. He was certainly no one's nonentity. He
often talked to me at length about his work.

"I do color paintings, portraits, for the Germans.
They bring me photos of their relatives, wives,
mothers and children. Everyone wants to have
pictures of their closest kin. The SS describe their
families to me with emotion and love—the color of
their eyes, their hair. I produce family portraits from
amateurish, blurry black-and-white photos. Believe
me, I would rather paint black-and-white pictures
of the children in the piles of corpses in the **Lazarett**
than the Germans' families. Give 'em pictures of the
people they murdered; let 'em take them home and
hang them on the wall, the sons of bitches."

The artist was especially distraught on this occasion.

—SAMUEL WILLENBERG, **Revolt in Treblinka,**
p. 96. © Copyright by Samuel Willenberg, 1984.
Lazarett was another name for the execution
facility in the Treblinka concentration camp.

THE SHIFTING METAPHOR

33

I LIKE THINGS I CAN SEE AS MUCH AS THINGS I CAN'T

Sunday was another fine clear day. No wind to speak of, and the fall colors in the valley sparkling in the sunlight. Small white-breasted birds hopped from one branch to the next, deftly pecking the red berries. I sat on the terrace, soaking it all in. Nature grants its beauty to us all, drawing no line between rich and poor. Like time—no, scratch that, time could be a different story. Money may help us buy a little extra of that.

The bright blue Toyota Prius rolled up the slope to my door at ten on the dot. Shoko Akikawa was decked out in a thin beige turtleneck and snug-fitting slacks of pale green. Around her neck, a modest gold chain gave off a muted glow. As on her past visit, her hair was perfectly done. When it swayed I could catch a glimpse of the lovely line of her neck. Today, though, she had a leather bag, not a purse, slung over her shoulder. She wore brown loafers. It was a casual outfit, yet she had clearly spent time choosing each piece. And the swell of her breasts was very attractive too. I had the inside scoop from her niece that "no padding" was involved. I felt quite drawn to those breasts—in a purely aesthetic way, of course.

Mariye was dressed in straight-cut faded blue jeans and white Converse sneakers, a 180-degree turnaround from the formality of her first visit. Her jeans had holes in them (strategically placed, of course). She had on the sort of plaid shirt a lumberjack might wear in the woods, with a thin gray windbreaker draped over her shoulders. Underneath the shirt, as before, her chest was flat. And, just as before, she had a sour expression on her face. Like a cat whose dish has been whisked away halfway through its meal.

Just as I'd done the previous week, I went into the kitchen, made a pot of tea, and brought it to the living room. Then I showed them the three dessan I had made.

Shoko seemed to like them. "They're all so full of life," she exclaimed. "So much more like Mariye than photographs."

"Can I keep them?" Mariye asked.

"Sure," I answered. "Once your portrait is finished. I may need them until then."

Her aunt looked worried. "Really? Aren't you being too— . . ."

"Not at all," I said. "They're of no use to me once the portrait's done."

"Will you use one of these dessan for your underdrawing?" Mariye asked.

"No." I shook my head. "I did them just to get a three-dimensional feel for who you are. The you who I put on canvas will be altogether different."

"Can you tell what that's going to look like?"

"No, not yet. The two of us still have to figure that one out."

"Figure out how I look three-dimensionally?" Mariye asked.

"That's right. A painting is a flat surface, but it still has to have three dimensions. Do you follow me?"

Mariye frowned. I guessed she might somehow associate the word "three-dimensional" with her flat chest. In fact, she shot a glance at the curves beneath her aunt's thin sweater before looking at me.

"How can somebody learn to draw this well?" Mariye asked.

"You mean like these dessan?"

She nodded. "Yeah, like dessan, croquis, things like that."

"It's all practice. The more you practice the better you get."

"I think there are a lot of people," she said, "who don't improve, no matter how much they practice."

She sure hit that one on the head. I had attended art school, but loads of my classmates couldn't paint their way out of a paper bag. However we thrash about, we are all thrown in one direction or another by our natural talent, or lack of it. That's a basic truth we all have to learn to live with.

"Fair enough, but you still have to practice. If you don't, any gifts or talents you do have won't emerge where people can see them."

Shoko gave an emphatic nod. Mariye looked dubious.

491

"You want to learn to paint well, correct?" I asked
her.

Mariye nodded. "I like things I can see as much as
things I can't," she said.

I looked in her eyes. A light was shining there. I
wasn't sure I understood exactly what she meant. But
that inner light was drawing me in.

"What a strange thing to say," Shoko said. "Like
you were speaking in riddles."

Mariye didn't respond, just studied her hands.
When she did look up a short while later, the light
was gone. It had only been there a moment.

Mariye and I went to the studio. Shoko had already
pulled out the same thick paperback—at least, it
looked identical to the one she had brought the previous week—and settled down on the sofa to read.
She seemed totally engrossed in the book. I was even
more curious than before as to what it might be, but
I didn't ask.

Mariye and I sat across from each other about six
feet apart, just as we had the last time. The only difference was that now I had an easel and canvas in front
of me. No paints or brush, though—my hands were
empty. My eyes hopped back and forth, from Mariye
to the canvas to Mariye again. All the while, the question of how best to portray her "three-dimensionally"
was running through my mind. I needed a **story** of
some sort to work from. It wasn't enough to just look
at the person I happened to be painting. Nothing

good could result from that. The portrait might be a passable likeness, but no more. To turn out a true portrait, I had to discover **the story that must be painted**. Only that could get the ball rolling.

We sat there for some time, me on the stool, Mariye on a straight-backed chair, as I studied her face. She stared back at me without blinking, never averting her eyes. She didn't look defiant so much as ready to stand her ground. Her pretty, almost doll-like, appearance sent people the wrong signal—at her core, she had a strong sense of herself, and her own unshakable way of doing things. Once she'd drawn a straight line, good luck getting her to bend it.

There was something in Mariye's eyes that reminded me of Menshiki, though I had to look closely to see it. I had felt the similarity before, but it still surprised me. Their gaze had a strange radiance—"a frozen flame" was the phrase that leapt to mind. That flame had warmth, but at the same time, it was cool and collected. Like a rare jewel whose glow came from deep within. That light expressed naked yearning when projected outside. Focused inward, it strove for completion. These two sides were equally strong, and at perpetual war with each other.

Did Menshiki's revelation that his blood might be running through Mariye's veins influence me? Perhaps that had led me to unconsciously link the two of them together.

Whatever the case, I had to transfer that glow in her eyes to the canvas, to capture how **special** it was. The core element in her expression, the thing that cut through her modulated exterior. Yet I still hadn't located the context that made such a transfer possible. If I failed, that warm light would come across as an icy jewel, nothing more. Where was the heat coming from, and where was it headed? I had to find out.

I sat there for fifteen minutes, gazing at her face, then at the canvas and back again, before finally giving up. I pushed the easel aside and took a few slow, deep breaths.

"Let's talk," I said.

"Um, sure," she answered. "What do you want to talk about?"

"I want to know more about you. If that's okay."

"Like?"

"Well, what sort of person is your father?"

Mariye gave a small smirk. "I don't know him very well."

"You don't talk?"

"We hardly see each other."

"Because he's busy with work?"

"I don't know anything about his work," Mariye said. "I don't think he cares about me that much."

"Doesn't care?"

"That's why he handed me over to my aunt to raise."

I took a pass on that one.

"How about your mother—can you remember her? You were six when she passed away, right?"

"I can only remember her in patches."

"What do you mean, in patches?"

"My mom disappeared all of a sudden. I was too

little to understand what dying meant, so I didn't really know what had happened. She was there and then she just **wasn't**. Like smoke."

Mariye was quiet for a moment.

"It happened so quickly, and I couldn't understand the reason," she said at last. "That's why I can't remember much about that part of my life, like right before and after her death."

"You must have been pretty confused."

"It's like there's this high wall that divides when she was with me and when she was gone. I can't connect the two parts together." She chewed her lip for a moment. "Do you get what I mean?"

"I think so," I said. "My sister died when she was twelve. I told you that before, right?"

Mariye nodded.

"She was born with a defective valve in her heart. She had a big operation, and everything was supposed to be okay, but for some reason there was still a problem. So she lived with a time bomb ticking inside her body. As a result, everyone in our family was more or less prepared for the worst. Her death didn't hit us like a bolt from the blue, like when your mother was stung by hornets."

"A bolt . . . ?"

"A bolt from the blue," I said. "A bolt of lightning that strikes from a cloudless sky. Something sudden and unexpected."

"A bolt from the blue," she said. "What characters is it written with?"

"The 'blue' is written with characters for 'blue sky.'

'Bolt' is really complicated—I can't write it myself. In fact, I've never written it. If you're curious, you should look it up in a dictionary when you get back home."

"A bolt from the blue," she repeated. She seemed to be storing the phrase in her mental filing cabinet.

"At any rate," I went on, "we all had an idea what might happen. When it actually did, though—when she had a sudden heart attack and died, all in one day—our preparations didn't make a bit of difference. Her death paralyzed me. And not just me, my whole family."

"Did something change inside you after that?"

"Yes, completely. Both **inside** and **outside**. Time didn't pass as it had before—it flowed differently. And, like you said, I had a problem connecting how things were before her death with the way they were after."

Mariye stared at me without speaking for a full ten seconds. "Your sister meant a lot to you, didn't she?" she said at last.

"Yes," I nodded. "She did."

Mariye studied her lap for a moment. "It's because my memory is blocked," she said, looking up, "that I have trouble recalling my mom. The kind of person she was, her face, the things she said to me. My dad doesn't talk much about her either."

All I knew about Mariye's mother was the blow-by-blow account Menshiki had given me of the last time they had had sex. It had been on his office couch—the moment of Mariye's conception, perhaps—and it was violent. Not a big help at the moment.

"You must remember something, even if it's not much. After all, you lived with her till you were six."

"Just the smell."

"The smell of her body?"

"No, the smell of rain."

"Rain?"

"It was raining then. So hard I could hear the drops hit the ground. But my mother was walking outside without an umbrella. So we walked through the rain together, holding hands. I think it was summer."

"A summer shower, then?"

"I guess so. The pavement was hot from the sun, so it gave off that smell. That's what I remember. We were high in the mountains, on some kind of observation deck. And my mother was singing a song."

"What kind of song?"

"I can't remember the melody. But I do remember some of the words. They were like, 'The sun's shining on a big green field across the river, but it's been raining on this side for so long.' Have you ever heard a song like that?"

It didn't ring a bell. "No," I replied. "I don't think so."

Mariye gave a little shrug. "I've asked different people, but no one knows it. I wonder why. Do you think maybe I made it up in my head?"

"Maybe she invented it there on the spot. For you."

Mariye looked up at me and smiled. "I never thought about it like that before. If that's true—it's pretty cool."

I think it was the first time I'd seen her smile. It

was as if a ray of sunlight had shot through a crack in an overcast sky to illuminate one special spot. It was that kind of smile.

"Could you recognize the place if you went there again?" I asked. "Back to that same observation deck in the mountains?"

"Maybe," Mariye said. "I'm not sure, but maybe."

"I think it's pretty cool that you carry that scene inside you."

Mariye just nodded.

After that, we just sat back and listened to the birds chirping. The autumn sky outside the window was perfectly clear. Not a wisp of cloud anywhere. We were each in our own inner world, pursuing our own random thoughts.

It was Mariye who broke the silence. "Why's that painting facing the wrong way?" she asked.

She was pointing at my oil painting (to be more precise, my attempted painting) of the man with the white Subaru Forester. The canvas was sitting on the floor, turned to the wall so that I wouldn't have to look at it.

"I'm trying to paint a certain man. It's a work in progress, but it's not progressing right now."

"Can I see it?"

"Sure. I've just started it, though. I have a long way to go."

I turned the canvas around and placed it on the easel. Mariye got up from her chair, walked over, and stood before it with her arms folded. The sharp gleam in her eyes had returned. Her lips were set in a straight line.

I had used three colors—red, green, and black—but still hadn't given the man a distinct shape. My initial charcoal sketch was now totally obscured. He refused to be fleshed out any further, to have more color added to his form. But I knew he was there. I had grasped the essence of who he was. He was like a fish caught in a net. I had been trying to pull him out of the depths, and he was fighting me at every turn. At that point in our tug of war I had set the painting aside.

"This is where you stopped?" Mariye asked.

"That's right. I couldn't find a way to push it past this stage."

"It looks pretty finished to me," she murmured.

I stood next to her and looked at the painting again from her angle. Could she really see the man lurking there in the darkness?

"You mean I don't need to add anything more?" I asked.

"Yeah, I think you should just leave it like this."

I swallowed. She was echoing what the man with the white Subaru Forester had said almost word for word. **Leave the painting alone. Don't touch it again.**

"Why do you think that?" I pressed.

Mariye didn't answer right away. Instead, she studied the painting some more. She unfolded her arms and pressed her hands to her cheeks. As if they were hot, and she was trying to cool them.

"This painting is more than powerful enough as it is," she said at last.

"More than powerful enough?"

"I think so."

"You mean a **not so good kind** of power?"

Mariye didn't answer. Her hands were still pressed to her cheeks.

"Do you know the man in the painting well?"

I shook my head. "No, to tell the truth he's a complete stranger. I ran across him a while back. In a faraway town when I was on a long trip. We never talked, so I don't know his name."

"I can't tell if the power is good or not. Maybe it could be either good or bad, depending on the situation. You know, like the way we see things changes depending on where we're standing."

"And you don't think I should let that power come to the surface, right?"

She looked me in the eye. "Suppose you did and it turned out to be a **not so good thing**, what would you do? What if it tried to grab you?"

She was right. If it turned out to be a **not so good thing**, or indeed an **evil thing**, and it reached for me, what would I do then?

I took the canvas from the easel and set it back down on the floor, facing the wall. The moment its surface was hidden, the tension in the studio released its grip. It was a tangible sensation.

Perhaps I should pack it up and shut it away in the attic, I thought. Just as Tomohiko Amada had stashed

Killing Commendatore there, to make sure no one could see it.

"All right, so then what do you think of that painting?" I asked, pointing to **Killing Commendatore** hanging on the wall.

"I like it," Mariye said immediately. "Who did it?"

"It was painted by Tomohiko Amada, the man who owns this house."

"It's calling out to me. Like a caged bird crying to be set free. That's the feeling I get."

I looked at her. "Bird? What kind of bird?"

"I don't know what kind of bird. Or what kind of cage. Or what they look like. It's just my feeling. I think maybe this painting's a little too difficult for me."

"You're not the only one. It's too difficult for me, too. But I'm sure you're right. There is a cry in this painting, a plea that the artist desperately wanted people to hear. I react the same way you do. But for the life of me, I can't figure out what that plea is."

"Someone is murdering someone else. Out of passion."

"Exactly. The young man has plunged a knife into the older man's chest, exactly as he planned. The man being murdered can't believe what's happening. The others are in total shock at what's taking place before their eyes."

"Can there be a proper murder?"

I thought for a moment. "I'm not sure. It depends how you define 'proper' and 'improper.' Many people regard the death penalty as a proper form of murder." Or assassination, I thought.

Mariye took a moment to respond. "It's funny, a man's being killed, and his blood is flying all over the place, but it's not depressing. It's like the painting is trying to take me someplace else. Someplace where things like 'proper' and 'improper' don't matter."

I didn't pick up a brush that day. Instead, Mariye and I sat there in the bright studio talking about whatever crossed our minds. I kept a close eye on her, though, filing each expression and mannerism away in my mind. That stock of memories would become the flesh and blood of the portrait I wanted to paint.

"You didn't draw anything today," Mariye commented.

"There are days like this," I said. "Time steals some things, but it gives us back others. Making time our ally is an important part of our work."

Mariye said nothing, just studied my eyes. As if she was peering into a house, her face pressed against the window. She was contemplating the meaning of time.

When the chimes rang as always at noon, Mariye and I moved from the studio to the living room. Shoko Akikawa was sitting on the sofa, wearing her black-rimmed glasses, reading her paperback. She was so deep in the book it was hard to tell if she was breathing.

"What are you reading?" I asked, unable to bear the suspense any longer.

"If I told you what it was," she said with a smile, marking her spot and closing the book, "it would jinx it. For some reason, every time I tell someone what I'm reading, I'm unable to finish. Something unexpected happens, and I have to break off partway through. It's strange, but it's true. So I've made it my policy not to reveal the title to anyone. I'd love to tell you about the book once I'm done, though."

"No worries. I'm quite happy to wait until you're finished. I could see how much you're enjoying it, so I got curious."

"It's a fascinating book. Once I get into it I can't stop. That's why I've decided to read it only when I'm here. This way, two hours pass before I know it."

"My aunt reads tons of books," Mariye chimed in.

"I don't have that much to do these days," her aunt said. "So books are how I get by."

"Do you have a job?" I asked.

She removed her glasses and gently massaged the crease between her eyebrows. "I volunteer at our local library once a week. I used to work at a private medical college in Tokyo. I was secretary to the president there. But I gave it up when I moved here."

"That was when Mariye's mother passed away, wasn't it?"

"At the time, I thought it would just be temporary.

That I would stay only until things got sorted out. But once I started living with Mariye it became hard to leave. So I've been here ever since. Of course, if my brother remarried, I would move back to the city."

"I'd go with you if that happened," Mariye said.

Shoko smiled politely but didn't say anything.

"Why don't you stay for lunch?" I asked the two of them. "I can whip up a pasta and salad in no time."

Shoko hesitated, as I knew she would, but Mariye seemed excited by the idea.

"Why not?" she told her aunt. "Dad isn't home."

"It's really no problem," I said. "I've got lots of sauce already made, so it's no more trouble to cook for three than for one."

"Are you sure?" Shoko said, looking doubtful.

"Of course. Please do stay. I eat alone all the time. Breakfast, lunch, and dinner, every day. I'd like to share a meal with others for a change."

Mariye looked at her aunt.

"Well, in that case we'll take you up on your kind invitation," Shoko said. "You're quite sure we're not imposing?"

"Not at all," I said. "Please make yourself at home."

The three of us moved to the dining area. They sat at the table, while I prepared the meal. I set the water to boil, warmed the asparagus-and-bacon sauce in a pan, and threw together a quick salad of lettuce, tomato, onion, and green peppers. When the water boiled, I tossed in the pasta and diced some parsley while it cooked. I took the iced tea from the fridge and filled three glasses. Mariye and her aunt watched me bustle about as if witnessing a rare and strange event. Shoko asked if there was something she could do. No, I replied, she should just relax—I had everything under control.

"You seem so at home in the kitchen," she said, impressed.

"That's because I do this every day."

I don't mind cooking at all. In fact, I've always liked working with my hands. Cooking, simple carpentry, bicycle repair, yard work. I'm useless when it comes to abstract, mathematical thought. Mental games like chess and puzzles are just too taxing for my simple brain.

We sat down at the table and began to eat. A carefree lunch on a sunny Sunday afternoon in autumn. And Shoko was a perfect lunchtime companion. She was gracious and witty, full of things to talk about and with a great sense of humor. Her table manners were elegant, yet there was nothing pretentious about her. I could tell she came from a good family and had attended the most expensive schools. Mariye left all the talking to her aunt and concentrated on her meal. Later, Shoko asked for my recipe for the sauce.

We had almost finished our lunch when the front doorbell gave a cheerful ring. It was no surprise to me, for just a moment earlier I thought I had heard the deep purr of a Jaguar engine. That sound—the polar opposite of the whisper of the Toyota Prius—had registered in that narrow layer between my conscious and unconscious minds. So it was hardly a "bolt from the blue" when the bell chimed.

"Excuse me for a second," I said, rising from my chair and putting my napkin down. Leaving the two of them at the table, I went to the front door. What would happen now? I didn't have a clue.

34

COULDN'T RECALL THE LAST TIME I CHECKED MY TIRES' AIR PRESSURE

opened the door, and there stood Menshiki.

He was wearing a white button-down shirt, a fancy wool vest with an intricate pattern, and a bluish-gray tweed jacket. His chinos were a light mustard color, his suede shoes brown. A coordinated and comfortable outfit, as always. His white hair glowed in the autumn sun. The silver Jaguar was behind him, parked next to the blue Toyota Prius. Side by side, the two cars resembled someone with crooked teeth laughing with his mouth wide open.

I gestured for him to enter. He was so tense his face looked frozen, like a plastered wall only half dry. Needless to say, I had never seen him like this before. He was always so cool, holding himself in check with his feelings packed out of sight. He had been that way even after an hour entombed in a pitch-black pit. Yet now he was as white as a sheet.

"Do you mind if I come in?" he said.

"Of course not," I answered. "We're almost through with lunch. So do come in."

"I really don't want to interrupt your meal," he said, glancing at his watch in what seemed a reflex motion. He stared at it for a long time, his face blank.

As if he had a quarrel with how the second hand was moving.

"We'll be done soon," I said again. "It's a very basic meal. Let's have coffee together afterward. Please wait in the living room. I'll make the introductions there."

Menshiki shook his head. "Introductions might be premature at this stage. I stopped by assuming they'd already left. I wasn't planning to meet them. But I saw an unfamiliar car parked in front and wasn't sure what to do, so I—"

"You came at the perfect time," I said, cutting him off. "Nothing could be more natural. Just leave everything to me."

Menshiki nodded and began to take off his shoes. Yet for some reason he seemed to have forgotten how. I waited until he had struggled through the procedure and showed him into the living room. He'd been there several times before, yet he stared at the room as though it was his first visit.

"Please wait here," I said, patting him on the shoulder. "Just sit down and relax. It shouldn't take more than ten minutes."

I left Menshiki sitting there by himself—though it worried me a bit—and went back to the dining area. Shoko and Mariye had finished their meal in my absence. Their forks rested on empty plates.

"Do you have a visitor?" Shoko asked in a worried voice.

"Yes, but it's all right. Someone from the neighborhood just happened to stop by. I asked him to wait in the living room. We're on friendly terms, so there's no need for formality. I'll just finish my meal first."

I ate what remained of my lunch. Then I brewed a pot of coffee while the two women cleaned up the dishes.

"Shall we have our coffee in the living room?" I asked Shoko.

"But won't we be intruding on you and your guest?"

I shook my head no. "Not in the slightest. It's a stroke of luck—this way, I can introduce you to each other. He lives on top of the slope on the other side of the valley, so I doubt you've ever met."

"What is his name?"

"Menshiki. It's written with the characters for 'avoidance' and 'color.' 'Avoiding colors,' in other words."

"What an unusual name!" Shoko exclaimed. "I've never heard anyone mention a Mr. Menshiki before. The addresses of people across the valley are close to ours, but there's little coming and going between the two sides."

We placed the pot of coffee, four cups, and some milk and sugar on a tray and carried it out to the living room. To my surprise, Menshiki was nowhere to be seen. The room was deserted. He wasn't on the terrace, either. And I doubted he was in the bathroom.

"Where did he disappear to?" I said to no one in particular.

"Was he here earlier?" Shoko asked.

"Until a few minutes ago."

His suede shoes were gone from the entranceway. I slipped on my sandals and opened the front door. The silver Jaguar was parked exactly where he had left it. So he hadn't returned home. The sun reflecting off the Jaguar's windows made it impossible to tell if anyone was inside. I walked over to check. Menshiki was sitting in the driver's seat, rummaging around for something. I tapped on the window, and he rolled it down. He looked lost.

"What happened?" I asked.

"I want to check the air pressure in my tires, but I can't find the gauge. It should be in the glove compartment, but it's gone."

"Is there some kind of rush?"

"No, not really. I was sitting there in your living room when it started to bother me. Couldn't recall the last time I checked."

"So there's no trouble with them?"

"No, nothing in particular. They seem normal."

"Then why don't you forget about the tires for now and come back in? The coffee is made, and two people are waiting."

"Waiting for me?" he said in a hoarse voice. "Are they waiting for me?"

"Yes, I told them I'd introduce you."

"Oh dear," he said.

"Why oh dear?"

"Because I'm not ready for introductions yet. Not emotionally prepared."

He had the baffled, fearful look of someone ordered to jump from the sixteenth floor of a burning building to a net that looked the size of a drink coaster.

"You should come," I said, not mincing words. "It's really not a big deal."

Menshiki nodded and got out, closing the car door behind him. He started to lock it before realizing how unnecessary that was (what thief would stray up here?), so he stuffed the key in the pocket of his chinos.

Shoko and Mariye were waiting in the living room. They rose to greet us as we entered. My introductions were simple and straightforward. A common human courtesy.

"Mr. Menshiki has also modeled for me. I painted his portrait. He happens to live nearby, and we've been friends since we met."

"I understand you live on the other side of the valley. Have you been there long?" Shoko inquired.

Menshiki blanched at the mention of his home. "Yes, I've been living there for a few years. Let's see, how many is it now—three years perhaps? Or is it four?"

He turned to me as if for confirmation, but I didn't respond.

"Can we see your home from here?" Shoko asked.

"Yes," Menshiki said. "But it's really nothing to brag about," he added. "It's awfully out of the way."

"It's the same on this side," Shoko said affably. "Simple shopping is a major expedition. Cell phone service and radios are hit-or-miss. And the road is terribly steep. When the snow is thick, it gets so slippery I'm afraid to take the car out. Luckily, it doesn't happen that often—just once, five years ago."

"You're right," Menshiki said. "It rarely snows here. It has to do with the warmth of the wind coming off the ocean. The ocean exerts a powerful influence on our climate. You see . . ."

"In any case," I broke in, "we should be thankful it snows so rarely here." I feared he was about to launch into a lecture on the structure and effects of the warm sea currents along the coast of Japan—that's how wound up he was.

Mariye was looking back and forth at her aunt and Menshiki throughout this exchange. She seemed to have formed no opinion about Menshiki as of yet. Menshiki, for his part, acted as though Mariye wasn't there, focusing on her aunt as though bewitched.

"Mariye here is letting me paint her portrait," I said to him. "I asked her to model for me."

"I drive her here every Sunday morning," Shoko said. "It's not far as the crow flies—from your eyes to your nose, you might say—but the road twists and turns so much we have to take the car."

Menshiki finally turned to look at Mariye Akikawa. But his eyes didn't focus on any part of her face—they buzzed about nervously like a fly in winter, searching for a place to land. Yet they never seemed to find one.

"These are what I've drawn so far," I said, coming to his aid. I handed him my sketchbook. "I haven't started painting yet—we've just wrapped up the preliminary stage."

Menshiki stared at the three dessan for a long time, devouring them with his eyes. As if the drawings of Mariye somehow meant more to him than Mariye herself. This wasn't true, of course—he simply couldn't bring himself to face her. The dessan were a substitute, nothing more. It was the first time he had been close to her, and he was having a hard time controlling his feelings. Mariye, for her part, regarded the floundering Menshiki as though he were some kind of strange animal.

"They're superb," Menshiki said. He turned to Shoko. "Each is so full of life. He's really captured her!"

"I totally agree," she said, beaming.

"All the same, Mariye is a very difficult subject," I said to Menshiki. "Painting her is a challenge. Her expression is constantly changing, so it takes time to grasp what's at the core. That's why I haven't gotten around to the actual painting stage yet."

"Difficult?" Menshiki said. He looked at Mariye a second time, squinting as though dazzled by her light.

"The three dessan should show very different expressions," I said. "The slightest facial movement radically transforms the whole atmosphere. When I paint her portrait, I have to get past those superficial differences to grasp the essence of her personality. Otherwise, I'd be conveying only part of the whole."

"I see," Menshiki said, dutifully impressed. He looked back and forth between the three sketches and Mariye, comparing them. In the process, his face, which had been so pale, began to regain some of its color. Red dots popped up at first, then the dots grew to blotches the size of ping-pong balls, then base-balls, until in the end his whole face had turned rosy. Mariye watched him, fascinated, but her aunt politely turned away. I grabbed the coffee pot and poured myself another cup.

I felt I had to break the silence. "I'm thinking of starting the actual portrait next week. You know, on canvas with real paint," I said to no one in particular.

"Do you have a clear image what it will look like?" asked Shoko.

"Not yet," I said, shaking my head. "I won't know in any concrete way until I'm sitting in front of the canvas with a brush in my hand. Hopefully, the in-spiration will hit me then."

"You painted Mr. Menshiki's picture as well, didn't you?" Shoko asked me.

"Yes, last month."

"It's a beautiful portrait," Menshiki said emphati-cally. "The paint has to dry a bit more before it can be framed, but it's hanging on the wall of my study. I'm not sure 'portrait' does it justice, though. It's a painting of me, but of something other than me, too. I don't know how to put it—I guess you could say it has **depth**. I never get tired of looking at it."

"You say it's you, yet it's not you at the same time?" Shoko asked.

"I mean it's a step beyond your typical portrait—it's deeper, more profound."

"I want to see it," Mariye said. They were the first words she had spoken since we had moved to the liv-ing room.

"But Mariye . . . you shouldn't invite yourself into someone's—"

"That's perfectly all right!" Menshiki said, cutting off her aunt's rebuke as if with a sharp hatchet. His tone was so jarring that we all—including Menshiki himself—were stunned.

"Please do come take a look," he continued after a moment's regrouping. "It's so rare for me to meet someone from the neighborhood. I live alone, so you needn't worry about disturbing anyone. Any time at all would be fine."

Menshiki's face was even redder by the time he finished. It appeared that we hadn't been the only ones shocked by the urgency in his voice.

"Do you like paintings?" Menshiki asked, this time directing his question to Mariye. His voice was back to normal.

Mariye gave a small nod.

"If it's all right with you, why don't I stop by again at this time next Sunday?" Menshiki said. "I could escort you to my home and we could all look at the painting together."

"But we shouldn't inconvenience you—" Shoko said.

"I want to see the painting!" Mariye was firm.

In the end it was agreed that Menshiki would come to pick up the two of them the following Sunday afternoon. I was invited too, but I declined, citing an important errand. The last thing I wanted was to get sucked in any deeper. From now on, let those who were involved look after things. I would remain the outsider, however the situation turned out. I would be the mediator, nothing more—though even that had not been my intention.

Menshiki and I accompanied the beautiful aunt and her niece outside to give them a proper send-off. Shoko looked for some time at the silver Jaguar parked next to her Prius. Like a dog lover appraising another person's dog.

"This is the latest model, isn't it?" she asked Menshiki.

"Yes, this is their newest coupe on the market," he answered. "Do you like cars?"

"No, it's not that. It's just that my late father drove a Jaguar sedan. I used to sit next to him, and every so often he'd let me hold the wheel. The Jaguar hood ornament takes me back to those times. Was it an XJ6? It had four round headlights, I think. And an inline six-cylinder 4.2-liter engine."

"That is the III series, I believe. A truly beautiful model."

"My father drove that car for ages, so he must have really liked it. Although he complained about the terrible mileage. And it had one minor malfunction after the other."

"That model in particular is a real gas guzzler. And the wiring was probably faulty. The electrical system has always been the Jaguar's Achilles' heel. But if it's running smoothly, and if you don't mind shelling out for gas, you can't beat a Jaguar. For driving comfort and handling, no other car matches it—it's got a charm all its own. Most people, though, are really turned off by things like gas consumption and mechanical glitches, which is why the Toyota Prius is the one flying off the lots."

"I didn't buy this car," Shoko said, as if by way of apology, gesturing toward her Prius. "My brother bought it for me because it's safe and easy to drive, and gentle on the environment."

"The Prius is an excellent car," Menshiki said. "I've thought of buying one myself."

Was he kidding? Menshiki behind the wheel of a Toyota Prius was as hard to picture as a leopard ordering a salade Niçoise.

"This is very rude of me," Shoko said, peering into the Jaguar's interior, "but would it be all right if I sat in it for a minute? I just want to try out the driver's seat."

"Of course," Menshiki answered. He coughed lightly, as if to bring his voice under control. "Sit there as long as you like. Take it for a spin if you wish."

I was flabbergasted by how interested she was in Menshiki's Jaguar. On the surface she was so cool and poised, not my image of a car person at all. Yet her eyes were shining when she climbed into the driver's seat. She snuggled into the cream-colored leather upholstery, studied the dashboard with care, and took the steering wheel in both hands. Then she placed her left hand on the gearshift. Menshiki took the car key from his pocket and passed it to her through the window.

"Turn it on if you like."

Shoko took the key, inserted it into the ignition next to the wheel, and rotated it clockwise. Instantly, the great feline awoke. She sat there entranced for a moment, listening to the deep purr of the engine.

"I remember this sound well," she said.

"It's a 4.2-liter V8 engine. Your father's XJ6 had six cylinders, and the number of valves and the compression ratio were different too, but they may well sound alike. Both are sinful, though—they squander fossil fuel like there's no tomorrow. Jaguars haven't changed a bit on that score."

Shoko flipped on the right-turn signal. I heard a cheerful clicking sound.

"This really brings back memories."

Menshiki smiled. "Only a Jaguar's turn signal sounds like this. It's unlike that of any other automobile."

"When I was young, I secretly practiced on the XJ6 to get my driver's license," she said. "The first time I drove another car I was totally confused—the parking brake wasn't where I expected. I had no idea what to do."

"I know just what you mean," Menshiki grinned. "The Brits are fussy about the funniest things."

"I think the interior smells a bit different than my father's car, though."

"Sadly, you're right. For a variety of reasons, Jaguar can't use the exact same materials on its newer models. The smell changed after 2002, when Connolly Leather stopped supplying their upholstery. In fact, the Connolly company went out of business at that point."

"How too bad. I loved that smell. I connect it to the smell of my father."

"To tell the truth," Menshiki said hesitantly, "I own another Jaguar as well, an older model. It may well have the same odor as your father's car."

"Is it an XJ6?"

"No, it's an E type."

"Does that mean it's a convertible?"

"Correct. It's a Series 1 roadster, made back in the mid-sixties. It still runs well, though. It's also equipped with a six-cylinder 4.2-liter engine. An original two-seater. The top has been replaced, of course, so it's not exactly in mint condition."

Most of this flew over my head—I know nothing about cars—but Menshiki's words seemed to have made a deep impression on Shoko. They clearly shared an interest, and a fairly specialized interest at that, in Jaguars. That made me feel a little calmer. No longer did I have to think up topics to help them through their first meeting. Mariye's boredom was palpable, though—she seemed even less into cars than me.

Shoko got out of the Jaguar, shut the car door, and handed the key to Menshiki, who returned it to the pocket of his chinos. Then she and Mariye got in the blue Prius. Menshiki closed the door after Mariye. I was struck by the different **thunk** it made as it closed, nothing like the Jaguar. In this world, what we think of as a single sound can have so many permutations.

Just as we know, from one note struck on the open string of a double bass, whether it's Charlie Mingus or Ray Brown.

"So we'll meet again next Sunday," Menshiki said.

Shoko gave Menshiki a big smile, took the steering wheel, and drove off. Menshiki and I waited until the squat rear of the Toyota Prius was out of sight before returning to the house. We sat in the living room sipping cold coffee. Neither of us spoke for some time. Menshiki looked exhausted. Like a long-distance runner who had just crossed the finish line.

"She's a beautiful girl," I said at last. "Mariye, I mean."

"You're right. She'll be even prettier when she grows up," Menshiki said. His mind seemed elsewhere.

"What did you think, seeing her up close?" I asked.

Menshiki smiled an uncomfortable smile. "I didn't get a very good look, to tell the truth. I was too nervous."

"But you must have seen something."

"Of course," he said, nodding. He paused for a long moment. "What did you think?" he asked at last, his eyes serious.

"What do you mean, what do I think?"

Menshiki's face flushed again. "Do you see any similarity between Mariye's features and mine? As an artist who has painted people's portraits for many years, I'm interested in your professional opinion."

I shook my head no. "You're right, I'm trained to take quick note of people's facial characteristics. But that doesn't mean I can tell whose child is whose.

Some parents and children don't look alike at all, while total strangers can appear almost identical."

Menshiki gave a long, deep sigh. It sounded wrenched from his entire body. He rubbed his palms together.

"I'm not asking for a definitive judgment. I'm just asking for your **personal impressions**. Even the most trivial ones. I'd like to know if you noticed something, anything at all."

I thought for a moment. "As far as facial structure goes, I don't see much concrete similarity. But your eyes do have something in common. In fact, it startles me every so often."

He looked at me, his thin lips pressed together. "You're saying there's something similar in our eyes?"

"Maybe it's because they reflect your true feelings. Curiosity, enthusiasm, surprise, suspicion, reluctance—I can see those subtle emotions in both your eyes and hers. Your faces aren't all that expressive, but your eyes really are the windows to your hearts. Most people are the opposite. Their faces are expressive, but their eyes aren't nearly so lively."

Menshiki appeared surprised. "Is that how my eyes look to you?"

I nodded.

"I was never aware of that."

"You couldn't control it if you tried. Maybe it's because your feelings are on such a tight leash that your eyes are so expressive. It's not that obvious, though— you have to pay really, really close attention to read them. Most people wouldn't notice."

"But you can."

"Reading faces is my profession."

Menshiki considered that for a minute. "So she and I have that in common. But you still can't tell if we're father and daughter, right?"

"I do have certain impressions when I look at people, and I value those. But artistic impressions and objective reality are separate things. Impressions don't prove anything. They're like a butterfly in the wind—totally useless. But how about you? Did you feel anything special?"

He shook his head several times. "I couldn't tell anything in one brief meeting. I need to see her more. I have to get used to being around her first."

He shook his head again, this time more slowly. He plunged his hands into his jacket pockets as though searching for something, then pulled them out again. As though he'd forgotten what he was looking for.

"No, maybe it's not the number of times," he went on. "It could be the more we meet the more confused I'll get, the farther from any conclusion. It's **possible** she's my daughter, but then it's possible she isn't. But either way makes no difference to me. Her presence alone allows me to consider that possibility, to physically experience that hypothesis. When that happens, I feel fresh blood coursing through my body. Maybe I've never understood the true meaning of being alive until now."

I held my peace. What could I say about the feelings he was experiencing, or about his definition of being alive? Menshiki glanced at his thin, expensive-looking wristwatch and awkwardly struggled to his feet from the sofa.

"I owe you my thanks. I couldn't have done a thing if you hadn't given me a push."

With these few words he stumbled toward the door, struggled a bit to put on his shoes, and stepped outside. From the door, I watched him climb in his car and drive away. When his Jaguar was out of sight, the peaceful quiet of a Sunday afternoon enfolded me once again.

The clock said a little after two p.m. I was dead tired. I pulled an old blanket from the closet, lay on the sofa, and slept with it tucked over me. It was past three when I awoke. The angle of the sunlight in the room had shifted somewhat. What a strange day! I couldn't be sure if I had moved forward or fallen behind, or if I was just circling over the same spot. My sense of direction had gone haywire. There was Shoko and Mariye, and then there was Menshiki. Each had a special magnetism. And I had landed smack in the middle of it all. Lacking any magnetism of my own to speak of.

However exhausted I might feel, though, Sunday was far from over. The hands of the clock had only just passed three. The sun was still in the sky. Loads of time remained before a new day dawned and Sunday became a thing of the past. Yet I didn't feel like doing anything. I had taken a nap, but my head was muddled. It felt like a ball of yarn had been crammed into the back of a narrow desk drawer, and now the drawer wouldn't close properly. Maybe this was the sort of day I should check the air pressure in my tires. Anyone feeling this blah should be able to rouse himself to do that much.

Come to think of it, though, I had never checked the air pressure myself. Whenever a gas station attendant said that the air in my tires "looked a little low," I always asked him to take care of it. Which means I don't own an air pressure gauge. In fact, I don't even know what one looks like. If it fits in a glove compartment, it can't be all that big. Nor so expensive as to require monthly payments. Maybe I should buy one, just to see.

When it began to get dark, I went to the kitchen, cracked open a can of beer, and began preparing dinner. In the oven, I broiled a piece of yellowtail that I'd marinated in sake lees, then sliced pickles, made a cucumber-and-seaweed salad with vinegar, and fixed some miso soup with radishes and deep-fried tofu. Then I sat down and ate my silent meal. There was no one there to talk to, and nothing in particular I could think of to talk about. Just when I was finishing my simple, solitary dinner, the front doorbell rang. There seemed to be a conspiracy afoot to interrupt me toward the end of every meal.

So this day hasn't ended after all, I thought. I had the premonition it would be a long Sunday. I got up from the table and walked slowly to the door.

35

YOU SHOULD HAVE JUST LEFT
THAT PLACE ALONE

I walked slowly to the door. Who could possibly be ringing the bell? Had a car pulled up in front without my knowledge? The dining area was toward the rear of the house, but it was a quiet night, so I should have heard the crunch of gravel and the rumble of an engine. Even the vaunted "silent" hybrid engine of a Prius. Still, my ears had picked up nothing.

No one would climb such a long, steep slope on foot at night on a lark. The road was unlit, and deserted. My house had been plopped down on top of an isolated mountain, with no neighbors close by.

For a moment, I thought it might be the Commendatore. But that didn't make much sense. I mean, he could come and go whenever he wanted, so why ring the bell?

I unlocked and opened the door without bothering to check who it was. Mariye Akikawa was standing there. She was wearing the same clothes she had worn that afternoon, only now a thin navy-blue down jacket covered her windbreaker. Naturally, it got chillier once the sun was down. She had a Cleveland Indians cap on her head (why Cleveland?) and a large flashlight in her right hand.

"Can I come in?" she asked. There was no "Good evening," no "Sorry for the surprise visit."

"Sure," I said. "Come on in." That was it. My mental desk drawer wasn't closing properly yet. That ball of yarn was still jammed in there.

I showed her into the dining room.

"I'm still eating dinner. Mind if I finish?" I said.

She nodded silently. She was free of all the tiresome social graces—they meant nothing to her.

"Want some tea?" I asked.

She nodded again. She took off her down jacket, removed her cap, and straightened her hair. I set the kettle to boil, and put some green tea in a small teapot. I wanted a cup of tea myself.

With her elbows on the table, Mariye watched me polish off the broiled yellowtail, miso soup, and salad as if she had come across something very strange. She could have been sitting on a rock in the jungle, watching a python swallow a baby badger.

"I marinated the yellowtail myself," I explained, breaking the silence. "It keeps a lot longer that way."

She didn't respond. I couldn't tell if my words had reached her or not. "Immanuel Kant was a man of punctual habits," I said. "So punctual that people set their clocks by when he passed on his strolls."

Absolutely meaningless, of course. I just wanted to see how she'd react to something so totally random. If she was really listening or not. Again, no response. The silence around us only deepened further. Immanuel Kant continued strolling through the streets of Königsberg, leading his regulated and taciturn life. His last words were "This is good" (**Es ist gut**). Some people can live like that.

I finished dinner and carried the dishes to the sink. Then I made tea. I returned with the teapot and two cups. Mariye sat there at the table watching me throughout. She was eyeballing me intently—like a historian meticulously checking the footnotes of a text.

"You didn't come by car, did you?" I asked.

At last she opened her mouth. "I walked," she said.

"All the way from your house, by yourself?"

"Uh-huh."

I waited for her to go on. But she didn't. We sat there across from each other at the table for a while without speaking. I'm pretty good at long silences, though. No accident I'm holed up by myself on top of a mountain.

"There's a secret passageway," Mariye said at last. "It's a long way by car, but not far if you take the passageway."

"I've walked all over this area but I've never seen anything like that."

"You don't know how to look," she shot back. "You really have to pay attention to find it. It's well hidden."

"You hid it, right?"

She nodded. "I've lived here since I was small. The whole mountain is my playground. I know every part of it."

"So the passageway is really well concealed."

She gave another firm nod.

"And you used it to come here."

"Uh-huh."

I sighed. "Have you had dinner?"

"I ate already."

"What did you eat?"

"My aunt isn't a very good cook," the girl said. Not a real answer to my question—it was clear she wanted to let the matter drop. Maybe she didn't want to recall what she'd eaten for dinner.

"Does your aunt know you came here by yourself?"

Mariye didn't reply. Her lips were set in a straight line. I chose to answer my own question.

"Of course she doesn't. What responsible adult would let a thirteen-year-old girl wander the mountains after dark? Right?"

There followed another period of silence.

"She's not aware of the passageway?"

Mariye shook her head several times. So her aunt didn't know.

"And you're the only one who knows about it?"

Mariye nodded several times.

"In any event," I said, "given where you live, once you left the passageway you probably went through the woods and past an old shrine to get here. Right?"

Mariye nodded again. "I know that shrine. And I know that someone used a big machine to dig up the pile of rocks behind it."

"Did you watch?"

Mariye shook her head. "I didn't see them digging.

I was at school that day. But I saw the tracks. The ground was covered with them. Why did you do it?"

"I had reasons."

"What kind of reasons?"

"If I tried to explain from the beginning it would take too long," I said. So I didn't try. The last thing I wanted was for her to find out that Menshiki was involved.

"It was wrong to dig it up like that," Mariye said, abruptly.

"Why do you say that?"

She gave what looked like a shrug. "You should have just left that place alone. Everyone else did."

"Everyone else?"

"It's been there like forever, but no one touched it until now."

The girl was right, I thought. Perhaps we shouldn't have touched it. Perhaps we should have behaved like "everyone else" had. It was too late to change that now, though. The stones had been moved, the pit exposed, the Commendatore set free.

"Were you the one who removed the lid?" I asked. "Let me guess: you looked inside, then you replaced the boards and the stones that held them down. Am I right?"

Mariye raised her head and looked me straight in the eye. As if to say: How did you know?

"The rocks on the lid had been rearranged. My visual memory is pretty good, always has been. I could see the difference right away."

"Wow," she murmured, impressed.

"But the hole was empty. Nothing but darkness and damp air, right?"

"A ladder was there too."

"You didn't climb down it, did you?"

Mariye shook her head vigorously. As if to say: No way!

"And now," I said, "you've come here at this time of night for a particular reason, haven't you? I mean, this isn't just a social visit, is it."

"A social visit?"

"You know, an 'I happened to be in the neighborhood so I thought I'd stop by' kind of thing."

She thought for a moment before shaking her head. "No, it's not 'a social visit.'"

"Then what is it?" I asked. "I'm more than happy to have you visit me, but if your aunt or your father found out, it could lead to a bizarre misunderstanding."

"What kind of misunderstanding?"

"There are all sorts of misunderstandings in this world," I said. "Some go far beyond what you and I can imagine. In this case, it could make it impossible for me to paint your portrait. That would bother me a lot. Wouldn't it bother you?"

"My aunt won't find out," she said emphatically. "I go to my room after dinner and she never follows me. It's like an agreement we have. I leave through my window and no one knows. No one's ever caught on."

"So you've been walking the mountain at night for a long time?"

Mariye nodded.

"Isn't it scary all by yourself after dark?"

"Other things are a lot scarier."

"Like what, for example?"

Mariye shrugged her shoulders slightly but said nothing.

"Your aunt may not be a problem, but how about your father?"

"He's not back yet."

"Even though today's Sunday?"

Mariye didn't answer. I guessed she wanted to avoid talking about her father.

"Anyway, you don't have to worry," she said. "No one knows when I leave the house. Even if they found out I'd never give your name."

"All right then, I'll stop worrying," I said. "But why did you come here tonight of all nights?"

"Because I wanted to talk to you about something."

"Like what?"

Mariye picked up her cup and took a sip of hot tea. She looked warily around the room as if to make sure no one would overhear. Of course nobody was there but the two of us. That is, unless the Commendatore had returned and was listening in. I looked around as well. But the Commendatore wasn't there. If he was, he hadn't assumed bodily form.

"Your friend who showed up this afternoon, the guy with the pretty white hair," she said. "What was his name? It was kind of weird."

"Menshiki."

"That's right, Mr. Menshiki."

"He's not really a friend. I met him just a short while ago."

"Whatever."

"So what is it about Mr. Menshiki?"

She narrowed her eyes and looked at me. "I think," she said, lowering her voice, "that man is hiding something. In his heart."

"What sort of thing?"

"I don't know. But I don't believe he showed up this afternoon by accident, like he said. I think he came for a very specific purpose."

"What purpose is that?" I asked, a little shocked by how observant she was.

She fixed me with her gaze. "I'm not sure. Don't you know?"

"I have no idea," I lied, praying that Mariye wouldn't see through my deception. I have never been a good liar. When I lie it's written on my face. But there was no way I could tell her the truth.

"For real?"

"For real," I said. "I had no idea he would show up today."

Mariye seemed to buy my story. Menshiki had not told me he would be coming, and his sudden visit had taken me by surprise. So I wasn't really lying after all.

"His eyes are weird," Mariye said.

"Weird in what way?"

"It's like he's always **scheming** about something. Like the wolf in 'Little Red Riding Hood.' When the wolf dresses up like the grandmother and lies in bed, you can tell it's him by his eyes."

Like the wolf in "Little Red Riding Hood"?

"So you had an adverse reaction to Mr. Menshiki, right?"

"Adverse reaction?"

"A negative impression. A feeling he might harm you."

"Adverse reaction," she said. She seemed to be storing the phrase in her mental filing cabinet. Alongside "a bolt from the blue," no doubt.

"It's not like that," Mariye said. "I don't think he's planning anything bad. I just think Mr. Menshiki with the pretty white hair is hiding something."

"And you sense it, right?"

Mariye nodded. "That's why I came to see you. I thought you might be able to tell me more about him."

"Does your aunt feel the same way?" I asked, trying to deflect her question.

"No," she answered, tilting her head to one side. "That's not what she's like. She seldom has an adverse reaction to people. And I think she's interested in him. He's a bit older, but he's handsome and well dressed and I guess very rich and living all by himself . . ."

"So you think she's taken to him?"

"I guess so. She really lit up when she talked to him. Her face, and her voice—it got higher. She wasn't like usual. I bet he felt the change too."

I said nothing, just poured us both a fresh cup of tea. I took a sip.

Mariye seemed to be turning something over in her mind. "I wonder, how did he know we were going to be here today?" she asked. "Did you tell him?"

"I don't think Mr. Menshiki came planning to meet your aunt." I chose my words with care, hoping to avoid another lie. "In fact, he tried to leave when he realized the two of you were here, but I talked him into staying. He **happened** to stop by when your aunt **happened** to be here, and when he saw her he got interested. Your aunt is a very attractive woman, you know."

Mariye didn't look entirely convinced, but she didn't push the issue any further. She just sat there frowning, elbows on the table.

"In any case, the two of you are going to visit his home next Sunday," I said.

Mariye nodded. "Yes, to see your portrait of him. My aunt seems to be really looking forward to it. To paying Mr. Menshiki a visit, I mean."

"I don't blame her for getting excited," I said. "After all, she's living in the mountains with no other people around. Not like in the city, where she'd have opportunities to meet all sorts of men."

Mariye pressed her lips together for a moment.

"My aunt used to have a boyfriend," she said, as if letting me in on a big secret. "A man she saw for a really long time. When she was a secretary in Tokyo. But a lot of things happened, and in the end they broke up. It hurt her a lot. Then my mother died, and she came to look after me. She didn't tell me any of this, of course."

"I don't think she's seeing anyone now, is she?"

Mariye shook her head. "I don't think so."

"So you're a little concerned that your aunt is interested in Mr. Menshiki, and that she may be experiencing the first stirrings of something. So you came to talk to me about it. Is that right?"

"Tell me, do you think he's trying to seduce her?"

"Seduce her?"

"I mean, that he isn't serious?"

"There's no way for me to tell," I said. "I don't know Mr. Menshiki that well. They just met this afternoon, so nothing has happened between them yet. When two people's feelings are involved like this, things can change in subtle ways. What begins as a small feeling can grow into something really big, or the opposite can happen."

"But I have a kind of hunch this time," she asserted.

I sensed that I should believe her "kind of hunch," baseless though it was. For I had a similar kind of hunch.

"So you're worried something could occur that might harm your aunt psychologically," I said.

Mariye gave a quick nod. "My aunt's not a very cautious person, and she's not used to being hurt."

"It sounds like you're the one looking after her, and not the other way around," I said.

"In a way," Mariye said seriously.

"How about you, then? Are you used to being hurt?"

"I don't know," Mariye said. "At least I'm not about to fall in love."

"You will someday, though."

"But not now. Not until my chest gets a little bigger anyway."

"That may happen sooner than you expect."

Mariye made a wry face. I guessed she didn't believe me.

I felt a seed of doubt sprout in my own chest. Would Menshiki draw close to Shoko Akikawa to establish a firm connection with Mariye?

After all, he had said to me, **I couldn't tell anything in one brief meeting. I need to see her more.**

Shoko would be an important intermediary—through her, Menshiki could see Mariye on a regular basis. After all, she was the one looking after the girl. To a greater or lesser extent, therefore, Menshiki had to place Shoko under his thumb. That shouldn't be too hard for a man of Menshiki's talents. Not child's play, perhaps, but close to it. I didn't like to think that Menshiki was harboring a plan of that sort. Yet perhaps the Commendatore had been right, and he was a man who couldn't help fabricating some scheme or other. From what I had seen, however, he wasn't that cunning.

"Mr. Menshiki's house is really impressive," I said to Mariye. "You may or may not like it, but it wouldn't hurt to take a look."

"Have you been there?"

"Only once. I went there for dinner."

"It's on the other side of the valley?"

"Right across from us."

"Can you see it from here?"

I pretended to think for a moment. "Yes, but it's far away, of course."

"Show me."

I led her to the terrace and pointed out Menshiki's mansion on top of the mountain across the valley. Bathed in the light from the garden lanterns, the building floated white in the distance like an elegant ocean liner sailing the night sea. Several of the windows were also lit up. The lights burning there were small and unobtrusive.

"That enormous white house?" Mariye exclaimed in surprise. She stared at me for a moment. Then, wordlessly, she turned back to the distant mansion.

"I can see it from my house, too," she said eventually. "The angle's a bit different, though. I've always wondered who would live in a place like that."

"It does stand out, that's for sure," I said. "Anyway, that's Mr. Menshiki's home."

Mariye spent a long time leaning over the railing looking at the house. A handful of stars twinkled above its roof. There was no wind, and a small, sharp-edged cloud hung there motionless. Like a paper cutout nailed to a plywood backdrop in a play. Each time the girl moved her head, her straight black hair glittered in the moonlight.

"Does Mr. Menshiki really live there all by himself?" Mariye asked, turning to me.

"Yes, he does. All alone, in that big house."

"And he's not married?"

"He told me he has never married."

"What kind of work does he do?"

"I'm not sure. Something connected to the information business, he said. Maybe having to do with tech. He doesn't have a regular job right now, though. He lives on the money he made from selling his old business, and from stock dividends and so forth. I don't know the details."

"So he doesn't work?" Mariye said, wrinkling her forehead.

"That's what he said. Seldom leaves his home, apparently."

He might well be standing on his terrace, watching the two of us through his high-powered binoculars just as we were watching him. What would run through his mind if he saw us standing side by side like this?

"You'd better head home," I told Mariye. "It's getting late."

"Besides asking about Mr. Menshiki," she said softly, as if confiding something, "I wanted to tell you I'm really happy that you're painting my picture. I can't wait to see it."

"I hope it turns out well," I said. Her words moved me more than a little. It was strange how much this girl opened up when painting was involved.

I walked her to the door. Mariye put on her tight-fitting down jacket and crammed her Indians cap down over her head. Now she looked like a boy.

"Shall I walk with you partway?" I asked.

"I'm fine. I know the path."

"See you next Sunday, then."

But instead of leaving, she paused for a moment with her hand on the doorframe.

"One thing bothers me," she said. "It's that bell."

"The bell?"

"I thought I heard it ringing on my way here. The same kind of jingling sound that the bell in your studio made."

I was at a loss for words. Mariye's eyes were on my face.

"Where was it exactly?" I asked.

"In the woods. It came from behind the shrine."

I listened to the dark. But I heard no bell. I heard no sound at all. Just the quiet of the night.

"Weren't you scared?" I asked.

Mariye shook her head. "If I leave it alone, there's nothing to be scared of."

"Wait here just a second," I told Mariye. I ran back to the studio. The bell was not where I had left it. It had vanished from the shelf.

36

WHAT I WANT IS NOT TO HAVE TO DISCUSS THE RULES OF THE GAME

fter seeing Mariye off, I went into the studio, turned on all the lights, and combed every inch of the room. But the old bell was nowhere to be found. It had vanished from sight.

When had I last seen it? The previous Sunday, on her first visit, Mariye had taken the bell down and shaken it. Then she had returned it to the shelf. I remembered that. But had I laid eyes on the bell since? I couldn't recall. I had hardly set foot in the studio all week. Not once had I picked up my brush. **The Man with the White Subaru Forester** had stalled, and I hadn't yet started Mariye's portrait. I was what you might call "between paintings."

Then, without my knowledge, the bell had disappeared.

But Mariye had heard it ringing behind the shrine when she passed through the woods. Could someone have returned it to the pit? Should I rush there now, see if I could hear the bell with my own ears?

Yet the prospect of hurrying off into the dark woods alone didn't appeal to me. Too many surprises in one day had worn me out. Whatever one might say, I had more than filled my quota of "unforeseen events."

I went into the kitchen, pulled out the ice tray, plunked a few cubes in a glass, and doused them with whiskey. It was only eight thirty. Had Mariye safely navigated the woods and returned home through her passageway? I felt sure she had. No need for me to worry. This mountain had been her playground since she was small, she had said. And she was a lot tougher than she looked.

I took my time working my way through two glasses of Scotch, munched a few crackers, brushed my teeth, and went to bed. For all I knew, I might be roused in the middle of the night by a ringing bell. Around two a.m., as before. Nothing much I could do about that. If it happened, I would deal with it then. But nothing happened. As far as I knew, anyway. I slept like a log until half past six the next morning.

When I awoke, it was raining outside. A chilly rain, signaling the approach of winter. Quiet and persistent. It reminded me of the rain that had been falling that day in March when my wife announced that our marriage was over. I hadn't faced her as she spoke. For the most part, I had looked out the window at the rain.

After breakfast, I put on my vinyl poncho and rain hat (both purchased on my trip, at a sporting-goods store in Hakodate) and walked into the woods. I didn't take an umbrella. I circled the shrine and removed half the boards covering the pit. I made a careful search with my flashlight, but it was empty. No bell, and no sign of the Commendatore. Just to make sure, I decided to descend the metal ladder to check. I had never entered the pit before. The rungs sagged and gave an ominous creak with each step down. In the end, however, I found nothing. It was just an uninhabited hole in the ground. Perfectly round, it might have been a well were it not so wide. Had its builders intended to draw water from it, they would have made its circumference much smaller. And the construction of the wall was too intricate. It was just as the landscaper had said.

I stood in the pit for some time, lost in thought. I didn't feel trapped since I could see a cleanly severed half-moon of sky above. I flicked off my flashlight, leaned my back against the damp, dark stone wall, and closed my eyes as the rain pattered overhead. **Something** was running through my mind, but I couldn't grasp what it was. One thought would link to another, which in turn would link to still another thought. That chain was bizarre somehow, though I couldn't say exactly why. It was as if I had been swallowed by the act of thinking, if that makes sense.

The pit was thinking too, I could tell. It was alive—I could feel it breathing. My thoughts and those of the pit were like trees grown together: our roots joined in the dark, our sap intermingled. In this condition, self and other blended like the paints on my palette, their borders ever more indistinct.

At a certain point, it felt as though the walls of the pit were beginning to close in. My heart made a dry sound as it expanded and contracted in my chest. I felt I could hear its valves open and close. The sensation chilled me, as if I were approaching the realm of the dead. That world didn't strike me as altogether unpleasant, but it was not yet my time to enter.

I returned to my senses with a start. I untangled myself from my train of thought, which had run on without me, then flicked on my flashlight and looked around. The ladder was still where it had been. The sky above my head was the same. I breathed a sigh of relief. For all I knew, the sky could have vanished and the ladder disappeared. Anything could happen in this place.

With great care, I climbed from the pit one rung at a time. Only when I had emerged and was standing on the wet ground did my breathing finally return to normal. It took even longer to get my heartbeat under control. I peered down into the pit one last time. With my flashlight, I illuminated every inch of the dirt floor. But it was just a normal, everyday kind of pit. It was not breathing or thinking, nor were its walls closing in. It just sat there in silence, absorbing the chilly mid-November rain.

I moved the boards back into place and set the rocks on top. I arranged them with care, making sure that they were exactly as they had been before. That way I would know if someone moved them. Then I stuck my rain hat back on my head and walked home along the same path I had come on.

As I walked through the woods, I wondered where the Commendatore had gone. I hadn't seen him for at least two weeks. Strangely, I missed having him around. Without realizing it, I had come to feel a certain kinship with the two-foot man with the tiny sword at his side, despite his odd way of speaking, his voyeurism when my girlfriend and I were making love, and the fact that I had no clear idea what he was. I hoped nothing bad had happened to him.

When I got home, I went straight to the studio, sat down on the ancient wooden stool (the stool Tomohiko Amada must have used when he was working), and studied **Killing Commendatore** hanging there on the wall. I often did that when I wasn't sure what to do—in fact, I studied it endlessly. It was a painting I never tired of, no matter how often I looked at it. It should have been displayed in a museum as a prized example of Japanese art, but instead, it graced the wall of this small studio, and I was the only one who could enjoy it. Before me, it had been hidden in the attic, unseen by anyone.

It's calling out to me, Mariye had said. **Like a caged bird crying to be set free.**

The more I studied the painting the more I realized Mariye had hit the nail square on the head—something was desperately struggling to escape that enclosed space. It longed for a place less confined, for freedom. It was the strength of that will that gave the painting its impact. Whether we understood the meaning of the bird and the cage or not.

I felt the urge to paint something that day. Powerfully. I could feel it mounting within me. Like the evening tide coming in. It was still too early, though, to work on Mariye's portrait. That could wait until next Sunday. And I didn't feel like going back to **The Man with the White Subaru Forester** either. As Mariye had pointed out, a dangerous force lurked beneath its surface.

A new canvas sat on the easel, ready for Mariye's portrait. I sat on the stool studying it for a long time. Yet nothing came to me—no image of what to paint. The blank stayed blank. What should be my subject matter? After a while, at last, the answer rose to my mind.

I stepped away from the easel and took out my big sketchbook. Then I sat on the floor, crossed my legs, leaned back against the wall, and began to draw a chamber of stone in pencil. Not my usual soft pencil but a much harder one. It was a sketch of the strange pit we had found under the pile of rocks in the woods. I had just come from there, so it was fresh in my mind, and I rendered it in as much detail as possible. I drew the intricately fitted wall of stones. I drew the ground around the pit, and the beautiful pattern of the wet fallen leaves. The stand of pampas grass that had once hidden the pit lay flattened by the backhoe.

As I sketched, the eerie sensation that I was merging with the pit returned. It wanted me to draw it. Accurately, and in great detail. In response, my hand moved without conscious guidance. It was a pure act of creation, and it brought with it a kind of joy. When I returned to my senses, I realized that a length of time had passed (I had no idea how much), and that the page in my notebook was covered with pencil lines.

I went to the kitchen, gulped down several glasses of cold water, reheated the coffee, and carried a cup back to the studio. I placed the open sketchbook on the easel and sat down to take a second look, this time from farther away. There was the pit in the woods, in realistic detail. It looked somehow alive. Even **more** alive than the real thing. I got off the stool and examined it up close, then studied it again from a different angle. Only then did it hit me how much it looked like a woman's genitals. The clump of pampas grass flattened by the backhoe resembled her pubic hair to a T.

I shook my head and smiled a wry smile. I mean, how Freudian can you get? I imagined some egghead critic fulminating on the drawing's psychological implications: "This black, gaping hole, so reminiscent of a woman's solitary genitalia, must be understood functionally, as a symbolic representation of the artist's memories and unconscious desires." Or something of the sort. Seriously!

Yet try as I might, I couldn't get the connection between the strange circular pit in the woods and a woman's sex out of my head. So when the phone rang a short while later, I had a hunch it would be my married girlfriend.

And it was.

"Hi," she said. "Some free time just opened up, and I was wondering if I might stop by."

I glanced at my watch. "Sounds good. Let's have lunch together."

"I'll pick up something simple on the way," she said.

"Great idea. I've been working since morning, so I haven't prepared anything."

She ended the call. I made the bed, picked my clothes up off the floor, folded them, and returned them to the chest of drawers. I washed the breakfast dishes in the sink and put them away.

Then I went to the living room, placed my usual record—Richard Strauss's **Der Rosenkavalier**, conducted by Georg Solti—on the turntable, and read on the sofa while I waited for her to arrive. What kind of book was Shoko Akikawa reading, I wondered? What could have so captivated her?

My girlfriend showed up at twelve fifteen. Her red Mini pulled up in front of my house and she got out, a paper bag from the grocery store in her arms. Although a quiet rain was still falling, she carried no umbrella. Wearing a yellow vinyl raincoat with a hood, she walked quickly to my door. I met her there, took the bag, and brought it to the kitchen. She removed the raincoat, exposing the brilliant green turtleneck underneath. Beneath the sweater were two very attractive bulges. Her breasts weren't as large as Shoko's, but they suited me just fine.

"Have you been at it all morning?"

"Yeah," I said. "But it's not a commission. I felt like drawing, so I came up with something on my own, just for fun."

"Just passing the time, huh?"

"Yeah, a bit like that."

"Are you hungry?"

"Not all that much."

"That's good," she said. "Why don't we eat afterward, then?"

"Fine by me," I said.

"You were awfully passionate today. Is there a special reason?" she asked. It was afterward, and we were lying in bed.

"I wonder," I said. What I might have said was, maybe it was because I spent the whole morning madly sketching a strange six-foot-wide hole in the ground and, partway through, my mind made a connection between the hole and a woman's vagina, which must have turned me on . . . But I couldn't.

"It was because I haven't seen you for so long," I said instead.

"You're sweet," she said, tracing a line on my chest with her fingertips. "But be honest—sometimes don't you want a younger woman?"

"No, I've never thought about that."

"Really?"

"Not once," I said. I was being truthful. Our sexual relationship was pure pleasure for me, and I had no desire to seek out anyone else. (My desire for Yuzu, of course, was of a wholly different order.)

I decided not to tell her about Mariye Akikawa. If she learned that a beautiful thirteen-year-old girl was modeling for me, it would only spark her jealousy. It seemed a woman at any age—thirteen, forty-one, you name it—felt she was facing a delicate time in her life. This was one thing my modest experience with the opposite sex had taught me.

"Still," she said. "Don't you think it's strange, the way women and men hook up?"

"Strange in what way?"

"I mean, look at us. We haven't known each other that long, yet here we are lying together naked, making love like this. Completely vulnerable, with no sense of shame. Don't you think it's weird?"

"Maybe you're right," I murmured.

"Try to think of it as a game. Maybe not only that, but a kind of game all the same. Otherwise what I'm saying won't make any sense."

"Okay, I'll try," I said.

"A game has to have rules, right?"

"Yeah, you need those."

"Baseball, soccer, all the sports have a thick rule book, right, where the rules are written down to the tiniest detail, and then umpires and players have to memorize them all. Without that, the game can't take place. Isn't that so?"

"You're absolutely right."

She paused, waiting for the image to sink in.

"So what I'm trying to say is, have we ever sat down and discussed the rules of **this game** that we're playing? Have we?"

I thought for a moment. "Possibly not," I said finally.

"Yet despite that, we are playing the game by a set of hypothetical rules. Right?"

"When you put it that way, I guess you have a point."

"So this is what I think," she said. "I'm playing the game according to my set of rules. And you're playing according to yours. The two of us **instinctively** respect each other's rules. As long as the two sets don't conflict and mess things up, we can go on like this without a hitch. Don't you agree?"

I considered what she had said. "Maybe you're right. We basically respect each other's rules."

"But you know, I think there's something even more important than respect and trust. And that's etiquette."

"Etiquette?"

"Etiquette's big."

"You may be right there," I agreed.

"If all those things—trust, respect, etiquette—stop functioning, the rules clash and the game breaks down. Then we either suspend the game and come up with a new set of rules we can both follow, or we end it and leave the playing field. The big question then would be which of those two routes we decide to follow."

That was precisely what had happened to my marriage. I had called a halt to the game and walked off the field. On that cold and rainy Sunday afternoon in March.

"So are you suggesting that we should talk out the rules of our relationship?"

"You don't get what I'm saying at all," she said, shaking her head. "What I want is **not** to have to discuss the rules of the game. That's why I'm able to be naked with you like this. You don't mind, do you?"

"Not a bit," I said.

"So that leaves us with trust and respect. And most of all etiquette."

"And most of all etiquette," I repeated.

She reached down and squeezed a part of my body.

"It's getting hard again," she whispered in my ear.

"Maybe that's because today is Monday," I said.

"What does Monday have to do with it?"

"Or maybe because it's raining. Or winter is coming. Or we're starting to see migrating birds. Or there's a bumper crop of mushrooms this year. Or my cup is a sixteenth full of water. Or the shape of your breasts under your green sweater turns me on."

She giggled. My answer appeared to have done the trick.

Menshiki called that evening. He thanked me for the day before.

I had done nothing worthy of his gratitude, I replied. All I had done was introduce him to two people. What developed after that, and how, had nothing to do with me—in that sense, I was a mere outsider. And I would like to keep it that way (though I had a premonition things might not work out so conveniently).

"Actually, I'm calling about something else," Menshiki said once the pleasantries were over. "I've received some new information about Tomohiko Amada."

So he was continuing his investigation. He might not be doing it himself, but arranging for such detailed work was certainly costing him a lot. Menshiki was a man who poured money into anything he thought necessary, sparing no expense. But why, and to what degree, was tracking down Tomohiko Amada's experiences in Vienna necessary to him? I didn't have a clue.

"What we've turned up may not have a direct connection with Amada's stay in Vienna," Menshiki went on. "But it overlaps with that time, and it's clear that it had a huge personal impact on him. So I thought you would like to hear about it."

"It overlapped with that time?"

"As I told you before, Tomohiko Amada returned to Japan from Vienna in early 1939. On paper, he was deported, but in fact he was rescued by the Gestapo. Officials from the foreign ministries of Japan and Nazi Germany had met in secret, and agreed that he be extradited but not charged with any crime. The failed assassination attempt had taken place in 1938, but it was linked to two other important events of that year: the **Anschluss**—Hitler's annexation of Austria—and **Kristallnacht**. The **Anschluss** took place in March, and **Kristallnacht** in November. Once they occurred, the brutality of Hitler's plan was obvious to everyone. Austria was firmly installed as a part of the Nazi war effort. An inextricable cog in the machine. Hoping to block this flow of events, students organized an underground resistance movement, and in the same year, Tomohiko Amada was arrested for his role in the assassination plot. Get the picture?"

"In a general sort of way, yes," I said.

"Do you like history?"

"I'm no expert, but I love books that deal with history," I said.

"A number of important events were taking place in Japan that year as well. Fatal, irrevocable events, which led to eventual disaster. Does anything spring to mind?"

I dusted off my store of historical knowledge, so long untouched. What had taken place in 1938? In Europe, the Spanish Civil War had intensified. German Condor bombers had flattened Guernica. But in Japan . . . ?

"Did the Marco Polo Bridge Incident take place that year?" I asked.

"That was the year before," Menshiki said. "On July 7, 1937. With the Marco Polo Bridge Incident, the war between China and Japan went into full swing. Then in December of that year, another serious event took place."

What had happened in December of 1937?

"The fall of Nanjing?" I asked.

"That's right. What's known today as the Nanjing

Massacre. After a hard-fought battle, Japanese troops occupied the city, and many people were killed. Some died in the fighting, others after the fighting ended. The Japanese army lacked the means to keep prisoners, so they killed the Chinese soldiers who surrendered as well as thousands of civilians. Historians disagree on exactly how many died, but no one can deny that a massive number of noncombatants were sucked into the conflict and lost their lives. Some say 400,000, others 100,000. But what difference is there really between 400,000 lives and 100,000?"

He had me on that one.

"So Nanjing fell in December, and many were killed. But what does that have to do with what happened to Tomohiko Amada in Vienna?" I asked.

"I'm getting to that," Menshiki said. "The Anti-Comintern Pact was signed by Japan and Germany in November of 1936, cementing their alliance, but Vienna and Nanjing were so far apart it's doubtful much news about Japan's war in China was getting through to Vienna. In fact, however, Tomohiko Amada's younger brother, Tsuguhiko, had been part of the assault on Nanjing as a private in the Japanese army. He had been drafted and assigned to one of the units fighting there. He was twenty, and a full-time student at the Tokyo Music School, now the Faculty of Music at the Tokyo University of the Arts. He studied the piano."

"That's strange," I said. "To my knowledge, full-time university students were exempt from the draft at that time."

"You're absolutely right. Full-time students were given a deferment until graduation. Yet for some reason Tsuguhiko was drafted and sent to China. In any case, he was inducted in June of 1937 and spent the next twelve months as a private second-class in the army. He was living in Tokyo, but his birth was registered in Kumamoto, so he was assigned to the 6th Division based there. That much is documented. After basic training, he was sent to China, and participated in the December assault on Nanjing. He was demobilized in June of the following year, and was expected to return to the conservatory."

I waited for Menshiki to continue.

"Not long after his discharge, however, Tsuguhiko Amada took his own life. He slit his wrists with a razor in the attic of the family home, which was where they found him. Right around the end of summer."

Slit his wrists in the attic?

"If it was toward the end of summer in 1938 . . . then Tomohiko was still an exchange student in Vienna when his brother Tsuguhiko slit his wrists, right?"

"That's correct. He didn't return home for the funeral. Commercial air travel was still in its infancy. You could only travel between Austria and Japan by rail and ship. There was no way he could have made it back in time."

"Are you suggesting that there's a connection between Tomohiko's involvement in the failed assassination and his brother's suicide? They seem to have happened almost simultaneously."

"Maybe yes, maybe no," Menshiki said. "That's in the realm of conjecture. What I'm reporting to you now are the facts our investigation was able to uncover."

"Did Tomohiko Amada have any other siblings?"

"There was an older brother. Tomohiko was the second son. Tsuguhiko was the third and last. The manner of his death was concealed, though, to protect the family's honor. Kumamoto's 6th Division was celebrated as a band of fearless warriors. If word had gotten out that their son had returned from the battlefield bathed in glory only to turn around and kill himself, they could not have faced the world. Still, as you know, rumors have a way of spreading."

I thanked Menshiki for updating me. Though what the new information meant in concrete terms escaped me.

"I'm planning to dig a bit deeper into this," he said. "I'll let you know if we turn up something more."

"Please do."

"So then I'll stop by next Sunday shortly after noon," Menshiki said. "I'll drive the Akikawas over to my place. To show them your painting. That's okay with you, right?"

"Of course. The painting is yours now. You're free to show it or not to whomever you like."

Menshiki paused. As if searching for just the right words. "To tell you the honest truth," he said. "Sometimes I'm very envious of you." There was resignation in his voice.

Envious? Of me?

What could he possibly be talking about? Why would Menshiki envy me? It made no sense. He had everything, while I had nothing to my name.

"What could you possibly be envious about?" I asked.

"I see you as the kind of person who doesn't really envy anyone. Am I right?"

I thought for a moment before replying. "You have a point. I don't think I've ever envied another person."

"That's what I'm trying to say."

All the same, I don't have Yuzu, I thought. She had left me for the arms of another man. There were times I felt abandoned at the edge of the world. Yet even then I felt no envy toward that other man. Did that make me strange?

After our phone call, I sat on the sofa and thought about Tomohiko Amada's brother slitting his wrists in the attic. It wasn't the attic of this house, that was for sure. Tomohiko had bought this place after the war. No, Tsuguhiko Amada had committed suicide in the attic of their family home. In Aso, no doubt. Nevertheless, the brother's death and the painting **Killing Commendatore** might be connected by that dark, secret room above the ceiling. Sure, it might have been pure coincidence. Or perhaps Tomohiko had his brother in mind when he hid the painting in the attic here. Still, why was Tsuguhiko compelled to take his own life so soon after returning from the front? After all, he had survived the bloody conflict in China and come home with all his limbs intact.

I picked up the phone and dialed Masahiko's number.

"Let's get together in Tokyo," I said. "I have to visit the art supply shop soon to stock up on paints. Maybe we could meet and talk then."

"Sure thing," he said, checking his schedule. Thursday just after noon was best for him, so we arranged to have lunch together.

"The art supply store in Yotsuya, correct?"

"That's the one. I've got to pick up fresh canvases, too, and I'm running out of linseed oil. It'll be quite a load, so I'll take the car."

"There's a quiet restaurant not far from my office. We could have a nice relaxed chat over lunch."

"By the way," I said, "divorce papers from Yuzu came in the mail, so I signed and returned them. It looks like our divorce will become official pretty soon."

"Is that so," Masahiko said in a subdued voice.

"What can you do? It was just a matter of time."

"Still, from where I stand it's a real shame. You guys seemed like such a good match."

"It was great as long as things were going well," I said. Just like an old-model Jaguar. A wonderful ride until the problems start.

"So what will you do now?"

"No big changes. Just keep on as I am for the time being. Can't think of what else to do."

"Are you painting?"

"Yeah, I've got a couple of paintings I'm working on. Not sure what will happen with them, but at least I'm at it."

"That's the way to go." Masahiko hesitated before adding, "I'm glad you called. There's something I want to discuss with you as well."

"Something good?"

"It's just the facts—I can't say if they're good or bad."

"Does it have to do with Yuzu?"

"It's hard to talk about over the phone."

"Okay, on Thursday then."

I ended the call and walked out to the terrace. The rain had stopped, and the cool night air was clear and bracing. I could see stars peeping from the cracks between the clouds. They looked like scattered crystals of ice. Hard crystals, millions of years old, never melting. Hard to their very core. Across the valley, Menshiki's house glimmered in the cool light of its lanterns.

As I looked at his house, I thought of trust, respect, and etiquette. Especially etiquette. As I expected, though, none of those thoughts led me to any definite conclusions.

37

EVERY CLOUD HAS
A SILVER LINING

It turned out to be a long haul from my mountaintop perch on the outskirts of Odawara to downtown Tokyo. I took several wrong turns en route, which ate up a lot of time. My old used car had no navigation system or electronic pass for the highway tolls. (I guess I should have been grateful it came with a cup holder!) It took me ages to find the Odawara-Atsugi Road, and when I moved from the Tomei Expressway onto the Metropolitan Expressway it was jammed, so I opted to get off at the Shibuya exit and drive to Yotsuya via Aoyama Avenue. Even the city roads were crowded, though—just choosing the correct lane was a huge pain in the ass. Parking the car wasn't easy, either. It seems as if, year after year, the world becomes a more difficult place to live.

By the time I picked up what I needed at the art supply store, loaded it into the trunk, drove to Masahiko Amada's office in Aoyama, and found a parking spot, I was exhausted. I felt like the country mouse visiting his city cousin. When I reached his office it was past one by my watch, which meant I was more than a half hour late.

I asked the receptionist to call Masahiko. He came right down. I apologized for being so tardy.

"Don't worry about it," he laughed. "My office can adjust, and so can the restaurant."

Masahiko took me to an Italian place in the neighborhood, located in the basement of a small building. Masahiko was obviously well known there, for no sooner had they seen his face than we were guided to a private room in the back. It was very quiet: the sound of voices did not reach us and no music was playing. A quite passable landscape painting hung on the wall. It showed a white lighthouse on a green peninsula under a blue sky. Super-ordinary scene, sure, but done well enough to let the viewer think, "Hey, that place might be nice to check out."

Masahiko ordered a glass of white wine, while I asked for Perrier.

"I've got to drive back after this," I explained. "It's quite a trek."

"No kidding," said Masahiko. "Still, it's a heck of a lot better than Hayama or Zushi. I lived in Hayama once, and driving back and forth to Tokyo in the summer was awful. The whole route was jammed with people heading to the ocean from the city. A round trip was a half day's work. Compared to that, driving in from Odawara is nothing."

The menus arrived and we ordered the prix fixe lunch: prosciutto as appetizer followed by asparagus salad and spaghetti with Japanese lobster.

"So you finally decided to do some serious painting," Masahiko said.

561

"Well, I'm living alone now, and I don't need commissions to get by. Maybe that's why the urge to paint my own stuff hit me."

Masahiko nodded. "Everything has a bright side," he said. "The top of even the blackest, thickest cloud shines like silver."

"Yeah, but getting up there to see it is no picnic."

"I was speaking more theoretically," Masahiko said.

"I think living on top of a mountain may be affecting me too. It's the perfect spot to focus on my art."

"Yeah, when no one's there to distract you and it's that quiet, you can really concentrate. A more normal person might get a bit lonely, but I figured you're the kind of guy who can handle it."

The door opened and the appetizer was brought in. We fell quiet as the plates were laid out.

"I think the studio has a lot to do with it as well," I said once the waiter had gone. "There's something about being in that room that makes me want to paint. At times it feels like the center of the whole house."

"If the house were human, it'd be the heart, perhaps."

"Yeah, or the consciousness."

"**Body and Mind,**" Masahiko said in English. "To tell the truth, though, it's hard for me to spend time in his studio. **His** smell has sunk in too deep. I can still feel him in the air. When I was a boy, he'd isolate himself in that room almost all day, painting away without a word to anyone. It was his sanctum, off-limits to a kid like me. I tend to steer clear of the studio when I'm there, even now. You should be careful too."

"Be careful? Why?"

"So you don't become possessed by his spirit. It's a strong one."

"Spirit?"

"Maybe 'psychic energy' is a better term. Or 'flow of being.' His is intense enough to sweep you away. At any rate, when someone like him spends a long time in a particular place, it soaks in his aura. Like particles of smell."

"And that's what could possess me?"

"Maybe 'possessed' isn't the best way to put it. 'Absorb his influence,' perhaps? It's like he invested that room with some special **power**."

"I wonder. I'm only looking after his home, and I never met him. So maybe it won't weigh on me as much."

"You're probably right," Masahiko said. He took a sip of white wine. "Being related to him may make me more sensitive to those things. And if it turns out that his 'aura' inspires you in your work, so much the better."

"So how's he doing these days?"

"Nothing in particular is wrong with him. He's past ninety, so I can't say he's the picture of health, and his mind is confused, but he can still manage to get around with a cane, his appetite's fine, and his eyes and teeth are in good shape. You know, his teeth are better than mine—never had a cavity!"

"How bad is his memory? Can he recall anything?"

"Not a whole lot. He doesn't recognize me. He's lost the concept of family, of father and son. Even the distinction between himself and other people may have blurred. Still, maybe it's easier when those things are swept away, and you don't have to think about them anymore."

I sipped my slender glass of Perrier and nodded. So Tomohiko Amada had forgotten even his son's face. Memories of student days in Vienna must have set sail for the far shore of forgetfulness some time ago.

"All the same, what I called his 'flow of being' is still strong," Masahiko said, as if in wonder. "It's strange: he remembers almost nothing, but his will is the same as always. It's obvious when you look at him. That psychic power is what makes him who he is. I feel a bit guilty sometimes that I didn't inherit that temperament, but there's nothing I can do about it. We're all born with different abilities. Being linked to someone by blood doesn't mean you have similar gifts."

I looked in his face. It was rare to see Masahiko bare his true feelings.

"It must be awfully hard to have such a famous father," I said. "I can't even imagine what it's like. My dad was nothing special, just a small businessman."

"There are some benefits to having a famous father, but there are times that it really sucks. I think the latter are a bit more frequent, actually. You're lucky you don't have to deal with that. You're free to be who you want."

"You look like the one with a free life."

"In a sense," Masahiko said. He turned his wine-glass around in his hand. "But in another sense, no."

Masahiko possessed a keen artistic sensibility of his own. He had taken a job with a medium-sized ad agency after finishing school. By now, his salary had increased, and he looked for all the world like a bachelor enjoying everything city life had to offer. I had no way of knowing if that was true, however.

"I was hoping to ask you a few things about your father," I said, broaching the reason for my visit.

"What sort of things? You know, I really don't know that much about him."

"I heard that he had a younger brother named Tsuguhiko."

"Yeah, that's true. That would be my uncle, I guess. But he died a long time ago. Before Pearl Harbor."

"I heard he committed suicide."

A shadow passed across Masahiko's face. "That's supposed to be a family secret, but it happened so long ago, and part of it's public knowledge now anyway. So I guess it's okay to tell you. He cut his wrists with a razor. He was only twenty."

"What made him do it?"

"Why do you want to know something like that?"

"I've been trying to learn more about your father. I stumbled across your uncle's story when I was looking through some documents."

"You want to learn more about my father?"

"I wanted to learn more about his paintings, but as I looked at his career I became more and more interested in his personal life. I'd like to know the kind of man he was."

Masahiko studied my face from across the table. "All right," he said. "You've taken an interest in my father's life. There may be some significance in that. Living in that house has created some sort of bond between the two of you."

He took a swallow of white wine before launching into his story.

"My uncle, Tsuguhiko Amada, was a student at the Tokyo Music School back then. A talented pianist, they say. He loved Chopin and Debussy, and high hopes were held for his future. Forgive me for sounding arrogant, but artistic talent seems to run in our family. To varying degrees, of course. However, in the midst of his studies my uncle was drafted. He should have received a student deferment, but his papers had been mishandled when he enrolled in the conservatory. If those forms had been properly filed, he could have put off military service until graduation, and probably avoided it altogether. My grandfather was a big landowner in the area, and influential in political circles. But there was a slip-up in the paperwork. It came as a great shock to my uncle. But once the system grinds into motion there's not a whole lot anyone can do to stop it. Protest was futile: the army grabbed him, gave him his basic training in Japan, and then loaded him onto a troop transport and shipped him off to Hangzhou. At the time, his elder brother Tomohiko—in other words, my father—was studying painting under a famous artist in Vienna."

I didn't say anything.

"Everyone knew that my uncle wasn't cut out for the rugged life of a soldier or the carnage of the battlefield—he was a high-strung young man, and physically weak. To make matters worse, the young men of southern Kyushu who made up the 6th Division were a rough group, known for their violence. My father agonized over the news that his brother had been drafted and sent off to war. My father was egotistic and highly competitive, a typical second son, but his younger brother was shy and retiring, the somewhat pampered baby of the family. As a pianist, he had to be careful to protect his hands. Even as a child, my father learned to look out for his little brother, who was three years younger, and shield him from the outside world. It became second nature to him—he was his brother's protector. But all he could do in faraway Vienna was sit and fret. The only information he got came in his brother's letters from the front.

"Of course those letters were strictly censored, but the two brothers were so close that the elder could read the younger's feelings between the lines. Moreover, the true meaning of those lines was skillfully camouflaged, so only he could figure it out. My uncle's regiment had fought their way from Shanghai to Nanjing, engaging in fierce battles in the towns and cities en route, and leaving a trail of murder and plunder in their wake. Those bloody events left my high-strung uncle with deep emotional scars.

"One of my uncle's letters described a beautiful pipe organ they had come across in a church in occupied Nanjing. It had survived the fighting in perfect shape. For some unfathomable reason, though, the long description of the organ that followed had been inked out. What military secrets could an organ in a Christian church possibly have compromised? The standards used by the censor attached to their regiment were impossible to fathom. As a matter of fact, it was common for him to black out the most innocuous and unthreatening passages of a letter while overlooking the parts that really might have put troops at risk. As a consequence, my father was left in the dark as to whether his brother had been able to play that organ or not.

"Uncle Tsuguhiko's year in the army ended in June of 1938," Masahiko continued. "Although he had arranged to reenter the conservatory right after his return, he went back to Kyushu instead and committed suicide in the attic of the family home. He sharpened a straight razor to a fine edge and slit his wrists. It must have taken tremendous resolve for a pianist to do that to his hands. I mean, if he had survived, he might never have been able to play again, right? They found him in a pool of blood. The fact that he had killed himself was kept a deep, dark secret. To the world, the official cause of death was heart failure or something like that.

"In fact, though, it was clear to everyone why Uncle Tsuguhiko had taken his own life—his war experience had ruined his nerves, and wrecked him psychologically. I mean, here was a delicate young man of twenty, whose entire world was playing the piano, thrown into the bloodbath of the Nanjing campaign, surrounded by heaps of corpses. Today we talk about post-traumatic stress disorder, but that phrase—even that concept—was unknown then. In that deeply militaristic society, people like my uncle were dismissed as lacking courage, or patriotism, or strength of character. In wartime Japan, such 'weakness' was neither understood nor accepted. So the family buried what had happened, as evidence of their shame."

"Did he leave a suicide note?" I asked.

"Yes, they found a personal testament in his desk drawer. It was quite long, closer to a memoir, really. In it, Uncle Tsuguhiko recorded his war experiences in excruciating detail. The only people who saw it were his parents—my grandparents, in other words— his eldest brother, and my father. When my father returned from Vienna and read it, he burned it while the other three watched."

I waited for him to go on.

"My father kept his lips sealed about what that testament contained," Masahiko continued. "It was the family's darkest secret: to use a metaphor, it was nailed shut, weighted with heavy stones, and sent to the bottom of the ocean. However, my father did tell me the gist of what was in it once, when he was drunk. I was in grade school, and it was the first time I learned that I had an uncle who committed suicide. To this day, I have no idea whether it was the alcohol that loosened my father's lips, or if he figured that I had to hear the story at some point."

Our salad plates were cleared, replaced by the spaghetti with Japanese lobster.

Masahiko took his fork and stared at it for a moment. As if inspecting an implement used for some special task.

"Hey man," he said. "This isn't really something I want to talk about when I'm eating."

"No problem. Let's talk about something else."

"Like what, for example."

"Something as far removed from your uncle's testament as possible."

So we talked golf as we ate our spaghetti. Of course, I had never played the game. No one around me had either. I didn't even know the rules. Masahiko, however, had taken it up in order to play with the people he did business with. And to get back into some kind of shape after years of inactivity. He had purchased a set of clubs, and spent his weekends on the golf course.

"You may not know this," he told me, "but golf is the oddest game you can imagine. As weird as it gets. You could say it's a sport unto itself. Yet I'm not even sure if it can be called a true sport. The funny thing is, once you get used to its weirdness you can't go back."

Masahiko went on and on about the strangeness of golf, telling me one off-the-wall story after another. A great conversationalist, he made our lunch extremely entertaining. We laughed together as we hadn't in ages.

Our plates were cleared away and coffee was brought in, although Masahiko opted for another glass of white wine.

"Anyway, back to my uncle's suicide letter," he said, his voice abruptly serious. "According to my father, Uncle Tsuguhiko wrote about being forced to behead a Chinese prisoner. He described it in painful detail. Of course, a common soldier like him didn't carry a sword. In fact, he had never touched a sword up to that point. I mean, he was a pianist, right? He could read a complex musical score, but wielding an executioner's sword was beyond him. But his commanding officer handed him one and ordered, 'Chop off his head!' The prisoner wasn't in uniform and had no weapon when he was picked up. Nor was he a young man. He claimed he was a civilian, not a soldier. But the army was grabbing any likely men they could find and dragging them in to be killed. If your palms were callused, you were deemed a peasant and might be released. If they were soft, however, it was assumed that you were a soldier who'd tossed his uniform to pass as a civilian, and you were summarily executed. Arguing the sentence was a waste of breath. The method of execution was either being gutted by a bayonet or decapitated by a sword. If a machine gun unit was in the area, prisoners might be lined up in a row and shot, but there was a general reluctance to 'waste' ammunition that way—bullets were always in short supply—so bayonets and swords were used. The bodies were collected and dumped in the Yangtze River, where they fed the many catfish who lived there. I don't know if it's fact or fiction, but it was said that some grew as big as ponies on that diet.

"My uncle took the sword from the officer, a

young second lieutenant who had just completed officer training school, and prepared to cut off the prisoner's head. Of course, he didn't want to do it. But it was unthinkable to refuse an order. Not something corrected by a simple reprimand. An order from an officer in Japan's Imperial Army was an order from the Emperor himself. My uncle's hands were shaking. He wasn't a strong man, and to make matters worse it was a crummy, mass-produced sword. The human neck isn't that easy to sever. His attempt failed. Blood sprayed everywhere, the prisoner thrashed about—it was gruesome."

Masahiko shook his head. I sipped my coffee.

"When it was finally over my uncle started puking. When there was nothing left he puked gastric juice, and when that was gone he puked air. His comrades ridiculed him. The officer called him a 'pitiful excuse for a soldier' and kicked him hard in the side with his army boots. No one sympathized. Instead, he was ordered to decapitate two more prisoners. This was for **practice**, to help him become **accustomed** to cutting off people's heads. A soldier's rite of passage, it was thought. Participating in such carnage made a man a 'true warrior.' But my uncle was never meant to be a warrior in the first place. He wasn't put on this earth for that. He was born to make beautiful music, to perform Chopin and Debussy. Not to chop the heads off other human beings."

"Are some people born to chop off heads?" I asked.

Masahiko shook his head again. "I can't answer that. But I do know there must be quite a few who are able to **get used to it**. People can become accustomed to almost anything, especially when they're pushed to the limit. It may become surprisingly easy then."

"Or when they're given justification for their actions."

"You're right there," Masahiko said. "In most cases, they're provided with some justification for what they do. I'm not confident that I'd be any different, to tell the truth. I might not be strong enough to stand up and say no if I were thrown into a system as violent as the military, even if I knew the order was horribly wrong or inhuman."

I thought of myself. Would I be any different if I were in his uncle's shoes? The image of the strange woman I had spent the night with in the port town in Miyagi popped into my head. The young woman who had handed me the belt of her bathrobe and asked me to strangle her in the middle of sex. I still remembered how the belt felt wrapped tight around my hands. Probably I would never forget.

"Uncle Tsuguhiko couldn't refuse his superior's order," Masahiko said. "He lacked the guts to do that. Yet later he was able to sharpen a razor and use it to kill himself. In that sense, I don't think he was weak at all. Only by taking his own life was my uncle able to recover his humanity."

"The news must have been a terrible shock to your father in Vienna."

"That hardly needs saying," Masahiko replied.

"I've heard that your father got caught up in some political events in Vienna that got him deported back

573

to Japan. Did those have any connection to his brother's suicide?"

Masahiko folded his arms and frowned. "It's hard for me to say. You see, my father never said a word about what happened."

"What I heard was that your father fell in love with a girl who belonged to a resistance organization, and that she was involved in a failed assassination attempt."

"Yes, I know about that. Apparently she was an Austrian student at the university, and they were planning to get married. But when the plot came to light, she was arrested and sent to the concentration camp at Mauthausen. She probably died there. My father was arrested by the Gestapo and forcibly repatriated as an 'undesirable alien' in early 1939. Of course, this didn't come from my father but from someone in the family—a credible source."

"Do you think someone somewhere prevented your father from speaking about what had happened in Vienna?"

"Yeah, I'm sure that's true. I'm sure authorities on both sides—Japan and Germany—laid down the law in no uncertain terms when they arranged his deportation. He knew he had to keep his mouth shut—that was the price he paid for saving his own neck. But I don't think he wanted to talk about those events, either. Otherwise he wouldn't have remained so close-mouthed when the war ended and the threat was gone."

Masahiko paused for a moment before continuing.

"I think it's entirely possible that Uncle Tsuguhiko's suicide played a role in my father's involvement in the anti-Nazi resistance in Vienna. The Munich Conference removed the threat of war for the time being, but it also strengthened the Berlin-Tokyo axis, and set the world moving in an even more dangerous direction. My guess is that my father was determined to try to put the brakes on that movement. He was a man who prized freedom above all else. Fascism and militarism ran against everything he believed. The death of his younger brother could only have strengthened those convictions."

"Do we know anything more?"

"My father never talked to anyone about his life. He did no interviews with the media, and left nothing written down for posterity. He was like someone who walks backward, erasing his own footsteps with a broom."

"He kept his silence as a painter too, didn't he," I said. "He exhibited none of his work from the time he returned from Vienna to the end of the war."

"Yeah, eight years in total, from 1939 until 1947. All that time, he stayed as far removed as possible from what we might call 'artistic circles.' He couldn't stand that crowd anyway, and their 'nationalist art' glorifying the war effort made him like them even less. Lucky for him, his family was well off, so he didn't have to worry about getting by. And, thankfully, he wasn't drafted to be a soldier during the war. In any case, once the postwar chaos had settled down, Tomohiko Amada reemerged, having metamorphosed into a purely Japanese-style painter. He had jettisoned his old style and adopted a totally new one."

"And thus was born a legend."

"That's right," Masahiko said. "The rest is legend." He waved his hand, as if shooing something away. As if the legend were a mote in the air, interfering with his breathing.

"As I hear you tell the story," I said, "I begin to think your father's student days in Vienna cast a shadow over his whole life. Whatever the exact circumstances may have been."

Masahiko nodded. "Yeah, I think that too. Those events changed the course of his life in a drastic way. The failure of the assassination plot must have led to a number of dreadful things. Things too horrible to speak of."

"Still, we don't know the details."

"No, we don't. I didn't know them growing up, and it's an even bigger riddle now. The man in question can't have a clue either."

Perhaps, I thought. People can forget what they should remember, and remember what by all rights and purposes they should forget. Especially when death approaches.

Masahiko polished off his second glass of white wine and glanced at his watch. He gave a slight frown.

"I've got to head back to the office," he said.

"Wasn't there something you wanted to tell me?" I asked, suddenly remembering.

He rapped his knuckles on the tabletop as if to echo my feeling. "You're right," he said. "There is something. But we spent all our time talking about my father. It'll have to be next time. It's nothing that urgent."

I looked at his face again as we were about to get up. "Why are you being so open with me?" I asked. "Showing me the skeletons in your family's closet."

He spread his hands on the table and thought for a minute. He scratched his ear.

"Let's see. For one thing, I'm getting a little tired carrying these 'family skeletons' around all by myself. Maybe I wanted to share them with someone. Someone who has nothing to gain from them, and who'll keep his mouth shut. In that sense, you're an ideal person to unburden myself to. Also, to tell the truth I'm feeling a little guilty where you're concerned, so this may be my way of trying to pay you back."

"Guilty?" I burst out. "In what way?"

Masahiko half closed his eyes. "I'd intended to tell you about that," he said. "But there's no more time today. My next appointment is one I can't miss. Let's meet again soon. Then we can talk all we want."

Masahiko paid the tab. "Don't worry," he said. "This much I can write off." I accepted with gratitude.

After that, I drove the Corolla station wagon back to Odawara. By the time I parked the dusty old heap in front of the house, the sun had almost reached the ridge of the western mountains. A large flock of cawing crows was winging across the valley, heading to their nests.

38

HE COULD NEVER BE A DOLPHIN

B y the time Sunday rolled around, I had a pretty good idea how to attack the canvas I'd set aside for Mariye Akikawa's portrait. I still wasn't sure exactly what form the painting would take. But I did know **how I should begin**. Those first steps—which brush to use, what color, the direction of the first stroke—had come to me out of nowhere: they had gained a foothold in my mind and, bit by bit, taken on a tangible reality of their own. I loved this process.

It was a chilly morning. The kind of morning that heralds the coming of winter. I brewed coffee, ate a simple breakfast, went to the studio, laid out what I needed to paint, and then stood before my easel, which held the empty canvas. In front of the canvas, however, sat my sketchbook, open to the detailed pencil drawing I had done of the pit in the woods. I had tossed it off several mornings earlier without giving it much thought. I had even forgotten I had drawn it.

Nevertheless, the longer I stood there facing the drawing, the more it sucked me in. The mysterious stone chamber in the woods, the secret opening. The sodden earth, the patchwork of fallen leaves. The sunlight filtering through the branches. As my imagination filled in the penciled sketch, I began to see it as a colorful painting. I could breathe in the air of the place, smell the grass, hear the birds singing.

The pit I had drawn with such precision in my big sketchbook was beckoning me, luring me toward something—or was it somewhere? **The pit was demanding that I paint it.** I seldom thought of painting landscapes. I mean, I'd done virtually nothing but portraits for nearly ten years. But maybe a landscape painting wasn't such a bad idea. **The Pit in the Woods.** This pencil sketch could be a first step in that direction.

I removed my sketchbook and closed it. The unblemished white canvas remained on the easel. The canvas that would soon be graced by my portrait of Mariye.

At a few minutes before ten, as before, the blue Toyota Prius rolled silently up the slope. The doors opened, and Mariye and her aunt Shoko stepped out. Shoko Akikawa was wearing a long, dark-gray herringbone jacket, a light-gray wool skirt, and patterned black stockings. Wrapped around her neck was a bright Missoni scarf. A chic late-fall outfit. Mariye was dressed much like before: a baggy varsity jacket, a windbreaker, jeans with holes in them, and dark-blue Converse sneakers. Her head was bare. The air was chilly, and a thin blanket of clouds covered the sky.

After a simple exchange of greetings, Shoko curled

up on the sofa and, once again, immersed herself in her thick paperback. Mariye and I left her there and went into the studio. I sat on the same wooden stool, Mariye on the same simple straight-backed chair. Six feet or so separated us. Mariye took off her jacket, folded it, and laid it next to her chair. Then she removed her windbreaker. Underneath was a blue short-sleeved T-shirt and, beneath that, a gray long-sleeved T-shirt. Her chest was as flat as ever. She ran her fingers through her straight black hair.

"Aren't you cold?" I asked. There was an old-fashioned kerosene space heater in the studio, but it was unlit.

Mariye gave a slight shake of her head. As if to say **No, not particularly.**

"I'll start painting today," I said. "You don't have to do anything. It's enough if you just sit there. You can leave the rest to me."

"I can't not do anything," she said, looking me straight in the eye.

"What does that mean?" I asked, my hands on my knees.

"Like, I'm living and breathing and thinking all kinds of stuff."

"Of course," I said. "Please, breathe as much as you want and think as many thoughts as you can. All I meant was, there's nothing special you have to do. I just want you to be yourself."

Yet Mariye continued to stare straight at me. As if my explanation was too simple to swallow.

"But I want to do something," she said.

"Like what?"

"I want to help you paint."

"I appreciate that, but what do you mean exactly? Help me in what way?"

"Mentally, of course."

"I see," I said. Yet I couldn't think of anything specific she could do "mentally" to help.

"I'd like to see things as you see them," she said. "Look at myself through your eyes while you're painting me. I think I'd understand myself better if I did that. And you'd probably understand me better, too."

"I'd love that," I said.

"Really?"

"Yes, really."

"It might get pretty scary sometimes."

"Knowing more about yourself, you mean?"

Mariye nodded. "If you want to know yourself better you have to bring in something different from someplace else."

"Are you saying you can't know yourself unless you add a third-person perspective?"

"A third-person perspective?"

"In other words," I explained, "to understand the relationship between A and B you might need C, a third point of view. What we call 'triangulation.'"

Mariye thought for a moment. "Maybe," she said with a shrug.

"Are you saying that what you bring in might be scary, depending on the situation?"

Mariye nodded.

"Have you had that scary feeling before?"

Mariye didn't respond.

"If I can draw you the right way, maybe you'll be able to see yourself through my eyes," I said. "If all goes well, of course."

"That's why we need pictures."

"You're right—that's why we need pictures. Or literature, or music, or anything of that sort."

If all goes well, I said to myself.

"So let's get started," I said to Mariye. Looking at her face, I started mixing the brown for the under-drawing. Then I selected the first brush I would use on the painting.

The work progressed slowly but smoothly. The painting would show her from the waist up. She was a beautiful girl, but beauty wasn't what I was after. Instead, I had to find what was hidden beneath the surface. What underlay her personality—what allowed it to subsist. I had to find that **something** and bring it to the canvas. It didn't have to be pretty. Sometimes it might even be ugly. In either case, though, I had to know her well enough to discover what that something was. Not through words or logic, but as a singular form, a composite of light and shadow.

I concentrated on layering lines and color on the canvas. Rapidly at times, at other times with pains-taking care. Mariye sat, unmoving, on the straight-backed chair, her expression never wavering. She had mustered her willpower, I sensed, and was sustaining it for as long as necessary. I could feel her strength. "I can't not do anything," she had said. And indeed, she was **doing something**. To help me, most likely. An unmistakable current of some kind was flowing between this thirteen-year-old girl and myself.

I recalled my sister's hands. She had taken my hand in hers when we entered the chilly darkness of the wind cave on Mt. Fuji. Her hand was small and warm—yet her fingers were surprisingly strong. A definite life force connected us. Each was giving something to the other, and at the same moment receiving something. It was an exchange limited to a particular time and place. It was bound to fade and disappear. But the memory remained. Memory can give warmth to time. And art can—when it goes well—give shape to that memory, even fix it in history. Much as Van Gogh inscribed the figure of a country mailman on our collective memory so well that he lives on, even today.

For the next two hours, we focused on our respective jobs without exchanging a word.

Thinning the paint with linseed oil, I began by roughing in her form in a single color. That would be the portrait's underdrawing. Mariye sat quietly in the chair, continuing to be herself. At noon, as they did every day, chimes rang in the distance, announcing that our time was up. I put down my palette and paintbrush, straightened my back, and stretched.

Only then did I realize how tired I was. I took a deep breath to break my concentration, whereupon Mariye finally let her body relax.

The monochrome outline of Mariye's head and shoulders was there on the canvas before me. This was the structure upon which the portrait would be built. It was skeletal, but at its core was the source of the heat that made her who she was. That was still hidden, but if I could grasp its general location I would be able to make adjustments further down the line. Then all that would be left was fleshing out the skeleton.

Mariye didn't ask anything about what I had painted, nor did she ask to see it. I said little on my part, as well. I was just too worn out. We left the studio together and moved to the living room without a word. Shoko was still absorbed in her paperback. She marked her spot, closed the book, removed her black-rimmed reading glasses, and looked up at us. I could see that she was a bit alarmed. Our fatigue must have been written on our faces.

"Did it go all right?" she asked in a slightly worried tone.

"We're only partway through the process, but we're right on schedule."

"That's so good to hear," she said. "Would you mind if I made some nice hot tea? I've already set the water to boil. And I know where you keep the tea leaves."

Taken somewhat aback, I glanced down at her. Her lips were curved in a refined smile.

"I fear I'm being a poor host, but yes, that would be wonderful," I said. I was dying for some hot tea, but getting up and going to the kitchen to boil water was beyond me. I was exhausted. It had been ages since I'd gotten so tired painting. It felt good, though.

Shoko returned to the living room ten minutes later with three cups and a pot on a tray. We sat there quietly, each drinking our black tea. Mariye hadn't uttered a word since we left the studio. Every so often she'd reach up to push the hair back from her forehead. She had put her heavy jacket on again. As if she needed it to protect her from something.

The three of us sat there politely sipping our tea (not one of us slurped) and enjoying the lazy flow of the Sunday afternoon. No one spoke. The silence was easy and unforced, as if in accordance with the laws of nature. At a certain point, I heard a familiar sound, like waves on a distant shore, a listless and reluctant, yet somehow obligatory, lapping. Soon, however, the sound took on the unmistakable rhythm of a well-tuned engine. An eight-cylinder, 4.2-liter engine with power to spare burning (most elegantly, of course) high-octane fossil fuel. I got up from my chair, went to the window, and watched the approach of the silver car through a crack in the curtain.

Menshiki was wearing a lime-green cardigan over a cream-colored shirt. His pants were gray wool. They were clean and wrinkle-free, as if just back from the cleaners. None of his clothes appeared to be new—

they all looked comfortably worn. That made them seem even cleaner. His hair, as always, was a glowing white. It seemed impervious to the seasons and the weather. I guessed that in summer or in winter, on sunny or cloudy days, its radiance would never fade. Only its tone would vary.

Menshiki got out of the car, closed the door, and looked up at the cloudy sky. He thought about the weather for a moment (at least that's how it looked to me), composed himself, and walked slowly to the front door. Then he rang the doorbell. Slowly and deliberately, like a poet selecting the precise word for a crucial passage. However you looked at it, though, it was just a common old doorbell.

I opened the door and showed Menshiki into the living room. Smiling, he greeted the two women. Shoko rose to welcome him. Mariye remained on the sofa, twirling her hair. She barely glanced his way. At my bidding, we all sat down. Would you like some tea, I asked Menshiki. Please don't bother, he replied, shaking his head several times and waving his hand in refusal.

"How is your work going?" he asked me.

Moving along as usual, I replied.

"Modeling is tiring, isn't it?" Menshiki asked Mariye. I couldn't remember him addressing her while looking her in the eye before. His tone was still a bit tense, but today at least he wasn't paling or blushing in her presence. His face looked almost normal. He was doing a good job controlling his emotions. I bet he'd been training hard to pull that off.

Mariye didn't answer. She seemed to mumble something, but it was entirely inaudible. Her hands were clasped tightly on her knees.

"You know she really looks forward to coming here Sunday mornings," Shoko remarked, breaking the silence.

"Modeling is hard work," I said, doing my humble best to back her up. "Mariye is doing a great job."

"I served as a model here for a while," Menshiki said. "I found it odd somehow. There were times it felt like my soul was being stolen from me." He laughed.

"It's not like that at all," Mariye said, in what was little more than a whisper.

The three of us turned in her direction.

Shoko looked as though she had popped something she shouldn't have into her mouth and bitten down on it. Menshiki's face registered unadulterated curiosity. I remained, as ever, the impartial observer.

"What do you mean?" asked Menshiki.

"Nothing's being stolen from me," Mariye said in a monotone. "I'm giving something, and I'm getting something in return."

"You're absolutely right," Menshiki said quietly. He seemed impressed. "I was being too simplistic. There has to be an exchange. Artistic creation can never be a one-way street."

Mariye was silent, her eyes fixed on the teapot on the table. She looked like a lone night heron motionless on the shore, glaring at the water's surface for hours on end. The teapot was simple white ceramic, the kind you can find anywhere. It was old (Tomo-

587

hiko Amada had used it), and eminently practical, but apart from a small chip on the rim, nothing about it warranted close examination. Mariye just needed something to stare at right then.

The room fell silent. Like a blank, white billboard.

Artistic creation, I thought to myself. Those words had a pull to them that drew all the silence in the vicinity into a single spot. Like air filling a vacuum. No, more like a vacuum sucking up all the air.

"If you're coming to my house," Menshiki said gingerly, facing Shoko, "then perhaps we should go in my car. I'll bring you back here afterward. The back-seat is a bit cramped, but the drive is so full of twists and turns—you'll find this much easier."

"Of course," Shoko said at once. "We'll ride in your car."

Mariye's eyes were still on the white teapot. She seemed deep in thought. Of course, I had no idea what was on her mind, or in her heart. I had no idea what the three of them would do for lunch, either. But Menshiki was smart. He had it all planned—there was no need for me to sweat the details.

Shoko sat in the passenger seat, while Mariye settled in the back. Adults in front, kids in back. The natural way of the world—no prior consultation necessary. I watched from my front door as the car slipped down the slope and out of sight. I went back into the house, took the teacups and teapot into the kitchen, and washed them.

When I finished, I placed Richard Strauss's **Rosenkavalier** on the turntable, stretched out on the sofa, and listened. **Der Rosenkavalier** had become my fallback when I had nothing else to do. A habit implanted in me by Menshiki. The music was somehow addictive, as he had warned. An uninterrupted stream of emotion. Musical instruments in colorful profusion. It was Strauss who boasted, "I can describe anything in music, even a common broom." Maybe he didn't say "broom"—it could have been something else. At any rate, there was something painterly about his music. Though what I was aiming for in my painting was very different.

When I opened my eyes a while later, there was the Commendatore. He was sitting in the leather easy chair across from me wearing the same Asuka-period clothing, his sword still on his hip. Perched on the chair, his two-foot frame looked quite demure.

"It's been a while," I said. My voice sounded strained and forced, as if coming from somewhere else. "How have you been?"

"As I have told my friends in the past, time is a concept foreign to Ideas," he said in a small but clear voice. " 'A while' thus lies outside my understanding."

"It's a customary phrase. Please don't let it bother you."

"I cannot fathom 'customary' either."

Fair enough. Where there is no "time" there can be no "custom." I stood up and walked to the stereo, lifted the needle, and returned the record to its sleeve.

"As you may have surmised," the Commendatore

said, reading my mind, "in a realm where time flows freely in both directions such things as customs cannot exist."

"Don't Ideas require an energy source of some kind?" I asked him. The question had been puzzling me for some time.

"It is a thorny question," the Commendatore answered, frowning dramatically. "All beings require energy—to be brought into this world and to survive. It is a principle that holds true throughout the universe."

"So what you're saying is, Ideas have to have a source of energy too. Right? In accordance with the universal principle."

"Affirmative! It is an undisputed fact. Universal law binds us one and all—there can be no exceptions. Ideas are felicitous insofar as we possess no form of our own. We materialize when others become aware of us—only then do we take shape. Though that shape is but a borrowed thing, for the sake of convenience."

"So then Ideas can't exist unless people are cognizant of them."

The Commendatore closed one eye and pointed his right index finger in the air. "And what principle can be deduced from that, my friends?"

It took a long moment to wrap my head around that one. The Commendatore waited patiently.

"This is what I think," I said at last. "Ideas take their energy from the perceptions of others."

"Affirmative!" the Commendatore said cheerfully. He nodded several times. "You have a good head on your shoulders. Ideas cannot exist outside the perceptions of others—those perceptions are our sole source of energy."

"So then if I think, 'The Commendatore doesn't exist,' you cease to exist. Right?"

"Negative! In theory, you have a point," the Commendatore said. "But only in theory. In reality, that is quite unrealistic. One is hard put to will oneself to cease thinking about a given matter. Namely, to determine to 'stop thinking' about something is itself a thought—as long as one follows that path, that something continues to exist. In the end, to stop thinking about something means to stop thinking about stopping thinking."

"In other words," I said, "it's impossible for people to escape Ideas unless they lose either their memory or their interest in Ideas."

"Truly, dolphins have that power," the Commendatore said.

"Dolphins?"

"Dolphins have the power to put the right or left half of their brain to sleep. Did my friends not know that?"

"No, I didn't."

"Affirmative! It is why dolphins have so little time for Ideas. It is why they stopped evolving, too. We Ideas tried our hardest, but I am sad to say that all of our efforts led nowhere. It was such a promising species, too. Proportionate to their size, they had the biggest brains of all the mammals until humankind reached its full development."

"So then you managed to establish a rewarding relationship with humans?"

"It is a known fact that, unlike the dolphin brain, the brain of the human species runs along a single track. Hence, an Idea that enters such a brain cannot be easily brushed aside. That allows us to draw energy therein, and thus sustain ourselves."

"Like parasites," I said.

"Nonsense!" said the Commendatore, wagging his finger like a schoolmaster scolding his wards. "When I say 'drawing energy,' I mean the tiniest amount. A shred so infinitesimal the members of my friends' species are unaware. Too small to affect health, or hinder lives in any way."

"But you told me that Ideas possess nothing like morality. Ideas are an entirely neutral concept, neither good nor bad. It all depends on how humans use them. In which case Ideas can have a beneficial effect in some cases, and a negative effect in others. Isn't that so?"

"$E = mc^2$ is neutral in itself, yet that Idea led to the creation of the atomic bomb. Then the bomb was dropped on Hiroshima and Nagasaki. In reality. Is that what you are trying to say, my friends?"

I nodded.

"My heart bleeds for you—figuratively, of course; we Ideas have no bodies, and hence no hearts. But then again, my friends, all is caveat emptor in this universe."

"What?"

"The Latin for 'buyer beware.' To wit, a vendor is

not responsible for how the buyer uses his wares. Can a shopkeeper determine what manner of man will wear the suit hanging in his window?"

"That argument sounds pretty fishy to me."

"$E = mc^2$ gave birth to the atomic bomb, but by the same token it spawned a host of good things as well."

"Like what, for instance?"

The Commendatore thought about this for a moment. He seemed to be having trouble coming up with a good example, however, for he said nothing, just vigorously rubbed his face with the palms of his hands. Then again, perhaps he simply saw no point in pursuing the discussion any further.

"By the way," I asked, suddenly remembering. "Do you have any inkling where the bell in the studio disappeared to?"

"Bell?" the Commendatore asked, looking up. "What bell?"

"The old bell you were ringing at the bottom of the pit. I put it on the shelf in the studio, but when I looked the other day it was gone."

The Commendatore shook his head in an emphatic no. "Oh, that bell. Negative! I have not laid hands on it recently."

"So who do you think might have taken it?"

"How should I know?"

"Whoever it was has started ringing it somewhere."

"Hmm. It is nothing to do with me. I have no use for it anymore. The bell was never mine alone. It belongs to the place, to be shared by everyone. So if it has disappeared, there must be a reason. No need to worry—it will show up sooner or later. Just wait."

"The bell belongs to the place?" I said. "You mean it belongs to the pit?"

"By the way," he said, not answering my question. "If my friends are waiting for Shoko and Mariye's return, it will not happen soon. At least not until nightfall."

"And do you think Menshiki has something up his sleeve?" I asked my final question.

"Affirmative! Menshiki has an ulterior motive for everything. Never wastes a move, that fellow. It is the only way he knows. Using both sides of his brain, all the time. He could never be a dolphin."

The Commendatore's form faded little by little, and then, like mist on a windless midwinter morning, it thinned and spread until it was completely gone. All that sat facing me now was an old empty armchair. His absence was so absolute, so profound, I had trouble believing that, until a moment earlier, he had been there at all. Perhaps I had been sitting across from empty space, nothing more. Perhaps I had only been talking to myself.

As the Commendatore had predicted, Menshiki's silver Jaguar took a long time to show up. The two beautiful ladies seemed in no rush to leave his home. I stepped onto my terrace and looked across the valley at the white house. But I could spot no one. To kill time, I went inside and started preparing dinner.

I made soup stock, parboiled the vegetables, and froze what I would not be using. I kept myself busy doing whatever I could think of, but when I finished, I still had time on my hands. I returned to the living room, put Richard Strauss's **Rosenkavalier** back on the turntable, stretched out on the sofa, and read a book.

Shoko was charmed by Menshiki. That much was certain. She looked at him differently than she looked at me. Her eyes shone. He was a most attractive middle-aged man, to say the least. A handsome and wealthy bachelor, well dressed and well mannered, a man who lived in the mountains in a huge mansion with four English automobiles stored in its garage. It was no mystery why so many women in this world might find him charming (to the same degree they might find me less than desirable). Yet it was equally certain that Mariye had a deep distrust of Menshiki. She was a girl of keen instincts. Perhaps she had intuitively divined that he was concealing the reasons for his behavior. Thus she maintained a careful distance. At least that was how it appeared to me.

What was going to happen? I was naturally curious, yet at the same time I had vague misgivings. My curiosity and those misgivings were therefore in direct opposition. Like an incoming tide meeting the outgoing current at the mouth of a river.

It was shortly after five thirty when Menshiki's Jaguar made its way back up the slope. As the Commendatore had predicted, it was already dark outside.

39

A CAMOUFLAGED CONTAINER, DESIGNED FOR A SPECIFIC PURPOSE

The Jaguar eased to a stop in front of my house, and Menshiki emerged. He walked around the car to open the door for Mariye and Shoko Akikawa, lowering the passenger seat so that Mariye could climb out of the back. The girl and the woman got into the blue Prius. Shoko rolled down the window and politely thanked Menshiki (Mariye, of course, turned the other way). Then the two drove home without stopping by to say hello. Menshiki watched them until they were out of sight, took a moment to (I assumed) recalibrate his mind and adjust his expression, and walked to my front door.

"I know it's late, but do you mind if I drop in for a few minutes?" he asked rather shyly.

"Sure, please do. I'm not busy right now," I said, showing him in.

We went to the living room; he sat on the sofa, while I sat in the easy chair that the Commendatore had just vacated. I thought I could feel the Commendatore's shrill voice still reverberating in the air.

"Thank you so much for today," Menshiki said to me. "I owe you a lot."

No thanks were necessary, I said. I really hadn't done anything.

"But if it hadn't been for your portrait—indeed, if it hadn't been for you, period—this chance would have passed me by. I would never have met Mariye face-to-face, never come this close to her. Everything has hinged on you—you're like the base of a folding fan. I'm concerned that you may not be enjoying that role, however."

"Nothing could make me happier than helping you out like this," I said. "But I must confess, it's hard to figure out how much is accidental and how much is planned. That part of it does bother me."

Menshiki thought for a moment. "You may not believe this," he said, nodding, "but I didn't plan any of this. Maybe it's not all pure coincidence, but almost everything has unfolded quite naturally."

"So I'm the catalyst that happened to set those events in motion? Has that been my role?" I inquired.

"Catalyst? Yes, maybe you could say that."

"To tell the truth, though, I feel more like a Trojan horse."

Menshiki looked up at me, as if squinting into a bright light. "What do you mean?"

"You know, the hollow wooden horse the Greeks built. They hid their warriors inside and presented it as a gift to the clueless Trojans, who dragged it inside their fortress. A camouflaged container, designed for a specific purpose."

Menshiki took a moment to respond. "In other

words," he said, choosing his words carefully, "you think I may have exploited you, used you as a kind of Trojan horse? To get close to Mariye?"

"At the risk of offending you, I do feel a little that way."

Menshiki narrowed his eyes, and the corners of his mouth curled in the beginnings of a smile.

"I guess that can't be helped. But as I just said, this has been a series of unexpected coincidences. To be honest, I like you. My affection for you is personal, and very natural. I don't find myself liking many people, so when it does happen I try to take it seriously. I would never exploit you for my sole convenience. I know I can be selfish, but I'd like to think that I'm able to draw a line between friendship and self-interest. You're not being used as a Trojan horse— not now, not ever. So please don't worry."

He didn't seem to be making this up—his words had the ring of truth.

"So did you have a chance to show them the painting?" I asked. "My portrait of you in your study?"

"Of course. That's why they came in the first place. They loved it. Though Mariye didn't say anything. She's a girl of few words, as you know. But I could tell how strongly she felt. It showed in her face. She stood in front of the portrait for a very long time. Just stood there, not speaking or moving."

In fact, I couldn't remember the portrait very well, though I had finished it only a few weeks before. That was my pattern—the moment I launched into a new painting, the one I had just finished slipped from my mind. Only a vague and general image remained. I did retain a physical memory, however, of the sense of achievement I got from working on it. That palpable sensation meant more to me than the completed work.

"Their visit sure lasted a long time," I said.

Menshiki gave an embarrassed shrug. "After they'd seen your painting, I gave them a light lunch and showed them around. A tour of my house and the grounds. Shoko seemed interested, you see. The time flew by."

"I bet they were impressed."

"Shoko was, I think," Menshiki said. "Especially by my Jaguar XKE. But Mariye didn't say anything. Maybe she didn't like my house. Or maybe she's not interested in houses in general."

I guessed she probably couldn't care less.

"Did you have a chance to talk to her?" I asked.

Menshiki shook his head no. "She opened her mouth two or three times at most. And what she said was almost meaningless. She generally ignores me."

I kept quiet. I had no special thoughts on the matter, but I could picture the scene. Whenever he tried to start a conversation with Mariye, she would clam up, just mumble a word or two. Once Mariye made up her mind not to speak, trying to reach her was like ladling water onto a parched desert.

Menshiki picked up an ornament from the table, a glossy ceramic snail, and inspected it from a variety of angles. The snail had been one of the very few decorative objects left in the house. Probably a piece of Dresden china. The size of a smallish egg. Purchased long ago, perhaps, by Tomohiko Amada himself. Menshiki gingerly returned the snail to the table. Then he raised his head and looked across at me.

"I guess it will take her a while to get used to me," he said, as if addressing himself. "I mean, we've only just met. She's a quiet child to begin with, and thirteen is said to be a difficult age, the beginning of puberty. All the same, being with her in the same room, breathing the same air—it was a precious experience, priceless really."

"So then your feeling hasn't changed?"

Menshiki's eyes narrowed slightly. "What feeling do you mean?"

"That you don't care to know if Mariye is your child."

"No, that hasn't changed a bit," Menshiki said without hesitation. He chewed his lip for a moment before continuing. "It's hard to explain. But when she's near, and I look at her face and watch her move, this odd feeling comes over me. The sense that somehow my life up to now may have been wasted. That I no longer understand the purpose of my existence, the reason I'm here. As if values I'd thought were certain were turning out to be not so certain after all."

"And for you these sorts of feelings are extremely odd, am I right?" For me, they were par for the course.

"That's right. I've never experienced them before."

"And they started after spending several hours with Mariye?"

"Yes. You must think I'm some kind of idiot."

I shook my head no. "Not at all. I felt the same way when I hit puberty and met a girl I liked."

Menshiki gave a small smile. There was something rueful in it. "That's when the pointlessness of all my accomplishments and successes, and all the money I've accumulated, hit me. That I'm no more than an expedient and transitory vehicle meant to pass a set of genes on to someone else. What other function do I serve? Beyond that, I'm just a clod of earth."

"A clod of earth." I tried saying the words. They had a strange ring.

"To tell the truth, I was down in the pit when that realization hit me. Remember, that pit we uncovered behind the shrine, underneath the pile of rocks?"

"How could I forget?"

"If you'd felt like it, you could have abandoned me there. Without food and water, my body would have shriveled and returned to the soil. I would have been no more than a clod of earth in the end."

I didn't know what to say, so I remained silent.

"It's enough for me," Menshiki said, "that the **possibility** exists that Mariye and I are related by blood. I feel no compulsion to find out if it's true or not. That mere possibility has sent a beam of light into my life—now I can look at myself in a new way."

"I think I understand," I said. "Maybe not every step in your reasoning, but the way you feel. What I don't get is what you're expecting from Mariye. In concrete terms."

"It's not that I haven't given that question any thought," Menshiki said. He looked down at his

601

hands. They were beautiful hands, with long fingers. "People devote a lot of energy to thinking about things. Whether they want to or not. Yet in the end we all just have to wait—only time can tell how events play out. The answers lie ahead."

I remained quiet. I had no clear idea what he had in mind, and no compelling desire to find out. Were I to know, my position might become even more difficult.

"I've heard Mariye is much more forthcoming with you," Menshiki said after a long pause. "That's what Shoko said, at least."

"That's probably true," I said cautiously. "We seem to be able to talk quite naturally when we're in the studio."

Of course, I didn't tell him that Mariye had come to visit me from the adjoining mountain through a hidden passageway. That was our secret.

"Do you think it's because she's gotten comfortable with you? Or because she feels some personal connection?"

"The girl is fascinated by painting, maybe artistic expression in general," I explained. "If a painting is involved, there are occasions—not always, mind you—when she's quite comfortable talking. She's not a typical child, that's for sure. When I taught her at the community center, she didn't speak much to the other kids."

"So she doesn't get along with children her own age?"

"Maybe. Her aunt says she doesn't make many friends at school."

Menshiki pondered that for a moment.

"She opens up with Shoko to some extent, I guess," he said.

"So it seems. From what I've heard, she's much closer to her aunt than she is to her father."

Menshiki merely nodded. His silence seemed charged with implication.

"What sort of man is her father?" I asked him. "Have you checked?"

Menshiki looked to the side and narrowed his eyes. "He was fifteen years older than she was," he finally said. "By 'she' I mean his late wife."

Of course, "late wife" meant Menshiki's former lover.

"I don't know how they got together, or why they married. I have no interest in those things," he said. "Whatever the case, though, it's clear he loved his wife dearly. Her death was a terrible shock. They say he was a changed man after that."

According to Menshiki, the Akikawas were a big landowning family in the area (much as Tomohiko Amada's family was in Kyushu). Although they had lost nearly half of their property in the land reform that followed World War Two, they retained many assets, enough that the family could get along comfortably on the income they produced. Yoshinobu Akikawa, Mariye's father, was the first of two children and the only son, so when his father passed away at an early age he became the head of the family. He built a house for himself at the top of the mountain they owned, and set up an office in one of their buildings in Odawara. From that office, he managed the family properties in the city and its environs: several commercial and apartment buildings, and a number of rental houses and lots. He also dabbled in real estate. In other words, while he kept the business going, he made no attempt to broaden its scale. The core of his enterprise consisted of looking after the family's assets when the need arose.

Yoshinobu married late in life. He was in his mid-forties when he tied the knot, and his daughter (Mariye) was born the following year. Then, six years later, his wife was stung to death. It was early spring, and she had been walking alone through a big plum grove they owned when she was attacked by a swarm of large hornets. Her death hit him hard. To wipe away anything that could remind him of the tragedy, as soon as the funeral was over he hired men to raze the plum trees, and yank their roots from the earth. What was left was a dreary and barren plot of land. It had been a beautiful grove, so its destruction was painful for many. Moreover, for generations those living nearby had been permitted to pick a portion of the abundant fruit to make pickled plums and plum wine. As a result, Yoshinobu Akikawa's barbaric act of retaliation deprived many local residents of one of the small pleasures they could look forward to each year. Still, it was his mountain, the plum grove was **his**, and no one could fail to understand his fury—at the hornets and the trees. As a consequence, those complaints were never voiced in public.

Yoshinobu Akikawa turned into a rather morose man after his wife's death. He hadn't been particularly social or gregarious to begin with, and now his introverted side only grew stronger. His interest in spiritual things deepened, and he became involved with a religious sect whose name was unknown to me. It is said that at one point he spent some time in India. At great personal expense, he built a grand hall for the sect's use on the outskirts of town, where he began spending much of his time. It's not clear exactly what takes place there. But it appears that a daily regimen of stringent religious "austerities" and the study of reincarnation helped him find a new purpose in life after his wife's death.

These activities reduced his involvement in the business, but his duties hadn't been all that demanding in the first place. There were three longtime employees more than capable of managing things when the boss failed to show up. His visits home became more infrequent. When he did return it was usually just to sleep. His relationship with his only daughter had, for some reason, grown more distant after his wife's death. Perhaps she reminded him of his dead wife. Or perhaps he had never really cared for children. In any case, as a result the child never really took to her father. The responsibility for looking after Mariye went to his younger sister, Shoko. She had taken leave from her job as secretary for the president of a medical college in Tokyo and moved to the house atop the mountain near Odawara on what she expected to be a temporary break to look after the child. In the end, though, the arrangement became permanent. Perhaps she came to love the girl. Or perhaps she couldn't stand idly by when her little niece needed her so much.

Having reached that point in his account, Menshiki stopped to touch his fingers to his lips.

"Do you happen to have any whiskey in the house?" he asked.

"There's about a half a bottle of single malt," I said.

"I don't want to impose, but could I have some? On the rocks."

"My pleasure. But aren't you driving?"

"I'll call a cab," he said. "No point in losing my license."

I went to the kitchen and came back with a whiskey bottle, a ceramic bowl of ice, and two glasses. In the meantime, Menshiki put the record of **Der Rosenkavalier** that I had been listening to on the turntable. We sat back and listened to the lush strains of Richard Strauss as we sipped our whiskey.

"Are you a devotee of single malt?" Menshiki asked.

"No, this was a gift. A friend brought it. Sure tastes good, though."

"I have a bottle of rare Scotch at home that a friend in Scotland sent to me. A single malt from the island of Islay. It's from a cask sealed by the Prince of Wales himself on his visit to the distillery there. I'll bring it on my next visit."

"You needn't make such a fuss on my account," I said.

"There's a small island near Islay called Jura," he said. "Have you heard of it?"

"No," I replied.

"It's practically uninhabited. More deer than people. Lots of other wildlife, too—rabbits, pheasants, seals. And one very old distillery. There's a spring of freshwater nearby, just perfect for making whiskey. If you mix the single malt with that water, the flavor is absolutely amazing. You can't find it anywhere else."

"It sounds delicious," I said.

"Jura is also known as the place where George Orwell wrote **1984**. Orwell rented a small house on the northern end of the island, really the middle of nowhere, but the winter took a terrible toll on his body. It was a primitive place, with none of the modern amenities. I guess he needed that kind of Spartan environment to write. I spent a week on that island myself. Huddled next to the fireplace each night, drinking that marvelous whiskey."

"Why did you spend a whole week in such an out-of-the-way place all by yourself?"

"Business," Menshiki said simply. He smiled.

Apparently, he wasn't going to let me in on what sort of business was involved. And I had no particular desire to find out.

"I really needed a drink today," he said. "To settle myself down. That's why I'm imposing on you like this. I'll come and pick up my car tomorrow, if that's all right with you."

"Of course, I don't mind at all."

We sat there awhile without talking.

"Do you mind if I ask something personal?" Menshiki broke the silence. "I hope you won't take offense."

"Don't worry, I'm not a guy who gets offended. I'll answer you if I can."

"You've been married, correct?"

I nodded. "Yes, I was married. As a matter of fact, I just mailed off the divorce papers, signed and sealed. So I'm not sure if I'm officially married now or not. Still, it's safe to say that I **was** married. For six years."

Menshiki was studying the ice cubes in his glass as if deep in thought.

"Sorry to pry," he said. "But do you have any regrets about the way your marriage ended?"

I took another sip of whiskey. "How does one say 'buyer beware' in Latin?" I asked.

" 'Caveat emptor,' " Menshiki said without hesitation.

"I have a hard time remembering how to say it. But I know what it means."

Menshiki laughed.

"Sure, I have regrets," I replied. "But even if I could go back and rectify one of my mistakes, I doubt it would change the outcome."

"Do you think there's something in you that's impervious to change, something that became a stumbling block in your marriage?"

"Perhaps it's my **lack** of something impervious to change that was the stumbling block."

"But you have the desire to paint. That must be closely connected to your appetite for life."

"There may be something I have to get past first before I can really get started with my painting, though. That's my feeling, anyway."

"We all have ordeals we must face," Menshiki said. "It's through them that we find a new direction in our lives. The more grueling the ordeal, the more it can help us down the road."

"As long as it doesn't grind us into the ground."

Menshiki smiled. He had finished his questions about my divorce.

I brought a jar of olives in from the kitchen to accompany our drinks. We nibbled on them while sipping our whiskey. When the record finished, Menshiki flipped it over. Georg Solti continued conducting the Vienna Philharmonic.

Menshiki has an ulterior motive for everything. Never wastes a move, that fellow. It is the only way he knows.

If the Commendatore was correct, what move was Menshiki making—or about to make—now? I hadn't a clue. Perhaps he was holding back for the moment, waiting for his opportunity. He said that he had "no intention" of exploiting me. Probably he was speaking the truth. Yet intentions were, in the end, just intentions. He was a savvy guy who had managed to survive and thrive in the most cutting-edge sector of the business world. If he was harboring an ulterior motive, even if it was dormant now, it would be next to impossible for me to avoid getting sucked in.

"You're thirty-six years old, right?" Menshiki said out of the blue.

"Yes, that's correct."

"That's the best age."

I didn't see it that way at all. But I didn't say so.

"I'm fifty-four. Too old to be fighting on the front lines in the business I was in, but still a little too young to be considered a legend. That's why you see me dawdling around like this."

"Some become legends in their youth, though."

"Sure, there are a few. But there's no great merit in that. In fact, it could be a real nightmare. Once you're considered a legend, you can only trace the pattern of your rise for the rest of your life. I can't think of anything more boring than that."

"Don't you ever get bored?"

Menshiki smiled. "I can't remember ever being bored. I've been too busy."

I could only shake my head in admiration.

"How about you?" he asked. "Have you ever been bored?"

"Of course. It happens a lot. In my case, however, boredom is an indispensable part of life."

"Don't you find it painful?"

"I guess I've gotten used to it. So it doesn't feel like pain."

"I bet that's because painting is so central to your existence. That's your core—your passion to create is born out of what you call boredom. Without that core, I'm sure you'd find boredom unendurable."

"So you're not working these days, are you?"

"That's right, I'm basically retired. I do a little computer trading on the stock markets, as I've told you, but that's not out of necessity. It's more like a game, a form of mental discipline."

"And you live in that big house all by yourself."

"Correct."

"And you still never get bored?"

Menshiki shook his head. "I have so many things to occupy my mind. Books I should read, music I should listen to. Data to gather, sort, and analyze. I'm used to staying active—it's a daily habit. I work out too, and when I need a change of pace, I practice the piano. And there's housework, of course. I haven't time to be bored."

"Don't you ever worry about growing old? About becoming a lonely old man?"

"No question, I will age," Menshiki said. "My body will decline, and I'll probably grow more and more solitary. But I'm not there yet. I have an idea what it will be like. But I'm the kind of guy who doesn't believe something until he's seen it. So I have to wait until it's sitting right in front of me. I'm not especially afraid of aging. I can't say I'm looking forward to it, but I am a little curious."

Menshiki slowly swirled the whiskey in his glass.

"How about you?" he asked, looking me in the eye. "Are you afraid of getting old?"

"I was married for six years, and it didn't turn out so well. I didn't paint a single painting for myself during all that time. I guess people would say I squandered those years. After all, I was turning out one painting after another of a sort I don't especially like. Yet, in a way, maybe I was fortunate to have gone through that. That's how I feel these days."

"I think I understand what you're trying to say. That there's a time in life when you have to discard your ego. Is that it?"

Perhaps, I thought. But maybe in my case it simply took me that long to discover what I'd been lugging around all that time. Had I dragged Yuzu along on that pointless, roundabout journey?

Am I afraid of growing old? I wondered to myself. Did I dread the advent of old age?

"I still have a hard time imagining it," I said. "It may sound foolish for a man in his mid-thirties to say this, but I feel as if my life is just beginning."

"That's not foolish at all," Menshiki said, smiling. "You're probably right—you're just getting started."

"You mentioned genes a few minutes ago," I said. "That you felt you're just a vehicle receiving a set of genes from one generation and transmitting it to the next. And beyond that duty, you're no more than a clod of earth. Right?"

Menshiki nodded. "That's what I said."

"But you don't find being a clod of earth particularly frightening, do you?"

"I may be a clod of earth," Menshiki said, laughing, "but as clods go I'm pretty good. It may sound conceited, but I think I may even be a superior clod. I've been blessed with certain abilities. Those have limits, I know, but they're abilities nonetheless. That's why I go all out in whatever I do. I want to stretch myself as far as I can, to see what I'm capable of. I have no time to be bored. That's the best way I know of keeping fear and emptiness at arm's length."

We drank until almost eight o'clock, at which point the bottle ran out. Menshiki stood up to leave.

"I should be on my way," he said. "I've imposed on you for too long."

I called for a taxi. "Tomohiko Amada's house" was all it took to identify our location. He was a famous man. The dispatcher said it would be fifteen minutes. I thanked him and hung up.

Menshiki used that time to tell me something.

"I told you earlier that Mariye's father had become deeply involved in a religious sect, didn't I?" he began.

I nodded.

"Well, it turns out that it's one of the new religions, and a shady one at that. I checked online and found out they've got a really bad track record. A number of civil suits have been filed against them. Their so-called doctrine is a pile of rubbish unworthy of the name 'religion.' Of course, Mr. Akikawa is free to subscribe to whatever beliefs he likes. That goes without saying. But he has sunk quite a lot of money into this group. His money, company money. He had considerable wealth in the beginning, was able to manage on the monthly rents he collected. But there was a clear limit to how much he could withdraw without selling property and other assets. Now he's way past that limit—he's sold a lot of those. Clearly, an unhealthy situation. Like an octopus trying to survive by devouring its own legs."

"Are you saying he's being preyed on by that cult?"

"Exactly. He's a real pigeon. When a group like that squeezes you, they take everything they can get. Right down to the last drop. Forgive me for saying so, but Mr. Akikawa's privileged upbringing may make him more vulnerable to that kind of thing."

"So you're concerned about this situation."

Menshiki sighed. "It's Mr. Akikawa's responsibility how he ends up. He's a mature adult, aware of his actions. It's not so simple for his family, though—they have no idea what's going on. Not that my worrying about them will make a bit of difference."

"The study of reincarnation," I said.

"It's a fascinating hypothesis," Menshiki said. He quietly shook his head.

The taxi finally arrived. Before getting in, he offered a most courteous thanks. His complexion and his decorum were a constant, no matter how much he drank.

40

I COULD NOT MISTAKE THE FACE

After Menshiki left, I brushed my teeth, climbed into bed, and fell asleep immediately. I drop off in no time at all under normal circumstances, and whiskey only accentuates that tendency.

In the middle of the night, however, a loud sound jolted me awake. I think the sound was real. Possibly, though, it took place in my dream. Its source could have been my own unconscious. Whatever its origins, it was a huge crash, as though an earthquake had struck. The impact lifted me into the air. That part was real, for sure, not a dream or a product of my imagination. I had been fast asleep, and now, an instant later, I was on the verge of tumbling from my bed, my mind on high alert.

According to the clock on the bedside table, it was past two. The time of night when the bell had usually rung. But I could not hear a bell. With winter approaching, there were no insect voices. A deep hush had fallen over the house. Outside, thick, dark clouds covered the sky. If I listened hard enough, I could hear the wind.

I felt for the lamp, switched it on, and slipped a sweater over my pajamas. I would take a quick look around the house. Something very strange had happened, or so it seemed. Had a wild boar crashed through one of the windows? Or had a small meteorite hit the roof? Probably not, but it was still a good idea to make sure. I was, after all, the caretaker of the house. And I would have a hard time falling back to sleep if I didn't find out. The crash had left me wide awake, my heart pounding.

I walked through the house flicking on lights, checking room by room. As far as I could tell, nothing was out of place. All was in order. It wasn't a big house, so I would have noticed if something was amiss. When I finished my inspection, I headed to the studio. I stepped through the door connecting it to the living room and reached for the wall switch. But some thing stopped me. **Don't turn on the light**, the thing whispered in my ear. In a small but clear voice. **Better to leave it dark.** Following its instructions, I removed my hand from the switch and closed the door behind me without a sound. Quieting my own breathing, I peered into the darkened studio.

As my eyes adjusted to the light, I became aware that someone else was in the room. The signs were unmistakable. And that someone was sitting on the wooden stool that I used when I was painting. At first, I thought it was the Commendatore. That he had materialized and returned. But this person was much bigger. The silhouette looming in the dark was that of a tall, gaunt man. The Commendatore was two feet tall, if that, but this man was close to six feet in height. He was sitting somewhat hunched over, as tall people often do. And not moving at all.

I didn't move either as I stood there looking at his back, with my own back pressed against the door-frame and my left hand near the light switch, just in case. There in the dark, in the middle of the night, we were frozen, like two statues. For some reason, I wasn't scared. My breathing was shallow and the sound of my heartbeat was hard and dry. But I felt no fear. Someone I had never seen before had come barging into my house in the middle of the night. For all I knew, it could have been a burglar. Or perhaps a ghost. Either should have frightened me. Yet for some reason, I felt neither danger nor dread.

Perhaps all the strange happenings I had been experiencing—starting with the appearance of the Commendatore—had made me immune to such weirdness. Yet there was more to it than that. What was the mysterious intruder doing there in the studio so late at night? My curiosity trumped my fear. He seemed to be lost in thought. Or maybe he was star-ing hard at something. The intensity of his focus was obvious, even to an observer. He had no idea that I had entered the room. Or, perhaps, my presence was beneath his notice.

I tried to quiet my breathing and control the pounding of my heart against my ribs as I waited for my eyes to adjust to the dark. After a while, I began to realize what he was regarding with such ferocity. It was something hanging on the opposite wall. Which meant it had to be Tomohiko Amada's painting **Killing Commendatore**. He was sitting stock-still on the wooden stool, bent slightly forward, staring at that painting. His hands were on his knees.

At last the dark clouds covering the sky began to part, and a shaft of moonlight entered the room. It was as if an ancient tombstone had been bathed in pure, silent water, baring the secrets carved on its surface. Then the darkness returned. But only for a short time. The clouds parted again, and a pale blue light filled the room for a full ten seconds. Now, at last, I could determine the identity of the person on the stool.

His white hair fell to his shoulders. It had been uncombed for some time, for wisps jutted in every direction. Judging from his bearing, he was quite old. And withered, like a dead tree. Once, he must have had a powerful and manly physique. But now he was skeletal, wasted by age and possibly illness. That much I could tell.

His face was so emaciated it took me a while to figure out who he was. But there, in the hushed moonlight, I finally realized. I had seen only a few photographs, yet I could not mistake the face. The profile of his aquiline nose and the powerful physical aura were undeniable proof. Though the night was cold, sweat streamed from my armpits. My heart pounded even faster and harder. It seemed impossible to believe, but there was no room for doubt.

The old man was Tomohiko Amada, the artist who had created the painting. Tomohiko Amada had returned to his studio.

41

ONLY AS LONG AS I
DIDN'T TURN AROUND

t couldn't be the flesh-and-blood Tomohiko
Amada. That "real" Tomohiko Amada was confined to a nursing home in Izu Kogen. He suffered from advanced dementia and seldom left his
bed. There was no way he could have come that far
under his own steam. What I was looking at, therefore, could only be his ghost. Yet as far as I knew,
Amada was still alive. Which meant I was looking at
his "living spirit." Of course, he could have drawn his
last breath just moments earlier. In which case, this
would indeed be his ghost.

Whichever the case, this was no hallucination. It
was far too real, too dense, for that. It projected an
unmistakable humanity and the workings of a conscious mind. Tomohiko Amada had, through some
special agency, returned to **his** studio, and was sitting
on **his** stool regarding **his** painting **Killing Commendatore**. He was staring straight at it—his eyes seemed
to cut through the dark. He was indifferent to my
presence. I doubt he even realized I was in the room.

As the clouds rolled by, the moonlight through the
window came and went, allowing me brief glimpses
of his silhouette. He was sitting so I could see his

profile, and wearing what could have been an old bathrobe or nightgown. His feet were bare. No stockings, no slippers. Disheveled white hair, jaw covered with a white grizzle. A haggard face, but clear and penetrating eyes.

I wasn't afraid so much as bewildered. The scene before me defied common sense. My hand hovered near the light switch on the wall. I had no intention of turning it on—I was just frozen in that posture. I didn't want to disturb Tomohiko Amada—be he ghost or phantasm—in any way. This studio was his proper place. Where he **truly belonged**. I was the intruder, with no right to interfere in whatever he wanted to do.

I waited until my breath calmed down and my body relaxed, then quietly backed out of the studio. I eased the door shut. Tomohiko Amada remained motionless on his stool throughout. Had I tripped over the table and sent the vase crashing to the floor, though, I doubt he would have noticed. His concentration was that fierce. The moon had broken through the clouds again, illuminating his skeletal frame. That last image engraved itself in my mind—embraced by the delicate shadows of night, that silhouette seemed to distill his entire life. **You must never forget this**, I told myself. I had to preserve in my memory what my eyes had seen, in all its detail.

I sat at the dining room table and drank glass after glass of mineral water. I really wanted a shot of whiskey, but the bottle was empty. Menshiki and I had drained it the previous evening. No other liquor was left in the house. There were a few bottles of beer in the fridge, but they wouldn't do the trick.

It was past four a.m. when sleep finally came calling. Until then, I just sat at the table while one thought after another passed through my head. I was too keyed up to be capable of any kind of action. All I could do was close my eyes and let my mind wander. Nothing cohered. For several hours, I followed those fragmented, meandering thoughts. Like a kitten chasing its tail.

When I grew tired, I mentally called up the image of Tomohiko Amada that I had seen mere hours before. To ensure its accuracy, I sketched it in my mind. I opened my imaginary sketchbook, pulled out my imaginary pencil, and drew the old man's silhouette. This was something I often did when I had time to spare. Actual paper and pencil weren't necessary. In fact, it was easier without them. Mathematicians go through a similar process, I imagine, when they picture a formula on an imaginary blackboard. Someday I might commit what I had seen to canvas.

I didn't really want to check the studio again. Of course, I was curious. Was Tomohiko Amada—or, more likely, his double—still there? Still sitting on his stool with his eyes riveted on **Killing Commendatore**? Sure, the possibility intrigued me. I had encountered a most rare and precious event, had seen it with my own eyes. Might it provide the key—several keys, actually—to help unravel the secrets of Tomohiko Amada's life?

All the same, I didn't want to interfere with what

he was doing. He had come so far, transcending space and reason, to reexamine his **Killing Commendatore,** poring over it to find—what? He had to have sacrificed much of his dwindling store of energy just to make it here. Drained his life force. Yet something had compelled him to return to the painting one last time, at whatever cost. To study it to his heart's content.

When I opened my eyes it was already past ten o'clock. Rare for an early bird like me. I washed my face, brewed coffee, and ate breakfast. For some reason, I was famished. I ate nearly double my usual amount. Three slices of toast, two boiled eggs, and a tomato salad. Not to mention two big cups of coffee.

I checked the studio after breakfast just to be sure, but of course Tomohiko Amada was gone. What remained was the empty, silent room in the morning. An easel with a canvas (my painting of Mariye Akikawa), a round stool in front of it, and the straight-backed chair Mariye used when she posed for me. **Killing Commendatore** hanging on the wall. The bell still missing from the shelf. The sky over the valley blue, the air cold and crystal clear. The piercing calls of birds, awaiting winter's arrival.

I picked up the phone and called Masahiko's office. His voice was sleepy, though it was almost noon. A clear case of the Monday-morning blahs. After our hellos, I casually inquired about his father. I wanted to know if he had died, and if the apparition I had seen was his ghost. If Tomohiko Amada had passed away the night before, surely his son would have been notified.

"How's your father?" I asked.

"I went to see him a few days ago. His mind has passed the point of no return, I'm afraid, but he's all right physically, I guess. At least he doesn't look like he's at death's door."

So Tomohiko Amada was still alive. What I had seen wasn't a ghost. It was the fleeting embodiment of a living person's will.

"It's a strange question, I know, but have you noticed anything unusual about your father recently?"

"My father?"

"Yeah."

"Why do you want to know that all of a sudden?"

I followed the script I had prepared. "To tell the truth, I had this weird dream last night where your father visited this place. I bumped into him while he was here. It felt very real. Real enough to make me jump out of bed. That's why I wondered if something had happened to him."

"Wow," he said. "That's wild. What was my father doing while he was there?"

"He just sat on the stool in the studio."

"That's all?"

"That's it. Nothing but that."

"By stool you mean that old three-legged chair, the round one?"

"Yeah, that's the one."

Masahiko thought for a moment.

623

"Maybe he is reaching the end," he said in a flat voice. "They say that in our last hours, our spirit returns to where we feel we've left something undone. From what I know of my father, that would be the studio."

"But from what you've told me, he has no memory left."

"Yes, memory in the conventional sense, anyway. But his spirit's still there. His brain just can't access it any longer. The circuit's broken—his mind isn't connected. But his spirit remains, behind the scenes. It's probably the same as ever."

"That makes sense," I said.

"Weren't you scared?"

"By the dream?"

"Yeah. I mean it sounds awfully real."

"No, I wasn't afraid. But it did feel very strange. Like the man himself was right there."

"Maybe it really was him," Masahiko said.

I didn't say anything. I couldn't let on that Tomohiko Amada had likely returned specifically to view **Killing Commendatore** (actually, **I** might have invited him—had I not unwrapped the painting, he might not have shown up). If I told his son, I would have had to explain the whole story, from the moment I stumbled across the painting in the attic to when I opened it without permission and, even more blatantly, chose to hang it on the studio wall. I knew I would have to let Masahiko know eventually, but I didn't want to raise the issue at this juncture.

"Anyway," he said, "last time we met I mentioned

there was a matter I needed to talk to you about? But we didn't have enough time then. Remember?"

"Yeah."

"So why don't I stop by one of these days and fill you in. Okay?"

"This house is yours, you know. Come whenever you like."

"How about this weekend? I'm thinking of visiting my father in Izu Kogen, so I could stop by on my trip back. It's right on the way."

I told him he was welcome anytime except Wednesday and Friday nights and Sunday morning. My art class was on Wednesday and Friday and Mariye's sitting was on Sunday.

He figured he'd be able to make it Saturday night. "I'll let you know beforehand," he said.

After our phone call, I went into the studio and sat on the stool. The wooden stool that Tomohiko Amada had occupied the night before. As soon as I sat down, it hit me—this stool was no longer **mine**. No, the long years Tomohiko Amada had spent sitting on it painting made it **his**, now and forever. To the uninformed, it looked like no more than an old dinged-up, three-legged chair, but it was infused with his will. I had borrowed it without permission, that was all.

I sat there and studied **Killing Commendatore** on the wall, as I had done countless times before. It rewarded multiple viewings—its depth allowed for so many different ways of looking at it. This time, though, I felt I wanted to inspect it from an entirely new angle. What was there that had made Tomohiko Amada return to it at the end of his life, to see it one last time?

I spent a long time sitting there, just studying the painting. I chose the same position, the same angle, even adopted the same posture that Tomohiko Amada's living spirit or alter ego had taken the night before, and tried to focus on it with the same intense concentration. Yet I couldn't find that **something** I had previously missed.

When I grew tired of thinking, I went outside. Menshiki's silver Jaguar was still parked in front of my house, at a slight remove from my Toyota Corolla station wagon. It had been sitting there all night, waiting quietly for its master's return, like an intelligent, well-trained pet.

I strolled on past the house, musing about **Killing Commendatore** in a vague sort of way. Walking the little path through the woods, I had the distinct impression that someone was spying on me from behind. As if Long Face had pushed up the square lid of his hole and was secretly observing me from the corner of the painting. I whipped around and looked back. But nothing was to be seen. No hole in the ground, no Long Face. Just a deserted leaf-strewn path wending through the quiet woods. This pattern repeated itself a number of times. But each time I spun around no one was there.

Then again, it might well be that the hole and

Long Face were there **only as long as I didn't turn around**. Perhaps they could tell when I was about to look back, and hid themselves at that moment. Like a child playing a game.

I passed through the woods to the very end of the path, the first time I'd gone that far. I figured the entrance to Mariye's secret passageway had to be nearby. Yet I couldn't locate it. "You really have to pay attention to find it," she had said, and it did seem to be well camouflaged. In any case, she had taken the passageway after dark to reach my place from the adjoining mountain, alone and on foot. Past the thickets and through the woods.

The path came to an abrupt end at a small, circular clearing. The overhanging trees thinned out, so I could see pieces of sky. I found a flat stone bathed in a small pool of light, sat down, and looked through the tree trunks at the valley below. I imagined that at any minute Mariye might pop up out of her secret passageway, wherever that was. But of course no one appeared. My only companions were birds, who hopped from limb to limb and then flew off again. They moved about in pairs, each chirping loudly to let the other know where they were. I had once read an article describing how certain birds mate for life, and how when one died, the survivor spent the rest of their days alone. It goes without saying that they never had to sign and seal official divorce papers sent by certified mail from a lawyer's office.

A truck selling fresh produce passed in the distance, its driver listlessly broadcasting his wares over its loudspeaker. No sooner was his voice out of ear-shot than there was a loud rustle in the bushes nearby. What was it? It didn't sound human. A wild animal was more likely. For a scary second I thought it might be a wild boar (boars and hornets were the most dangerous things in the area), but then the sound abruptly stopped.

I stood up and started walking back to the house. When I passed the small shrine I checked the pit, just to make sure. The planks were in place, the stone weights neatly arranged on top. They hadn't been moved, as far as I could tell. Fallen leaves covered the boards. They had lost their bright colors and turned sodden in the rain. So young and fresh in spring, their quiet death had come now, in late autumn.

As I stared at the planks, I began to feel that Long Face might poke his elongated, eggplant-shaped head out of the pit at any minute. But the planks didn't budge. Obviously. Long Face's hole was square, not round, and was smaller and more personal in scale. Moreover, **this** hole was home to the Commendatore, not Long Face. Or at least home to the Idea that had borrowed the Commendatore's form. It had been the Commendatore that had rung the bell to call me here, and had made me open the pit.

Everything started with this pit. After Menshiki and I had pried open the lid with a backhoe, strange things had started happening one after another. Then again, it might have all begun when I had found **Killing Commendatore** in the attic and removed it from its packaging. That was the correct sequence. Or perhaps the two events acted in tandem. **Killing Commendatore** could have been what called the Idea to the house. The appearance of the Commendatore could have been my reward for liberating the painting. Try as I might, I couldn't tell what was the cause, and what was the result.

Menshiki's Jaguar was gone when I got back to the house. He had probably come by taxi to pick it up. Or else sent one of the people who worked for him to collect it. Whichever the case, my mud-spattered Toyota Corolla was left there, parked forlornly outside my front door. Menshiki had been right—I should check the tires one of these days, though I hadn't bought an air pressure gauge and probably never would.

I went to the kitchen to start making lunch, but no sooner had I picked up a knife than I realized I was no longer ravenously hungry. Instead, I was very sleepy. I got a blanket, stretched out on the living room sofa, and promptly drifted off. I had a dream, a short one. It was clear and very vivid. But I couldn't remember anything about it. Just that it was clear and vivid. It felt as though a fragment of real life had slipped into my sleeping mind by mistake. Then the moment I awoke, it fled like a quick-footed animal, leaving no trace behind.

42

IF IT BREAKS WHEN YOU DROP IT, IT'S AN EGG

The next week flew by. I spent my mornings focused on my painting, and my afternoons reading, taking walks, and doing whatever housework needed to be done. One day blended into the next. My girlfriend showed up on Wednesday and we spent the afternoon making love. The constant creaking of my old bed really cracked her up.

"It's going to fall to pieces before long," she predicted during a pause in our exertions. "There'll be nothing left but splinters—we won't be able to tell if they're wood or pretzel sticks."

"Maybe we should try to make love more quietly."

"Maybe Captain Ahab should have hunted sardines," she said.

I thought about that for a moment. "Are you saying some things in this world can't be changed?"

"Kind of."

A short time later, we were back on the rolling seas, in pursuit of the great white whale. Some things really can't be changed so easily.

·   ·   ·

Each day, I worked a little on Mariye Akikawa's portrait. My initial sketch had established the skeleton, and now I was filling it out. I tried combining various colors to come up with the right tone for the background. Her face had to sit naturally over that foundation. These tasks tided me over as I waited for her next visit to the studio on Sunday. Some parts of my job were carried out while the model was present, while other preparatory work had to be done before the model's arrival. I loved both. I could take my time mulling over the various elements, and experiment to find just the right color, just the right style. I enjoyed the hands-on nature of this work, and the challenge of creating an environment from which the subject would spring to life.

While preparing Mariye's portrait, I began working on a different canvas—a painting of the pit behind the shrine. The pit had etched itself in my mind with such force that I didn't need it in front of me. I painted the scene in minute detail. The style was purely realistic, the viewpoint objective. I avoided objective representation in my art (except, of course, the portraits that were my "day job"), but that didn't mean I couldn't do it. When I wanted to, I could paint so precisely that the result could be mistaken for a photograph. I used that hyperrealistic style occasionally to change my mood, or refresh the fundamentals of my craft. I never showed those paintings to anyone, though—they were for my private enjoyment, nothing more.

In this way, the pit in the woods began to appear before me, more vivid and alive with each passing day. A mysterious round aperture half covered by thick planks. This was the pit that had given birth to the Commendatore. There were no human figures in the painting, however, just a black hole. Fallen leaves covered the earth surrounding it. A scene of perfect tranquility. Yet it felt as if someone (or something) might come crawling out of that hole any minute. The longer I pictured the scene, the stronger that premonition grew. Looking at it made my spine tingle, although I was the one who had painted it.

I worked like this every day, spending all morning alone in the studio. Palette and brush in hand, I moved back and forth between **A Portrait of Mariye Akikawa** and **The Pit in the Woods**—two more different paintings would be hard to imagine—as the mood struck me. I applied myself to the canvases while sitting on the same stool Tomohiko Amada had occupied in the dead of night the previous Sunday. Perhaps because my focus was so great, the dense presence I had felt the next morning had at some point disappeared. The old stool was once again a mere piece of furniture, there for my use. It seemed that Tomohiko Amada had gone back to where he belonged.

There were nights that week when I opened the studio door a crack to peek inside. But no one was ever there. Not Tomohiko Amada, not the Commendatore. Just an old stool parked in front of two easels. The moon cast its dim light over the objects in the room. All was quiet. **Killing Commendatore** hung on one wall. My unfinished work, **The Man with the White Subaru Forester,** was turned around so no one could see it. The two paintings I was working on, **A Portrait of Mariye Akikawa** and **The Pit in the Woods,** sat side by side on two easels. The smell of oil paint, turpentine, and poppyseed oil hung in the air. It never left, no matter how long the windows were left open. It was a special aroma, one I breathed every day, and would probably go on breathing for the rest of my life. I inhaled the air of the studio as if to confirm its presence, then quietly closed the door.

Masahiko called Friday night to say he was coming the next afternoon. He'd buy fresh fish from the market nearby, so I needn't worry about dinner. I could look forward to a special treat.

"Anything more I should bring?" he asked. "I can pick up what you want on my way."

"Can't think of anything," I answered. Then I remembered. "Now that you mention it, I'm out of whiskey. A friend and I polished off what you brought last time. Could you pick up another bottle? Any brand is okay."

"I like Chivas myself. Would that do?"

"You bet," I said. Masahiko had always been picky about food and drink. I was a different story. I ate and drank whatever was put in front of me.

When our phone call ended, I went to the studio, took **Killing Commendatore** down from the wall, carried it to my bedroom, and covered it. It wouldn't do to have Tomohiko Amada's son see the painting his father had hidden in the attic. For the time being, at least.

Now a visitor to the studio would see only **A Portrait of Mariye Akikawa** and **The Pit in the Woods**. I stood there looking back and forth at the two works in progress, comparing them. An image rose to my mind: I could see Mariye walking behind the shrine to the pit. I had a distinct sense that **something** might begin then. The lid was half open. The darkness was calling. Was Long Face there waiting for her? Or the Commendatore?

Could these two paintings be connected in some way?

Since moving to this house, I had been painting almost nonstop. I had completed Menshiki's portrait on commission, then started **The Man with the White Subaru Forester** (brought to a halt when I had just begun to add color), and now was working on **A Portrait of Mariye Akikawa** and **The Pit in the Woods** in tandem. It struck me that the four paintings might fit together to form the beginning of a story of some kind.

Then again, perhaps I was documenting the story through my painting. That's what it felt like, anyway. Had someone given me the role or the right to be that chronicler? If so, **who**? Why was I chosen, of all people?

Masahiko's black Volvo station wagon came trundling up the slope shortly before four o'clock on Saturday afternoon. He loved the toughness and reliability of those old boxy cars. He'd driven this one seemingly forever, put a ton of miles on it, yet showed no inclination to trade it in for a new one. On this occasion, he brought along the special carving knife he used for fish. As always, it was razor sharp. In my kitchen, he used it to prepare the large, fresh sea bream he had just bought in Itoh. Masahiko had always been good with his hands, a man of many talents. Without a wasted motion, he filleted the fish, sliced the flesh into sashimi, and boiled the bones for broth. He lightly grilled the skin to nibble on with our drinks. I just stood there, enjoying the show. Who knows, he might have been a famous chef had he taken that route.

"Actually, it's best to let sashimi sit a day until the flesh softens and the flavor comes out, but what the hell," he said, deftly plying the knife. "You can handle it, right?"

"No problem—I'm not picky," I said.

"You can eat any leftovers tomorrow."

"Will do."

"Hey, do you mind if I crash here tonight?" Masahiko asked. "I'd like to stay the evening so we can hang out and drink without feeling rushed. Drinking and driving is no good, right? I can sleep on the sofa in the living room."

"Sure," I said. "It's your house, after all. Stay as long as you like."

"Are you sure some woman won't show up in the middle of the night?"

"No plans as of now," I replied, shaking my head.

"Okay, then I'll stay."

"You don't have to crash on the sofa—there's a bed in the guest room."

"No, I prefer the sofa. It's a lot more comfortable than it looks. Slept like a baby on it back in the old days."

He pulled out a bottle of Chivas Regal, cut the seal, and opened it. I brought ice from the refrigerator and two glasses. The gurgle of whiskey pouring into the glass was music to my ears. Like an old friend opening his heart to me. We sipped the whiskey as we finished preparing dinner.

"It's been a hell of a long time since you and I drank like this," Masahiko said.

"It sure feels that way. I remember us putting back a lot."

"I put back a lot, you mean," he said. "You never drank that much."

I laughed. "Maybe not from your point of view, but it was a lot for me."

I never got totally drunk. I always fell asleep first. But he was a different kind of drinker. Once he settled in for the long haul, he went all the way.

We sat across from each other at the table, sipping whiskey and eating the seafood. For starters, we shared the eight raw oysters he had bought with the sea bream. Then we dug into the sashimi. It was a bit too firm, as he had predicted, but it was delicious nonetheless, especially with the whiskey. By the end, we had polished it all off. We were already pretty full. The only other food was the crispy fish skin, small chunks of wasabi mixed with sake lees, and a dish of tofu. We topped off the meal with the soup he had prepared.

"I haven't had a feast like this in ages," I said.

"You can't eat like this in Tokyo," he said. "Living around here wouldn't be half bad. Fresh fish anytime."

"I bet you'd find life here boring eventually, though."

"Are you bored?"

"Am I? I guess I've never found boredom that painful. And besides, there's quite a lot going on here."

That was for sure. I had met Menshiki soon after my arrival in early summer, we had dug up the pit behind the shrine, then the Commendatore had made his appearance, and finally Mariye Akikawa and her aunt Shoko had entered my life. I had a girlfriend, a housewife in her sexual prime, who came to comfort me. Tomohiko Amada's living spirit had paid me a visit. There was hardly time to be bored.

"I might not be bored here either," Masahiko said. "Did you know I used to be into surfing? I rode the waves all up and down this coast."

That was news to me, I told him. He'd never mentioned it before.

"I've been thinking of leaving Tokyo, of going back to that kind of life. I'd check out the ocean when I woke up, then grab my board and head out if the surf was up."

The idea of that kind of life left me cold.

"What about your job?" I asked.

"I only need to go to Tokyo twice a week to take care of business. Most of my work is done on computer anyway, so it wouldn't be that hard to live outside the city. The world's changing, right?"

"I wouldn't know."

He looked at me in amazement. "This is the twenty-first century, man. Haven't you heard?"

"I've heard talk."

After dinner, we moved to the living room to continue drinking. Autumn was almost over, but it wasn't so cold that we needed to light a fire.

"So then, how's your father doing these days?" I asked.

Masahiko let out a small sigh. "Same as always. His mind is shot. Can't tell the difference between his balls and a pair of eggs."

"If it breaks when you drop it, it's an egg," I said.

He laughed. "People are strange creatures, aren't they? I mean, my father was as solid as a rock until just a few years ago. Mind as clear as the night sky in winter. To an almost disgusting degree. And now his memory is like a black hole. This dark, unfathomable hole that popped up out of nowhere in the middle of the cosmos."

Masahiko shook his head.

"Who was it that said, 'The greatest surprise in life old age'?" he asked.

I couldn't help him with that one. I'd never heard the saying. But it was probably true. Old age must be an even bigger shock than death. Far beyond what we can imagine. The day someone tells you that you're flat-out useless, that your existence is irrelevant—biologically (and socially)—in this world.

"So tell me about this dream you had of my father," Masahiko asked me. "Was it really as lifelike as you said?"

"Yeah, so lifelike it hardly seemed a dream."

"And he was in the studio?"

I took him to the studio.

"Your father was sitting there," I said, pointing to the stool in the middle of the room.

Masahiko walked over to the stool. "Just sitting?" he asked, placing his palm on its seat.

"That's right. He wasn't doing anything."

In fact, his father had been staring at **Killing Commendatore** on the wall, but I didn't tell him that.

"My father loved this stool," he said. "It was just a common old thing, but he never got rid of it. He sat on it to paint, and to think."

"It's relaxing to sit on," I said. "You'd be surprised."

Masahiko stood there with his hand on the stool, lost in thought. But he didn't sit down. After a minute, he turned his attention to the two canvases facing it. **A Portrait of Mariye Akikawa** and **The Pit in the Woods,** my two works in progress. He examined them slowly and carefully, like a doctor looking for a trace of shadow on a patient's X-ray.

"These are great," he said. "Really interesting."

"Both of them?"

"Yes, both. When you place them side by side like this, you feel a strange kind of movement between them. Their styles are totally different, but you get a sense they're somehow linked."

I nodded. I'd been thinking the same thing for a few days, in a vague sort of way.

"It seems to me that, little by little, you're finding a new direction," he went on. "Like you've finally emerged from a deep forest. You should take this really seriously, old friend."

He raised his glass and took a swallow of whiskey. The ice cubes tinkled.

I felt an urge to show Masahiko his father's **Killing Commendatore**. What would he have to say about it? His comments might provide a valuable clue. But I suppressed the impulse. Something was holding me back.

It's still too early, it said. Still too early.

We left the studio and went back to the living room. The wind had picked up—through the window I could see thick clouds edging their way north. The moon was hidden from view.

"So about what brought me here," Masahiko said, not wasting any more time. He seemed to be steeling himself for what he was about to say.

"It sounds like something that's not easy to discuss," I said.

"You're right, it's hard. **Quite** hard, in fact."

"But it's something that I need to know."

Masahiko rubbed his hands together. Like a man preparing to lift a heavy object.

"It's about Yuzu," he said, cutting to the chase. "She and I have met up a number of times. Before you left this spring, and afterward, too. She calls me when she wants to talk, and then we meet somewhere. She asked me not to tell you. I hated hiding it from you, but, well, I promised her."

I nodded. "It's important to keep our promises."

"Yuzu and I were friends too, you know."

"I know," I said. Masahiko put great stock in friendship. It could be a weakness of his.

"She had another man. Apart from you, that is."

"I know that too. **Now,** at least."

He nodded. "It started about six months before you walked out. Their relationship, that is. It hurts me to tell you this, but the guy is someone I know. A colleague of mine at work."

I let out a small sigh. "I imagine he's really handsome, right?"

"Yeah, you got it. Classic features. An agency scouted him in high school, and he modeled part-time for a while. He's that good-looking. And, well, it seems that I was the one who introduced them."

I didn't say anything.

"At least that's how it worked out," Masahiko said.

"Yuzu always had a thing for handsome men. It was almost pathological. She knew it too."

"You're not bad-looking yourself," he said.

"Thanks, man. Now I can sleep better tonight."

We didn't speak for a time. Finally, he broke the silence.

"Anyway, he's a really good-looking guy. A nice guy, too. I know this doesn't help you very much, but he's not violent, or a womanizer, or vain about his looks. He's not that type."

"That's nice to hear," I said. My voice was tinged with sarcasm, though I hadn't meant it to sound that way.

"It all started in September a year ago," Masahiko said. "He and I were out together when we bumped into Yuzu, and since it was about noon, the three of us stopped for lunch nearby. Believe me, I had absolutely no idea things would turn out this way. He's five years younger than she is."

"So the two of them didn't waste much time."

Masahiko gave a small shrug. Things must have progressed very quickly indeed.

"The guy talked to me about what was going on," he said. "Your wife did as well. It put me in a very difficult position."

I kept quiet. Anything I said would just make me look foolish.

Masahiko was silent for a moment. Then he spoke. "The fact is, Yuzu is pregnant."

I was speechless for a moment. "Yuzu? Pregnant?"

"Yeah, seven months gone already."

"She did it on purpose?"

"I don't know," Masahiko said, shaking his head. "But she's planning to have the baby. After seven months there's not much choice, is there."

"She always told me she wasn't ready for kids."

He winced slightly. "There's no chance the child could be yours, is there?" he said, looking into his glass.

I did a quick mental calculation. "No. I don't know the legal side of it, but biologically the chances are zero. I left eight months ago, and we haven't seen each other since."

"That's good," Masahiko said. "At any rate, she asked me to tell you she's going to have a baby. And that it shouldn't cause you any problems."

"But then why tell me at all?"

He shook his head. "I guess she's informing you out of courtesy."

I said nothing. **Out of courtesy?**

"I've been waiting for the chance to apologize for all this. I knew what was going on between Yuzu and my colleague, and I kept it from you. It was inexcusable. Under any circumstances."

"Then was letting me stay in this house your way of making amends?"

"Not at all—there's no connection between that and Yuzu. My father lived and painted in this house for a great many years. I figured you could keep that tradition alive. It's not something I could have asked anybody else, not like that at all."

Again, I said nothing. He sounded sincere.

"In any case," Masahiko continued, "you signed and sealed the divorce papers you received and sent them back to Yuzu, right?"

"More precisely, to her lawyer. So our divorce

should be official by now. I guess those two will choose a date for their own wedding now that's taken care of."

And go on to have a happy marriage. A tall, hand-some man, a small child, and little Yuzu. The three of them strolling happily through the park on a sunny Sunday morning. Heartwarming.

Masahiko added some ice and poured us more whiskey. He took a swig from his glass.

I went out to the terrace and looked across the valley at Menshiki's white house. Lights were on in some of the windows. What was Menshiki doing at this minute? What was he thinking about?

The night air was chilly. The leafless branches quivered in the wind. I went back to the living room and sat down.

"Can you forgive me?"

"It's not like you meant to hurt me," I said, shaking my head.

"I for one am sorry it turned out this way. You and Yuzu looked so well matched, and you seemed happy together. It's sad that it fell apart."

"You drop them both—the one that breaks is the egg," I said.

Masahiko laughed weakly. "So how are things now? Is there a woman in your life?"

"Yeah, there's someone."

"But not the same as Yuzu?"

"It's different. I've been looking for the same thing in women my whole life. Whatever that is, Yuzu had it."

"And you can't find that in anyone else?"

"Not so far," I said, shaking my head again.

"You have my sympathy," Masahiko said. "So what is it exactly that you've been looking for?"

"It's hard to put into words. I feel as if I lost track of something along the way, and have been searching for it ever since. Don't you think that's how everyone falls in love?"

"I don't think you can say 'everyone,'" he said with a slight frown. "You may actually be in the minority. But if you can't find the right words, why not paint it? You are an artist, after all."

"If you can't say it, paint it. That's easy to say. Not so easy to do, though."

"But it may be important to try, don't you think?"

"And perhaps Captain Ahab should have set out after sardines."

Masahiko laughed. "Sure, from a safety standpoint. But that's not how art is born."

"Hey, give me a break. Mention art, and the conversation comes to a screeching halt."

"Looks like we need some more whiskey," he said, shaking his head. He poured us another drink.

"I can't drink too much. I've got to work tomorrow morning."

"Tomorrow is tomorrow. Today is all we have right now," Masahiko said.

I found this idea strangely compelling.

"Can I ask you a favor?" I said to Masahiko. Our conversation was wrapping up, and we were about to get ready for bed. The hands on the clock pointed to a little before eleven.

"Sure, anything at all."

"I'd like to meet your father. Could you take me with you the next time you go to Izu?"

Masahiko regarded me as he might a strange animal. "You want to meet my father?"

"If it's not too much trouble."

"It's no trouble at all. But my father's in no shape to talk to you. He's quite incoherent. His mind is chaotic—a mud swamp, really. So if you have any expectations—if you're hoping to gain some insight into the person known as Tomohiko Amada—you'll only be disappointed."

"No, I'm not expecting anything like that. I just want to take one good look at him, that's all."

"But why?"

I took a breath and looked around the room. "I've been living in this house for six months now," I said. "Sitting on the stool he sat on, painting in his studio. Eating off his dishes, listening to his records. I feel his presence all over the place. That's why I have to meet the flesh-and-blood Tomohiko Amada. Once is enough. It doesn't matter a bit if we can't talk to each other."

"Then it's all right," Masahiko said, seemingly persuaded. "He won't be thrilled to see you, but he won't be ticked off either. He can't tell one person from another, you see. So there's no problem if you come along. I plan to visit the nursing home again pretty soon. According to the doctor, he doesn't have much longer—the end could come at any time. So join me on my next visit, if you're free."

I brought a spare blanket, pillow, and futon and made up a bed on the sofa in the living room. I looked around the room to make sure the Commendatore wasn't there. If Masahiko woke up in the middle of the night and saw him—two feet tall and dressed in ancient Asuka garb—he'd freak out. He'd figure he had become a real alcoholic.

Besides the Commendatore, there was **The Man with the White Subaru Forester** to worry about. I had turned the painting around so no one could see it. Still, I had no idea what strangeness might happen without my knowledge in the middle of the night.

So I wasn't kidding when I wished Masahiko a sound sleep.

I gave him a spare pair of pajamas to wear. He and I were more or less the same size, so there was no problem with the fit. He took off his clothes, put on the pajamas, and climbed under the bedding I had laid out. The air in the room was a bit chilly, but he looked snug and warm under the covers.

"You're sure you're not angry?" he asked before I left.

"No, I'm not angry," I answered.

"It must hurt a little, though."

"Maybe a little." I had the right to be a little hurt, I thought.

"But the cup is still one-sixteenth full."

"You've got it there," I said.

I turned off the living room light and retired to my bedroom. Before long I had fallen asleep, together with my slightly wounded feelings.

43

IT COULDN'T END LIKE
ANY OTHER DREAM

When I woke it was already light outside. Thin gray clouds covered the sky from end to end, but the sun's benevolent rays still quietly filtered through. It was not quite seven.

I washed my face, turned on the coffee maker, and went to check the living room. Wrapped in blankets, Masahiko was fast asleep on the sofa. He appeared unlikely to wake up any time soon. The almost empty bottle of Chivas Regal sat on the table. I managed to tidy up the bottle and glasses without disturbing him.

I must have drunk quite a lot the night before, but I wasn't a bit hungover. My mind was as sharp as it was every morning. No heartburn, either. I've never had a hangover in my life. Why, I don't know. Probably it's just the way I was born. One night's sleep and all traces of alcohol vanish from my system, however much I drink. I eat breakfast and I'm ready to go.

I toasted two slices of bread, fried two eggs, and ate them while listening to the news and weather on the radio. The stock market was fluctuating wildly, a new parliamentary scandal had been uncovered, and a terrorist bombing in the Middle East had killed and wounded many people. Nothing to brighten my day. Yet none of these events was likely to affect my immediate circumstances. For now, at least, they were limited to distant places and people I had never met. I felt bad, but there was nothing I could do. The weather forecast promised nothing new either. Not a particularly gorgeous day, but not particularly awful either. Overcast, but no rain. Maybe not, anyway. But the forecasters and media types were clever—they never used vague words like "maybe." No, they stuck with convenient terms for which no one could be held accountable, like "probability of precipitation."

When the news and weather ended, I turned off the radio and cleaned up the breakfast dishes. Then I sat down again at the table, drank a second cup of coffee, and thought. Most people would have used that time to read the Sunday paper, but I didn't subscribe. So I just sipped my coffee, looked at the magnificent willow tree outside the window, and thought.

First, I thought about my wife, who, I had been told, was about to give birth. Then it hit me—she wasn't my wife any longer. No connection between us remained. Not contractual, not personal. From where she stood, I was now in all likelihood a virtual stranger, a person of no special consequence. It felt weird. Until a few months ago we had eaten breakfast together, shared the same soap and towel, walked around naked in front of each other, slept in the same bed. Now our lives bore no relationship to each other.

As I followed this train of thought, gradually I began to feel a stranger to myself as well. I placed my hands on the table and studied them for a while.

These were my hands, no doubt. Right and left a symmetrical pair. I used these hands to paint, to cook, to eat, sometimes to caress a woman's body. But this morning, for some reason, they didn't look like my hands at all. They had become a stranger's hands—the palms, the backs, the fingernails.

I quit studying my hands. And thinking about the woman who had formerly been my wife. I got up from the table and went to the bath, where I removed my pajamas and took a hot shower. I carefully washed my hair and shaved in the bathroom sink. When I finished, I thought about the baby Yuzu was about to have—the baby who was not my child—again. I didn't want to, but there was nothing I could do about it.

She was about seven months pregnant. Seven months ago had been the second half of April. Where was I then, and what was I doing? I had left home and set out on a long, solitary trip in mid-March, driving my antique Peugeot 205 more or less at random all across Hokkaido and northeastern Japan. By the time my trip ended and I returned to Tokyo it was already early May. In late April I had crossed over from Hokkaido to Aomori in northern Honshu on the ferry that ran from Hakodate to Oma on the Shimokita Peninsula.

I pulled the simple diary I had kept out of a desk drawer and checked. At that time I had been traveling in the mountains of Aomori, far from the sea. Although it was well into the second half of April, it was still cold, and snow was everywhere. Why on

earth had I chosen such a cold place? I couldn't remember the precise location, but I did recall a small,
almost deserted lakefront hotel where I had stayed
for a few days. It was an unprepossessing old building made of concrete, where they offered simple (but
not bad) meals and amazingly cheap rates. There was
even a small outdoor hot springs bath in a corner of
the garden that was available twenty-four hours a day.
The hotel had just reopened for the spring season, and
I was practically the only guest.

For some reason, my recollections of that trip were
vague. All I recorded in the notebook I used as a diary
were the names of the places I visited, where I stayed,
what I ate, the distance I had driven, and how much I
spent. It was a brief, very hit-and-miss record. I could
find no mention of my thoughts and feelings, or anything else along those lines. I guess there was nothing
to write about. One day just flowed into another,
with no distinction between them. I had jotted down
the names of the places, but couldn't remember much
about any of them. Many times, even their names had
been left out. Looking back, I could only recall that
feeling of repetition: the same scenery day after day,
the same food, the same weather ("cold" and "not so
cold" were my only categories).

The little sketchbook I had carried did a better job
of bringing the trip back to life. (I carried no camera,
so I hadn't taken a single photograph. Instead, I had
sketched.) Even so, there weren't that many sketches
to look at. When I had spare time, I had just whipped
off simple drawings of what was before my eyes with

an old pencil or ballpoint pen. Flowers and plants on the roadside, dogs and cats, mountain peaks, things like that. Now and then I would sketch someone I met along the way, but I almost always gave those pictures to whomever I had drawn.

Beneath the diary entry for April 19 I had written the words "Dream last night." That was all. I had been staying at the small lakefront hotel on that date. The words were underlined with a thick pencil. It must have been a special kind of dream to warrant such emphasis. It took me a while to remember what the dream had been about. When the memory returned, though, it arrived all at once.

The dream had come to me shortly before dawn that day. It was vivid, and very erotic.

In the dream I was back in the apartment in Hiroo. The one Yuzu and I had shared for six years. There was a bed, and my wife was sleeping in it. I was looking down at her from the ceiling. In other words, I was hovering above her. I didn't find that at all out of the ordinary. In fact, the me in the dream found floating in the air to be perfectly normal. Nothing unnatural about it. Of course, I had no idea I was dreaming. What was happening felt totally real.

Quietly, so as not to wake Yuzu, I descended from the ceiling to stand at the foot of the bed. I was sexually aroused, powerfully so. I hadn't made love to her for ages. Bit by bit, I peeled back the quilt covering her. She was fast asleep (had she taken a sleeping pill before retiring?) and showed no signs of waking up, even when I removed the quilt. She never even twitched. This made me more daring. Taking my time, I slipped off her pajama bottoms, then her panties. Her pajamas were a pale blue, her tiny cotton panties pure white. Still she did not wake. There was no resistance, no sound.

I gently parted her legs and caressed her vagina with my finger. It was warm and wet, and opened to my touch. As if it had been waiting for me. I couldn't stand it any longer—I slipped my erect penis inside. Or, from another angle, that part of her actively swallowed my penis, immersing it in what felt like warm butter. Yuzu did not open her eyes, but she sighed and let out a small moan. As if she had been impatient for this to happen. Her nipples were as hard as cherry pits when I touched them.

She might be deep in a dream, I thought. If she was dreaming of someone, though, it was surely not me. For a long while now she had resisted sex with me. Whatever dream she might be having, though, whoever she was mistaking me for, it was too late to turn back, for I was already inside her. It could be a terrible shock if she woke up in the midst of the act and saw who it was. She might well be furious. If that were to happen, I would deal with it then. Now all I could do was take it to the limit. My desire raged like a river through a broken dam, carrying me along.

At the beginning, I moved my penis slowly, trying not to arouse her so much as to wake her up, but, naturally, the pace quickened as I went on. I could tell from the way her body welcomed me that she wanted me to be more forceful. Soon, though, I reached the moment of climax. I wanted to remain inside her, but I couldn't control myself any longer. It had been ages since we had last had sex, and, though asleep, she was responding to our lovemaking with more passion than ever before.

My ejaculation was violent, and repeated. Again and again, semen poured from me, overflowing her vagina, turning the sheets sticky. There was nothing I could do to make it stop. If it continued, I worried, I would be completely emptied out. Yuzu slept deeply through it all without making a sound, her breathing even. Her sex, though, had contracted around mine, and would not let go. As if it had an unshakable will of its own and was determined to wring every last drop from my body.

I woke up at this point. I had indeed ejaculated. My underwear was drenched in semen. I quickly slipped it off to avoid soiling the bed, carried it to the sink, and washed it. Then I went out through the hotel's back door to bathe in the hot springs. As the bath was entirely exposed to the elements, with no ceiling or walls, I was freezing by the time I reached it. Once I got in, however, the water warmed me to the core.

I soaked there alone in the predawn hush, listening to the water drip as steam melted the ice, replaying the dream over and over in my head. The memory was so vivid and physical it didn't feel like a dream at all. I had **actually** visited the Hiroo apartment and had **actually** made love to Yuzu—that was the only way I could think about it. My hands remembered the touch of her silky skin and my penis could still feel her vagina. It had clung to my penis, had embraced it with a violent passion (true, Yuzu may have mistaken me for someone else, but it was me nonetheless). She had wrung me out, taking every last drop of my semen for her own.

I could not help but feel a kind of shame for having such a dream (if dream indeed it was). After all, I had raped my own wife in my imagination. I had undressed and entered her while she was sleeping, without her consent. In the eyes of the law, a man who does that to a woman—even his wife—is guilty of sexual assault. In that sense, my conduct was far from praiseworthy. Still, objectively speaking, **it was a dream**. Something experienced in sleep. I had not created it on purpose. I had not written the script.

Yet in it I had played out my truest hopes and desires. There was no question on that score. Had I been placed in a similar situation in real life—not in a dream—I might well have acted the same. I might have stripped and forcibly entered her. I wanted Yuzu's body, longed to penetrate it. I was possessed by that desire. I had been able to realize it in exaggerated form in my dream (conversely, only in a dream could it have been realized).

As I continued on my solitary journey, this "real" erotic dream provided me with a provisional kind of happiness. You might say it buoyed me up. By recalling it, I could feel that I was a living creature organically connected to the world. Linked to my surroundings not through logical or conceptual thought, but carnally, through my body.

At the same time, though, the thought that someone else—some other man—was **actually** enjoying Yuzu as I had in my dream was agony. That someone was caressing her stiffened nipples, removing her tiny white panties, and thrusting himself into her until he came, again and again. When I imagined that, it felt as though I were torn and bleeding inside. Nothing (as far as I could remember) had ever made me feel that way before.

That was the strange dream I had experienced shortly before dawn on April 19. Noted in my diary as "Dream last night" and thickly underlined in pencil.

It was right around that time that Yuzu had conceived. Of course, the precise date could not be known. But it would not be odd if it were that day.

The similarity between my situation and the story Menshiki had told me was striking. The difference was that he had made love to a flesh-and-blood woman on his office sofa **in reality**. That had not taken place in a dream. And it had been right around then that she had conceived. Immediately thereafter she had married a man of substantial means, and had subsequently given birth to Mariye. Menshiki's belief that Mariye might be his child therefore had a basis in fact. It was a long shot, perhaps, but at least it was possible. My lovemaking with Yuzu, on the other hand, had taken place in a dream. I was in the mountains of Aomori, while Yuzu was (probably) in the heart of Tokyo. Thus her child could not possibly be mine. That was the only logical conclusion. The odds were not low, they were zero. **If, that is, one was thinking logically.**

But my dream was too vivid to be so easily dismissed on logical grounds. Moreover, the pleasure I had felt during our lovemaking was greater, and far more memorable, than at any time during our six years of marriage. When I came again and again inside her, the fuses in my brain seemed to have all blown at once, melting what had been distinct layers of reality into a single heavy, turbid mass. As in the primal chaos of the earth.

So graphic an occurrence must have consequences—it couldn't end like any other dream. I felt that strongly. It had to be connected to **something**. To have some sort of impact on the present.

Masahiko woke up shortly before nine. He padded into the dining room in his pajamas and drank a cup of hot black coffee. No breakfast, thanks, he said—just coffee, if you don't mind. There were bags under his eyes.

"Are you okay?" I asked.

"I'm fine," he said, rubbing his eyelids. "I've had much worse hangovers. This is mild."

"Why don't you stick around for a while?" I said.

"Don't you have a guest coming?"

"That's at ten. There's still time. And there's no problem if you're here when they arrive. I'll introduce you. They're both very attractive."

"Both? I thought there was just one model."

"Her aunt is her chaperone."

"Her chaperone? So they still do things the old-fashioned way in this neck of the woods? Like in a Jane Austen novel. They don't wear corsets and ride in a horse-drawn carriage, do they?"

"Not a horse-drawn carriage. A Toyota Prius. And no corsets. When I'm painting the girl, the aunt sits in the living room and reads for the whole two hours. 'Aunt' makes her sound old, though—she's pretty young."

"What sort of books is she into?"

"I don't know. I asked, but she wouldn't tell me."

"No kidding," he said. "Oh yeah, speaking of books, remember the character in Dostoevsky's **The Possessed,** the guy who shoots himself with a pistol just to prove how free he is? What's his name? I figured you might know."

"Kirillov," I said.

"That's right, Kirillov. I've been trying to remember, but it keeps slipping my mind."

"Why do you want to know?"

"No special reason," Masahiko said, shaking his head. "He popped into my head, and when I tried to recall his name, I couldn't. It's been bugging me.

Like a fish bone caught in my throat. But man, those Russians. They come up with the weirdest ideas, don't they?"

"There are lots of characters in Dostoevsky who do crazy things just to prove that they are free people, unconstrained by God and society. Though looking at Russia back then, maybe they weren't so crazy after all."

"Then how about you?" Masahiko asked. "You and Yuzu are formally divorced, which means you're now a lawfully unwedded man. So what comes next? Even if it wasn't your choice, freedom is still freedom, right? Why not run out and do something crazy, now that you have the opportunity?"

I laughed. "I'm not planning anything at present. Sure, I may be free for the moment, but that doesn't mean I've got to go out and prove it to the world, does it?"

"So that's how you look at it," Masahiko said in a disappointed tone. "But hey, you're a painter, right? An artist. Artists flaunt the rules left and right—they make a great show of it. But you've always walked the straight and narrow. The path of reason, I guess. So why not let loose now, throw off the restraints and do something wild?"

"Like murdering an old moneylender with an axe?"

"Yeah, that might work."

"Or falling for a prostitute with a heart of gold?"

"Even better."

"I'll think about it," I said. "But you know, it seems to me that reality itself has a screw loose somewhere.

That's why I try to keep at least myself in line as much as possible."

"Well, I guess that's one way of looking at it," Masahiko said resignedly.

It's more than just "one way of looking at it," I wanted to tell him. Indeed, it felt like everything around me was becoming unscrewed—that reality was losing its grip. If I lost my grip too, then the craziness would get completely out of hand. But I couldn't tell Masahiko the whole story at this stage of the game.

"At any rate, I've got to be going," he said. "I'd love to meet the two women, but I've got work waiting for me back in Tokyo."

Masahiko finished his coffee, got dressed, and drove off in his boxy jet-black Volvo. Baggy eyes and all. "Glad we finally had a chance to talk," were his parting words.

One thing that morning completely stumped me. Masahiko's knife, the one he'd brought to prepare the fish, had gone missing. It had been carefully washed, and neither of us remembered touching it afterward, but we searched the kitchen high and low and still couldn't find it.

"Forget it," he said. "It's probably out for a walk. Grab it for me when it comes back. I'll pick it up on my next visit—I don't use it all that often."

I'll keep looking, I told him.

I checked my watch once the Volvo was out of sight. The Akikawas would be showing up before long. I removed the bedding from the living room sofa, and flung the windows wide open to let fresh air in. The sky was still faintly overcast and gray. There was no wind.

I took **Killing Commendatore** from my bedroom and hung it back where it had been on the studio wall. Then I sat down on the stool to examine the painting one more time. Red blood still gushed from the Commendatore's chest, while Long Face's sharp eyes still glittered in the lower left-hand corner of the canvas. Nothing had changed.

Even as I studied **Killing Commendatore**, though, I couldn't erase Yuzu from my mind. It had been no dream, of that much I felt sure. **I had truly visited our apartment that night.** I was as sure of that as I was that Tomohiko Amada had visited the studio several days before. Like him, I had overcome the laws of physics by some means to make my way to our Hiroo apartment, penetrate her, and discharge my semen inside her body. People can accomplish anything, I thought, if they want it badly enough. There are channels through which reality can become unreal. Or unreality can enter the realm of the real. If we desire it that strongly. Deep in our heart. But that didn't mean that we were free. It might demonstrate quite the opposite.

If I had the chance, I wanted to ask Yuzu if **she** had experienced a similar dream in late April of this year. If she had dreamed shortly before dawn that I had come to ravish her while she was fast asleep (or else somehow deprived her of her freedom). In other words, was my dream something I alone experienced, or was it a two-way street? That's what I wanted to confirm. Yet if the dream was one we had shared, wouldn't she view me as sinister, a villain? Could such a presence exist within me? I hated to think of myself in that way.

Was I free? As far as I was concerned, the question was wholly irrelevant. What I needed now more than anything was a firm reality to hold on to. A solid foundation on which to stand. Not the sort of freedom that allowed me to rape my own wife in my dreams.

44

THE TRAITS THAT MAKE A PERSON WHO THEY ARE

Mariye didn't speak that morning. She just sat there, the perfect model, in the simple straight-backed chair, and gazed at me as if at some distant landscape. Since my stool was taller than her chair, she was looking up at a slight angle. I made no special attempt to talk to her. There was nothing I had to say, nor did I feel any particular need. So I plied my brush across the canvas in silence.

I was painting Mariye's portrait, yet I could sense elements of my dead sister Komi and my former wife Yuzu creeping into the work. This wasn't intentional—they worked their way in quite naturally. Perhaps I was searching within Mariye for reminders of those two women, so important to me, whom I had lost. I couldn't say if this was healthy or not. But that was the only way I could paint at the time. No, to say "at the time" is off the mark. When I thought about it, I had operated like this from the very beginning. Giving form to what eluded me in reality. Inscribing secret signals only I could decipher.

Whatever the case, I was able to push Mariye's portrait forward with relative ease. Step by step, it moved steadily toward completion. Like a river, it followed the contours of the land, pooling in the hollows until it overflowed the final barrier to stream unobstructed to the sea. I could feel it circulate through my body, like blood.

"Can I come visit you later," Mariye said in a small voice just before we finished our morning's work. The lack of inflection made it sound like an assertion, but it was a clear question.

"You mean through your secret passageway?"

"Yes."

"I don't mind at all, but around what time?"

"I don't know yet."

"I don't think you should come after dark," I said. "You can never tell what's in these mountains at night."

All sorts of weird things could be lurking out there: the Commendatore, Long Face, the man with the white Subaru Forester, Tomohiko Amada's living spirit. Even the incubus that was my sexual alter ego. Yes, depending on the circumstances, I might turn into one of those sinister creatures that prowled the night. The thought gave me a chill.

"I'll try to come before dark," Mariye said. "I want to talk to you about something. Just the two of us."

"I'll be waiting."

We wrapped up for the day not long after the noon-hour chimes sounded.

Shoko was sitting on the sofa, once again focused on her reading. She appeared to have almost finished

665

the thick paperback. Taking off her glasses, she noted her place with a bookmark and looked up at us.

"We made good progress today," I told her. "One or two more sessions and we should be done. I'm sorry to be taking so much of your time."

Shoko smiled. It was a beautiful smile. "Not at all," she answered. "Mariye seems to enjoy sitting for you, and I so look forward to seeing the finished portrait. And this sofa is the perfect place to read. I'm never bored in the slightest. In fact, it's a welcome change of pace for me to come here—I always feel better afterward."

I wanted to ask her how their visit to Menshiki's house had gone the previous Sunday. Had his fine mansion impressed her? What had she thought of him as a person? But asking questions like that would have been a breach of etiquette—I had to wait for her to raise the subject first.

Once again, Shoko had dressed for the occasion. It was most definitely not what a regular person would put on to visit a neighbor on a Sunday morning. A perfectly pressed camel hair skirt, a fancy white silk blouse with a big ribbon, and a dark blue-gray jacket with a gold pin adorning the collar. The pin had a jewel embedded in it, which I took to be a real diamond. The whole outfit seemed rather too fashionable to wear behind the wheel of a Toyota Prius. But who was I to say? Toyota's director of marketing would likely have a very different opinion.

Mariye was dressed as usual. The same old varsity jacket, her hole-studded jeans, and a pair of white sneakers even dirtier than the ones she usually wore (the backs of these were stomped flat).

When they were heading out the door, Mariye looked back and gave me a wink, a secret sign that said "See you later." I flashed a quick smile in response.

When Shoko and Mariye had gone, I went to the living room, lay down on the sofa, and slept. I had no appetite, so I skipped lunch. It was a brief nap, about thirty minutes, deep and dreamless. I was grateful for that. It was more than a little scary to think what I might do in my dreams, and even scarier to think **what I might become.**

My mood that Sunday afternoon was as unfocused as the weather. It was a quiet, slightly overcast day with no wind to speak of. I read a little, listened to a little music, cooked a little, but nothing helped me work out my feelings. It promised to be one of those afternoons where nothing gets resolved. Giving up, I ran a hot bath, got in, and soaked for a long time. I tried to remember the names of the characters in Dostoevsky's **The Possessed**. I was able to come up with seven, including Kirillov. For some reason, since my high school days I've had a knack for memorizing lengthy Russian names. Maybe now was a good opportunity to go back and reread **The Possessed**. I was free, with time on my hands and nothing that had to be done. The perfect conditions for reading long Russian classics.

I thought about Yuzu some more. Her belly

would probably be showing after seven months. I pictured how that would look. What would she be doing now? What would she be thinking? Was she happy? Of course, I had no way to know any of those things.

Perhaps it was as Masahiko had said. Perhaps, like a nineteenth-century Russian intellectual, I should do something out-and-out crazy just to prove I was a free man. But what? Something like . . . spend an hour shut up at the bottom of a pitch-black pit? **That** was what Menshiki had done. True, his actions might not fit the category "out-and-out crazy." But they were definitely beyond the pale, to put it mildly.

It was after four when Mariye showed up. The doorbell rang, I opened the door, and there she was. She slipped through the half-open door like a wisp of cloud and looked around warily.

"No one's here."

"Nobody's here, that's true," I said.

"Someone was here yesterday."

That was a question. "Yes, a friend of mine stayed over," I said.

"A man."

"Yes, a man. A male friend. But how did you know?"

"There was an old car I'd never seen before parked in front of your house. It looked like a black box."

That would be Masahiko's ancient Volvo station

wagon, what he called his "Swedish lunch box." Convenient for hauling reindeer carcasses.

"So you came yesterday."

Mariye nodded. It appeared that she was using her passageway to come and check on the house whenever she had time. She'd probably been doing this since long before my arrival. After all, it was her playground. Or "hunting ground" might be more accurate. I was just someone who had chanced to move in. In which case, could she have come face-to-face with Tomohiko Amada at some point? I had to ask her about that sometime.

I led her into the living room. We sat down together, she on the sofa, me in the armchair. I offered her something to drink, but she said no.

"The guy who stayed over is a friend from my college days," I said.

"A good friend?"

"I think so," I said. "In fact, he may be the only person I can call a true friend."

Such a good friend that he could introduce his colleague to my wife and keep me in the dark when they started sleeping together—a situation that had led to my just concluded divorce—without casting a cloud over our relationship. To call us friends would hardly be stretching the truth.

"Do you have any good friends?" I asked her.

Mariye didn't answer. In fact, she didn't bat an eye, just acted as if she hadn't heard what I'd said. I guessed it was something I shouldn't have asked.

"Mr. Menshiki isn't a good friend of yours," she said. I knew it was a question, though her intonation was flat. **Do you mean Mr. Menshiki isn't a good friend of yours?** was what she meant.

"As I've told you," I said, "I haven't known Mr. Menshiki long enough to call him a real friend. I started talking with him after I moved here, and that was only six months ago. It takes longer than that for people to become close. Still, he strikes me as a very interesting person."

"Interesting."

"How can I explain? His disposition strikes me as a little different than the average guy. Maybe more than a little, actually. He's not an easy person to figure out."

"Disposition."

"Personality. The traits that make a person who they are."

Mariye stared at me for a while. As if selecting the exact words she ought to use.

"He can see my home from his deck—it's right across the valley."

It took me a moment to respond to that. "Yes, you're right. That's the lay of the land. But he can see my house just as clearly. Not yours alone."

"Still, I think that man is **spying on** us."

"What do you mean, spying on you?"

"He's got something like a pair of big binoculars on the terrace, though he hides them with a cover. They're on a kind of tripod. He can see us really clearly if he uses those."

So the girl found him out, I thought. Watchful, observant. Eyes that missed nothing of importance.

"So you think that Mr. Menshiki has been observing you through those binoculars?"

Mariye gave a terse nod.

I took a deep breath, then let it out. "Still, that's just a guess on your part, right? They don't necessarily mean he's peeking into your house. He could be observing the moon and stars."

Mariye's gaze didn't waver. "I've had this feeling like I'm **being watched**," she said. "For a while. But I didn't know who was watching me, or from where. But now I know. It's **that person,** for sure."

I took another long, slow breath. Mariye's supposition was on the money. Menshiki was watching her through his high-powered military binoculars on a nightly basis. Yet to my knowledge—and this was not to defend Menshiki—his motives for being a peeping Tom were far from nefarious. He just wanted to see the girl. This beautiful thirteen-year-old girl who might be his biological daughter. For that reason, and that reason alone, he had purchased the mansion on the other side of the valley. Wresting it from the family living there and booting them out. Yet I couldn't reveal that to Mariye.

"Let's say you're right," I said. "But then what's his motive? Why is he so fixated on your home?"

"I don't know. Maybe he has a crush on my aunt."

"Has a crush on your aunt?"

She gave a brief shrug of her shoulders.

671

Mariye couldn't imagine she was the target. She hadn't yet reached the stage where she could see herself as an object of male desire. I found it strange, yet I didn't dare call her version of events into question. If that was how she read the situation, better perhaps to let it ride.

"I think Mr. Menshiki is hiding something," Mariye said.

"What, for example?"

"My aunt is seeing Mr. Menshiki," she said, not answering my question. "They met twice this week." Her tone suggested that she was passing on highly sensitive state secrets.

"On dates?"

"I think she went to his house."

"Alone?"

"She left a little after noon and didn't return until late."

"But you can't be sure she went to Mr. Menshiki's, can you?"

"I can tell," she said.

"How can you tell?"

"My aunt doesn't leave the house that much," she said. "Sure, she'll volunteer at the library or go shopping, but then she doesn't take a long shower, or paint her nails, or put on perfume and her fanciest underwear."

"You really have sharp eyes, don't you," I said, impressed. "You see everything. But are you sure the man she's meeting is Mr. Menshiki? Couldn't it be someone else?"

Mariye narrowed her eyes at me. She gave a small shake of her head. As in, **Do you think I'm that stupid?** After all, under the circumstances it was unlikely to be anyone but Menshiki. And Mariye was anything but stupid.

"So your aunt spends quite a bit of time at Mr. Menshiki's house, just the two of them together."

Mariye nodded.

"And the two of them—how should I put this?— are engaged in what we might call a very intimate relationship."

She nodded again. "Yes, a very intimate relationship," she said, her cheeks turning a faint pink.

"But you're in school all day. Not at home. So how can you know these things?"

"I can tell. I can tell that much from a woman's face."

But I couldn't tell. Yuzu had carried on an extended affair while we were living together, and I was clueless. Looking back, I should have been able to figure out that much. How could a thirteen-year-old girl pick up on something I couldn't that quickly?

"So things really moved fast between those two, didn't they," I said.

"My aunt's no dummy—there's nothing wrong with her head. But her heart has a weak spot. And Mr. Menshiki is stronger than normal people. A lot stronger—she's no match for him."

She's probably right, I thought. Menshiki did have some special power. Once he made his move, it would be almost impossible for an average person to resist.

Myself included. I doubted he would find it difficult to make a woman his, if that was his goal.

"So you're worried about your aunt, right? That Mr. Menshiki is using her for some reason."

Mariye swept her hair back with her hand, exposing her ear. It was small and white, and its shape was lovely. She nodded.

"But it's not that easy to stop a relationship of this sort once it's gotten started," I said.

Not that easy at all, I said to myself. It would move forward, crushing everything in its path, like the Hindus' great wheel of karma. There could be no turning back.

"That's why I had to talk to you," Mariye said. Then she looked me square in the eye.

When it began to get dark, I took my flashlight and walked Mariye almost as far as her passageway. She said she had to be home by dinner. They usually ate around seven.

She had come to ask me for advice. Yet I hadn't been able to offer anything useful. All I could tell her was to wait and see how things developed. I knew Menshiki and Shoko might be having sex, but they were two unmarried and consenting adults. What was I supposed to do? Sure, I had some background information, but I couldn't reveal it, not to Mariye, and not to her aunt. That meant that I couldn't give useful advice to anyone. I was like a boxer trying to fight with his best arm tied behind his back.

Mariye and I walked side by side through the woods, hardly exchanging a word. We had gone partway along the path when she reached down and took my hand. Her hand was small, but its grip was unexpectedly firm. I was surprised at first, but then I had often walked this way with my sister, so it didn't put me off. Instead, it felt normal, a kind of return to my youth.

Mariye's hand was very smooth to the touch. Warm but not at all sweaty. She must have been thinking about something, for her hand squeezed mine and relaxed, squeezed and relaxed, depending, I guess, on what she was thinking. My sister had done the same thing back in the old days.

When we reached the shrine, she let go of my hand and, without a word, circled around to the back. I followed her.

The pampas grass still bore the tread marks of the backhoe. Within lay the silent pit. Its cover was made of sturdy boards, weighted down by a row of stones. I shone my flashlight on them to confirm that they hadn't been moved. They hadn't.

"Is it okay if I look in?" Mariye asked me.

"Just look."

"Just look," Mariye said.

I set some of the stones to the side and removed one of the boards. Mariye knelt and peered through the opening. I trained the flashlight on the floor of the pit. Of course, nobody was there. Only a metal ladder leaning against the wall. If one so chose, one could use it to climb down and then back up again.

It would be next to impossible to get out without the ladder, although the pit was less than nine feet deep. The walls were just too smooth and slick to be scaled.

Holding her hair back with one hand, Mariye stared inside the pit for a long time. Intently, as if searching for something in the dark. I had no idea what was down there to capture her attention.

"Who built this?" she asked, looking up at last.

"I don't know. At first I thought it might be a well, but now I'm not so sure. I mean, who would dig a well in such an out-of-the-way place? Anyway, it looks very old. And it's very well put together. It must have taken a long time to build."

Mariye looked at me steadily without saying anything.

"This area has been your playground for quite a while, hasn't it?" I said.

She nodded.

"But you didn't know this pit was behind the shrine until recently."

She shook her head. No, she hadn't known.

"You found it and opened it, didn't you?" she asked.

"That's right, I may have been the one who discovered it. I didn't know it was a pit, but I figured **something** had to be under that pile of rocks. The person who arranged for the rocks to be moved and the pit to be opened, though, was Mr. Menshiki." I wanted to let her in on this much, at least. It was better to be honest.

A bird cried in the trees. It was a sharp, piercing

call, as if to warn its fellow creatures. I looked up but couldn't catch sight of it. All I could see were the layered branches of the leafless trees. And beyond those the evening sky of approaching winter, flat, expressionless, and gray.

Mariye winced slightly. But she didn't respond.

"It's hard to explain," I said. "I felt as if the pit was demanding that someone open it. And that I had been bidden to perform that task."

"Bidden?"

"Invited. Called upon to."

She looked up at me. "It wanted you to open it?"

"Yes."

"**This pit** asked you to open it?"

"It could have been anyone, perhaps. Maybe I just happened to be around."

"But it was Mr. Menshiki who actually did it."

"Yes. I brought him here. I couldn't have uncovered it without him. The rocks were too heavy to move by hand, and I didn't have the cash to bring in heavy equipment. It was a fortunate coincidence."

"Maybe you shouldn't have done it," she said after a moment's thought. "I think I told you that before."

"So you think I should have left it as it was?"

Mariye didn't answer immediately. She stood up and brushed the dirt off the knees of her jeans. Not once but several times. She and I replaced the board, and the stones that held it down. Once again, I committed their location to memory.

"Yes, I think so," she said at last, lightly rubbing her palms against each other.

"I think this place may have had some kind of religious background. There might be legends or stories connected to it."

Mariye shook her head. She didn't know of any. "Maybe my father knows something."

The whole area had been owned by her father's family since before the Meiji period. The adjoining mountain was also in their hands. He might have a good idea of what the pit and shrine meant.

"Could you ask him?"

Mariye winced slightly. "I'll try," she said in a small voice. She hesitated. "If I have a chance."

"It would be a big help if we knew who built it when, and for what purpose."

"Maybe they shut up something inside, and put heavy stones on top to make sure it didn't get out," she offered.

"So you think maybe they heaped on the stones to prevent whatever it was from escaping, and then built the little shrine to ward off its curse?"

"Maybe."

"And then we went and pried it open anyway."

Mariye gave a small shrug.

I accompanied her to where the woods ended. She'd go on from there by herself, she said. The darkness was no problem—she knew the way. She wanted no one to see the passage that led to her home. It was a shortcut that she alone should know. So I turned back, leaving her there. Only a glimmer of light remained in the sky. The cold blackness was descending.

The same bird made the same piercing call when I passed before the shrine. This time, though, I didn't look up. I headed straight home, leaving the shrine behind. As I prepared dinner I sipped a glass of Chivas Regal and water. There was only enough left in the bottle for one more drink. The night was deathly silent. As if the clouds were absorbing every living sound.

You shouldn't have opened the pit.

Perhaps Mariye was right. I should have steered clear of the pit. It seemed that everything I did these days was off the mark.

I imagined Menshiki making love to Shoko. The two of them naked, entwined on a big bed in a room somewhere in that sprawling white mansion. That event was taking place in another world, of course, one that bore no connection to me. Yet the thought of the two of them together left me bereft. As if I were standing in a station watching a long, empty train pass by.

Finally, I fell asleep and my Sunday ended. A deep dreamless sleep, undisturbed by anyone.

45

SOMETHING IS ABOUT TO HAPPEN

O f the two paintings I was working on, **The Pit in the Woods** was the one I knocked off first. It was Friday afternoon when I finished it. Paintings are strange things: as they near the end they acquire their own will, their own viewpoint, even their own powers of speech. They tell the artist when they are done (at least that's the way it works for me). A spectator to the process—if one is present—can't tell the difference between a painting in process and a completed painting, for the line is virtually invisible to the naked eye. But the artist knows. He or she can hear the painting say, **Hands off, I'm done**. The artist has only to heed that voice.

So it was with **The Pit in the Woods**. At a certain point, it announced itself finished and refused my brush. Like a sexually satisfied woman. I took the canvas from the easel and leaned it against the wall. Then I sat down on the floor and regarded it at length. My painting of a half-covered hole in the ground.

I couldn't pin down my motive for painting it, or its meaning. It had just grabbed me. I couldn't come up with anything beyond that. These things happen. When something strikes me in that way—a landscape, an object, a person—I pick up my brush and am off to the races. No meaning, no motive. I just go where my gut tells me, pure and simple.

But wait, I thought. This time was different. This wasn't mere impulse. **Something** had demanded that I paint this painting. Urgently. That was why I had finished it so quickly—whatever it was, that demand had fired me up, sent me to my easel, and propelled me forward, like a hand on my back. Or maybe the pit was the agent, pushing me to draw its portrait, leaving me to guess its motive. In the same way that Menshiki, likely in pursuit of some larger plan, had enlisted me to paint his portrait.

Judged in a fair and objective way, the painting wasn't bad. I couldn't tell whether it could be called a work of art or not. (Not to make excuses, but I hadn't begun with that goal in mind.) From the standpoint of pure technique, though, it was a success. The composition was flawless, and I had captured both the light streaming through the trees and the colors of the fallen leaves. It was realistic right down to its tiniest detail, yet, nevertheless, a mysterious, symbolic aura hovered over it.

As I sat there staring at the finished work, a feeling came over me, what might be called a **premonition of impending movement**. On the surface at least, it was just as its title said: a landscape painting of the pit in the woods. It was so accurate, in fact, that "reproduction" might be closer to the truth. As someone who had been developing his craft, however imperfectly, for so long, I had the artistic skill to reproduce an exact likeness of the scene on canvas. I had not painted the scene so much as I had **documented** it.

Nevertheless, that **premonition** was there. Something was about to take place within that landscape. The painting was telling me that. Then I realized. What I had been trying to get across, or what that **something** had been trying to get me to paint, was precisely that premonition, those signs.

Sitting there on the floor, I straightened my back and looked at the painting anew.

What was about to happen? Was someone or something about to come crawling out from the darkness that lay beneath the half-open cover? Or, conversely, was someone about to climb down into the hole? Though I looked long and hard, I couldn't guess what would take place. I only knew some sort of movement was about to occur. The strength of my premonition left no doubt.

Why did the pit so badly want me to paint it? To try to tell me something? To warn me? It was a game of riddles. So many riddles, and not a single answer. I wanted to show the painting to Mariye and hear what she had to say. Maybe she could see what I couldn't.

Friday was the day I taught drawing near Odawara Station. Mariye was one of the students, so she would be there. Perhaps I could have a word with her afterward. I hopped in my car and headed to town.

There was still plenty of time when I arrived, so I parked and went to get my customary cup of coffee. No gleaming, functional Starbucks for me—my coffee shop was untouched by time, a back-alley spot run by a man on the cusp of old age who served a jet-black, muddy brew in a cup that weighed a ton. Jazz from a former era played on the ancient speakers. Billie Holiday, Clifford Brown, and other classics. As I still had time to spare when I finished my coffee, I wandered down the shopping street. I was low on coffee filters, so I bought a pack. I found a used-record store, and browsed through their old LPs. I realized I hadn't listened to anything other than classical music for a very long time. Tomohiko Amada's shelves contained no other kinds of records. If I listened to the radio, it was only to catch the news and weather on the AM dial (my location meant almost no FM reception).

I had left my records and CDs—not that there were a lot of them—in the Hiroo apartment. It would have been painful to sort out which books and records belonged to Yuzu and which to me. Impossible, really. Who did Bob Dylan's **Nashville Skyline** belong to? How about the Doors album with "Alabama Song" on it? What difference did it make who had shelled out the money? We'd shared the same music for a period of time, lived our life together listening to it. Even if we had been able to divide the records, we could never have separated the memories attached to them. I had to leave them all behind.

I looked for **Nashville Skyline** and the first album by the Doors, but couldn't find either. They may have been available on CD, but I wanted to hear them on an old-style phonograph. There was no CD player in Tomohiko Amada's house anyway. And no cassette deck. Just a couple of record players. Tomohiko Amada likely had no interest in new technology. He'd probably never come within six feet of a microwave oven.

In the end, I bought two records. Bruce Springsteen's **The River** and a collection of duets by Roberta Flack and Donny Hathaway. Both were old favorites of mine. At some point in my life, I had given up on new music. Instead, I listened to the old stuff over and over again. Books were the same. I reread books from my past, often more than once, but ignored books that had just come out. Somewhere along the way, time seemed to have come to a screeching halt.

Perhaps time really had stopped. Then again, maybe it kept nudging forward despite the fact that evolution, or anything resembling it, had ended. Like a restaurant approaching closing time that has stopped taking orders. And I was the only one who hadn't figured it out.

The shop assistant put the two records in a bag, and I paid. Then I went to a nearby liquor store to buy some whiskey. I wasn't sure what to get, but finally settled on Chivas Regal. It was a little more expensive, but would be a big hit with Masahiko the next time he stopped by.

My starting time for class was approaching, so I stashed the records, coffee filters, and whiskey in my car and entered the building where classes were held. The kids were first, starting at five o'clock. Mariye was part of that group. But I couldn't spot her. This was a first. She was passionate about the class, had never skipped it before, as far as I knew. Her absence unsettled me. I found it somehow alarming, even threatening. Was she all right? Was she ill, or had something unexpected happened to her?

Nevertheless, I carried on as though nothing was wrong, assigning simple exercises, offering comments on each child's drawing, giving advice. When class ended, the children went home and the adult class began. It too passed without incident. I exchanged good-natured pleasantries with the people there (hardly my strong point, but I can do it when required). After that, I had a brief meeting with the workshop organizer about future plans. He had no idea why Mariye was absent. There had been no word from her family.

After work, I went to a nearby noodle shop and ate a hot bowl of tempura soba. This too was my weekly habit. Always the same shop, and always tempura soba. One of life's little pleasures. Then I drove back to my house on the mountain. It was almost nine when I arrived.

I couldn't tell if anyone had tried to contact me while I was gone, for there was no answering machine (such a "clever" device probably numbered among Tomohiko Amada's bêtes noires). I gave the simple, old-fashioned telephone a long look, but it didn't speak. It just sat there, in black silence.

I had a long soak in a hot bath. Then I poured what was left of the original bottle of Chivas Regal into a glass, added two ice cubes from the fridge, and took the drink to the living room, where I sipped it while listening to one of the records I had just bought. At first, it seemed somehow **inappropriate** to be playing anything other than classical in my mountaintop domicile. The air in the room had been conditioned to that type of music for a very long time. Still, I was playing my music, so that now, song by song, a familiarity overcame the feeling of inappropriateness. As I listened, I could feel my body start to relax. I must have been tense without being aware of it.

The A side of the Roberta Flack and Donny Hathaway record had ended and the first song on the B side ("For All We Know," a really cool performance) had just begun when the phone rang. The clock said 10:30. Who on earth would be calling me so late? I didn't want to answer. Yet the ring sounded urgent. I put down my glass, rose from the sofa, lifted the needle off the record, and picked up the phone.

"Hello?" It was Shoko Akikawa.

I greeted her.

"I'm so terribly sorry to be phoning this late," she said. I had never heard her sound so anxious. "But I needed to ask you something. Mariye didn't show up at art class today, did she?"

No, I replied, she didn't. The question was a strange one. Normally, Mariye came straight from school (the public junior high in the area) in her uniform. When class ended, her aunt picked her up in the car, and the two went home together. That pattern never varied.

"I haven't seen Mariye anywhere," Shoko said.

"Haven't seen her?"

"She's missing."

"Since what time?" I asked.

"Since this morning, when she left for school. I offered to drive her to the station, but she said she'd walk. She likes walking. Much more than riding in the car. So I give her a lift when she's running late, but otherwise she walks down the hill to the bus stop and takes the bus to the station. This morning she left the house at seven thirty, as usual."

Shoko said all this in a single breath, then stopped. I could hear her trying to control her breathing. I used the pause to put what she had just told me into some kind of order.

"Today is Friday," Shoko continued. "When school lets out on Fridays, she goes directly to art class. And then I pick her up afterward. But today Mariye said she'd take the bus home instead. So I didn't go. When she says something like that, it's pointless to argue. But she still gets back by seven or seven thirty. Then she has dinner. But tonight, it turned to eight and then eight thirty and she still hadn't returned. So I called the center and asked whether she had come to class or not. They checked and said she hadn't shown up. That's when I got really worried. Now it's ten thirty and she's still not back. I've heard nothing. That's why I'm calling you—I thought perhaps you might know something."

"I haven't a clue where she is," I said. "I was rather surprised when I showed up for class and Mariye wasn't there. She's never skipped before."

Shoko gave a deep sigh. "My brother's not back yet. I don't know when to expect him—he hasn't contacted me. I'm not sure if he'll return tonight or not. I'm here all alone, and I don't know what to do."

"She was wearing her school uniform when she left this morning, correct?"

"Yes, she left in her uniform, with a bag over her shoulder. The same as always. A blazer and skirt. I don't know if she ever made it to school, though. It's late, so there's no way to check. But I'm quite sure she got there. The school contacts us if there's an unexplained absence. She was carrying enough money for a single day's expenses, no more. I make her take a cell phone just in case, but it's been shut off all day. She doesn't like cell phones. She'll use hers to call me, but she usually keeps it off the rest of the time. I've warned her about that over and over, begged her not to turn it off, explained that we may need to reach her if something important comes up, but she doesn't—"

"Has this ever happened before? Her coming home late?"

"This is the first time, really. Mariye is very dependable. She has no close friends she hangs out with, and once she's agreed to do something, she follows through, even though she doesn't like school all that much. She won a prize for perfect attendance in elementary school. She always comes straight home after school. She never loiters along the way."

Mariye's aunt was clearly in the dark about her nighttime forays.

"Was there anything she said or did this morning that was out of the ordinary?"

"No, nothing. It was a regular morning. The same as always. She drinks a glass of warm milk, eats a slice of toast, and heads out the door. Every day is identical. I made her breakfast today as I usually do. She didn't say a great deal. But that's normal. She can talk a blue streak once she gets started, but most of the time, you can't get much out of her."

I was beginning to worry. It was almost eleven at night, and it was pitch dark outside. The moon was hiding behind the clouds. What on earth had happened to Mariye Akikawa?

"I'll wait one more hour. If Mariye still hasn't contacted me by then, I'll call the police," Shoko said.

"That's a good idea," I said. "And let me know if there's anything I can do. Any time is all right—please don't hesitate, no matter how late it is."

Shoko thanked me and hung up. I drained what was left of the whiskey and washed the glass in the sink.

After that I went to the studio. I turned on all the lights and stood there in the bright room, taking another lingering look at my unfinished **Portrait of Mariye Akikawa** on the easel. It was close to done— only a little work remained. It showed a version of what a quiet thirteen-year-old girl would ideally look like. Yet there were other elements too, aspects of her that could not be seen, that made her who she was. What I was attempting in all my painting—though not, of course, in the portraits I did on commission— was to try to capture those things which lay outside my field of vision and communicate their message in a different form. Mariye was, in that sense, a most fascinating subject. There was just so much that was hidden, like a trompe l'oeil. And now as of this morning she herself had disappeared. As if swallowed by that very trompe l'oeil.

I turned to look again at **The Pit in the Woods** leaning against the wall. I had just completed it that afternoon. I could feel that painting calling out to me too, though in another way, and from a different direction, than **A Portrait of Mariye Akikawa**.

Something is about to happen. I felt this again as I looked at the landscape. Until that afternoon it had been a premonition of sorts, but now it was encroaching on reality. **The movement was already under way.** Mariye's disappearance and the pit in the woods were linked in some way. I could sense it. By finishing the painting I had set the gears in motion. And Mariye's vanishing act was the likely result.

Yet I could tell Shoko none of this. All that would do was confuse her even more.

I went back to the kitchen and rinsed the whiskey taste from my mouth with several glasses of water. When that was done, I picked up the phone and called Menshiki. I called three times before he picked up. I detected a slight edge to his voice, as if he were waiting for an important call. That it was me on the line seemed to surprise him. It only took a second, though, for the edge to disappear and the voice to turn cool and collected, as always.

"I'm very sorry to call so late," I said.

"Not at all. I stay up late, and I've got plenty of time. I'm always happy to hear your voice."

Skipping the normal pleasantries, I gave him a brief report of Mariye's disappearance. The girl had left home for school in the morning but hadn't returned. Nor had she shown up at my painting class. The news seemed to throw Menshiki for a loop. He took a moment to reply.

"And you have no idea where she might have gone, right?" he asked me.

"None at all," I replied. "It came out of left field. How about you?"

"I have no idea either, of course. She barely says a word to me."

There was no anger or regret in his voice. He was simply relating the way she treated him.

"That's just how she is—she's like that with everybody," I said. "But Shoko is at her wit's end. Mariye's father isn't home either, so she's all alone and unsure what to do."

Menshiki paused again. It was rare to see him at a loss for words—in fact, I had never witnessed it before.

"Is there anything I can do?" he said at last.

"I know it's sudden," I said, "but is there any chance you could drop by now?"

"To your home?"

691

"Yes. There's something in this connection that I need to talk to you about."

Menshiki took a moment to respond. "All right," he said. "I'll leave right away."

"Are you sure you don't have to take care of a matter there first?"

"It's not big enough to call a 'matter.' It's just a trivial thing," he said. He cleared his throat. He seemed to be checking his watch. "I can be there in about fifteen minutes."

When the phone call ended, I got ready to go out. I laid out a sweater and my leather jacket, and placed the big flashlight within easy reach. Then I sat on the sofa and waited for the purr of Menshiki's Jaguar rolling up the hill.

46

PEOPLE ARE POWERLESS BEFORE A STURDY, TOWERING WALL

Menshiki arrived at eleven twenty. The moment I heard his Jaguar, I slipped on my leather jacket and headed out the door. He stepped from the car wearing a padded, dark-blue windbreaker, narrow-cut black jeans, and leather sneakers. A light scarf was draped around his neck. His mane of white hair glowed in the dark.

"If it's okay, I'd like you to come with me to check out the pit in the woods," I said.

"Of course," Menshiki said. "Do you think it's connected to Mariye's disappearance?"

"I'm not sure. But I've had a premonition for a while that something bad was going to happen. Something connected to that pit."

Menshiki asked no more questions after that. "Fine," he said. "Let's go take a look."

He opened the trunk of his Jaguar and pulled out what looked like a lantern. Then he closed the trunk and set off with me toward the woods. Neither moon nor stars were out, so it was very dark. There was no wind.

"Sorry to ask you to venture out so late," I said. "But it seemed safer to have you come along. If something went wrong, I might not be able to handle it alone."

He patted my arm. As though to encourage me. "It's no trouble at all—I'm happy to do what I can."

We picked our way through the trees, shining the flashlight and lantern on our feet to avoid tripping over the roots. The only sound was the crunch of dry leaves underfoot. Otherwise it was dead silent. I sensed the animals of the woods silently watching us from their hiding places. The dark depths of midnight give rise to illusions like that. Had someone seen us, they might have mistaken us for a pair of grave robbers on their way to ransack a tomb.

"There's just one thing I'd like to ask," Menshiki said.

"What's that?"

"Why do you think Mariye's disappearance and the pit might be connected?"

I explained that she and I had visited the pit together not long before. That she had already known about its existence. That the whole area was her playground. That nothing happened here without her knowledge. Then I told him what she had said: **You should have left the place as it was. You should never have opened it up.**

"When she stood in front of the pit she seemed to have experienced something," I said. "A special feeling . . . I guess you could call it spiritual."

"And she was drawn to it?"

"Yes. She was leery, but at the same time something about the pit was drawing her in. That's why I worry it might have played a role. That she might be down there, unable to get out."

Menshiki thought for a moment. "Did you tell her aunt this?" he asked. "Does Shoko know?"

"No, I haven't said anything yet. If I mentioned the pit to her, I'd have to go back to the beginning. To how we opened it, and why you were involved. It would turn into a very long story, and I doubt I could explain myself very well."

"Yes, it would cause her a lot of needless worry."

"It would be even more awkward if the police got involved. If they grew interested in the pit."

Menshiki looked at me. "Are they investigating already?"

"She hadn't contacted them yet when I talked to her. But she could have put in a search request by now. After all, it's getting pretty late."

Menshiki nodded several times. "Yes, it's only natural. It's almost midnight, and a thirteen-year-old girl hasn't come home. No one knows where she's gone. What can her family do but call the cops?"

I could tell from his tone that Menshiki wasn't too thrilled that the police would be entering the picture.

"Let's keep the pit between ourselves if we can," he said. "The fewer people know, the better. Otherwise we could run into problems." I agreed.

The biggest problem for me was the Commendatore. It was almost impossible to explain the significance of the pit without bringing him—as an Idea, no less—into the mix. Yes, as Menshiki said, mentioning the pit would only make things worse. (And even if I did reveal the existence of the Commendatore, who would believe me? They'd just question my sanity.)

We emerged from the trees in front of the small shrine and circled around to the back. Stepping across the clump of pampas grass, whose plumes still lay cruelly flattened by the backhoe's treads, we arrived at the pit. The first thing we did was shine our lights on the boards covering the hole and the row of stones that held them down. I checked the placement of the stones. The change was subtle, but I could tell they had been moved. Someone had come after Mariye and me, removed the stones and several boards, and then, when they left, tried to return everything to its original position. My eyes could spot that slight difference.

"Someone moved the stones," I said. "There are signs that the pit has been opened."

Menshiki glanced at me. "Do you think it was Mariye?" he asked.

"I wonder. It's not a place anyone would stumble upon, and apart from you and me, she's the only one who knows about it. So the chances are good it was Mariye."

The Commendatore knew about the pit, of course. After all, that was where he had come from. Yet in the end he was an Idea. He had no fixed shape. He wouldn't have had to move those heavy stones if he wanted to go back inside.

We removed the stones and took the boards away.

Once again, the hole was exposed. It was perfectly round and not quite six feet across, but it looked bigger now, and blacker, too. I imagined that the darkness was what created the illusion.

Menshiki and I leaned over the hole and directed our lights inside. No one was there. There was nothing at all. Just that empty cylindrical space surrounded by the same stone wall. There was one difference, however. The ladder had vanished. The collapsible metal ladder that the landscaper had considerately left behind after moving the pile of boulders. I had last seen it leaning against the wall of the pit.

"Where did the ladder go?" I wondered out loud.

It didn't take us long to find it lying on its side some distance away in a stand of pampas grass that the backhoe hadn't flattened. Someone had taken it from the hole and chucked it there. It wasn't heavy, so moving it required no great strength. We returned the ladder to the hole and leaned it back against the wall.

"I'm going down to take a look," Menshiki said. "Maybe I'll find something."

"Are you sure you'll be okay?"

"Don't worry, I've been down there before."

Menshiki descended the ladder with ease, lantern in hand.

"By the way, do you know the height of the Berlin Wall?" he asked as he descended.

"No."

"Ten feet," he said looking up at me. "It varied depending on the location, but that was the standard height. A little taller than this hole is deep. It was about a hundred miles long, too. I saw it with my own eyes. When Berlin was still divided into East and West. A pitiful sight."

When Menshiki reached the bottom, he inspected the pit in the light from his lantern. Even then, though, he kept on talking to me.

"Walls were originally erected to protect people. From external enemies, storms, and floods. Sometimes, though, they were used to keep people in. People are powerless before a sturdy, towering wall. Visually and psychologically. Some walls were constructed for that specific purpose."

Menshiki broke off at that point. Holding his lantern aloft, he examined every inch of the wall and the ground. Intently and carefully, like an archaeologist poring over the inner sanctum of an Egyptian pyramid. His lantern was stronger than my flashlight, so it illuminated a much wider area. He seemed to have found something on the floor of the pit, for he knelt down and examined it closely. I couldn't make it out from above, though. Menshiki said nothing. Whatever it was, it must have been very small. He stood up, wrapped it in his handkerchief, and deposited it in the pocket of his windbreaker. He looked up at me.

"I'm coming out," he said, raising his lantern into the air.

"Did you find something?" I asked.

Menshiki didn't answer. Carefully, he ascended the ladder. Each rung gave a dull creak under his weight. I kept close watch, my flashlight trained on him. The vantage point made me realize how well his daily routine had trained his body. Not a motion was wasted. Each muscle played its role perfectly. When he was back on the ground he gave a big stretch and then brushed the dirt from his trousers with care. Not that there was much to brush off.

"You can feel how intimidating the height of those walls is from down there. You really feel powerless. I saw something similar in Palestine a while ago. Israel erected a twenty-five-foot concrete wall there, with high-voltage wires running along the top. That wall is almost three hundred miles long. I guess the Israelis figured ten feet was too low, but that's enough to do the job."

He set the lantern down. Now the ground around our feet was illuminated.

"Come to think of it, the walls of the solitary cells in Tokyo prison measure about ten feet as well," Menshiki said. "I don't know why they made them so high. All you had to look at were those blank walls, day after day. Nothing else to lay your eyes on. No pictures or anything like that, of course. Just those damned walls. You start feeling like you've been thrown into a pit."

I listened in silence.

"I did some time in that place a while back. I haven't told you about that, have I?"

"No, you haven't." My girlfriend had told me he had spent time in prison, but of course I didn't mention that.

"I figure I should be the one to tell you. You know how gossips love to twist facts to spice up their stories. So it's better if I give it to you straight. It's not pretty, but this might be a good time to tell you. In passing, so to speak. Do you mind?"

"Not at all. Tell me."

"I'm not making excuses," he said after a moment's pause, "but I've done nothing to feel guilty about. I've tried my hand at many things in my life. Borne many risks. Still, I'm not stupid, and I am cautious by nature, so I've always been careful to avoid anything illegal. I know where to draw the line. In this case, though, I happened to take on a partner who was careless. Because of him, I suffered a great deal. That experience taught me never to join forces with anyone again. To take responsibility for myself and no one else."

"What were you charged with?"

"Insider trading and tax evasion. What they call 'economic crimes.' I was indicted and tried, but in the end they found me not guilty. All the same, the investigation was grueling, and I spent a pretty long time in prison. They found one reason after another to keep me locked up. I was in there for so long that now being surrounded by walls makes me a little nostalgic. As I said, I had done nothing to warrant punishment. My hands were clean. But the prosecutors had already concocted their scenario, and in it, I was guilty as sin. They had no desire to go back and rewrite it. That's how bureaucracies work. It's practically impossible to change something once it's been decided. Going against the current means that someone, somewhere down the line, has to take responsibility. As a result, I spent a long time in solitary."

"How long?"

"Four hundred and thirty-five days," Menshiki said, as if it were nothing. "A number I'll never forget, no matter how long I live."

It wasn't hard to imagine what spending that much time in solitary meant.

"Have you ever been confined in a small space for a long time?" Menshiki asked me.

"No," I said. My experience being locked in the back of the moving van had given me a bad case of claustrophobia. Now I couldn't even ride in an elevator. I'd fall apart if I were confined as he had been.

"I learned how to endure it," Menshiki said. "I spent the days training myself. In the process, I learned several foreign languages. Spanish, Turkish, and Chinese. They limit how many books you can keep in solitary, but those restrictions don't apply to dictionaries. In that sense, it's the ideal place to study languages. I'm blessed with good powers of concentration, so when I was focused on a language I could forget the walls. There's a bright side to everything."

Even the darkest, thickest cloud shines silver when viewed from above.

Menshiki continued. "What terrified me was the thought of earthquake and fire. Trapped like that, I could never have escaped. Imagining myself crushed or burned to death in that tiny space scared me so much sometimes I couldn't breathe. That was the one fear I couldn't overcome. It woke me up some nights."

"But you got through it."

"Of course. I'd be damned if I'd let those bastards

beat me. Or let their system grind me down. If I had signed the papers they laid in front of me, I could have walked out of my cell and returned to the world. But signing them would have meant my utter defeat. I would have admitted to crimes I hadn't committed. So I decided to treat the experience as an ordeal sent from above, an opportunity to test my strength."

"Did you think about your time in prison when you spent that hour alone down in the pit?"

"Yes. I need to return to that experience once in a while—it's my starting point, so to speak. Where the person I am today was formed. It's easy to get soft when life is comfortable."

What a peculiar guy, I thought again. How would another person react to treatment that harsh— wouldn't they try to forget it as soon as possible?

As if remembering, Menshiki reached into the pocket of his windbreaker and pulled out something wrapped in a handkerchief.

"I found this at the bottom of the pit," he said. He unfolded the handkerchief, took out a small plastic object, and handed it to me.

I examined it under my flashlight. It was a black-and-white penguin, barely half an inch long, with a tiny black strap attached to it. The kind of thing that schoolgirls like to attach to their cell phones and schoolbags. It was clean and looked quite new.

"It wasn't there the first time I went into the pit," Menshiki said. "I'm sure of that."

"So it must have been dropped by someone after-ward, when they were down there."

"I wonder. It looks like a cell phone ornament. And the strap isn't broken. So someone had to unhook it first. Doesn't that suggest it wasn't dropped—that whoever left it did so intentionally?"

"You mean they entered the pit just to leave it there?"

"Or dropped it down from above."

"Why would anyone do that?" I asked.

Menshiki shook his head. As if he couldn't understand either. "It's possible that whoever it was left it as a charm or talisman. That's just a guess, though."

"You mean Mariye?"

"Probably. After all, it's doubtful anyone else was near the pit."

"So she left it as a kind of charm?"

Menshiki shook his head again. "I don't know," he said. "It's hard to read a thirteen-year-old girl—their minds can come up with all sorts of stuff, can't they?"

I looked again at the tiny penguin in my hand. Now it struck me as a charm or amulet of some kind. An aura of innocence clung to it.

"Then who pulled out the ladder and dragged it over there? What was the reason for that?" I said.

Menshiki shook his head again. He had no idea either.

"Anyway," I said, "let's call Shoko when we get back and find out if Mariye has a penguin charm on her cell phone. She should know one way or the other."

"You hold on to the penguin for now," Menshiki said. I nodded and put it in my trouser pocket.

We replaced the boards, leaving the ladder resting against the wall of the pit. When we put the stones back I registered their exact positions in my mind. Then we headed home through the woods along the same path we had come on. I glanced at my watch—it was already past midnight. We said nothing, just shone our lights on our feet. We were both lost in thought.

As soon as we got back, Menshiki went to his Jaguar, opened the big trunk, and placed the lantern inside. Then he shut the trunk and, as if finally allowing himself to relax, leaned against it and looked up at the sky. The black sky in which nothing was visible.

"Do you mind if I come in for a few minutes?" he said. "It'd be hard for me to relax at home."

"By all means. I don't think I can sleep yet either."

Menshiki's eyes were still fixed on the sky. He seemed lost in thought.

"I can't explain why," I said, "but I can't get rid of this feeling that something bad is happening to Mariye. And that she's nearby."

"But not in the pit, right?"

"I guess not."

"What kind of bad thing?" Menshiki asked.

"That I don't know. But I feel she's in some kind of physical danger."

"And that the danger is lurking **somewhere close to here**, right?"

"Right," I said. "Near here. And it bothers me that the ladder was removed from the pit. Who took it, and why did they hide it in the grass? What does it all mean?"

Menshiki stood up and gave me another pat on the shoulder. "You're right. I don't know either. But worrying about it won't get us anywhere. Let's go inside."

47

"IT IS NOW FRIDAY, IS IT NOT?"

The moment we walked in the house I threw off my leather jacket and called Shoko. She picked up on the third ring.

"Anything new?" I asked.

"Mariye still hasn't called." I could hear her struggling to breathe normally.

"Have you contacted the police?"

"No, not yet. It still feels too early somehow. I keep thinking she'll come wandering in the door . . ."

I described the plastic penguin we had found at the bottom of the pit. Without detailing how we'd found it, I asked if Mariye carried such an object with her.

"Yes, Mariye had a penguin attached to her cell phone. It was a penguin, I'm sure . . . yes. A penguin. Without doubt. A tiny plastic figurine. She got it in a donut shop. It came free with her order, but she treasured it. As if it were a kind of protective charm."

"And she carried her phone wherever she went, correct?"

"Yes. It was turned off most of the time, but she always had it with her, yes. She didn't receive calls, but occasionally she'd call to let me know when something came up." Shoko paused for a moment. "Did you find it somewhere?"

I struggled to come up with an answer. If I told the truth, I'd have to tell her about the pit in the woods. If the police got involved, I would have to explain it to them as well—in a way they could swallow. Since the penguin was something she carried, they would comb the pit, even search the whole woods for further evidence. I would get the third degree, and Menshiki's past would be brought into it. I couldn't see how any of that would help. As Menshiki had said, it would just complicate things.

"I found it in the studio," I said. I hated to lie, but I had to. "When I was sweeping the floor. I thought that it might be Mariye's."

"Yes, it's hers. I'm sure," said the girl's aunt. "But then what should I do? Should I call the police?"

"Have you heard from your brother—I mean, Mariye's father?"

"No, I haven't been able to reach him," she said hesitantly. "I have no idea where he is. He's not some-one who follows a regular schedule—I'm never sure if he's coming home or not."

The situation sounded complicated, but now wasn't the time to worry about that. I simply told her to inform the police of Mariye's disappearance. It was after midnight, and the date had changed. It was possible that Mariye had been in some kind of accident. She said she'd call them right away.

"So Mariye still isn't answering her cell phone?"

"No, she isn't answering, though I've called her

many times. It seems to be turned off. Or the batteries are dead. One or the other."

"She left this morning for school, and she's been missing ever since. Right?"

"That's right."

"Which means she should be in her school uniform, correct?"

"Yes, she should be. A navy-blue blazer and vest, a white blouse, a knee-length plaid skirt, white socks, and black loafers. Oh, and a plastic shoulder bag with the school's name and emblem on it. She wasn't wearing a coat."

"Didn't she have another bag for her art supplies?"

"She keeps that in her locker at school. She uses it when they have art class, and then takes it to your class on Fridays. She doesn't bring it from home."

That was the outfit she always wore to my class—blue jacket, white blouse, tartan plaid skirt, plastic shoulder bag, and a white canvas bag with her paints and brushes. I could picture her perfectly.

"Was she carrying anything else?"

"No, not today. So I doubt she was going very far."

"Please call me if you hear anything," I said. "Any time of the day or night."

She said she would.

I hung up the phone.

Menshiki was standing beside me throughout this conversation. Only after I put down the phone did he shed his windbreaker. Underneath was a black V-neck sweater.

"So the penguin was Mariye's after all," Menshiki said.

"Seems so."

"In which case, it's likely that she went into the pit at some point—we don't know when—and left her treasured penguin there. That's what we have so far."

"So you think she left it there on purpose, as a protective talisman."

"Probably."

"But if that's so, who or what was it protecting?"

Menshiki shook his head. "I'm not sure. But it was clearly her lucky charm. So she must have left it behind for a reason. People don't part with things they value so easily."

"Unless it's to protect something they value more than themselves."

"For example?" Menshiki said.

Neither of us could answer that one.

We sat there in silence. Slowly but surely, the hands of the clock inched ahead. Each tick pushed the world that much further forward. Outside the window stretched a vast darkness. Nothing moved there. It seemed nothing could.

I suddenly recalled what the Commendatore had said about the missing bell. "The bell was never mine alone. It belonged to the place, to be shared by everyone. So if it disappeared there must have been a reason for it."

Belonged to the place?

"Just maybe Mariye didn't leave this penguin in the pit. Couldn't the pit be connected to some other location? Perhaps it isn't a sealed-off space but a conduit of some kind. If that's the case, it might be able to summon all sorts of things."

That is what I had been thinking, but said aloud it sounded ludicrous. The Commendatore might have understood. But not anyone from **this world**.

A deep silence settled over the room.

"So what could the bottom of the pit be connected to?" Menshiki said at last, as if addressing himself. "Remember, not so long ago I spent an hour alone down there. In the dark, without a light or a ladder. I tried to use the silence to focus my mind. To extinguish my physical existence and become pure consciousness. I figured if I could do that, I could transcend those stone walls and go wherever I liked. I used to try the same sort of thing when I was in solitary. But I couldn't find a way out of the pit. In the end, those walls allowed me no escape."

Perhaps the pit chose whom it wanted, I thought. The Commendatore had come to me when he left the pit. Chosen me as his lodgings, so to speak. Mariye too might have been chosen. But the pit hadn't chosen Menshiki—for whatever reason.

"In any case," I said, "we're agreed—we won't tell the police about the pit. At **this** stage, anyway. Still, we're clearly concealing evidence if we keep our mouths shut about finding the penguin there. If they find that out, we could be in a sticky position."

Menshiki thought for a moment. "So we'll keep our lips sealed—that's all there is to it!" he said at last. "You found it on your studio floor. We'll go with that."

"Maybe one of us should be with Shoko," I said. "She's home by herself with no idea what to do. Lost and confused. She's heard nothing from Mariye's father. Doesn't she need someone there?"

Menshiki furrowed his brow. "I'm in no position to do that," he said at last, shaking his head. "Her brother and I are total strangers, so if he came back . . ."

Menshiki lapsed into silence.

I had nothing to say either.

Menshiki sat there, lightly drumming his fingers on the arm of the sofa. Whatever he was thinking brought a slight flush to his cheeks.

"Would you mind if I stayed a little longer?" he asked a while later. "Shoko may try to get in touch with us."

"By all means, please do," I said. "I don't think I'll be going to bed any time soon. Stay as long as you like. You can sleep here too. I'll lay out some bedding for you."

Menshiki said he might take me up on my offer.

"Shall I make coffee?" I asked.

"Sounds good," Menshiki said.

I went to the kitchen, ground the beans, and started the coffee maker. When the coffee was ready, I took it out to the living room. Then Menshiki and I drank it together.

"I think I'll build a fire," I said. The room had grown markedly colder once midnight passed. It was already December. An appropriate time for the first fire of the season.

I filled the cast-iron grate in the fireplace with the small stack of firewood I had set aside in the corner of the living room. Then I inserted paper under the grate and lit a match. The wood appeared to be dry, for it caught right away. I was worried that the fireplace might back up—Masahiko had said it was set to go, but you never knew until you used it. A bird could have nested in the chimney. Fortunately, however, it worked beautifully. We moved our chairs in front of the fireplace and sat there in the warmth.

"Nothing beats a wood fire," Menshiki said.

I thought of offering him some whiskey but changed my mind. Tonight we should stay sober. Who knows, we might have to drive somewhere. So we listened to records and watched the flames dance. Menshiki selected a Beethoven violin sonata and put it on the turntable. Georg Kulenkampff on violin, with Wilhelm Kempff on piano. Perfect music for an early-winter night before a fire. It was hard to enjoy it, though, with Mariye out there shivering in the cold.

Shoko called half an hour later. Her brother had just come home and had already contacted the police. They would be there any moment to investigate. (The Akikawas were an old and wealthy family in the area, so the possibility that it was a kidnapping was making them move quickly.) There was no word from Mariye, and calling her cell phone still didn't work.

They had contacted every likely person they could think of (there weren't that many) with no luck. No one knew where Mariye had gone.

"Let's hope she's all right," I said. I asked her to let me know if there was any progress, and hung up the phone.

We sat before the fire and listened to another record. Richard Strauss's Oboe Concerto. Menshiki plucked that off the shelf as well. It was the first time I had heard it. We sat there side by side as it played, watching the fire and thinking our solitary thoughts.

At one thirty, I suddenly grew terribly sleepy. I could barely keep my eyes open. I've always been an early-to-bed, early-to-rise kind of guy, so late nights are hard on me.

"Go ahead and turn in," Menshiki said, looking directly at me. "Shoko may call again, so I'll stay up a while longer. I don't need much sleep. I can skip a night without any problem. Always been that way. So please don't worry about me. I'll keep the fire burning. I can watch it while I listen to music. Do you mind?"

Of course not, I said. I brought in another load of firewood from the shed outside the kitchen and stacked it next to the fireplace. More than enough, I thought, to last until morning.

"Well then, I'm off to bed," I said to Menshiki.

"Sleep tight," he answered. "Let's rotate. I'll probably sleep for a bit around daybreak. Could you lend me a blanket or something?"

I went and got the blanket Masahiko had used, a

down duvet, and a pillow, and arranged them on the sofa. Menshiki thanked me.

"I have whiskey if you'd like some," I added.

Menshiki gave a brusque shake of his head. "No, no alcohol for me tonight. We don't know what could happen."

"If you get hungry, please help yourself to the food in the fridge. There's not much, but there's crackers and cheese at least."

"Thanks," Menshiki said.

Leaving him there, I retired to my room. I slipped under the covers, flicked off the bedside light, and tried to go to sleep. Yet sleep didn't come. I was exhausted, but a tiny bug was whirring in my brain. This happens sometimes. I gave up, switched the light back on, and got out of bed.

"What might be the problem, my friends?" the Commendatore said. "You cannot sleep?"

I looked around the room. There he was, sitting on the windowsill, clad in the same white garment. Strange pointy-toed shoes, a miniature sword by his side. His hair neatly tied back. As always, a perfect replica of the Commendatore who was stabbed to death in Tomohiko Amada's painting.

"You're right, I can't sleep," I said.

"There is indeed a great deal happening these days," said the Commendatore. "No wonder people struggle so to drift off, to no avail."

"It's been a long time, hasn't it," I said.

"I cannot attest to that. I think I told my friends before, but 'long time' is lost on us Ideas. We cannot fathom 'It's been a long time,' or 'Sorry not to have written in so long.'"

"Still, your timing is perfect. There's something I need to ask you."

"And what, then, is the question?"

"Mariye Akikawa went missing this morning, and everyone is out looking for her. Where on earth could she have gone?"

The Commendatore cocked his head to one side and thought for a moment.

"As my friends know," he said, choosing his words carefully, "the human realm is ruled by three elements: time, space, and probability. Ideas, by contrast, must remain independent of all three. I cannot, therefore, concern myself with matters of the sort that my friends have just described."

"I can't entirely follow you—is the problem that you can't foresee the outcome?"

The Commendatore didn't answer.

"Or is it that you know, but can't tell me?"

The Commendatore narrowed his eyes in thought. "I am not evading responsibility—Ideas have our own constraints."

I stiffened my back and looked him square in the face.

"Let's get things straight. I must save Mariye Akikawa. She may be in great danger, and needing my help. She has likely wandered into a place from which she cannot escape. That's the feeling I get, anyway.

Still, I'm at a loss how to find her. And I think her disappearance is linked in some way to the pit in the woods. I can't give you a rational explanation, but I'm quite sure there's a connection. Now, you spent a very long time confined in that same hole. I have no idea what led you to be shut up there. Nevertheless, whatever may have been the case, Menshiki and I brought in heavy equipment, moved the pile of boulders, and opened the pit. We **set you free**. That's true, isn't it? Thanks to us, you are now able to move throughout time and space, with no restriction. Appear and disappear as you like. You can even watch me making love to my girlfriend. All this is as I say, isn't it?"

"Affirmative, my friends. Affirmative!"

"I'm not demanding that you tell me precisely how Mariye can be saved. I'm not asking the impossible— I can see that the world of Ideas has its own restrictions. But can't you give me a hint? After all I've done for you, don't you think you owe me at least that much?"

The Commendatore gave a deep sigh.

"An indirect, roundabout hint is enough. I'm not trying to accomplish anything earthshaking here, like putting a stop to ethnic cleansing or global warming, or saving the African elephant. All I'm trying to do is find one thirteen-year-old girl who's likely caught somewhere, in some small, dark place, and return her to this world."

The Commendatore sat there for a long time lost in thought, his arms folded. He seemed to be having second thoughts.

"Affirmative, my friends," he said, with resignation. "When you speak in such a fashion, there is not much I can do. I will give my friends but a single hint. Yet be warned—**several sacrifices** may be required. Are you willing nonetheless?"

"What sort of sacrifices?"

"I cannot speak much of that yet. But they will be inevitable. Metaphorically speaking, **there will be blood**. That is an inevitable fact. What sorts of sacrifices are involved should grow clearer as time passes. Someone may have to risk his life."

"I don't care. Give me the hint."

"Affirmative!" the Commendatore said. "It is now Friday, is it not?"

I checked my bedside clock. "Yes, it's still Friday. No, wait a minute, it's Saturday already."

"On Saturday morning, before noon, my friends will receive a phone call," the Commendatore said. "For an invitation somewhere. No matter the circumstances, my friends must not decline that invitation. Do you understand?"

I mechanically repeated what he had just said. "Someone will call me this morning and invite me somewhere. I must not decline."

"Hold those words close," said the Commendatore. "For it is the only hint I am able to share. It traverses the narrow line that divides 'public' and 'private' parlance."

With those final words, the Commendatore began to fade away. Before I knew it, his form had disappeared from the window ledge.

I turned off the bedside lamp and this time fell

asleep with relative ease. The whir of insect wings in my head was gone. A moment before I went under, I imagined Menshiki sitting in front of the fire, absorbed in his thoughts. I guessed he would keep the fire burning all night. I had no idea what those thoughts might be, of course. He was a strange man. But it went without saying that his life was bounded by time, space, and probability. Like everyone else's in this world. None of us could escape those constraints, as long as we lived. Each of us was enclosed by sturdy walls that stretched high in the air, surrounding us on all sides. Probably.

"Someone will call me this morning and invite me somewhere. I must not decline." I parroted the Commendatore's words one more time in my head. Then I slept.

48

THE SPANIARDS SIMPLY COULDN'T NAVIGATE THE ANGRY SEAS OFF THE IRISH COAST

I woke shortly after five. It was still dark outside. I slipped a cardigan over my pajamas and went to check the living room. Menshiki was sleeping on the sofa. He hadn't been asleep for long—the fire was out but the room was still warm. The stack of firewood had shrunk. He was sleeping peacefully on his side, breathing quietly with the duvet draped over his body. Not snoring at all. His manners governed even the way he slept. The room seemed to be holding its breath so as not to disturb him.

Leaving him there, I went into the kitchen and brewed coffee. I made some toast as well. Then I carried the toast and coffee into the dining area and sat there, munching and sipping, as I read my book. It was about the Spanish Armada. About the unfolding of the brutal conflict upon which Queen Elizabeth and Philip II had staked the fortunes of their nations. Why did I feel compelled to read an account of that late-sixteenth-century sea battle off the coast of Great Britain at that particular moment? All I knew was that, once I started reading, I couldn't stop. It was an old book I had found on Tomohiko Amada's shelf.

While standard accounts claim that faulty strategy

caused the Armada's decimation by the English fleet, a defeat that changed the course of history, this book argued that most of the damage was caused not by direct fire from English cannon (volleys by both sides, it appeared, missed their targets to fall harmlessly into the ocean), but by shipwreck. Accustomed to the calm waters of the Mediterranean, the Spaniards simply couldn't navigate the angry seas off the Irish coast, and thus ran vessel after vessel against the dark reefs.

As I followed the sad fate of the Spanish navy and sipped my second cup of black coffee, the sky gradually brightened in the east. It was Saturday morning.

Someone will phone you, my friends, this morning, and invite you somewhere. You must not decline.

I mentally repeated what the Commendatore had told me. Then I looked at the phone. It preserved its silence. But it would ring at some point, I was sure of that. The Commendatore was not one to lie. All I could do was be patient and wait.

I thought of Mariye. I wanted to call her aunt to find out if she was safe, but it was still too early. I should wait until seven o'clock at least. Her aunt would contact me if Mariye was found. She knew how worried I was. No word from her meant no progress. So I sat at the dining table reading about the invincible Armada and, when I tired of reading, staring at the phone. But the phone maintained its silence.

I called Shoko shortly after seven. She answered immediately. As if she had been sitting beside the phone, waiting for it to ring.

"We haven't heard from her. She's still missing,"

she said right away. She sounded as if she'd had little (or maybe no) sleep. Fatigue filled her voice.

"Are the police looking?" I asked.

"Yes, two officers came last night. We gave them photographs of Mariye, described what she was wearing . . . We explained that she isn't the kind of girl who would run away or stay out late partying. They spread the word, and by now I'm sure it's been broadcast to all the precincts. I've asked them not to make the search public yet, of course."

"But nothing so far, correct?"

"That's right, no leads up to this point. I'm sure they're working very hard on it, though."

I did my best to console her and asked her to let me know the moment something did turn up. She promised she would.

When our call ended, Menshiki had already risen and was scrubbing his face in the bathroom sink. After brushing his teeth with the toothbrush I had set aside for him, he sat across from me at the dining room table and drank his black coffee. I offered him toast, but he declined. Sleeping on the sofa had mussed his luxuriant hair a bit more than usual, but then his "usual" was super neat. The man sitting there was the same coolheaded, well-groomed guy as always.

I related my conversation with Shoko. "This is just my gut feeling," he said when I finished, "but I doubt the police will be very much help."

"Why is that?"

"Mariye is no typical teenager, and her disappearance is no typical disappearance. I don't think she was kidnapped, either. That means the usual police methods are likely to hit a wall."

I didn't offer an opinion. But I figured he was right. We had been given an equation with multiple functions but almost no solid numbers. To make any progress, we had to nail down as many numbers as possible.

"Shall we go take another look at the pit?" I asked. "Who knows—there might be some change."

"Let's go," Menshiki said.

We were operating under the tacit assumption that **nothing else was to be done.** I knew that the phone could ring, and that Shoko Akikawa or the person behind the "invitation" the Commendatore had mentioned might be on the other end. But I was pretty sure neither would call this early. Call it a vague premonition on my part.

We put on our jackets and headed out. It was a sunny day. A southwesterly wind had swept away the cloud cover of the previous night, leaving behind a sky almost unnaturally high and transparent. Indeed, when I raised my eyes to the sky, I had the feeling that up and down had been reversed, and that I was peering down into a spring of clear water. I could hear the faint drone of a long train running along a faraway track. When the air was like this, you could pick up distant sounds on the wind with great clarity. That's the sort of morning it was.

Without exchanging a word, we cut through the

woods and around the little shrine. The plank cover of the pit was exactly as we had left it the night before. Nor had the stones holding it down been moved. When we took off the boards, the ladder was still leaning against the wall, its position unchanged. No one was in the pit. This time, Menshiki didn't offer to go down to search the floor. The bright sunlight made that unnecessary—we could see that nothing had changed. The pit looked altogether different in the light of day than it had at night. There was nothing at all unsettling about it.

We replaced the lid and rearranged the stones that held it down. Then we walked back through the woods. In front of my house, Menshiki's spotless silver Jaguar sat reticently beside my dusty, unpretentious Toyota Corolla.

When he reached his car, Menshiki came to a halt. "I think I'll head home," he said. "I'll just be in your way if I presume on your hospitality any longer, and there's nothing I can do now anyway. Do you mind?"

"Of course not. Please go home and rest. I'll let you know right away if there's any change."

"Today is Saturday, isn't it?"

"That's right. It's Saturday."

Menshiki reached into his windbreaker pocket and pulled out his key. He stood there staring at it for a moment, thinking. Trying to make his mind up about something, perhaps. I waited for him to reach a conclusion.

"There's one thing I should probably tell you," he said at last.

I leaned on the door of my Corolla as he figured out what to say.

"It's actually quite personal, so I wasn't sure if it was appropriate, but then I thought perhaps I should, for courtesy's sake. I don't want to cause any needless misunderstandings . . . Anyway, the thing is, Shoko and I have become—what's the correct word?—quite intimately involved."

"You mean you and she are lovers?" I asked, cutting to the chase.

"Exactly," Menshiki replied after a moment's pause. I thought I saw a faint blush rise to his cheeks. "You may think it quite hasty."

"No, the speed isn't the problem."

"That's correct," Menshiki acknowledged. "The speed is not the problem."

"The problem is—" I began.

"My motives, you were going to say. Am I correct?"

I didn't respond. Yet it was clear that my silence meant yes.

"You should know," he said, "that none of this was planned from the beginning. It was an entirely natural development. In fact, it happened without me being conscious of it. You may find that hard to believe, of course."

I sighed. Then I spoke frankly. "All I know is that if you started with that plan in mind, it would have been pretty easy to carry out. I'm not being sarcastic, either."

"You're probably right," Menshiki said. "I recognize that. Easy, or at least not all that difficult. **Perhaps.** But that's not how it was."

"So are you saying that you met Shoko Akikawa for the first time and fell in love right off the bat, or something like that?"

Menshiki pursed his lips as if embarrassed. "Fell in love? No, I can't make that claim. To be honest, the last time I fell in love—I think that's probably what it was—was ages ago. I can't even remember what it was like. But I can say with confidence that I find myself powerfully attracted to Shoko, as a man is attracted to a woman."

"Leaving Mariye out of the picture?"

"That's hard to know. Mariye was the reason for our first meeting, after all. But had Mariye never existed, I think I still would have been attracted to her aunt."

I wondered about that. Would a man whose mind was as complicated as Menshiki's be so "powerfully attracted" to a woman as simple and easygoing as Shoko Akikawa? Still, I was in no position to judge. The workings of the human heart are impossible to predict. Especially when sex is involved.

"I understand," I said. "At any rate, thank you for speaking so honestly. Honesty is always best, I think."

"I hope you're right."

"To tell you the truth, Mariye already knew. That you and Shoko had begun that sort of relationship. In fact, she came to talk to me about it. A few days ago."

The news seemed to catch Menshiki by surprise.

"She's a perceptive child," he said. "We tried our best not to let her find out."

"Yes, a **very** perceptive child. But she didn't find out from you. It was the things her aunt said and did that tipped her off."

Shoko was a well-brought-up, intelligent woman, but while she could conceal her feelings to a degree, her mask was bound to slip sooner or later. Menshiki was aware of that, no question.

"If that's the case . . . do you think Mariye's disappearance is connected to her discovery of our relationship?"

I shook my head. "I can't tell for sure. But I can tell you that you and Shoko ought to talk through everything together. She's beside herself with worry, and she's confused. She must be in need of your encouragement and support. Urgently in need."

"You're right. I'll contact her the minute I get home."

Menshiki wasn't finished. Something else appeared to be on his mind.

He sighed. "To tell the truth, I don't think I've fallen in love. I'm not cut out for that. Haven't been from the beginning. I don't know why I feel as I do. Would I have been so attracted to Shoko if not for Mariye? The connection between the two of them isn't clear to me at all."

I said nothing.

"But I swear I didn't plan any of it in advance. Can you believe me?"

"Mr. Menshiki," I said. "I can't explain why, but I think you're an honest man at heart."

"Thank you," he said. The corners of his mouth edged upward. It was a somewhat uncomfortable smile, but not an altogether unhappy one.

"Can I go on being honest?" he said.

"Of course."

"Sometimes I think I'm empty," he confessed. The smile still lingered on his lips.

"Empty?"

"Hollow inside. I know it sounds arrogant, but I've always operated on the assumption that I was a lot brighter and more capable than other people. More perceptive and discerning, with greater powers of judgment. Physically stronger, too. I figured I could succeed at whatever I turned my mind to. And I did. Put my hands on whatever I wanted to possess. Being locked up in Tokyo prison was a clear setback, of course, but I considered that an exception to the rule. When I was young, I saw no limits to what I could achieve. I thought I could attain a state close to perfection. Climb and climb until I reached a height where I could gaze down on everyone else. But when I passed fifty, I looked at myself in the mirror and discovered nothing but emptiness. A zero. What T. S. Eliot called a 'straw man.'"

I couldn't think of anything to say.

"My whole life may have been a mistake up till now," Menshiki went on. "I feel that way sometimes. That I took a wrong turn somewhere. That nothing

I've done has any real meaning. That's why I told you I often find myself envying you."

"Envying what, for example?"

"You have the strength to wish for what you cannot have. While I have only wished for those things I can possess."

I assumed he was talking about Mariye. She was the one thing that had evaded his grasp. Yet there wasn't much I could say about that.

Menshiki slowly got into his car. Then he rolled down the window, said goodbye, and drove off. When his car was out of sight I went back into the house. It was just past eight.

The telephone rang at shortly after ten. The call was from Masahiko.

"I know it's sudden," he said, "but I'm on my way to Izu to see my father. Would you like to come along? You mentioned the other day that you'd like to meet him."

Someone will phone my friends tomorrow morning and invite you somewhere. You must not decline.

"That's great. I'd love to go."

"I just got on the Tokyo-Nagoya Expressway. I'm at the Kohoku parking area now. I think it'll take me about an hour to reach you. I'll pick you up and we can drive to Izu Kogen."

"Did something happen to your father?"

"Yeah, the nursing home called. Seems he's taken

a turn for the worse. So I'm going to check on him. I'm more or less free today anyway."

"Are you sure it's all right if I go along? Aren't times like this for family only?"

"Don't worry. It's perfectly okay. No other relatives will be there, so the more the merrier." He hung up.

I put down the phone and scanned the room. Was the Commendatore around? But he was nowhere to be seen. Prophecy dispensed, he had disappeared. Probably to a realm where the dictates of time, space, and probability did not apply. Nevertheless, there had been a morning phone call, and I had been invited somewhere. So far, at least, that prophecy had been accurate. It bothered me to leave with Mariye still unaccounted for, but I couldn't do much about that. The Commendatore had instructed me, "No matter the circumstances, my friends must not decline that invitation." I could leave Shoko in Menshiki's hands. After all, she was his responsibility, to some extent.

I sat back in the easy chair in the living room and resumed the story of the invincible Armada as I waited for Masahiko. Almost all the Spanish soldiers and seamen who had managed to escape their shipwrecked vessels and crawl onto the shores of Ireland more dead than alive were murdered by those who lived along the coast. The poverty-stricken locals had slaughtered them for their possessions. It had been the Spaniards' hope that, as fellow Catholics, the Irish might show them mercy, but they were out of luck. Religious solidarity was no match for the fear of starvation. Sadly, the Spanish ship carrying the war chest holding the gold and silver intended to buy off England's powerful nobility sank as well. No one knew where all that wealth had gone.

It was shortly before eleven in the morning when Masahiko's old black Volvo pulled up in front of my house. I was still thinking about all those gold coins lying at the bottom of the sea as I threw on my leather jacket and headed out the door.

The route Masahiko chose took us from the Hakone Turnpike to the Izu Skyline highway and then down from the Amagi highlands to Izu. He explained that this way would be faster—that the weekend meant the coastal roads would be jammed—but nevertheless our route was crowded with people out on excursions. The leaf-viewing season had not yet ended, and many of those on the road were weekenders unfamiliar with mountain driving, so the trip took a lot longer than expected.

"Is your father really in bad shape?" I asked.

"He's not long for this world, that's for sure," Masahiko said lightly. "A matter of days, to be more precise. Age has whittled him down to almost nothing. He has trouble eating, and pneumonia is a constant threat. But the patient's orders are that under no circumstances are IV lines and feeding tubes to be used. In other words, he demands that he be allowed to go quietly once he can no longer eat. He arranged this with his lawyer when he was still mentally competent, signed the forms and everything. So there will be no interventions. That means he could go at any time."

"So I guess you have to be prepared for the worst."

"That's about right."

"It must be rough."

"Hey, it's a big deal when someone dies. I can hardly complain."

The old Volvo was equipped with a tape deck, and the glove compartment was stuffed with cassettes. Masahiko stuck his hand in, grabbed one, and inserted it without checking to see what it was. It turned out to be a collection of hits from the 1980s. Duran Duran, Huey Lewis, and so on. When ABC's "The Look of Love" came on, I turned to him.

"Sure feels like time has stopped in this car," I said.

"I don't like CDs. They're too shiny—they'd scare crows away if I hung them outside my house, but they're hardly something to listen to music on. The sound is tinny and the mixing is unnatural. Having no A and B sides is a drag too. That's why I still drive this car—so I can listen to my cassettes. Newer models don't have tape decks, right? Everyone thinks I'm nuts. But I'm stuck. I have a huge collection of songs I recorded off the radio and I don't want them to go to waste."

"Man, I never thought I'd hear ABC's 'Look of Love' again in this lifetime."

"Don't you think it's amazing?" Masahiko said, casting me a quizzical glance.

We went on talking about the music of the eighties, songs we'd heard on the radio, as we tooled through the mountains of Hakone. The blue slopes of Mt. Fuji loomed around each curve.

"You and your dad are quite a pair," I said. "The father listens only to records, and the son is stuck on cassettes."

"You should talk. You're just as behind the times. Worse than us, maybe. I mean, you don't even have a cell phone. And you hardly ever go online, right? I've always got my cell phone with me, and anything I need to know, I Google. I design stuff on my Mac at work. Socially, I'm light-years ahead of you."

Bertie Higgins's rendition of "Key Largo" came on. An interesting selection indeed for a guy claiming to be socially evolved.

"Are you seeing anyone these days?" I asked, changing the subject.

"You mean, like a woman?"

"Yeah."

Masahiko gave a small shrug. "I can't say it's going all that well. As usual. And things have gotten even rockier since I made this weird breakthrough."

"What kind of breakthrough?"

"That the right and left sides of a woman's face don't match up. Did you know that?"

"People aren't perfectly symmetrical," I said. "Whether it's breasts or balls, the size and shape of the two sides are always going to be different. Every artist knows that much. That lack of symmetry is one of the things that makes the human form so interesting."

Masahiko shook his head several times without taking his eyes off the road. "Of course I know that.

But what I'm saying is a little different. I'm talking about personality, not form."

I waited for him to go on.

"About two months ago, I took a photo of this woman I was seeing with a digital camera. A close-up of her face from the front. I put it on the big office computer. Then I managed to divide the screen down the middle and look at the two halves of her face separately. Removing the right half to look at the left, and vice versa . . . You get the idea, right?"

"Yeah, I get it."

"That's when I realized that her left side and her right side looked like two separate people. Like Two-Face, the bad guy in **Batman**."

"I missed that one."

"You should watch it sometime. It's pretty good. Anyway, it freaked me out a bit. I should have left things alone at that point, but I went ahead and tried reversing each side to make a composite face. That way, I could double the right side to create a complete face, and do the same with the left side. Computers make that sort of stuff easy. What I was left with was images of what could only be seen as two women with two totally distinct personalities. It shocked me. I mean, there were actually two women inside every woman I met. Have you ever looked at women that way?"

"Nope," I said.

"I tested my idea on several other women. Took head shots and created left- and right-side composites on the computer. That made it even clearer. That women literally have two faces. Once I knew that, I found I couldn't figure out women at all. For example, if I was with a woman and we were having sex, I didn't know if it was her right side or her left that I was embracing. If it was the right side, then where had the left side gone—what was it doing, and what was it thinking?—and if it was the left side, then what was the right side thinking? Once I reached that point, things got really messy. Get what I'm saying?"

"Not completely, but I can see that it must be messy."

"You bet. Really messy."

"Did you try it on men's faces?"

"Yeah, I did. But it didn't work the same way. The only drastic changes were with women's faces."

"Maybe you should go see a psychologist or therapist about this," I said.

Masahiko sighed. "You know, I've always believed myself to be a totally normal sort of guy."

"That could be a dangerous belief."

"To believe that I'm normal?"

"I think it was F. Scott Fitzgerald who wrote that one should never trust people who claim they're normal. It's in one of his novels."

Masahiko thought about that for a moment. "So even a commonplace man is irreplaceable?"

"I guess that's another way of putting it."

Masahiko thought for a while, his hands on the steering wheel.

"At any rate," he said, "could you try it just once and see?"

"You know I've been a portrait painter for a long time. So I think I'm more skilled than most when it comes to examining faces. You could even say I'm an expert at it. But I've never thought that the difference between the right and left sides reflected a disparity in personality. Not once."

"But almost all the subjects you painted were men, correct?"

Masahiko had a point. I'd never been commissioned to paint a woman. For whatever reason, my portraits were all of men. The only exception was Mariye Akikawa, and she was more child than woman. And I hadn't finished her portrait, either.

"Men and women are different," Masahiko insisted. "Completely."

"So then let me ask you," I said. "Are you claiming this personality difference on the right and left sides applies to almost all women?"

"Yeah, that's my conclusion."

"So then do you find yourself attracted to one side or the other? Or do you find you like both sides **less**?"

Masahiko pondered this question for a moment. "No," he said at last. "That's not how it works. It's not that I prefer one side to the other. That I find one side cheerful and the other gloomy, or that one side is prettier. The problem is at another level: it's simply that the two sides are **different**. It's that **sheer fact** that shakes me up. Sometimes it scares me."

"It sounds to me like a kind of obsessive-compulsive disorder," I said.

"It sounds like that to me too," Masahiko said. "Just listening to myself. But it's **the truth**. I ask you, just check it out for yourself."

I promised him I would. But I had no intention of following through. That could only add to my troubles. My life was messy enough as it was.

Then we talked about Tomohiko Amada. About Tomohiko Amada in Vienna.

"My father said he heard Richard Strauss conduct one of Beethoven's symphonies," Masahiko said. "With the Vienna Philharmonic, of course. He said it was out of this world. That's one of the few stories he told me about his days in Vienna."

"What else did he say about his time there?"

"Nothing at all remarkable. He mentioned the food, the drink, the music. Stuff like that. He really loved music, you know. That was all he talked about. He never mentioned painting or politics or things of that sort. Or women either."

Masahiko paused before continuing.

"Maybe someone should write my father's biography. It could be a really interesting book. But the reality is, no one will ever take a shot at it. Why? Because there's hardly any personal information out there. My father had no friends, his family members were virtual strangers—he just spent his time shut away by himself on a mountain, painting. His only acquaintances, if you could call them that, were a handful of art dealers. He hardly spoke to anyone. He wrote no letters. So if someone did try to write his biography, they'd have almost nothing to work with. It's not just that there are a few holes in his life story, it's that his life is riddled with them. Think of Swiss cheese with more holes than cheese."

"All he's leaving behind is his work."

"You're right, his paintings and almost nothing else. That's probably the way he wanted it."

"And you. You're a part of his legacy too," I said.

"Me?" Masahiko looked at me in surprise. Then he turned back to the road. "You're right there. If I stop to think of it, I'm part of his legacy too. Not a particularly shining part, though."

"But irreplaceable."

"True enough. Run of the mill, but nonetheless irreplaceable," Masahiko said. "You know what I think sometimes? That you should have been Tomohiko Amada's son. If that were the case, things would have gone so much more smoothly."

"Give me a break!" I said with a laugh. "No one was fit for that role!"

"Maybe not," Masahiko said. "But you might have been his spiritual successor, if you can call it that. You're a lot more qualified in that area than I am— that's my gut feeling anyway."

Killing Commendatore popped into my mind. Was that painting something I had "inherited" from

Tomohiko Amada? Had he led me to that attic room to discover it? Was he using it to demand something of me?

Deborah Harry was singing "French Kissin' in the USA" on the car stereo. It was hard to think of less appropriate background music for our conversation.

"I guess it must have been tough having a father like Tomohiko Amada," I said bluntly.

"I reached a point years ago where I had to make a clean break and move on with my life," Masahiko said. "Once I had done that, it wasn't as hard on me as everyone thought. I make a living from art as well, but the scale of my father's talent and the scale of mine are so dramatically different. When the gap is that huge, it stops being a problem. My father's fame as an artist doesn't hurt anymore. What hurts is the kind of human being he was, the fact that until the very end, he never opened up to me, his own son. That he didn't pass a single bit of information about himself on to me."

"So he showed nothing of his inner world, even to you?"

"Not a glimpse. His attitude was: 'I gave you half my DNA, so what more do you want? The rest is up to you.' But a relationship is based on more than DNA. Right? I never asked him to act as my guide through life. I didn't demand that. But it still should have been possible to have something like a father-son conversation once in a while. He could have filled me in just a little on what he had experienced, what he thought. Even bits and pieces would have helped."

I listened quietly to what he had to say.

When we stopped at a long red light, Masahiko took off his dark Ray-Ban sunglasses and wiped them with his handkerchief.

"My guess," he said, turning in my direction, "is that my father is hiding heavy secrets of some kind, personal secrets he has borne entirely alone and intends to take with him when he drifts from this world. It's like there's this metal safe in his heart where he stored them. He locked them all in there, and then he either threw the key away or hid it somewhere. Now he can't remember where he stashed it."

In that case, the unsolved riddle of what had taken place in Vienna in 1938 would be buried in darkness. Then again, perhaps **Killing Commendatore** itself was the hidden key. The idea struck me all of a sudden. Were that true, it would explain why, at the end of his life, Tomohiko's living spirit had returned to his mountaintop to confirm the painting's existence.

I swiveled around to look in the backseat. Just maybe, the Commendatore was sitting there. But the seat was empty.

"Is something wrong?" Masahiko said, glancing behind him.

"No, nothing at all," I said.

When the light turned green, he stepped on the accelerator.

49

FILLED WITH JUST
AS MANY DEATHS

On our way to check in on his father, we stopped
at a roadside restaurant so that Masahiko could
use the toilet. We were shown to a table next to
the window, where we ordered coffee. As it was already noon, I ordered a roast beef sandwich, too. Masahiko asked for the same thing. Then he headed for
the men's room. While he was gone I stared blankly
out the window. The parking lot was packed with
cars. Most had come with families. The number of
minivans really stood out. All minivans look identical
to me. Like cans of tasteless biscuits. There was an observation deck at the end of the lot where people were
using small digital cameras and cell phones to snap
photos of Mt. Fuji, which towered right in front of
them. It's dumb, I know, but I've never really gotten
comfortable with phones taking pictures. I'm even
less cool with cameras making phone calls.

While I was sitting there looking at nothing in
particular, a white Subaru Forester turned off the
road and into the lot. I don't know much about cars
(and the Subaru Forester is hardly distinctive), but I
could tell at a glance that it was the model the man
with the white Subaru Forester had been driving. It

trolled up and down the rows before finally nosing into an empty space. Sure enough, the logo on the spare-tire cover read SUBARU FORESTER. It appeared to be the same model as the car I had seen in the little seaside town in Miyagi Prefecture. I couldn't make out the license plate, but the more I looked, the more I was sure it was the same car I had seen that spring. Not just the same model. I mean the **exact same car.**

My visual memory is sharper than most—and more durable. As a result, I could tell that the stains and other markings were strikingly similar to those of **that car** as I remembered it. I could hardly breathe. But just when I was straining to identify the driver as he stepped out, a large tour bus pulled into the lot and blocked my view. Unable to move past the jam of cars, it just sat there. I jumped up and hurried out of the restaurant. I rushed around the bus, which had stopped dead in its tracks, and approached the spot where the white Subaru Forester was parked. But the car was empty. Its driver had gone off somewhere. He might be in the restaurant, or perhaps was taking pictures on the observation deck. I scanned the area but couldn't spot the man with the white Subaru Forester anywhere. Of course, the driver could have been someone else.

I checked the license plate. Sure enough, it read "Miyagi Prefecture." On the rear bumper was a sticker with a picture of a marlin on it. It was the same car, no question. **That man had come here.** A chill ran down my spine. I decided to search for him. I wanted to see his face one more time. To figure out why I couldn't finish his portrait. Perhaps I had overlooked something basic about him. First, though, I memorized the license plate number. It might prove useful. Then again, it might be of no use at all.

I walked around the parking lot, keeping an eye out for someone who resembled him. I checked the observation deck. But the man with the white Subaru Forester was nowhere to be seen. A man of middle age, deeply tanned, with a salt-and-pepper crew cut. On the tall side. When last seen, wearing a battered black leather jacket and a Yonex golf cap. I had whipped off a quick sketch on my memo pad and shown it to the young woman sitting across from me. "You're really good at drawing!" she had enthused.

Once I was sure no one matching his description was outside, I looked inside the restaurant. I circled the place, but he was nowhere to be seen. The seats were almost full. Masahiko was back at our table, drinking his coffee. The sandwiches hadn't shown up yet.

"Where'd you disappear to?" he asked me.

"I thought I saw someone I knew. So I went outside to check."

"Did you find them?"

"No. Probably a case of mistaken identity," I said.

After that, I kept a close eye on the white Subaru Forester outside. Yet if the man in question did come back, what should I do? Go out and talk to him? Tell him I was sure I had bumped into him twice this past spring in a small coastal town in Miyagi? **Is that so? Well, I don't remember you,** he'd probably shoot back.

Well then, why are you following me? I would ask. **What are you talking about?** he would reply. **Why the hell would I be tailing someone I don't even know?** End of conversation.

In any event, the driver of the white Subaru Forester never went back to his car. It just sat there in the lot, short and squat, silently awaiting its owner's return. We finished our sandwiches and coffee, but he still hadn't shown.

"We'd better be going," Masahiko said, glancing at his watch. "We don't have a whole lot of time." He picked up his Ray-Bans from the table.

We stood, paid the bill, and walked out. Then we climbed into the Volvo and drove out of the jammed parking lot. I wanted to wait for the man with the white Subaru Forester to return, but meeting Masahiko's father had to be my top priority. The Commendatore had driven home that message with absolute clarity: **My friends will be invited somewhere. You must not decline that invitation.**

I was left with the fact that the man with the white Subaru Forester had shown up once again. He had known where to find me and had made it clear that **he was there.** His intent was obvious. His appearance could be no accident. Nor, of course, was the tour bus that had hidden him from view.

To reach the facility where Tomohiko Amada was being cared for, we had to leave the Izu Skyline and drive down a long, winding road. The area had recently been turned into a summer retreat for city folk: we passed stylish coffee shops, fancy inns built to resemble log cabins, stands selling local produce, and small museums aimed at passing tourists. Each time we went around a curve, I gripped the door handle and thought of the man with the white Subaru Forester. Something was blocking me from finishing his portrait. A key element, something that made him who he was, had escaped me. A missing piece of the puzzle, as it were. This was new for me. I always gathered together everything I knew I would need before I started a portrait. In the case of the man with the white Subaru Forester, though, I had not been able to do that. Probably the man himself was standing in my way. He didn't like having his portrait painted, for whatever reason. In fact, he seemed dead set against it.

At a certain point, the Volvo turned off the road and passed through a big, open steel gate. The gate was marked only by a very small sign. Someone could easily drive right by if they weren't paying attention. It appeared to be an institution that didn't feel compelled to announce its presence to the world. Masahiko stopped at the small guardhouse beside the gate and gave his name and the name of the resident he was visiting to the uniformed security guard on duty. The guard made a phone call to confirm the resident's identity. Once through the gate, we entered a dense grove of trees. Most were tall evergreens, which cast a chilly shadow. We drove up the freshly paved road to the circle set atop the rise, where cars could be parked. A bed of ornamental cabbages surrounding a circle of bright red flowers sat at the center. The flowers were being tended with care.

Masahiko drove to the far end of the circle and parked his car in one of the visitor spots. Two other cars had preceded us. A white Honda minivan and a dark blue Audi sedan. Both were sparkling new—between them his Volvo looked like an aged workhorse. Masahiko, however, didn't seem to mind a bit (his Bananarama cassette tape took clear precedence). Below, the Pacific Ocean gleamed dully in the early-winter sun. A few midsized fishing vessels were plying its waters. A small humped island sat just offshore, and beyond it the Manazuru Peninsula. The hands of my watch pointed to 1:45.

We got out of the car and walked toward the entrance. The building looked quite new. It was a clean and stylish concrete structure, yet nothing was distinctive about it. Perhaps the architect who designed it lacked imaginative oomph. Or else the client, considering its function, had demanded that the building be as simple and conservative as possible. It was three stories high, and quite square—a structure made up entirely of straight lines. The blueprints could have been drawn up with a single ruler. The ground floor was mainly glass, to create as bright an impression as possible. Jutting out from the front of the building was a large wooden balcony with about a dozen deck chairs, but it was winter, so no one would be sunbathing, however bright and pleasant the day. The cafeteria had glass walls that soared from floor to ceiling. I could see five or six people inside, all well along

in years, from the look of them. Two were in wheel-
chairs. I couldn't tell what they were doing. Perhaps
watching television on the big screen on the wall.
They weren't playing leapfrog, that's for sure.

Masahiko walked through the entranceway and up
to a young woman stationed at the front desk. She
was round-cheeked and friendly, with beautiful long
black hair. A name tag was affixed to her dark blue
blazer. She seemed to know Masahiko by sight, for
the two of them chatted for a few minutes. I stood
a short distance away and waited for them to finish. A large vase sat in the entranceway, overflowing
with a lavish assortment of fresh flowers, arranged,
I assumed, by an ikebana expert. At a certain point,
Masahiko signed the guest register with a pen and,
consulting his watch, added the precise time. He left
the desk and walked over to me, hands in pockets.

"My father's condition seems to have stabilized,"
he said. "Apparently, he was coughing all morning
and very short of breath, so they worried that he was
developing pneumonia. But they got his cough under
control a short while ago, and now he's fast asleep."

"Is it really okay for me to go in with you?"

"Of course," Masahiko said. "You came all this
way to see him, didn't you?"

He and I took the elevator to the third floor. The
corridor there was also simple and conservative. Decoration kept to a bare minimum. The one exception,
as if by way of concession, was a row of oil paintings hanging on the long, white wall. All were coastal

landscapes. They seemed to be a series by a single artist, who had painted spots along the same stretch of coast from a number of angles. They weren't especially well done, but at least the artist had been generous in his use of paint, and I could applaud the way his paintings disrupted the strict minimalism of the architecture. The rubber soles of my shoes squeaked ostentatiously on the smooth linoleum floor. A little old white-haired lady in a wheelchair pushed by a male attendant passed us in the corridor. She stared straight ahead, her gaze so fixed and rigid it did not even flicker when we went by. As if she was determined not to lose sight of a crucial sign suspended in the air before her.

Tomohiko Amada was in a big room at the very end of the corridor. The name card on the door had been left blank. Most likely to protect his privacy. He was, after all, famous. The room was the size of a small hotel suite, with a basic set of living room furniture in addition to the bed. A folded wheelchair rested against the bed's foot. A large southeast-facing window looked out over the Pacific Ocean. It was a magnificent, unobstructed view. A hotel room with a view like that would cost an arm and a leg. No paintings hung on the walls. Just a mirror and a round clock. A medium-sized vase filled with purple cut flowers sat on the table. There was no odor at all. Not of a sick old person, nor of medicine, nor of flowers, nor of sun-drenched curtains. Nothing. That's what surprised me most—the room's utter lack of smell. It was so striking I thought something had happened to my nose. How could odor be erased so completely?

Tomohiko Amada was fast asleep near the window, oblivious to the view outside. He slept on his back facing the ceiling, his eyes tightly shut. Bushy white eyebrows overhung his aged eyelids like a natural canopy. Deep wrinkles furrowed his forehead. His quilt was pulled up to his neck—I couldn't tell if he was breathing or not. If he was, they were extremely shallow breaths.

I knew right away that this was the mysterious old man who had visited my studio. I had seen him for only a moment or two in the shifting moonlight, but the shape of his head and his wild, white hair left no doubt: it had been Tomohiko Amada. The fact didn't surprise me in the least. It had been clear all along.

"He's dead to the world," Masahiko said to me. "We'll just have to wait for him to wake up. If he wakes up, that is."

"All the same, it's a blessing that he's sleeping peacefully," I said. I glanced at the clock on the wall. It said five minutes before two. I suddenly thought of Menshiki. Had he called Shoko Akikawa? Had there been any developments in Mariye's case? Right now, however, I had to focus on Tomohiko Amada.

Masahiko and I sat across from each other on matching chairs, sipping the canned coffee we had bought from the vending machine in the corridor, while we waited for Tomohiko Amada to wake up. In the meantime, Masahiko told me a few things about

Yuzu. That her pregnancy was progressing nicely. That her due date was sometime in the first half of January. That her handsome boyfriend was thrilled about becoming a father.

"The only problem—from his perspective, anyway—is that she seems to have no intention of marrying him," Masahiko said.

"Huh?" I couldn't believe what I had just heard. "You mean she plans to be a single mom?"

"Yuzu intends to have the baby. But she doesn't want to marry the father, or live with him, or share custody of the child . . . that seems to be the story. He can't figure out what's going on. He assumed they'd be properly married once the divorce was final, but she completely rejected his proposal."

I thought about that for a moment. The more I thought, though, the more confused I got.

"I can't wrap my head around it," I said. "Yuzu always said she didn't want kids. Whenever I said I thought the time was right, she said it was still too early. So why does she want a child so badly now?"

"Maybe she didn't plan on a baby, but changed her mind once she got pregnant. Women can do that, you know."

"Still, it'll be tough to look after the child all by herself. Hard to hang on to her job, for one thing. So why not marry him? He is the child's father, right?"

"Yeah, he doesn't understand either. He thought they were getting along just great. And he was happy a child was coming. That's why he's so confused. He asked me about it, but I'm stumped too."

"Have you talked to Yuzu directly?" I inquired.

Masahiko frowned. "To tell you the truth, I'm trying hard not to get too sucked in. I like Yuzu, but he's my colleague at work. And of course you and I have been friends for ages. I'm in a tough spot. The more I become involved, the less I know what to do."

I didn't say anything.

"I always enjoyed seeing the two of you together— you seemed like such a happy couple," Masahiko said, looking perplexed.

"You said that before."

"Yeah, maybe I did," Masahiko said. "But it's the truth."

After that, we sat there without speaking, looking at the clock on the wall, or the ocean outside the window. Tomohiko Amada lay on his back in a deep sleep, not moving a muscle. He was so still, in fact, that I worried whether he was alive or not. No one else seemed concerned, though, so I figured his stillness was normal.

Watching him lying there, I tried to imagine how he might have looked as a young exchange student in Vienna. But of course I couldn't. This was an old man with furrowed skin and white hair, experiencing the slow but steady annihilation of his physical existence. All of us are, without exception, born to die, and now he was face-to-face with that final stage.

"Aren't you planning to contact Yuzu?" Masahiko asked me.

"Not at present, no," I said, shaking my head.

"I think it might be a good idea for you two to get

together and talk things over. Have a good heart-to-heart, so to speak."

"Our formal divorce proceedings were handled through our lawyers. That's the way Yuzu wanted it. Now she's about to give birth to another man's child. Whether she wants to marry him or not is her problem. I'm in no position to say anything about it. So what exactly are the **things** we should talk over?"

"Don't you want to know what's going on?"

I shook my head no. "I don't want to know any more than I have to. It's not like what took place didn't hurt."

"Of course," Masahiko said.

All the same, to be honest there were times I couldn't tell if I had been hurt or not. Did I really have the right? I wasn't clear enough about things to know. Of course, people can't help feeling hurt in certain situations, whether they have the right to or not.

"The guy is a colleague of mine," Masahiko said after a pause. "He's a serious guy, hard worker, good personality."

"Yeah, and handsome, too."

"True. Women love him. Only natural, I guess. Sure wish they flocked to me like that. But he has this tendency that always left us all shaking our heads."

I waited for him to go on.

"You see, we've never been able to figure out why he's chosen the women he has. I mean, he always has lots of women to pick from, and yet he comes up with these losers. I'm not talking about Yuzu, of course. She's probably the first good choice he's made. But the women before her were real disasters. I still can't figure it out."

He shook his head, remembering those women.

"He almost got married a few years back. They'd printed the invitations, reserved the venue for the ceremony, and were heading off to Fiji or someplace like that for their honeymoon. He'd gotten leave from work, bought the airplane tickets. The bride-to-be wasn't at all attractive. When he introduced us, I remember being shocked by how homely she was. Of course, you can't judge a book by its cover, but from what I could see, her personality was nothing special, either. Yet for some reason he was head over heels in love. Anyway, they seemed poorly matched. Everyone who knew them felt that way, though no one said so. Then, just before the wedding, she skipped out. In other words, it was **the woman** who split. I couldn't tell if that was good or bad for him, but all the same it blew my mind."

"Was there some kind of reason?"

"Not that I know of. I felt sorry for the guy, so I never asked. But I don't think he ever understood why she did what she did. I mean she just **ran**. Couldn't stand the thought of marrying him. Something must have bothered her."

"So what's the point of your story?"

"The point is," Masahiko said, "it still may be possible for you and Yuzu to get back together. Assuming that's what you want, of course."

"But she's about to have another man's child."

"Yeah, I can see that might be a problem."

We fell silent again.

Tomohiko Amada woke up shortly before three. His body twitched at first. Then he took a deep breath—I could see the quilt over his chest rise and fall. Masahiko stood and went to his father's bedside. He looked down on his face. The old man's eyes slowly opened. His bushy white eyebrows quivered in the air.

Masahiko took a slender glass funnel cup from the bedside table and moistened his father's lips. He mopped the corners of his mouth with a piece of what looked like gauze. His father wanted more, so he repeated the process several times. He seemed comfortable with the job—it appeared that he had done it many times before. The old man's Adam's apple bobbed up and down with each swallow. Only when I saw that movement was I sure he was still alive.

"Father," Masahiko said, pointing at me. "This is the guy who moved into the Odawara house. He's a painter who's working in your studio. He's a friend of mine from college. He's not too bright, and his beautiful wife ran out on him, but he's still a great artist."

It wasn't clear how much Masahiko's father comprehended. But he slowly turned his head in my direction as if following his son's finger. His face was blank. He seemed to be looking at something, but that **something** carried no particular meaning for him. Nevertheless, I thought I could detect a surprisingly clear and lucid light deep within those bleary eyes. That light seemed to be biding its time, waiting for that which might hold real significance. At least that was my impression.

"I doubt he understands a word I say," Masahiko said. "But his doctor instructed us to talk to him in a free and natural way, as if he was able to follow. No one knows how much he's picking up anyway. So I talk to him normally. That's easier for me too. Now you say something. The way you usually talk."

"It's nice to meet you, Mr. Amada," I said. I told him my name. "Your son has been kind enough to let me live in your home in Odawara."

Tomohiko Amada was looking at me, but his expression hadn't changed. Masahiko gestured: **Just keep talking—anything is okay.**

"I'm an oil painter," I went on. "I specialized in portraits for a long time, but I gave that up and now I paint my own stuff. I still accept occasional commissions for portraits, though. The human face fascinates me, I guess. Masahiko and I have been friends since art school."

Tomohiko Amada's eyes were still pointed in my direction. They were coated by a thin membrane, a kind of layered lace curtain hanging between life and death. What sat behind the curtain would fade from view as the layers increased, until finally the last, heavy curtain would fall.

"I love your house," I said. "My work is steadily progressing. I hope you don't mind, but I've been listening to your records. Masahiko told me that was all right. You have a great collection. I enjoy the operas especially. Oh yes, and recently I went up and looked in the attic."

I thought I saw a sparkle in his eyes when I said the word "attic." It was just a quick flash—no one would have noticed it unless they were paying attention. But I was keeping close watch. Thus I didn't miss it. Clearly, "attic" had a charge that caused some part of his memory to kick in.

"A horned owl has moved into the attic," I went on. "I kept hearing these rustling sounds at night. I thought it was a rat, so I went up to check during the day. And there the owl was, sitting under the beams. It's a beautiful bird. The screen on the air vent has a hole, so it can go in and out at will. The attic makes a perfect daytime hideout for a horned owl, don't you think?"

The eyes were still fixed on me. As if waiting to hear more.

"Horned owls don't cause any damage," Masahiko put in. "In fact, they're said to bring good luck."

"I love the bird," I added. "And the attic is a fascinating place too."

Tomohiko Amada stared at me from the bed, not moving a muscle. His breathing had turned shallow again. That thin membrane still coated his eyes, but the secret light within seemed to have brightened.

I wanted to talk more about the attic, but Masahiko was beside me, so there was no way I could bring up what I had found there. It would only prick Masahiko's curiosity. So I let the topic hang in the air while Tomohiko Amada and I stared into each other's eyes.

I chose my words with care. "The attic suits owls, but it might suit paintings too. It could be a perfect place to store them. Japanese-style paintings, especially—they're really tricky to preserve. Attics aren't damp like basements—they're well ventilated, and you don't have to worry about sunlight. Of course, there's always the danger of wind and rain getting in, but if you wrap it up carefully enough a painting should keep for quite a while up there."

"You know, I've never even looked in the attic," Masahiko said. "Dusty places creep me out."

I was watching Tomohiko Amada's face. His gaze was fixed on me as well. I felt him trying to construct a coherent line of thought. Owl, attic, stored paintings . . . these familiar words all needed to be strung together. In his current state, this was no easy thing. No easy thing **at all**. Like trying to pick through a labyrinth blindfolded. But I sensed that making those connections was important to him. **Extremely** important. I stood by quietly watching him concentrate on that urgent yet solitary task.

I considered bringing up the shrine in the woods, and the strange pit behind it. To describe to him the steps that had led to it being opened, and the shape of its interior. But I changed my mind. I shouldn't give him too much to think about at one time. His level of awareness was so diminished that even one topic placed a heavy burden on his shoulders. What little he had left hung by a single, easily severed thread.

"Would you like more water?" Masahiko asked, funnel cup in hand. But his father didn't react. It was as if he hadn't heard his son's question. Masahiko drew nearer and asked again, but when his father still didn't respond, he gave up. The son was invisible in his father's eyes.

"Dad seems to have taken a real shine to you," Masahiko marveled. "He can't stop looking at you. It's been quite a while since anyone or anything held his interest like this."

I continued to look into Tomohiko Amada's eyes.

"It's strange. When I talk to him he won't turn to me, no matter what I say, but in your case he won't turn away. His eyes are riveted on you."

I couldn't help notice a mild envy in Masahiko's voice. He wanted his father to **see** him. That had probably been a common theme in his life, ever since childhood.

"Maybe he smells paint on me," I said. "The smell may be triggering his memories."

"You're right, that could be it. Come to think of it, it's been ages since I touched actual paint."

Regret no longer tinged his words. He was back to being the same old easygoing Masahiko. Just then, his cell phone began buzzing on the table.

Masahiko looked up with a start. "Damn, I forgot to turn the thing off. Cell phones are against the rules in this place. I'll have to go outside. You don't mind, do you?"

"Of course not," I said.

Masahiko picked up the cell phone and walked to the door. "This may take a while," he said, checking the caller's name on his screen. "Please talk to my father while I'm gone."

He was already whispering into the phone as he left, closing the door quietly behind him.

Tomohiko Amada and I were now alone. His eyes remained fixed on my face. No doubt he was struggling to figure out who I was. Feeling a bit suffocated, I circled the foot of his bed and went to the southeast-facing window. Bringing my face close to the glass, I looked out at the wide expanse of ocean. The horizon seemed to be pushing up against the sky. I followed the line where the sky met the water from end to end. No human being could draw a line so beautiful, whatever ruler they might use. Below that long, straight line, countless lives were thriving. The world was filled with so many lives, and just as many deaths.

Something else had entered the room—I felt its presence. I turned around and, sure enough, Tomohiko Amada and I were no longer alone.

"Affirmative, my friends. The two of you are alone no more," said the Commendatore.

50

IT WILL INVOLVE ORDEAL
AND SACRIFICE

Affirmative, my friends. The two of you are alone no more," said the Commendatore.

The Commendatore was sitting on the same upholstered chair that Masahiko had occupied a moment earlier. He hadn't changed a bit: same getup, same hairstyle, same sword, same tiny physique. I stared at him without saying anything.

"The friend of my friends will not return anytime soon," the Commendatore said, raising his right forefinger as though to pierce the sky. "His phone call promises to be a long one. So please do not worry. Instead, converse with Tomohiko Amada for as long as you desire. There are questions that my friends would like to ask him, are there not? How many he can answer, however, is a matter for debate."

"Did you send Masahiko away?"

"Certainly not," the Commendatore said. "I fear my friends have overestimated my powers. They are of a lesser sort. But company men are always at someone's beck and call. Those poor men have no weekends."

"Have you been here the whole time? Did you come with us in the car?"

The Commendatore shook his head. "Negative. It is a dreadfully long way from Odawara, and I am prone to carsickness."

"But still you came. Though you weren't invited, correct?"

"Affirmative! I was not invited. Technically, at least. But I was needed. There is a fine line between being invited and being needed, my friends. But leaving that aside, this time it was Tomohiko Amada who needed me. And I thought I could be of use to my friends as well."

"Of use to me?"

"Indeed. I am somewhat beholden to you, my friends. You freed me from that place beneath the ground. It was thanks to you that I was able to rejoin the world as an Idea. As my friends asserted. So it is only proper that I repay that debt. Even Ideas can fathom the import of moral obligation."

Moral obligation?

"Oh well, never mind. **Something like that**," the Commendatore said, reading my mind. "In any case, my friends wish with all your heart to track down Mariye Akikawa and bring her back from the other side. Affirmative?"

I nodded. Yes, that was true.

"Do you know where she is?" I asked.

"Indeed, I met her not long ago."

"Met her?"

"We exchanged a few words."

"Then please tell me where she is."

"I know, but cannot speak."

"You cannot say?"

"I do not have the right."

"But you just said that you came here today to help me."

"Affirmative, I said that."

"But still you can't tell me where Mariye is?"

The Commendatore shook his head. "That is not my role. I am most regretful."

"Then whose role is it?"

The Commendatore pointed his right forefinger directly at me. "It is your role, my friends. You, yourself. My friends must tell yourself where Mariye Akikawa is. It is the only path that leads to her."

"I have to tell myself?" I said. "But I haven't the faintest idea where she is."

The Commendatore gave a long sigh. "My friends know. But my friends do not yet know that they know."

"That sounds like a circular argument to me."

"Negative! It is not circular. My friends will know in due course. In a place that is not here."

Now it was my turn to let out a sigh.

"Please tell me one thing. Was Mariye kidnapped? Or did she wander off on her own?"

"That is something my friends can only know after my friends have found her and brought her back to this world."

"Is she in great danger?"

The Commendatore shook his head. "Determining what constitutes great danger is a role that humans, not Ideas, must play. If my friends truly wish to bring her back, however, my friends must find the road and move quickly."

Find the road? What road was he talking about? I looked at the Commendatore for a moment. It was as though he was playing a riddle game. Assuming his riddles had answers, that is.

"So what is it that you are offering me by way of assistance?"

"What I can do for my friends," the Commendatore said, "is to send you to a place wherein my friends encounter yourself. But that is not as easy as it may sound. It will involve considerable sacrifice, and an excruciating ordeal. More specifically, the sacrifice will be made by the Idea, while the ordeal will be endured by my friends. Do I have your approval?"

What could I say? I hadn't a clue what he was talking about.

"So what is it exactly that I have to do?"

"It is simple," the Commendatore said. "My friends must slay me."

51

NOW IS THE TIME

t is simple," the Commendatore said. "My friends must slay me."

"Slay you?" I said.

"Slay me, as in **Killing Commendatore**—let the painting be your model."

"I should slay you with a sword—is that what you mean?"

"Precisely. As luck would have it, I happen to have a sword with me. It is the real thing—as I told my friends once before, if it cuts you, then you will bleed. It is not full-sized, but I am not full-sized either, so it should suffice."

I stood at the foot of the bed facing the Commendatore. I wanted to say something but had no idea what it should be. So I just stood there, rooted to the spot. Tomohiko Amada was staring in the Commendatore's direction too, from where he lay stretched out on the bed. Whether he could make him out or not was another story. The Commendatore was able to choose who could see him, and who couldn't.

At last I pulled myself together enough to pose a question. "If I kill you with that sword, will I learn where Mariye Akikawa is?"

"Negative. Not exactly. First, my friends must dispose of me. Wipe me off the face of this earth. A chain of events will follow that could well lead my friends to the girl's location."

I struggled to decipher what he meant.

"I'm not sure what sort of chain of events you're talking about, but can I be certain they will lead me in the direction you anticipate? Even if I kill you, there's no guarantee. In which case, yours would be a pointless death."

The Commendatore raised one eyebrow and stared at me. Now he looked like Lee Marvin in **Point Blank**. Super cool. There wasn't the ghost of a chance that the Commendatore had seen **Point Blank,** of course.

"Affirmative! It is as my friends say. Maybe the chain of events will not flow so smoothly in reality. Maybe my hypothesis is based on mere supposition and conjecture. Just maybe, there are too many maybes. But there is no alternative. There is not the luxury of choice."

"So if I kill you, will you be dead to **me**? Will you vanish from my sight forever?"

"Affirmative! As far as my friends are concerned, I shall be dead and gone. One of the countless deaths an Idea must undergo."

"Isn't there a danger that the world itself will be altered when an Idea is killed?"

"How could it be otherwise?" the Commendatore said. Again, he raised one eyebrow, Lee Marvin–style. "What would be the meaning of a world that did **not** change when an Idea was extinguished? Can an Idea be so insignificant?"

"But you think I should still kill you, even though the world would be altered as a result."

"My friends set me free. And now my friends must kill me. Should my friends fail in that task, the circle would remain open. And a circle once opened must then be closed. There are no other options."

I looked at Tomohiko Amada, lying on the bed. His eyes seemed to be trained on the chair where the Commendatore was sitting.

"Can Mr. Amada see you?"

"It is about now that he should be seeing me," the Commendatore said. "And hearing our voices too. A few moments hence, he will begin to grasp the import of our discourse. He is marshaling all his remaining strength to that end."

"What do you think he was trying to convey in **Killing Commendatore?**"

"That is not for me to say. My friends should ask the artist," the Commendatore said. "Since he is right before you."

I sat back down in my chair and drew close to the man stretched out on the bed.

"Mr. Amada, I found the painting you stored in the attic. I am quite sure you meant to hide it. You would not have wrapped it so thoroughly had you planned to show it to anyone. But I unwrapped it. I know that may displease you, but my curiosity got the better of me. And once I discovered how superb

765

Killing Commendatore was, I couldn't let it out of my sight. It is a great painting. One of your best, no question. At this moment, almost no one knows of its existence. Even Masahiko hasn't seen it yet. A thirteen-year-old girl named Mariye Akikawa has, though. And she went missing yesterday."

The Commendatore raised his hand. "Please, let him rest. His brain is easily overtaxed—it cannot handle more than this at one time."

I stopped talking and studied Tomohiko Amada's face. I couldn't tell how much had sunk in. His face was still expressionless. But when I looked more closely I could see a glitter in the depths of his eyes. Like the glint of a sharp penknife at the bottom of a deep spring.

I began talking again, this time with frequent pauses. "My question is, what was your purpose in painting that picture? Its subject matter, its structure, and its style are so different from your other works. It makes me think you were using it to communicate a very personal message. What is the painting's underlying meaning? Who is killing whom? Who is the Commendatore? Who is the murderer Don Giovanni? And who is that mysterious bearded fellow with the long face poking his head out of the ground in the lower left-hand corner?"

The Commendatore raised his hand again. I drew up short.

"Enough questions," he said. "It will take a while for those to permeate."

"Will he be able to answer? Does he have enough strength left?"

"No," the Commendatore said, shaking his head. "I doubt my friends will obtain answers. He does not have the energy for that."

"Then why did you have me ask?"

"What my friends imparted were not questions, but information. That my friends had found **Killing Commendatore** in the attic, that its existence was known to my friends. It is the first step. Everything begins from there."

"Then what is the second step?"

"When my friends slay me, of course. It is the second step."

"And is there a third step?"

"There should be, of course."

"Then what is it?"

"Have you still not yet figured this out, my friends?"

"No, I haven't."

"By reenacting the allegory contained within that painting, we shall lure Long Face into the open. Into this room. By dragging him out, my friends shall win back Mariye Akikawa."

I was speechless. What world had I stepped into? There seemed no rhyme or reason to it.

"It is a hard thing, without question," the Commendatore intoned. "Yet there is no alternative. Hence my friends must dispatch me now, without further ado."

. . .

We waited for the information I had given Tomohiko Amada to complete its journey to his brain. That took some time. Meanwhile, I tried to put to rest some of my doubts by peppering the Commendatore with questions.

"Why," I asked, "did Tomohiko Amada remain silent about what had happened in Vienna even after the war had ended? I mean, no one was standing in his way at that point."

"The woman he loved was brutally executed by the Nazis," the Commendatore answered. "Slowly tortured to death. Their comrades were slain in a similar fashion. In the end, their plot was a wretched failure. Only through the offices of the Japanese and German governments did he barely escape with his life. The experience savaged him. He had been arrested and detained by the Gestapo for two months. They subjected him to extreme torture. Their violence was unspeakable, but they took care not to kill him, nor to leave any physical scars. Yet their sadism left his nerves in tatters—and as a result, something within him was extinguished. Placed under the strictest orders, he bowed to the inevitable and remained silent. Then he was forcibly repatriated to Japan."

"Not long before," I said, "Tomohiko Amada's younger brother had taken his own life, probably because of the trauma of his own war experience. He had been part of the Nanjing Massacre, and committed suicide right after his discharge from the army. Correct?"

"Affirmative. Tomohiko Amada lost many loved

ones in the whirlpool of those years. He himself was sorely damaged. As a result, his anger and grief put down deep roots. The hopeless, impotent realization that, no matter what he did, he could not stand against the torrent of history. As the sole survivor, he must also have felt an immense guilt. Hence he never spoke a word of what happened in Vienna, even after the gag was removed. It is as though he was unable to speak."

I looked at Tomohiko Amada's face. But I could detect no reaction as yet. I couldn't tell if he heard us or not.

I spoke. "Then at some point—we don't know exactly when—he created **Killing Commendatore**. An allegorical painting that expressed all he could not say. He put everything into it. A brilliant tour de force."

"He took that which he had been unable to accomplish in reality," the Commendatore said, "and gave it another form. What we might call 'camouflaged expression.' Not of what had in fact happened, but of **what should have happened**."

"Nevertheless, he bundled the painting up tight and hid it in the attic, out of public view," I said. "Although he had radically transformed the events, they were still too raw to reveal. Is that what you mean?"

"Precisely. It distills the pure essence of his living spirit. Then, one day, my friends happened upon it."

"So are you saying all of this began when I brought the painting out into the light? Is that what you meant by 'opening the circle'?"

The Commendatore said nothing, just extended his hands palms up.

Not long after, we noticed Tomohiko Amada's face turning pink. (The Commendatore and I had been watching him closely for any change.) At the same time, as if in response, the small, mysterious light that had been flickering deep in his eyes began to rise slowly to the surface. Like an ascending deep-sea diver gauging the effects of the water pressure on his body. The veil covering Amada's eyes also lifted, until, finally, both were wide open. The person lying before us was no longer a frail, desiccated old man on the verge of death. Instead, he was someone whose eyes brimmed with a determination to hang on to this world as long as he could.

"He is gathering his remaining strength," the Commendatore said to me. "Recovering as much of his conscious mind as he is able. But the more he regains mentally, the greater the physical torment. His body has been secreting a special substance to blot out that pain. It is thanks to the existence of such a substance that people can die in peace, not in agony. When consciousness returns, so does the pain. Nevertheless, he is trying to recover as much as he can. This is a mission he must fulfill here and now, however great the suffering."

As if to reinforce the Commendatore's words, Tomohiko Amada's face began to contort with agony. Age and infirmity had eaten away at his body until it was ready to shut down—he could feel that now. There was no way to avoid it. The end of his allotted time was fast approaching. It was painful to watch him suffer. Instead of calling him back, I might better have let him die a peaceful, painless death in a semiconscious haze.

"But he chose this way himself," the Commendatore said, again reading my mind. "It is painful to witness, but beyond our control."

"Won't Masahiko be returning soon?" I asked the Commendatore.

"Negative. Not for some time," he said with a small shake of his head. "His call was work related, something important. He will be gone a considerable time."

Tomohiko's eyes were wide open. They had been sunk within their wrinkled sockets, but now his eyeballs protruded like a person leaning out of a window. His breathing was deeper, and more ragged. It rasped as it passed in and out of his throat. And he was staring straight at the Commendatore. There was no doubt. The Commendatore was visible to him. Amazement was written in his face. He couldn't believe what was sitting in front of him. How could a figure produced by his imagination appear before him in reality?

"Negative, that is not the case," the Commendatore said. "What he sees and what my friends see are completely different."

"You mean you don't look the same way to him?"

"My friends, keep in mind that I am an Idea. My form changes depending on the person and the situation."

"Then how do you look to Mr. Amada?"

"That is something even I do not know. I am like a mirror that reflects what is in a person's heart. Nothing more."

"But you assumed this form for me on purpose, didn't you? Choosing to appear as the Commendatore?"

"To be precise, I did not choose this form. Cause and effect are hard to separate here. Because I took the form of the Commendatore, a sequence of events was set in motion. But at the same time, my form is the necessary consequence of that very sequence. It is hard to explain using the concept of time that governs the world you live in, my friends, but it might be summed up as: **All these events have been determined beforehand.**"

"If an Idea is a mirror, then is Tomohiko Amada now seeing what he wishes to see?"

"Negative! He is seeing what he **must** see," the Commendatore corrected me. "It may be excruciating. Yet he must look. Now, at the end of his life."

I examined Tomohiko Amada's face again. Mixed with the amazement, I could discern an intense loathing. And almost unendurable torment. The return to consciousness carried with it not only the agony of the flesh. It brought with it the agony of the soul.

"He is squeezing out every last ounce of strength to ascertain who I am. Despite the pain. He is striving to return to his twenties."

Tomohiko Amada's face had turned a fiery red. Hot blood coursed through his veins. His thin, dry lips trembled, he gasped violently. His long, skeletal fingers clutched at the sheets.

"Stop dithering, my friends, and kill me now, while his mind is whole," the Commendatore said. "The quicker, the better. He may not be able to hold himself together much longer."

The Commendatore drew his sword from its scabbard. It was just eight inches long, but it looked very sharp indeed. Despite its dimensions, it was a weapon capable of ending a person's life.

"Stab me with this," the Commendatore said. "We shall re-create the scene from **Killing Commendatore**. But hurry. There is no time to dawdle."

I looked back and forth from the Commendatore to Tomohiko Amada, struggling to make up my mind. All I could be remotely sure of was that Tomohiko Amada was in desperate need, and the Commendatore's resolve was firm. I alone wallowed in indecision, caught between the two of them.

I felt the rush of owl wings, and heard a bell ring in the dark.

Everything was connected somewhere.

"Affirmative! Everything is connected somewhere," said the Commendatore. "And my friends cannot escape that connection, however my friends may try. So steel yourself, and kill me. There is no room for guilt. Tomohiko Amada needs your help. By slaying me, my friends can save him. Make happen here what should have happened in the past. Now is the time. Only my friends can grant him salvation before he breathes his last."

I rose from my chair and strode to where the Commendatore was seated. I took his unsheathed sword in hand. I was past the point of determining what was just and unjust. In a world outside space and time, all dualities—before and after, up and down—ceased to exist. In such a world, I could no longer perceive myself as myself. I and myself were being torn apart.

The instant I took the sword in hand, however, I realized its handle was too small. It was a miniature sword for a tiny hand. There was simply no way could I kill the Commendatore with it, however keen its blade. The realization brought with it a sense of relief.

"The sword is too small. I can't grip it," I said to the Commendatore.

"That is a shame," he said with a sigh. "Well, there is nothing to be done. We must use something else, although that means diverging further from the painting."

"Something else?"

The Commendatore pointed to a small chest of drawers in the corner of the room. "Look inside the top drawer."

I went to the chest and slid open the uppermost drawer.

"Within is a knife for filleting fish," the Commendatore said.

Sure enough, a knife lay atop a small stack of neatly folded washcloths. The knife that Masahiko had used to prepare the sea bream he had brought to my home. An eight-inch blade honed to a razor's edge. Masahiko always kept his tools in perfect shape. This knife was no exception.

"Now take that knife and plunge it into my chest,"

said the Commendatore. "Sword or knife, what is the difference. We can still reenact the scene in **Killing Commendatore**. But we must make haste. There is little time."

I took the knife in hand. It was as heavy as stone. The tip of the blade shone cold and white in the light streaming from the window. The knife had vanished from my kitchen and come to wait for me here, in the chest of drawers. Masahiko had sharpened the blade, as it turned out, for the sake of his own father. There seemed no way to avoid my fate.

I still couldn't come to a decision. Nevertheless, I stepped behind the Commendatore's chair, gripping the knife tightly in my right hand. From his bed, Tomohiko Amada stared at us with eyes as big as saucers. As if watching history unfold before his eyes. His mouth was open, exposing his yellowed teeth and whitish tongue, a tongue that lolled in his mouth as though trying to form words. Words this world would never hear.

"My friends do not have a violent bone in your body," the Commendatore said, as if to admonish me. "It is obvious. My friends are not built to kill. But sometimes people must act against their nature, to rescue something important or for some greater purpose. Now is one of those times. So kill me! I am not big, as my friends can see, and I will not resist. I am merely an Idea. Just insert the tip of the knife into my heart. What could be more straightforward?"

The Commendatore pointed his tiny index finger at the spot where his heart was. But the thought of that heart inevitably recalled my sister's. I could remember her operation as if it were yesterday. How delicate and difficult it had been. Saving a malfunctioning heart was a formidable task. It required a team of specialists and gallons of blood. Yet destroying a heart was **so easy**.

"Such thinking will get us nowhere," the Commendatore said. "If my friends wish to save Mariye Akikawa, then do the deed. Even if my friends do not want to. Trust me. Jettison all feelings, and close your mind. But not your eyes. My friends must keep them open."

I stepped behind the Commendatore and raised the knife. But I couldn't bring it down. Sure, it might be only one of a thousand deaths for an Idea, but it was still extinguishing a life as far as I was concerned. Was this not the same order the young lieutenant had given Tsuguhiko Amada in Nanjing?

"Negative! It is not the same," said the Commendatore. "My friends are doing this at my behest. It is I who am asking my friends to kill me. So that I may be reborn. Be strong. Close the circle at once."

I closed my eyes and thought of the girl I had throttled in the love hotel in Miyagi. Of course, she and I had been pretending. I had squeezed her throat gently, so as not to kill her. I had been unable to do it long enough to satisfy her. Had I continued, I might indeed have strangled her to death. On the bed of that love hotel, I had glimpsed the deep rage within myself for the first time. It had churned in my chest like blood-soaked mud, pushing me closer and closer to real murder.

I know where you were and what you were doing, the man had said.

"All right, now bring it down," the Commendatore said. "I know my friends can do it. Remember, my friends will not be killing me. My friends will be slaying your evil father. The blood of your evil father shall soak into the earth."

My evil father?

Where did that come from?

"Who is the evil father of my friends?" the Commendatore said, reading my mind. "I believe your path crossed with his not long ago. Am I mistaken?"

Do not paint my portrait any further, the man had said. He had pointed his finger at me from within the dark mirror. It had pierced my chest like the tip of a sharp sword.

Spurred by that pain, I reflexively closed my heart and opened my eyes wide. I cleared all thought from my mind (as Don Giovanni had done in **Killing Commendatore**), buried my emotions, made my face a blank mask, and brought the knife down with all my might. The sharp blade entered the Commendatore's tiny chest precisely where he had pointed. I felt the living flesh resist. But the Commendatore himself made no attempt to fend off the blow. His fingers clutched at the air, but apart from that he did not react. Still, the body he inhabited did all that it could to avoid its looming extinction. The Commendatore was an Idea, but his body was not. An Idea may have borrowed it for its own purposes, but that body would not meekly submit to death. It possessed its own rationale. I had to overcome that resistance through brute force, severing its life at the roots. "Kill me," the Commendatore had said. But I was actually dispatching another **someone**'s body.

I wanted to drop the knife, drop everything, and run from the room. But the Commendatore's words echoed in my ears. "If my friends wish to save Mariye Akikawa, then do the deed. Even if my friends do not want to."

So I pushed the blade even farther into the Commendatore's heart. If you're stabbing someone to death, there's no halfway. The tip of the knife emerged from his back—I had run him through. His white garment was dyed crimson. My hands were drenched in blood. But the blood did not spew into the air as it did in **Killing Commendatore**. This is an illusion, I tried to convince myself. I was murdering a mere phantom. My act was purely symbolic.

Yet I knew I was fooling myself. Perhaps the act was symbolic. But it was no phantom that I was killing. Without question, my victim was made of flesh and blood. It may have been barely two feet tall, a fabrication created by Tomohiko Amada's brush, but its life force was unexpectedly strong. The point of my blade had broken the skin and several ribs on its way to the heart, then passed through to the back of the chair. No way that was an illusion.

Tomohiko Amada's eyes were open even wider

now, riveted on the scene unfolding before him. My murder of the Commendatore. No, for him it must have been the murder of someone else. Who was he seeing? The Nazi official whose assassination he had helped plot in Vienna? The young lieutenant who had given his brother a Japanese sword and ordered him to behead three Chinese prisoners in Nanjing? Or that evil **something**, something more fundamental, that lay at the root of those events? I could only guess. I could not read the expression on Tomohiko Amada's face. Though his mouth gaped open, his lips were motionless. Only his tongue continued its futile quest to form words of some kind.

At last, the strength left the Commendatore's neck and arms. His whole body went slack, like a marionette whose strings had been cut. I responded by pushing the knife even farther into his heart. All movement in the room came to a standstill; the scene was now a frozen tableau. It stayed that way for a long time.

Tomohiko Amada was the first to move. Once the Commendatore had lost consciousness and collapsed, the strength to focus his mind evaporated. He sighed deeply and closed his eyes. Slowly and solemnly, like lowering the shutters. As if to confirm: **Now I have seen what I needed to see.** His mouth was still open, but his lolling tongue was tucked out of sight. Only his yellow teeth were visible, like a ramshackle fence circling an empty house. His face was free of pain. The torment had passed. He looked peaceful and relaxed. I guessed he was back in the twilight world, where thought and pain did not exist. I was happy for him.

I finally relaxed my arm and drew the blade from the Commendatore's body. Blood spewed from the wound. Exactly as in **Killing Commendatore**. The Commendatore himself spilled lifelessly into the chair. His eyes were open, his mouth contorted in agony. His ten tiny fingers clawed the air. Dark blood pooled around his feet. He was dead. How much blood had come from that tiny body!

Thus did the Commendatore—or the Idea that had taken his form—meet his end. Tomohiko Amada had sunk back into his deep sleep. Standing next to the Commendatore's body, Masahiko's bloody knife in my right hand, I was the only conscious person left in the room. My labored breathing should have been the only sound. Should have been. But something was moving. I sensed it as much as I heard it, to my alarm. **Keep your ears open**, the Commendatore had told me. I did as he had instructed.

Something is in the room. I could hear it moving. Bloody knife in hand, I stood frozen like a statue, scanning the room, searching for the source of the sound. Out of the corner of one eye, I spotted something near the far wall.

Long Face was there.

Killing the Commendatore had lured Long Face into this world.

52

THE MAN IN THE
ORANGE CONE HAT

The scene in the room now matched the lower left-hand corner of Tomohiko Amada's **Killing Commendatore**. Long Face had poked his head out of a hole, and was raising its square cover with one hand as he peeked at what was taking place. His hair was long and tangled, and a thick black beard covered much of his face. His elongated head was shaped like a Japanese eggplant, narrow with a jutting chin and bulging eyes. The bridge of his nose was flat. For some reason, his lips glistened like a piece of fruit. His body was small but well proportioned, as if a normal person had been shrunk in size. Just as the Commendatore made you think of a scaled-down copy of a human being.

The big difference between the Long Face in **Killing Commendatore** and here was his expression— now he looked stunned as he stared at the lifeless body of the Commendatore. His mouth gaped in disbelief. How long had he been watching us? I had no idea. I had been so focused on snuffing out the Commendatore's life, and gauging Tomohiko Amada's reaction to his death, that I had been oblivious to the odd-looking man in the corner of the room. Yet

I bet he hadn't missed a thing. After all, that was the scene in **Killing Commendatore**.

Long Face remained completely still, there in the corner of our tableau. As if assigned a fixed position. I moved slightly to see how he would respond. But Long Face didn't react. He maintained the same position he had in the painting—one hand holding up the square lid, his eyes round as he gawked at the slain Commendatore. He didn't even blink.

As the tension drained from my body, I moved from my own assigned position. I edged cautiously toward Long Face, deadening my footsteps like a cat, the bloody knife in one hand. I could not let him slip back underground. To save Mariye Akikawa, the Commendatore had given his life to re-create the scene in the painting, and drawn Long Face out into the open. I must not allow that sacrifice to be in vain.

Yet how could I wrest from Long Face what I needed to know about Mariye? I was at a loss. **Who** or **what** was Long Face? How was his presence linked to Mariye's disappearance? What the Commendatore had told me was more riddle than information. One thing was clear, though: I had to get my hands on him. I could figure the rest out later.

The lid that Long Face was holding was about two feet square, made of the same lime-green linoleum as the rest of the floor. When closed, it would blend in perfectly, perhaps even disappear altogether.

Long Face did not move a muscle as I approached. He seemed rooted to the spot. Like a cat in the headlights. Or maybe he was just fulfilling his designated role—to maintain the composition of the painting for as long as possible. Whichever, it was lucky for me. Otherwise, he would have sensed me behind him and slipped back underground for good. Once the lid had been closed, I doubted it would open again.

I crept behind him, softly laid down the knife, and snatched his collar with both hands. He was wearing drab, snug-fitting clothes. Work clothes, from the look of it. Clearly different from the fine cloth of the Commendatore's garments. These looked rough to the touch and were covered in patches.

Jolted from his trance, Long Face thrashed about, desperately attempting to flee down his hole. I held tight to his collar. There was no way I was going to let him escape. I gathered my strength and tried to yank him all the way out. He fought back, grabbing the sides of the hole with both hands. He was much stronger than I'd anticipated. He even tried to bite my arm. What could I do—I slammed his eggplant-shaped head against the corner of the opening. Then I did it again, this time more violently. The second blow knocked him out cold. I could feel his body go limp. At last I could drag him out into the light.

Long Face was a little bigger than the Commendatore. Two and a half feet tall was my guess. He was wearing what a farmer might have worn in the fields, or a manservant sweeping the yard. A stiff, rough jacket over baggy work pants cinched at the ankles. His belt was a thick piece of rope. He wore no shoes, and his soles were thickly callused and stained black with dirt. His long hair showed no sign of having been recently washed or combed. Half his face was covered by a black beard. The other half was a sickly white. Nothing about him looked clean, yet, strangely, his body had no odor.

Based on appearance, I figured the Commendatore belonged to the aristocracy of his time, while Long Face was lower-class. Perhaps he was dressed the way commoners did back then. Or maybe Tomohiko Amada had imagined, **This is how people might have dressed in the Asuka period.** Historical accuracy, however, was beside the point. What I needed to do was squeeze from this man with the strange face any information that would lead me to Mariye.

I rolled Long Face over onto his stomach and tied his hands behind him with the belt of a bathrobe hanging close by. Then I dragged his motionless body to the center of the room. Because of his size, he wasn't very heavy. About the weight of a medium-sized dog. I grabbed a curtain tie and bound one of his legs to the bed. Now he had no way to flee.

Stretched out unconscious in the bright afternoon light, Long Face just looked pitiful. Gone was the weirdness that had alarmed me when he had poked his head up out of his hole, observing events with those glittering eyes. I could find nothing sinister about him. He didn't look bright enough to be evil. Instead, he looked honest in a dull-witted sort of way. And timid, too. Not like someone who concocted plans and made decisions, but, rather, the type who meekly followed his superiors' orders.

Tomohiko Amada was still stretched out on the bed, his eyes closed. He was completely still. I couldn't tell, looking at him, if he was alive or dead. I leaned down and put my ear less than an inch from his mouth. His breathing was faint, like a distant surf. He wasn't dead yet, just sleeping on the floor of his twilight world. I felt relieved. I didn't like the idea of Masahiko returning from his phone call to find that his father had died in his absence. Tomohiko's face, as he lay on his side, looked far more peaceful and satisfied than before. Maybe witnessing the slaying of the Commendatore (or someone else he wished to see killed) had put some of his painful memories to rest.

The Commendatore was slumped in his cloth chair. His eyes were wide open, and I could see his tiny tongue curled behind his parted lips. Blood was still seeping from the wound in his chest, but the flow was weaker than before. His right hand flopped life-lessly when I took it. Although his skin retained some warmth, it felt remote and somehow detached. The kind of detachment life acquires as it moves steadily toward its own end. I felt like straightening his limbs and placing him in a proper-sized coffin, one made for a small child. I would lay the coffin in the pit behind the shrine, where no one could bother him again. But all I could do now was gently close his eyes.

I sat in the chair and watched Long Face on the floor as I waited for him to regain his senses. Outside the window, the broad Pacific sparkled. A few fishing boats were still plying the waters. I could see the sleek fuselage of an airplane shining in the sun as it slowly made its way south. A four-prop plane with an antenna jutting up from its tail—probably an anti-submarine aircraft from the Japanese Maritime Self-Defense Force base in Atsugi. Some of us were quietly going about our business on a Saturday afternoon. I, for one, was in a sunlit room in an upscale nursing home, having just slain the Commendatore and fished out and tied up Long Face in my quest to find a beautiful thirteen-year-old girl. It takes all kinds, I guess.

Long Face didn't regain consciousness for some time. I checked my watch again.

What would Masahiko think if he came back now? The Commendatore in a pool of blood, Long Face bound and unconscious on the floor. Both in the unfamiliar garb of an ancient time, neither standing even three feet tall. Tomohiko Amada comatose on the bed, a faint but satisfied smile (if that's what it was) on his lips. A square, black hole gaping in a corner of the room. How could I explain what had led to this scene?

Of course, Masahiko didn't come back. He was tied up in a work-related phone call of great importance, as the Commendatore had said. He would be dealing with it for some time yet. Everything had been arranged in advance. No one would bother us. I sat on the chair, eyeing the unconscious Long Face. I had whacked his head pretty hard on the edge of the hole, but it shouldn't take him that long to come to. He'd have a fair-sized lump on his head, that's all.

At last, Long Face woke up. He twisted and turned a bit on the floor, and uttered a few incomprehensible words. Then, slowly, he opened his eyes a crack. Like a child looking at something scary—something he didn't want to see, but must.

I went and knelt beside him.

"There's very little time," I said, looking down at him. "I need you to tell me where I can find Mariye Akikawa. If you do, I'll untie you, and you can go back."

I pointed to the square hole in the corner. The lid was still raised. I couldn't tell if he understood what I was saying or not. But I decided to keep talking. All I could do was give it a shot.

Long Face violently shook his head back and forth several times. I couldn't tell if he was saying that he didn't know anything, or that my language was foreign to him.

"If you don't tell me, I'll kill you," I said. "You saw me stab the Commendatore, I bet. Well, there's no big difference between one murder and two."

I pressed the bloody blade of my knife against his dirty throat. I thought of the fishermen and the pilot of the southbound airplane. **We all have jobs we have to do.** And this was mine. I wasn't going to kill him, of course, but the knife was real, and very sharp. Long Face quivered in fear.

"Wait!" he gasped in a husky voice. "Stay your hand."

His way of speaking was strange, but I could understand him. I eased off on the knife.

"Where is Mariye Akikawa?" I pressed him. "Come on, spit it out!"

"No, sir, I do not know. I swear it."

I studied his eyes. They were big and easy to read. He seemed to be telling the truth.

"All right then, tell me, what are you doing here?" I asked.

"I am enjoined to verify and record these events. I do only what I am told to do. You have my word."

"Why must you verify them?"

"Because I was so bidden. I know nothing beyond that."

"So what on earth are you? Another kind of Idea?"

"Goodness no! I am a Metaphor, nothing more."

"A Metaphor?"

"Yes. A mere Metaphor. Used to link two things together. So please, untie my bonds, please, I beseech you."

I was getting confused. "If you are as you say, then give me a metaphor now, off the top of your head."

"I am the most humble and lowly form of Metaphor, sir. I cannot devise anything of quality."

"A metaphor of any kind is all right—it doesn't have to be brilliant."

"He was someone who stood out," he said after a moment's pause, "like a man wearing an orange cone hat in a packed commuter train."

Not an impressive metaphor, to be sure. In fact, not really a metaphor at all.

"That's a simile, not a metaphor," I pointed out.

"A million pardons," he said, sweat pouring from his forehead. "Let me try again. 'He lived as though he were wearing an orange cone hat in a crowded train.'"

"That makes no sense. It's still not a true metaphor. Your story doesn't hold. I'll just have to kill you."

Long Face's lips trembled with fear. His beard may have been manly, but he was short on guts.

"My sincerest apologies, sir. I am yet but an apprentice. I cannot think of a witty example. Forgive me. But I assure you that I am the genuine article, a true Metaphor."

"Then who is your superior—who commands you?"

"I have no superior, per se. Well, perhaps I do, but I have never laid eyes on him. I only follow orders—acting as a link between phenomena and language. Like a helpless jellyfish adrift on the ocean. So please do not kill me. I implore you."

"I can spare your life," I said, my knife still on his throat. "But only if you agree to guide me to where you came from."

"That is something I cannot do," Long Face said in a firm voice. It was the first time he had used that tone. "The road I took to get here is the Path of Metaphor. It is different for each one who traverses it. It is not a single road. Thus I cannot guide you, sir, on your way."

"Let me get this straight. I must follow this path alone, and I must discover it for myself—is that what you're saying?"

Long Face nodded vigorously. "The Path of Metaphor is rife with perils. Should a mortal like you stray from the path even once, you could find yourself in danger. And there are Double Metaphors everywhere."

"Double Metaphors?"

Long Face shuddered with fear. "Yes, Double Metaphors lurking in the darkness. The most **vile** and dangerous of creatures."

"It's all the same to me," I said. "I'm already mixed up in a whole lot of craziness. So it's no skin off my nose if the craziness grows or shrinks. I killed the Commendatore with my own hands. I don't want his death to be in vain."

"I see I have no choice. So let me offer you a word of warning before you set out."

"What kind of warning?"

"Take a light of some kind with you. You will pass through many dark places on your way. You will come across a river. It is a metaphorical river, but the water is very real. It is cold and deep, and the current is strong. You cannot cross without a boat. You will find a boat at the ferrying spot."

"How about after I cross the river—what should I do then?"

Long Face rolled his bulging eyes. "The world that awaits you on the other side, like this one, is subject to the principle of connectivity. You will have to see for yourself."

I checked Tomohiko Amada's bedside table. Sure enough, a flashlight was there. A facility like this one was sure to store one in each room in case of fire or earthquake. I flicked it on. The light was strong.

The batteries weren't dead. I slipped on my leather jacket, which I had draped over a chair, and started for the hole in the corner, flashlight in hand.

"Please, sir," Long Face begged. "Will you not loosen my bonds? I fear what may transpire should I be left in this state."

"If you're a true Metaphor, untying yourself should be easy. Aren't Concepts and Ideas and others like you able to move through space and time?"

"No, you overrate me. I am blessed with no such marvelous powers. Concepts and Ideas are Metaphors of a much higher order."

"Like those with orange cone hats?"

Long Face looked stricken. "Please do not mock me, sir. My feelings can be hurt too, you know."

After a moment's hesitation, I decided to untie his hands and feet. I had bound them so tightly they took time to undo. Now that we had talked, he didn't appear to be such a bad fellow. True, he didn't know where Mariye was, but he had volunteered other information. I doubted that he would interfere or cause me any harm if I untied him. And I certainly couldn't leave him bound and trussed where he was. Should anyone find him like that, it would only make things worse. When I finished, he sat there for a moment, rubbing his chafed wrists with his tiny hands. Then he felt his forehead. It appeared a lump had already sprouted.

"Thank you, sir. Now I can return to my world."

"Go ahead," I said, gesturing to the hole in the corner. "I'll follow later."

"I shall now make my departure. Please ensure that the lid is securely closed when you follow. Otherwise, someone might trip and fall in. Or grow curious and climb down. Then I would be held responsible."

"Understood. I will make sure it's closed."

Long Face trotted to the hole and climbed inside. Then his head and shoulders popped up again. His saucer eyes had an eerie glow. As they did in **Killing Commendatore**.

"I wish you a safe journey," Long Face said to me. "I hope you can find **What's-her-name**. Was it Komichi?"

"No, her name isn't Komichi," I said. A chill ran down my spine. My throat turned to sandpaper. I couldn't speak for a moment. "The name was Mariye Akikawa. Do you know something about Komichi?"

"No, I know nothing at all." Long Face seemed to realize that he'd let drop something he shouldn't. "The name just slipped into my clumsy metaphorical brain. A simple mistake. Forgive me, please, sir."

Long Face vanished down the hole. Like smoke in the wind.

I stood there for a moment, plastic flashlight in hand. Komichi? How could my sister's name come up here, of all places? Could she be connected to this strangeness? But I had no time to ponder that question. I switched the flashlight on and entered the hole, feetfirst. It was dark below, and there seemed to be a long path sloping downward. That was odd, too, come to think of it. The room was on the third floor, so the second floor should be directly beneath.

I trained the flashlight on the path, but couldn't make out where it led. I lowered the rest of my body inside and closed the lid tight behind me. Now everything was black.

The darkness was so complete that my five senses were useless. As if the links between my body and my mind had been severed, and no information was passing between them. It was the strangest feeling. As if I were no longer myself. Nevertheless, I had to go on.

"If my friends wish to save Mariye Akikawa, then do the deed."

Those had been the Commendatore's words. He had made the sacrifice. Now it was my turn to face the ordeal. I had to push forward. With the flashlight my only ally, I stepped down into the inky blackness of the Path of Metaphor.

53

MAYBE A FIREPLACE POKER

The blackness enfolding me was so thick, so complete, it seemed to have a will of its own. It felt like walking on the ocean floor, where not even a particle of light could penetrate. Only the yellow beam of my flashlight connected me to the world, and barely, at that. The passageway descended at a steady angle. The surface beneath my feet was hard and smooth—it felt like walking down a tunnel bored into solid rock. The ceiling was so low I had to stoop to keep from hitting my head. The air was chilly and odorless, and the total lack of smell disturbed me. Perhaps even the air was different here than above ground.

How long would my flashlight hold out? Its beam was strong and steady for now, but when the batteries failed (as they would eventually) I would be stranded in the dark. And if I were to believe Long Face, dangerous Double Metaphors were lurking out there, ready to pounce.

The palm of my hand that held the flashlight was sweaty from the tension. My heartbeat was a dull, hard thump. It sounded threatening, like a drumbeat would to someone lost in the jungle. Long Face had warned me: "Take a light of some kind with you. You will pass through many dark places on your way." So not everything in this passageway was pitch black. I wished it would brighten soon. I wished too that the ceiling would rise. I had always felt panicky in dark, constricted spaces. If this continued for much longer, I would soon have trouble breathing.

To calm myself, I tried to focus on other things. I needed to find something, anything, to occupy my mind. What popped into my head was an open-faced grilled cheese sandwich. Why a grilled cheese sandwich? Go figure. That's what came up first, for whatever reason. Perfectly melted cheese on a square of beautifully browned toast. Sitting on a pure white plate. So real I could reach out and touch it. And beside it a cup of piping-hot coffee. Coffee as black as a moonless night. A window opening onto a tall willow, on whose supple branches a small flock of chirping birds perched precariously, like a troupe of tightrope walkers. Everything at an immeasurable distance from where I was now.

Then, for some reason, I thought of the opera **Der Rosenkavalier**. I would listen to it as I sipped my coffee and nibbled my grilled cheese sandwich. That jet-black vinyl disk, released by Decca Records in Great Britain. I placed the heavy record on the turntable and gently lowered the needle. Georg Solti conducting the Vienna Philharmonic. The music elegant, intricate. When Richard Strauss had boasted he could describe even a broom musically, he was in his heyday. But was it a broom? I still couldn't

795

remember. Perhaps it was an umbrella, or then again maybe a fireplace poker. In any case, how could one describe a broom in music? Or a hot grilled cheese sandwich, or someone's callused feet, or the difference between a simile and a metaphor? Could music really depict those things?

Richard Strauss conducted the same orchestra in prewar Vienna. (Was it before the **Anschluss**? After?) The program on this given day was Beethoven's 7th, a resolute yet quiet and well-groomed symphony, squeezed between its bright, uninhibited older sister (the 6th) and its bashful and beautiful younger sister (the 8th). A youthful Tomohiko Amada was in attendance. A pretty young woman sat beside him. Most likely, he was in love with her.

I imagined the city of Vienna on that day. The waltzes, the sweet Sacher tortes, the red-and-black swastikas fluttering from the roofs.

I could feel my thoughts veering off in a pointless direction. Or, more accurately perhaps, in a directionless direction. Yet I was powerless to rein them in. They were no longer under my control. It's no simple matter to hold on to your mind in total blackness. Your thoughts become a tree of riddles whose branches trail off into the dark. (A metaphor.) Nevertheless, I had to focus on **something** to hold myself together. Any old **something** would do. Otherwise, I would start to hyperventilate.

One absurdity after another sauntered through my mind as I pushed down the endless slope. The passageway was as straight as an arrow, with no bends or forks. However far I walked, nothing changed—not the height of the ceiling, or the depth of the darkness, or the quality of the air, or the angle of the slope. My sense of time was foggy, but based on how long I had been walking, I must have been deep underground. Yet in the end, that "depth" had to be a fabrication. After all, I had entered this tunnel from the third floor of a building. The darkness too had to be fabricated. Everything was either concept or metaphor, nothing more. That's what I told myself, anyway. The problem was that the darkness enfolding me was real darkness, the depth pressing down on me real depth.

Just when my neck and back were firing off warning signals about my hunched-over posture, a dim light appeared ahead. Then came a series of twists and turns. With each, my surroundings grew a little brighter, as if the night sky was giving way to day. Now I could make out where I was. I switched off my flashlight to conserve the batteries.

It was growing light, but still I smelled nothing, heard nothing. Then, at last, the cramped passage abruptly ended, and I stepped out into the open. Yet I could see no sky above me, only what looked like a milky-white ceiling, far overheard. A pale glow covered everything, as if the world was lit by a host of luminous insects. It felt odd. Yet it was a relief to say goodbye to the darkness, and to be able to walk upright again. I could relax a bit.

Outside the tunnel, the ground was rough underfoot. There was no path, only a barren, rocky plain that stretched as far as the eye could see. The downward slope had ended, and I was walking up a gentle rise. I picked my way forward, unsure of my direction. I checked my watch, but its hands held no meaning. One glance told me that much. In fact, nothing I carried—key ring, wallet, driver's license, loose change, handkerchief—promised to be of any use at all.

The incline grew steeper and steeper. After a while, I was literally crawling up the slope on my hands and knees. If I could only reach the top, then maybe I could see where I was. I pushed on without pausing to catch my breath. The only sound was the sound I was making, and even that seemed artificial, not like real sound at all. There was nothing alive that I could see. Not a tree, not a clump of grass, not a solitary bird. Not even a puff of wind. Only I moved—all else was still. It was as if time itself had come to a halt.

I finally reached the top of the rise. I could see in all directions from there, as I had anticipated. Yet my view was limited. For there was a whitish mist that hung over everything. All I could make out was what amounted to a lifeless wasteland, a craggy, barren wilderness that stretched in every direction. There was no true sky, just that milky-white ceiling. I felt like an astronaut who had crashed, and landed on an uninhabited planet. Well, at least there was some light, and air that I could breathe. I should be grateful for those.

I could find no sign of life. Finally, though, I was able to make out a faint sound. I thought it might be a hallucination at first, or possibly coming from my own body. Yet it gradually became clear that the noise was continuous, and caused by some kind of natural phenomenon. In fact, it sounded like flowing water. Perhaps it was the river that Long Face had spoken of. Bathed in the pale light, I picked my way down the bumpy slope in the direction of the sound.

The sound of water made me terribly thirsty. Come to think of it, I had been walking a very long time with nothing to drink. Yet I had been so anxious that water had never crossed my mind. Now I craved it desperately. But was the water in that river—if that was where the sound was coming from—drinkable? It might be thick with mud, or filled with dangerous toxins. Or perhaps it was metaphorical water, which my hands could not scoop up. Oh well, I would find out when I got there.

The noise grew louder and clearer as I went along. It sounded like a fast-flowing river, tumbling through rocks. Yet I still could not see it. As I headed toward the sound, the ground on both sides of me rose until I was walking between two rock walls about thirty feet in height. The path cut between those towering cliffs, though its serpentine twists and turns made it impossible to know what lay ahead. It was not a man-made trail. Rather, it appeared to have been fashioned by the forces of nature. From what I could tell, the river lay at its end.

I hurried along the walled path. I passed no tree, no blade of grass. Not a living thing. The silent cliffs were all that I could see. A sterile, monochrome world. It was as if an artist had lost interest in painting a landscape, and had abandoned it before adding the colors. I could barely hear my own footsteps. The rocks seemed to absorb sound.

At a certain point the path, which had been flat for the most part, began to slope upward again. It took some time, but at last I reached the crest, which ran like a spine along the top of the cliffs. When I leaned forward, I could see the river. Now the rush of water was even more audible.

The river was not especially wide. Maybe fifteen or twenty feet across. But its current was swift. I couldn't tell its depth. Judging from the whitecaps it sent up here and there, boulders and other hidden obstacles lay beneath the surface. The river carved a straight line through the rocky terrain. I crossed the ridge and headed down the slope in its direction.

When I reached the river, and saw it rushing past from right to left, I felt much better. At the very least, a large quantity of water was on the move. It had originated somewhere and was flowing somewhere else, following the contours of the land. In a place where nothing stirred, and no wind blew, the sound of rushing water reverberated around me. No, this world was not wholly absent of motion. That fact alone gave me some comfort.

The moment I reached the river, I knelt on the bank and scooped up water in my cupped hands. It was pleasantly cold. The river seemed snow-fed. Its water was crystal clear and appeared pure. Of course, I couldn't tell by looking at it if it was safe to drink.

It might contain a deadly poison. Or bacteria that would ravage my body.

I sniffed the water in my hands. It had no odor (that is, if my sense of smell was still functioning). I took a sip. It had no flavor (that is, if I hadn't lost my sense of taste). I braced myself and swallowed deeply. I was too thirsty to resist, whatever the consequences. The water was indeed entirely tasteless and odorless. It might be real or fabricated, but thankfully, it would quench my thirst.

I knelt there, blissfully gulping mouthful after mouthful. I was thirstier than I had realized. Yet it was strange somehow to drink water lacking in taste and odor. Cold water when we are thirsty is **delicious** more than anything else. Our body sucks it in greedily. Our cells rejoice, our muscles regain their strength. Yet drinking the water from this river brought none of those feelings. It did no more than quench my thirst at a simple, physical level.

When I had drunk my fill, I stood up and looked at my surroundings one more time. Long Face had said that there would be a boat landing somewhere along the riverbank. That one of the boats could ferry me to the other side. There I would (probably) find information relating to Mariye Akikawa's whereabouts. But I could see nothing that looked like a landing, either upstream or downstream. I would have to search for it. A boat was crucial. Fording the river unaided was too dangerous. "The water is cold and deep, and the current is strong. You cannot cross without a boat," Long Face had told me. But which way should I turn to find that boat? Upriver or downriver? I had to choose one or the other.

Then I remembered Menshiki's given name, "Wataru," written with the kanji for traversing water. "The **wataru** in my name is the character that means 'to cross a river,'" Menshiki had said, when he introduced himself. "I don't know why I was given that name. I've never had much to do with water." A short while later he had added, "By the way, I'm lefthanded. If I'm told to go left or right, I always choose left. It's become a habit."

It was a random comment quite disconnected to what we were talking about—I couldn't figure out why he would blurt out something like that. Which is probably why it stuck in my mind.

Maybe his comment had no special significance. It could have been mere happenstance. Yet (according to Long Face) this was a land built upon the conjunction of phenomena and expression. I ought to be able to handle the **happenstance** of any hints that came in my direction. I stood before the river and made up my mind. I would go left. If I took the unconscious tip that "colorless" Menshiki had provided and followed the tasteless, odorless river downstream, it might provide a further hint of some sort. Then again, it might not.

As I walked along the riverbank, I wondered what, if anything, lived in the water. It didn't seem likely anything did. I couldn't confirm this, of course. Nevertheless, I could see no signs of life. What organism would live in water that had neither taste nor odor? The river appeared wholly concentrated on its own identity. "I am river," it said. "I am that which flows." Certainly it possessed the form of a river, but beyond that **state of being** there was nothing. Not a thing floated on its surface, not a twig, not a blade of grass. It was simply a great quantity of water cutting across the land.

I pushed on through that boundless, cottony mist. It gently resisted me as I moved, like a filmy curtain of white lace. After a while, my gut began to react to the water I had drunk. It didn't feel unpleasant or ominous, but neither was it cause for rejoicing. A neutral feeling, whose true nature eluded my understanding. I felt I was being somehow changed, as if I were no longer the same person. It was a strange sensation. Could the water be turning me into someone physically adapted to this world?

For some reason, though, I was able to stay calm. I thought, optimistically, that there could be no real harm. My optimism had no firm basis. Nevertheless, I had passed without mishap through the narrow pitch-black passageway. With neither map nor compass, I had crossed a rocky wilderness to find this river. I had quenched my thirst with its water. I had avoided a close encounter with a lurking Double Metaphor. Dumb luck? Or perhaps it was predetermined. Whichever the case, I was heading in a good direction. So I thought. Or at least so I tried to convince myself.

Finally, a vague shape appeared through the haze. It was not a natural object—its straight lines meant it had to be human-made. As I drew nearer I saw that it was a boat landing. A small wooden jetty extending from the shore. Turning left had been the correct decision. Then again, it was possible that, in a world governed by connectivity, things would shift to accommodate whatever action I chose. Apparently, Menshiki's unconscious hint had helped steer me through to this point.

I could see the figure of a man, shrouded in the mist. He was tall. In fact, after the tiny Commendatore and Long Face, he looked like a giant. He was standing very still at the end of the jetty, as if lost in thought, leaning against some kind of dark machine. The swift-flowing river bubbled over his feet. He was the first human being I had encountered in this land. Or human-shaped being, perhaps. I approached him with trepidation.

I couldn't see him clearly, so I took a chance and called out, "Hello!" through that cottony veil. But there was no reply. He just adjusted his posture slightly. I could see his dark silhouette shift in the mist. Perhaps my voice hadn't reached him. The sound of the river might have blotted it out. Or the air in these parts might not carry sound very well.

"Hello!" I said again, moving somewhat closer. In a louder voice this time. Still, he didn't speak. All I could hear was the unbroken rush of water. Perhaps he couldn't understand what I was saying.

"I can hear you. And I do understand," he said, as if reading my mind. His voice was deep and low, befitting his height. But it was also flat, utterly devoid of feeling. Just as the river was devoid of odor and taste.

54

ETERNITY IS A VERY LONG TIME

T he tall man standing before me had no face. He did have a head, of course. It sat on his shoulders in a normal way. But the head lacked a face. Where a face should have been was blank. A milky blankness, like pale smoke. His voice emerged from within that emptiness like wind from a deep cavern.

The man was wearing what looked like a dark raincoat. The coat ended just short of the ground, so I could see the tips of his boots peeking out. Its buttons were fastened up to his neck. It was as if there was a storm on the horizon, and he had dressed for it.

I stood there, rooted to the spot, unable to speak. From a distance, he had reminded me of the man with the white Subaru Forester, or Tomohiko Amada the night he had visited my studio. Or again, the young man who slayed the Commendatore with his sword in **Killing Commendatore**. All were similarly tall. A closer look, however, told me he was none of them. He was just the **faceless man**. A broad-brimmed black hat was pulled low over his eyes. The brim half concealed the milky emptiness.

"I can hear you. And I do understand," he repeated. I didn't see his lips move, of course. He had none.

"Is this the boat landing?" I asked.

"Yes," the faceless man replied. "This is the boat landing. Only from here can one cross the river."

"I must travel to the other side."

"As must all."

"Do many come?"

The man did not reply. My question was sucked into the void. There followed an interminable silence.

"What is on the other side?" I asked. The white mist over the river concealed the far shore.

I could feel the faceless man studying my face from within the emptiness. "What is on the other side depends on what you are seeking. It is different for everyone."

"I am trying to locate the whereabouts of a young girl named Mariye Akikawa."

"So that is what you seek on the other side, correct?"

"Yes. That is what I seek. That is why I have come."

"And how was it, then, that you were able to find the entrance?"

"I killed an Idea that had taken the form of the Commendatore. I killed him with a carving knife in a nursing home in Izu Kogen. I did so with his permission. His death summoned Long Face, the Metaphor who opened the hole to the underground passageway. I forced him to let me in."

The man fixed his empty countenance on me for some time. He didn't speak. Had he understood me or not? I couldn't tell.

"Was there blood?"

"A great deal," I answered.

"Actual blood, I take it."

"So it seemed."

"Look at your hands."

I looked. But no trace of blood remained. Perhaps it had been washed away when I drank from the river. There ought to have been a lot, though.

"No matter," the faceless man said. "I have a boat, and I will ferry you across. But there is one condition."

I waited to be told what that might be.

"You must pay me an appropriate fee. That is the rule."

"And if I can't pay, am I unable to cross to the far shore?"

"Yes. You would have to remain here for eternity. The river is cold and deep, and the current is strong. And eternity is a very long time. That is no figure of speech, I assure you."

"But I have nothing to pay you with."

"Show me what is in your pockets," the faceless man said, in a quiet voice.

I emptied my jacket and pants pockets. My wallet containing slightly less than 20,000 yen. My credit card, my bank card, my driver's license, and a gas station discount coupon. My key ring with three keys on it. A cream-colored handkerchief and a disposable ballpoint pen. Five or six coins. And that was it. Minus the flashlight, of course.

The faceless man shook his head. "I'm sorry, but I see nothing that can pay for your passage. Money has no meaning here. Don't you have something else?"

I had nothing more in my possession. A cheap

watch was on my left wrist, but time had no value here either.

"If you give me paper, I can portray your likeness. My skill as a painter is the only other thing I carry with me."

The faceless man laughed. At least I think he did. A faint trill echoed in the emptiness.

"In the first place, I have no face. How can you sketch the likeness of a man with no face? Can you draw a void?"

"I am a professional," I said. "I have no need of a face to draw your portrait."

I wasn't at all sure I could pull it off. But I figured it was worth a shot.

"I would be most interested to see what you come up with," the faceless man said. "Unfortunately there is no paper in these parts."

I looked down at the ground. Perhaps I could scratch something on its surface with a stick. But it was solid rock. I shook my head.

"Are you certain that is all you carry with you?"

I carefully searched a second time. The pockets of my leather jacket were empty. Completely. I did find something small tucked in the bottom of one of my jeans pockets, though. A tiny plastic penguin. Menshiki had picked it up from the floor of the pit and given it to me. It had an even tinier strap, which Mariye had used to fasten it to her cell phone. It was her lucky charm. Somehow, it had fallen into the pit.

"Show me what is in your hand," the faceless man said.

I opened my hand, revealing the figurine.

The faceless man stared at it with empty eyes.

"This will do," he said after a moment. "I will accept this as payment."

Should I hand it over or not? It was Mariye's precious lucky charm, after all. It wasn't mine. Could I just give it away? What if something bad happened to her as a result?

But I had no choice. If I failed to turn it over, I would never reach the opposite shore, and if I didn't reach the shore, then I would never find Mariye. The Commendatore's death would have been in vain.

"I will give you the penguin as my fare of passage," I said. "Please take me to the other side of the river."

The faceless man nodded. "The day may come when you can draw my likeness," he said. "If that day arrives, I will return the penguin to you."

The faceless man strode to the end of the wooden jetty and stepped down into the small boat moored there. It was a rectangular vessel, shaped like a pastry box. Barely six feet long and narrow, and made of heavy wooden boards. I doubted it could carry many passengers at a time. There was a thick mast in the middle of the boat, at the top of which stood a metal ring about four inches in diameter. A sturdy rope was threaded through that ring. The rope stretched across the river to the far shore in a straight line—it barely sagged at all. It appeared that the boat ran back and forth along that rope, which kept it from being swept away by the swift current. The boat looked as if it had been in use for ages. It had no visible means of propulsion, or even a proper prow. It was just a shallow wooden box floating on the water.

I followed the faceless man into the boat and seated myself on the horizontal plank that ran from side to side. He leaned against the thick mast with his eyes closed, as if waiting for something. Neither of us spoke. After a few minutes, as if it had made up its own mind, the boat began its slow departure. I had no idea what was propelling us, but we were moving silently toward the far shore. There was no sound of an engine, nor of any other machinery. All I could hear was the steady slapping of water against the hull. We moved at roughly the pace of someone walking. Our boat was dashed from side to side by the current, but the sturdy rope prevented us from being washed downstream. It was just as the faceless man had said—no one could cross the river without a boat. He leaned calmly against the mast, unperturbed even when it felt like our craft might capsize.

"Will I be able to find Mariye Akikawa when we reach the other side?" I asked, when we were about halfway across.

"I am here to ferry you across the river," the faceless man said. "To help you navigate the interstice between presence and absence. After that, it's up to you—my job is done."

Not long after, we hit the jetty on the far shore with a small bump. The faceless man's posture, however, did not change. He leaned against the mast, as if confirming some sort of internal process. When that was done, he expelled a great, empty breath and stepped up onto the jetty. I followed him out of the boat. The jetty and the winch-like mechanism attached to it were the same as those on the opposite bank. So similar, in fact, it felt as if we had made a round-trip, and ended back where we started. That feeling disappeared, however, the moment I stepped onshore. For the ground on this side was normal earth, not solid rock.

"You must proceed alone from here," the faceless man announced.

"But I don't know which path to take. Or which direction to go."

"Such things are inconsequential here," came the rumble from the milky void. "You have drunk from the river, have you not? Now each of your actions will generate an equivalent response, in accordance with the principle of connectivity. Such is the place you have come to."

With these words, the faceless man adjusted his wide-brimmed hat, turned on his heel, and walked back to his boat. Once he was aboard, it returned as it had come, following the rope to the other side. Slow and sure, like a well-trained animal. The faceless man and the boat were one as they vanished into the mist.

I decided to leave the jetty behind and walk downstream along the bank. I could have gone in any direction, but it seemed best to follow the river. That way, there was water to drink when I got thirsty. A short while later, I turned to look back at the jetty, but it was already cloaked in white mist. As though it had never existed.

The farther I walked, the wider the river became, and the gentler the current. There were no more whitecaps, and the sound of rushing water had practically disappeared. Why hadn't they put the pier here, instead of where the flow was so swift? True, the distance would have been greater, but the crossing would have been so much easier where the water was calm. All the same, this world probably operated according to its own principles, its own way of thinking. Even greater danger might lurk beneath the placid surface.

I searched my pockets. Sure enough, the penguin was gone. That the protective charm had been lost (most likely for all eternity) was hardly reassuring. Perhaps I had made the wrong choice. Yet what other option did I have? I could only hope Mariye would be all right without it. At this point, hope was all I had.

I made my way along the riverbank, the flashlight from Tomohiko Amada's bedside in one hand. I kept it turned off. This dusky world was not so dim as to require a light. I could see where I was walking, and for about twelve or fifteen feet ahead. The river flowed to my left, slow and silent. Once in a while, I could glimpse the far shore through the haze.

The farther on I pushed, the more the ground beneath my feet came to resemble a path. Not a well-defined path, yet something that fulfilled the function of a path. There were vague signs that people had passed this way before. Gradually, the path was leading me away from the river. At a certain point, I drew up short. Should I stick to the river? Or allow this **presumed path** to take me in another direction?

After some thought, I elected to follow the path and leave the river behind. I had a feeling it would lead me somewhere. **Now each of your actions will generate an equivalent response, in accordance with the principle of connectivity,** the ferryman had said. This path could well be an example. I decided to follow the plausible suggestion, if that's what it was, that had been presented to me.

The farther I moved from the river, the more the path turned uphill. Eventually, I realized I could no longer hear the rush of water. The slope was easy and the path almost straight, so my steps fell into a steady rhythm. The mist was melting away, but the light remained pale and somewhat opaque. There was no way to tell what lay ahead. I kept my eyes on my feet, and my breathing regular and systematic.

How long had I been walking? I had lost all sense of time. All sense of direction, too. And the thoughts running through my head were distracting me. I had so much to figure out, yet my thoughts had become so terribly fragmented. When I tried to focus on one thought, a new thought would appear to gulp it down, and my mind would careen in the wrong direction. Each time, I lost track of what I had just been thinking about.

I was so distracted, in fact, that I almost bumped right into **that**. I tripped on something, and raised my eyes as I was regaining my balance. In that instant, the air around me was transformed—I could feel it on my skin. I snapped back to reality. An enormous black mass loomed directly ahead. My jaw dropped in surprise. What was it? It took a moment to register that a huge forest stood in my path. It had materialized without warning in a terrain that, until that point, had had no vegetation, not a single leaf or blade of grass. No mystery, then, why I was so shocked.

It was a forest—no question there. A tangle of branches with thick leaves that formed a solid wall. Within the forest was darkness. More accurate than forest, perhaps, might have been "sea of trees." I stood before it and listened, but could hear nothing. No birdsongs, no branches rustling in the wind. A complete absence of sound.

I was afraid to step inside the forest. Instinctively. The trees were too dense, the darkness inside too deep. I had no way to gauge the scale, or how far the path would continue. It might well split into a labyrinth of side trails. If I got lost in that maze, my chances of escaping were practically zero. Still, I had no other real options. The path I had chosen headed straight into the forest (or, more accurately, was sucked into it, like train tracks are sucked into a tunnel). It made no sense, having come this far, to turn around and head back to the river. Who knows, the river might not even be there anymore. No, I had made my choice, and now I had to live with it. I would press on, at whatever cost.

Mustering my courage, I stepped into the trees. It was impossible to tell the time of day—it could have been dawn, or midday, or evening. The half-light never seemed to vary, no matter how much time passed. Then again, time might not exist in this world. In which case, this dusk could persist, day in and day out, forever.

Sure enough, it was dark inside. The layered branches above my head blocked out almost all light. Yet I left my flashlight off. Once my eyes adjusted, I could see enough to walk, and I didn't want to waste the batteries. I plunged through the forest, trying hard to empty my mind. Any thoughts would likely lead me to an even darker place. The path continued its gentle rise. All I could hear were my own footsteps, and those were more and more faint, as if their sound was slowly being sucked away. I hoped my thirst wouldn't return. By this time, the river would be far indeed. No chance of heading back for a drink, however thirsty I got.

How long did I walk? The forest was deep and dark, the view unchanging. The light never changed, either. My footsteps were all I could hear, and barely at that. The air was tasteless and odorless, as always. Thick trees walled both sides of the path. I could see nothing else. Did anything live here? Perhaps not. I had noticed no birds or insects.

Yet I could feel something watching me—the sensation was clear and very unpleasant. Sharp eyes were being trained in my direction from behind the wall of foliage. Every movement I made was under surveillance. My skin burned, as if under a magnifying glass in the sun. **What was I doing there?** they demanded. This was their domain, and I was a lone invader. Yet I never actually saw any of those eyes. I may have imagined them. Fear and suspicion can fashion eyes in the dark.

Then again, Mariye had felt Menshiki's eyes on her from across a valley, and through a telescope, no less. She had guessed that someone was keeping constant watch on her. And she was right. Those eyes were no fantasy.

Nevertheless, I decided to dismiss the eyes I felt scrutinizing me. There was no way that they were real. They had to be hallucinations, created by my fears. I needed to think that way. I had to make it through the great forest (though its actual size was a mystery). While retaining as much of my sanity as possible.

Luckily, there were no side trails. Thus I wasn't forced to make a choice that might take me into a maze that led nowhere. No thorny thickets blocked my way. All I had to do was push forward along a single path.

I couldn't tell how long I had been walking, yet I didn't feel especially tired. Perhaps I was under too much stress to register fatigue. Just when my legs were getting a little heavy, however, I spied a yellow point of light in the distance. At first, I thought it was a firefly. But I was mistaken. The light didn't move, or flicker on and off. Its fixed position suggested that it was human-made. The farther I went, little by little, the light grew larger and brighter. There could be no doubt. **I was approaching something.**

Was it something good, or something bad? Would it help or harm me? Whichever, I was out of options. For better or for worse, I had to find out what that light was. If I didn't have the guts to do that, I never should have embarked on this journey in the first place. Step by step, I advanced toward the light.

Then, just as suddenly as it had appeared before me, the forest ended. The trees that had lined the path on both sides vanished, and before I knew it, I had stepped out into a broad clearing. The clearing was the shape of a half-moon, and perfectly level. Now I could see the sky once more, and view my surroundings in that dusky light. Directly across from me rose a sheer cliff, and at the base of that cliff was the open mouth of a dark cave. The yellow light I had been following streamed directly from that opening.

The gloomy sea of trees was behind me, the towering cliff (much too steep for me to climb) straight ahead. The mouth of the cave opened directly before me. I looked up at the sky a second time, then around at my surroundings. Nothing looked like a path. My next move had to be to enter the cave—there was no alternative. Before going in, I took several deep breaths, to brace myself. By moving forward, I would generate a new reality in accordance with the principle of connectivity. So the faceless man had said. I would navigate the interstice between presence and absence. I could only entrust myself to his words.

Warily, I stepped into the cave. Then it struck

me—**I had been here before**. I knew this cave by sight. The air inside was familiar, too. Memories came flooding back. The wind cave on Mt. Fuji. The cave where our young uncle had taken Komichi and me during our summer break, back when we were kids. She had slipped into a narrow side tunnel and disappeared for a long while. I had been scared to death that she was gone for good. Had she been sucked into an underground maze for all eternity?

Eternity is a very long time, the faceless man had said.

I walked slowly through the cave toward the yellow light, deadening my footsteps and trying to quiet my pounding heart. I rounded a corner, and there it was: the source of the light. An old lantern with a black metal rim, the sort that coal miners once carried, hanging on a thick nail driven into the stone wall. A fat candle burned inside the lantern.

Lantern, I thought. The word had come up not long before. It was part of the name of the anti-Nazi underground student organization that Tomohiko Amada was presumed to have joined. Things seemed to be converging.

A woman was standing beneath the lantern. I didn't see her at first because she was so tiny. Less than two feet tall. Her black hair was coiled atop her head in a neat bun, and she wore a white gown from some ancient time. Its elegance was apparent at a glance. Another character lifted from **Killing Commendatore**. The beautiful maiden who looks on in horror, her hand over her mouth, as the Commendatore is slain. In Mozart's **Don Giovanni,** she is Donna Anna. The daughter of the Commendatore.

Magnified by the light of the lantern, her sharp black shadow trembled on the wall of the cave.

"I have been awaiting you," the miniature Donna Anna said.

55

A CLEAR CONTRAVENTION
OF BASIC PRINCIPLES

have been awaiting you," said Donna Anna. She was tiny, but her voice was clear and bright.

Nothing could have surprised me by that point. It even seemed natural for her to be there waiting for me. She was a beautiful woman, with an innate elegance, and the way she spoke had a majestic ring. She might be only two feet tall, but she clearly had that special something that could captivate a man.

"I will be your guide," she said to me. "Please be so kind as to take that lantern."

I unhooked the lantern from the wall. I didn't know who had put it there, so far beyond her reach. Its circular metal handle allowed it to be hung on a nail or carried by hand.

"You were waiting for me?" I asked.

"Yes," she said. "For a very long time."

Could she be another form of Metaphor? I hesitated to pose such a bold question.

"Do you live in these parts?"

"Live here?" she said, casting a dubious glance in my direction. "No, I am **here** to meet you. And I'm afraid I don't understand what you mean by 'these parts.'"

I gave up asking questions after that. She was Donna Anna, and she had been waiting for me.

She wore the same sort of ancient garb as the Commendatore. In her case, a white garment, most likely made of fine silk. Draped in layers over the top half of her body, with loose-fitting pantaloons below. Though her shape was therefore hidden, I guessed she was slender but strong. Her small black shoes were fashioned of leather of some kind.

"Then let us commence," Donna Anna said to me. "Not much time remains. The path is narrowing as we speak. Please follow me. And be so good as to hold the lantern."

I followed in her wake, holding the lantern above her head. She walked toward the back of the cave with quick, practiced steps. The candle's flame fluttered as we moved, casting a dancing mosaic of shadows on the pitted walls.

"This looks like a wind cave on Mt. Fuji that I once visited," I said. "Is that possible?"

"All that is here **looks like** something," Donna Anna declaimed without turning around. As though she were addressing the darkness ahead.

"Do you mean to say nothing here is the real thing?"

"No one can tell what is or is not the real thing," she stated flatly. "All that we see is a product of connectivity. Light here is a metaphor for shadow, shadow a metaphor for light. You know this already, I believe."

I didn't think I knew, at least not all that well, but I refrained from inquiring further. That could only lead to more knotty abstractions.

The cave grew narrower the farther back we went. The roof became lower too, so that I had to stoop as I walked. Just as I had done in the Mt. Fuji wind cave. Finally, Donna Anna drew to a halt and turned to face me. Her small, flashing eyes stared up into mine.

"I can guide you this far. Now you must take the lead. I will follow, but only to a certain point. After that, you are on your own."

Take the lead? I shook my head in disbelief—from what I could see, we had reached the very back of the cave. A dark stone wall blocked our way. I passed the lantern across its face. But it appeared that we had hit a dead end.

"It seems we can't go any farther," I said.

"Please look again. There should be an opening in the corner to your left," Donna Anna said.

I shone the lantern on that section of the cave wall once more. When I stuck my head out and looked more closely, I could make out a dark depression on the far side of a large boulder. I squeezed myself between the wall and the boulder to inspect it. It certainly did appear to be an opening. I remembered my sister slipping into an even narrower crack.

I turned back to Donna Anna.

"You must enter there," the two-foot-tall woman said.

I looked at her lovely face, wondering what to say. On the wall, her elongated shadow flickered in the lantern's yellow light.

"I am fully aware," she said, "that you have been terrified of small, dark places all your life. In such places, you can no longer breathe normally. I am correct, am I not? Nevertheless, you must force yourself to enter. Only in such a manner can you grasp that which you seek."

"Where does this opening lead?"

"I do not know. The destination is something you yourself must determine by following your own heart."

"But fear is in my heart as well," I said. "That's what worries me. That my fear will distort what I see and push me in the wrong direction."

"Once again, it is you who determines the path. You are the one who chose the proper route to reach this world. You paid a great price for that, and have crossed the river by boat. You cannot turn back now."

I looked again at the opening. I shuddered to think I would have to crawl into that dark, cramped tunnel. Yet that was what I had to do. She was right—I couldn't turn back now. I placed the lantern on the ground and took the flashlight from my pocket. A lantern would be much too cumbersome in that tiny space.

"Believe in yourself," Donna Anna said, her voice small but penetrating. "You have drunk from the river, have you not?"

"Yes, I was very thirsty."

"It is good that you did so," Donna Anna said. "That river flows along the interstice between presence and absence. It is filled with hidden possibilities that only the finest metaphors can bring to the surface. Just as a great poet can use one scene to bring another new, unknown vista into view. It should be obvious, but the best metaphors make the best poems. Take good care not to avert your eyes from the new, unknown vistas you will encounter."

Tomohiko Amada's **Killing Commendatore** might be seen as one such "unknown vista." Like a great poem, the painting was a perfect metaphor, one that launched a new reality into the world.

I switched on the flashlight and checked its beam. It was bright and unwavering. The batteries should last for some time yet. I removed my leather jacket. It was too bulky to fit into such a tight space. That left me wearing a light sweater and jeans. The cave wasn't especially cold, but neither was it all that warm.

Bracing myself, I crouched until I was almost on all fours and squeezed headfirst into the opening. Inside I found what appeared to be a tunnel sunk into solid rock. It was smooth to the touch, as if worn by water over the course of many years. There were almost no jagged or protruding edges. As a result, despite its narrowness, I was able to progress more easily than I had expected. The rock was cool and slightly damp. I inched forward on my stomach like a worm, the flashlight illuminating my way. I figured that the tunnel must have functioned as a waterway at some point in the past.

The tunnel was about two feet high and three feet across. Crawling was the only option. It looked like it would go on forever, a dark, natural pipe that expanded and contracted by small degrees. Sometimes it curved to the side. At other times it sloped up or down. Thankfully, though, there were no abrupt rises or falls. Then it hit me. If this was an underground conduit, water could flood the tunnel at any moment, and I would surely drown. My legs stopped moving, paralyzed by fear.

I wanted to turn around and go back the way I had come. But it was impossible to reverse course in such a cramped space. The tunnel seemed to have grown even narrower. Crawling backward to where I had begun was out of the question. Terror engulfed me. I was literally nailed to the spot. I couldn't move forward, and I couldn't retreat. Every cell in my body cried out for fresh air. Forsaken by light, I felt powerless and alone.

"Do not stop. You must push on." Donna Anna's command was irrefutable. I couldn't tell if I was hearing things or if she was really behind me, urging me on.

"I can't move," I gasped, squeezing out the words. "And I can't breathe."

"Make fast your heart," said Donna Anna. "Do not let it flounder. Should that happen, you will surely fall prey to a Double Metaphor."

"What are Double Metaphors?" I asked.

"You should know the answer to that already."

"I should know?"

"That is because they are within you," said Donna Anna. "They grab hold of your true thoughts and feelings and devour them one after another, fattening themselves. That is what Double Metaphors are. They have been dwelling in the depths of your psyche since ancient times."

Unbidden, the man with the white Subaru Forester entered my mind. I didn't want him there. But there was no way around it. It was he who had pushed me to throttle that young woman, forcing me to look into the darkness of my own heart. He had reappeared more than once, to make sure I would remember that darkness.

I know where you were and what you were doing, he was announcing to me. Of course he knew everything. Because he lived inside me.

My heart was in chaos. I closed my eyes and tried to anchor it, to hold it in one place. I ground my teeth with the effort. But how should I go about securing my heart? Where was its true location, anyway? I looked within myself, searching one place after another. But it didn't turn up. Where could it be?

"Your true heart lives in your memory. It is nourished by the images it contains—that's how it lives," a woman said. This time, however, it was not Donna Anna speaking. It was Komi. My sister, dead at age twelve.

"Search your memory," said that dear voice. "Find something concrete. Something you can touch."

"Komi?" I said.

There was no answer.

"Komi, where are you?" I said.

Still no reply.

There in the dark, I searched my memory. Like

rummaging through an old duffel bag. But it seemed to have been emptied. I couldn't even recall exactly what memory was.

"Turn off your light and listen to the wind," Komi said.

I switched off the flashlight. But I couldn't hear the wind, though I tried. All I could make out was the restless pounding of my heart, a screen door banging in a gale.

"Listen to the wind," Komi repeated.

Once again, I held my breath and focused. This time, I could hear, lying beyond my heartbeat, a faint humming. A wind seemed to be blowing somewhere far away. A wisp of a breeze brushed my face. Air was entering the tunnel ahead. Air I could smell. The unmistakable odor of damp soil. The first odor I had encountered since setting foot in this Land of Metaphor. The tunnel was leading somewhere. To a place I could smell. In short, to the real world.

"All right then, on you go," said Donna Anna. "There isn't much time left."

With my flashlight turned off, I crawled on into the blackness. As I moved forward, I tried to draw even the slightest whiff of that real air into my lungs.

"Komi?" I asked again.

There was no answer.

I ransacked my store of memories. Komi and I had raised a pet cat. A smart black tomcat. We named it Koyasu, though why we gave it that name escapes me. Komi had picked it up as a kitten on her way home from school. One day, however, it disappeared. We scoured our neighborhood looking for it. We stopped countless people and showed them Koyasu's photograph. But in the end the cat never turned up.

I crawled on, the image of the black cat vivid in my mind. I tried to imagine my sister and me together, searching for it. I strained my eyes to catch a glimpse of the cat at the end of the dark tunnel. I pricked my ears to hear its mewing. The black cat was solid and concrete, something I could touch. I could feel its fur, its warmth, the firmness of its body—even hear it purr—as if it were yesterday.

"That's right," Komi said. "Just keep remembering like that."

I know where you were and what you were doing, the man with the white Subaru Forester called out of nowhere. He wore a black leather jacket and a golf cap with the Yonex logo. His voice was hoarse from the sea wind. Caught by surprise, I recoiled in fear.

I tried to find my memories of the cat. To draw the fragrance of damp earth into my lungs. I seemed to recall that smell from somewhere. From a time not so far away. But I couldn't remember, try as I might. Where had it been? As I struggled to recall, once again, my memories began to fade away.

Strangle me with this, the girl had said. Her pink tongue peeked out at me from between her lips. The belt of her bathrobe lay beside her pillow, ready to be used. Her pubic hair glistened like grass in the rain.

"Come on," Komi urged me. "Call up a favorite memory. Hurry!"

I tried to bring back the black cat. But Koyasu

was gone. Why couldn't I remember him? Perhaps the darkness had snatched him away while I was distracted. Its power had devoured him. I had to come up with something else, and fast. I had the horrid sense that the tunnel was tightening around me. It seemed alive. **There is not much time**, Donna Anna had said. Cold sweat trickled from my armpits.

"Come on now, remember something," Komi's voice said behind me. "Something you can physically touch. Something you can draw."

Like a drowning man clutching a buoy, I latched onto my old Peugeot 205. My little French car. I remembered the feeling of the steering wheel as I toured northeastern Japan and Hokkaido. It felt like ages ago, yet I could still hear the rattle of that primitive four-cylinder engine, and the way the clutch growled when I shifted from second into third. For a month and a half, the car had been my constant comrade, my only friend. Now it was probably sitting in a scrap yard somewhere.

The tunnel was definitely narrowing. My head kept banging against the roof. I reached for the flashlight.

"Do not turn on the light," Donna Anna commanded.

"But I can't see where I'm going."

"You must not see," she said. **"Not with your eyes."**

"The hole is closing in. If I go on I won't be able to move."

There was no answer.

"I can't go any farther," I said. "What should I do?"

Again no answer.

I could no longer hear Donna Anna and Komi. I sensed they were gone. All that remained was a deep silence.

The tunnel continued to shrink, making it even harder for me to advance. Panic was setting in. My limbs felt paralyzed—just drawing a breath was growing difficult. A voice whispered in my ear. **You are trapped**, it said. **This is your coffin. You cannot move forward. You cannot move backward. You will lie buried here forever. Forsaken by humanity, in this dark and narrow tomb**.

I sensed something approaching from behind. A flattish thing, crawling toward me through the dark. It wasn't Donna Anna, nor was it Komi. In fact, it wasn't human. I could hear the scraping of its many feet and its ragged breathing. It stopped when it reached me. There followed a few moments of silence. It seemed to be holding its breath, planning its next move. Then something cold and slimy touched my bare ankle. The end of a long tentacle, it seemed. Sheer terror coursed up my back.

Could this be a Double Metaphor? That which stemmed from the darkness within me?

I know where you were and what you were doing.

I couldn't recall a thing. Not the black cat, not the Peugeot 205, not the Commendatore—everything was gone. My memory had been wiped clean a second time.

I squirmed and twisted, frantically trying to escape the tentacle. The tunnel had contracted even farther—I could barely move. I was trying to force myself into a space smaller than my body. That was a clear contravention of basic principles. It didn't take a genius to figure out it was physically impossible.

Nevertheless, I kept on thrusting, pushing myself forward. As Donna Anna had said, this was the path I had chosen, and it was too late to choose another. The Commendatore had died to make my quest possible. I had stabbed him with my own hands. His body had sunk in a pool of blood. I couldn't allow him to die for nothing. And the owner of that clammy tentacle was trying to get me in its grips.

Rallying my spirits, I pressed on. I could feel my sweater unravel as it caught and tore on the rock. I awkwardly squirmed ahead, loosening my joints like an escape artist slipping his bonds. My pace was no faster than that of a caterpillar. The narrow tunnel was squeezing me like a giant vise. My bones and muscles screamed. The slimy tentacle slithered farther up my ankle. Soon it would cover me, as I lay there in the impenetrable dark, unable to move. I would no longer be the person I was.

Jettisoning all reason, I mustered what strength I had left and forced myself into the ever-narrowing space. Every part of my body shrieked in pain. Yet I had to push forward, whatever the consequences. Even if I had to dislocate every joint. However agonizing that would be. For everything around me was the product of connectivity. Nothing was absolute. Pain was a metaphor. The tentacle clutching my leg was a metaphor. All was relative. Light was shadow, shadow was light. I had no choice but to believe. What else could I do?

The tunnel ended without warning, spitting me out like a clump of grass from a clogged drainpipe. I flew through the air, utterly defenseless. There was no time to think. I must have fallen at least six feet before I hit the ground. Luckily, it wasn't solid rock, but relatively soft earth. I curled and rolled as I fell, tucking in my head to protect it from the impact. A judo move, done without thinking. I whacked my shoulder and hip on landing, but I barely felt it.

Darkness surrounded me. And my flashlight was gone. I seemed to have dropped it when I tumbled out. I remained on all fours, not moving. I couldn't see anything. I couldn't think anything. I was only aware, and barely at that, of a growing pain in my joints. Every tendon, every bone wailed in protest at what it had been put through during my escape.

Yes—I had escaped that dreadful tunnel! The realization hit me at last. I could still feel the eerie tentacle sliding over my ankle. I was grateful to have eluded that thing, whatever it was.

But then, where was I now?

There was no breeze. But there was smell. The odor I had caught a whiff of in the tunnel was everywhere. I couldn't recall where I had encountered it before. Nevertheless, this place was dead quiet. Not a sound anywhere.

I needed to find my flashlight. I carefully searched the ground where I had fallen. On all fours, in a widening circle. The earth was moist. I was scared that I might touch something creepy in the dark, but there was nothing, not even a pebble. Just ground so perfectly flat it must have been leveled by human hands.

After a long search, I finally found the flashlight lying about three feet from where I had landed. The moment my hand touched its plastic casing was one of the happiest of my life.

But I didn't switch it on right away. Instead, I closed my eyes and took a number of deep breaths. As if I were patiently unraveling a stubborn knot. My breathing slowed. My heartbeat did, too, and my muscles began to return to normal. I slowly exhaled the last deep breath and switched on the flashlight. Its yellow light raced through the darkness. But I couldn't look yet. My eyes had grown too used to the dark—the tiniest light made my head split with pain.

I shielded my eyes with one hand until I could open my fingers enough to peer through the cracks. From what I could see, I had landed on the floor of a circular-shaped room. A room of modest size, with walls of stone. I shone the flashlight above my head. The room had a ceiling. No, not exactly that. Something more like a lid. No light seeped through.

I realized where I was: in the pit in the woods, behind the little shrine. I had crawled into the tunnel in Donna Anna's cave and tumbled out onto the floor of this stone chamber. I was in a real pit in the real world. I had no idea how that could have happened. But it had. I was back at the beginning, so to speak. But why was there no light? The lid was made of wooden boards. There were cracks between those boards, through which some light should enter. Yet none did.

I was stumped.

At least I knew where I was. The smell was a dead giveaway. Why had it taken me so long to figure out? I carefully examined my surroundings with my flashlight. The metal ladder that should have been standing there was gone. Someone must have pulled it out and carted it off. Which meant there was no means of escape.

What I found strange—it should have been strange, I guess—was that I could find no trace of the opening, no matter how hard I looked. I had exited the narrow tunnel and fallen onto the floor of this pit. Like a newborn baby pushed out in midair. Yet I couldn't find the aperture. It was as if it had closed after it spit me out.

Eventually, the flashlight's beam illuminated an object on the ground. Something I recognized. It was the old bell the Commendatore had rung—hearing it had led me to discover the pit. Everything had begun with this bell. I had left it on the shelf in the studio— then at some point it had vanished. I picked it up and examined it under the flashlight. It had an old wooden handle. There could be no doubt—it was **that bell**.

I stared at it for some time, trying to understand. Had someone brought it back? Had it returned under its own power? The Commendatore had told me the bell belonged to the pit. What did that mean— belonged to the pit? But I was too tired to figure out the principles that might explain what was taking place. And there was no pillar of logic I could lean on.

I sat down, back against the stone wall, and switched off the flashlight. I had to figure out how to escape from this pit. I didn't need light for that. And it was important to conserve the batteries.

So what should I do now?

56

IT APPEARS THAT SEVERAL BLANKS NEED FILLING IN

A number of things made no sense. Most troubling of all was the total absence of light. Someone had sealed the pit's opening. But who would do such a thing, and why?

I prayed that someone (whoever it was) hadn't piled boulders on top of the lid, returning it to how it had been in the beginning. That would mean my chances of getting out were practically zero.

A thought struck me—I clicked on the flashlight and checked my watch. It read 4:32. The second hand was circling the face, doing its job. Time was passing, no doubt about it. At least I was back where time flowed at a set pace, and in a single direction.

Yet what was time, when you got right down to it? We measured its passage with the hands of a clock for convenience's sake. But was that appropriate? Did time really flow in such a steady and linear way? Couldn't this be a mistaken way of thinking, an error of major proportions?

I clicked off the flashlight and, with a long sigh, returned to absolute darkness. Enough pondering time. Enough pondering space. Thinking about stuff like that led nowhere. It only added to my stress. I had to think about things that were concrete, things I could see and touch.

So I thought about Yuzu. She was certainly something I could see with my eyes and touch with my hands (if I was ever given that opportunity again). Now she was pregnant. This coming January, the child—not my child, but that of some other man—would be born. That situation continued without my involvement, in a place far removed from me. A new life with which I had no connection would enter this world. Yuzu had asked nothing of me. So why was she refusing to marry the father? I couldn't figure it out. If she planned to be a single mother, odds were she'd have to quit her job at the architectural firm. I doubted that a small business like that could extend a lengthy maternity leave to a new mother.

I could find no convincing answers to these questions, though I tried. I was stumped. And the darkness made me feel even more powerless.

If I ever got out of this pit, I would put aside my hesitations and go see Yuzu. No question about it, I was hurt when she left me for someone else. It angered me, too (although it took me a very long time to realize that). But why carry around my resentments for the rest of my life? I would go meet her and we could talk things out. I needed to know, from Yuzu herself, what she was thinking, and what she wanted. Before it was too late. Once I made that decision, I felt a little easier. If she wanted to be friends, well, maybe I could give it a shot. It wasn't beyond the realm of possibility, at least. Perhaps we could resolve things that way. If I managed to get out of the pit, that is.

After this I fell asleep. I had shed my leather jacket before entering the tunnel (what fate lay in store for that jacket of mine?), and the cold was starting to get to me. The thin sweater I had on over my T-shirt had been so shredded by the walls of the tunnel that it was a sweater in name only. Moreover, I had returned to the real world from the Land of Metaphor. In other words, I was back where time and temperature played their proper roles. Yet my need for sleep won out. I drifted off, sitting there on the ground, leaning against the hard stone wall. It was a pure sleep, free of dream or deception. A solitary sleep beyond anyone's reach, like the Spanish gold resting on the floor of the Irish Sea.

It was still pitch black when I woke up. I couldn't see my finger when I waved it in front of my face. The darkness blotted out the line between sleep and wakefulness as well. Where did one end and the other begin, and which side was I on? I dragged out my bag of memories and began flipping through them, as if counting a stack of gold coins: the black cat that had been our pet; my old Peugeot 205; Menshiki's white mansion; the record **Der Rosenkavalier;** the plastic penguin. I was able to call up memories of each, in great detail. My mind was working okay—the Double Metaphor hadn't devoured it. It's just that I had been in total darkness for so long that I was having trouble drawing a line between the world of sleep and the waking world.

I switched on the flashlight, covered it with my hand, and read my watch in the light leaking between my fingers: 1:18. Last time I looked, it was 4:32. Could I have been sleeping in such an uncomfortable position for nine hours? That was hard to believe. If that were true, I should be a lot stiffer. It seemed more reasonable to assume that, unbeknownst to me, time had traveled backward three hours. But I couldn't be certain either way. Being immersed in the dark for so long had obliterated my sense of time.

In any case, the cold had grown more penetrating. And I had to pee. Badly. Resigning myself, I shuffled to the other side of the pit and let it all out. It was a long pee that the ground quickly absorbed. A faint smell of ammonia lingered, but only for a moment. Once the need to pee had been taken care of, hunger stepped in to take its place. By slow and steady degrees, it seemed, my body was readapting to the real world. Perhaps the effects of the water I had drunk from the River of Metaphor were wearing off.

I had to get out of the pit as soon as possible. I felt that more urgently now. If I didn't, it wouldn't take long to starve to death. Human beings can only sustain life if provided with food and water—that was a basic rule of the real world. And my present location had neither. All I had was air (though the lid was closed, air seemed to be leaking in from somewhere). Air, love, and ideals were important, no argument there, but you couldn't survive on them alone.

I pulled myself off the ground and attempted to scale the pit's smooth stone wall. I tried from a number of spots, but, as I expected, it was a waste of energy. The wall was less than nine feet high, but it was straight up and down, with nothing at all to grab onto. It would take superhuman ability to climb, and even if I reached the top, there was still that heavy lid to deal with. I would need a solid foothold to push that aside.

I sat back down, resigned. Only one option presented itself. I could ring the bell. As the Commendatore had done. But there was one big difference between the Commendatore and me. He was an Idea, while I was a flesh-and-blood human being. An Idea never felt hunger, while I did. An Idea wouldn't starve to death, whereas I would, relatively quickly. The Commendatore could ring the bell for a hundred years (though the concept of time was foreign to him) and not get tired, while my limit without food and water was probably three or four days. After that, I wouldn't have the strength, though the bell was light.

So I began ringing the bell there in the dark. There was nothing else to do. Of course I could call out for help. But the pit was in the middle of a deserted woods. Since the woods was the private property of the Amada family, under normal circumstances there would be no one around. To make matters worse, the cover of the pit had been sealed tight. I could shout at the top of my lungs and no one would hear. My voice would just grow hoarse, and I would become even thirstier. At least shaking the bell was better than nothing.

Moreover, there was something out of the ordinary about the bell's ring. It seemed to have some special power. In physical terms, it wasn't very loud. Yet I had heard it from my distant bed in the middle of the night. The autumn insects had fallen silent the moment they heard that ringing. As if commanded to stop their racket.

So I sat there at the bottom of the pit, my back against the stone wall, and rang the bell. I shook my wrist from side to side and emptied my mind as best I could. When I got tired, I took a break and then started again. As the Commendatore had done before me. It wasn't hard to clear my mind. When I listened to the bell I felt, quite naturally, that I didn't have to think about anything else. The ringing sounded different in the dark than in the light. I'm pretty sure that difference was real. I was stuck in a black hole with no way out, but as long as I was shaking the bell, I felt neither fear nor anxiety. I could forget cold and hunger, as well. For the most part, I could even set aside my need to analyze what was taking place. This was a welcome change, as you can imagine.

When I tired of ringing the bell, I dozed off leaning against the stone wall. When I awoke, I switched on the flashlight and checked my watch. Time, I discovered, was behaving in a very haphazard manner. Of course, this may have had more to do with me than the watch. No question there. But that haphazardness was fine with me. I just went on mindlessly ringing the bell, then falling asleep, then waking up to ring the bell again. An endless repetition. With the repetition, my consciousness grew ever more thin and rarified.

Not a single sound made its way into the pit. I couldn't hear the birds, or the wind. What could explain that? This was supposed to be the real world. I was back in a place where people felt hunger, and the need to pee. The real world ought to be filled with all kinds of noises.

I had no idea how much time had passed. I had given up checking my watch. The passing of days made even less sense than the passage of minutes and hours. How could it be otherwise in a place that lacked day and night? Not just time, either—I was losing contact with my own self. My body had become a stranger to me. I was finding it harder and harder to understand what my physical existence meant. Or perhaps I didn't care to understand. All I could do was keep ringing that bell. Until my wrist was almost numb.

After what felt like an eternity (or after time had surged and ebbed like waves pounding the shore), and my hunger became unbearable, finally I heard something above my head. It sounded as if someone had grabbed hold of a corner of the world and was trying to peel back its skin. But the sound didn't strike my ear as real. I mean, how could anyone do that? And if they succeeded, what would follow? A fresh new world, or an endless nothing? In truth, though, I didn't care one way or the other. The final result would probably be more or less the same.

There in the dark, I closed my eyes and waited for the peeling of the world to conclude. But the world wasn't to be peeled so easily, it seemed, and the din only mounted. Maybe it was real, after all. An actual object undergoing a process that produced an actual physical sound. Steeling myself, I opened my eyes and looked up. I trained the beam of my flashlight on the ceiling. Someone was up there making an awful racket. I didn't know why, but it was an ear-splitting grinding noise.

I couldn't tell if the sound threatened me, or was being made **on my behalf**. Whichever the case, I just sat there at the bottom of the pit shaking my bell, waiting to see how things would turn out. At last, a thin sheet of light shot through a crack between the boards and into the pit. Like the broad, sharp blade of a guillotine gliding through a mass of gelatin, it swept down through the darkness to land on my ankle. I dropped the bell and covered my face to protect my eyes.

Next, one of the boards was moved to the side and even more sunlight flooded in. Though my eyes were closed and my palms were pressed against them, I could feel the darkness turn to light. Then new air flowed in from above. It was fresh and cold, and filled with the fragrance of early winter. I loved that smell. I remembered how I had felt as a child wrapping a scarf around my neck on the first cold morning of the year. The softness of the wool against my skin.

843

Someone was calling my name from the top of the pit. At least, it seemed to be my name. I had forgotten I had one. Names possessed no meaning in the world where I had been for so long.

It took me a while to connect the **someone** calling my name with Wataru Menshiki. I shouted back. But no words emerged. All I could produce was a sort of growl, a signal that I was still alive. I wasn't sure my voice was strong enough to reach him, but at least I could hear it. The strange, harsh call of some imaginary beast.

"Are you all right?" Menshiki called down.

"Menshiki?"

"Yes, it's me," Menshiki said. "Are you hurt?"

"No, I'm all right," I said. My voice had returned. "I think," I added.

"How long have you been down there?"

"I don't know. It just happened."

"Can you climb the ladder if I lower it to you?"

"I think so," I said. Probably.

"Wait just a minute. I'll go get it."

My eyes began to adjust to the sunlight as I waited. I still couldn't open them all the way, but at least I didn't have to cover them with my hands. As luck would have it, it wasn't that bright. I could tell it was daytime, but the sky was probably blanketed with clouds. Or else dusk was approaching. At last, I heard the metal ladder being lowered.

"Please give me a little more time," I said. "My eyes aren't used to the light, so I have to be careful."

"Of course, take all the time you want," said Menshiki.

"Why was the pit so dark? There was no light at all."

"I covered it two days ago. It looked like someone had been monkeying with the lid, so I brought a heavy tarp from my house and tied it down with metal pegs and twine so it wouldn't budge. I didn't want a child to slip and fall in. I checked first to be sure no one was inside. It was empty then, I'm sure of it."

It made perfect sense. Menshiki had covered the lid. That's why it had been so dark.

"There were no signs that anyone had tampered with the tarp. It was just as I left it. So how did you get in? I don't understand," Menshiki said.

"I don't understand either," I said. "It just happened."

There was nothing more I could tell him. And I had no intention of trying to explain, either.

"Shall I come down?" Menshiki asked.

"No, please stay where you are. I'll come up."

I could keep my eyes half open now. Mysterious images were churning behind them, but at least my mind was functioning. I lined up the ladder against the wall, put my foot on the lowest rung, and tried to push myself up. But my legs were weak. They didn't feel like my legs at all. Still, I was able to gingerly climb up the ladder, one rung at a time. The air grew fresher the closer I got to the surface. I could hear birds chirping.

When I reached the top, Menshiki took my wrist in an iron grip and pulled me out. He was much stronger than I expected. Strong enough that I gave myself over to his hands without a second thought. Gratitude was all I felt. Out of the hole, I flopped onto my back and looked up at the dim sky. Sure enough, it was covered by gray clouds. I couldn't tell the time of day. Tiny pellets of rain struck my cheeks and forehead. I found the irregular way they landed on my face exhilarating. I had never realized what a blessing rain could be. It was so full of life. Even the first cold rain of winter.

"I'm starving. And thirsty. And cold. I'm freezing," I said. That's all I could get out. My teeth were chattering.

Menshiki guided me through the woods, his arm wrapped around my shoulder. I was having a hard time putting one foot in front of the other—by the end, he was pulling me along. He was a lot more powerful than he looked. Those daily workouts of his were paying off.

"Do you have the key?" Menshiki asked.

"It's under the potted plant to the right of the front door. Probably." The "probably" was necessary. Nothing in this world could be stated with absolute certainty. I was still shaking with cold. The chattering of my teeth was so loud I could barely hear myself talk.

"You'll be happy to hear Mariye returned home safe and sound early this afternoon," Menshiki said. "What a relief. I got a call from Shoko about an hour ago. I'd been calling you, but no one ever picked up.

That worried me, so I came over. I could hear the faint ring of a bell coming from the woods. So on a hunch, I came out and removed the tarp."

The view opened up as we emerged from the trees. I could see Menshiki's silver Jaguar parked demurely in front of my house. It was as spotless as ever.

"Why is your car always so beautiful?" I asked Menshiki. Not a fitting question under the circumstances, perhaps, but something I had long wanted to ask.

"I don't know," he said in a disinterested tone. "Maybe it's because I wash it when I have nothing else to do. From front to back. Then once a month, a pro comes and waxes it. And my garage protects it from the elements. That's all."

That's all? If my poor Toyota Corolla wagon heard that, after six months spent languishing in wind and rain, its shoulders would sag in dismay. It might even pass out.

Menshiki took the key from under the flowerpot and opened the door.

"By the way, what day of the week is it?" I asked him.

"Today? Today is Tuesday."

"Tuesday? Are you sure?"

Menshiki double-checked his memory. "I put out the empty bottles and cans yesterday, so it must have been Monday. Therefore today is Tuesday, without a doubt."

It had been Saturday when I had visited Tomohiko Amada's room. So three days had passed. It wouldn't have surprised me had it been three weeks, or three months, or even three years. I made a mental note. I rubbed my jaw with my palm. But there was no three-day stubble. Instead, my chin was smooth. What explained that?

Menshiki took me to the bath straightaway. He put me in a hot shower and brought me a fresh change of clothes. The clothes I had been wearing were tattered and filthy. I rolled them up in a ball and threw them in the garbage. There were red contusions all over my body but no visible injuries. I wasn't bleeding.

Then he led me to the kitchen, sat me down, and slowly fed me water. By the end I had drained a big bottle of mineral water. While I was drinking he found several apples in the fridge and peeled them. I just sat there, admiring his skill with a knife. The plate of peeled apples looked beautiful, elegant even.

I ate three or four apples in all. It was a moving experience—I had never realized how delicious apples were. I wanted to thank their creator for inventing such a marvelous fruit. When I finished the apples, Menshiki dug up a carton of crackers and gave it to me. I emptied the box. The crackers were a bit soggy, but they still tasted like the best in the world. In the meantime, he boiled water, made tea, and mixed it with honey. I drank a number of cups. The tea and honey warmed me from the inside.

There wasn't much in my fridge. It was, however, well stocked with eggs.

"How about an omelet?" Menshiki asked.

"I'd love one," I said. I needed to fill my stomach—anything would do.

Menshiki took four eggs from the fridge, broke them in a bowl, whipped them with chopsticks, and added milk, salt, and pepper. Then he whipped them again. It was clear he knew what he was doing. Then he turned on the gas, chose a small frying pan, and melted some butter in it. He located a spatula in one of my drawers and deftly cooked the omelet.

His technique was remarkable, as I would have expected. He could have been featured on a TV cooking show. Housewives across the nation would have sighed with envy. When it came to omelets—when it came to **anything,** I should say—Menshiki was precise, efficient, and incredibly stylish. I could only look on in admiration. He slid the finished omelet onto a plate and gave it to me with a dollop of ketchup.

The finished omelet was so beautiful I wanted to sketch it. But instead I grabbed my knife and started eating. The omelet wasn't just pretty to look at—it was delicious.

"This omelet is perfection," I said.

Menshiki laughed. "Not really. I've made better."

What sort of omelet could that have been? One that sprouted wings and flew from Tokyo to Osaka in under two hours?

When I had polished off the omelet, he took my plate to the sink. At last my stomach felt comfortable. Menshiki sat down across the table from me.

"Can we talk a little?" he asked me.

"Certainly," I said.

"Aren't you tired?"

"Maybe so. But we have lots to talk about."

Menshiki nodded. "It appears that several blanks need filling in."

If they can be filled in, I thought.

"Actually, I stopped by Sunday afternoon," Menshiki said. "I'd called many times but you never picked up, so I was a little worried. I got here around one."

I nodded. I had been **somewhere else** around then.

"I rang the bell and Tomohiko Amada's son came to the door. Masahiko, is that right?"

"Yes, Masahiko Amada. An old friend. He owns this house, and he's got a key so he can get in when I'm not here."

"He was—how should I put this—very worried about you. He said the two of you were visiting his father's room in the nursing home last Saturday when all of a sudden, you disappeared."

I nodded, but didn't say anything.

"He said you vanished into thin air while he was out of the room making a phone call. The nursing home is in Izu Kogen, so the nearest station is too far to reach on foot. But there were no signs that anyone had called a taxi. And the receptionist and the security guard hadn't seen you leave, either. Masahiko called your home later, but no one answered. He was so alarmed that he drove all the way here to check. He was concerned about your safety. Worried something bad had happened to you."

I sighed. "I'll try to explain things to Masahiko.

His father's in bad shape, and I only added to his worries. How is his father, by the way? Did he say anything?"

"It seems he's been in a coma. Hasn't regained consciousness at all. His son has taken a room near the home. He was on his way back to Tokyo when he stopped by here."

"I should call him right away," I said, shaking my head.

"That's true," Menshiki said, placing his hands on the table. "But first I think you need to come up with a coherent story about where you've been and what you've been doing the past few days. Including an explanation of how you disappeared from the nursing home. No one's going to buy it if you tell them you just woke up and found yourself back here."

"You're right," I said. "But how about you? Can you buy my story?"

Menshiki thought for a moment. His brow was puckered, as if he was having trouble deciding what to say. "I've always been a man who thought along rational lines," he said at last. "That's how I was trained. To be honest, though, I can't be logical where the pit behind the shrine is concerned. Anything could happen there and it wouldn't feel strange in the least. Spending an hour inside the pit brought that home all the more. That place is more than just a hole in the ground. But I doubt anyone who hasn't experienced it could understand."

I couldn't find the right words to respond, so I stayed silent.

"I think you should take the position 'I don't re-member anything' and then stick with it," Menshiki said. "I don't know how many people will believe you, but from what I can see, that's your only option."

I nodded. Yes, that could well be my only option.

"There are some things that can't be explained in this life," Menshiki went on, "and some others that probably **shouldn't** be explained. Especially when put-ting them into words ignores what is most crucial."

"You've experienced that, correct?"

"Of course," Menshiki said with a small smile. "More than once."

I drained what was left in my teacup.

"So Mariye wasn't hurt at all?" I asked.

"She was muddy and scratched up, but had no serious injuries. Not much more than a skinned knee. Just like you."

Just like me? "Where was she these past few days?"

Menshiki looked perplexed. "I'm pretty much in the dark about that, too. What I do know is that she returned home a short while ago. Dirty and banged up. That's all I was told. Shoko was in such a state she couldn't explain much over the phone. You should probably ask her yourself when things have settled down. Or, if possible, ask Mariye directly."

I nodded. "You're right. I'll do that."

"Don't you think you should get some sleep?" Menshiki asked.

No sooner had these words left his mouth than sleepiness hit me. I had slept deeply while I was in the pit (at least I think I had), but now I could barely keep my eyes open.

"Yes, you're right. I think I'll go lie down," I said, looking at the backs of his clasped hands, perfectly aligned on the table.

"Have a good sleep. That's what you need right now. Is there anything else I can do for you?"

I shook my head. "No, I can't think of anything. But thanks."

"Then I'll take off. Please don't hesitate to call me for whatever reason. I should be at home for the next little while." He slowly rose to his feet. "Thank goodness Mariye got home safely. And that I was able to help you out of a tough spot. To tell the truth, I haven't had much sleep these days either. So I think I'll go home and rest."

With that he left. As always, I heard the solid **thunk** of his car door slamming shut, and the engine starting up. I waited until the car was out of earshot before heading for bed. When my head hit the pillow, I remembered the old bell (I had left it and the flashlight in the pit!) for a split second. Then I descended into a deep sleep.

57

SOMETHING I HAVE
TO DO EVENTUALLY

I awoke at two fifteen. Again surrounded by total darkness. For a split second, I was under the illusion that I was still in the pit, but I realized my mistake right away. There was a clear difference between the darkness here and there. Above ground, there was always a vestige of light, even on the blackest night. Not like underground, where no light could enter. It may have been two fifteen, but the sun was still in the sky, albeit on the other side of the planet. That was the size of it.

I turned on the light, went to the bathroom, and drank glass after glass of cold water. The house was hushed. Too hushed, in fact. I listened carefully, but could hear nothing. No breeze. No insect voices, since it was winter. No night birds. No bell. Come to think of it, I had first heard the bell ringing at precisely this time of night. The time when events outside the normal are most likely to occur.

I was no longer sleepy. I was wide awake. Draping a sweater over my pajamas, I headed for the studio. I hadn't set foot in there since returning home. And I was concerned about the paintings I had left. Especially **Killing Commendatore**. Menshiki had said that

Masahiko had visited the house in my absence. If he had gone into the studio, he might have stumbled upon it. He would have known right away that it was his father's work. Fortunately, however, I had covered it. I'd worried about leaving it exposed, so I had taken it down from the wall and wrapped a sheet around it to hide it from inquisitive eyes. If the sheet hadn't been removed, Masahiko ought not to have seen it.

I walked in and flipped on the wall switch. The studio was dead quiet as well. Needless to say, no one was there. Not the Commendatore, not Tomohiko Amada. I was all alone.

Killing Commendatore was where I had left it on the floor, the sheet still in place. It didn't seem that anyone had touched it. I couldn't be sure, of course. But nothing suggested otherwise. I unwrapped the painting. It looked the same as always. There was the Commendatore. And Don Giovanni, who had run him through with his sword. And the shocked servant, Leporello. And the beautiful Donna Anna, covering her mouth in astonishment. And in the lower left-hand corner of the painting, poking his head through the square opening, the creepy-looking Long Face.

In truth, I had been harboring some misgivings. Might the painting have been altered by the series of events in which I had played a part? Long Face deleted from the scene, for example, because I had shut the lid? Or the Commendatore killed, not with a sword, but with a carving knife? Yet search as I might, I could find nothing changed. Long Face still poked his grotesque face out of his hole, the raised lid in one hand. His saucer eyes still surveyed the scene. The Commendatore was still impaled on a long sword, blood spewing from his heart. The painting remained a perfectly composed work of art. I admired it for a while, then put the sheet back over it.

I turned to look at the two paintings I was working on. They sat side by side on two easels. One, **The Pit in the Woods**, was wider than it was tall. The other, **A Portrait of Mariye Akikawa**, was taller than it was wide. I looked at them carefully. Both were exactly as I had left them. Nothing had been changed. One was finished, while the other awaited a final go-around.

Then I turned **The Man with the White Subaru Forester**, which had been facing the wall, sat on the floor, and took another good look at it. The man with the white Subaru Forester stared back at me from behind the thick layers of paint, which I had applied with my palette knife in several colors. He had no concrete shape, but I could see him there nonetheless. He was looking straight at me with the piercing eyes of a nocturnal bird of prey, his face empty of expression. He was dead set against the completion of his portrait—the exposure of his true form to the world. Against being hauled from the dark into the light.

But I was determined to reveal who he was. I had to drag him out into full view. However much he might resist. The time might not yet have come. But when it did, I had to be ready to follow through.

I returned to **A Portrait of Mariye Akikawa**. It was far enough along that I didn't need Mariye to model for me anymore. Only a series of final, technical operations remained. Then the portrait would be basically done. I thought it might turn out to be my most accomplished work to date. At the very least, it would capture the freshness of that beautiful thirteen-year-old girl. I was confident of that. But I knew I would never take those last steps. By leaving it unfinished I was shielding something within her, even though I didn't know what that something was. That much was clear.

I needed to look after a few things right away. I had to call Shoko and hear the full story of Mariye's return. I had to call Yuzu and tell her I wanted to see her to talk things out, as I'd resolved at the bottom of the pit. That it was time for us to meet. Then, of course, I had to talk to Masahiko. To explain how it was that I had vanished suddenly from his father's room at the nursing home, and tell him where I had been for the three days I was missing and unaccounted for (though what I would say—what was **possible** to say—escaped me).

Clearly, I couldn't call any of them now. I had to wait for a more appropriate time. That would come in due course—assuming, that is, that time was behaving normally. I drank a glass of warm milk that I heated on the stove and nibbled some biscuits as I sat and looked out the window. It was pitch black outside. No stars were out. Daybreak was still a while off. It was the time of year when nights were the longest.

How should I pass the time? The proper thing

would be to climb back into bed. But I wasn't at all sleepy. I didn't feel like reading or working. With nothing better to do, I decided to run a bath. While the bathtub was filling, I lay on my back and stared at the ceiling.

Why had it been necessary to pass through that underground world? To make that trip, I had been forced to kill the Commendatore with my own hands. He had sacrificed his life, and I had been compelled to endure one ordeal after another in a world of darkness. There had to have been a reason. The underground realm was full of unmistakable danger, and real fear. Down there, the most outlandish occurrences weren't strange at all. By successfully navigating that realm, I seemed to have freed Mariye **from somewhere**. At least she had returned home safely. As the Commendatore had foretold. But what connected my experiences underground and her safe return? Were they somehow parallel?

Perhaps the river water I had ingested was an important piece of the puzzle. It could have altered something in me. I felt that at an intuitive and physical level, though it made no rational sense. Thanks to that change, I had passed through a tunnel clearly too small for my body. Cheered on by Donna Anna and Komi, I had managed to overcome my deep-rooted claustrophobia. No, Donna Anna and Komi could have been **a single entity**, Donna Anna at one moment, Komi at the next. Together, perhaps, they had shielded me from the dark powers, and protected Mariye Akikawa at the same time.

But where had Mariye been confined? Had she been confined in the first place? When I had given her penguin charm (though "given" didn't really cover it) to the faceless man, had I harmed her? Or, conversely, had the charm in some shape or form protected her in the end?

The questions only mounted.

Perhaps I would understand the events of the past few days better once I met Mariye in person. I would have to wait. True, things might be no clearer even after we talked. Mariye might recall nothing. Or she might remember, but (like me) be unwilling to share her story.

At any rate, I had to see her once more in this real world, and have a good long talk. We needed to share our stories about what had happened to us. If at all possible.

But was **this the real world?**

I looked around. So much was familiar. The breeze through the window carried a familiar smell, the sounds outside were familiar sounds.

Just because it looked like the real world at first glance, however, didn't mean that was necessarily the case. It might be no more than my assumption. I might well have descended through one hole in Izu and traveled the underworld only to be spit out three days later through the wrong hole in the mountains of Odawara. There was no guarantee that the world I had left and the world I had returned to were one and the same.

I rose from the sofa, stripped off my clothes, and

stepped into the bathroom. Once again, I soaped and scrubbed every inch of my body. I thoroughly washed my hair. I brushed my teeth, swabbed my ears with cotton, trimmed my nails. I shaved (though there wasn't much beard to shave). I put on another set of clean underwear. A freshly ironed white cotton shirt and a pair of khaki pants with a sharp crease. I strove to make myself look as acceptable as I could to the real world. But the night still hadn't ended. Outside was pitch black. So black I felt morning might never arrive, not for all eternity.

But morning did come. I brewed some fresh coffee and made some buttered toast. The fridge was almost bare. Two eggs, some sour milk, and a few limp vegetables. I made a mental note to go shopping later.

I was washing the coffee cup when it struck me that I hadn't seen my girlfriend in some time. How long had it been? I couldn't count the exact number of days without checking my calendar. But I knew quite a while had passed. So many things had been going on—a number of them literally not in this world— that I hadn't noticed her failure to contact me.

Why was that? She called me at least twice every week. "How's it going?" she would say. I couldn't call her, though. She couldn't give me her cell phone number, and I didn't use email. When I wanted to see her, I had to wait for her call.

Sure enough, my girlfriend did call around nine that morning, when she was still in the back of my mind.

"I've got to talk to you about something," she said, skipping the pleasantries.

"Fine, let's talk," I said.

I leaned against the kitchen counter, phone to my ear. The clouds outside were starting to break up, and the early-winter sun was peeking through the gaps. The weather at least was improving. From the sound of it, though, what she had to say wasn't going to be all that pleasant.

"I think it's best if we don't see each other again," she said. "It's too bad, but . . ."

Her tone was flat and dispassionate. I couldn't tell if she really felt it was too bad or not.

"There are a number of reasons," she said.

"A number of reasons," I echoed.

"To begin with, I think my husband is catching on. He's noticed some signs."

"Signs," I repeated.

"Women leave certain signs in situations like this. Like they start paying more attention to their makeup and their clothes, or change their perfume, or start a serious diet. I've tried to be careful, but even so."

"I see."

"The main thing is, we can't go on like this."

"Like this," I repeated.

"With no future. No hope of resolution."

She had it there. Our relationship had no "future," no "hope of resolution." The risks were too large if we continued as we were. I didn't have all that much to lose, but she had a family and two teenage daughters attending private school.

"There's more," she went on. "I'm having a serious problem with my daughter. The older one."

Her elder daughter. If I remembered correctly, she was the obedient child who never talked back to her parents and got good grades.

"A serious problem?"

"She can't get out of bed in the morning."

"Can't get out of bed?"

"Hey, will you please stop repeating everything I say?"

"Sorry," I apologized. "But what is her specific problem? She can't get out of bed?"

"That's right. It's been going on for about two weeks. She doesn't try to get up. She doesn't go to school. She just lies in bed in her pajamas all day. Doesn't answer when spoken to. I take food to her, but she barely touches it."

"Has she seen a counselor?"

"Of course," she said. "There's a school counselor. No help at all."

I thought for a minute. But there was nothing I could say. I'd never even met the girl.

"So that's why I can't see you," she said.

"Because you have to stay home and look after her?"

"There's that. But that's not all."

She didn't go on, but I understood how she felt. She was terrified, and blaming herself as a mother for our affair.

"It's really too bad," I said.

"It's fine for you to say that, but it's even worse for me."

She could be right, I thought.

"There's one last thing I wanted to tell you," she said. She took a quick, deep breath.

"What's that?"

"I think you can become a really good artist. Even better than now."

"Thank you," I said. "That gives me some confidence."

"Goodbye."

"Take care," I said.

When our phone call ended, I went to the living room, stretched out on the sofa, and thought about her as I looked at the ceiling. We had been together so many times, yet never had I thought of painting her portrait. Somehow, that feeling had never arisen. Instead I had sketched her over and over again. In a small sketchbook with a thick pencil, so quickly I hardly removed pencil from paper. In most she was naked, and posing lewdly. Spreading her legs to show her vagina, for example. Or I sketched her in the act of making love. Simple drawings but still very real. And very vulgar. She loved looking at them.

"You're really good at drawing naughty pictures, huh? You toss them off, but they're super dirty."

"It's just for fun," I said.

I drew her again and again, then threw the drawings away. Someone might see them, and it didn't make sense to keep them. Still, maybe I should have secretly held on to at least one. To prove to myself she had really existed.

I got up slowly from the sofa. The day was only beginning. There were many conversations ahead.

58

LIKE HEARING ABOUT THE
BEAUTIFUL CANALS OF MARS

called Shoko Akikawa. It was just after nine thirty. A time when most people are already up and about. But no one picked up the phone. It rang on and on until the answering machine kicked in. **We're sorry, but we can't come to the phone right now. Please leave your message after the tone** . . . I left no message. She must be scrambling to deal with her niece's disappearance and sudden return. I kept calling at intervals, but no one answered.

I thought of calling Yuzu after that, but I didn't want to bother her while she was working. I could call during her lunch break. With luck, I would get to have a brief talk with her. It wasn't like our conversation would be a long one. I would simply ask if we could meet sometime soon—that was the gist of it. A yes-or-no question. If the answer was yes, we would set a date and a place to meet. If it was no, that was that.

Then, with a heavy heart, I called Masahiko. He picked up right away. He let out a huge sigh when he heard my voice.

"Are you home now?" he asked.

I told him I was.

"Can I call you back in a couple of minutes?"

Sure, I said. He called fifteen minutes later. He seemed to be using his cell phone on the roof of an office building, or someplace like that.

"Where the hell have you been?" he said, his voice uncharacteristically stern. "You disappeared from my father's room without a word—no one knew where you were. I drove all the way to Odawara looking for you."

"I'm really sorry," I said.

"When did you get home?"

"Last night."

"So you were traipsing around from Saturday afternoon until Tuesday night? Where did you go?"

"To be honest, I have no memory of where I was or what I was doing," I lied.

"So you just woke up and found yourself back home—is that it?"

"Yeah, that's it."

"For real? Are you serious?"

"There's no other way to explain it."

"Sorry, man. I can't buy it. Sounds fake to me."

"Come on, you've seen this sort of thing in movies and novels."

"Give me a break. Whenever they pull that amnesia bit I turn off the TV. It's so contrived."

"Alfred Hitchcock used it."

"You mean **Spellbound**? That's one of his second-rate films," Masahiko said. "So tell me what **really** happened."

"I don't know myself at this point. Like there are

these fragments floating around, and I can't figure out how to piece them together. Maybe my memory will return in stages. I'll let you know if that happens. But I can't tell you anything right now. I'm sorry, but you'll have to wait a little longer."

Masahiko paused to digest what I had just said. "All right then, let's call it amnesia for now," he said in a resigned voice. "I gather your story doesn't involve drugs or alcohol or a mental breakdown or a femme fatale or abduction by aliens or anything along those lines."

"No. Nothing illegal or contrary to public morals."

"Public morals be damned," Masahiko said. "But clue me in on one thing, would you?"

"What's that?"

"How did you manage to slip out of the nursing home Saturday afternoon? They keep a really strict eye on who comes and goes. A number of famous people are staying there, so they're paranoid about leaks. They've got a receptionist stationed at the entrance, a guard on-site twenty-four seven, and security cameras. All the same, you managed to vanish in broad daylight without being spotted or caught on film. How?"

"There's a secret passage," I said.

"Secret passage?"

"An exit no one knows about."

"How did you find that? It was your first time there."

"Your father let me know. Or I should say, he gave me a hint. In a very indirect way."

"My father?" Masahiko said. "You must be kidding. His mind's as mushy as boiled cauliflower these days."

"That's one of the things I can't explain."

"What to do," Masahiko said with a sigh. "If it were anyone else I'd say, 'Cut the crap.' But it's you, so I guess I have to put up with it. Put up with this crazy, no-good bum who spends his whole life painting."

"Thanks," I said. "By the way, how's your father doing?"

"When I got back to the room after my phone call, you were nowhere to be seen and Dad was unconscious and barely breathing. I panicked, man. I couldn't figure out what was going on. I knew it wasn't your fault, but I couldn't help blaming you anyway."

"I really am sorry," I said. I wasn't kidding, either. Still, I felt a wave of relief that there was no trace of the Commendatore's body, or of the pool of blood on the floor.

"Yeah, you should be sorry. Anyway, I rented a room nearby to be with him, but his breathing stabilized and his condition improved slightly, so I came back to Tokyo the next afternoon. Work was piling up. I'm heading back this weekend, though."

"It's hard on you."

"There's nothing to be done. Like I told you, dying is a major undertaking. It's the person dying who has it hardest, though, so I really can't complain."

"Is there anything I can do?" I asked.

"No, there's nothing," Masahiko said. "But it would help if you didn't dump any more problems on me . . . Oh yeah, I almost forgot. When I was at your house on my way back to Tokyo your friend Menshiki stopped by. The handsome, white-haired guy in the snazzy silver Jaguar."

"Yes, I met him after that. He said you were there, and that you and he had talked."

"Just a few words at your doorstep. He seemed like an interesting guy."

"A **very** interesting guy," I said, putting it mildly.

"What does he do?"

"Not much of anything. He's so loaded he doesn't have to work. He trades stocks and plays the currency market online, but it's more like a hobby for him, a profitable way to kill time."

"That's really cool," Masahiko said, impressed. "It's like hearing about the beautiful canals of Mars. Where Martians row gondolas with golden oars. While imbibing honeyed tobacco through their ears. Warms my heart just hearing about it . . . Oh yeah, while we're at it, did you ever find the knife I left at your place?"

"Sorry, but no, I haven't come across it," I said. "I don't have a clue where it went. I'll buy you a new one."

"Don't sweat it. It probably had a bout of amnesia, just like you. It'll wander back before too long."

"Probably," I said. So the knife hadn't remained in Tomohiko Amada's room either. It had vanished somewhere, just like the Commendatore's corpse and the pool of blood. It might show up here, though, as Masahiko had said.

Our conversation ended there. We vowed to get together again soon and hung up.

After that, I drove my dusty old Corolla station wagon down the mountain to the shopping plaza. I went to the supermarket, where I toured the aisles with the neighborhood housewives. From the looks on their faces, they weren't thrilled by their morning shopping. Not a whole lot of excitement in their lives. No ferryboat rides in the Land of Metaphor, that's for sure.

I tossed what I needed—meat, fish, vegetables, milk, tofu, the whole lot—into my shopping cart and paid at the register. I saved five yen by bringing my own bag. Then I went to a discount liquor store and bought a twenty-four pack of Sapporo. Back home, I arranged most of what I had purchased in the fridge, including six cans of beer. I wrapped what needed to be frozen in plastic and stuck it in the freezer. I set a big pot of water on the stove and parboiled the asparagus and broccoli for salads. I boiled a few eggs, too. In the process, I managed to kill most of the morning. Nevertheless, there was still time to spare. I considered following Menshiki's example and washing my car, then realized it would get dirty again in no time flat, and tossed the idea. Parboiling vegetables was much more productive.

·   ·   ·

I called Yuzu's architectural firm shortly after noon. Actually, I wanted to wait until my feelings had settled down before talking to her, but at the same time I didn't want to delay acting on what I had decided in the darkness of the pit, even for a single day. Otherwise, something might cause my feelings to change. Yet the receiver weighed a ton in my hand. A cheerful-sounding young woman answered. I gave her my name, and asked to talk to Yuzu.

"Are you her husband?" she chirped.

Yes, I replied. To be precise I wasn't, of course, but there was no reason to go into details over the phone.

"Please hold on," she said.

I waited for quite a long time. I had nothing in particular to do, so I stood there leaning on the kitchen counter, receiver to my ear, biding my time until Yuzu came to the phone. A big black crow passed right in front of the window. Its glossy feathers gleamed in the sunlight.

"Hello," said Yuzu.

We exchanged a simple greeting. I had no idea how a just-divorced couple was supposed to address each other, how much distance was appropriate. So I kept it as brief and conventional as possible. How have you been? I've been fine. And you? Like a summer shower, our words were sucked up the moment they struck the parched soil of reality.

I mustered my courage. "I thought we should get together and talk about a number of things face-to-face," I said.

"What sorts of things are you talking about?" Yuzu asked. I hadn't expected that response (why hadn't I?), so I was at a loss for words. What did I mean by "things"?

"I . . . I haven't thought it through that far," I stammered.

"But you want to talk about a number of things, correct?"

"That's right. It occurred to me that we ended up like this without ever having talked."

She thought for a moment. "To tell the truth," she said, "I'm pregnant. I'm happy to see you, but don't be shocked to see how big my belly's grown."

"I know. Masahiko told me. He said you asked him to."

"That I did," she said.

"I don't know how big you've gotten, but I'd like to see you in any case. If it's not too much of an imposition."

"Can you wait a moment?" she asked.

I waited. She appeared to be leafing through her appointment book. Meanwhile, I tried hard to remember what kind of songs the Go-Go's sang. I doubted they were as good as Masahiko had claimed, but then maybe he was right, and my view was perverse.

"Next Monday evening is good for me," Yuzu said.

I did the calculation in my head. Today was Wednesday. So Monday was five days away. The day Menshiki took his empty bottles and cans to the pickup spot. A day I didn't have to teach drawing in town. That meant I was free—no need to check my schedule. What did Menshiki wear when he took out his garbage, I wondered.

"It's good for me too," I said. "Just give me a time and place and I'll be there."

She named a coffee shop not far from the Shinjuku Gyoen-mae Station. The name brought back memories. It was not far from her office, and we had met there often when we were still living together as a married couple. After she finished work, usually before we went out someplace for dinner. There was a little oyster bar a short distance away, which offered fresh oysters at a reasonable price. She loved eating their small oysters loaded with horseradish, and washed down with chilled Chablis. Was the restaurant still in the same spot?

"Can we meet there shortly after six?"

I said that'd be fine.

"I'll try not to be late."

"That's all right. I'll wait."

"Okay, see you then," she said, and hung up.

I stared at the receiver in my hand for a moment. So I would see Yuzu again. My estranged wife, soon to bear another man's child. The place and time had been set. Our conversation had gone without a hitch. Yet had I done the right thing? I wasn't at all sure. The receiver still weighed heavy in my hand. Like a phone built back in the Stone Age.

When it came down to it, though, could anything be completely correct, or completely incorrect? We lived in a world where rain might fall thirty percent, or seventy percent, of the time. Truth was probably no different. There could be thirty percent or seventy percent truth. Crows had it a lot easier. For them, it was either raining or not raining, one or the other. Percentages never crossed their minds.

Talking to Yuzu had left me at loose ends. I sat in the dining room for an hour, mostly looking at the clock on the wall. I would see her on Monday and we would talk about "a number of things." We hadn't seen each other since March. It had been a chilly Sunday afternoon then, rain quietly falling. Now she was seven months pregnant. A major change in her life. I, on the other hand, was still just me. True, I had drunk the water of the Land of Metaphor only a few days earlier, and had crossed the river that divided presence and absence, but I wasn't sure if the experience had changed me or not.

Finally, I called Shoko again. But no one came to the phone. Instead it switched to the answering machine. I gave up and sat down on the sofa. I had made all my calls, and nothing more needed to be done. I hadn't set foot in the studio in what felt like ages, and part of me wanted to get back to my easel, but I couldn't think of anything in particular that I wanted to paint.

I put Bruce Springsteen's **The River** on the turntable. Then I lay on the sofa, closed my eyes, and listened. When the A side of the first LP had finished, I turned it over and listened to the B side. Albums like **The River** have to be heard in this fashion. After "Independence Day" wraps up the A side, you take the record in both hands, turn it over, and carefully lower the stylus. "Hungry Heart" fills the room. What was the point of listening to **The River** any other way? In my personal opinion, when CDs strung together the sides of records like **The River,** they spoiled the experience. The same was true of **Rubber Soul** and **Pet Sounds**. Great music should be presented in its proper form. And listened to in a proper manner.

Whatever the case, the E Street Band's performance was a knockout. The band revved up the singer, and the singer inspired the band. As I zoned in on the music, I could feel my worries fading.

I was lifting the needle from the first record when I realized that, perhaps, I should give Menshiki a call. We hadn't spoken since the day before, when he had rescued me from the pit. Yet somehow I didn't really feel like it. This happened on occasion. He was a fascinating guy, but there were times I really didn't want to talk to him. The gap between us was vast. Why should that be? At any rate, I didn't feel like hearing his voice at that particular moment.

So I gave up. I'd call him later. After all, the day had just begun. I put the second record of **The River** on the stereo. But just when I was settling back to listen to "Cadillac Ranch" ("All gonna meet down at the Cadillac Ranch"), the telephone rang. I lifted the needle and went into the dining room to answer it. I figured it was Menshiki. As it turned out, it was Shoko.

"Have you been trying to reach me this morning?" she began.

That's right, I replied, I had tried on several occasions. "I heard yesterday from Mr. Menshiki that Mariye had returned home, so I wondered how she was."

"Yes, she came back safe and sound. Yesterday afternoon. I called you a number of times to let you know but there was no answer, so I tried contacting Mr. Menshiki. Did you go somewhere?"

"Yes, I had to look after urgent business some distance from here. I got back last night. I wanted to contact you earlier, but there was no phone where I was, and I don't carry a cell phone," I said. It wasn't a complete lie.

"Mariye returned all by herself yesterday afternoon, covered in mud. But no serious injuries, thank goodness."

"Where was she all that time?"

"We don't know yet," she said in a hushed voice. As if afraid that her phone was tapped. "Mariye won't tell us what happened. We had filed a missing person's report, so the police came and asked her all sorts of questions, but she wouldn't tell them anything. Not a single word. So they gave up and left, saying that they'd come back when she'd had more time to recover. That at least she had made it home, and that she was safe. But she won't tell either her father or me anything. You know how stubborn she can be."

"But she was covered in mud, correct?"

"Yes, her whole body. Her school uniform was torn up too, and her arms and legs were scratched.

We didn't have to take her to the hospital, though—none of her injuries was that serious."

Just like me, I thought. Muddy, clothing in tatters. Could we have wormed our way back to this world through the same narrow tunnel?

"And she won't speak?" I asked.

"No, not a single word since she came home. Not just words, either—she hasn't made a sound. As if someone had stolen her tongue."

"Do you think some kind of trauma might have left her in shock? Taken away her voice?"

"No, I don't think so. I think she's made up her mind not to say anything, a vow of silence, if you will. She's done this kind of thing before. When she's furious about something, for example. Once she's made up her mind like this she tends to stick to it—that's the sort of child she is."

"There's no question of criminal acts, right? Like kidnapping, or unlawful confinement?"

"I can't tell. The police say they'll come back to ask more questions once she's had a chance to calm down, so maybe we'll find out then," Shoko said. "But I do have a favor to ask, if it's not too much of an imposition."

"What might that be?"

"Would you try to talk to her? Just the two of you? There may be things she'll only open up to you about. She might reveal more about what happened if you're there."

I stood there with the receiver in my right hand,

considering her suggestion. If Mariye and I were alone together, what was there to discuss? I couldn't begin to imagine. I had my own riddles to unravel and she (most likely) had hers. If we laid one set of riddles over the other, what answers could possibly emerge? Still, I had to see her. There were things we had to talk about.

"Of course. I'd be happy to," I said. "Where would you like me to go?"

"Oh no, please let us come to you, as always. I think that's best. If you don't mind, of course."

"No, that's fine with me," I said. "I'm free all day. Please come when it's convenient for you."

"Would it be all right if we came now? She's home from school today. If she's willing, of course."

"Please tell her she doesn't have to talk. That there are things on my end that I'd like to tell her," I said.

"Very well. I'll tell her exactly that. I'm dreadfully sorry to keep imposing on you like this," said the beautiful aunt. Then she quietly hung up the phone.

The phone rang again twenty minutes later. It was Shoko.

"We'll be coming at three o'clock," she said. "Mariye has said she's willing. Well, she gave a small nod, is more accurate."

I said I would expect them at three.

"Thank you so much," she said. "I'm at my wit's end. I don't understand what's going on, or what I should be doing."

I wanted to tell her I felt the same way, but I didn't. That's not the response she was seeking.

"I'll do what I can. I can't be sure if it will work, but I'll try my best," I said. Then I hung up.

I stole a look around the room as I put down the receiver. On the off chance that the Commendatore might be in the vicinity. But he was nowhere to be seen. I missed him. The way he looked, and his odd way of speaking. But I would never lay eyes on him again. With my own hand, I had driven a knife through his tiny heart. The razor-sharp carving knife Masahiko had brought to my house. All for the purpose of rescuing Mariye from someplace. I had to find out where that **someplace** was.

59

UNTIL DEATH SEPARATED US

B efore Mariye arrived, I took another look at her portrait, so close to done. I could picture exactly what it would look like if I ever finished it. Sad to say, though, I never would. There was no way around that. I had no good explanation for why I couldn't complete the painting. No logical argument. Just the strong feeling that **it had to be that way**. The reason, I expected, would reveal itself in stages. What was clear now was that I was fighting a very dangerous opponent. I had to be on my toes every second.

I went out to the terrace, sat in a deck chair, and stared across the valley at Menshiki's white mansion. Handsome, colorless Menshiki, he of the white hair. "We only talked for a moment at your door, but he seemed like an interesting guy," Masahiko had said. "**A very** interesting guy," I had corrected him. At this stage of the game, though, I would have to say **a very, very, very** interesting guy.

A few minutes before three, the familiar blue Toyota Prius rolled up the slope and parked in its usual spot in front of my house. The engine stopped, the driver's door opened, and Shoko Akikawa got out. Most elegantly, pivoting in her seat, knees tight together. A moment later, Mariye emerged from the passenger's seat. Most reluctantly, her movements slow and sluggish. The morning clouds had sailed off somewhere, and the sky was the clear blue of early winter. The soft hair of the two women danced in the cold wind coming off the mountain. Mariye brushed the hair from her eyes in an impatient gesture.

Mariye was in a skirt, unusual for her. A wool skirt of navy blue, it reached her knees. Beneath was a pair of dark blue tights. Her white blouse was covered by a cashmere V-neck sweater. The sweater was a deep purple, the color of grapes. Her shoes were dark brown loafers. In that outfit, Mariye looked like a well-brought-up child from a well-off family, a healthy, pretty, utterly conventional girl. You could see nothing eccentric about her. Just that her chest was almost flat.

Shoko was wearing snug light-gray slacks. Gleaming black low-heeled shoes. A long white cardigan, fixed with a belt around her waist. Her breasts stood out proudly beneath the cardigan. She was carrying a black purse made of what looked like enamel. The sort women commonly carry, though their contents have always mystified me. Mariye appeared a bit at a loss with no pockets to plunge her hands into.

They were so different in age and stage of maturity, this young aunt and her niece, yet both were so lovely. I observed their approach through the parted curtains. When they walked side by side, the world brightened a little. As when Christmas and New Year's arrive in tandem each year.

The doorbell chimed, and I went to open the door. Shoko greeted me politely, and I ushered them inside. Mariye said nothing. Her lips were set in a straight line, as if someone had stitched them together. She was a strong-willed girl. Once she made up her mind about something, she never backed down.

As before, I led them to the living room. Shoko launched into a string of apologies, but I cut her off. This was no time for social niceties.

"If you don't mind, could you leave Mariye and me alone for a while?" I said, getting straight to the point. "I think that's best. Please come back in about two hours. Would that be possible?"

"Oh, well, certainly," the young aunt said. She seemed a little flustered. "If it's all right with Mariye, then it's all right with me."

Mariye gave a slight nod. It was all right with her.

Shoko Akikawa consulted her small silver watch.

"Then I'll come back at five o'clock. I'll be waiting at home, so please call if you need anything."

I told her we would.

Looking worried, Shoko paused uncertainly, clutching her black purse. Then she appeared to make up her mind, for she took a deep breath, smiled a bright smile, and left. There was the sound of the Prius's engine starting (I couldn't really hear it, but I assume it did), and the car disappeared down the slope. Mariye and I were left alone in the house.

The girl sat on the sofa and looked down at her lap, her lips still set in a stubborn line and her knees pressed together. Her pleated blouse was neatly ironed.

A deep silence followed. Finally, I spoke up.

"You don't have to say a word," I began. "You can stay quiet as long as you want. So try to relax. I'll do the talking—all you have to do is listen. All right?"

Mariye raised her eyes and looked at me. But she didn't speak. Nor did she nod or shake her head. She merely stared in my direction. Her face showed no emotion. I felt as if I were gazing at the full moon in winter. Perhaps she had made her heart like the moon for the time being. An icy mass of rock floating in the sky.

"First, I need your help with something," I said. "Can you come with me?"

I rose and headed to the studio. A moment later she got up and followed. The room was chilly, so I lit the kerosene stove. When I pulled back the curtains, the mountainside was bright in the sun. Mariye's portrait-in-progress was sitting on an easel, close to finished. She glanced at it but then quickly looked away, as if she had glimpsed something she shouldn't have.

I crouched down, removed the cloth I had draped over **Killing Commendatore**, and hung the painting on the wall. I asked Mariye to sit on the stool to observe it more closely.

"You've seen this painting before, right?"

Mariye gave a small nod.

"It's called **Killing Commendatore**. At least that's what was written on its wrapping. It's one of Tomohiko Amada's most perfect works, though we don't know exactly when he painted it. It's beautifully composed and masterfully drawn. Each character is fully realized and utterly convincing."

I paused for a moment, waiting for my words to sink in.

"Yet this painting was wrapped up and closeted away in the attic of this house," I went on, "where no one would ever see it. When I stumbled upon it and brought it downstairs, it had been gathering dust for a very long time. Apart from the artist, you and I are probably the only people who have ever looked at it. Your aunt could have too on your first visit, but for some reason it didn't catch her eye. I don't know what made Tomohiko Amada hide it in the attic. It's such a brilliant work, one of his true masterpieces, so why would he keep it from the world?"

Mariye didn't respond. She sat on the stool, her eyes fixed on **Killing Commendatore**.

I continued. "As if on cue, weird things have happened one after another since I stumbled on this painting. First, Mr. Menshiki went out of his way to make my acquaintance."

Mariye nodded slightly.

"Then I uncovered that strange hole behind the shrine in the woods. I heard a bell ringing in the middle of the night and traced it to that spot. It was coming from beneath a pile of stones. They couldn't be moved by hand—they were too big and too heavy. So Menshiki arranged for a landscaper to come in with his backhoe. I didn't understand why Menshiki would go to such lengths, and I still don't. At any rate, the stones were moved at great cost of time and money. Underneath them was a hole. A round pit about six feet across, made of smaller stones tightly set together in a perfect circle. Who built it, and for what purpose, is a mystery. Of course you know about the pit."

Mariye nodded.

"The Commendatore came out of that opened pit. This guy."

I went up to the painting and pointed to the figure. Mariye looked at him. But her expression didn't change.

"He looked exactly the same as you see here, same face, same clothes. But he was only two feet tall. Very compact. And with a peculiar way of speaking. For some reason, I seem to be the only person able to see him. He called himself an 'Idea.' And said he had been stuck in that pit. In other words, Mr. Menshiki and I had set him free. Do you get what he meant by 'Idea'?"

Mariye shook her head no.

"It's hard for me, too. The way I understand it, an idea is a type of concept. But not all concepts are ideas. Love, for example, is not an idea. But ideas are what make love possible. Without ideas, love cannot exist. This discussion can go on forever, though. And to tell you the truth, I'm not even sure of the correct definitions. Anyway, an idea is a concept, and concepts have no physical shape. They are pure abstractions. Nevertheless, this Idea temporarily borrowed the form of the Commendatore in the painting to make itself visible to me. Do you follow me so far?"

"Pretty much," Mariye broke her silence for the first time. "I met him too."

"You did?" I exclaimed. I looked at her in stunned silence. Then I recalled what the Commendatore had said to me in the Izu nursing home. **I met her not long ago**, he had told me. **We exchanged a few words**.

"So you met the Commendatore too."

Mariye nodded.

"When? Where?"

"At Mr. Menshiki's," she said.

"What did he say?"

Mariye clamped her lips together again. To signal, it seemed, that she didn't want to talk any more for the moment. I didn't push her further.

"Other characters in this painting have appeared as well," I said. "For example, the man in the lower left-hand corner of the painting, the bearded guy with the strangely shaped face. Right here."

I pointed to Long Face.

"I call him 'Long Face,' and he's a weird one, all right. He's about two and a half feet tall. He slipped out from the painting too—I caught him holding up the cover of his hole just as he is doing here, and he helped me reach the underground world. I had to get a bit rough, though, before he gave me directions."

Mariye looked at Long Face for some time. But she didn't say anything.

I continued. "I walked through that dim world, climbing hills, crossing a rapid river, until I met the pretty young woman you see right here. This person. I call her 'Donna Anna,' after the character in Mozart's opera **Don Giovanni**. She's also very small. She led me to a tunnel in the back of a cave. Then she and my dead sister helped me worm my way through to where it ended. If they hadn't cheered me on I never would have made it—I'd have been trapped in the underworld forever. My hunch—though of course it's pure guesswork—is that Donna Anna in this painting may be the young woman Tomohiko Amada loved when he was a student in Vienna. She was executed as a political prisoner seventy years ago."

Mariye looked at Donna Anna in the painting. Her face still as impassive as the white winter moon.

Then again, Donna Anna could have been Mariye's mother, stung to death by a swarm of hornets. Perhaps she was the one who had protected Mariye. Depending on who was looking at her, Donna Anna might embody many things. Of course, I didn't say this out loud.

"Then we have this man here," I said. I turned the painting leaning against the wall around so we could see its front. It was my portrait in progress, **The Man with the White Subaru Forester**. On the surface, it was just thick layers of paint, three colors in all. Behind those layers, though, was the Subaru Forester guy. I could see him. Though other people couldn't.

"I showed you this before, didn't I?"

Mariye gave a firm nod, but said nothing.

"You told me it was finished as it was."

Mariye nodded again.

"I call the person portrayed here—or the person I must eventually portray—'the man with the white

Subaru Forester.' I ran across him in a small coastal village in Miyagi Prefecture. Our paths crossed twice. In a very mysterious and meaningful way. I have no idea what sort of person he is. I don't even know his name. But a moment came when I realized I had to paint him. I was compelled to. I started painting him from memory, but had to stop when I reached a certain point. So I painted over him like this."

Mariye's lips were still set in a straight line.

Then she shook her head from side to side.

"That man is really scary," she said.

"That man?" I said. I followed her eyes. They were fixed on **The Man with the White Subaru Forester**. "Do you mean the painting? Or the man?"

She gave another firm nod. Despite her fear, she seemed unable to look away.

"Can you see him?"

She nodded. "I can see him behind the paint. He's standing there looking at me. Wearing a black cap."

I turned it around and set it back, face against the wall.

"You have the ability to see the man with the Subaru Forester standing there. Most people don't," I said. "But I think it's better if you don't look at him anymore. There's probably no need at this stage."

Mariye nodded as if in agreement.

"I don't know if the man with the white Subaru Forester is of this world or not. It's possible that someone, or something, merely borrowed his form. In the same way an Idea borrowed the form of the Commendatore. Or it could be that I saw part of myself reflected in him. But when I was surrounded by real darkness, it was no mere reflection, believe me. It was a tangible, living, moving **thing**. The people in that land call it a 'Double Metaphor.' I do plan to finish the painting someday. But not yet—it's still too early. And too dangerous. Some things shouldn't be recklessly dragged into the light. But I may not be . . ."

Mariye was looking straight at me without saying a word. I found it difficult to continue.

"Anyway, thanks to the help of many people, I was somehow able to cross the underworld and squeeze through a narrow, black tunnel to make my way back to this world. At virtually the same moment, you were freed **from somewhere**. I can't believe that was a mere stroke of luck. On Friday, you disappeared somewhere for four days. Then on Saturday I disappeared for three days. On Tuesday, we both **returned**. There has to be a connection. My guess is that the Commendatore connected us. And now he's gone from this world. He fulfilled his role and moved on. Only you and I are left. We're the only ones who can close the circle. Do you believe what I'm saying?"

Mariye nodded.

"That's what I wanted to tell you. Why I asked to talk to you alone."

Mariye's eyes were trained on my face.

"No one else would believe me," I went on, "even if I told the truth. They'd think I was nuts. I mean the story just doesn't fly—it's too far removed from reality—though I figured you'd believe me. And then I'd have to show them **Killing Commendatore**.

Without that painting, nothing I said would make sense. But I don't want anyone else to see it. Only you."

Mariye kept looking at me. She didn't speak. But I could see the sparkle slowly returning to her eyes.

"Tomohiko Amada invested everything, all of himself, in this painting. It's filled with his emotion. As though he painted it with his own blood and flesh. Truly a once-in-a-lifetime work of art. He did it for himself, but also for those who were no longer of this world, a kind of requiem to their memory. To purify the blood they had shed."

"Requiem?"

"A work to bring peace to the spirits of the dead and heal their wounds. That's why he didn't expose it to public view. The critical reception, the accolades, the financial rewards—they had no meaning. He wanted none of those things for this painting. It was enough for him to know that he had created it, and that it existed somewhere. Even if it was wrapped up in paper and hidden in an attic where no one would ever see it. I want to respect his feelings."

The room was quiet for a while.

"You've played around here since you were small, right? Using that secret passageway of yours. Isn't that so?"

Mariye nodded.

"Did you ever meet Tomohiko Amada?"

"I saw the old guy. But I never talked to him. I just hid and looked at him from far away. When he was painting. I mean, I was trespassing, right?"

I nodded. The image was all too real. Mariye in the shrubbery, peeking into the studio. Tomohiko Amada on his stool, intently wielding his brush. The thought that he was being observed a million miles from his mind.

"You asked me to help you with something," Mariye said.

"So I did. There's one thing," I said. "I'd like you to help me wrap up these two paintings and hide them in the attic where no one can see them. **Killing Commendatore** and **The Man with the White Subaru Forester**. I don't think we need them right now. That's where I could use your help."

Mariye nodded but didn't say anything. Truth be told, this was a task I really didn't want to do alone. More than help, I needed someone to act as observer and witness. Someone tight-lipped, whom I could trust to share the secret.

I went to the kitchen and got some twine and a utility knife. Then Mariye and I packed up **Killing Commendatore**. We wrapped it carefully in the same brown washi, the traditional Japanese paper it had been in before, bound it with twine, draped it in a white cloth, and then tied it again. Firmly, to make it difficult for anyone to unwrap. The thick paint on **The Man with the White Subaru Forester** wasn't quite dry, so we wrapped it more loosely. Then we carried the two paintings to the closet of the guest bedroom. I climbed to the top of the stepladder, raised the trap door to the attic (much like Long Face had pushed up the square lid to his hole, come to think of it), and climbed up. The air was chilly there, but a pleasant kind of chilly. Mariye handed the paintings up to me. **Killing Commendatore** went first, followed by **The Man with the White Subaru Forester**. I leaned them next to each other against the wall.

All of a sudden, I sensed I had company. I gulped. Someone was there—I could feel a presence. Then I saw the horned owl. Probably the same owl I had seen the first time. The night bird was perched on the same beam as before, still as a statue. He didn't seem particularly concerned when I moved in his direction. Also like the first time.

"Hey. Come up and see something," I whispered to Mariye. "Something very cool. Try not to make any noise."

Looking curious, Mariye mounted the ladder and crawled through the opening into the attic. I pulled her up the last step with both hands. The floor of the attic was covered with a fine white dust, but she didn't show any concern that it would get on her wool skirt. I sat down and pointed out the horned owl to her. She knelt beside me and looked at the bird, entranced. It was very beautiful. Like a cat that had sprouted wings. "It's been living here the whole while," I whispered to her. "It goes out to hunt in the forest in the evening, and flies back in the morning to sleep. That's its entrance there."

I pointed at the air vent with the hole in its screen.

Mariye nodded. I could hear the faint sound of her breathing.

We sat there side by side without speaking, looking at the owl. Showing little interest in us, the owl sat there quietly, a model of discretion. The owl and I had a tacit understanding that we would share the house. One of us was active during the day, the other at night—in that way, the domain of consciousness was shared equally, half and half.

Mariye reached over and took my hand in hers. Her head came to rest on my shoulder. I gently squeezed her hand back. Komi and I had spent long hours together like this. We were close as brother and sister. Our feelings had flowed back and forth in a very natural way. Until death separated us.

I could feel the tension drain from Mariye's body. Little by little, that part of her that had become so rigid was beginning to unclench. I stroked her head on my shoulder. Her soft, straight hair. When my hand touched her cheek, I realized she was crying. The tears were so warm it felt as if blood was spilling from her heart. I continued to hold her like that. The girl had needed to cry. But she hadn't been able to. Probably for a very long time. The horned owl and I kept watch over her as she wept.

The rays of the afternoon sun angled through the hole in the broken vent. White dust and silence surrounded us, nothing more. Dust and silence that seemed to have been passed down from antiquity. We could hear no wind. On his beam, the horned owl mutely preserved the wisdom of the forest. A wisdom also bequeathed from the distant past.

Mariye wept for a long time. She made no sound, but the trembling of her body told me she was still crying. I kept stroking her hair. As if she and I were heading upstream along the river of time.

60

IF THAT PERSON HAD
PRETTY LONG ARMS

I was at Mr. Menshiki's house," Mariye said. "The
whole four days." She had stopped crying, and was
talking again.

She and I were in the studio. Mariye was perched
on the round stool, her knees touching as they peeked
out from beneath her skirt. I was leaning on the windowsill. I could see how pretty her legs were. Her
bulky tights couldn't hide that. When she matured a
bit more, those legs would attract the gaze of many
men. By then, her chest would have filled out too.
Now, however, she was just a lost and confused girl,
wavering on the threshold of adulthood.

"You were at Mr. Menshiki's?" I asked. "I'm not
sure I understand. Can you fill me in a little?"

"I needed to know more about him, so I went
to his house. I had to find out why he was watching our home through those binoculars every night.
I think he bought the big house across the valley just
to do that. To spy on us. I couldn't understand why
he would do something like that. I mean, it was so
not normal. I thought there had to be some kind of
reason."

"So you went to pay him a visit?"

Mariye shook her head no. "I didn't pay him a visit. I snuck in. Secretly. And then I couldn't get out."

"You snuck in?"

"Yes, like a burglar. I didn't plan it like that, though."

When her morning classes ended on Friday, Mariye slipped out the back door of the school. If a student was unexpectedly absent in the morning, the school called their family. But no phone call was made when a student missed his or her afternoon classes. There was no clear reason for this policy—that's just the way things were done. Mariye had never skipped out before, so she figured if she got caught she could talk her way out of trouble. She hopped on a bus and got off close to where she lived. But instead of heading home, she turned up the opposite slope, toward Menshiki's house.

At first, Mariye had no intention of sneaking in. The idea never crossed her mind. Yet she wasn't planning to ring Menshiki's doorbell and invite herself in, either. The fact was, she went there with no plan in mind. She was simply drawn to the white mansion like a metal filing to a powerful magnet. She couldn't solve the mystery of Menshiki's behavior merely by standing outside his wall. She knew that much. Yet she couldn't stifle her curiosity. Her legs carried her to his gate under their own volition.

It was a very long climb. When she turned and looked back, she could see the ocean sparkling between the mountains. His house was surrounded by a high wall with a sturdy electrically operated gate positioned at the entrance. Security cameras were set on each side. One of the gate's pillars had a security company's logo stuck to it. She had to approach with care. She hid behind some bushes and took stock of the situation. She could spot no movement, either inside or outside the house. No one entered or left, and no noise of any kind came from within.

After wasting half an hour hanging around with nothing to do, she had given up and was preparing to leave when she saw a van roll up the hill. A minivan, from a parcel delivery service. It stopped in front of the gate, a door opened, and a uniformed young man jumped out, clipboard in hand. He walked to the gate and rang the bell. There was a brief exchange with someone over the intercom. When the big wooden gate started to slowly swing in, the young man hurried back to his van and drove inside.

Mariye had no time to think things through. The moment the van entered, she leapt from the bushes and sprinted as fast as she could through the closing gate. It was pretty close, but she managed to slip through a split second before it shut. The security cameras might have picked her up. But no one came out to challenge her. Dogs, though, were a scarier proposition. A guard dog might be prowling the grounds. She hadn't considered that before racing in. The instant the gate closed behind her, though, the possibility occurred to her. A property this extensive could easily have a Doberman or a German shepherd running loose. A big dog like that would be a problem. Mariye was afraid of dogs. But as luck would have it, none appeared. She heard no barking, either. Now that she thought of it, there had been no talk of a dog when she and her aunt had paid their visit.

Having made her way inside the wall, she hid behind some shrubs and appraised her situation. Her throat was dry. I stole in here like a burglar, she thought. I'm breaking the law—this is trespassing, no doubt about it. The cameras have recorded proof of my guilt.

Had she made the right move? She wasn't sure. When she had seen the delivery van pass through the gate, her response had been automatic. She'd had no time to consider the possible consequences. Now's my one and only chance, she'd thought, and acted on the spur of the moment. Her body had moved before her mind clicked in. Yet for some reason, even now, she had no second thoughts.

From her hiding place she saw the delivery van roll back up the driveway. Once again, the gate slowly swung open and the van passed through. If she was going to leave, now was the time. Just run out before the gate closed. Return to the world of safety. She wouldn't be a criminal. But she didn't move. Instead, she remained there, hidden in the shadows, and watched the gate close again. Intently biting her lower lip.

She waited there for precisely ten minutes, measuring the time on her small Casio G-Shock watch. When the ten minutes were up, she emerged from the shrubbery. Bending low so the cameras would have difficulty spotting her, she hurried down the gentle slope toward the front door of the house. It was two thirty.

What if Menshiki discovered her? She thought about that for a moment. Well, she decided, if that happened she'd wriggle out of it somehow. Menshiki seemed to have a keen interest (or something like that) in her. So if she told him she'd just come to say hi and, seeing the gate open, had walked in, and made it all seem like a kid's game, he would trust her. He wants to believe in something, she thought, so he'll swallow what I say. The problem was, where did his "keen interest" come from, and did he have good intentions, or was he dangerous?

The front door of the mansion was around the bend, at the bottom of the sloping driveway. There was a bell beside the door. Needless to say, she didn't push it. Instead, she moved clockwise around the building, hiding behind trees and shrubs, hugging the concrete wall and giving the roundabout where guests parked a wide berth. A two-car garage sat to the left of the entranceway. Its door was rolled down and locked. A little farther on sat a stylish little building that looked like a cottage. That must be the guest-house, she thought. Beyond that was a tennis court. She had never seen a home with a tennis court before. Who did Mr. Menshiki play tennis with? The court, however, appeared to have been long ignored. It had no net, its all-weather surface was strewn with leaves, and the white lines were so faded they were almost invisible.

All the windows facing the mountainside were

small and tightly shuttered, so nothing inside could be seen. As before, the house was absolutely quiet. No barking dogs. From time to time she could hear birds chirping high in the trees, but that was all. At the back of the house was another garage. Also with space for two cars. It seemed to have been added after the house was built. Menshiki sure could store an awful lot of cars!

The slope behind the house had been turned into a large Japanese-style garden. She could see a descending flight of steps, and below that a path weaving through a number of large rocks. The azalea bushes were pruned to perfection, the pine branches overhead an array of bright greens. What looked like an arbor lay just beyond. A reclining chair where one could stretch out and read sat under the arbor. Beside it was a coffee table. Lanterns and lights were scattered here and there.

Mariye worked her way around the house to the back. The house's broad deck looked from there out over the valley. She had walked out onto that deck on her first visit. It was from there that Menshiki kept watch on her home. The second she set foot on it she knew that was true. She felt it in her bones.

Mariye squinted as she looked over at her home. It was right across from her. So close it seemed a person could reach out and touch it (if that person had pretty long arms, that is). From this vantage point, the house looked utterly defenseless. At the time it was built, there had been no homes on this side of the valley. Only recently (though more than ten years ago) had building restrictions been eased and houses erected on this slope. That was why, when her home was designed, no attempt had been made to shield it from those across the way. That made it a sitting duck for prying eyes. A high-powered telescope or even a pair of good binoculars would give one a clear view of what was going on inside. The window to her bedroom was a perfect example. To be sure, she was a cautious girl. She always closed the curtain before taking off her clothes. But that didn't mean there were no unguarded moments. What had Menshiki seen?

Mariye descended the outside steps to the next floor where the study was, but the windows were shuttered there too. She couldn't peek in at all. So she kept walking down to the lowest level. Most of that floor was occupied by a large utility area. She could see a washing machine, a place for an ironing board, a room that seemed to be set aside for a live-in maid, and, on the far end, a sizable gym containing five or six exercise machines. Unlike the tennis court, these appeared to be well used. They all looked clean and well oiled. A heavy punching bag hung from the ceiling. Compared with the upper floors, this floor was less tightly guarded. Many of the windows lacked curtains, so she could peer inside. Nevertheless, both the windows and the sliding glass doors were securely locked from within. Here too the security company had pasted their stickers to scare off intruders. An alarm would sound in their offices if anyone tried to force their way in.

The mansion was huge. She found it impossible to

believe that a single person could inhabit such a big space. It must be a lonely life. The concrete walls were thick, and every precaution had been taken to block anyone from gaining entry. True, there was no guard dog (maybe he didn't like dogs either), but apart from that every antiburglar device under the sun had been employed.

What should be her next step? Nothing came to mind. There was no way to get inside, and no way to breach the wall to get out. Menshiki was home, she knew that. He had pushed the button that opened the gate and taken delivery of the parcel. And he lived there by himself. Once a week, a cleaning service came, but apart from that the house was off-limits to outsiders. That was his basic principle—he had told them that on their visit.

Since she couldn't gain access to the house, she had to find a place to hide outside. If she kept poking around she might locate a likely spot. After a long search, she finally came across what seemed to be a small storage shed at the far corner of the garden. The door was unlocked. Inside were a bunch of garden tools and stacked bags of fertilizer. She slipped in and sat down on the bags. The shed was far from inviting. But at least the security cameras wouldn't find her here. And it was unlikely anyone would show up. Sooner or later, things would change. All she could do was wait.

Although she was stuck in one place, she felt full of energy. After her shower that morning, she had noticed swellings on her chest in the mirror. It was an exciting development. Of course, she might be deluding herself. It could just be wishful thinking. She had inspected her chest from a number of angles, and touched it with her hands. There did seem to be two soft protuberances that had not been there before. Her nipples were still tiny (a far cry from her aunt's, which resembled olive pits), but there was a hint they might be about to sprout.

Mariye passed her time in the storage shed thinking about her budding breasts. She pictured how they might look when they grew. What would it feel like to live your life with really big ones? She imagined strapping on the kind of underwire bra her aunt used. That day was still miles away, however. After all, her periods had only begun that spring.

She was a little thirsty, but she could bear that. She consulted her chunky G-Shock watch. It was five minutes past three. Her painting class was on Fridays, but she'd been planning to skip that anyway. She hadn't brought her bag of painting supplies with her. Yet her aunt was sure to worry if she didn't get home by dinnertime. She could come up with a good excuse later.

She seemed to have fallen asleep. It was hard to believe that she could have slept in this place, and under these circumstances. Yet she had managed to drop off without realizing it. It hadn't been for very long. Ten or fifteen minutes. Maybe less. But a deep sleep, nonetheless. She was disoriented when she awoke, her mind at loose ends. For a moment she didn't know where she was or what she was doing. It seemed she had been dreaming. A vague dream, something to do with full breasts and milk chocolate. Her mouth was filled with saliva. Then it hit her. I snuck into Menshiki's, she remembered, and now I'm hiding in his storage shed.

A noise had roused her. A repetitive, mechanical noise. To be more precise, a garage door clattering open. The door of the garage near the entrance. Menshiki was probably in his car and about to head off somewhere. Mariye hurried from the shed and ran around to the front, making as little sound as possible. When the door was fully open the clattering stopped. She heard a car start up, and then the front of Menshiki's silver Jaguar slowly emerged. Menshiki was sitting in the driver's seat. The driver's window was down, and his pure white hair glowed in the afternoon sun. She watched from behind the shrubbery.

Had Menshiki looked to his right, he could have glimpsed her there in the shadows. The shrubs were too small to provide full cover. But his eyes were trained straight ahead. Hands on the wheel, he seemed lost in thought. The Jaguar moved up the driveway, passed around the curve, and disappeared. The remote control–activated metal door began to clatter down again. The second before it closed, Mariye raced from her hiding place and slipped under the door. Like Indiana Jones in **Raiders of the Lost Ark**. Another reflex action. Without really thinking, she had decided to gain access to the house through the garage. The automatic door hesitated when it sensed her slide underneath, then resumed its descent until it was tightly shut.

Another car was in the garage. A stylish blue convertible with a beige hood, the sports car her aunt had admired on their previous visit. Mariye couldn't care less about cars, so she'd barely glanced at it then. It had a very long nose, and, here too, the Jaguar crest. Even someone who knew as little about cars as Mariye could tell it was worth a lot of money. A collector's piece, in all likelihood.

A person could pass into the house through a door in the garage. She tried the knob with some trepidation, but it turned easily. She sighed with relief. Few people would lock a door like that during the day, but Menshiki was such a cautious man she couldn't be sure. Perhaps something had been on his mind to make him forget. She'd been lucky.

She walked through the door and into the house. Should she take her shoes off or keep them on? In the end, she decided to carry them with her. Leaving them on the doorstep didn't seem like a good option. The house was hushed when she entered. As if everything in it was holding its breath. Menshiki was gone, and she was positive no one else was there. I'm alone in this huge house, she thought. For the next little while, I am free to go wherever, and do whatever, I want.

Menshiki had given them a basic guided tour on their first visit. She remembered it well enough. The general layout was fixed in her head. She entered the big living room that took up almost the entire first floor. From there, one could go out to the broad deck through a sliding glass door. She hesitated, though. Menshiki might have activated the security system before leaving. If he had, an alarm would go off when she tried to slide it open. A light would flash in the agency's office. They would phone the house to check. A password would be necessary to end the alert. Mariye stood before the sliding door, black loafers in hand, pondering the situation.

Finally, she reached the conclusion that Menshiki hadn't set the alarm. The fact that he had left the inner door in the garage unlocked suggested that he wasn't heading off on a long trip. Odds were he had gone shopping, or was running some sort of errand. Mariye made up her mind. She unlocked the door, slid it open, and waited to see what would happen. No alarm went off, and the security agency did not phone. She heaved a sigh of relief (had security guards found her there she couldn't have joked her way out of it) and stepped out onto the deck. Putting down her shoes, she went over to the binoculars and removed their plastic cover. They were too heavy to hold, so she tried balancing them on the railing, but that didn't work very well. Looking around, she noticed what looked like a stand leaning against the wall. It resembled a camera tripod and was the same olive color as the binoculars. The binoculars could be screwed onto the stand. She stuck them together, pulled up the low metal stool left nearby, sat down, and looked through them. Now using the binoculars was easy.

Moreover, they were positioned so that she couldn't be observed from the other side of the valley. This had to be how Menshiki spent much of his time.

She was shocked at how clearly the inside of her house could be seen. Everything was a notch brighter—one of the binoculars' special features, she assumed. Some of the curtains in the rooms facing the valley hadn't been drawn. The view within was so distinct she felt she could reach out and touch what she was looking at. A vase of flowers, for example, or even a magazine on the table. Her aunt should be home at this hour. But she couldn't locate her anywhere.

It was weird to look inside her own house from such a distance, and in such naked detail. It felt as if she had become one of the dead (how was unclear) and now was viewing her home from their vantage point. She had belonged there for so long, yet it was hers no more. She knew it so intimately but could never go back. It was a strange, dissociated sensation.

She trained the binoculars on her own room. It faced in her direction, but the curtain was drawn. Shut tight, without a crack. Her familiar curtain, with its orange pattern. The orange bleached by the sun. She couldn't see behind it. But her shadow was probably visible at night, when the light was on. How visible, though, could only be known after dark. Mariye panned across the house, looking for her aunt. She ought to be there. But she was nowhere to be seen. Perhaps she was preparing dinner in the kitchen in the back. Or resting in her room. Wherever she was, she wasn't visible from this angle.

Mariye felt a powerful urge to go back to that house. Right away. She longed to sit in her familiar chair at the dining room table and sip hot tea in her very own cup. To watch her aunt preparing dinner in the kitchen. How wonderful that would be, she thought. Until that point, she had never imagined missing her home this way. Not for a second. To her, the house had always been an ugly, barren monstrosity. She had hated living there. In fact, she was impatient for the day when she was old enough to move into her own place, one that suited her. Yet now, looking at its interior from the other side of the valley through the clear lens, she wanted to return at any cost. **It was where she belonged.** Where she would be protected.

Just then she heard a faint droning sound. Prying her eyes from the binoculars, she saw something black circling above her. A large bee with a long body, probably a hornet. The kind of hostile, aggressive hornet with a sharp stinger that had killed her mother. Mariye ran back into the house, forcefully slid the door shut, and locked it. The hornet buzzed around the door for a while, as if to pen her in. It struck the glass several times, then finally gave up and flew away. Mariye gave a great sigh of relief. Her heart was pounding, her breathing ragged. Nothing scared her more than hornets. Her father had lectured her time and again how dangerous they were. Mariye had looked at many photographs so that she knew exactly how they looked. In the process, she had conceived the terrifying idea that she, like her mother, would be stung to death. She might well have the same allergic reaction. One couldn't escape death, but it should come later—she wanted to know what it felt like to have full breasts and a woman's nipples at least once before she died. It would really suck if hornets killed her before she had that chance.

It was better to stay in the house a while, for safety's sake. That savage insect would still be flying about. Moreover, it appeared to be targeting her. She decided to search inside the mansion and forget about going outside for the time being.

Her first step was to tour the sprawling living room. She could see no particular change since her first visit. There was the big Steinway grand piano. A small stack of musical scores was piled on top of it. A Bach invention, a Mozart sonata, one of Chopin's études, that sort of thing. Nothing that required advanced technical skill. Still, being able to play them at all was impressive. Mariye could tell that much. She had taken piano lessons when she was younger. (She hadn't gone very far—art was what had grabbed her.)

A number of books were scattered on the coffee table's marble top. Judging from the bookmarks stuck in them, all were in the process of being read. One was on philosophy, one was historical, and two were novels (one of which was in English). She recognized none of the titles and had heard of none of the authors' names. She flipped through several, but they weren't her thing. The master of the house loved difficult books and classical music. Between those pursuits, he looked into her home across the valley through high-powered binoculars.

Was he just a perv? Or was there a logical reason or purpose for his behavior? Did he have the hots for her aunt? Or for her? Or for both of them? (Was such a thing possible?)

Next she went to take a look at the lower levels. First she made her way to Menshiki's study. His portrait hung on the wall. She stood in the middle of the room and studied it for a moment. Of course, she had seen it before (that had been the purpose of their first visit). This time, though, the longer she looked at it, the more it felt as if Menshiki were there with her. So she turned away from the painting. Trying her best to ignore it, she went over to inspect his desk. There was a state-of-the-art Apple desktop computer, but she didn't switch it on. She knew without trying that it was secured. There would be no way she could gain access. Not much else was on the desk. There was a deskpad calendar with almost nothing written on it. Just a few incomprehensible symbols and numbers here and there. He would have input his daily schedule into the computer, and then shared it with his other devices. All would be locked. Mr. Menshiki was a cautious man. He would leave no traces.

The other things on the desk were the sort of work-related materials you would expect to find in anyone's study. The pencils were all of the same length, and sharpened to a fine point. Paper clips were arranged according to size. The white memo pad waited patiently for someone to write on it. The digital clock faithfully clicked off the time. The desk was in such perfect order it was frightening. Unless he's a well-made android, Mariye thought to herself, something sure is funny about Mr. Menshiki.

As she expected, every desk drawer was locked. That was only natural. No way he would neglect securing them. The study held little else that she wanted to see. She had no special interest in the shelves of books, or the CD collection, or the new, obviously expensive stereo system. Those did no more than reflect his range of tastes. They didn't help her understand who he was as a person. They had no connection to the secret he was (most likely) concealing.

Mariye left the study and walked down the dim hallway, checking the rooms as she went. All were unlocked. None had been included in the house tour. She and her aunt had only been shown the living room, the study, the dining room, and the kitchen (she had also used the guest bathroom on the first floor). Mariye opened the doors to these unknown rooms one by one. The first was Menshiki's bedroom. As the so-called master bedroom (she assumed), it was very big. It had a walk-in closet and a private bathroom. Its large bed was neatly turned out, with a quilted duvet. Since there was no live-in maid, she assumed Menshiki had made the bed. If so, its neatness didn't surprise her. A pair of plain dark brown pajamas lay next to the pillow, also neatly folded. A number of prints hung on the wall. A set by a single artist, from the looks of it. A half-read book rested on the bedside table. He certainly was an avid reader. The window faced the valley, but it wasn't very large and its blinds had been drawn.

She opened the door to the big walk-in closet. Rows of clothes were hanging there. Lots of jackets and blazers, but not many suits. Not many neckties, either. She guessed he seldom needed to dress for formal occasions. All the shirts had plastic covers, and appeared to have just come back from the cleaners. Shoes and sneakers were lined up on shelves in neat rows. Coats of varied thicknesses occupied another part of the closet. Everything in the closet was looked after with care and reflected the good taste of its owner. Indeed, the whole closet could have been featured as it was in a menswear magazine. There were not too many clothes, nor too few. Moderation governed everything.

His drawers contained socks, handkerchiefs, and underwear. All were pressed and folded, and arranged in perfect order. There were more drawers for his jeans, polo shirts, sweatshirts, and so forth. One large drawer had been entirely given over to a colorful array of beautiful sweaters. None had patterns. Yet Mariye could find nothing in any of these drawers to help her unravel Menshiki's secret. Everything was immaculate and divided according to its function. Not a speck of dust was on the floor, and all the picture frames were level on the walls.

Mariye did reach one clear conclusion about Menshiki, however: this man would be impossible to live with. No normal person could meet his standard.

Her aunt was something of a neat freak, but even she wasn't this meticulous.

The next door opened onto what appeared to be the guest room. It had a double bed, made up and ready to be used. A writing desk and office chair sat near the window. There was also a small television set. But there was no sign that anyone had ever slept there—the room felt as if it had been forsaken for eternity. Mr. Menshiki was not in the habit of entertaining guests, it seemed. Instead, this room was apparently to be used in emergencies (though she couldn't imagine what those might be).

The room next door was more like a storeroom. It had no furniture, and at least ten cardboard boxes were stacked on the green carpet. Judging by their weight, they contained documents. Each had a label, with markings in ballpoint pen. All were carefully sealed with tape. Mariye imagined they were filled with work-related documents. Those might contain important secrets. But they were business secrets, not the sort of thing that she was after.

None of these rooms was locked. Though their windows faced the valley, their blinds were closed. No one was there to delight in the bright sunlight and the majestic view. They were dimly lit and smelled of abandonment.

The fourth room fascinated her. Not so much the room itself, though. The furnishings were sparse—just a single straight-backed chair and a small, plain wooden table. No pictures graced the bare walls. Without decoration of any kind, it felt barren and empty.

A room no one ever used. Yet when she checked the walk-in closet, she found an assortment of women's clothes hanging there. Not a huge number. But everything a woman would need, more or less, for a stay of several days. Mariye guessed the clothes had been set aside for someone who came to visit Menshiki on a regular basis. She scowled. Did her aunt know a woman like that was in the picture?

She quickly realized her mistake, however. The clothes were all out of style, designs from a different era. The dresses and skirts and blouses sported name brands, and were very fashionable and expensive, but not the sort that women wore these days. Mariye wasn't that up-to-date on current trends, but even she could tell that much. They had probably been in style before she was born. And all were permeated with the smell of mothballs. It appeared that the clothes had been hanging there for quite some time. They were being well looked after, though. She saw no moth holes. And the colors hadn't faded, which meant that care had been taken not to expose them to extreme heat or cold. The dresses were size 5. That indicated that the woman was about five feet tall. And very slender, looking at the skirts. She wore a size 5 shoe.

An assortment of women's undergarments, socks, and nightgowns were stored in the closet drawers. All were in plastic bags to ward off dust. She pulled a few out to examine. The bras were a 32C. Mariye pictured the shape of the breasts they had held. Slightly smaller than her aunt's, she estimated (it was impossible to guess the shape of the nipples, of course). The panties were dainty and elegant. Some were on the sexy side. All in all, they spoke of a woman of some means, who shopped in lingerie boutiques while savoring the thought of embracing the man she loved. They were made of silk and lace and had to be washed by hand in lukewarm water. Not the sort of panties one wore to weed the garden. Here too the odor of mothballs was strong. She folded the panties up carefully, returned them to the plastic bag, and put it back in the drawer.

This was the wardrobe of a woman whom Menshiki had been seeing some time before—fifteen or twenty years ago, most likely. That was the conclusion Mariye drew. Then something had happened that caused the woman to leave her stylish clothes—her size 5 dresses, size 5 shoes, and 32C bras—behind. She had never come back. Why would she have left such an expensive collection behind? If they had separated for some reason, wouldn't the normal thing have been to take the clothes with her? Mariye couldn't figure it out. Moreover, Menshiki had preserved that small collection with such care. Like the river sprites of the Rhine, who took pains to preserve their legendary gold for posterity. He probably visited this room on occasion to look at the clothes and take them in his hands. When the seasons changed, he would replace the mothballs (she couldn't imagine him letting anyone else do this).

Where was that woman today? Perhaps she had

915

married another man. Or died of illness, or in some kind of accident. Nevertheless, he held her in his memory, even now.

(Of course, Mariye had no way of knowing that woman was her mother, and I could find no compelling reason to tell her. That right, I thought, belonged to Menshiki alone.)

Mariye pondered this new knowledge. Should she think more generously of a man who had treasured the memory of a woman for so long? Or was the fact that he had preserved her clothing with such care a little creepy?

Mariye was still thinking this through when, all at once, she heard the garage door clattering up. Menshiki had come home. She had been so absorbed in the clothes that she hadn't heard the front gate open, or the car in the driveway. She had to get away as quickly as possible. She needed to find a safe place to hide. Then she realized. Something of **vital importance**. Panic grabbed her.

She had forgotten her shoes on the deck. And the binoculars were out of their case and attached to their stand. The hornet had scared her so much that she had fled into the house without covering her tracks. Everything was out in the open. When Menshiki went out to the deck and saw those things (as he would sooner or later), he would know right away that someone had invaded his home in his absence.

The black loafers would tell him that the invader was a girl. Menshiki was no dummy. It wouldn't take long for him to figure out it was Mariye. He would comb the house, searching every nook and cranny, until he found her hiding place. It would be child's play for him.

There wasn't time enough to run outside up to the deck, collect her shoes, and put the binoculars back where they belonged. She was certain to bump into Menshiki somewhere along the way. She couldn't think of a next step. Her heart pounded, her breathing became labored, her limbs froze with fear.

The car engine stopped and the garage door started clattering shut. Any minute now Menshiki would enter the house. What should she do? What should she . . . Her mind was a blank. She sat on the floor, her head in her hands and her eyes squeezed shut.

"It is best to remain where you are," someone said.

Was she hearing things? No, she wasn't. Pulling herself together, she opened her eyes. There was a little old man no more than two feet tall, perched on a low chest of drawers. His salt-and-pepper hair was tied in a bun on top of his head. He wore white garments from a bygone age and carried a tiny sword at his waist. Naturally, she thought she was hallucinating. Her panic was making her imagine things that weren't there.

"No, this is no hallucination," the little old man said in a small but resonant voice. "I am the Commendatore. And I am here to aid my young friends."

61

I HAVE TO BE A BRAVE, SMART GIRL

T his is no hallucination," the Commendatore repeated. "There are sundry opinions as to whether I exist, but a hallucination I am not. I have come to aid my friends. You are in need of aid, are you not?"

"My friends" referred to her, Mariye assumed. She nodded. His manner of speech was strange indeed, but what he said was true. She needed help, no question there.

"My friends cannot retrieve your shoes from the deck," the Commendatore said. "And it is best to forget the binoculars as well. But quell your fears. I will strive my utmost to ensure that Menshiki does not go there. For the time being, at least. Once the sun sets, however, I cannot prevent him. When darkness falls, he will venture out to watch the home of my friends. This is his custom. We must fix the problem before that happens. Can my friends understand the import of my words?"

Mariye could only nod. Somehow, she did understand.

"My friends must hide in this closet awhile," said the Commendatore. "Be as quiet as a mouse. Give no sign that you are here. When the time is propitious I will let you know. Until then, do not move or make a sound. No matter what happens. Do my friends understand?"

Mariye nodded again. Was this a dream? Could he be an elf or sprite of some kind?

"I am neither dream nor sprite," the Commendatore read her thoughts. "I am an Idea, and thus lack shape of my own. It would be very inconvenient if my friends could not see me, so I have taken the form of the Commendatore for the time being."

Idea, the Commendatore . . . Mariye repeated the words in her mind without voicing them. He can tell what I am thinking. Then she remembered. He was a figure in that very wide Japanese-style painting by Tomohiko Amada that she had seen in his studio. Somehow he had slipped out of the painting and come here. That explained his tiny size.

"Affirmative," the Commendatore said. "I am borrowing the form of that character. The Commendatore—I myself do not know his significance. But I am called by that sobriquet now. Wait here in silence. I will come for my friends at the proper time. Do not fear. These raiments will shelter you."

These raiments will shelter me? What did that mean? But he did not respond to her unspoken question. A moment later he was gone. Vanished into thin air, like vapor.

Mariye did as the Commendatore said. She quieted her breathing and didn't move a muscle. Menshiki was home—she had heard him enter the house. He seemed to have been shopping, for she could make out the rustle of paper bags. Her breathing almost stopped when his slippered feet padded slowly past the room where she was hiding.

The closet door was a Venetian blind, so some light seeped upward through the slats. But only a tiny bit. The closet would grow very dark when the daylight faded. She could see only the carpeted floor through the cracks. The closet was cramped, and filled with the sharp odor of mothballs. With walls on all sides, there was nowhere to hide. And no way to escape. The lack of an escape route scared her to death.

The Commendatore had promised to come and get her when the right time came. She had no choice but to believe him. He had said, "These raiments will shelter you," too. He must have meant the clothes there in the closet. Old clothes worn by some unknown woman, likely before Mariye was even born. How could they protect her? She reached out and stroked a dress with a flower pattern. The pink cloth was soft to the touch. She let her fingertips linger for a while. She couldn't explain why, but there was something comforting about it.

I bet this dress would fit, Mariye thought. Its owner wasn't that much bigger than me. I can wear a size 5. Of course my chest hasn't filled out yet, so I'd have to figure a way to conceal that. But I could wear most of these clothes if I wanted to, or if I had to for some reason. The thought made her heart skip a beat.

Time was passing. Slowly but surely, the room was

growing darker. Evening was approaching, minute by minute. She looked at her watch. But she couldn't read it in the gloom. She pressed a button and the face lit up. It was almost four thirty. The sun would be going down soon. The days were getting shorter. And when night did come, Menshiki would head out to the deck. It would take him but a second to realize that someone had invaded his home. She had to find some way to deal with the shoes and binoculars before that happened.

Mariye waited impatiently for the Commendatore to arrive, her heart in her mouth. Yet he never did. Perhaps there had been some kind of hitch. Menshiki might have left him no opening. She hadn't a clue how extensive the actual powers of a person—or an Idea—like the Commendatore were, in fact, or how far she could depend on him. Yet he was her only hope. She had nowhere else to turn. Mariye sat holding her knees on the floor of the closet, staring through the slats at the carpet. From time to time she reached up to stroke the flowery dress. As though it were a lifeline of some kind.

When the room had grown quite dark, she heard footsteps in the hall a second time. Once again, they were slow and soft. The footsteps came to an abrupt halt in front of the room where she was hiding. As if whoever it was had sniffed out something. A moment later she heard the door open. There could be no doubt. Her heart froze in her mouth. Then she heard the person (Menshiki, she presumed—no one else was in the house) step inside and gently close the door behind him. It clicked shut. **The man is in the room. For sure.** Like her, he held his breath and listened carefully, trying to pick up the slightest sign. She could tell. But the man did not turn on the light. Instead he carried out his search in the dark. Why? Anyone else would have switched on the light the moment they came in. It baffled her.

Mariye stared at the floor through the slats. If he came close enough, his toes would come into view. She couldn't see them yet. Yet his presence felt very real. It was definitely a man. Moreover, that man (it had to be Menshiki!) was staring at the closet door in the dark. He had picked up signs of something. Something different than usual. Next he would open the door. It couldn't be otherwise. It would be easy, since of course it wasn't locked. All he had to do was reach out, grab the knob, and pull.

The footsteps drew even closer. Fear gripped her. Cold sweat dripped from her armpits. I should never have come, she thought. I should have stayed home like a good girl. In my dear home across the valley. There is something really scary about this place. Something I should never have approached so recklessly. Some kind of consciousness operated here. The hornets were a part of it. Now she was within arm's reach of that **something**. She could see the toe of a slipper through the blinds. She could tell that the slipper was brown and made of leather, but it was too dark to see anything more.

Mariye instinctively reached up and grabbed the

dress. The size 5 dress with the flower pattern. **Please help me! Protect me!** she prayed.

The man stood in front of the closet's double doors for some time. He didn't make a sound. She couldn't even hear him breathe. Still as a stone statue, he stood there gauging the situation. The silence grew heavier, the dark more impenetrable. She huddled on the floor, quivering. Her teeth chattered faintly. Mariye longed to shut her eyes and ears. To put her mind in a totally different place. But she didn't. She somehow knew how dangerous that would be. She must never give in to fear, however great. Never abandon her senses. Never stop thinking. With her ears pricked and her eyes fastened on the toes of the leather slippers, she fiercely clutched the hem of the soft pink dress.

The clothes would protect her. The whole wardrobe was her ally. The size 5 dresses, the size 5 shoes, the 32C bras—they would enfold her in a cloak of invisibility. I am not here, she told herself. **I am not here.**

How much time passed? She had no way of knowing. Time was no longer uniform, nor did it flow in sequence. Nevertheless, a fixed period seemed to have elapsed. At one point, the man had been on the verge of opening the door. Mariye felt that strongly. She braced herself. When it opened he would see her. She would see him. Then what? She had no clue. **Perhaps it's not Menshiki at all**—the thought popped into her head. **But then who could it be?**

Yet the man never opened the door. After some

hesitation, he pulled back his hand and moved away. Why had he changed his mind at the last minute? **Something** must have held him back. He stepped out into the hallway and closed the door behind him. The room was empty again. For certain. It was no ruse. She was alone. She was certain of that. Mariye closed her eyes and expelled all the air she had been holding in a great sigh.

Her heart was still pounding. Like a tom-tom— that's how a novelist might describe it. What was a tom-tom, anyway? She had no clear picture. She had been in great peril. At the very last moment, however, something had intervened to protect her. Even so, this place was too dangerous—that much was obvious. Whoever it was, that **someone** had sensed her presence. Beyond a doubt. She couldn't hide in this room forever. This time, she had squeaked through. Next time she might not be so lucky.

She kept waiting. The room grew even darker. But she didn't make a sound. She was fearful, she was anxious, but she persevered. The Commendatore would not forget her. She believed what he had told her. She had no other options—she had to rely on the little guy with the funny way of talking.

Then, before she knew it, the Commendatore was there.

"My friends must leave immediately," he whispered. "Now, at this very moment. Wake up, it is now time."

Mariye was at a loss. It was hard to stand up. When she imagined leaving the closet she was assaulted by a new fear. Even greater dangers might await her in the world outside.

"Menshiki is in the shower," the Commendatore said. "You know what a clean person he is. So he should linger there awhile. But he will come out by and by. This is the one and only chance that my friends will have. Make haste!"

Marshaling her strength, Mariye pulled herself to her feet. She pushed the door of the closet open. The room was dark and empty. Before she stepped out, she turned to take one last look at the clothes hanging there. She inhaled the smell of mothballs. She might never see these clothes again. For some reason, they had become so close to her, so dear.

"My friends must go now," said the Commendatore. "There is not much time. Go into the hallway and turn left."

With her bag over her shoulder, Mariye walked out the door and down the corridor. She ran up the stairs, cut across the big living room, and slid open the glass door to the deck terrace. The hornet might still be around. Or he might have retired for the night. He could be the kind of insect that wasn't fazed by the dark. But she couldn't dwell on that now. She stepped out, unscrewed the binoculars from their stand, and returned them to their plastic cover. She folded the stand and leaned it back against the wall. Her nerves made her hands fumble, so it took longer than she had expected. Then she picked her black loafers up off the deck. All the while, the Commendatore sat on the stool and watched her. The hornet never showed itself. To Mariye's great relief.

"Well done," said the Commendatore, with a nod. "Now go back inside, shut the door, and descend the stairs to the very bottom."

Down two flights of stairs? That would mean plunging into the depths of the house. Wasn't she trying to escape?

"There is no chance of escaping now," the Commendatore said, reading her mind. He shook his head from side to side. "The gate is strictly barred. My friends are constrained to hide a while longer. I beseech you to listen."

Mariye had no choice but to believe the Commendatore. She hurried through the living room and down the two flights of stairs.

The maid's room was at the bottom. Beside it was the laundry room and next to that a storeroom. At the end of the hallway was the gym with its row of exercise machines. The Commendatore pointed to the maid's room.

"This is your hiding place," he said. "Menshiki seldom ventures into that room. He descends once a day to do his laundry and to exercise, but he almost never enters there. It is unlikely he will find my friends, should you remain quiet. The room has a sink and a refrigerator. In case of earthquake, an ample store of food and mineral water has been set aside. So my friends will not starve. There is enough to live in relative safety for a number of days."

A number of days? Mariye asked (albeit without speaking) incredulously, her shoes in hand. I must remain **here** that long?

"Affirmative. It is a shame, but my friends are obliged to stay here for such a time," the Commendatore said, shaking his tiny head. "This house is kept under tight guard. In more than one way. This is a fact I cannot alter. An Idea's powers are limited, I am sad to say."

"How long will I have to stay here?" Mariye asked in a small voice. "I have to go home soon. My aunt will worry about me. If I'm missing too long, she'll have to report it to the police. Then there'll be a real mess."

The Commendatore shook his head. "A million pardons, but this is outside my control. My friends must wait here."

"Is Mr. Menshiki dangerous?"

"A very hard question to answer," the Commendatore said. He made an exaggerated frown. "Menshiki himself is not an evil man. He is a decent sort, one could say, with abilities that exceed those of most people. There is even a hint of nobility in him, if one looks hard enough. Yet there is a gap in his heart, an empty space that attracts the abnormal and the dangerous. It is there that the problem lies."

Mariye wasn't clear what all of this meant, of course. **The abnormal?**

"Who was the person standing outside the closet door?" she asked. "Was that Menshiki?"

"It was Menshiki, but at the same time it was not Menshiki."

"Is he aware of any of this?"

"Most likely," the Commendatore said. "Most likely. But there is nothing he can do about it."

The abnormal and the dangerous? Perhaps the hornet she had seen was one of the forms those things took, Mariye thought.

"Affirmative. Beware of those hornets. They are most virulent creatures," the Commendatore read her mind.

"Virulent?"

"They have the power to kill my friends," the Commendatore explained. "For now, my friends have no choice but to stay here. Do not go outside."

"Virulent," Mariye repeated in her mind. The word sure had a sinister ring.

Mariye opened the door of the maid's room and went in. It was little larger than Menshiki's bedroom closet. There was a kitchenette with a fridge, a hot plate, a small microwave oven, and a sink and faucet. There was also a bed and a tiny bathroom. The bed was bare, but there were blankets, quilts, and a pillow on the shelf, and a simple table and chair for meals. Only a single chair, though. A small window faced the valley. She could look out across it through a crack in the curtain.

"It is best to make as little noise as possible," the Commendatore said. "Do my friends understand?"

Mariye nodded.

"You are a brave girl, my friends," said the Commendatore. "A touch reckless, perhaps, but brave nonetheless. It is an admirable quality. But while you are here, you must be **very** alert. Never be caught off guard. This is no ordinary place. Sinister things are skulking out there that could cause you harm."

"Skulking?"

"Prowling about, in short."

Mariye nodded. In what way was this "no ordinary place," and what sort of sinister things were skulking? She wanted to know, but couldn't think how to ask. Where to begin? There was just so much she couldn't understand.

"I may not be able to come again," the Commendatore said, as if imparting a secret. "There is another place I must go, and another task I must look after. A very important task, if I may say. So I fear I cannot help my friends any further. Hereafter, my friends must manage on your own."

"But how can I escape this place by myself?"

The Commendatore narrowed his eyes and looked squarely at Mariye. "Be sure your ears are open and your eyes are peeled. And keep your wits about you. It is the only way. Then you will know when the right moment comes. As in, 'Aha, now is the time!' You are a brave, smart girl, my friends. Just stay alert."

Mariye nodded. I have to be a brave, smart girl, she thought.

"I wish my friends all the very best," the Commendatore said, encouraging her. Then, as if by afterthought, "And worry not, my friends. Your chest will soon fill out."

"Enough to fill a C-cup bra?"

The Commendatore gave an embarrassed shrug.

"I fear I am a mere Idea. I know not how the under-garments of women are measured. But all the same, I can assure you that your breasts will grow. No need to worry. Time is the remedy for your concerns. It is the key for all things that possess form. True, time does not last forever, but as long as you have it, it is remarkably efficacious. So look forward to the future, my friends!"

"Thank you," Mariye said. It was certainly good to hear. She needed every bit of support to be the brave girl she knew she had to be.

Then the Commendatore vanished. Again, like vapor into thin air. The silence around her deepened the moment he was gone. The thought that she might never see him again left her sad and lonely. I have no one to rely on now, she thought. She sprawled out on the bare mattress and stared at the ceiling. It was low, and made of white plasterboard. In its exact center was a fluorescent light. But of course she couldn't turn it on. That was a definite no-brainer.

How long would she be stuck in this room? It was almost dinnertime. If she wasn't home by seven thirty, her aunt would call the arts-and-culture center. They would inform her that she'd been absent that day. The thought hurt. Her aunt would be hysterical, terrified that something bad had happened to her. Somehow, she needed to let her know she was all right. Then she remembered—there was a cell phone in the pocket of her school blazer. She had left it turned off.

She pulled it out and switched it on. The words "Low Battery" flashed on the screen. A split second later the screen went black. Her phone was dead. She could hardly blame the phone: she hadn't used it in ages (she seldom needed it in her daily life, and had little interest in—or affection for—cell phones), so no surprise the battery was drained.

She heaved a sigh. She should have recharged it once in a while at least. Just in case something happened. But there was no use crying over spilt milk. She stuck the cell phone back in her blazer pocket. But something had caught her attention, and she pulled it out again. The plastic penguin attached to it was gone! It had been her lucky charm since she had won it on points at a donut shop. The strap must have broken. But where on earth could she have dropped it? It was hard to imagine. She hardly ever took it out of her pocket.

At first, she felt uneasy without her lucky charm. Then she thought some more. Her own carelessness was probably to blame for losing it. But a new kind of talisman had appeared in its place—that closetful of clothes—and those clothes had protected her. And that little man with the funny way of talking, the Commendatore, had led her to this place. So **something**, she thought, is still looking out for me. No need to mope about the missing penguin.

Mariye wasn't carrying much. Wallet, handkerchief, change purse, house key, and a half a pack of Cool Mint gum—that was about it. Her shoulder bag contained pencils and pens and a few school textbooks. None were likely to be very useful.

She slipped out of the maid's room and went to

check the storage room. As the Commendatore had said, it was stocked with provisions in case of earthquake. The ground was comparatively stable in this mountainous part of Odawara, so an earthquake shouldn't be that serious. The great Kanto earthquake of 1923 had devastated the city of Odawara, but here in the hills, the damage had been relatively minor (she'd done a summer project in grade school on the impact of the earthquake on the Odawara region). Nevertheless, it would be very difficult afterward to get food and water way up here. Thus Menshiki had taken pains to stock up on both. His caution knew no bounds.

She selected two bottles of mineral water, a box of crackers, and a bar of chocolate and carried them back to her room. She was pretty sure Menshiki wouldn't miss such a small amount. However meticulous he might be, he wouldn't keep tabs on how many bottles he had stored. The water was necessary because she didn't want to turn on the tap in her room if at all possible. That would make the pipes in the house gurgle. It is best to make as little noise as possible, the Commendatore had said. She had to be careful.

Mariye returned to the maid's room and locked the door from the inside. In a sense, it was a useless gesture, since Menshiki had keys to all the rooms in the house. Yet it might earn her a little time. At the very least, it eased her mind a bit.

She wasn't hungry at all, but she ate a few crackers and drank some of the water just to check. The crackers were mediocre, as was the water. She checked the labels—neither had reached its best-before date. I'm okay, she thought. I won't starve.

Outside was now completely dark. She pulled the curtain back a little farther and looked across the valley. She could see her house. She couldn't see what was going on inside without the binoculars, but she could tell lights were burning in some of the rooms. If she looked hard, she might be able to observe someone moving around. Her aunt was there, freaking out, she was sure, because she hadn't come home. Wasn't there a way to call her? Menshiki must have a phone somewhere. All she had to do was say, "Please don't worry. I'm all right," and hang up. If she kept it short, Menshiki probably wouldn't find out. But her room had no phone, nor had she seen one in that part of the house.

Could she escape under cover of darkness? Find a ladder somewhere and scale the wall to freedom? She recalled seeing a fold-up ladder in the garden shed. Then she recalled the Commendatore's words: **This place is kept under tight guard. In more than one way.** She was pretty sure that "tight guard" didn't refer to the security company's alarm system alone.

I should believe the Commendatore, Mariye thought. This is no normal place. Many things are lurking about. I have to be super cautious. Super patient. This is no time to be rash or willful. I should sit back and wait for the right opportunity, like the Commendatore said.

You will know when the right moment comes. As in, "Aha, now is the time!" You are a brave, smart girl, my friends. Just stay alert.

That's right, I have to be a brave, smart girl. Survive all this in good shape and then watch my breasts get bigger and bigger.

So she thought as she lay there on the bare mattress. All around was growing darker. She could tell that darkness of a different order was about to arrive.

62

ONE CAN STUMBLE INTO
A LABYRINTH

Time followed its own principles, paying no heed to her thoughts. She lay there on the bare mattress in her little room, watching it sluggishly shuffle past. She had nothing else to do. It would be nice to have a book to read, she thought. But there were no books at hand, and even if there had been she couldn't switch on the light. All she could do was lie there in the dark. She had found flashlights and spare batteries in the storeroom but had decided to use those as little as possible.

The night deepened, and she fell asleep. She was nervous and apprehensive in such an unfamiliar place, and she wanted to stay awake, but at a certain point fatigue overcame her and she dropped off. She simply couldn't keep her eyes open. The coverless bed was cold, so she took a quilt and blankets from the closet, wrapped herself up in them like a Swiss Roll, and closed her eyes. There was no space heater in the room, and she couldn't use the central system for obvious reasons.

(A note here on the time frame: Menshiki would have left to visit me while Mariye was asleep. He stayed over and went back the following morning. In other words, he wasn't at home that night. The house was empty. But Mariye had no way of knowing that.)

Mariye woke up once that night to use the bathroom, but didn't flush the toilet. During the day was one thing, but in the still, wee hours of the morning the sound of running water could attract attention. Menshiki was without question a cautious and meticulous individual. He would notice even the slightest change. So why risk discovery?

Her watch said two in the morning. Saturday morning, that was. Friday had passed. When she peeped through the curtain she could see her home across the valley. The lights in the living room were blazing. It was after midnight and she still hadn't returned, so the people there—at night that would mean her father and her aunt—were unable to sleep. I've done an awful thing, Mariye thought. She even felt sorry for her father (very rare for her). I shouldn't have been so reckless—it wasn't my intention. This is what I get for acting so impulsively.

Yet whatever her regrets, however much she might blame herself, she couldn't transport herself across the valley. She was not a crow. She couldn't sprout wings and fly through the air. Nor could she disappear and reappear like the Commendatore. She was confined within her still-growing body, and shackled by time and space. Hers was a clumsy, awkward existence. Look at her chest—as flat as a board. Her breasts still pancakes that had failed to rise.

Naturally, Mariye was scared alone there in the dark. Her powerlessness pained her. She wished the Commendatore were there. She had so many things to ask him. Whether he answered them or not, at least she would have someone to talk to. To be sure, his way of speaking was odd, somewhat different from modern Japanese, but she could still understand his general meaning. But he might never come back. "There is another place I must go, and another task I must look after," he had told her. She was desolate to have lost him, perhaps forever.

From outside the window came the resonant cry of a night bird. It sounded like an owl, perhaps a horned owl. They were cloistered in the dark forests, honing their wisdom. I must be as wise as they are, she thought. Be a smart, brave girl. But sleep overtook her a second time. She couldn't keep her eyes open. Pulling the bedding around her once again, she lay down on the mattress and closed her eyes. It was a deep and dreamless sleep. When she woke up it was already growing light outside. Her watch said half past six.

The world was welcoming a new Saturday.

Mariye spent all that day holed up in the maid's room. In place of breakfast, she had more crackers, a few chocolates, and mineral water. She crept into the gym and borrowed several issues from a small mountain of Japanese editions of **National Geographic**. She guessed Menshiki read them when he was working out on his exercise bike, since they were stained here and there with what appeared to be his sweat.

She read through them several times. There were articles on the habitat of the Alaskan wolf, the mysteries of the rising and ebbing of the tides, the life of the Inuit, and the gradual shrinking of the Amazon rain forest. Not Mariye's usual reading material by any means, but now, with nothing else to look at, she read them over and over until she had them practically memorized. She bored holes in the illustrations with her eyes.

When she tired of reading, she napped. On occasion, she looked through the curtain at her home across the valley. I wish I had that telescope now, she thought. Then I'd really be able to see inside, even watch people moving around. She wanted to be back inside her room with the orange curtains. Scrub every inch of her body in a nice hot bath, change into fresh pajamas, and curl up in her warm bed with her cat.

Just after nine in the morning, she heard the sound of someone coming down the stairs. The footsteps of a man in slippers. Menshiki, most likely. His way of walking was somehow distinctive. She wanted to peek through the keyhole, but the door didn't have one. She huddled over her knees in a corner of the room, her body rigid. Escape would be impossible if he opened the door and came in. The Commendatore had said that shouldn't happen, and she had taken him at his word. But nothing was a hundred percent sure thing in this world. Making herself as invisible as possible, she thought of the clothes in the closet and prayed, **Don't let anything happen to me.** Her throat was as dry as cotton.

Menshiki seemed to have brought down his dirty laundry. He probably washed a day's worth of clothes at this time each morning. He tossed them in, added detergent, set the timer and mode, and turned the washer on. She could tell by listening that his movements were practiced. She was surprised how well she could hear. The washer began to churn. Menshiki then moved to the gym and began working out on his exercise machines. That seemed to be his ritual—to work out while his clothes were spinning in the washer. While listening to classical music. She could hear strains of Baroque music coming from the speakers attached to the gym's ceiling. It sounded like Bach, or Handel, or Vivaldi. Mariye didn't know much about classical music, though, so it could have been any one of those three.

Mariye spent a full hour with her ears tuned to the churn of the washer, the systematic whirring of the exercise machines, and the music of either Bach, Handel, or Vivaldi. It was a nerve-wracking hour. True, Menshiki probably wouldn't notice that his pile of **National Geographics** was short a few issues, or that his stash of crackers and chocolate in the storeroom was shrinking bit by bit. She had taken only a tiny fraction of what he had laid away. Nevertheless, there was no telling what might happen. She had to guard against carelessness. To stay on her toes.

Eventually, a buzzer went off and the washer stopped. Menshiki walked slowly back to the laundry room, took the clothes from the washer, put them in the dryer, and turned it on. The dryer began to turn.

Satisfied that all was in order, Menshiki ambled up the stairs. It appeared that his workout had ended. Now he would probably take a long shower.

Mariye closed her eyes and sighed with relief. Menshiki would likely come back down in an hour or so. To remove his clothes from the dryer. Yet the most dangerous period had passed. At least it felt that way. He hadn't sensed her hiding there in the room. Hadn't felt her presence at all. She could breathe more freely now.

Then who had it been in front of the closet? The Commendatore had said it was Menshiki, but then again it wasn't him at all. What had that meant? She couldn't understand what he had been trying to say. It was just too difficult for her. Whatever the case, that **someone** had been able to tell that she (or at least a person) was in the closet. They had sensed her there, no doubt. Yet, **for some reason**, that someone was unable to open the closet door. What could that reason have been? Had that assembly of beautiful old clothes really protected her?

She longed to ask the Commendatore. But he had gone off somewhere. There was no one left who could explain things to her.

Menshiki did not set foot outside the house all that Saturday. As far as she knew, the garage door hadn't opened, nor had a car engine started up. He had come down to pick up his laundry, and then walked slowly back up the stairs. That was it. No one had visited the house at the top of the hill where the road came to an end. No parcels or registered documents had been delivered. The doorbell had remained silent. She had heard the telephone ring twice. The ring was faint and distant, but she could still make it out. It was picked up on the second ring the first time, and the third ring the time after that (that was how she knew Menshiki was in the house). The town garbage truck crawled up the slope to the melody of "Annie Laurie" and then crawled back down again (Saturday was garbage pickup day). Otherwise, she heard no sounds. The house was perfectly still.

The morning passed, afternoon rolled on, and soon evening was drawing near.

(A second note on the time frame: While Mariye was hiding in the maid's tiny room, I killed the Commendatore in the Izu nursing home, tied up Long Face, and descended into the underworld.)

But she never found the perfect time to escape. She had to be patient and wait for "the right moment," the Commendatore had told her. **You will know when the right moment comes. As in, "Aha, now is the time!"**

However, the "right moment" never came. Mariye grew more and more tired of waiting. Patience was not her strength. How long, she wondered, must I stay holed up here?

Menshiki began playing the piano not long before nightfall. Apparently, he kept the living room window open when he practiced, so Mariye could hear the music in her hiding place. It sounded like Mozart. One of his sonatas, in a major key. She had noticed the score on the piano. Menshiki ran through the slow-paced movement, then went back to repeat several sections, adjusting his fingering until he was satisfied. It was difficult, though, and he seemed to be having trouble balancing the sound. For the most part, Mozart's sonatas aren't all that hard, but a pianist who tries to master one can stumble into a labyrinth. That labyrinth, however, didn't seem to faze Menshiki in the least. Mariye listened to him patiently walk back and forth over the thorny passages. He practiced that way for about an hour. At the end, he closed the lid with a bang. She sensed he was frustrated. But not all that much. Rather, it was a moderate, elegant frustration. Even when he was alone (or at least, when he thought he was alone) in his sprawling mansion, he kept a tight rein on his feelings.

What followed was a repeat of the previous day. The sun set, the sky darkened, and the crows flew cawing back to their nests in the mountains. One by one, the lights of the houses across the valley went on. The Akikawas' lights did too, and stayed lit even after midnight. Those lights signaled to Mariye just how worried her family was. At least it felt that way to her. It hurt not to be able to ease their pain.

In stark contrast, not a single light went on at To-mohiko Amada's house (in short, the house I inhab-ited). To all appearances, it looked abandoned. Night came, yet it remained black. It seemed that no one was home. Mariye thought it strange. Where had her teacher gone? Did he know that she was missing?

At a certain hour, sleep again attacked Mariye. The sandman showed no mercy. Shivering in her school blazer, she wrapped herself in blankets and quilts and closed her eyes. I wish my cat were here, she thought as she drifted off. For some reason, her cat—it was a she—seldom mewed or yowled. She only purred. Mariye could have kept her with her without fear of discovery. But of course she wasn't there. Mariye was all alone. In a small pitch-black room with no means of escape.

Sunday morning dawned. When Mariye opened her eyes it was still quite dark. Her watch said before six. The days were getting shorter. Rain was falling outside. A hushed, winter rain. She didn't realize it was raining until she noticed water dripping off the branches. The air in the room was chilly and damp. If only she had a sweater, she thought. All she was wearing under her blazer was a thin knitted vest, a cotton blouse, and beneath that a T-shirt. An outfit for a warm afternoon. A wool sweater would sure come in handy.

Then she remembered—she'd seen a sweater in **that closet**. An off-white cashmere that looked nice and warm. She could trot up the stairs and get it. Put it under her blazer, and she'd be warm as toast. But slipping out the door and climbing the stairs was just too dangerous. **Especially to that room.** She had to make do with what she had on. After all, this cold wasn't unbearable. Nothing like the brutal cold the Inuit had to deal with. This was the outskirts of Odawara, in early December.

Yet the rainy winter morning chilled her to the bone. She could feel the icy damp seep into her body. So Mariye closed her eyes and turned her thoughts to Hawaii instead. When she was small, she and her aunt, and her aunt's old school friend, had visited Hawaii. They rented a small surfboard for her on the beach at Waikiki, and she played in the waves—when she tired of that, she basked in the sun on the white sand. It was so warm, and so harmonious. High above her, the fronds of the palms swayed in the trade winds. White clouds sailed out to sea. She lay there and sipped a glass of lemonade, so cold her temples hurt. Mariye remembered the trip in detail. Would she ever see a place like that again? She'd give anything for that chance.

Once again, a little after nine, Menshiki came padding down the stairs in his slippers. The washer started, the classical music kicked in (this time it sounded like a Brahms symphony), and the rhythm of the exercise machines began. This lasted a full hour. A perfect repeat of the day before. Only the composer was different. The master of the house was certainly a creature of habit. He transferred the laundry from the washer to the dryer, and returned exactly an hour later to pick it up. He didn't come downstairs after that, and showed no interest at all in the maid's room.

(Another note on the time frame: Menshiki went to my home that afternoon, where he bumped into Masahiko and they had a brief conversation. For some reason, though, Mariye was again unaware that he had left the house.)

Menshiki's unwavering routine was useful to Mariye. She could prepare herself emotionally, and plan her movements in advance. Unexpected events would have made it much harder on her nerves. She had grown familiar with Menshiki's pattern, and adapted herself to it. He almost never went out (at least to her knowledge). He worked in his study, washed his own clothes, cooked his own meals, and, in the evening, sat down in front of his Steinway and practiced. Sometimes there was a phone call, but those were infrequent. She could count them on her fingers. For some reason, he didn't seem to like phones all that much. He appeared to take care of his work-related communications—she had no idea how extensive they were—on the computer in his study.

Menshiki took care of the basic cleaning, but once a week he had a cleaning service come to him. Mariye remembered him mentioning that on their previous visit. I don't mind doing it myself, he had said. Cleaning can cheer me up, just like cooking. But it was clearly beyond him to keep such a big house tidy on his own. Thus the need for professional help. He had said he left the house for half a day when they came. What day of the week would it be? Maybe that's when I can make my getaway, Mariye thought. People will be bringing equipment, so the gate should be opening and closing as their vehicles come and go. Menshiki should be absent. So getting out might not be all that hard. That could be my one and only chance.

Yet there was no sign that the cleaners were coming. Monday was much the same as Sunday. Menshiki was making good progress with Mozart: his mistakes were fewer, and the whole piece was coming together musically. He was a careful and patient man. Once he set a goal, he stuck to it. Mariye had to admit she was impressed. Even if he could make it through without a hitch, though, how pleasing would his Mozart be to the ear? Listening to what was coming from upstairs, she had her doubts.

She was surviving on crackers, chocolate, and mineral water. She also polished off an energy bar full of nuts. And a can of tuna fish. Since she had no toothbrush, she brushed her teeth with mineral water, using her finger. She read issue after issue of the Japanese version of **National Geographic**. In the process, she learned about a number of further topics: the man-eating tigers of Bengal; the lemurs of Madagascar; the shifting topography of the Grand Canyon; natural-gas extraction in Siberia; the life expectancy of the penguins of Antarctica; the world of the highland nomads of Afghanistan; the grueling initiation rituals of New Guinean youth. She learned the basics about AIDS, and Ebola. Such miscellaneous information about nature might prove useful one day. Then again, it might be entirely useless. Whatever the case, no other books were on hand. She devoured back issues of **National Geographic** like there was no tomorrow.

Once in a while, she would slip her hand under her T-shirt to check the status of her breasts. But they didn't appear to be growing at all. If anything, they seemed to be getting smaller. She was also concerned about her period. According to her calculations, the next was due in about ten days. She had found nothing related to that condition in the storeroom. (Plenty of toilet paper was stockpiled in case of earthquake, but no sanitary napkins or tampons. It seemed that women and their needs didn't register with the owner of the house.) She'd be in big trouble if it started while she was in hiding. Probably, though, she would have escaped by then. **Probably.** It was hard to imagine putting up with another ten days of this.

The cleaners finally showed up on Tuesday morning. She could hear the lively chatter of women in the upper garden as they unloaded equipment from the back of their van. Menshiki had not done his laundry that morning, nor performed his exercise routine. In fact, he hadn't come downstairs at all. She had wondered if this could be why (Menshiki wouldn't change his daily schedule without a reason), and, sure enough, it was as she had guessed. Menshiki had probably driven his Jaguar out the gate at the same moment the cleaners' big van pulled in.

Mariye rushed to tidy up the maid's room. She gathered the empty water bottles and cracker packets and put them in a garbage bag, which she set out in a visible place. The cleaners would look after it. She neatly folded the blanket and quilt and returned them to the closet. She took care to erase every trace of her presence. Now no one could tell that someone had been living there for days. Then she slung her bag over her shoulder and crept up the stairs. Timing her moves, she darted through the hallway without attracting the cleaners' attention. Her heart pounded at the thought of the dangers of **that room**. At the same time, though, she missed the clothes hanging in its closet. She wanted to go back for one last look. Touch them with her hands. But there was no time for that. She had to hurry.

She slipped through the front door undetected, and ran up the curved driveway. The gate had been left open, as she had anticipated. It made no sense for anyone working there to open and close it each time they passed through. Her face as she stepped out onto the road was a picture of normality.

Should I really be able to leave this easily? she thought outside the gate. Shouldn't I have to pay a higher price? Go through some sort of painful rite of passage, like the teenage tribesmen of New Guinea? Endure a ritual like that as a badge of courage? Those thoughts did not linger, however. They were dwarfed by the liberation she felt at having made her getaway.

The day was overcast, with low-lying clouds that threatened cold rain at any minute. But Mariye's face was raised to the sky. As if she were on the beach at Waikiki, gazing up at the swaying palm trees. She took several deep breaths, giddy with her good fortune. I am free, she thought. My feet will take me anywhere I want to go. My nights spent trembling in the dark are over. That fact alone made her grateful to be alive. It had been only four days, but now the world appeared so fresh, each tree, every blade of grass charged with such wonderful vitality. She found the smell of the wind exhilarating.

Yet this was no time to dawdle. Menshiki could have forgotten something and come driving back at any time. I should get away from here, she thought, and fast. Adopting what she hoped was a nonchalant expression, Mariye tried to smooth her wrinkled school uniform (she had been sleeping in it for days) and straighten her hair to avoid arousing suspicion as she trotted down the mountain.

At the foot of the slope, she turned up the road on the other side. But she did not take her usual route home—rather, she headed for my place. She had something in mind. But the house was empty. She rang the bell repeatedly, but no one came to the door.

Giving up, she went around to the back and took the path through the woods to the pit behind the little shrine. Now, however, a blue plastic sheet covered the pit. The sheet hadn't been there before. It was held firmly in place by cords attached to stakes driven into the ground. Stone weights were lined up on top. It was no longer possible to peek inside. In her absence, someone—who, she didn't know—had sealed it. Probably they considered it a safety hazard. She stood in front of the pit and listened for a while. But she heard nothing.

(My note: The fact she didn't hear the bell could have meant that I hadn't arrived yet. Or possibly that I had fallen asleep.)

Cold drops of rain began to fall. I should go home,

she thought. My family is worried about me. But how could she explain the last four days? She had to think of something. She couldn't let on that she had been hiding at Menshiki's all that time—that was out of the question. It would create an even bigger mess. The police had probably been notified of her disappearance. If they knew that she had broken into Menshiki's home, she'd be charged with trespassing. She would be punished.

What if she claimed that she had fallen into the pit by accident, and had been unable to get out for four days? That only when her teacher—**me**, in other words—came by was she able to climb to safety. Mariye had expected me to play along with this scenario. But I hadn't been home, and the pit's opening had been secured with a plastic tarp. Thus her plan fell through. (Had that scenario unfolded, I would have had to explain to the police why Menshiki and I had brought in heavy equipment to uncover the pit, which might have led to even thornier problems.)

Claiming temporary amnesia was the only other story she could think of. Nothing else came to mind. She would say that those four days were a blank. That she couldn't remember a thing. That when she came to, she was lying alone on the mountain. She would stick with that—there was no other way. She had seen a TV show that hinged on that idea. She wasn't sure if people would swallow an excuse like that. The police and her family would grill her. They might send her to a psychiatrist or counselor of some kind. Even so, a claim of amnesia was the only option. She would have to mess up her hair, splatter mud on her legs and arms, and add a few scattered cuts and bruises to make it look as if she had spent all that time in the mountains. It would be an act she would have to carry through to the very end.

And in fact that was what she did. It was hardly a masterful performance, but she could come up with no alternative.

This was what Mariye revealed to me. She had just finished her account when Shoko Akikawa returned. I heard her Toyota Prius pull up in front of my house.

"I think you should keep quiet about what really happened," I said to Mariye. "Don't tell anyone but me. It will be our secret."

"Of course," Mariye said. "Of course I won't tell anyone. Even if I did, they wouldn't believe me."

"I believe you."

"Does this mean the circle is closed?"

"I don't know," I said. "Maybe not all the way. But I think we can rest easy. The dangerous part is over."

"The virulent part."

"That's right," I said. "The virulent part."

Mariye studied my face for a full ten seconds. "The Commendatore," she said in a small voice. "He really exists."

"That's right," I replied. "He really does." And I killed him with these hands. **Really.** But of course I couldn't tell her that.

951

Mariye gave a single nod. I knew she would keep our secret. It was a secret we would share forever.

I wished I could have told Mariye that the clothes that had protected her from that **something** had been worn by her late mother before she married. But I couldn't. I didn't have the right. Neither did the Commendatore. There was but one person in the world who did, and that was Menshiki. But he would never exercise it.

We all live our lives carrying secrets we cannot disclose.

63

BUT IT'S NOT WHAT
YOU'RE THINKING

Mariye and I had a secret. An important secret shared by the two of us alone. I described my time in the underworld, and she told me exactly what had happened to her at Menshiki's mansion. We wrapped up the two paintings, **Killing Commendatore** and **The Man with the White Subaru Forester,** as tightly as we could and stored them in the attic of Tomohiko Amada's house. Nobody else knew about that, either. The owl did, of course, but it wasn't going to talk. It would hold our secret in perfect silence.

Mariye came to visit from time to time (she hid it from her aunt, using her secret passageway). We put our heads together to try to figure out what our experiences had in common, comparing the timelines right down to the smallest detail.

At first, I worried that Shoko would suspect that Mariye's four-day disappearance and my three-day "long-distance trip" were somehow related, but the idea seems never to have entered her head. Nor did the police direct their attention to that coincidence. They were ignorant of the passageway, so they dismissed my home as just another house on the next ridge over. Since I did not number among the Akikawas' "neighbors," they never came to interview me. Nor did it appear that Shoko had told them I was painting Mariye's portrait. She probably didn't see it as relevant. Had the police put Mariye's absence and my trip together, I could have been placed in a delicate situation.

I never completed my portrait of Mariye Akikawa. It was almost done, but I feared where finishing it might lead. Menshiki, for one, would move heaven and earth to put his hands on it. That much was clear, no matter what he might say to the contrary. I had no intention, however, of letting him install the painting in his private "sanctuary." That could be dangerous. So in the end I left it unfinished. Mariye, however, loved the painting ("It shows how I think these days," was how she put it), and wanted to keep it near her if possible. So I readily gave it to her in its unfinished state (along with the three sketches I had promised earlier).

"I think it's cool," Mariye said. "It's a work in progress, and I'm a work in progress too, now and forever."

"None of us are ever finished. Everyone is always a work in progress."

"How about Mr. Menshiki?" Mariye asked. "He looks very finished to me."

"I think he's a work in progress too," I said.

Menshiki was far from being a completed human being. From what I could tell, anyway. That is why, night after night, under cloak of darkness, he reached out to Mariye Akikawa across the valley on his high-powered binoculars. He couldn't help himself. That secret allowed him to maintain some sort of personal equilibrium. It was for him the equivalent of the long balancing pole that tightrope walkers carry.

Of course, Mariye was aware that Menshiki was peeking into her house. But she never revealed it to anyone (apart from me). She never told her aunt. What possessed him to do something like that? It mystified her. Yet for some reason she didn't feel like pursuing it any further. All she did was keep her curtain closed. The sun-bleached orange curtain stayed tightly shut at all times. She also made sure that the light in her room was off when she changed for bed at night. Elsewhere in the house, however, his voyeurism didn't bother her. Sometimes she even thought she enjoyed it. Perhaps she found some meaning in the fact that **she alone** knew what was going on.

According to Mariye, Shoko and Menshiki were still seeing each other. Her aunt would jump in the car and drive off to his house once or twice a week. Their relationship appeared to be sexual (Mariye hinted at this in a very roundabout way). Her young aunt never said where she was going, but Mariye knew. When she came back, her complexion was rosier than usual. In any case—whatever the nature of that peculiar void within Menshiki—Mariye was powerless to interfere in their affair. She could only let them continue on as they were. All she wished was not to be drawn into whatever was going on between the two of them. That she be allowed to stand at a safe distance, outside the whirlpool of their relationship.

I doubted that she could pull that off. Without realizing it, she would be sucked in sooner or later, to a greater or lesser degree. From the periphery, unavoidably toward the center. Menshiki was wooing Shoko Akikawa, but always with Mariye in mind. Whether he had planned it all from the start or not, he couldn't help himself—that's the kind of man he was. And, like it or not, I had brought them together. He had met Shoko in this house. That's what he had wanted. And when Menshiki wanted something, the guy knew how to put his hands on it.

Mariye wasn't sure what Menshiki would do with that closetful of shoes and size 5 dresses. She guessed he would keep them—whether they were stored in that closet or in another place. However his relationship with Shoko Akikawa turned out, he wouldn't be able to discard them, or burn them. That was because the wardrobe had become a part of his psyche. The clothes would be forever enshrined within his spiritual sanctuary.

I decided to quit teaching my painting class near Odawara Station. "I'm sorry, but I need to focus on my art," was how I put it to the director. He took it in stride. "It's a shame," he said. "Everyone says you're a wonderful teacher." His words didn't sound altogether false, either. I thanked him, and promised to stick it out till year's end. By then, he had located a good replacement, a retired high school art instructor in her mid-sixties. She struck me as a very nice woman, with eyes that resembled those of an elephant.

Menshiki called from time to time. No practical matter was ever involved—we just chatted. Each time he would ask if there had been any change in the pit behind the shrine, and each time I would tell him no, there hadn't. That was the honest truth. The blue plastic sheet was still stretched across the opening. I went to check sometimes when I was out for a walk, but never saw any sign that it had been tampered with. The stones holding it down hadn't been moved either. There were no more strange or suspicious events connected to the pit. I never heard the bell in the middle of the night, nor did the Commendatore (or anything else) emerge from it. It was just a big hole sitting quietly in the middle of the woods. The clump of tall pampas grass flattened by the backhoe was growing back, concealing the area around the pit once again.

As far as Menshiki knew, I had been in the pit the whole time I was missing. True, he couldn't explain how I had gotten inside. Yet he had found me there—that was an indisputable fact. As a result, he never connected Mariye's disappearance and mine. He could only see the overlap of the two events as some kind of strange coincidence.

Discreetly, I probed to see if he had an inkling that someone had been hiding in his house for four days. But he had seen no telltale signs. He was wholly in the dark. In which case, whoever had been standing outside the closet in the **forbidden chamber** was most likely not him. But then who had it been?

Although Menshiki called, he no longer came by for visits. Perhaps he no longer needed to hang out now that Shoko was in his grasp. Or maybe he had lost interest in me. Or both. It didn't matter to me one way or the other (though there were times I missed the sound of his Jaguar V8 purring up the slope).

Nevertheless, the occasional phone calls (always before eight in the evening) suggested that Menshiki felt we should stay connected in some way. Perhaps the fact that he had revealed to me that he **might** be Mariye's biological father weighed on his mind to some extent. I don't think he worried that I would blurt it out—to either Mariye or Shoko Akikawa—somewhere down the line. He was sure I would guard his secret. He could read me well enough to know that, like he could read all people. Yet it was **so foreign** to Menshiki to have bared his heart to anyone, whoever they might be. He had an iron will, but maybe even he found it exhausting to keep secrets to himself all the time. He must have really needed me on his side when he made his confession. And I had struck him as relatively harmless.

Whether or not he had exploited me from the beginning, however, I still owed him my gratitude. It was he who had rescued me from the pit. Had he not come along, if he hadn't lowered the ladder and then yanked me up to the surface, I would have become a dried-up corpse. In a sense, then, Menshiki and I had each placed our lives in the other's hands. That meant that our accounts were even.

Menshiki just nodded when I told him that I had given **A Portrait of Mariye Akikawa** to Mariye in its unfinished state. I guess he no longer needed the painting that much, though he had commissioned it. Or he saw no meaning in an unfinished work. Or his mind was on other things.

A few days after Menshiki and I had this conversation, I put a simple frame on **The Pit in the Woods**, placed the painting in the trunk of my Corolla, and took it to his house. This was the last time we would meet face-to-face.

"This is for saving my life. Please accept it," I said.

He seemed to like the painting a lot. (I thought it was pretty good myself.) He offered to pay me for it, but I turned him down. I had received too much money from him as it stood. There was no need for further obligations on either side. We had become neighbors who lived across the valley from each other, no more, and I wanted to keep it that way.

Tomohiko Amada passed away the Saturday of the week I was rescued from the pit. He had been in a coma for three days, and in the end his heart simply stopped beating. It shut down quietly and naturally, like a locomotive pulling into the last station. Masahiko was by his side throughout. He called me soon after.

"He went peacefully," he said. "That's the way I would like to go. I thought I could even detect a smile."

"A smile?" I asked.

"Maybe it wasn't a true smile, strictly speaking. But that's the way it looked. To me, anyway."

"I'm very sorry about your father," I said, choosing my words, "but I'm glad he went peacefully."

"He was semiconscious until midweek, but he didn't seem to want to leave any parting words," Masahiko said. "I guess he had no regrets—he lived his ninety years to the fullest, doing what he wanted to do."

You're wrong, I thought. He had regrets. In fact, he bore a very heavy burden. Yet only he knew what that burden was. Now there was no one left who knew, and it would remain like that forever.

"I'm afraid I'll be out of touch for a while," Masahiko said. "Dad was famous in his own way, which means I have to take care of all kinds of things. I'm the son and heir, so I can't say no. Let's get together and talk after things have settled down a little."

I thanked him for taking the trouble to let me know, and we hung up.

Tomohiko Amada's death cast an even deeper hush over my home. But that was only natural. He had lived there for a long time, after all. I shared the house with that silence for several days. It was intense, but not unpleasant. You could call it a pure silence, in that it was not connected to anything else. A chain of events had come to an end. That's how it felt, anyway. It was the kind of hush that comes when matters of major importance are finally resolved.

One night about two weeks after Tomohiko Amada's death, Mariye came to talk to me, stealing to my house in secret like a cautious cat. She didn't stay very long. Her family was keeping close watch on her, so she didn't have the freedom to come and go that she had enjoyed before.

"My breasts seem to be getting bigger," she said. "My aunt and I went shopping for a bra. The stores carry something called a 'beginner's bra.' Did you know that?"

No, I said, I didn't. I glanced at her chest but saw nothing new beneath her green Shetland sweater.

"I don't see much difference," I said.

"That's because the padding is thin. If it were any thicker, people would see the change right away and think you stuffed something inside. So you start thin and then work up from there. It's more complicated than I thought."

Mariye told me that a female police officer had questioned her at length about where she had been those four days. The questioning had been gentle most of the time, yet on occasion the woman had become very firm. But Mariye had stuck with her story: she could remember only that she'd been roaming the mountain and had gotten lost. The rest was a complete blank. She thought she'd survived on the mineral water and chocolate she always carried in her schoolbag. That was all she would say. Otherwise, she kept her mouth clamped shut. She was good at keeping quiet. Once the police were sure that she had not been kidnapped and held for ransom, they took her to a hospital to have her cuts and bruises examined. They wanted to know if she had been sexually abused in any way. When it was clear that no abuse had taken place, the police lost interest. She was just another runaway kid who had gone missing for a couple of days. Hardly a rare occurrence.

Mariye threw away everything she had been wearing during that time: her dark blue blazer, checked skirt, white blouse, knitted vest, loafers—everything. She bought a whole new set of school clothes to replace them. She wanted to start fresh. Then she went back to her life as if nothing had happened. The only difference was that she quit attending the painting class (she was too old for the children's class anyway). She hung my (unfinished) portrait of her on her wall.

It was hard to imagine what kind of woman she would grow up to be. Girls of that age can change in the blink of an eye, physically and emotionally. I might not even be able to recognize her in a few years. I was thus very happy to have painted her picture (unfinished though it was) as she was at thirteen, freezing her image in time. In this real world of ours, after all, nothing remains the same forever.

I called my former agent in Tokyo and told him I wanted to go back to portrait painting. He couldn't have been happier. They were always short of skilled artists.

"But you told me you were through with the business, didn't you?" he said.

"I changed my mind," I answered. Why exactly, I didn't say. He didn't ask, either.

I wanted to live without thinking about anything for a while, to let my hands move on their own, churning out normal, "commercial" portraits one after the other. In the process, I could gain some financial stability. I didn't know how long I could keep that up. I couldn't predict the future. But for the time being, at least, that's what I wanted. To use my hard-won skills without calling up any complicated thoughts. To avoid getting mixed up with Ideas, or Metaphors, or anything along those lines. To keep a safe distance from the messy private affairs of the wealthy, mysterious man who lived across the valley. Not to be dragged into any more dark tunnels for having brought hidden masterpieces into the light. More than anything, that's what I desired.

I met Yuzu. We talked over coffee and Perrier at a café not far from her office. Her belly wasn't as big as I had imagined.

"You're not planning to marry the father?" I asked her right off the bat.

She shook her head. "No, not at the present time."

"Why?"

"I just feel that's for the best."

"But you plan to have the child, right?"

She gave a little nod. "Of course. Can't turn back now."

"Are you living with him?"

"No, I'm not. Since you left I've lived alone."

"How come?"

"For one thing, we're not divorced yet."

"But I sent you the divorce papers a while ago, signed and sealed. So I assumed we were already divorced."

Yuzu was quiet for a moment. "To be honest, I never submitted them," she said at last. "I couldn't somehow, so I let them sit. You and I have been legally married all this time. That means the baby will legally be your child, whether we get divorced or not. You won't bear any responsibility for it, of course."

I couldn't grasp what she meant. "But biologically speaking, the baby is his, correct?"

Yuzu looked me in the eye. "It's not that simple," she said at last.

"What do you mean?"

"How can I put this? I'm not a hundred percent certain the baby is his."

Now it was my turn to look her in the eye. "Are you saying you don't know who got you pregnant?"

She nodded. **I don't know.**

"But it's not what you're thinking," she said. "I wasn't sleeping around. I can only have a sexual relationship with one man at a time. That's why I stopped sleeping with you. Right?"

I nodded.

"I felt sorry for you, though."

I nodded again.

"But I was careful to use protection with him. I didn't want a child. You know how I felt. I was ultracautious about those things. And yet I got pregnant, just like that."

"There can always be slipups, no matter how careful we try to be."

"Women know when something like that happens," Yuzu said, shaking her head. "We have a sixth sense that tells us. I don't think men have it."

Of course, I didn't.

"At any rate, you're planning to have the baby," I said.

Yuzu nodded.

"But you never wanted one. At least as long as we were together."

"That's true," she said. "I didn't want one with you. I didn't want one with anybody."

"And yet now you're going to go ahead and bring a child into the world without knowing who the father is. Why didn't you have an abortion? You could have done so earlier."

"I thought about it, of course. And part of me wanted one."

"But you didn't."

"This is how I think these days," Yuzu said. "This is my life, sure, but in the end almost all that happens in it may be decided arbitrarily, quite apart from me. In other words, although I may presume I have free will, in fact I may not be making any of the major decisions that affect me. I've come to think my pregnancy is an example of that."

I listened to her without saying anything.

"I know this sounds fatalistic, but it's what I have **truly** come to feel. Honestly and deeply. So then I thought, if that's how things work, why not have the child and raise it on my own. See it through, and find out what happens. That's come to seem terribly important."

"There's just one thing I need to ask," I said, diving in.

"What is it?"

"It's a simple question, one that requires a mere yes or no. I won't say anything more."

"No problem. Ask away."

"Can I return to you—would you take me back?"

Her brow furrowed slightly. She looked me hard in the face for a moment. "Do you mean you wish to live once more as husband and wife?"

"If that's possible."

"I'd like that," she said quietly. There was no hesitation in her voice. "You are still my husband, and your room is as you left it. You can come back anytime you wish."

"Are you still seeing the other man?" I inquired.

Yuzu quietly shook her head. "No, that's over."

"Why?"

"I didn't want to allow him parental rights—that's the main reason."

I said nothing.

"It seems to have come as a great shock to him.

Only natural, I guess," she said. She rubbed her cheeks with her hands.

"But you would allow me?"

She rested her hands on the table and once again looked at me closely.

"You've changed a little, haven't you? Your features, or maybe your expression?"

"I don't know how I look, but I have learned a few things, I think."

"I may have learned a few things myself."

I picked up my cup and drained what was left of my coffee.

"Masahiko's father just passed away," I said, "so he's got a lot to deal with right now. When things have settled down for him, I'll pack my bags and return to our apartment in Hiroo, probably sometime early in the New Year. Assuming that's all right with you, of course."

She studied my face. As if gazing at a landscape she had missed for a very long time. Finally, she reached across the table and gently covered my hand with hers.

"I'd like to give it another try," she said. "In fact, I've been thinking that for a while."

"I've been thinking the same thing," I said.

"I don't know if it will work out or not."

"I don't know either. But it's worth a shot."

"I'm about to have a baby without knowing who the father is. Is that going to be all right with you?"

"I don't have a problem with that," I said. "I know you're going to think I'm crazy, but there's a possibility that I could be the baby's father—potentially. That's my feeling, anyway. I could have somehow gotten you pregnant, mentally, from a distance. As a concept, using a special route."

"As a concept?"

"That's one hypothesis."

Yuzu considered that for a minute. "If that's true," she said, "then that's one heck of a hypothesis."

"Perhaps nothing can be certain in this world," I said. "But at least we can believe in something."

She smiled. That was the end of our conversation that day. She took the subway home, while I climbed into my dusty old Toyota Corolla station wagon and drove back to my home on the mountain.

64

AS A FORM OF GRACE

I t was several years after I moved back in with my wife that, on March 11, a huge earthquake devastated northeastern Japan. I sat in front of the television as, one after another, coastal villages and towns from Iwate all the way down to Miyagi were laid to waste before my eyes. That was the very same region I had driven through in my old Peugeot 205. I had encountered the man with the white Subaru Forester in one of those towns. Yet now all I could see were the remains of communities leveled by a tsunami that had fallen on them like some giant beast, leaving nothing in its wake but drowned wreckage. Try as I might, I could find no visible connection to **that town**. Since I couldn't remember the name of the place, I had no way of learning how much damage it had suffered, or how it had been changed.

I couldn't bring myself to do anything—I just sat staring at the TV screen for days on end in stunned silence. I was transfixed. I prayed to find something, anything, connected to my memories. If I failed, I feared, something stored within me, something very important, would be lost for good, carried off to some distant, unknown place. I wanted to hop in my car and drive to the stricken region. See for myself what had survived the disaster. That was out of the question, of course. The main roads had been torn to pieces, which meant that towns and villages were cut off from the world. Electricity, gas, water—all lifelines had been severed. Farther south, on the coast of Fukushima (where I had abandoned my Peugeot when it gave up the ghost), several nuclear reactors were in meltdown. It was impossible to venture into that part of the country.

I had not been a happy man when I had traveled there. It had been a lonely, painful, thoroughly wretched period in my life. I think I was lost in a number of ways. Nevertheless, the trip had allowed me to spend time among unfamiliar people, and witness their lives. I had not imagined then how valuable that would turn out to be. In the process— usually unconsciously—I had discarded some things and picked up others. By the time I passed through all those places I had become a somewhat different person.

I thought of **The Man with the White Subaru Forester** hidden in the attic of the Odawara house. Had that man—whether he belonged to the real world or not—still been living in the same town when disaster struck? What about the skinny young woman with whom I had spent that strange night. Had they and the other inhabitants been able to escape the earthquake and tsunami? Were they still alive? What was the fate of the love hotel and the roadside restaurant?

When five o'clock came around, I would go to pick up our daughter at the nursery school. This was my designated role (my wife having gone back to work at the architectural firm). On an adult's legs, the school was a ten-minute walk away. Then the two of us would slowly stroll home, hand in hand. If the weather was good, we would stop by a park on the way to sit on a bench and watch the neighborhood dogs pass by. Our daughter wanted a little dog of her own, but no pets were permitted in our apartment building, so she had to make do with looking at them in the park. Every so often, someone would let her pet their small, unthreatening dog.

Our daughter's name was Muro. Yuzu had chosen it. She had seen the name in a dream shortly before the baby was born. In the dream, she had been in a large Japanese-style room that looked out over a spacious and beautiful garden. There was a low, old-fashioned writing desk, and on top of that a sheet of white paper. On the paper a single character, 室 (Muro), had been written in bright black ink. The calligraphy was magnificent. That was Yuzu's dream. It stayed stuck in her mind even after she awoke. Thus, she decided, Muro had to be the baby's name. I was fine with that, of course. After all, she was the one having the baby. The idea that the calligrapher might be Tomohiko Amada popped into my head. But that was just a passing thought. When you came right down to it, it was only a dream, nothing more.

I was happy the child was a girl. I had grown up with my younger sister Komi, so I found it relaxing to have a little girl around. It felt as natural as could be. I was happy, too, that she came into this world with her name already settled. Names are important, whatever one might say.

When we got home, Muro and I watched the news together. I tried to shield her from shots of towns being swallowed by the tsunami. I thought the images were too disturbing for a young child. I was quick to cover her eyes when they came on the screen.

"Why, Daddy?" Muro asked me.

"Because you're still too young."

"But it's real, isn't it?"

"Yes, it is. It's really happening somewhere far from here. But just because it's real doesn't mean you have to see it."

Muro thought about that for a while. But of course she couldn't wrap her head around what I had said. She couldn't understand tsunamis and earthquakes yet, or the meaning of death. All the same, I blocked her vision whenever the tsunami appeared on the screen. Understanding something and seeing it are two different things.

One time, I saw the man with the white Subaru Forester on TV. Or at least I thought I did. They were shooting a large fishing vessel stranded on a bluff some distance from shore, and **he** was standing nearby. Like an elephant keeper beside an elephant that had outlived its usefulness. But that shot was quickly followed by another. I couldn't be sure if it was really the man with the white Subaru Forester or not. But to me the tall fellow in the black windbreaker and black cap with a Yonex logo could be no one else.

His image came and went. There was only a brief second before the camera angle shifted.

Besides watching news about the earthquake, I painted "commercial" portraits on commission to shore up our finances. It was something I could do without thinking—when I sat before the canvas, my hands moved almost automatically. I had been seeking just that sort of life. And that's what people had been seeking from me. The work provided a steady income. I needed that too. I had a family to take into account.

Two months after the earthquake, my old home in Odawara burned down. The house on the mountain where Tomohiko Amada had spent half his life. Masahiko called with the news. He had been tearing his hair out over how to look after it once I had left, and it turned out his fears were well founded. It had caught fire just before dawn at the end of the May holidays, and although firemen had rushed to the scene, the old wooden structure had almost burned to the ground by the time they arrived (the fire trucks had trouble navigating the steep and twisting road). Luckily, it had rained the night before, so flames hadn't spread to the surrounding trees. The fire department investigated, but to no avail. It might have been an electrical short circuit, but then again it could have been arson.

The first thing that came to mind when I heard the news was **Killing Commendatore**. It must have been incinerated along with the house. Same with **The Man with the White Subaru Forester**. And the record collection. Had the owl in the attic managed to escape?

Killing Commendatore was without a doubt one of Tomohiko Amada's best works, its demise a great loss to Japan's art world. Yet only a few people had laid eyes on it. Just Mariye Akikawa and me. Shoko Akikawa, very briefly. Its creator, Tomohiko Amada, of course. After that, possibly no one. Now it was gone forever, swallowed by the flames. I couldn't shake the feeling that I was somehow to blame. Shouldn't I have made public Tomohiko Amada's hidden masterpiece? Instead, I had bundled it up and stuck it back in the attic. Now it was just a pile of ashes. (I had carefully copied the characters who appeared in it in my sketchbook, all that remained of **Killing Commendatore**.) As a self-respecting artist myself, the idea pained me. The painting was so wonderful, I thought. Perhaps I had committed a crime against art itself.

Yet it also struck me that it might have been a work that **had to be lost**. Tomohiko Amada had poured just too much of his passion, his soul, into it for it to be exposed to public view. It was filled with his spirit. Thus, although it was a superb painting, it possessed some sort of vicious power—it could summon things from **the other side**. By discovering it, I had set a cycle of some kind in motion. Dragging a painting like that out into the light could well have been a big mistake. Wasn't that what the artist himself had thought? Wasn't that why he had hidden it in the attic, away from view? If so, then I had respected his wishes. Whichever the case, it had been lost to the flames, and there was no way anyone could turn back time to recover it.

I didn't regret the loss of **The Man with the White Subaru Forester** for a moment. I knew I would tackle that subject again in the future. By then, though, I would have become a more resolute man, and an artist of greater integrity. When it came time to create my own art again, I should be able to paint **The Man with the White Subaru Forester** from a whole new angle. Perhaps that work would become my own **Killing Commendatore**. If that happened, it would be the greatest legacy I could receive from Tomohiko Amada.

Mariye called me right after the fire, and we talked for half an hour about the little old house it had left in ashes. That house had been important to her. Not so much the building, perhaps, as the world it encompassed, and the time when it was an essential part of her life. That would include Tomohiko Amada, back in the days when he still lived there. Whenever she saw him, the painter was always immersed in his work. From Mariye's experience, an artist was someone who holed up for days painting in his studio. She had watched Amada through the window of that house. Now it was gone, and she had lost that world forever. I shared her sadness. That house held deep meaning for me as well, though I had lived there less than eight months.

At the end of our call, Mariye told me that her breasts were much bigger than before. By now, she was in her second year of high school. I had not seen her once since my departure. Our relationship consisted of an occasional phone call. I didn't particularly want to revisit the house, nor had I any compelling reason to go there. It was always Mariye who called me.

"They haven't filled out yet, but they're definitely growing," she whispered confidentially. It took me a while to register what she was talking about.

"Just as the Commendatore prophesied," she said.

That's wonderful, I said. I considered asking if she had a boyfriend, but decided against it.

Her aunt was still seeing Menshiki. She had revealed that to Mariye at some point. That they were **very close indeed**. And that they might get married before too long.

"Would you live with us if that happened?" her aunt had asked.

Mariye had pretended she hadn't heard. She was good at that.

I found the idea a bit unsettling. "Are you intending to live with Mr. Menshiki?" I asked her.

"I don't think so," she said. "But I'm not so sure."

Not so sure?

"I thought you had some pretty bad memories of his house," I said, my bafflement showing.

"All of that happened when I was a kid. It seems so long ago. And there's no way I'm going to live alone with my father."

So long ago?

It felt like yesterday to me. When I said that to Mariye, though, she didn't respond. Perhaps she wanted to forget those days, and what had taken place then. Or maybe she already had. Now that she was older, she might even have started to develop an interest in Menshiki, however slight. Maybe she had come to see something special in him, a blood tie of some sort.

"I really want to see what happened to that closet-ful of clothes," Mariye said.

"That room attracts you, doesn't it?"

"That's because those clothes protected me," she said. "But who knows, I may live on my own when I go to college."

Sounds good to me, I said.

"So what's the situation with the pit behind the shrine?" I asked.

"No change," Mariye replied. "The blue plastic sheet's still on it, even after the fire. Leaves will cover it eventually. Then maybe no one will know it's even there."

The little old bell would be lying on the floor of the pit. Together with the flashlight I had taken from Tomohiko Amada's room at the nursing home.

"Have you seen the Commendatore?" I asked.

"No, not once. It's hard to believe he really existed."

"He did, all right," I said. "You'd better believe it."

All the same, I figured that, little by little, that realm would disappear from Mariye's mind. Her life would grow busier and more complicated as she moved into her late teens. She would no longer have time to consider crazy things like Ideas and Metaphors.

Every so often, I found myself wondering about the plastic penguin. I had given it to the faceless man as payment for ferrying me across the river. There had been no alternative, given the swiftness of the current. I could only pray that little penguin was watching over Mariye from somewhere—probably as it shuttled back and forth between presence and absence.

I still can't be sure about the identity of Muro's father. A DNA test would tell me, but I have no desire to know the result. Perhaps we'll find out somewhere along the way. The truth may be revealed. But what meaning would that "truth" carry? Muro is my child in the legal sense, and I love her deeply. I treasure the time we spend together. I couldn't care less who her biological father is or isn't. The question is inconsequential. It can change nothing.

I went to Yuzu in a dream as I wandered from town to town in northeastern Japan. I made love to her while she was asleep, stealing into her dream and impregnating her, so that nine months and a few days later she bore a child. I love this idea (although I hold it in secret). That child's father is me as Idea, or perhaps me as Metaphor. Just as the Commendatore visited me, or as Donna Anna guided me through the dark, so did I, in some alternate world, deposit my seed in Yuzu's womb.

But I will not become like Menshiki. He has built his life by balancing the possibility that Mariye Akikawa is his child with the possibility that she isn't. It is through the subtle and unending oscillation between those two poles that he seeks to find the meaning of his own existence. I have no need, though, to challenge my life in such a troublesome (or, at the least, unnatural) way. That is because I am endowed with the capacity **to believe**. I believe in all honesty that something will appear to guide me through the darkest and narrowest tunnel, or across the most desolate plain. That's what I learned from the strange events I experienced while living in that mountaintop house on the outskirts of Odawara.

Killing Commendatore may have been lost forever in the flames that hour before dawn, yet its beauty and power live within me even now. I can call up the images of the Commendatore, Donna Anna, the faceless man, and the rest with perfect clarity. They look so tangible, so real, I feel as though I could reach out and touch them. Contemplating them affords me perfect tranquility, as though I were watching raindrops fall on the surface of a broad reservoir. That soundless rain will fall forever in my heart.

I will probably live the rest of my life in their company. My little daughter Muro is their gift to me. A form of grace. I am convinced of this.

"The Commendatore was truly there," I say to Muro as she lies sleeping. "You'd better believe it."

A NOTE ABOUT THE AUTHOR

Haruki Murakami was born in Kyoto in 1949 and now lives near Tokyo. His work has been translated into more than fifty languages, and the most recent of his many international honors is the Hans Christian Andersen Literature Award, whose previous recipients include J. K. Rowling, Isabel Allende, and Salman Rushdie.

www.harukimurakami.com